THE BLACK TIDE
&
THE BIG
FOOTPRINTS

Also by Hammond Innes

FICTION

TRAVEL

HISTORY

Hammond Innes was born in Sussex in 1913. He was the author of thirty international bestsellers, all reissued by Pan. He also wrote a superb history of the Conquistadors, two books of his world travels and sailing, and an evocative illustrated book on East Anglia. It was in the early fifties, with books like *The Lonely Skier*, *Campbell's Kingdom*, *The White South* and *The Wreck of the Mary Deare*, all of them filmed, that he achieved international fame.

HAMMOND INNES

THE BLACK TIDE
&
THE BIG
FOOTPRINTS

PAN BOOKS

The Black Tide first published 1982
by William Collins and first published by Pan Books 1998
The Big Footprints first published 1997
by William Collins and first published by Pan Books 1996

This omnibus edition published 2002 by Pan Books
an imprint of Pan Macmillan Ltd
Pan Macmillan, 20 New Wharf Road, London N1 9RR
Basingstoke and Oxford
Associated companies throughout the world
www.panmacmillan.com

ISBN 0 330 41818 1

1 3 5 7 9 8 6 4 2

A CIP catalogue record for this book is available from
the British Library.

Phototypeset by Intype London Limited
Printed and bound in Great Britain by
Mackays of Chatham plc, Chatham, Kent

THE BLACK TIDE

To
MARJORY AND IAN

In admiration, for reasons that
will be apparent to all their
many friends

CONTENTS

PART ONE

PRELUDE TO POLLUTION

CHAPTER ONE

It was New Year's Eve. The last weather forecast had given wind south-westerly force 5 increasing to 6 with poor visibility in sleet or snow showers. Between Land's End and the Scillies, and already into the north-bound traffic lane, the tanker *Petros Jupiter*, with 57,000 tons of crude for the Llandarcy refinery in South Wales, made a long slow turn to starb'd, finally settling on to a course of 95°.

Her cargo had been resold late that afternoon, but delay in obtaining signature on certain documents had meant that it was not until 22.54 that her master was informed of the transaction and instructed to alter course for Rotterdam. Less than an hour later, at 23.47, the alarm bells sounded on the bridge.

Like many of the early VLCCs, the *Petros Jupiter* was just about worn out. She had been built for the Gulf Oil Development Company in the sixties, at the height of the Japanese expansion in shipbuilding. Her design life at maximum efficiency was about eight years and GODCO had sold her to a Greek company in 1975. She was now in her seventeenth year and, since rounding the Cape, steam leaks had been creating an almost permanent fog in the engine-room with the evaporator barely able to produce sufficient distilled water to replace the loss. The log would show that on two previous occasions loss of distilled water had been so great that the automatic cut-out on the single boiler had been tripped.

For ships taking the inside route between Land's End and the Scilly Islands the northbound traffic lane is the one nearest to the mainland. But the *Petros Jupiter* had been on the outer edge of the lane when she had made the turn to starb'd, and being on a slow-steam voyage she was moving at barely 11½ knots through the water, so that when the alarm bells sounded and the single high pressure boiler cut out, bringing both the steam turbines to a halt, she was still not clear of Land's End.

Engine-room staff immediately switched to auxiliary power to keep the alternators going and to provide electricity, but power to drive the ship could not be restored until the accumulation of leaks in the steam pipework had been repaired and the loss of distilled water for the boiler reduced. The ship gradually lost way until finally she lay broadside to the waves, rolling sluggishly.

There she remained for over two hours, during which time she drifted about three miles in the general direction of Land's End. By then emergency repairs had been completed and at 02.04 she was under way again. And then, at 02.13, the unbelievable happened: the secondary reduction gear, the gear that drove the single propeller shaft, was stripped of its teeth. A journalist would write later that it had made a very expensive sound, which was the phrase used by Aristides Speridion, the Greek second engineer, who had been at that end of the engine-room when it happened.

With the secondary reduction gear useless, there was no way the *Petros Jupiter* could proceed and at 02.19 the master contacted Land's End coastguard station on VHF to inform the watch officer of the situation and enquire about the availability of a tug.

The tanker was now lying helpless, wind-rode and wallowing heavily, her hull broadside to the sea, which were big and breaking. If she had been fully loaded she might still have survived, but half her cargo had been off-loaded at Corunna and she was riding quite high out of the water, her huge slab-sided hull acting as a giant sail.

Her position at this time was 8½ miles from Land's End with the Longships light bearing 058°. The wind was still south-westerly, still increasing, and the barometer was falling. The latest forecast was for southwest 7 increasing to gale 8, veering later with a possible temporary increase to strong gale 9.

The coastguard officer on watch at Land's End told a reporter later that at this point, in the early hours of the morning with the threat of another *Torrey Canyon* on his hands, he very much wished he still had his SAR radar capability so that he could have monitored the tanker's drift. Unfortunately, the radar had been dismantled when the new coastguard station for the South West on Pendennis Point, at the entrance to Falmouth, had been completed. Even so, it did not take him long to figure out that the *Petros Jupiter* would need to have a tow line on board within the next four to five hours if she was not to be driven on to the rocks at Land's End. He informed the master accordingly, warning him not to place too much reliance on his anchors and only to use them when the depth of water was shallow enough to give him a good scope of chain. At 02.23 he alerted the Falmouth station officer of the tanker's situation enquiring, on behalf of the master, whether there was a tug stationed in the vicinity. Fortunately the Dutch tug based on Falmouth was in port.

Nevertheless, almost another hour went by before the master finally requested the coastguards to inform Lloyd's that tug assistance was required. This delay may have been due to the *Petros Jupiter* contacting other ships in the vicinity. It would certainly explain why she did not speak direct on W/T with Telecom International at the Land's End radio station, all their messages being routed through Land's End coastguard station on VHF.

The tug left immediately, steaming out past Pendennis Point at 03.27 with an ETA at the probable position of the drifting tanker of about 06.30. By then Falmouth coastguards had alerted the Naval Flag Officer, the Sennen lifeboat had been put on stand-by and the duty officer at the Department of Trade's Marine Division, Sunley House, High Holborn, had been informed and had immediately called the retired admiral who headed the Marine Pollution Control Unit.

As anticipated by the forecast, the weather was now worsening rapidly so that by 04.00 the wind was force 8, gusting 9, and the tug, out from under the lee of the Lizard and punching westward into heavily breaking seas, was forced to reduce speed. Shortly before 05.00 the tug master contacted the *Petros Jupiter* and informed her master that owing to heavy seas his ETA would now be 07.30 or even later.

By then the tide had turned, wind and tide pushing the ship in a north-easterly direction. Falmouth coastguards, plotting the shifting direction of the tidal stream between Land's End and the Scillies, calculated that with a wind drift of approximately one knot the ship would go aground in the vicinity of the Longships about an hour before the tug could reach her. This warning was passed to the master and the advice repeated to let go his anchors when he was in a depth that would give him sufficient scope of chain. In the weight of wind and, with the seas now big, the chain would almost certainly snap, but there was just a chance that the anchors might hold long enough for the north-going tide to take the tanker clear of the Longships and, with the extra fetch provided by Whitesand Bay, the tug might still get a line on board before she struck.

Meanwhile, the secretary of the Sennen lifeboat, in consultation with his cox'n, had decided to launch. The time of launch was 04.48 and the lifeboat reached the casualty at 06.07. By then the *Petros Jupiter*, with two anchors down and her bows pointed in the general direction of the Wolf Rock, was barely a mile from the Longships. An hour later, as dawn began to break, first one anchor chain, then the other parted, and the lifeboat, which was lying in the lee of the tanker's stern, reported the grey granite tower of the lighthouse just visible through mists of wind-blown spray and driving snow. It was very close, the cox'n radioed.

It was a dark, cold dawn, full of scudding clouds. A Sea King helicopter from RNAS Culdrose, hovering overhead, taking photographs and checking for pollution, gave the distance between the tanker's stern and the lighthouse as barely 500 metres. The pilot also reported that he could see no sign of the tug. This information was passed to the MPCU at Sunley House, which was now fully manned and already operating on the assumption of a major disaster, alerting tugs and aircraft fitted with spraying equipment and arranging for the transportation of stock-piled dispersants to Land's End.

The *Petros Jupiter* struck at 07.23, but not on the Longships. By then she had drifted clear of the lighthouse and the sunken ledges on which it was built, and with the wind veering, and the direction of the tidal stream already changing, she went on to the shallow reef south-west of the Shark's Fin, swung round and finished up with her stern almost touching the flat of the rock known as Kettle's Bottom.

The tug did not reach the casualty until almost an hour later, and though the wind had eased by then, the seas were still very confused and it was another hour and a half before a line was got across to the tanker's bows. The first attempt to tow her off was made shortly after 10.00.

Meantime, on the other side of England, at Colchester, where the Casualty Room at Lloyd's Intelligence Services kept a 24-hour watch, the Casualty Reporting Officer, informed by Land's End coastguards that the *Petros Jupiter* was on the rocks with two ruptured tanks spilling oil, began notifying all those organizations which took the service. This included, of course, the media, so that it was on the BBC 8 o'clock news and all subsequent broadcasts. Information about the casualty was also transmitted by telex from the Communications Room on the same floor direct to the Lloyd's of London building in the City for posting on the Board, so that underwriters entering the Room for the start of business after the New Year's Day holiday would see it there.

The lead underwriter for the *Petros Jupiter* cover was Michael Stewart. He headed three of the top marine insurance syndicates, a position he had inherited on the death of his father just over a year ago. He was still relatively young, only just turned fifty, but he had a good track record and was generally regarded as having his father's underwriting flair. He heard the news on the radio and immediately phoned his Claims Manager. Holiday or no holiday, he was anxious to get things moving – the Salvage Association in particular.

Michael Stewart's syndicates were not deeply

involved in the *Petros Jupiter*, for though he had agreed to continue the cover following the change of ownership in 1975, he had increased the extent of the re-insurance. But it was still his responsibility as the lead underwriter and it looked as though this was going to be the second casualty in two months with which his name would be associated.

The first had been the *Aurora B*, a 120,000-ton tanker belonging to GODCO. She had simply disappeared somewhere off Ceylon. Gulf Oil Development Company vessels had always been operated at such a high standard, and had always had such an outstanding record, that his father had allocated to his most favoured syndicate a greater proportion of the total premium, and consequently a greater proportion of the liability, than was normal. His son had seen no reason to change the practice. The GODCO policies had an excess of £500,000 to be met by the Company and, as a result, Syndicate OX71 had done very well out of this line of underwriting over the years.

In the case of the *Aurora B*, it wasn't just one syndicate that was heavily involved. In dealing with the re-insurance that spread OX71's liability round the market, he had allocated a larger than normal percentage to his two other syndicates. The *Petros Jupiter*, on the other hand, was no longer a GODCO vessel. But though he could comfort himself that at least he had had the sense to reduce his syndicates' involvement, it was still basically a GODCO policy and he was still the lead underwriter.

The loss was thus a blow to his pride, as well as

to his pocket, for there was nothing to indicate on that bank holiday morning that the stranding was anything other than an accident. It was just another disastrous tanker casualty that Lloyd's, and his own syndicates in particular, could have done without.

PART TWO

AFTERMATH OF A WRECK

CHAPTER ONE

Twelfth Night and it was after lunch, after the fog had lifted, that the first oil-sodden bodies began to come ashore. I had just left the rough board table where I did my writing and was out with spade and pick breaking up a little patch of new ground above the cottage. The air was cold and very still, a high hanging over us with the pressure close on 1040 and the sea lying like pewter against a white, opaque sky, no horizon and the remains of a westerly swell barely creaming the base of the Brisons.

From the new ground, where I was planning to grow sorrel and lamb's lettuce, possibly some bush tomatoes close under the rocks that sheltered it, I looked straight down on to the sloping roof of our cottage, and beyond it, beyond the rock outcrop that looked like the head of an elephant, the grey granite tower of the Longships lighthouse was just beginning to emerge, a dim, blurred finger still wreathed in mist.

And almost alongside it, that bloody tanker looking like a ghost ship, the fog still swirling about it.

I stopped digging and lit my pipe, thinking once again about how it must have been up on the tanker's bridge that night almost a week ago when the gale had stranded her on Kettle's Bottom. A faint breeze stirred the peat smoke of our cottage chimney and the fog rolled back from the Longships so that the wreck, the rocks that held her pinned at the stern and all the attendant ships were suddenly revealed in startling clarity against the white miasma glimmering now in pale sunlight. The *Petros Jupiter* was all of three miles away, but in that strange watery brightness every detail of her seemed magnified, so that even at that distance I could identify the salvage equipment littering her deck, the pumps, compressors, hose and coils of rope and wire.

Incredibly, because of the unseasonable quietness of the weather during the days following the gale, she was still intact and, except that she was down by the stern and her after deck almost awash, she might have been anchored there. All this side of the wreck the sea was a flat oily brown. I left my spade and went up to the knoll above the elephant head rock. When I had been out to the wreck on the Friday the spillage had all been to seaward and I was hoping it would prove to be some trick of the iridescent light. But it wasn't. It was oil all right. Two anti-pollution vessels were spraying close inshore along Whitesand Bay and the slick ran in a long dirty line from the tanker right across the bay until it disappeared from sight below the cliffs on which I was standing.

Karen must have been looking at it, too. From the door of the cottage you could see straight down the rocky pathway to the little patch of sand wedged into the rocks of the gully where we kept our inflatable. The anguish of her cry cut the stillness. She was out of the door, searching wildly and calling to me: 'Trevor! Trevor!' She looked up to where I stood. 'D'you see it?'

'See what?' I called down to her, though I knew damn well what she'd seen.

She turned. 'There! On the sand.' Her voice was high like the screech of a gull. We had been expecting this for almost a week now. 'By that rock.' She was standing in the cold, watery sunlight, her left hand shading her eyes, her right stretched out, pointing down into the cove.

From where I stood I couldn't see it, the little cove blocked from my view by the top of the elephant rock.

'I can see it moving.' She had turned, looking up at me again, the smooth rounded beauty of her face shattered by the violence of her emotions – a fishergirl's face, I had described it in a magazine piece, with the high-necked fisherman's jersey she wore in winter and the blue scarf tied in a bandeau round her head. And then she was running, her feet flying on the grass slope to the path.

'Careful!' I shouted. She was a big girl and running

like that, at such a crazy pace, I was afraid she'd go flying head first down among the rocks.

But it was no good. She took no notice. She never did. Once her emotions took charge, nothing stopped her. The cottage, the birds, everything – our whole way of life, it was all hers. She was so impossibly lovable, so damnably difficult, and now I was running after her, and it seemed to me, in exasperation, I'd always been adapting myself, excusing myself, ever since she'd faced me, holding on to the handlebars of her bike, eyes wide and spitting like a cat. That had been at the back end of Swansea docks, our first meeting, and a gang of teenagers using a puppy for a football. They'd broken its back and instead of going after them, I'd got hold of the jerking little rag of a body and put it out of its misery with a hand chop to the back of its neck. The teenagers were Arab, and she had thought I was one of them.

Now, as I joined her on the little V-shaped patch of sand, she was in the same sort of mood. 'Look at it!' She thrust the feebly flapping bird at me. Her hands were wet and covered with oil, her dark brown eyes gone almost black with anger.

The bird lifted its head, squirming and opening its beak. It was a razorbill, but only recognizable by the strangely bulbous shape of its beak. The beautiful black and white plumage was coated with a thick film of heavy, black oil. No sound came and its movements were so feeble that it was almost certainly near the point of death.

'How many more?' Her voice trembled on the edge

of hysteria. 'Last time – remember? November it was. The night we had that bonfire on the beach. Mrs Treherne's little boy found it flapping in the shallows, and the very next day they began coming ashore.' Her breath smoked in the cold air, her eyes wide and very bright. 'Dead birds, dead fish – I can't take it.' Her lips were trembling, tears of anger and frustration starting. 'Spilling their filthy oil, ruining our lives, every-thing . . . I can't take it. I won't take it.' And then, gripping hold of me, holding my arm so tight I could feel her fingernails through the thick sweater, 'We've got to do something, fight back . . .'

'I'm doing what I can, Karen.' I said it gently, keeping a tight hold on myself, but she thought I was on the defensive.

'Talk, talk, talk, nothing but talk. That silly little committee of yours—'

'There's an Under-Secretary coming with our MP this evening. I told you, be patient. It's a big meeting. The press and the media, too. We're trying for the same rules and sea routes that the French established after the *Amoco Cadiz*, and tonight . . .'

'Tonight he'll say yes; tomorrow, at Westminster, he'll have forgotten all about it.' She said it bitingly, her eyes contemptuous. She looked down at the razorbill. 'Remember that first time? And last March, how many was it we took into the cleansing station – twenty-seven? All those people working for hours. Three hours to clean each bird. And they all died, every one of them.' The bird lay passive now, no longer struggling. 'We've got to stop them – do something – make them realize.'

'Do what?' I asked. 'What can we do that we're not doing?'

'Bomb that bloody ship, set the oil ablaze. Destroy it. That's what. Make the government act. And if the government won't do it, then do it our bloody selves.'

'But I've told you . . .' It was ridiculous, arguing there in that tiny cove with the waves lapping at our feet and Karen still clutching that limp bundle of oil-soaked feathers. I had told her before that it wouldn't work. The experts had said it wouldn't, that the effect would be to produce an even worse *mousse*, a thick mess of black, long-lasting globules of tar, big as cow pats. But she wouldn't listen.

'Just do something,' she screamed at me. 'Or are you afraid?'

'Of what?' My voice had risen, the lilt that was always there increasing – I could hear it. 'Why should I be afraid?'

But she backed away from that, her eyes wide, sensing the violence of my reaction if she put it into words. Only I knew, we both knew, what had been on the tip of her tongue. Once the blood's mixed it can always be thrown in your face. And the sensitivity, the stupid bloody helpless sensitivity . . . 'You want me to do something . . .' I said it slowly, keeping a tight hold on myself. 'But what? I'm not Cornish, you know. Indeed, to the local people we're both of us foreigners. So what is it you want? What do you expect me to do?'

She shook her head quickly. 'No good asking me. Work it out for yourself.' She was staring at me then as though she hated me. I could see it in her eyes. They were blazing as she said, 'This is a man's job.' And then, standing there, the bird held in her two hands and spitting the words out – 'But I'll tell you this, Trev, if I were a man . . .'

'Go on,' I said, for she had suddenly stopped. 'If you were a man you'd do what?'

'Set fire to it myself.' Her teeth were gritted. 'I'd do something . . .'

'And how do you set fire to an oil slick? Use a box of matches like you'd light a fire, or a torch of newspapers? Oil doesn't burn that easily, not crude mixed with sea water.'

'Of course it doesn't. I'm not that stupid. But there are other things, that old paraffin flame-thrower thing Jimmy Kerrison was using a few years back to burn the weeds off his drive. Don't tell me that wouldn't set the stuff alight. Or a bomb, like that man Hals in Africa – that got results.'

'It got him the sack.'

'But he forced them to act, didn't he? And that American, flying his own slick patrol. All over the world there are people fighting back. If you won't do anything . . .'

'Oh, for God's sake.' I didn't take her seriously and suddenly she seemed to give up, standing there very still with a frozen look on her face. 'Perhaps it's my fault,' she breathed. 'I shouldn't have persuaded you—' She was gazing seaward. 'Tourists seemed the

21

only pollution we had to fear. I never thought of oil. Oh yes, I know you warned me. But it was all so clean, so perfect – so very, very beautiful. Something I'd always dreamed of, brought up in Swansea, amongst all the squalor—' She was staring down at the bird. 'Here, you take it.' She thrust it into my hands so violently that its muscles contracted in an effort to beat its wings and it turned its head and stabbed at my hand with its powerful beak. 'I'm going up to the cottage. I'm going to bed. And I'm going to stay in bed until that slick's dispersed. I don't want to see it. I don't want to know about it. This time I'm going to pretend it isn't there. And when it's gone, when you've stirred yourself out of your lethargy and done something about it—'

'I've told you, I'm doing what I can. All of us, we're all doing everything—'

'Balls! You're in love with the sound of your own voices, you and Jimmy and that fellow Wilkins. A visit from a junior minister and you're over the moon, so full of your own importance you forget—'

'Shut up!'

'I won't shut up. I'm telling you the truth for once.'

We were shouting at each other and I was so angry I could have hit her. The bird was struggling and I took hold of its neck and wrung it. Anything to stop her yelling and put the wretched thing out of its misery, but my hands slipped on the oil and I botched it, so that I had to finish it off by slamming its head against a rock.

She flew at me then, shouting at me to stop, and I

had to hold her off. I held her off until the bird was dead and then I flung the mangled corpse of it back into the sea. 'Now go to bed,' I told her. 'Bury your head in the sand and don't come out until it's all over and the slick gone.'

She didn't move for a moment, standing there, staring at me as though seeing me for the first time. 'You bastard!' she said quietly. 'I'll show you.' And she turned and walked slowly off up the path, back to the cottage.

I stayed there for a moment, thinking back over all that had been said, wishing I could have handled it differently. But it had been building for several days now, ever since the *Petros Jupiter* had stranded within sight of our home. I was out of understanding, totally exhausted by her emotional behaviour and her refusal to accept that everything was being done that could be done. She was so impractical. She knew about ships. She'd been brought up with them, her father a crane driver in the docks, but she'd never understood the sea, how cruel it could be – not until she had come to live here.

My gaze lifted from the lifeless razorbill sloshing back and forth like an oily rag in the suck and thrust of the wavelets to the edge of the slick, pushing a dirty brown tongue round the rocks that hid the tanker from view. Something moved in the film of oil, a wing flapping. I turned away in disgust, climbing the path slowly, but not to the cottage. I struck away to the right, across the knoll above the elephant rock, striding out furiously as I reached the top.

I was cursing under my breath – not at Karen, not entirely, but at the whole sodding bloody mess, the way our idyll of a simple life was breaking up under the pressure of outside events. I could remember so clearly the day we had first seen Balkaer snugged into the grass and wild flowers and rocks above the cove, so remote, so peaceful on that still, sunny day in early spring two years ago. Doubtless that was why it was being offered at such a reasonable price. For a quick sale, they had said, but it was really the lack of any amenities. Who wants a cottage perched on an exposed coast with no services and the nearest track for vehicles over 500 metres away? Only people like ourselves. Karen from the dust and polyglot overcrowding of a Welsh port, and me with my earliest memories of a tiny hospital on the edge of the desert. For us that Atlantic coast, its soft salt air, the solitude of the cottage perched above the cove, it was all irresistible. We had put our deposit down that afternoon, moved in a week later, and for almost a year we had been sublimely happy. The tourists hadn't bothered us as much as we had feared, I had sold several magazine pieces and had started on a book, *Mate of the Balkaer*. And then, at the tail end of a March gale, the first oil had come ashore and we had spent hours clearing up the beach.

That was when I discovered how unreasonable Karen could be, how taut her nerves were under that beautiful, smooth, rain-soft skin. The birds that came ashore that first time were all dead and whenever she found one she'd hold it out to me in mute accusation. Perhaps she didn't mean it that way, but that's how it had seemed to me. And though she said she remembered my warning, I doubt if she really remembered what I had told her that day when we had stood in the cottage doorway and decided Balkaer was what we wanted. Three years tramping round the world, then two on the Gulf-Karachi-Bombay run; I knew the sort of men who manned the smaller, older vessels. There'll be engineers, I had told her, who'll pump the bilges out whatever the regulations, tanker skippers who'll turn a blind eye to tank cleansing at sea, even order it, and sooner or later Cornwall will have another oil spillage disaster like the *Torrey Canyon*. But she was happy, dreaming dreams. She hadn't been listening, she hadn't really taken it in. And then, when it happened . . .

I had slowed my pace, staring ahead beyond the white sand sweep of the bay, beyond the road slanting down to Sennen and its cluster of houses, to Land's End and the rocks off, and that tanker sitting there, stern-on to the rocks and leaking oil. The slick now stretched in a great smooth, brown, greasy layer right across the bay, the spraying vessels moving through it with scarcely a ripple like two water beetles. I was thinking back to the other spillages then. The first one hadn't been too bad, a minor slick that had stayed offshore. But the second, which had happened sometime in the early hours of the morning, had been very different – bigger, longer-lasting, heavy, black glutinous oil that stuck to the rocks like glue, and because it was spring and the start of the breeding season many more birds had been involved. A shift of wind had brought them ashore, some of them still very much alive so that we had spent time and money getting them to the cleansing centre.

Now, here, staring me in the face, was the thing I had dreaded. I wondered how much of her cargo they had managed to pump out. Three small tankers festooned with fenders had been working in relays to lighten her all through the quiet weather period. Doubtless they'd tell us at the meeting tonight. But the glass had started to fall and now that the sky was visible I could see mares' tails showing high up to the south-west. If it started to blow ... I stopped and stared back along the coast to Cape Cornwall and beyond. In the stillness and the cold slanting sunlight it all looked green and fresh, everything washed clean as though waiting for the spring. But for us it wouldn't be a spring like our first spring. If it were going to blow and she broke up, if the *Petros Jupiter* split open, spilling the rest of her oil, all that lovely shoreline would be polluted, the marine life killed off and birds that should be nesting coming ashore again as oil-sodden bundles. It would drive Karen out of her mind.

Bloody stupid, incompetent bastard! I was thinking of the master, risking a ship like that so close to Land's End just for the sake of a few miles and a tiny saving in bunker fuel. Or had it been deliberate? First the boiler out of action, then the secondary reduction gear stripped. If it wasn't an accident, then the chief engineer would have to be in on it – one of the engin-eers, anyway. Would any man in his senses deliberately cause a tanker breakdown close off such a notorious headland? But then if the money was right . . .

I shrugged. No doubt the Enquiry would produce the answer and we'd probably be told tonight when it would be held.

I walked as far as Sennen, where I had a word with Andy Trevose, the lifeboat's relief cox'n. One of the salvage boys had told him in the pub that if the weather held there was a chance they'd float the *Petros Jupiter* off on Monday's tide. Apparently she'd been given enough buoyancy for'ard to lift most of her hull clear of the rocks. Only her stern remained fast on Kettle's Bottom. He also told me there was a rumour the second engineer had jumped a foreign trawler off Porthcurno and disappeared.

The sun had set by the time I got back to Balkaer, night closing in and the mares' tails gone, the sky clear again and beginning to turn that translucent green that indicates cold. The door was on the latch, but Karen wasn't there. I thought at first she had gone up to see old Mrs Peever. She did that sometimes when she was upset about something. Or Jean Kerrison perhaps. Jean was more her own age and they got on well enough. It would have been natural considering what had happened and the mood she was in.

It wasn't until I went out to the stone cleit I'd built above the path to get peat to bank up the fire that I thought of looking down into the cove. I saw her then, out in the rubber dinghy. She was paddling it along the edge of the slick, not using the outboard, though she had it mounted. I called to her and she looked up, but she didn't wave. I thought she was out there to pick up any live birds caught in the slick and I went back into the cottage, banked up the fire and got my things. The meeting was at six in Penzance and Jimmy had said he would pick me up at the bottom of the lane at five-fifteen.

I called to her again as I left, but she didn't answer. The light was fading as I went off up the path to the lane, but I wasn't worried about her. She knew how to handle the inflatable and, like me, she enjoyed being on her own sometimes. It's not easy when people are cooped up in a lonely little Cornish tin-miner's cottage in winter. You tend to get on each other's nerves, however much you're in love. Even so, if it hadn't been for that bloody tanker . . . But Karen would get over it. They'd get the tanker off and then, when the spring came – everything would look different in the spring.

So I comforted myself. I was really quite cheerful as I approached the lane, the black mood dissipated by the walk to Sennen. It would be the same for Karen, I thought. I didn't realize how her emotions had been working on her imagination this past week, what depths of passion and desperation had been building up inside her.

Jimmy was already waiting for me in his battered blue van and I didn't think any more about her as we drove across the moor to Penzance. He farmed a few acres, pigs and chickens mainly, but mostly he made his living out of the tourists, renting two cottages he owned in Sennen, so that he had a vested interest in the coastal environment.

The meeting, which was in the Town Hall, proved to be a much bigger affair than anything Wilkins, the secretary of our Preservation Society, had so far been able to organize locally. Just about every organization involved was represented, and since it was open to the public the place was packed. The local MP was in the chair and the chief speaker was the Under-Secretary for the Marine Division of the Department of Trade whose theme, of course, was that everything was being done that could be done. He pointed out that his own emergency information room, his Ops Room, which was on the top floor of the Marine Division's HQ in Holborn, had been activated and continuously manned since January 1, the day the *Petros Jupiter* had been stranded. The local anti-pollution plan had been put into operation immediately, including the setting up of a pollution operation control room at Land's End; the oil company involved had had tankers and pumps available for transferring cargo within fourteen hours; and the owners and Lloyd's had had salvage teams, ships and equipment on the spot the following day. Of the 57,000 tons of crude oil carried in the ship's tanks, 39,000 had already been pumped out. It was estimated that no more than 9,000 tons had leaked into the sea and this was being dissipated by spraying from the ships everyone could see from Land's End. 'With luck the salvage operators hope to have the *Petros Jupiter* off the rocks tomorrow or the day after.'

Andy Trevose, a few feet in front of me and talking to another Sennen Cove fisherman, suddenly got to his feet. 'Tedn't laikly th'all get 'er off'n tamorrer.'

'The salvage operators assure me—'

'Then th'are kidding themsel', an' thee – t'll be blawing tamorrer, d'you see.'

'Have it your own way,' the Under-Secretary said mildly. 'I'm not an authority on local weather and I can only repeat what the salvage operators have told me. They are optimistic – very optimistic – of getting the ship off on tomorrow's tide.' And on that he sat down.

His speech, which had lasted almost half an hour, was followed by a question and answer session. Here he was at his best, combining an air of authority with a touch of humour that had the effect of softening his slightly offhand manner and making him more human. Yes, he thought the Minister would be giving close consideration to the setting up of some sort of committee to reconsider the question of tanker routes in the sea area between the Scillies and Land's End. This in answer to a question by the representative of the International Tanker Owners' Pollution Federation. Both Nature Conservancy and the local representatives of the inshore fishermen pressed him hard on this point, but all he would say was, 'I will convey your observations to the Minister.'

Nobody seemed to think this was good enough. The demand was for a tightening of regulations in the waters between Land's End and the Scillies, and regular patrols to ensure that tankers and other bulk carriers of dangerous cargoes reported in as they had to on the French side off Ushant. And, similarly, they wanted them routed outside the Scillies. The Under-

Secretary said, of course, it would take time, that there were a great number of interests to be considered, as well as the whole legal question of the freedom of the seas. At this point he was shouted down, first by local fishermen and their wives, then by some of the coastal farmers; finally a group of boarding house operators led by Jimmy joined in. There was so much noise for a time that even the local MP couldn't get a hearing.

In the end the Under-Secretary departed with nothing settled, only his promise that he would convey the feelings of the meeting most forcefully. It was by then almost eight-thirty. Jimmy and I, and several others from the Whitesand area, talked it over in the bar of a nearby pub. Most of us felt nothing had been achieved. Andy Trevose said he reckoned nothing would be done until we got a disaster as big as the *Amoco Cadiz*. 'An' tedn't no use pretending – tha'll put paid to the inshaaw fishing for a generation.' And he went off to phone his wife.

When he returned we had another round, and then Jimmy and I left. It was very still by then with wisps of sea fog trailing up from the direction of the harbour. 'Looks like the man from London could be right.' Jimmy was crouched over the wheel, straining to see the road. 'If this weather holds they've a good chance of getting her off.' The mist was thick on the moor, but when we reached his house the barometer was already falling. It was as we were standing there, staring at it, that Jean handed me a printed card. 'Give that to Karen, will you? I said I'd try and find it for her, but it's so long since we used it . . .'

'Used what?' I asked.

'That flame weedkiller. But it's very simple and I told her how it worked.'

'You told her—' I was staring down at the instructions card, my mind suddenly alerted, seeing Karen out in the cove and remembering there had been something beside her in the dinghy, something with a bell-shaped end like a blunderbuss resting on the bows. It must have been the flame guard, but the light was so dim by then I hadn't been able to see it clearly. 'When was this? When did she borrow it from you?'

'This afternoon. She was up here . . . Oh, it would have been about three – well before tea anyway.'

'God Almighty!' I breathed. 'You gave her that thing?'

'It's all right,' she added quietly. 'I explained it all to her, how to pressurize the tank and get the flame ignited. I even lent her a pump and some meths.'

'She didn't say why she wanted it?'

'No.'

'You didn't ask her?'

'Why should I? It's for burning off weeds.'

I turned to Jimmy then and asked him to drive me down to the end of the lane, and when we got there he insisted on coming down the path with me to the cottage. The mist had thickened, a blank wall of vapour blocking the beam of my torch. 'What are you worried about?' he asked. 'She wouldn't be fooling about with it at this time of night.'

'She didn't want it for weeds,' I said.

'What then?'

'That oil slick.'

'Oh, I see.' He laughed. 'Well, you can relax. Even if she did get it going it wouldn't do much good. That's pretty heavy stuff that slick.'

The cottage loomed, a darker grey in the fog. No sign of a light. The door was locked and I was shouting for Karen before I had even got it open. But there was no answer. The cottage was still and dead, wrapped in the fog, and only the faintest glow from the peat fire in the big chimney place. 'Karen! Karen!' I searched quickly. There was nobody there. Then I was running, stumbling through the fog, down into the cove. The little stone boathouse was empty, the door hanging open and no sign of the inflatable anywhere on the sands, only the marks where she had dragged it into the water.

I stood stock still for a moment, my heart hammering and trying to think, trying to prove to myself that what I feared couldn't be, that she couldn't be such a fool. But I knew she could. The fog swirled to a breath of wind and I turned, the path and the cottage suddenly clear in the long-throwing beam of my torch. Andy Trevose! That would be the quickest. Drive to Sennen and get Andy to take me out in his boat. I called to Jimmy, climbing the path in long strides, not bothering to lock the cottage, heading for the van, and behind me Jimmy said, 'You think she's going to use that flame-thrower on the slick?'

'Yes,' I panted.

'But I told you, that stuff's too heavy—'

'The ship then – something. She wanted to make

a gesture, blow the thing up. I'm afraid she'll hurt herself.'

We reached the van. 'Sennen?' he asked as he started the engine.

'Yes, Andy Trevose.' He should be back by the time we got there.

'She's probably stranded on the sand somewhere. If the outboard broke down . . . Shall I stop for Jean?'

'No. Hurry.'

But he stopped all the same, to tell her where we were going, and then we were feeling our way up on to the Sennen road, with the mist closed down and getting thicker. It seemed an age, both of us peering into the murk and the refracted beam of the headlights, but at last we were down by the hard and pulling up at the Trevose cottage near the lifeboat station. Andy was back and he had his oilskins on. 'Seen your wife?' he asked. 'Is Karen home?'

'No.'

'She was here,' he said. And his wife, behind him, added, 'Karen came up from the quay abaht eight-thirty, asked me what Andy thawt would be the result of the meeting, and when Ah told her he'd promised to phone she asked to stay. She was that urgent to knaw what happened.'

'And when you told her, what did she say?'

'Nothing much. She'd been very withdrawn, all the taime we were waiting. Very edgy-laike, knaw what I mean. And then, when Ah tauld her nothing had been decaided, she laughed. I knew it, she says, the laugh a little wild and her voice a bit high laike. Very white, she was. Very tuned-up – laike she wanted to scream but was managing to throttle it back.' She gave a big, full-breasted shrug. 'Tha's all. She went out then.'

'She didn't say where she was going?'

'No. The only thing she said was, *Ah'll show 'em*. At least, Ah think that was it. She was muttering to herself as she flung out of the door. I ran after her, but the mist had thickened and she was already gawn.'

'Rose thinks she'd be off to the ship', Andy said, and his wife nodded. 'Tha's right. Ah don't know why, but tha's what Ah think.'

And Andy Trevose in oilskins and sea boots. 'You were going to take your boat out,' I said. 'You were going to look for her?'

'Aye, but not my boat. The ILB, I think.'

I thanked him, glad I didn't have to waste time trying to convince him of the urgency of it. 'You'll need oilskins,' he said as we started down towards the lifeboat station, a single street light shining dimly and a cold breeze swirling the mist over the roofs of the cottages. Away to the south-west the Longships' explosive fog signal banged twice and far away I could just hear the moaning of the Seven Stones' diaphone. 'Rack'n we'll take the inshore boat,' he said. 'Tha'll be quicker.' He had the key of the lifeboat house and after issuing Jimmy and myself with lifejackets, oilskins and seaboots, he motioned us to take the stern of the high speed rubber boat and the three of us dragged it out and ran it down into the water.

Visibility was virtually nil as we went out from under the stone breakwater on a compass bearing,

Andy crouched in the stern over the big outboard, Jimmy and I in the bows. I have only a vague recollection of the passage out, my mind concentrated on Karen, trying to visualize what she was doing, where she would have got to by now. Maybe Jimmy was right. Maybe she was just lost in the fog. But the double bang from the Longships light made it seem unlikely. Andy hadn't thought she was lost. He'd put on his oilskins as soon as Rose had told him, prepared to go out after her alone. I could just see him, a dark shadow in the stern leaning forward away from the engine, a VHF handset to his ear.

Through The Tribbens it was only about a mile and a half from Sennen to Kettle's Bottom, and before we had gone half that distance the five minute fog signal from the Longships was audible even above the roar of the outboard. Another ten minutes and Andy was throttling back, listening out on his walkie-talkie. 'Tha's one of the tugs. Rack'ns he's seen a laight by the starn o' that tanker. Farg cawms an' goes, he says. He's got a searchlight trained on 'er an' he'll keep it so till we get thar.'

He opened up the throttle again and we bounced across what appeared to be a small tide rip. The tide would be ebbing now, pulling us down towards the rocks. There was movement in the fog, an iridescent glimmer of light. The light was there for a moment, then it was gone, the fog closed up again.

'Getting close now,' Andy shouted, leaning forward and passing me the big torch. 'As soon as 'ee see the wreck—' He shouted a warning and swung the boat over in a hard turn. The slop of wavelets running over rocks slid by to port, just visible in the beam of the torch. The fog signal on the Longships cracked out, sharp and very clear, and in the same instant the land-ward-facing fixed red peered at us through thinning mist like some demented Cyclops, and to the right of it the shadowy shape of the stranded tanker showed black in silhouette against the brightening beam of a searchlight.

I don't know how far away the wreck was – four, five hundred yards, three cables perhaps. But it was near enough for me to see that all the huge length of her was clear of the water, save for the stern, which was right against the rocks and sunk so low that the deck was awash. It was only a few seconds that we saw her clearly, then the fog closed in again. But it was still long enough for me to see a rubber boat snugged against the after rail and a figure moving along the sloping deck pinpointed by a flickering light.

I shouted. But at that distance and with the engine running . . . what the hell did she think she was doing? It had to be her. Nobody else would be out to the wreck in a fog like this. I turned to Andy. 'Did you get a bearing?' I screamed at him.

He nodded. ''Bout three-one-O. We're in among the rocks.' He had cut the engine right down, manoeuvring slowly. 'Gi' us some laight.' I switched on the torch again, swinging the beam of it in a wide arc. Ripples everywhere, the white of little waves breaking as the tide ripped the shallows.

'Was that a torch she had?' Jimmy asked. But he

knew it wasn't. There had been no beam and a faint, flickering light like that, it could only be that damned flame-thrower. The beam from the tug's searchlight was growing, the fog like a luminous curtain getting brighter all the time. Then suddenly it was swept away completely and we had a clear view of the tanker again, a little nearer now, her decks deserted, no sign of anyone. Had I dreamed it, that figure with the ghostly flame? But then I saw her, coming out from the shadow of the superstructure, a small shape high up the sloping deck and holding out ahead of her that tiny flame of light.

There was an open hatch and my eyes, staring through the cold humidity of the atmosphere, were beginning to water. It had to be a hatch, the entry hatch to one of the fuel tanks, and a void opened up inside me, my breath held and my body trembling. Oh God, no! And nothing I could do, no way I could stop her. I saw her reach it and she paused, crouched down on the deck. 'She's pumping,' Jimmy breathed. 'She's pumping up the pressure, building up the flame.'

She stood up, the flame much brighter as she pushed it forward. That's what I shall never forget, that I could see her pushing that flame towards the hatch and nothing I could do to stop her. I may have screamed. I don't know. We were too far away, the engine roaring, and nothing I could do, nothing. I could see her, but I couldn't stop her. The mist closed in and I sat there, my mouth open, dumb and appalled, waiting.

And then, as the silhouette of the tanker faded to

a shadow, it came – a great whoosh of flame burning the fog to a blazing incandescent fire that shot upwards with a terrible roaring sound.

The engine was idling again and we sat there, stunned and in a state of shock as the heat of it hit us through the fog glare. And the noise – it was a roar like a thousand trains going through a tunnel, a great eruption of sound.

I remember Jimmy suddenly yelling, 'It's gone. The whole bloody ship's gone, my God!' And Andy muttering close behind me, 'Tha'll show 'em, arl raight, poor gal.' His hand gripped my arm, a touch of sympathy. 'She'll be remembered a long taime for this.'

I didn't move. I didn't say anything. I was thinking of Karen, wondering if she'd really known what she was doing, what the result would be. But she must have. She must have known. Oil and air, the fumes an explosive mixture. She wasn't a fool. She'd known. Christ! And I'd let her go. I'd seen her, down there in the cove in the dim evening light, the flame-thrower there, in the bows, and I'd waved to her, and gone off up the path to that useless meeting.

The heat was burning up the fog now. I could see the bright white heart of the fire and the great billowing cloud of smoke rising like a volcanic eruption. I couldn't see the wreck, only the rocks of the Kettle's Bottom all red with the glare. Either it was sunk or else the smoke and flames had engulfed it completely. The effect was terrifying, the thunderous roar, the whole appalling conflagration seeming to burst up from the surface of the sea as though fuelled by some

underwater vent. Lightning flashed in the smoke and
I sat there, thinking of Karen, trying to imagine . . . I
think I must have been crying, for my eyes became
crusted with salt and I could feel my mouth trembling.
But the intensity of the heat burned up my tears, so
that I stared, dry-eyed, at the pyre she had made for
herself.

I should have known. After three years – God! I
should have known. And we'd been here almost two
– two years living in expectation, waiting for just such
a catastrophe.

The heat was scorching my face and there was
wind. Jimmy's hand gripped my arm. 'Hold it!' he said
urgently. 'Nothing you can do.' I realized then that I
had been struggling to my feet. 'Nothing at all.' His
face was close to mine. 'Not now. Just sit there . . .'

Just sit, do nothing. The tanker blazing and Karen's
body – her lovely, soft body burned to nothing. Had
it been quick? An explosion like that, such a holocaust
of flame – she wouldn't have known? Surely to God it
wouldn't have hurt? I tried to imagine myself there
beside her when it happened, but it was no use – my
mind couldn't grasp what it would have been like,
what the impact of it would have been on flesh and
bone. The nerves . . . it would have been her nerves
that took the full shock of it, reacting like a seismo-
graph, shrieking information to the brain in that split
second of exploding flames.

My head was turned, still facing the lurid heat-
glow. But it was over the stern now. Andy had swung
the inflatable away from it. The wind was growing,

whipping the surface of the water to spray, and it was cold – cold air being sucked in by the rising heat of the flames.

I don't know what happened after that, my mind seemed to blank out, so that I wasn't conscious of anything until we were inside the Sennen breakwater and carrying the ILB up to the boathouse. The sea mist was almost gone, torn to shreds, and out where the ship had been there was nothing but billowing smoke lit by a red internal glow. The fog signal on the Longships banged again, the red light glaring fixedly. Somebody was talking to me, asking questions, and I became aware of a small crowd gathering. There was a police car there and a young helicopter pilot I knew.

'It was your wife, was it, sir – the young woman they saw went out to blow up the ship? Can you give me her name please, her full name . . .' And another voice, a camera reporter from one of the TV companies that had been waiting to film the ship being hauled off the rocks, said, 'What the hell did she do it for, going out to a wrecked oil tanker with a thing like a miniature flame-thrower? Did she want to kill herself?'

His eager, hungry little eyes stared up at me, the camera cradled on his arm. I could sense his excitement. 'Did you see her? Was she really out there?' And then, as I told him to go to hell, he stepped back, the camera raised, and his mate switched a spotlight on, suddenly blinding me. 'Just tell it to us in your own words, Mr Rodin. Why did she do it?'

I started towards him, but Andy stopped me. I

thought better of it then. At least it was a chance to tell people . . . 'Are you recording this?' I asked him.

'Yes. You tell us. Now.' And I heard the whirr of the camera. So I told them – I told them what the quiet and beauty of Balkaer had meant to Karen, to us both – and how cheap flag-of-convenience ships, badly officered, badly equipped, were destroying the coastline, ruining everybody's lives. 'And that tanker spilling oil. Nothing came of the meeting tonight, only an assurance they'd get her off tomorrow. But Karen knew . . . she knew the pressure was falling and a storm due. She knew they'd do nothing, so she . . .' I heard the hesitation in my voice – 'so she must have made up her mind—' I couldn't go on, my voice caught on a sob, my words unintelligible. 'She just – decided – she'd do it herself. Set the slick alight. Nobody was going to do anything, so she'd—' I was conscious of the silence around me, everybody hanging on my words, the camera whirring. 'That's all,' I muttered. 'She didn't realize – she didn't mean to kill herself – only to save the coast and the seabirds.' I heard him say 'Cut' and the camera stopped.

'Thanks,' he said. 'You'll wring a lot of hearts with that stuff. Pity your wife isn't here too.' He gave my arm a quick pat. 'Sorry. Terrible shock for you. But thanks. Thanks a lot.'

I shook my head, feeling dazed, the world going on around me and myself not part of it. The camera crew were packing up. The police officer was at my elbow again, asking more questions, writing it down.

'You say she didn't mean to blow the ship up and herself with it?'

I turned my head, seeing his eyes blue like gemstones in the beam of a car's headlights. 'She was killed,' I said dully. 'It was accidental.'

It didn't mean anything to me now. It was as though talking to the camera had got the shock of it out of my system for the moment.

'She loved life,' I told him. 'Why should she want to kill herself? She went out there with only one thought, to burn up that oil slick.'

He took it all down, then he read the statement back to me and I signed it, resting the paper on the warm bonnet of the police car. After that I was able to get away, back to the Trevose cottage. I didn't go in, I just stood outside by the parked van. I wanted to get away, to be with Karen – back to the cottage, to the memories . . . all I'd got left.

Jimmy says I didn't utter a word all the way back, except to ask him to drive me straight down to the bottom of the lane. He wanted me to stay the night with them, of course, but I wouldn't. 'I'll be all right.' I thanked him and got my torch out of the back. Then I was going down the path to Balkaer, alone now and on my own for the first time since it had happened.

The chickens stirred in their shed at my approach and in the dark cleft of the cove the suck and gurgle of waves lapping against the rocks came to me on an updraught of wind. There were no stars, the night dark and the sky overcast. It would be blowing from the sou'west by morning. The cottage door was unlocked, the peat fire glowing now in the wide chimney, the place warm and snug, but terribly empty, as though it knew she wouldn't be back.

I remember thinking – *it will always be empty like this now.* But there was movement on the far side, under the table. I lit the lamp and in its bright flame I saw five of the cardboard boxes they'd given us to carry the oil-soaked birds when driving them to the cleansing centre. It hit me then. It hit me so hard that I just sat down, a sort of strangled cry coming from inside me, tears falling. I was remembering that scene down in the cove with her holding the wretched bird out to me. If only her tongue could be scolding at me again. Anything rather than this deadly quiet.

And that night, lying alone in the big untidy bed, my eyes wide and staring into the dark, the loneliness of it unbearable. Without Karen what was there to life? She was all I had, all I'd ever had. She was this cottage, Balkaer, the life we'd been leading. It was her idea – the way we lived, everything. Without her it had no meaning. I was back to the nothingness of my existence before we met. Ever since I'd stowed away on that dhow in Dubai, got myself across to Gwadar and up to Peshawar by way of Quetta, ever since then I'd been tramping the world, living out of suitcases, owning nothing, belonging nowhere – no one belonging to me. Only Karen had ever belonged . . .

The wind was rising. In the end I couldn't stand it, lying there staring into the dark, listening to the wind and seeing her figure moving along the sloping deck of that tanker, the flickering flame held out in

front of her, and then the flash of the explosion, the
roaring holocaust that had followed. Poor darling!
Poor wonderful, adorable, emotional darling! If only
I'd gone down into the cove, instead of waving and
climbing the path and leaving her there. She must have
tried to ignite the slick with that garden flame-thrower
right after I had left. And when she'd failed, she'd
motored across the bay to Sennen to wait with Rose
to hear the result of the meeting.

I should have known. If I hadn't been so angry . . .
God! If – if – if . . . I flung off the bedclothes and got
the bottle of Armagnac I kept for emergencies at the
back of the kitchen cupboard. It was the last of
the bottles I had brought with me when I had finally
come ashore to become self-employed instead of a
salaried ship's officer. There wasn't much of it left, but
it was over the remains of that bottle, sitting in the
rocking chair with two oiled-up cormorants and three
razorbills in boxes under the table beside me, listening
to the roar of the wind outside, the crash of the rollers
in the cove below, sensing the movement of the stone
walls round me in the gusts, that I began to come to
terms with what had happened. Times like this we'd
have had each other – talking together, working
together, going to bed together, making love; one way
and another we'd always kept the gales at bay, locking
ourselves into our own little world and shutting out
the wind.

But now there was only myself. And with Karen
gone I was intensely conscious of every battering blast
of wind, so that the cottage seemed no longer a

protection, the wind entering it and the waves beating at its foundations. And my love out there by the Kettle's Bottom. Tomorrow or the next day, a week, a fortnight maybe, somewhere along the coast they'd find the charred remains of her floating in the sea, or smashed up on the rocks – and I'd be expected to identify her. Or would that rounded, full-breasted form have been reduced to ashes? If it had been cremated beyond recognition . . . I could see her still, sitting in the wing chair on the opposite side of the chimney piece. We had bought that chair in a gale, junk from a nearby homestead that had gone for nothing, no dealers there, and she had laboriously re-covered it with material from an old Welsh *cardden* that had belonged to her mother.

I could see her now, sitting there like a ghost with one hand propping her chin, the other holding a book, or sitting staring intently at the fire as I read aloud to her what I had written during the day. She was doing the typing for me, of course – she was a trained typist – but I think it was my reading to her that developed her interest in books. She had never been much of a reader before, but then she started borrowing from the travelling library, always wildlife books or stories about animals. Sometimes she would borrow a book about Wales, but mostly it was wildlife, and because much of what I was writing was about the birds and seals that visited our coast, she became in a sense my sounding box, our relationship deeper, more intimate, so that now, for the moment, I could still see her, sitting there in that empty chair.

That was really the start of it, that was when I saw the pattern of my life, how it all added up – so that what had been without purpose before suddenly became purposeful.

It's hard to explain, for in the hours I sat there, sleepless, with the noise of the front coming in out of the Atlantic steadily increasing, I went through several stages. I had already passed through shock and had reached the point of feeling sorry for myself when I came down seeking the comfort of the Armagnac. But then, as the fire of it gave me courage to face my loss and the loneliness that would follow, I came to feel that Karen wasn't dead, that she still existed, not in her own body but in mine – that she had become part of me.

It was a strange feeling, for my thinking immediately became different. It was as though death had opened the door for me so that life had a new meaning, a new dimension – all life, not just human life. I was beginning to think like her. I suddenly felt at one with the Greenpeace movement and all those people who had tried to stop the harp seal killers of Canada or to prevent the slaughter of the dolphins by the fishermen off Iki.

The world as I drank seemed to be shrieking aloud the cruelty of humans – not just to themselves, but to all living things. Greed, and a rage against nature. Karen was right. A rogue species. She'd read that somewhere. And about vested interests, too. There'd always be vested interests, always be reasons for not interfering, for allowing another species to be wiped out, for letting them cut down another rain forest, pollute another stretch of coast, another sea, an ocean even, with oil or nuclear waste. She'd seen it. Now I was seeing it. And I hadn't reasoned it out – it was just suddenly there in my mind, as though she had put it there.

A gust shook the walls, the wind tugging at the door and a sheet of spray lashing at the windows. The peat fire glowed and I saw her face in it, the long black hair let down and burning like a torch. Slumped in the old rocker, I relived the moment, the holocaust, confusing the peat-glow and seeing her body shrivel in the heat of it, and with that hallucinatory sight the anger that was there, deep inside me, boiled over, vengeance then my only thought. An eye for an eye, a life for a life. Somebody had put that bloody ship on the rocks, somebody had been responsible – for the pollution, for Karen's death.

Speridion? Another gust, the cottage trembling, and I spoke the name aloud. Aristides Speridion. And he'd got away in a boat. That's what the marine consultant, an oil pollution specialist from Cardiff, had said at the meeting, that the second engineer of the *Petros Jupiter* was missing and they'd traced him through a Penzance fisherman to a stolen dinghy and a Breton fishing boat. I'd hunt him down. I'd kill the bastard. The wind howled and I emptied my glass, hugging that thought to me.

A bloody little Greek – they were always Greek. I'd find him and I'd get the truth out of him, and if he was responsible, if he'd deliberately caused that damned tanker to go on the rocks . . .

Dawn was breaking as I finished the last of the bottle and began to dress. The razorbills were dead by then, only the cormorants still alive, and the room was very dark, a lot of noise. There always was a lot of noise with a gale blowing out of the west and a big sea running. Lloyd's! That was what was in my mind now as I shaved and dressed. With an insurance claim in, Lloyd's would know where the man had gone to earth if anybody did. Lloyd's of London – I'd phone them as soon as I had banked up the fire and got myself some breakfast.

CHAPTER TWO

I didn't bother to clear up, I just got my anorak, picked up the containers holding the two live cormorants and shouldered my way out into the gale. One night. One single night. A split moment of time, and now everything had changed, my whole life. Clear of the cottage the wind took hold, thrusting me up the path. It was blowing a good force 9 and I could hardly breathe, the collar of my anorak whipping against my chin with a harsh whirring sound, and the waves thundering below me, the cove a white maelstrom of broken water thrown back by the rocks.

It was quieter when I reached the lane, a grey, miserable morning with ragged wisps of cloud flying in the wind, the moors all hidden. A herring gull sailed past my head, a scrap of paper blown by the gale. She would have liked that – one bird at least without oil on its feathers.

The blue van was parked in the yard of the Kerrisons' place and I found Jimmy cleaning out the chicken roost at the back of the outbuildings. I handed him the cardboard containers holding the cormorants. 'The last thing she did,' I said.

'Okay, I'll see they get to the cleansing centre.'

'Can I use your phone?'

He nodded and took me through into the house. Jean called down to see if I was all right. The phone was at the foot of the stairs and she leaned over the banisters to ask if I could use a cup of coffee. I answered her automatically, trying to remember the departmental details given in Lloyd's Nautical Year Book. I didn't want underwriters or salvage experts; I wanted the people who dealt with fraudulent claims. But I couldn't remember what the section was called, only that it was located outside London.

By the time I had been through Directory Enquiries and Lloyd's of London switchboard I was sweating, my nerves on edge, tiredness coming in waves. Colchester, the girl said – Intelligence Services. And she gave me the number.

'You all right, Trevor?' It was Jean, looking anxious and holding a cup of coffee out to me.

'Yes, I'm all right.' There were beads of sweat on my forehead. 'It's very warm in here, nice and warm after being outside.'

'Come and sit down then. You can phone after you've had your coffee.'

'No. No thanks. I'll get this over, then I'll sit down for a moment.' I dialled the Colchester number, mopping the sweat from my forehead, and when I told the girl I was enquiring about the engineer of the

Petros Jupiter she put me through to a quiet, friendly-sounding voice: 'Ferrers, Special Enquiries Branch. Can I help you?' But as soon as I asked him whether it was negligence, or if the tanker had been put ashore deliberately, his manner changed. 'Have you any reason to suppose it was deliberate?'

'The engineer,' I said. 'A Greek named Speridion. He took a dinghy from Porthcurno. They say he was picked up by a Breton fishing boat.'

'It doesn't prove anything,' the voice said. 'A man who's been shipwrecked . . .' There was a pause, and then the inevitable question. 'May I know your interest in the matter? Are you representing anyone in particular?'

'No. Only myself.' I told him my name then and where I was speaking from, and he said 'Trevor Rodin', repeating it slowly. 'It was your wife . . .' The voice trailed away, embarrassed, and I heard him say, 'I'm sorry.' After that there was a long silence. And when I asked him for information about the engineer, where he lived, or where the fishing boat had taken him, he said, 'I can't answer that. There's nothing through yet. Why not try the police, or maybe the solicitors . . .' He hesitated, 'May I have your address please?'

I gave it to him, also the Kerrisons' telephone number. 'Could you ring me here if it turns out to be a scuttling job?'

'What makes you think it might be?'

'He's fled the country, hasn't he?' And when he

didn't answer, I said, 'Well, hasn't he? Somebody put that bloody tanker on the rocks.'

'That's a matter for the courts.' His voice sounded suddenly a little distant. Silence then. I thought he'd cut me off, but when I said 'Hullo', he answered at once. 'Just a moment.' A long pause. Then he went on, 'Sorry – I've got a telex here, and I was just looking at a newspaper report of what happened last night . . . you've been a ship's officer, I see. Gulf, and Indian Ocean. You know Mina Zayed?'

'The Abu Dhabi port?'

'Yes.'

'Is that where he's headed?'

'It's where the tanker was loaded. Do you know it?' And when I told him I'd been into it only once since it was built, he said, 'Well, that's more than most ships' officers have.' And he asked me whether I was ever in London.

'No,' I said. 'Not for a long time.' But then I remembered about the book and the publishers I had sent it to. I'd have to sort that out, think about what I was going to do. 'Maybe now . . .' I murmured.

'You'll be coming to London then?'

'I expect so.'

'When?'

'I don't know – soon. It depends.'

'Well, let me know.' He repeated the number I had given him, promised to phone me if they heard anything definite, then hung up.

I drank the rest of my coffee there by the phone, wondering why he wanted to know if I'd be in London.

There was nothing I could tell him. I took the empty cup through into the kitchen. Jean was there, looking a little tearful as she insisted I lunch with them. 'You're going to leave Balkaer now, aren't you?'

I nodded. There was a sort of extra-marital closeness between us. Perhaps it was her mixed Romany blood, but she always seemed to know what was in my mind. 'Yes, time to leave now.' Time to go back to the superficial companionship of officers' quarters on some tramp.

'Back to sea?'

I nodded, not relishing the thought.

'What about the book?'

I shook my head. It was over a month since I had sent it to the publishers and not a word. 'It'll be back to the Gulf again, I suppose. But first—' I stopped there, my hands trembling, my mind on that engineer. I couldn't tell her what I planned to do. I couldn't tell anybody. 'I'll take a break first.' My voice sounded faint, little more than a mumble. 'Try and sort things out.'

She put the saucepan down carefully and caught me by the arm. 'Two wrongs don't make a right, Trevor. They never did.' And she added, 'I know how you feel, but . . . just leave it be, love. The thing's done. Leave it be.' And then, without waiting for an answer, she said, 'Now go on down to the cottage, clean things up and come back here for lunch just after twelve. Cold ham and salad. And I'll do you some meringues.' She knew I liked meringues.

'All right,' I said.

But instead of going back to Balkaer, I went with Jimmy in his van to the cleansing station. We helped there for a while, getting back just in time for lunch. And afterwards I stayed on, enjoying the warmth of their company, the cosy heat of the coal fire. The wind had dropped, but there was still cloud over the moors and it got dark early. I didn't think about it when they switched the television on for the news, but then, suddenly, I was sitting up, electrified, seeing it all over again through the eyes of the camera – the red glow of the blazing tanker and the ILB coming into the slipway, the three of us caught against the furnace glare of the burning oil with ragged wisps of fog in the background, and myself, dazed and speaking slowly, as though in a trance, trying to answer their questions, telling them what had happened. The wind was blowing in my hair and my face had the pallor of death in the hard glare of the spotlight.

Back at the cottage, with the aftermath of the gale beating into the cove, it was my own TV shadow, my wild, ghostly appearance that stayed in my mind, not the words I had spoken. I was tired by then, so emotionally exhausted that I fell asleep by the fire. I spent most of the night there and in the morning, when I went up to the top, above the elephant rock, and looked across to the Longships, all that remained of the *Petros Jupiter* was the blackened bridge housing half sunk and leaning drunkenly against the Kettle's Bottom.

It was a bright, sparkling morning, the sort of morning that would have had Karen bubbling with that almost childishly excited Welsh enthusiasm of hers. I walked on, across the fields and down the road into Sennen, and there I found the story of what she had done plastered all over the papers with eye-witness accounts and statements from the salvage boss and pollution experts, also from several politicians.

Reading about it, I found it all strangely remote, as though it hadn't been Karen out there, but somebody else. Reporters came and a girl from the local radio station with a portable tape recorder. But by then I was in a daze, answering their questions automatically. It didn't seem real, any of it, the seas now rolling in unobstructed to break on the Shark's Fin, only the top of the hull's twisted wreck just showing at low water and no slick, the oil all burned up or driven ashore. It only seemed real when I was back at Balkaer. Then the emptiness of the cottage was like a constant nagging ache. Or when I was down in the cove. Wreckers from far and wide were prowling the shores of Whitesand Bay, searching all the headlands. They were picking up bits and pieces of the *Petros Jupiter* as far north as Cape Cornwall.

I began to get a stack of mail, letters from all sorts of people, conservationists chiefly, though some of them attacked me for encouraging Karen to sacrifice herself unnecessarily or accused me of standing by while she committed suicide. They were from women mainly, the bulk of them praising what she had done. Saturday, the mail included several invitations to speak at conservationist meetings and a letter from the publishers. This I saved until after my return from

Penzance, where I saw the agents and put Balkaer up
for sale. The letter was signed Ken Jordan, Senior
Editor. He wanted me to go up to London and see
him, but with Karen gone, the cottage for sale, that
part of my life was ended. It didn't seem important
any more, the book no longer meaning very much to
me. And on the Sunday, which was sunny with an
easterly breeze, families wandered down the path from
the lane to stand and point, and giggle in embarrassment when I told them to bugger off. There was even
a man who pushed open the cottage door to take
pictures of the interior. He was quite upset when I
slammed it in his face. Because he had seen Balkaer
on TV in his own home he seemed to think in some
curious way that he owned the place.

And then, about dusk, when all the gawpers and
souvenir hunters had gone, there was a knock at the
door and I opened it to find a man dressed in a sheepskin jacket and a polo-necked sweater standing there.
He had a fur cap rammed tight down on his bullet
head.

I recognized him at once, though it must have been
three years or more since I had last seen him; those
broad powerful shoulders, the beer-barrel belly, the
little pig eyes and the round heavy face. He was of
that breed of Englishman that has made Brits a word
of contempt.

I didn't ask him in. I just stood there, waiting. The last
time I'd seen him was at a shipboard party on a Liberian
tanker waiting to load at Bahrain. 'Remember me?'

I nodded. I had met him several times, on different ships, in different ports, and in hotel bars where he was always flush with money, always buying rounds of drinks. The word was that he was front man for a drug-smuggling ring.

'Len Baldwick,' he said, holding out a big paw. 'Can I have a word with you?'

'What about?'

'You. The future.' The small grey eyes were watching me, the whites as clear as if he'd never touched a drop of alcohol in his life. 'You'll be thinking of a ship now?'

'Will I?'

He ducked his head, pushing his way in. 'Saw you on the telly.' He unzipped the sheepskin jacket, pushing the fur cap to the back of his head. 'Peat fire, eh? You always were a bit simple-like. I told you, way back, didn't I – being honest and licking the arses of the owners don't pay. Now look where it's got you. You lost your wife. She's gone and you're on your own. You got nothing, laddie, nothing at all.'

'What the hell do you want?' Any ordinary man I'd have thrown out. But he was well over six foot, massive as a rock. 'Why are you here?'

'To offer you a job.' And he went on to explain that he was head-hunting for a consortium going into the tanker business. 'Oil money,' he explained, drooping an eyelid. 'You know how it is. Bubbles out of the arse of any Muslim in the Gulf. These people are starting their own fleet, see, an' while crew's no problem, it's not so easy to find officers. The right sort, that is.' He was watching me out of the corner of his eyes. 'The money's good. Double British rates.' He hesitated. 'And a bonus at the end.'

'End of what?' I asked. 'What's the bonus for?'

He shrugged. 'For getting the ship there. End of voyage bonus.' He was standing with his legs apart, staring at me. 'Air passage out, of course. Everything provided.'

The two years since I'd come to England fell away. I was back in the Gulf, back in a world where promises are seldom met, nothing is what it seems and men like Baldwick scavenge the hotels and clubs fomenting bar talk that is the never-never land of salesmen's dreams. Nothing would have induced me to accept an offer from him, but I didn't tell him that. I excused myself on the grounds that I had written a book and would be seeing the publishers shortly.

'Jesus!' he exclaimed and burst out laughing. 'I come here offering you the job of first officer on a hundred thousand tonner, and you talk about a bloody book. You out of your mind?'

'No,' I said. 'Just a question of values. I know what I want to do with my life.'

'Pollution. On the telly you was talking about pollution and crooked tanker owners, the need for government to introduce new laws.' He hesitated, eyeing me speculatively. 'Maybe these people can help.' He said it tentatively and I nearly burst out laughing it was so damned silly. Baldwick of all people on the side of the angels! Quick as a flash he sensed my reaction. 'So you won't even discuss it?'

I shook my head.

'I come all the way from Bristol to make you an offer most men would jump at—'

'Then why haven't they? Why come to me?'

'I told you. I saw you on the telly.' And he added, 'These people, they understand about pollution. They can afford to run their ships so there won't be any. The idea is to improve the tanker image, and they'll put pressure on any government that doesn't behave sensibly.'

'What pressure?' I asked.

'How the hell do I know? Political pressure, I imagine. Anyway, Pieter Hals is one of the skippers. He wouldn't have signed on if he hadn't believed they were serious about it.'

Hals was the man who had stood on the deck of a flag-of-convenience tanker in the Niger River with a bomb in his hand threatening to blow it up, and himself with it, if the effects of a collision weren't remedied before he sailed. She was scored along one side and leaking oil. The account I had read had commented that he was wilder than the Greenpeace movement or the union leader in Brest who'd called his men out to stop a Greek cargo vessel sailing with an oil leak in the stern gland. 'Who are these people?' I asked.

He shook his head, laughing and telling me he wasn't here to gossip about the consortium, just to offer me a job and if I didn't want it, what the hell did it matter to me who the owners were. 'They operate in the Gulf, of course, and they want ships' officers, deck as well as engineers.' He stood there for a moment, feet apart, with his back to the fire watching me out of his bright little button eyes. 'Tonight I'll be in Falmouth,' he said. 'I'll be talking to the captain of the *Petros Jupiter*. He'll be looking for another job I wouldn't wonder.' He waited, and when I didn't say anything, he nodded. 'Okay, suit yourself.' He pulled a business card from his wallet, took out what looked like a real gold pen, and after copying some entries from a leather diary on to the back of the card, he handed it to me. 'If you change your mind, those are my immediate movements.' The card described him as Consultant. On the back he had written down dates and telephone numbers for Liverpool, Nantes, Marseilles, Dubai.

He stood there a moment longer, pointedly surveying the stone-walled room and the junk furniture. Then he turned and zipped up his fleece-lined jacket. I opened the door for him and as he was going out he paused, looking down at me. 'You're not a company man any longer. You want a berth, you got to go out into the market and face all the other ships' officers that's out of a job.' His little eyes were cold, his lips a hard line. 'I'm warning you, Rodin, you'll find the going rough. A VLCC – you never had anything like that. It's the chance of a lifetime for a man like you.' He stood there a moment longer, staring down at me as though to check that his words had sunk in. Then he nodded. 'Okay. It's your loss. But if you change your mind, ring me before I leave for France.'

He left then and I stood there, watching him as he

climbed the path, leaning his body into it, and thinking how odd it was, the power of the media. First the publishers, conjured out of the blue because of the publicity, and now Baldwick, appearing like some evil genie and talking of pollution as though oil slicks could be eliminated by rubbing a few gold coins together.

I went back into the cottage, to another night of loneliness with only the memory of Karen for company. The next day I had a service for her in the local church.

There was still nothing to bury. Nothing had been found of her, nothing at all, so it was just a sort of memorial service to a girl who had immolated herself in protest against oil pollution. Most people seemed to regard it as a futile gesture, but they were kind and they turned up in force. The environmentalists made a bit of a demo out of it, the local press were there and two BBC men from Bristol. The little church was packed and it was raining.

The service was very moving, I think because of all the people and the strength of feeling that reached out to me. And afterwards, when one of the reporters started questioning me about her motives, I was in such an emotional state that I just let my feelings rip, telling him I'd get the bastard who put the *Petros Jupiter* on the rocks, killing Karen, killing the birds, ruining our bit of Cornwall. 'If the government won't stop it, I will.' There was a camera running, everybody staring, and when somebody asked me if I meant to take on the oil companies I answered him, 'No, the ship owners – the tanker owners – the bastards that switch names, companies, ownership – the whole stinking, sodding mess of corrupt tanker dealing . . .' Somebody pulled me away then, Andy I think. I was in tears, coming out of the church, straight from the service. And that night they had a brief flash of that interview on *Nationwide*. I watched it in the lounge of a Penzance hotel over a farewell drink with the Kerrisons, shocked as much by the haggard look of my face, and the tears streaming down it, as by the violence of my words. Then they drove me to the station and I caught the night train to London.

It was five days since it had happened, five miserable days alone at the cottage. On the Saturday, when I had seen the estate agents in Penzance, I had told them they could deal with the contents when they liked, but to leave the cottage until the spring, when the evenings would be drawing out and the daffodils in bloom in the sheltered patch behind the elephant rock. It would sell better then. But though it wouldn't be on the market immediately, the mere fact of having arranged to sell it had had the effect of making me feel an interloper, the place we had striven for and loved so much suddenly no longer part of my life. It added to the bitterness of my departure as the wheels rattled me eastwards through the night.

I hadn't bothered about a sleeper. I sat up all the way, dozing fitfully, thinking about the *Petros Jupiter* and what I'd do to that dirty little Greek when I caught up with him. It was either that or start thinking about Karen, and I couldn't face that, not any more. Not after that service. I felt drained, too nervously exhausted to plan ahead. I didn't even think about the letter from the publishers. That meant thinking constructively, about my writing, about the future. I didn't want to think about the future. I didn't want to face up to a future alone. And so I sat there, my mind drifting on the edge of consciousness, nerves taut and the wheels hammering the name Speridion into my tired brain. *Aristides Speridion. Aristides Speridion.*

Dawn broke, cold and grey, the wind blowing out of the north, a curtain of sleet beginning to whiten the roofs of the buildings backed on to the railway. It was much too early to ring the solicitors when we pulled into Paddington, so I took the Circle Line to Liverpool Street, checked my two cases into a lock-up and just had time to buy some papers before catching the next train for Colchester.

Except for a brief paragraph in the *Telegraph* headed OIL SLICK DEMO AT CORNISH CHURCH, the *Petros Jupiter* seemed to have dropped right out of the news. The lead story in all the papers was the arrest of four more terrorists at the GB Shahpur Petro-Chemical Company's offices in the City. They were charged with being implicated in the Piccadilly Underground explosion that had killed eleven people just before Christmas.

Feeling drowsy as the train ran into the flat Essex countryside, I went into the buffet for some coffee. There was a queue and, while I was waiting, the guard came through checking tickets. The buffet car was full, every seat occupied, and when I finally got my coffee I took it through into the next coach and sat down in an almost empty first class compartment. There was one occupant only, a neat elderly man with rimless half-glasses who sat hunched in an overcoat in the far window seat reading the *Economist*. He was making notes and on the seat beside him several articles on insurance lay on top of a slim black leather briefcase. Outside the windows, the drizzle had turned to snow, a thick driving veil of white. I held the paper cup in both hands, sipping the hot coffee and wondering whether I was wasting my time travelling all the way down to see Ferrers when it would have been so much simpler to phone. Quite probably Lloyd's Intelligence Services wouldn't know anything more than had already been released to the press. And if they did, would he tell me?

One thing I was sure about, however . . . if they did know anything more, then I had a far better chance of getting it out of him if I saw him personally. Also, by going to their offices I could see the set-up, form some idea of what their sources of information were. I knew they had agents all over the world, but though I had been conscious of the extraordinary global network controlled by Lloyd's of London ever since I had become a ship's officer, I had no real idea how the organization worked, least of all how its Intelligence Service operated. And from Colchester of all places! Why not London?

The answer to that was supplied by the man opposite me. As we neared Colchester he put his *Economist* carefully away in his briefcase and began gathering his things together. I asked him if he could direct me to Sheepen Place and he looked at me quickly with a little smile. 'Lloyd's Shipping Press?'

'No, Intelligence Services,' I said.

He nodded. 'Same thing. You're a ship captain, are you?'

I shook my head. 'Mate only, though I've got my master's certificate. I left the sea a few years back.'

'Ah, you work for marine solicitors, eh?' He glanced out of the window. 'Snowing quite hard now. My wife's meeting me with the car. We can give you a lift.' And when I said I could get a taxi, that I didn't want to take them out of their way, he said, 'No trouble. It's quite close. Within walking distance.' He gave a little laugh. 'Except that it's not a good day for walking, eh?'

The train was slowing now, and as we took our place in the corridor, I asked him why such a vital part of Lloyd's should be tucked away in an East Anglian coastal town. He looked at me, frowning. 'I suppose because members of Lloyd's traditionally live in East Anglia. The best of 'em, anyway,' he added, smiling. 'In the great days of the railways Liverpool Street was a handy way of getting out into the country. Now a lot of the big insurance companies, some of the largest of the Lloyd's brokers, have moved their administrative organizations out of the City, to Colchester, Ipswich, even as far north as Norwich. Costs are a lot less than in the City and staff don't have to commute so far.' The train jerked to a stop and we got out into a bitter wind.

It was much colder than it had been in London,

the snow small-flaked and hard like ice. The car his wife was driving was a brand-new Mercedes, their background a whole world away from mine. We drove down under the railway bridge, the road curving away to the right. The snow was heavier now, the Town Hall tower, which marked the centre of Colchester, only just visible on its hill. The insurance man turned from answering his wife's queries about a frozen tap and said, 'You know, I envy you ships' officers who handle marine solicitors' enquiries. Not only does it take you all over the world, but you're dealing all the time with case histories, all the exciting side of insurance. Whereas people like me, we make money, of course, but broking, looking after Names, dealing with accounts, finances, that sort of thing – it's all very humdrum, you know. Down here I've got an office employs between two and three hundred, and all the time flogging back and forth to London.' We were on a new road, crossing a big double culvert where the Colne ran between banks of snow. 'Across the A12 roundabout, then left and left again at the next,' he said to his wife, and she answered sharply, 'I know where it is, Alfred.'

He waved a hand to the ruins of a colossal flint and tile wall that climbed away from us as the car swung. 'That's the outer remains of Camulodunum, the Roman centre of East Anglia.' Sheepen Place appeared on a name-plate edged with snow, an industrial estate doubling back towards the A12 roundabout and the meadow land beyond. The car slowed, turned right into the entrance of a printing works. 'Don't forget the ramps,' he said. 'Two of them.'

'I haven't forgotten.' She almost stalled the car as we bumped over the first, which showed only as the slightest hump in the wind-drifted snow. A board announced Lloyd's Shipping Press and I saw there was a three-storey brick building beyond the printing works. No mention of Intelligence Services.

'You've not been here before?' He was watching for the next ramp, not looking at me, and I guessed it was just an idle question.

'No,' I said.

'Anybody in particular?'

'A Mr Ferrers.'

We bumped over the second ramp. The Shipping Press building was stretched over the car park on steel pillars. 'What department?'

'Special Enquiries.'

He nodded. 'Ah yes, of course, Marine Frauds.' He turned in his seat, eyeing me curiously as the car slid to a stop outside the plate glass entrance doors. 'Which particular marine casualty are you investigating – or aren't you at liberty to say?'

I hesitated. 'I've come to see him about the *Petros Jupiter*.'

He nodded. 'That was an odd one, eh?' He turned to his wife. 'Remember, Margaret? A young woman – she blew it up and herself with it.'

'Yes, I remember, Alfred.'

'An odd way to end your life.'

'She didn't—' I began, but then I stopped myself.

Better leave it at that. No good trying to explain about oil slicks and pollution and seabirds dying. I began to get out and he said, 'Intelligence Services is on the second floor.'

I thanked him. I thanked them both and stood there in the bitter wind until their car was out of sight round the other side of the building. Now that I was here I wasn't quite certain how to proceed. A muddy Triumph pulled into a parking place and a big fair man in a rumpled suit and no top-coat got out. I pushed open the plate glass door. There was a lift and some stairs and it was warm. I took the stairs. The swing doors facing the lift on the first floor were clearly marked Shipping Press. Through glass panels I could see men working at their desks, some in their shirt sleeves. It was an open-plan office covering virtually the whole floor and there were visual display units scattered about so I knew the operation was computerized.

The swing doors on the second floor were completely anonymous, no mention of Intelligence Services. As on the floor below, the offices were open-plan with a lot of electrical equipment, VDUs and telex machines, particularly on the far side where the wind, blowing straight in off the North Sea, drove the snow in near-horizontal white lines across the large, clear, sheet-glass windows. The lift doors opened behind me. It was the big fair man in the rumpled suit, and as he was pushing past me, he paused briefly, holding the swing doors open with his shoulder. 'Looking for somebody?'

'Ferrers,' I said.

'Barty Ferrers.' He nodded and I stepped inside. 'Expecting you?' He was already slipping his jacket off.

'Yes,' I said and gave him my name.

The big, open-plan floor was very warm. A lot of men there, most of them in their shirt sleeves, the desks flat tables littered with books and papers. A few women on the far side and one girl sitting with seven or eight men at a big table with a card on it marked Casualty Room.

I could see he was a bit doubtful and I said quickly, 'It's about the *Petros Jupiter*.'

His eyes widened then, a sudden glint of recognition. 'Yes, of course. The *Petros Jupiter*.' He gave me a sympathetic pat on the shoulder. 'I'm Ted Fairley. I run Lloyd's Confidential Index.' He gave me a big jovial smile. 'That's the prudent insurers' index to vessels of doubtful virtue.' He turned and surveyed the room. 'Can't see Barty at the moment. But Tim Spurling, the other half of the Marine Fraud twins, he's there.' He had his jacket off now and I followed him between the crowded tables. 'Barty contacted you, did he?'

'No. Was he going to?'

'Yes, I think the legal boys want to talk to you.' He stopped at a desk with a typewriter and a litter of books and tossed his jacket on to the empty chair. 'That's my square foot or so of lebensraum. Casualty History on one side, Casualty Reporting on the other. Very convenient and never a dull moment. Ah, there's

Barty.' He veered towards an area of the floor jutting out to the north and full of the clatter of telexes and operators keying information into visual display units. 'Information Room,' he said over his shoulder. 'This is where our two thousand agents all over the world report in by telex. Barty!' He had to raise his voice against the clatter.

Barty Ferrers wasn't in the least what I had expected. He was a plump, jolly-looking man with a round, babyish face and thick horn-rimmed glasses that were bifocal. He looked up from the telex he was reading, and when he realized who I was, his eyes seemed to freeze behind the thick glasses. They were pale blue, the sort of cold blue eyes that Swedes often have. 'What the hell are you doing here?' I started to explain, but he cut me short. 'Never mind. I've been trying to get you at that Sennen number.'

'The ship was wrecked deliberately then?'

'We don't know that.'

'Why were you phoning me then?'

'Marine solicitors. They want to see you.'

'Why?'

He shook his head. 'Can't talk here. First – read that.' He handed me a telex slip one of the operators had passed across to him. 'Came in last night.'

It was from Lloyd's agent at La Rochelle and dated the previous day, January 11:

VAGUE D'OR LOCKED INTO TRAWLER BASIN HERE TWO DAYS AGO. CAPTAIN HAS NO INFORMATION ARISTIDES SPERIDION. MAN TAKEN ON BOARD OFF

PORTHCURNO IS SHIP'S ENGINEER HENRI
CHOFFEL. THIS MAN LEAVES IMMEDIATELY FOR
PARIS EN ROUTE BY AIR TO BAHRAIN. THIS IS
CERTAIN AS ALL NECESSARY BOOKINGS MADE
LOCALLY.

The telex then went on to describe Choffel as short
with dark hair –

POSSIBLY PIED NOIR, SPEAKS FRENCH WITH AN
ACCENT, AQUILINE FEATURES, AGE 46, WIFE DEAD.
DAUGHTER ONLY. ADDRESS 5042 LES TUFFEAUX,
PARNAY, NEAR SAUMUR-ON-LOIRE. HOLDS FRENCH
PASSPORT.

Time and occupation right, the Breton fishing boat,
too. I was remembering a list I had read in one of the
papers giving the names of French boats operating off
the Cornish coast. I was almost certain one of them
had been the *Vague d'Or*. Only the man's name was
different. 'He must have had two passports,' I said.

Ferrers nodded, handing me another telex. 'This
just came in.' It was from Bahrain:

SUBJECT OF QUERY ARRIVED BAHRAIN YDAY
MORNING. WENT STRAIGHT ABOARD FREIGHTER
CORSAIRE, BUT NOT AS ENGINEER, AS PASSENGER.
CORSAIRE NOW TAKING ON FUEL PREPARATORY TO
SAILING.

So by now he would have gone. Ferrers took the

telexes from me and passed them to one of the operators with instructions to transmit the information to Forthright & Co. 'They're the solicitors.' He gave me a quick, searching glance, then jerked his head towards the far corner of the floor. 'We don't encourage visitors,' he said as we got away from the clatter of the telexes. 'So I'd be glad if you'd keep it to yourself that you've been here.'

'It doesn't give the ship's destination,' I said.

'No, but I can soon find that out.' He pushed past a man with an armful of the *Lloyd's List*, and then we were in his little corner and he had plonked himself down at a table with a VDU on it. 'Let's see what the computer says.' While his fingers were busy on the keyboard he introduced me to Spurling, a sharp-featured, sandy-haired man with a long freckled face and bushy sideburns. What the computer said was INSTRUCTION INCORRECT. 'Hell!' He tried it again with the same result. 'Looks as though our fellow in Bahrain got the name of the ship wrong.'

Spurling leaned over his shoulder. 'Try the French spelling – with an "e" at the end, same as in his telex.'

He tried it and immediately line after line of print began coming up on the VDU screen, everything about the ship, the fact that it was French and due to sail today, also its destination, which was Karachi. He glanced up at me and I could see the wheels turning. 'That ship you were mate on, plying between Bombay and the Gulf – based on Karachi, wasn't she?'

I nodded.

'And the crew, Pakistani?'

'Some of them.'

'So you speak the language.'

'I speak a little Urdu, yes.'

He nodded, turning his head to stare at the windows and the driving lines of snow. 'Choffel,' he murmured. 'That name rings a bell.' He turned to Spurling. 'Remember that little Lebanese freighter they found waterlogged but still afloat off Pantelleria? I suddenly thought of her in my bath this morning. Not in connection with Choffel, of course. But Speridion. Wasn't Speridion the name of the ship's engineer?'

Spurling thought for a moment, then shook his head. 'Speridion, Choffel – not sure.' He was frowning in concentration as he lit a cigarette from the butt of his last and stubbed out the remains in the tobacco tin beside his in-tray. 'It's quite a time back. Seventy-six, maybe seventy-seven.' He hesitated, drawing on a cigarette. 'The crew abandoned her. Skipper's name, I remember—'

'Never mind the skipper. It's the engineer we want.'

'It'll be on the file. I'm certain I put it on the file.' He reached over to a small steel cabinet, but then he checked. 'I need the ship's name. You know that. Just give me the name . . .'

But Ferrers couldn't remember the name, only that there had been a Greek engineer involved. From what they said I gathered the cabinet contained confidential casualty information that included the background of ships' officers and crew members known to have been involved in fraud. Then Spurling was muttering to himself, still frowning in concentration: 'A crook Lebanese company owned her. Can't recall the company's name, but Beirut. That's where the ship was registered. A small tanker. I'm sure it was a tanker.' And he added, 'Pity you can't remember the name. Everything in that file is listed under the name of a ship.'

'I know that.'

'Then you'd better start searching again.'

'I've been through two years of casualty records already this morning. That's seventy microfiches.'

'You love it.' Spurling grinned at me, nodding to a shelf full of thick loose-leafed volumes on the wall behind us. 'All our casualty records are micro-filmed and filed in those binders. The VDU there acts as a viewing box and you can get a print-out at the touch of a button. It's Barty's own personal toy. Try the winter of seventy-five, seventy-six.'

'Back to where we first started keeping records?' Ferrers got slowly to his feet. 'It'll take me an hour to go through that lot.'

Spurling smiled at him wickedly. 'It's what you're paid for, isn't it?'

Ferrers gave a snort. 'May I remind you we're supposed to be keeping tabs on over six hundred vessels for various clients.'

'They'll never know, and if you pull the information Forthright want out of the box who's to say you're wasting your time?' Spurling looked at me and dropped an eyelid, his face deadpan. 'Come to think of it, I doubt if it was winter. They were several days in an open boat. Try March or April, seventy-seven.

She had her tanks full of arms, that's why you remember her.'

Ferrers nodded, reaching down the second volume from the far end of the shelf. I watched him as he searched quickly through the fiche pockets, extracted one and slipped it into the scanning slot. Immediately the VDU screen came alive with information which changed quickly as he shifted from microfilm to microfilm. And when he had finished with that fiche, I put it back in its pocket for him, while he began searching the next. Each fiche, measuring about 6 × 4 inches, was imprinted with rows of tiny little microfilms hardly bigger than pinheads.

He was over half an hour, working first forwards through 1977, then backwards into '76. He worked in the silence of total concentration, and with Spurling's attention divided between his typewriter and the telephone, they seemed to have forgotten all about me. At one point Spurling passed me a telex giving the latest report on the *Petros Jupiter* salvage situation. Smit International, the Dutch salvage people, had announced their intention of withdrawing from any further attempt to salvage the wreck. Their divers had only been able to operate for two days since the explosion, a total of 8½ hours. But apparently this had been sufficient to establish the general condition of the wreck, which was now lying in three sections to the north of Kettle's Bottom with only the skeletal remains of the superstructure awash at low tide. The effect of the explosion, followed by the intense heat generated by the ignition of the five tanks containing oil, had been such that they regarded any attempt to salvage the remains of the vessel as quite profitless. And they added that, in its present position, they did not consider it a danger to shipping. Further, all tanks were now completely ruptured and empty of oil.

There were three sheets of the telexed report and I had just come to the end of it when Ferrers suddenly exclaimed, 'Got it! The *Stella Rosa*. March 20, 1976.' Spurling looked up and nodded, smiling. 'Of course. The *Stella Rosa*.'

'Outward bound from Tripoli to Algiers.' Ferrers was reading from the scanner, his face close to the screen. 'Arms for the Polisario – Sam-7s and Kalashnikovs.' He straightened up, pressing the button that gave him the print-out, and when he had it, he passed it to Spurling. But by then Spurling had the *Stella Rosa* file out and was running quickly through it; 'Skipper Italian, Mario Pavesi from Palermo. Ah, here we are. Second engineer Aristides Speridion. No address given. Not among the survivors. First engineer – now we have something – guess who? None other than Henri Choffel, French. He was picked up and is described here as suspect on his past record. He was chief engineer of the *Olympic Ore* and is thought to have been implicated in her sinking in 1972. At the Enquiry into the sinking of the *Stella Rosa* he claimed it was Speridion who opened the sea cocks.' He passed the file to Ferrers. 'Good hunch of yours.'

Ferrers gave a little shrug. 'No indication then that Speridion got away in a boat?'

Spurling shook his head. 'No. And no record that

he managed to land on Pantelleria. All it says is – *no indication that he is still alive.*'

'So Choffel knew he was dead. He must have known otherwise he wouldn't have used the man's name. And to use Speridion's name he'd need his papers.' Ferrers was staring down at the file. 'I wonder what really happened to Speridion? It says here – *At the Enquiry held at Palermo Chief Engineer Henri Choffel stated that he and two of his men tried to stop the flow of water into the engine-room, but the cocks on the sea water inlet to the cooling systems had been opened and then damaged. Speridion had been on duty. Choffel thought he had probably been paid to sink the ship by agents of the Moroccan government.*' Ferrers shook his head, sucking in air through his teeth. 'And on the *Petros Jupiter* he was using the name Speridion. That means it's almost certainly sabotage.'

'And if he did have the Greek's papers and the police start looking into the *Stella Rosa* sinking—' Spurling hesitated. 'It could be murder, couldn't it?'

I thought he was jumping to conclusions. But perhaps that was because I had been thinking all the time in terms of Speridion. Choffel was something different, something new. It took time for my mind to switch. But murder as well as sabotage . . . 'God Almighty!' I said. 'Nobody who'd killed his second engineer, and then accused him of sabotaging the ship, would dream of using the man's name.'

'Wouldn't he?' Spurling had turned to his type-writer, the file beside him. 'If I let you loose on that filing cabinet, you'd be surprised at the stupidity of some of the marine frauds and the damn fool things men do. They're amateurs, most of them, not professionals. Remember the *Salem*, sunk off the West African coast right within sight of a BP tanker. They never seem to realize it takes time to sink a really big ship. I tell you, they do the craziest things.'

'If they didn't,' Ferrers said, 'there isn't a member of any marine syndicate at Lloyd's who'd be making money. They'd be losing their shirts instead.' He turned as Fairley appeared at his elbow, a telex in his hand.

'Just come in,' he said. 'Michael Stewart's box. Anything we can tell him about the *Howdo Stranger*. It's gone missing.' He placed the telex on Spurling's typewriter. 'I've checked the Confidential Index. Nothing. Hardly surprising. It's owned and run by Gulf Oil Development.'

'A tanker then?' Spurling picked up the telex and began reading it.

Fairley nodded. 'About the same size as the *Aurora B*, the GODCO ship that went missing two months ago.' He leaned over Spurling's shoulder, checking the telex. 'This one's 116,000 tons. She had a full cargo for Japan. Same destination, you see. And loaded out of the same port, Mina Zayed.' He straightened up with a shrug. 'She's ten years old, but she'd just passed survey A1, yet now, suddenly, she fails to report on schedule.'

'Where?' Ferrers asked.

'Estimated probable position somewhere southwest of Sri Lanka.'

'And the radio schedule.'

'Twice weekly. Same as *Aurora B*.'

'Okay,' he said. 'I'll look up the *Aurora B* details, let them have a print-out of that. Then we'll see what else we can cobble together.'

Standing there, totally ignored now, I was surprised at the speed with which their attention had switched, Spurling already hunched over the VDU checking with the computer, Ferrers reaching for the nearest binder, searching for the fiche on which the microfilmed details of the *Aurora B* casualty had been stored. 'Two of them can't have blown up.' Fairley pushed a hand up through his fair hair, which was now as rumpled as the rest of him. 'Two GODCO tankers in two months, it's not possible.'

'What about the *Berge Istra* and the *Berge Vanga*?' Ferrers said without looking round. 'Norwegian and just as good a stable as GODCO.'

Spurling looked up from the telex he had been reading and said, 'She left the Abu Dhabi port of Zayed 18.00 hours January 5.' He turned to Fairley. 'When did she miss her radio schedule?'

'Yesterday afternoon. It's in the telex.'

'Yes, but it doesn't give the time.'

'I checked the *Aurora B* schedule,' Fairley told him. 'She was reporting in at 14.00 hours Tuesdays and Fridays.'

'So this one could be the same time, but Mondays and Thursdays.' Spurling had the *Lloyd's Maritime Atlas* open at the Indian Ocean page and was pencilling figures on a slip of paper. 'That's it then. West or south-west of Sri Lanka. Just about where the *Aurora*

B missed her schedule. Previous schedule would have been roughly between Muscat and Karachi, so if she really is a casualty, then it could have happened anywhere between there and Sri Lanka.'

Fairley nodded. 'You're thinking it could be fraud.'

'We've had radio frauds before. It became quite fashionable a couple of years back.'

'That was cargo,' Ferrers said over his shoulder. 'Cargo that didn't exist, shipped in vessels that didn't exist or else had their names borrowed for the occasion. And all of them owned by companies Lloyd's wouldn't consider insuring. But GODCO. That's something entirely different.' His machine suddenly rolled out a sheet of paper, which he tore off and handed to Spurling. 'That's the *Aurora B* casualty information. Not very much to go on.' He suddenly seemed conscious of the fact that I was still standing there. 'I'd better run you up to the station. You're not supposed to be here and this doesn't concern you.'

'You've nothing more you can tell me about the *Petros Jupiter*?' I asked.

'No, nothing.'

'Except,' Spurling said, 'that the lead underwriter for the *Petros Jupiter* is the same as for these two tankers. Same solicitors, too.'

'That's confidential,' Ferrers cut in sharply.

No question now of getting anything more out of them. Ferrers hustled me out of the building and into his car, driving fast, in a hurry to get back. I envied him his total involvement. He really seemed to enjoy it. 'We're just back-room boys really, but when it's a

case of fraud – well, it gets quite exciting at times.'
We were crossing the Colne, now a black gut between
the white of snow-plastered buildings. 'Our job is to
feed information to the marine solicitors, in extreme
cases to the police.' He grinned at me as we slithered
on the roundabout. 'When Lloyd's is faced with marine
crooks, then it's our wits against theirs and every case
different. It's teamwork mainly, and sharp memories,
a bloody good filing system and a computer.'

He skidded the car to a standstill outside Colchester station booking hall, then scribbled a name and
a telephone number on one of his cards and handed it
to me. 'Forthright & Co., they're the marine solicitors
for the three syndicates run by Michael Stewart.' He
pushed open the door for me. 'A Mr Saltley. Give him
a ring while you're in London. He wants to speak to
you.'

'About the *Petros Jupiter*?'

He hesitated. But all he said was, 'Just give him a
ring, that's all.' And he added, leaning across to talk
to me as I pocketed his card and stepped on to the
hard-packed snow, 'He's a nice guy is Michael Stewart.
Lives only a few miles away, and if this tanker really
has gone missing, then he's in trouble. That's what I
hear anyway. So go and see Saltley, will you.' He
drove off then, slamming the door shut as the Cortina's
wheels churned the snow, and I went into the station
wondering why he thought I could help when all I was
interested in was the *Petros Jupiter*.

CHAPTER THREE

It **was** just after twelve-thirty when I got back to London. It had been a slow journey with several stops and as I made my way to a call box I was feeling tired and cold, my mind still on the *Petros Jupiter*, knowing I would have to move fast if I was to catch up with Choffel in Karachi. I hadn't much money, and an advance on the book was the only chance I had of raising the air fare.

But when I phoned the publishers the man who had written to me had already left for lunch. I made an appointment for three that afternoon, and then, because it was still snowing and I didn't imagine the sort of lodging I could afford would have a phone, I rang Forthright & Co. Again I was out of luck, Saltley's secretary informing me he was out and she didn't know when he would be back. She tried to discourage me from ringing later, but when I told her my name, she seemed to brighten up. Mr Saltley, she said, would definitely like to see me, and as soon as possible. He was attending a twenty-first birthday luncheon party at the Savoy and would be back by four at the latest. Could I ring again then?

I had some food at the station buffet, then got my suitcase out of the lock-up and took the tube to Stepney Green. Outside the station the Mile End Road seemed strangely quiet, the sound of the traffic muffled by a dirty carpet of salted slush. I crossed the road and headed south for a boarding house I had used before. It was in a long street of terraced houses down towards the river, and when I knocked at the door, it was opened by the same big-bosomed, bold-eyed landlady. I had forgotten her name until she reminded me. It was Mrs Steinway. She put me in the basement, which was the only room she had vacant and, after settling in and having a quick cup of tea with her, I walked back through the snow to Stepney Green station and took a train to South Kensington.

Jordans, the publishers to whom I had sent my book, were a small firm specializing in wildlife and natural history. It was just after three when I reached their office in Queen's Gate, one of those white porticoed buildings almost opposite the Natural History Museum. A pretty little girl with a streaming cold took me up to Ken Jordan's office on the first floor, which was little bigger than a partitioned cubicle, the ceiling showing part of the ornate plaster design of a larger room. There was a window looking across to the Museum and the walls were lined with bookshelves that overflowed into stacked heaps on the floor.

Jordan proved to be a rather intense individual

with sandy hair and eyes too close together, his face long and the lips turned up at the corners in what appeared to be a perpetual smile. He had my typescript on the desk in front of him, on top of an untidy litter of books, letters and galleys, and as soon as I was seated, instead of talking about my book he went into a long monologue about the one I ought to write. 'You owe it to your wife.' He said that several times. He wanted me to start again, writing the whole story of Balkaer from Karen's point of view . . .

'Write it in the first person. Imagine you're really your wife, everything from her angle, right?' His pale, rather protuberant eyes stared at me urgently. 'I'm sure you can do it. Her feelings as she's cleaning up those half-dead birds, what she thinks about the government, the oil companies, the men who run the tankers, how the idea gradually forms in her mind – immolation, a spectacular, suicidal gesture—'

'It wasn't suicide,' I said quickly.

'No, no, of course not.' He gave a high little laugh, almost a giggle. 'But that's how the public see it now. And it's the public that buy books. So you give them what they want, use your imagination. A little invention. Dramatize it. Build it up.' And then he had the nerve to ask me whether she had tried it before.

'How do you mean?' I could hear the hostility in my voice, feel anger building up inside me.

'Just that. Had she tried it before—' He stopped there and opened the folder, leafing through the pages Karen had typed so carefully. 'That oil slick you described. Not the first one.' He found the page he was looking for. It was near the end. 'The one in November. Now, if she tried to set fire to it and failed . . . you see what I'm getting at? It would make it so much more dramatic – her feelings when it didn't work, the sense of anti-climax.' He paused, staring at me. 'A nice build-up, you see, to the end of the book – very exciting, very moving . . . the reader having been through it all before when it didn't work, and then, the next time, knowing it's for real, that she's going to kill herself.'

'She didn't mean to,' I said again. 'She wasn't thinking of suicide, only of setting light—'

'No, but you see what I'm getting at. So dramatic, eh? And that's what you want, isn't it, to make the point she was trying to make? The news story, that's over, finished now. What we want is something much more personal, something deeply moving.' He was leaning forward, his voice quiet and persuasive. 'I'm sure you can do it, Mr Rodin. It's just a question of putting yourself in your wife's – er, sea boots—' he smiled, trying to lighten his words – 'seeing it as she might have seen it, and building the whole thing up, dramatizing it, making it exciting, sensational even – it needs fictionalizing, you see.'

'You aren't interested then in what I've already written?'

'No.' He shook his head. 'No, not really.' And he added quickly as I began to get to my feet, 'It's nicely written. Don't misunderstand me. You can write. But these are difficult times. I don't think we could sell it, not now. But the book I've just outlined . . . I'm sure we could sell that. It has excitement, emotional involvement, action – it could be a very moving book. We could try one of the Sundays too. It could make a good two or three-part serial.'

'But not if I wrote it the way I saw it, the way it really happened?'

He shook his head. 'No.' He banged the typescript shut. 'What we're talking about is a first book. Trevor Rodin. Nobody's heard of you, you see. You're new, unknown. So we've got to give it depth, excite people, give the reader something to get his teeth into – *husband writes the full intimate story of his wife's final, terrible decision.* See what I mean? It's moving. It would tear at their hearts—'

'No.' I was on my feet now, staring down at him, hating him for his callous rejection of all those months of work, for the way he was trying to get me to twist the truth to fit his own idea of what was marketable.

'Please,' he said, leaning forward again and gazing urgently up at me. 'Don't misunderstand me – I'm only trying to help. Our job as publishers is to produce books that authors like you write, and then to market them. Each book is a joint venture as it were, the author investing his time and his expertise, the publisher his money. It costs money to launch a book and my job is to see that the final product in each case is something people will want to buy.' And he added, 'Take my advice, Mr Rodin – I have some experience – write it the way I have suggested, from your wife's point of view, building it up to the point where she is so emotionally desperate she goes out to blow the ship up, and herself—'

'It was an accident,' I said angrily. I could see so clearly what he was driving at, and there was a part of me that was prepared to accept that he was right, that this was the way to handle it if it was to capture the imagination of the public. But it wasn't the truth, it wasn't the way it had happened. 'She didn't mean to kill herself.'

'How do you know? You can't be sure what was in her mind.' And he added, 'A little author's licence . . . what difference does it make? Or can't you do it? Is that the trouble, that you don't feel you're a good enough writer—'

'I could do it,' I said angrily. 'But I won't.' I reached across his desk and picked up the typescript. If I stayed in that untidy office any longer I knew I'd be tempted. Everything seen through her eyes, using my imagination – I'd always wanted to be a writer and I needed the money. Of course I could do it, the scenes already flashing through my mind. But in the end my memory of Karen would be blurred, the reality of her and what she had tried to do lost in a ghost creature of my own imagination.

'You won't do it then?'

'No.'

'I'm sorry.' He pushed his chair back and stood facing me. 'If you change your mind—'

'I shan't.'

'But if you do, don't leave it too long. A few months and there'll be another tanker on the rocks spilling oil somewhere else.' He held out his hand, limp and cold, and I left him, hurrying down the stairs and out into the street, clutching the typescript. The pavements were tight-packed ice and the ornate Victorian edifice of the Museum facing the Cromwell Road was picked out in thick white snowlines.

I was so angry I felt like flinging the typescript into the snow-clogged gutter. I had been sure they would take it, ever since I had received Jordan's letter. I had been so certain I would come out of that meeting with a contract and a cheque for the advance that I hadn't even checked the tramp rates or looked at the Shipping Index; I hadn't the slightest idea what the chances of a berth were for anyone who had been ashore as long as I had.

My breath smoked in the cold air and I became conscious of the traffic building up, moving sluggishly through the snow as London headed for home early. It seemed to be getting colder by the minute, the wind north-westerly now, the snowflakes like glass flying in horizontal lines past my face. How disappointed Karen would have been, all those evenings spent listening to me as I had read passages aloud in the lamplight, all the typing! She had felt at times almost as involved with it as I was. And now . . . How long would it be before the *Corsaire* reached Karachi? Or had the ship already arrived? Perhaps she would be anchored outside with all the other freighters waiting for a berth . . . But then I remembered the new harbour. It would be finished now and once the *Corsaire* docked, Choffel could disappear into the labyrinth of the bazaars. Or maybe he'd find a berth on some vessel headed for Japan, Australia, some distant part of the world beyond my reach.

The man's escape and the book's rejection became fused in my mind, the anger of despair gripping me as I tramped through the snow, the cold eating into me. And then suddenly there was a new thought in my head. Dramatize it, the man had said, so that's what I'd do. I'd re-write it, the whole story, her death, everything. And the end of it would be my search for Aristides Speridion or Henri Choffel, or whatever he might be calling himself when I caught up with him. I'd find him somehow. I'd find the bastard, and when I'd done with him, then I'd write it all down, just as it happened – for Karen's sake, for the sake of all those birds, for my own peace of mind. And reaching that decision, the emptiness, the hopeless feeling of depression was gone, determination taking hold.

I don't know why, but I was suddenly remembering my mother, conscious of the same obstinate streak that had made her go it alone, bring up a child on a nurse's pay in post-Mau Mau Nairobi, and later in the Gulf, in Dubai, where she had died of pulmonary pneumonia from overwork. I could hardly remember what she looked like, only that she was small and neat, and that she'd a lot of guts, a lot of nervous energy that had burned her up before she was forty. That and the climate, and the men she couldn't resist.

Back at South Kensington station, I went straight to a call box and rang Forthright. Saltley was back from his luncheon at the Savoy, but he was on the phone. I hadn't enough change to hang on, so I rang off and stood there, feeling very alone as I watched the milling crowd of office workers hurrying to get home before railway lines froze and roads became impassable. They were all so busy, so engrossed in their own worlds. I tried again a few minutes later and the girl said he was still talking. I had to ring twice more before she was finally able to put me through and a quiet, rather abrupt voice said, 'Saltley here.'

Ferrers had clearly briefed him about me, and of course he had read the papers. He said he'd like to see me as soon as possible, but he had a rather urgent case on and would be tied up for a couple of hours at least. I suggested that perhaps I could see him at his office the following morning, but he said he would be preparing a brief and in court most of the day. He hesitated, then told me that, because of the weather, he had arranged to stay the night at his club. 'You a sailing man, by any chance?'

'I had the loan of a boat once in Karachi,' I told him. 'A dinghy really.'

He seemed relieved. 'Then at least you won't be entirely out of your depth.' And he suggested I had supper with him at the Royal Ocean Racing Club in St James's Place. 'Seven-thirty suit you? And if the bar's crowded, then we'll go into the Fastnet Room and talk there.'

I had two and a half hours to kill. I went into the Science Museum, which being a government building was pleasantly warm, and stayed there until it closed, idling the time away activating all the working models, the steam engines and looms and laser beams. There was hardly anybody left when they pushed us out into the night. The wind had dropped, the air still and deathly cold. I took the Underground to St James's Park, bought an evening paper and read it over a cup of coffee in a cafeteria off Victoria Street. The City page carried the year's results of the Norwegian subsidiary of a large British shipping company. They had half their ships laid up and had been operating at a loss throughout the second half of the year.

I wished to God I hadn't seen it, for it did nothing to lift my morale as I went out into the frozen streets of London again. They had a dead look now, hardly any traffic. I walked up to St James's Park. There wasn't a soul there. It was as though I were the ghost of somebody who had returned after some terrible science fiction disaster. The water was a black pit under the bridge. The ducks and wild geese stood motionless on the ice, the flat white covering of snow scuffed with the imprint of their feet. The scene matched my mood. I could no longer conjure the soft Welsh lilt of Karen's voice, or see her standing there beside me. I was alone now, intensely, intolerably alone, with only anger and hatred for company.

I stayed there, keeping a frozen vigil with the birds, until Big Ben boomed out the quarter after seven. Then I walked slowly across the Mall and up past the Palace to St James's Street. I seemed to be the only human being left alive. A taxi crept past me as I turned into St James's Place. The Royal Ocean Racing Club was right at the end, past the Stafford Hotel where the taxi was now trying to turn. Somebody entered the Club ahead of me, the portholes of the inner doors momentarily revealed, two brass-rimmed eyes staring out at a dirty heap of snow piled against the railings.

Saltley was waiting for me in the bar, which was up the stairs past a nasty looking picture of the Fastnet Rock in a gale. It was a bright, cheerful place full of members locked into London by the state of the roads. He came forward to greet me, small, almost gnome-like, with pale, straw-coloured hair and thick glasses through which a pair of sharp, intensely blue eyes peered owlishly. He was younger than I had expected, mid-thirties, perhaps a little more, and as though to put me at my ease he said his odd appearance – those were the words he used, giving me a lopsided grin – was due to Swedish forebears, the name, too, originally Swedish, but bastardized to Saltley by dumb Anglo-Saxons who couldn't get their tongues round it. The way he put it I thought he probably knew my father had been a Scot.

Even now I don't know Saltley's Christian name. Everybody seemed to call him by his surname, his friends shortening it to Salt or Salty, even Old Salt, but what his initials C. R. stood for I still don't know. It didn't take me long in the atmosphere of that club to realize why he had asked me if I were a sailing man. The conversation as we stood drinking at the bar was general, the talk all about sailing, ocean races mainly – last season's and the Southern Cross series in Australia which had just finished with the Sydney–Hobart.

It was only when we went into the dining-room

that his attention focused on me personally. Those blue eyes, that crooked, very sensitive mouth, the soft, quiet voice – instead of finding out what it was he wanted to see me about, I found myself telling him about my life with Karen and the strange urge that had taken hold of me very early in life, trying to explain why I had wanted to become a writer. I told him something of my background, too, the way I had been brought up. 'So you never knew your father?' He said it very quickly, reaching for the wine bottle.

'No.' Fortunately we had a table to ourselves, the background noise of conversation drowning my words as I added with that mixture of belligerence and frankness that I could never quite conceal, 'And my mother never married.'

He filled my glass, smiling lopsidedly at me. 'That worry you?' He drank slowly, watching me and letting the silence run on. Oddly enough I felt no hostility toward him, no anger at the expert way in which he had manoeuvred me into blurting out more than I had intended. 'It shouldn't,' he said. 'Not now. But, of course, things were different in the fifties. Something we're apt to forget. We live in the present and our memories are short. But scars – deep, emotional scars – they remain in all of us, rooted there and producing gut reactions.' He cut into his steak, concentrating on his food for a moment. 'So you ran pretty wild as a kid?'

I nodded.

'Where?'

'I told you, Nairobi, Dubai . . .' I stopped there,

remembering a scene on the waterfront, a little Baluch boy they'd drowned.

'And Karachi?' he asked. 'Ferrers said something about Karachi.'

I nodded.

'That was after your mother died.'

'Yes.'

'You were fourteen then. Was it to contact your father's old regiment that you jumped a dhow headed for Karachi?' He was suddenly looking straight at me.

'I went to Gwadar,' I said.

'Ah yes.' He nodded. 'Dubai–Baluchistan – the old pearls and slaves route. Quite a journey for a kid of fourteen on his own, down the Gulf, out through the Straits of Hormuz to Gwadar, then to Karachi and almost the length of West Pakistan to Peshawar.'

I stopped eating then, wondering how the hell he knew all that. 'It was a long time ago,' I said.

He gave me a little apologetic smile. 'I've had somebody checking up on you.'

'Why?'

He didn't answer that. And when I asked him what else he had found out about me, he said, 'Your father was a lieutenant in the Khyber Rifles. After Partition he joined the Trucial Oman Scouts. He was stationed near Sharjah. That's how he met your mother. She was a nurse, an Anglo-Indian, I think.'

'If you know all that,' I said angrily, 'then you'll know that he was killed in the Muscat war. You'll also no doubt know that my mother's mother, my grandmother, was from the North West Frontier, an

Afridi.' And I added, the tone of belligerence back in my voice, 'My mother was hot-blooded, very beautiful, a wonderfully exciting person – but it's nothing to do with you what she was. Nothing to do with the *Petros Jupiter* either.'

'I'm sorry.' He gave a shrug and the same little apologetic smile. 'Force of habit. I make my living asking awkward questions.' The strange, bony features were touched suddenly with humour, the eyes smiling at me. 'Please – don't let your food get cold.' He waved his hand at my plate and switched the conversation to dinghy sailing. He navigated now for a man with a Class I ocean racer, but he'd started in dinghies.

It was after we had finished eating, sitting over our coffee, that he finally came to the point. 'I think you know roughly what my job is, but probably not much about the way marine solicitors operate.' And he went on to explain that there were only about a dozen firms in the City specializing in the legal side of marine insurance. At Forthright they concentrated on hull insurance. There were other firms that concentrated on cargoes. 'But as I say, there are only a handful of us trying to sort out all the legal problems that occur when there is an incident – fire, collision, fraud, anything concerning ships or their cargoes that results in an insurance claim. It's very specialist and often there is a great deal of money involved. We're so specialist, in fact, that we're involved worldwide, not just the London market.' He suddenly got to his feet. 'Sorry, you haven't got a drink. Brandy or port?'

'Rum, if I could,' I said, and he nodded. 'Good idea. Help keep the cold out.'

The bar was crowded and while he was getting the drink, I was wondering why he was taking all this trouble, what possible use I could be to such a specialized firm of solicitors operating in the City. I said as much when he handed me my drink and sat down again. He smiled. 'Yes, well, let me explain. We have forty or so partners. I'm never certain what the exact number is. They're solicitors, all of them. They each have their own clients, their own reputations. Then there are a number of trainees, a mass of articled clerks, lots of secretaries. In addition, we employ over a dozen ship captains, men who can go off to any port in the world where we have a problem and by their training and long experience can ask the right questions of the right people and assess what the answers are worth. Some of them develop a remarkable nose for ferreting out the truth. And, of course, each claim being different, and therefore requiring an individual approach, we use any method we feel may be necessary to protect our clients' interests. And that,' he added with a slight emphasis in his voice, 'sometimes includes the employment of people whom we consider have special qualifications for getting at the truth of a particular case.'

He sipped his port, the blue eyes watching me behind the thick-lensed glasses. 'You know Karachi. You speak Urdu. And you've been a ship's officer. I think you're the man I need.'

'For what?' I asked.

He laughed. 'If I knew I wouldn't need you, would I?'

'But it's not the *Petros Jupiter*.'

'No, it's not the *Petros Jupiter*. It's another ship. In fact, it's two now.' And when I told him I was only interested in the *Petros Jupiter*, he said, 'Yes, of course. I understand that.' He was leaning forward, still watching me. 'That's why I wanted to meet you. Ninety per cent of the time I'm just a hardworking solicitor slogging through the paperwork. But there's ten per cent of the time I'm operating by the seat of my pants, sleuthing out the truth like some amateur detective. That's the fun side – or it can be when you get it right and a hunch pays off.' He stopped there. 'It's not the ship you're interested in. It's the engineer, isn't it?' He said it tentatively, not looking at me now. 'Did Ferrers tell you he's changed his name, flown to Bahrain and is now on board a small freighter bound for Karachi?'

'Yes, he showed me the telex. It was from the Lloyd's agent in La Rochelle where the fishing boat landed him.'

'Suppose we were to send you to Karachi, everything paid, and a fee . . . You fly out, you'd be there about the time the *Corsaire* arrives.' He looked at me then. 'That's what you want, isn't it? You want to talk to Aristides Speridion who now calls himself Henri Choffel.' I nodded and he smiled. 'One of our partners would be interested in that, too. He's handling the *Petros Jupiter* case.' He paused then, watching me. 'Well, what do you say?'

I didn't answer immediately. In fact, I was thinking

of Baldwick and his proposition. This, in a way, was even odder. Saltley misinterpreted my silence. 'Sorry,' he said. 'Afraid I've put it to you very abruptly. Let me fill you in a bit. First, the seat of the pants side of it. Back in November the *Aurora B* disappeared. We don't know where. All we know is she missed her radio schedule when she should have been west of Sri Lanka and hasn't been heard of since. Now, just a few days ago, another VLCC, the *Howdo Stranger*, misses her schedule.'

'I was with Ferrers when the news came through,' I said. 'They both missed their schedules in the same area.'

He nodded. 'With a twice-weekly radio schedule it's just guesswork where they disappeared. But yes, the same area roughly. Both insured at Lloyd's, and the lead underwriter in each case Michael Stewart. He's a member here and a friend of mine. In fact, I was at his daughter's twenty-first today. We both started our racing together, you see, in the Lloyd's yacht *Lutine*.' He shook his head sadly. 'Not the best day to pick for a party. And the poor fellow wrote the slip for the *Petros Jupiter* as well, all three of them for the same syndicate, including the Sinister Syndicate, which is hard luck on the girls. He took quite a slice of it for them.'

I suppose he sensed I didn't really understand what he was talking about, for he said, 'You know how Lloyd's work do you? The Members – Names, we call them – operate in syndicates. There are around twenty thousand Names and their personal financial commitment is total. Each is limited in the extent of the premium income he, or she, can underwrite, but if things go wrong, then there's no limit at all to the amount they may be called upon to pay out, even to the point of complete bankruptcy.' And he added, 'One of the syndicates involved here is a rather special one. It's a marine syndicate composed entirely of Members' wives and daughters. My wife's a member of it, so is Mike's, and now his daughter Pamela. She's one of his regular racing crew, and her birthday being on New Year's Eve, the party today was really more to celebrate the start of her underwriting.' He smiled wryly. 'Virgins Unlimited, or the Sinister Syndicate, those are the tags the syndicate has got stuck with and I'm afraid it may prove more apt than intended. They could be facing a very big loss on these three vessels if all the claims are substantiated. And that won't do Mike's reputation any good. He might not even survive it.'

And then abruptly he switched back to the missing ships. 'GODCO – that's the company that owns the two missing VLCCs – operates right through the Gulf. They have offices not far from here, in Curzon Street of all places. But the centre of their operation is Dubai. If you went out, I'd see you had letters of introduction to Gulf Oil executives, the Lloyd's agents of course, also some very useful contacts I've built up over the years. But,' he added, 'that's on the official level. Much more important, I feel, is what you, with your knowledge of Urdu, might pick up unofficially, in the docks, or the bazaars, also in hotel bars. I'm thinking of Karachi, you see. I don't know why, but ever since this second GODCO tanker went missing I've had a feeling . . .' He hesitated, staring at me, then gave a little shrug and picked up his drink.

'You think it's sabotage?' I asked.

'It has to be, doesn't it? Two GODCO ships in two months. They haven't lost a VLCC in eight years. But even if I'm right, I've still got to prove it.'

'And the *Petros Jupiter*?' I asked. 'Who owned her?'

'A Dutch company.'

'I thought it was Greek.'

'It was, but they sold her a few months back. We'll be checking on the Dutch company, of course, but I'm told it's a perfectly reputable outfit.' He didn't know its name or anything about it. Another partner, a man named Pritchard, was handling the *Petros Jupiter*. And he explained that he'd been fully occupied recently preparing a briefing for arbitration in the matter of a £30 million claim where it was suspected that navigational negligence was a contributing factor in the loss of a giant tanker. But now, with the *Howdo Stranger* failing to keep its radio schedule, Stewart was pressing him to begin a full scale investigation of the *Aurora B* claim. That meant, not one, but two new casualties added to his work load. 'Look,' he said, 'I've made you a proposition. You go away and think about it. Tomorrow come along to our offices and have a look through the files.' And he added, with a quick little smile, so that I knew he was baiting the hook for me, 'The *Petros Jupiter*'s cargo was re-sold on the spot market the day before she was wrecked and the skipper's statement makes it clear that his instructions to alter course for Rotterdam reached him when he was midway between Land's End and the Scillies.' And he added, 'I can arrange for you to see that statement. In fact, the whole file, if you like.'

That was how, on the following morning, with the snow still falling and half England a no-go area because of blocked roads, I came to be sitting in the offices of Forthright & Co., marine solicitors, at Saltley's desk, with the *Petros Jupiter* file in front of me. All I had been given on arrival were the papers relating to the *Aurora B* claim. There was nothing on the *Howdo Stranger*. At least, that was what I was told by the only girl I could find who knew her way around the files. Saltley's secretary hadn't made it to the office, nor had half the Forthright staff, so that the whole place had a slightly deserted air, particularly the reception area, which must have cost a fortune in rental it was so vast. A matronly, grey-haired woman in tweeds, standing in as receptionist because neither of the girls at the two big desks had arrived, took me down a long corridor through fire doors to Saltley's empty office. 'Phone me if you want anything.' She gave me the number to dial on the internal phone, then shut the door on me so that I felt like a prisoner being locked into his cell.

It didn't take me long to go through the *Aurora B* file – the failure to meet her radio schedule on November 7, details of loading at Mina Zayed, condition and rating of vessel, information about the recent installation of anti-explosion precautions, all the basic, humdrum details on which any assessment of what might have caused the vessel's mysterious disappearance would depend. There was nothing about crew, no photograph, nothing – which was odd as GODCO always photographed and dossiered crew personnel before every voyage. I knew that because I had shipped a man once who had refused to sail on a GODCO tanker at the last moment because he wouldn't be photographed. In the end, he told me the reason he was camera-shy was that he was bigamously married and afraid that his first wife, whom he described as a right bitch, might see it and come after him. Why we all leap so readily to fanciful conclusions I am not sure, but until then I was convinced that he was either one of the train robbers still on the run, or else a murderer.

There was an internal and an external telephone on the desk. I lifted the external receiver and asked the switchboard operator for a line. She didn't ask who I was or who I was going to ring at the office's expense, she just gave me the line. But when I got through to the GODCO offices in Curzon Street and asked for the current voyage *Aurora B* crew details and pictures, they said all crew information was held at their Dubai offices. They gave me the number and the man to contact.

I might not have followed it up, except that I had asked for the *Petros Jupiter* file and the girl had come back to say that it was with Mr Pritchard and he was asking who I was and why I wanted it. While I waited, hoping he'd let me see it, I asked the switchboard if it was possible to get me the Dubai number and in a matter of minutes I was through to the GODCO Marine Superintendent's office. The man in charge of crew dossiers said that copies of all information concerning the *Aurora B* and the *Howdo Stranger* crews, including copies of the crew pictures, had been despatched airmail to London two days ago. But when I rang the London office again the man I had spoken to before finally admitted their staff was so depleted that morning that he couldn't tell me whether the crew details had arrived or not.

After that there was nothing for me to do but sit there waiting in that empty office. It was an odd feeling, as though I was suspended in limbo – the frozen world outside, and here, encased in concrete and glass, an organization that fed upon disaster, encapsulating the realities of existence, the gales, the sand storms, the oiled-up beaches, the furnace heat of raging fires, into typed reports and telex messages compressed and neatly filed between plastic covers. Cargoes, ships, dockside greed and boardroom chicanery, the remote cold-bloodedness of owners whose decisions were based on money, not humanity, it was all there, neatly filed and docketed – remote, unreal. Legal cases, nothing more.

The previous night, just as I was leaving, Michael Stewart had come into the club with his wife and daughter. They had been to the theatre, but when Saltley introduced me to him I could see the evening had not been a success. The man was under intense strain. And that morning I had spent the first hour or so visiting two shipping offices close to the Baltic Exchange in St Mary Axe. Rates were low, a lot of vessels still laid up and the chances of employment very slight unless you happened to be in a place where the need of a ship's officer was urgent.

Humans, not files – that was the real world. In the circumstances I could count myself lucky I'd had two offers of a job and hadn't had to go looking for either of them. There was a tap at the door and a sharp-faced man with a little brushed-up moustache sidled in, a file under his arm. 'Rodin?' He had a tired voice that matched the weary look on his face. He gave the impression of having seen too much of the wrong side of life.

I nodded and he said his name was Pritchard. His eyes, which were dark, had a nervous sort of clock-work tick, shifting back and forth, left and right, avoiding contact, but at the same time examining me closely. 'Salt told me you'd be asking for the *Petros Jupiter* file. Any particular reason, apart from your wife's involvement?'

'Isn't that sufficient?' I disliked the darting eyes, his lack of sensitivity, the coldness of his manner.

He put the file down on the desk in front of me, flipped open the plastic cover and pointed to the most recent item, a telex. 'That arrived this morning.' And he stood over me while I read it, watching me closely all the time, waiting no doubt to see how I would react to the news.

The telex was from the Lloyd's agent at Karachi. The *Corsaire* had docked that morning at first light.

PASSENGER CHOFFEL NOT ON BOARD. TRANS-
SHIPPED TO DHOW HORMUZ STRAITS 11.00 GMT
YESTERDAY. CORSAIRE'S CAPTAIN UNABLE TO
IDENTIFY DHOW'S NATIONALITY. NO NAME. NO
FLAG. SKIPPER SPOKE SOME ENGLISH, NO FRENCH.
ALL ON BOARD PROBABLY ARAB. ADVISE CONTACT
AGENTS UAE PORTS.

So he'd gone, got clear away. The chances of
finding him now . . . I closed the file and sat staring at
the phone. I could do as the Karachi agent advised,
start ringing round the ports of the United Arab Emirates. But how would the Lloyd's agent in Abu Dhabi,
Dubai, Doha, Bahrain or Kuwait know what dhow it
was? There were so many in the Gulf.

'You've seen all you want?'

I nodded.

'Your only interest then was Choffel?' He was
leaning over me, his eyes darting.

'Yes.'

'Pity!' He hesitated. 'I never had a case like this
before. Stranding is one thing. We might have been
able to claim negligence in their employment of a man
like Choffel, particularly as he had assumed a different
name. In any case, both the ship and its cargo could
have been salvaged. That was what the Dutch said.
But then your wife's action . . . quite unprecedented. It
introduced a new dimension altogether.'

'She's dead,' I said.

The words meant nothing to him. 'There's no

policy I've ever seen covers that sort of thing. You couldn't call it sabotage, could you?'

I stared at him, disliking him intensely. No use telling him I'd seen her die, watched the ship go up, and the man who'd caused her death running free somewhere in the Gulf. I opened the file again, leafing through the thick wad of papers. It was similar to the *Aurora B* file, but much fuller, of course, since the vessel had been there on the rocks for all to see. Salvage reports were interspersed with newspaper cuttings and both shore and marine pollution assessments . . .

'Salt said you might be going out there for us.'

'Yes. I might.' But where? Where would that dhow have taken him? Where the hell would he have gone? Dubai? Dubai was at least 100 miles from the Straits. Ras al Khaimah perhaps, or Khor al Fakkan, which was outside the Gulf on the shores of the Arabian Sea, or Muscat even. There were so many places and all of Arabia for him to get lost in. Iran and Pakistan, too. The dhow might have headed north to the coasts of either of those countries, or to one of the islands in the Gulf.

'If you do go out there for Saltley—' I was searching back through the file as he went on, picking his words carefully: 'He'll be employing you on behalf of his own clients, to try and discover what happened to the *Aurora B* and this new one that's disappeared.' Another, longer pause. I wasn't really listening. I had reached a wadge of newspaper clippings and was living again that night when I'd gone out with Andy in the ILB. 'But you'll keep me informed, won't you? If you do find Choffel, I mean. That's why you're going, isn't it? And if you find him, then try and get a written statement out of him.'

He was leaning right over me, his voice insistent, and I felt like throwing the file at him. Couldn't he understand what I was feeling, reading through those cuttings? And his voice going on again, cold, incisive: 'It could be worth quite a lot to you. I'm sure my clients would not be ungrateful. There's usually a reward, something quite substantial, when an insurance claim is refuted. And the claim here is in the order of eleven million, so we're not talking about—'

I looked up at him then, hating him for his stupidity. 'What the hell are you talking about?' My voice sounded high and uncontrolled. 'Money! I'm not going after him for money.'

He had the grace then to say he was sorry, a muttered apology as he turned away and opened the door. I think he was suddenly a little scared of me. 'I'll leave the file – you might like to look through it . . .' The clockwork eyes darted back and forth. 'I'm sorry,' he said again. 'I didn't quite realize . . .' The door closed, and he was gone, leaving me alone with those macabre cuttings.

A lot of the newspaper reports I hadn't seen before. They were spread over several days, and there were pictures. For factual details the *Telegraph* coverage seemed the best, and both the *Telegraph* and *The Times* had run long articles on the problems of pollution. And then I came upon this, from a weekly magazine: *Was she a nut-case, or just a totally imprac-*

tical young woman determined to set fire to the slick? Or was it done in full command of her senses, an act of great courage undertaken with one aim in mind – to shock the country into taking action to deal with the terrible and growing menace that successive governments have swept under the carpet? And there was a headline I thought Karen would have appreciated – GIRL'S TANKER PYRE SAVES SEABIRDS. The pictures, too – the whole front page of the *Sun*, a night shot with the mist lit by flames, a photograph of Karen inset on one side and one of myself on the other, a clip probably from the TV interview after I'd come back with Andy, my hair plastered over my face, my mouth open and shouting, my eyes wild.

I glanced at them all, pausing here and there to read. And then I had passed beyond that terrible Twelfth Night, back to cuttings that reported the effects of the stranding, the damage to the environment, the probable cost of pollution control, the proportion of the insurance claim to be borne by the London market, Lloyd's in particular. There were pictures from two of the Sunday papers of the wreck and the salvage ships taken from the air. And then I was looking at a picture of the crew being landed at Sennen Cove. They looked Chinese, all except the officers whose names were given in the caption below. *Aristides Speridion, Second Engineer.* It was the first time I had seen a picture of the man. He had a lined, rather sad face, squarish with a dark moustache and dark hair, and a hooked nose so that he might have passed as a member of almost any of the

Mediterranean races. He was wearing a sweater under his uniform reefer and his ears stuck out prominently on either side of the peaked cap, which he wore pushed up on to the back of his head and at a jaunty angle as though he was pleased with himself and to hell with everybody else. The picture also revealed that, if this were the full complement, officers and crew numbered only fifteen.

I was sitting with my chin in my hands, my elbows on the desk, concentrating all my mind on absorbing and retaining the image of the man I now knew to be Choffel, and then suddenly my attention was caught by the face of a bystander right on the edge of the crowd to the left of the picture – a big man, half a head taller than any of the others, broad-shouldered, thick-set. He was in profile, but even so I could see the heavy set of the jaw, the big jowls and the round bullet head. The size of the man alone, the way he stood, the arms slack but the body balanced and alert – I didn't need a caption to tell me who it was. Baldwick! And the date of that cutting was January 3, which meant he had come from Bristol immediately the news of the stranding broke. Why? That Sunday when he had come to Balkaer . . . he hadn't said anything about having been in Sennen nine days before.

I leaned back, staring out of the window with its rime of snow, wondering why he had been there. Was it Choffel he had been after? At Balkaer all he had said was that he'd be in Falmouth that evening, to see the captain of the *Petros Jupiter*. No mention of the second engineer, no reference to the fact that he had been there, in Sennen, when the whole crew were brought ashore. In any case, it wasn't the captain who'd put the engines out of action. No, it had to be Choffel, and if I was right, then the one man who knew where the little bastard would be now was Baldwick. The card he had given me was in my pocket, but when I rang the Liverpool number he had scribbled on the back of it he had already left – for France, the hotel said, but they had no forwarding address.

His next destination was Nantes, a river port on the Loire, so probably Choffel had given him the names of possible ships' officers he knew who needed money and were not too particular how they came by it. I phoned the Nantes number. It was the Hôtel du Commerce. Yes, Monsieur Baldwick had a reservation, but he do not arrive yet. His room there was booked for two nights.

I leaned back again, staring out at the darkening sky, thinking about Len Baldwick and a story I had once heard of his early life in Sheffield, from a little rat-faced Sparks I'd met at an oil man's flat in Basra. He'd been a shop floor convener in a privately owned steelworks then, a paid-up card-holding Communist, the man had said, and to his certain knowledge Baldwick had set fire to the home of a well-known Labour supporter who had accused him of intimidation. Was that what he'd done to Choffel, intimidated him? Had he fixed it all, the *Vague d'Or*, the *Corsaire*, the dhow in the Hormuz Straits? Was he the link by which I could catch up with the man?

My hand reached slowly out to the internal phone,

trembling slightly as I lifted the receiver and dialled the grey-haired woman's extension. Phone me, she had said, if you want anything . . . and Saltley the night before trying to insist that I went out to Karachi for him. The woman answered. I took a deep breath and asked her to contact their usual travel agents and have them book me on the next flight to Nantes. She didn't argue. She just took it in her stride as though a sudden request like that from a total stranger was the most natural thing in the world. All she said was, 'Return or single, Mr Rodin?'

'Single,' I said. I thanked her and put down the receiver, and after that I just sat there, not caring what Saltley would say, only wondering what the hell I was letting myself in for.

It must have been about ten minutes later that the door was pushed open and he came bustling in, a briefcase in one hand, a file of papers in the other, his face still pink with the cold outside and his overcoat glistening with melted snow. A bright red woollen cap was perched incongruously on his head. 'So you're going to Nantes.' He dumped his papers and briefcase on the desk. 'Mrs Shipton asked me to tell you they've booked you on tomorrow's flight.' He glanced at his watch, then passed me my anorak from the chair where I had thrown it. 'We'll be late, I'm afraid. I said one o'clock and it's that already.' He hurried me out, along a corridor that led to another set of lifts, explaining as we went that after I had left his club the previous night Michael Stewart had suggested we had lunch with him in the Captain's Room at Lloyd's.

'That's if you were going to work for us. I take it you are?'

'So long as I have a free hand,' I said.

He gave me a quick hard look. 'The *Petros Jupiter*?'

I nodded.

The lift came. 'I don't think we'll object to your running the enquiries in tandem. I know Mike won't. He knows now he slipped up on the *Petros Jupiter*. He should never have written the slips. As good as told me so last night. But it's the other two claims . . . if he has to meet those—' He gave a little shrug. We were out into Lime Street, picking our way diagonally across the grey, churned-up slush of the roadway and into the great arched portals of Lloyd's itself.

I couldn't help it. I suddenly felt overwhelmed, a sense of excitement, of awe almost. All my life, ever since I had gone to sea, I'd always heard of Lloyd's. It had always been there in the background, to initiate enquiries into any misadventure, any slip-up in navigation, to survey the ship, check seaworthiness, pay for damage, arrange salvage, the cargo too – and here I was entering the building, being taken to lunch in the Captain's Room. A waiter took our coats, a magnificent figure in long scarlet greatcoat, black-collared and cuffed, the whole elaborate archaic paraphernalia topped off with a gold-banded tall black hat. The grandeur and opulence of that entrance; it was more like a museum, except the undercover roadway went through to the offices of the Baltic Exchange. 'I said

I'd pick him up at his box,' Saltley said. 'Give you an opportunity to see the Room.'

We went through swing doors into a high room floored in black, white and grey marble, half a dozen flags flanking a stained glass window at one end, and at the other a scarlet-coated waiter sitting at a desk. Saltley said good morning to him, produced a plastic pass card and went on through revolving doors that were posted as *Private – for the use of Members and their associates*, through into a lofty, galleried room the size of a football field filled with dark-suited men armed with papers, books and files. They stood about, talking softly or hurrying between the ranks of 'boxes' that were the underwriters' pitches and looked like old-fashioned, high-backed pews, except that the men sitting in them were writing busily or looking up information in the books and ledgers that were stacked on the shelves.

'It goes on like this all day,' Saltley said over his shoulder as he pushed his way to the far end of the Room. 'Most of the fellows you see rushing about are brokers and their clerks busy getting underwriters to sign the slips that give insurance cover to whatever the business is they're handling. Looks a madhouse, but the box arrangement is the most space-saving way of handling such a huge volume of business.'

The wall to the left was papered with telex sheets and typed information, the Stock Exchange news running into weather forecasts and sports results. There were three lifts, but Saltley turned away from them, threading his way quickly between ledger-piled boxes, heading out from under the balcony into the centre of the Room. Michael Stewart's box was in the far corner. There were three men in it and a queue of three or four clerks waiting upon him with papers ready in their hands. He handed over to one of the others and came hurrying across. I saw him glance at Saltley, who gave a little nod, then he was greeting me. 'We'll have a quick drink first. I've sent my daughter up to grab a table. She insisted on lunching with us.' His hand was on my arm, steering me to the lifts near the Lime Street entrance, and I was remembering my meeting with the girl the previous night. She had been quite plain-looking with a squarish face, very little make-up and no jewellery; a big, sensible girl with strong hands and a nice smile. 'You've seen the files, have you? Got all the information you need?' His voice sounded tense. 'That's the Casualty Board, incidentally.' He nodded to two short display panels opposite the lifts peppered with yellow pages of typescript secured with bulldog clips. 'That's where all the bad news is posted. The Ulcer Board, a friend of mine calls it. Every year, it seems, the casualties get worse. When are you leaving?'

'Tomorrow morning,' Saltley answered for me. 'He's flying to Nantes.'

'Nantes! Why Nantes?'

'A contact,' I told him. I turned to Saltley. 'A hunch really.' I knew he'd understand that.

'And after Nantes?' Stewart asked.

'One of the Gulf ports. Dubai most probably since that seems to be my man's present base. But from my knowledge of him I'd say he operates in any port of the Gulf where there's drugs or arms or something equally nasty to be shipped. At the moment he's head-hunting officers for a consortium starting up in the tanker business. I think he's recruited Choffel.'

'And you're going to let yourself be recruited, that it?' His assumption came as a shock, though I suppose the thought had been there at the back of my mind. We were in the lift then and he was smiling, his manner suddenly easier and more relaxed. He turned to Saltley. 'Looks like you've picked a flier.' And then to me: 'You don't waste time. How did you hear this man was recruiting ships' officers?'

I explained briefly and by then we had reached the second floor and were out into a big room with high narrow windows. It was very crowded, the waitresses bustling from table to table with trays of drinks. 'Ah! There's Pam, and she's got a table.' His face had brightened, his manner suddenly almost boyish. 'Best of running a boat, even daughters do as they're told.'

Pamela Stewart was holding the fort at a table in a large annexe guarded by white pillars. There was an oil painting above her head of the Room cleared of boxes with a diamond-spangled ball in formal swing. She jumped to her feet, her eyes lighting, and in that instant she looked quite lovely, brimming over with youth and vitality. Perhaps it was her presence, the way she leaned forward, her eyes on me all the time, but before I had even finished my Bloody Mary I had filled them in on Baldwick and how he and Choffel were a possible lead. And over lunch, in one of the

wooden cubicles of the solid, rather old-fashioned restaurant they called the Captain's Room after the room
in the old Lloyd's Coffee House where the insurance
business had all started, I even talked about my book.
And all the time I was conscious of Pamela's brownish-
green eyes watching me intently. She was dressed in a
close-knit woollen dress, very plain with a high neck.
It was the colour of autumn gold and there was a
golden eagle clutching a round globe of some deep-
red stone at her throat.

And afterwards, when we had finished our coffee,
she insisted on taking me down to the Nelson Exhibition on the Gallery floor. It was a beautiful room,
all rich woodwork and flanked by glass display cabinets full of Nelson letters and a lot of silver. There was
an alcove to the left with a big oil canvas of Nelson
by a painter called Abbott, and at the far end Hardy's
golden Trafalgar sword was displayed in a separate
case below some more Nelson letters and a Hopner
print of him. And then I was leaning on the only other
glass table case in the room, staring at the log of HMS
Euryalus covering the period 23 May to 11 March
1806. It was open at the page recording Nelson's
England expects signal.

'Something I want you to understand . . .' She
wasn't looking at the log book. She hadn't commented
on it, or on anything else in the room. The visit to the
exhibition was just an excuse, and now, with her back
to the priceless relic, leaning her handsomely shaped
body against the case containing Hardy's sword, she
went on in a quiet, very throaty voice, 'We're in

trouble, and after listening to you today, over drinks and during lunch, I've got a sort of feeling . . . I don't know how to put this. But it's like you are our only hope, if you see what I mean.'

She checked there, swallowing hard as though she was struggling to suppress some deep emotion. Then she went on, her voice more controlled. 'If these claims stick, particularly the *Aurora B* and the *Howdo Stranger* claims, then I think Daddy's finished. He's underwriting the premium maximum and the family has always taken a lot of the GODCO insurance. I'm not affected, of course. I didn't start underwriting till this month. But Mother's been one of his Virgins for years, so both of them are in very deep.' She put her hand out and gripped hold of my arm. 'This is what I want you to understand. It's not the money. The money doesn't matter so much. We'll survive, somehow. But I don't think you quite understand what this means to my father. He's the third generation. His father, and his father's father, they were both underwriters here at Lloyd's. In marine insurance they were the tops. It was their life, their *raison d'être*. They lived and breathed Lloyd's, totally dedicated to the Society.' And she added, 'You might even say obsessed. That's how Daddy is. It's his life, his whole world.' She smiled. 'That and sailing,' she said, endeavouring to lighten the emotional intensity with which she had been speaking. 'I didn't want you to feel . . .' She paused, shaking her head. 'I don't know how to put this. Our backgrounds must seem very different.'

'You know nothing about my background.'

'Oh, yes, I do.' And when I laughed and told her not to make erroneous comparisons, she said quickly, 'Last night, after you'd gone, Salty showed us a dossier on you somebody had got out for him – where you'd been, what you'd done. Daddy was impressed. So was I. Especially what you did after your mother died. Did you really go right through Baluchistan and the North West Frontier, to the Khyber and up into the Murree Hills – on your own, when you were only fourteen?'

'Yes. But it wasn't like it is today.'

She didn't seem to hear. 'And then – this morning – I went to the Overseas League and looked through the newspaper files. I'm only just back from Gib – we've got our boat down there, you see – so I didn't know the details, about the *Petros Jupiter*, I mean. I'm sorry. It must have been quite terrible for you – seeing it.'

'Yes, but I'll get him.' I said it without thinking, but all she did was nod her head, accepting it as though that were the inevitable sequel to what had happened. There was a long silence. Finally she said, 'What I wanted to explain . . .' She shook her head. 'No, it's too difficult.' A moment's pause and then she went on, 'We're just people, you see. Like anyone else really. I know we've got money, a big house, cars, a yacht – but it doesn't mean anything. Not really. What I mean is . . . well, when you're racing, in a force 8 gale with a big sea running, you don't worry then about whether you've got more money than the next guy – you're too tired, too battered, too bloody scared sometimes.' She gave me that warm smile, the eyes large and fixed on mine, her hand touching my arm. 'I just wanted you to understand. I'm afraid Salty may have got you into something . . .'

'I got myself into it,' I said. I could feel her fingers through my jacket. 'So no need for you to worry.'

'Yes, of course.' She took her hand away, shifting her position, her mood suddenly changing. 'Daddy will be back at his box now. And I have a boy I promised to see who's desperate to crew with us in the Med this year.' She gave a quick little laugh. 'I'm not sure yet whether it's me or the boat he's interested in. Can you find your way back to Forthright's?'

She left me almost immediately, and I didn't think about her again until that night. I was all set then, tickets, traveller's cheques, contacts, everything the marine solicitors could provide me with – a contractual letter, too. And then, alone on the hard iron bedstead in that dingy basement, unable to get to sleep, I found myself thinking about her. God knows, there'd been nothing sexy about her. Quite the reverse, in fact. Just a nice, plain English girl, hooked on sailing and probably half in love with her father. And yet . . .

There wasn't a sound to disturb my thoughts. A little room in the East End of London and I might have been in space. Everything deathly still, frozen into silence. No sound of the sea now, no gulls screaming, no rollers thundering. The stillness of death, and my thoughts not on Karen, but on a lump of a girl propped against a case with a gold sword in it belonging to Captain Hardy of the *Victory* and talking endlessly about how they were just ordinary folk, while I stared at her tits and wondered what she'd do if I grabbed hold of them, in Lloyd's of all places!

The next thing I knew it was daylight and the sun was streaming in out of a hard clear sky. It was still shining three and a half hours later when I took off from Heathrow in a half-empty Fokker Fellowship, flying over an England that was mantled deep in snow and brilliantly white. It was only when we were over the Channel and approaching the coast of France that we ran into cloud.

PART THREE

THE ROAD TO DUBAI

CHAPTER ONE

The clouds were thinning when we landed at Nantes, fitful gleams of sunlight flickering on wet tarmac, and in the city itself the French moved quickly, huddled in topcoats, for it was cold with an east wind blowing down the river. Baldwick was out when I reached the Hôtel du Commerce, and not expected back until evening. I scribbled him a note, and after checking into a room, took a taxi to the address of the Lloyd's agent. His name was Louis Barre and he had a small, untidy office looking out over the quay to a glimpse of the river through the superstructure of a cargo vessel.

'Mistair Rodin?' He was on his feet, waving a telex at me as I entered. 'Zis arrive thees morning to say you are coming to me. Sit down, sit down please.' He waved me to a chair. 'You want to know about Choffel, eh? The *Petros Jupiter*. I have made enquiries.' He was large and energetic, bouncing up and down on the balls of his feet as he talked, jiggling a bunch of keys in the pocket of his jacket. 'He is what I think you call my patch.' His English was quick, almost staccato, the words ejected like grape pips through half-closed teeth. 'It is a big river, the Loire, but Nantes is not like a seaport. It is more . . . what is the word? More a port of the region. Along the quay here we know many people, and Choffel, he has a house at Parnay, a few kilometres beyond Saumur, so it is not difficult for me to find out about him.'

He bounced across to the door of the outer office, rattled some French at the girl who had shown me in, then turned back to me: 'She has now finished typing the report. You like coffee while you read it? Milk, sugar?' I said I'd like it black and he nodded. '*Deux noirs*,' he said and handed me a single sheet of type-script. 'It gives the background, all I can discover about him. If you want more, then we drive to Parnay and talk to his daughter. She is secretary at a clinic in Saumur. But today she is at home because she has a bad cold.'

The report was in the form of notes and typed in English:

Dossier of Henri Albert Choffel, ship's engineer: Age 46. Medium height, appearance swarthy, black waved hair, large ears, nose like hawk. Address: 5042 Les Tuffeaux, Parnay. Place of birth – no information.

First employed in the locality by Réaux et Cie as replacement for engineer who is sick on board the coaster *Tarzan* in 1959. Married Marie Louise

Gaston from Vertou in 1961. One child, a daughter, Guinevere. Continued in employment with Réaux until 1968 when he became chief engineer of the bulk carrier *Olympic Ore*. This vessel is Greek-owned at that time and sailing on Panamanian flag-of-convenience. She is sunk in 1972.

After that there is no information about Choffel until 1976, except that he buys the house at Parnay and his wife dies in February 1973, after a transplant of the kidney operation. It is her husband who gives the kidney.

In 1976 Choffel's name occurs in connection with the *Stella Rosa*. This is a small Lebanese vessel sunk off Pantelleria and Choffel is chief engineer. The enquiry, which was in Palermo, exonerated Choffel from any involvement in the sabotage of the sea cocks. But the ship is gun-running for the Polisario and on his return to Nantes in March 1977 his connection with these two ships, the *Olympic Ore* and the *Stella Rosa*, makes it difficult for him to gain employment as chief engineer. He is, in any case, not a Frenchman, though he has been naturalized for over twenty years. This is evident from his papers, which are already French when he is first employed by Réaux in 1959. This leads me to believe he may have been from North Africa originally. I can enquire of the relevant department of government if this information is required.

In 1978 I understand he tried to establish a

small mushroom business at his home in Parnay, but this does not seem to have succeeded as he is back in Nantes looking for employment on a ship early in 1979. I can discover no information concerning this man in Nantes between June 1979, when he shipped out as third engineer on the Colombian-registered cargo ship, *Amistad*, and this year when he is second engineer on the *Petros Jupiter*. I have not so far made enquiries of his daughter, but will do so if it is thought necessary.

(SIGNED) LOUIS BARRE

The coffee arrived and I read the report through again, conscious all the time of the Frenchman's impatience. It told me very little I didn't already know, except about Choffel's personal life, but that was no concern of mine. The *Stella Rosa* – nothing new there. And no information about the sinking of the *Olympic Ore*. I wished I had asked about that at Colchester, but there had been so much information to absorb. All the report amounted to was confirmation of a doubtful record. I finished the Nescafé, concentrating on the last part of the report. Why mushrooms? Why spend a year or more a long way up the river at Parnay? And the daughter – would she know where he had gone? If they were close, which was possible with his wife dead, then she might have had a letter.

'What is it?' Barre suddenly exploded. 'You are not satisfied? There is something more you think your people require?'

I hesitated. The man had done his best. But it was disappointing. 'Choffel left the *Corsaire* in the Straits of Hormuz, did you know that?'

'Yes. I have a telex from Pritchard two days ago to that effect. He is trans-shipped to a dhow.'

'But you don't know where he is now.'

He stared at me as though I had said something outrageous. 'Pritchard ask only for background information. He does not ask me where he is gone, what his plans are. How could I possibly tell him that? A man like Choffel, on the run as you say, does not shout his destination from the rooftops.'

'His daughter might know. It's almost a week now. He could have written.'

'You want to question her, she is at her house today. Or I take you to Réaux.' He produced the names of several individuals who had given him background information. 'You wish to question them yourself?'

I shook my head. I didn't see how that would help.

'So why do you come?' he demanded angrily. 'Why don't you stay in London till you receive my report?'

I hesitated. 'Did any of them mention a man named Baldwick in connection with Choffel? Len Baldwick. He's at the Hôtel du Commerce.'

He shook his head. 'What is he? What is he doing here?' And when I told him, he said, 'But if he is recruiting these types, why Nantes? Why not Brest or Marseilles, some big seaport where he has more chance of finding what he want?'

'That's something I hope to discover this evening.'

'So that is why you come here, to see this Englishman who is staying at your hotel?'

'Partly.' I was looking down at the sheet of typing
again. 'How do you know Choffel's daughter is at
home today?'

'I phone the clinic in Saumur this morning.'

'But not her home.'

'No.'

'Can we phone her now?'

'She is not on the phone.'

'You think she knows where her father is?'

He didn't answer that, his sharp eyes staring and
a frown on his face. 'So! That is why you are here.' He
leaned forward, his elbows on the desk, the knuckles of
his hands pressed into his cheeks, looking straight at
me. 'It is not the man's background that interests you,
it is where you can find him. Why? You are not the
police. You cannot arrest him. Even if you discover
where he is—' He stopped there, silent for a moment,
his eyes still fixed on me. 'All right then. Okay.' He
suddenly bounced to his feet. 'I take you to see her. It
is only two hours, a bit more per'aps according to the
traffic. And there is a little restaurant I know just
beyond Angers where we can eat.'

He had a Renault 20 and he drove fast, the radio
on all the time so that conversation was almost impossible. I leaned back and closed my eyes, lulled by the
husky voice of a singer crooning a French love song,
wondering about the girl, what she would be able to
tell me. And in the evening I would be meeting Baldwick. The thought depressed me – that and Barre's

hostility. I could feel it in the silent intensity of his driving. He didn't understand, of course. He hadn't connected me with the woman who had blown the ship up. And it had been tactless of me not to conceal my disappointment at his report. Two years living an isolated existence with just one other human being – I had forgotten the pressures of everyday life, the sensitivity of men whose pride was part of their individual armour against the world. Rationalization, self-justification . . . God! How tired I was! How very, very tired!

The drone of the engine, the voice singing, the sky dark and the wind blattering at the car in gusts . . . I had a feeling of remoteness, my mind transported, drifting in a daze. Emotional exhaustion perhaps, or just the loneliness. Sitting there, my eyes closed, my cap pushed back, my body enveloped in the heat from the engine – heavy lorries thundering by, the flash of headlights in the murk . . . Christ! What a filthy lousy day! And here I was being driven by a stranger, a Frenchman, through a land gripped in winter, to meet the daughter of a man I'd sworn to kill . . . Guinevere – a name from Arthurian legend, was that important? Would she have heard from him? He could be in the desert now, or at sea, or buried in the teeming masses of some Arab town. Dubai, Sharjah, Ras al Khaimah, Khor al Fakkan – the Emirate names passing through my mind like a refrain – and Muscat, too, El Ain . . . all the names of all the places I had ever visited in the Gulf. Where would it be – where would I catch up with him? And when I did, would I really kill him? Would I have the guts?

And then, after a long time, I saw his newspaper picture face twisted in pain, the wide stare, the shocked surprise and the blood spurting. What had I used? In God's name, was it a knife, or was it my bare hands? My teeth were bared and gritted, my fingers wet and feeling flesh, squeezing, squeezing, and I was cursing as the tongue came out and his eyes glazed . . .

'Angers,' Barre said and I blinked my eyes and sat up.

We were off the dual carriageway, driving into the centre of a city. 'I'm sorry,' I murmured. 'I must have fallen asleep.'

'You're tired, I think. You were talking to yourself.' He switched off the radio. 'We are coming now to one of the great châteaux of France.' He turned off to the right, away from the river which he said was the Maine, and above us I saw a line of great black-banded towers. 'A pity you don't have time to view the tapestries of the Apocalypse – this city has some of the most remarkable tapestries in the world.' He talked then about the Angevin kings and the Plantagenet connection until we stopped at a little hotel in Bohalle for lunch.

What I had said while I was asleep in the car I don't know, but all through the meal, it seemed, he avoided the purpose of our journey, putting himself out to be entertaining as though I were somebody to be treated with care. It was only at the end, over the last of the wine and some excellent local cheese, that he suddenly said, 'That girl, what are you going to say to her, have you thought?'

I gave a little shrug. What the hell was I going to say to her? 'Does she know her father wrecked a tanker?'

'It's not certain. There's no proof yet. But of course she knows he's under suspicion. It is in all the papers. And yesterday the local press print a statement from the skipper of the *Vague d'Or*.' And he added, 'Is better you leave it to me, eh? She may not have any English and if I talk to her—'

'Ask her if she's heard from her father, if possible get his address.'

'And how do we explain ourselves? She might talk to me, but with two of us there – I don't know.' He was frowning. 'I think if I were her I would be asking some questions before giving any answers.'

We were still discussing it as we drove out of Bohalle, the road now hugging the bank of the Loire, through Les Rosiers, St Clément-de-Levées and St Martin-de-la-Place. At Saumur, with its fairy château perched above the river, we crossed over to the south bank and almost immediately the road was bounded by shallow limestone cliffs along which conventional house fronts had been built as façades to what were apparently troglodyte dwellings. 'Les Tuffeaux,' Barre said, and talked for a moment about the mushroom industry that had grown side by side with the wine business in caves carved out of the limestone to provide the building material for medieval churches.

He stopped at a riverside café to enquire the way

and afterwards we turned right at Souzay to join a narrow road close under the cliffs. Mushrooms, he said, were a by-product of the Cavalry School at Saumur. 'What you call horse shit,' he added, laughing. It was a long, very narrow road and the Choffel house was at the end, in a little cul-de-sac where there was a cave half-hidden by a drooping mass of vegetation, the entrance sealed off by an iron door with a dilapidated notice announcing Vin à Vendre. We parked there and walked back. The figures 5042 were painted black above the rough plaster porch and from a rusty little iron gate opposite that led into a small rose garden there was a fine view over tiled rooftops to the broad waters of the Loire glinting in a cold shaft of sunlight.. Dark clouds hung over the northern bank where the vineyards gave way to forest.

I had no preconceived mental picture of Choffel's daughter. I expected her to be dark, of course, but I hadn't really thought about it, my mind on how I could persuade her to give us the information I needed. It came as a shock, when she opened the door, to find there was something vaguely familiar about her. She was about twenty, well-rounded with black hair cut in a fringe that framed a squarish face and I had the feeling I had seen her before.

Barre introduced us and at my name she turned her head, staring at me with a puzzled frown. Her eyes were large and dark like sloes, very bright, but that may have been because of her cold. She looked as though she was running a temperature. Barre was still talking, and after a moment's hesitation, during which her eyes remained fixed on my face, she let us into the house. 'I have told her we are here about the *Petros Jupiter* insurance, nothing else,' Barre whispered as she ushered us into what I suppose would be called the parlour in that sort of house. It was a comfortably furnished room and almost the first thing I noticed was a photograph of her father, the same dark features and prominent nose I had seen in the newspaper pictures, but clean shaven and bare-headed, the crinkly black hair carefully smoothed down, and he was smiling self-consciously, dressed in his engineer's uniform. Standing beside it, in an identical silver frame, was the photograph of a young woman with the most enormous eyes staring out of a long, gaunt face. She had a broad, pale brow and a mass of curly brown hair. 'My family,' the girl said to me in English, and then she had turned back to Barre, speaking in French again, the tone of her voice sharp and questioning.

It was a strange room, more than half of it natural rock that had been plastered over and then decorated. This and the colour of the walls, which was a pale green, gave it a certain coldness, and with just the one window it had an almost claustrophobic feel to it. I heard my name mentioned and Guinevere Choffel was repeating it, staring at me again, her eyes wide, a shocked look that was mixed with doubt and confusion. 'Why are you here? What do you want?' Her English was perfect, but with something of a lilt to it, and she said again, 'Why are you here?' her voice

dropping away to a note of despair. 'It was an accident,' she breathed. 'An accident, do you hear?'

She knew! That was my first reaction. She knew
about Karen, what had happened. And the reason I
was here, she must have guessed that, for she didn't
believe me when I said I represented Forthright & Co.,
the marine solicitors dealing with the case, and needed
her father's address so that we could arrange for him
to make a statement. 'No. It's something else, isn't it?'
And in the flash of her eyes, the sound of her voice, I
had that sense of familiarity again, but stronger now.
And then it dawned on me. She was like Karen in a
way, the same sort of build, the same high colouring
against the raven black hair, that lilt in the voice; that
emotional quality, too, the voice rising and those dark
eyes bright with the flash of her anger: 'You don't
understand. You don't know my father or you
wouldn't think such a thing.' She pulled a handkerchief
from the pocket of her skirt and turned away to blow
her nose. 'He's had a hard life,' she mumbled. 'So
many things gone wrong, and not his fault – except
that once.' This last was swallowed so that I almost
lost it. And then she had turned and was facing me
again, her voice rising: 'Now you're here, blaming him.
It's been the same, always, you understand. Always.
Do you know what it's like, to be accused of things
you don't do? Well, do you?' She didn't wait for an
answer. 'No,' she said, her voice higher still and trembling. 'Of course you don't. It's never happened to
you. And now you come here, asking me, his daughter,
to tell you where he's gone. You think I would do that

when you have already passed judgment on him?' She seemed to take a grip of herself then, speaking slowly and with emphasis, 'It's not his fault the ship is wrecked. You must believe that. Please.'

'You saw him in La Rochelle, did you?' Or perhaps he had only had time to contact her by phone.

'In La Rochelle?' She stared at me.

'In the trawler basin there, when he arrived in the *Vague d'Or.*'

'No, I don't go to La Rochelle. Is he in La Rochelle?' She sounded surprised.

'He didn't contact you?'

'No, how could he? I didn't know.' She was still staring at me, breathing heavily. 'La Rochelle, you say?' And when I explained, she shook her head. 'No, I don't see him there, or anywhere. I didn't know he was in France.'

'But you've had a letter from him?'

'No, not since—' she checked herself. 'No. No letter.'

'But you've heard from him. You know where he is.'

She didn't answer that, her lips tight shut now.

'Do you know a man named Baldwick?' I thought there was a flicker of recognition in her eyes. 'He's in Nantes. Has he phoned you, or sent you a message?'

She lifted her head then, the dark eyes staring into mine. 'You don't believe me, do you? You've made up your—' She shook her head. 'You had better go please. I have nothing to tell you, nothing at all, do you hear?' Her voice, quieter now, the lilt stronger, had an undercurrent of tension in it. 'She was your wife, I suppose. I read about it in an English paper.' And when I didn't answer, she suddenly cried out, 'She did it – herself. You cannot blame somebody who wasn't there.' I could smell her fear of me then as she went on, 'I'm sorry. But it's her fault. Nothing to do with my father.'

'Then why didn't he stay in England? If he'd waited for the Enquiry—'

'It's nothing to do with him, I tell you.' And then, vehemently, almost wildly – 'It's the chief engineer. He's the man you should ask questions about, not my father.'

'Is that what he's told you?'

She nodded.

'You have heard from him then,' I said.

'Of course. He wrote me as soon as he landed in Cornwall.'

'Did he tell you he was planning to get away in a Breton fishing boat, that he didn't dare face the Enquiry?'

'No, he didn't say that. But I was glad – glad when I knew. For his sake.' She must have been very conscious of my hostility, for she suddenly shouted at me, 'What do you expect him to do? Wait to be accused by a chief engineer who isn't sick, but drunk and incompetent? It's happened before, you know. Why should he wait, an innocent man, to be accused again?' She was standing quite close to me, looking up into my face, her eyes wide and desperate. 'You don't believe me?'

'No,' I said.

And then she did something so unexpected it shocked me deeply. She spat in my face. She jerked her head and ejected her germ-laden spittle straight into my face. '*Maquereau!* You're like all the rest. When you've got a man down you kick his teeth in. My father is the finest, most generous, kindly man I know, and you use him, all of you, as though he is nothing but a turd under your feet. I hate you. I hate the whole world.' Tears were streaming down her face and she rushed to the door, pulling it open and screaming, 'Get out! D'you hear? *Allez!* And tell your friends, everybody, that he is clear of you all now. He's free, and you'll never find him. Never.'

The door banged behind us.

'Is not a very rewarding visit, eh?' Barre said with a chuckle as we walked back to the car. He seemed to enjoy my discomfort, and then as we drove back down to the main road he said, 'Nothing is what it seems to be, isn't it so? The man you regard as a terrorist, others think of in ideological terms. So what about Choffel, eh? You see him as a wrecker, a man who has deliberately caused a tanker to go on to the rocks, but to his daughter he is a kindly, generous man who would not hurt a soul and you are the enemy.' He glanced at me quickly. 'How do you think he sees himself?'

I hadn't considered that. 'I've had other things to think about,' I told him.

'That is not an answer.' He waited a moment, then said, 'But why does he do it?'

'Money,' I said. 'What else?'

'There are other reasons – anger, frustration, politics. Have you thought about those?'

'No.'

He gave a little shrug and after that he didn't ask any more questions. It was a filthy drive, night falling and the traffic heavy after we had passed through Saumur. He seemed withdrawn then. A dusting of sleet gradually laid a white coating over everything. He had the radio on, the windscreen wipers clicking back and forth – my eyes closed, my mind drifting into reverie, no longer thinking about the girl, but about my meeting with Baldwick. It loomed closer every minute and I had no idea where it would take me, what I was letting myself in for. Suppose I was wrong? Suppose he hadn't recruited Choffel? Then it would be to no purpose and I could find myself involved in something so crooked that not even my letter of agreement with Forthright's would protect me.

It was just on six when we pulled up at the entrance to my hotel. 'I'm sorry you don't get what you want,' he said. 'But the girl was frightened. You realize that.' And he sat there, staring at me, waiting for me to say something. 'You frightened her,' he said again.

I started to open the door, thanking him for the trouble he had taken and for the lunch he had insisted on buying me, but his hand gripped my arm, holding me. 'So! She is right. It was your wife. I had forgotten the name. I did not connect.' He was leaning towards me, his face close, his eyes staring into mine. '*Mon Dieu!*' he breathed. 'And you have no proof, none at all.'

'No?' I laughed. The man was being stupid. 'For God's sake! The chief was sick, or so he says. Choffel was in charge, and for the secondary reduction gear to go right after an engine failure ... that ... that's too much of a coincidence. He was quite close to it when it happened. He admitted that.' And then I was reminding him that, at the first opportunity, the man had stolen a dinghy, got aboard a Breton fishing boat, then flown out to Bahrain to board a freighter bound for Karachi and had finally been picked up by a dhow in the Hormuz Straits. 'His escape, everything, organized, even his name changed from Speridion back to Choffel. What more do you want?'

He sat back then with a little sigh, both hands on the wheel. 'Maybe,' he murmured. 'But she's a nice girl and she was scared.'

'She knew I was right. She knew he was caught up in some crooked scheme—'

'No, I don't think so.' But then he shrugged and left it at that. '*Alors!* If there is anything more I can do for you—' He barely waited for me to get out before pulling away into the traffic.

There was a note for me at the desk. Baldwick was back and waiting for me in the hotel's bar-restaurant. I went up to my room, had a wash in lukewarm water, then stood at the window for a moment staring down at the shop-lit street below, where cars moved sluggishly in a glitter of tiny snowflakes. Now that the moment of my meeting with Baldwick had come, I was unsure of myself, disliking the man and the whole stinking mess of Arab corruption on which he

141

battened. A gust of wind drove snowflakes hard like sugar against the window and I laughed, remembering the girl. If it were true what Barre had said, that she'd been frightened of me ... well, now I knew what it felt like. I was scared of Baldwick, of thrusting my neck into his world, not knowing where it would lead. And the girl reminding me of Karen. God damn it! If I was scared now, how would it be when I was face to face with her father?

I turned abruptly from the window. It wasn't murder. To kill a rat like that ... Why else was I here, anyway? In Nantes. At the same hotel as Baldwick. And she'd known about Baldwick. I was certain of it, that gleam of recognition when I mentioned his name. She'd associated him with her father's escape. And Baldwick in Sennen when that picture had been taken of the *Petros Jupiter*'s crew coming ashore. To recruit a man like Choffel meant he'd been told to find an engineer who was an experienced wrecker.

I shivered, the room cold, the future looming uncertain. Another gust rattled the window. I made an effort, pulled myself together and started down the stairs.

The bar-restaurant looked out on to the street, the windows edged with a dusting of ice crystals, the snow driving horizontally. The place was cold and almost empty. Baldwick was sitting at a table pulled as close as possible to a moveable gas fire. He had another man with him, a thin-faced man with a dark blue scarf wrapped round a scrawny neck and a few strands of hair slicked so carefully over the high bald dome of his head that they looked as though they were glued there. 'Albert Varsac,' Baldwick said.

The man rose, tall and gaunt. '*Capitaine* Varsac.' He held out a bony hand.

'First mate on a coaster's as far as you ever got.' Baldwick laughed, prodding him with a thick finger. 'That's raight, ain't it? You never bin an effing captain in yer life.' He waved me to a seat opposite. 'Got your message,' he said. His eyes were glassy, his mood truculent. He shouted for a glass, and when it came, he sloshed red wine into it and pushed it across to me. 'So you changed your mind, eh?'

I nodded, wondering how far I would have to commit myself in order to catch up with Choffel.

'Why?' He leaned forward, his big bullet head thrust towards me, the hard bright eyes staring me in the face. 'You good as told me ter bugger off when I saw you down at that little rat hole of a cottage of yours. Get a't, you said. I don't want anything to do wi' yer bloody proper-propositions. Raight?' He wasn't drunk, but he'd obviously had a skinful, the north country accent more pronounced, his voice a little slurred. 'So why're you here, eh? Why've you changed yer mind?' His tone was hostile.

I hesitated, glancing at the Frenchman who was gazing at me with drunken concentration. 'The reason doesn't matter.' My voice sounded nervous, fear of the man taking hold of me again.

'I got ter be sure . . .' He said it slowly, to himself, and I suddenly sensed a mood of uncertainty in him. In that moment, as he picked up the bottle and thrust it into Varsac's hands, I glimpsed it from his point of view, engaging men he didn't know for some crooked scheme he didn't dare tell them about or perhaps didn't even know himself. 'You piss off,' he told the Frenchman. 'I wan' ter talk to Rodin 'ere alone.' He waved the man away, an impatient flick of a great paw, and when he'd gone, he called for another bottle. 'Now,' he said. 'Let's 'ave it. Why're you here?' He was leaning forward again, the hard little eyes boring into me, and I sat there for what seemed an age, staring at him speechless, not knowing what to say, conscious only that it wasn't going to be easy. The bastard was suspicious.

'The book,' I said finally, my voice no more than a whisper. 'The publishers turned it down.'

'The publishers?' He stared at me blankly. Then, suddenly remembering, he opened his mouth and let out a great gust of laughter. 'Turned it da'n, did they? That bleedin' book of yours. An' now you come runnin' ter me.' He sat back, belching and patting his stomach, a smug, self-satisfied gleam in his eye. 'Wot makes yer think I still got a job for yer, eh?'

There was a sort of cunning in the way he said it, but his acceptance of my explanation gave me confidence. 'The desk said you were booked out to Marseilles in the morning,' I said. 'If you'd got all the officers you needed, you'd be headed for Dubai, not Marseilles. And you didn't get the master of the *Petros Jupiter*, only the engineer.'

I was taking a chance in saying that, but he only grinned at me. 'Been makin' enquiries, have yer?'

'Where's the ship?' I asked. I thought he might be drunk enough to tell me. 'Abu Dhabi, Dubai—'

The grin faded. 'Yer don't ask questions, mate. Not if yer wantin' a job a't o' me. Got it?' He leaned forward, the glassy eyes staring. 'You've no idea, have you – no idea at all what a man like me 'as ter do ter turn an honest silver thaler.' There was sweat on his forehead, his eyes glazing, and he was breathing deeply so that I thought for a moment he was going to pass out on me. 'But this is different.' He seemed to pull himself together. 'The men I need – they got ter be . . .' His voice trailed away and he was silent for a while, staring down at his glass as though thinking something out. Finally he lifted his head, looking straight at me as he said, 'I got ter be careful, see.' His eyes held mine for a long moment, then he refilled our glasses. 'You sold that cottage of yours?'

'Not yet,' I said. 'I've told them not to put it on the market till the spring.'

He lifted his glass, swallowing half of it at a gulp as though it were beer. 'Won't fetch much, will it?' He wiped his mouth with the back of his hand, smiling. 'Yer wife dead and yer book in the dustbin, in a bit of a mess, ain't yer?' His eyes creased, smiling at me as though somebody in a bit of a mess was what life was all about. 'Got anything tucked away?'

He said it casually, but I sensed that the question was important. 'How do you mean?'

'You got enough to get here . . .' He sat there, waiting.

'Just enough,' I said. 'That's all.'

'No return ticket?'

I shook my head.

'Christ, man! You took a chance.' He nodded. 'So you're out o' bread an' no way of getting back to the U-kay, no prospect of finding work there anyway?'

I didn't say anything and he grinned at me. 'Orl raight, so I still got a berth for a second mate.' He leaned forward, peering into my face. 'But wot makes you think you're the man for the job?'

'Depends what it is,' I said. But he wouldn't tell me that, or who the owners were, not even the name of the ship. It was double rates and an end of voyage bonus, so what was I worrying about? 'You want the job or don't you?'

I knew then that I had no alternative. To find Choffel I would have to commit myself. 'Yes,' I said.

'You got any money at all, apart from what you'll get from that cottage?'

'Enough to pay the hotel bill, that's all.' I didn't know whether he was fishing for a bribe or not.

'No dole money, no redundancy?'

'I don't qualify.'

'So you got nothing. An' now yer wife's gone . . .' He thumped the table, gloating at me. 'You got nothing at all, have you?' He sat back, smiling and lifting his glass in his big fist. 'Orl raight, Trevor – yer on. Nantes–Paris, then Paris–Dubai, an' after that you wait until we're ready for you, everything laid on – hotel, swimming, booze, girls, anything you want. Just one thing though—' He reached out a big hand and gripped my arm. 'No tricks. An' remember – it's 'cos of me you're getting the job. Understand?'

I nodded. I hadn't been in the Gulf all those years not to recognize the glint in his eyes. 'How much?' I asked.

'Voyage money will be paid in advance. You hand me half of it, okay?' And he added, 'You'll still be getting full second mate's pay. And you keep the bonus.' The bonus would be five hundred quid, he said – 'So you don't ask questions, see.'

And so it was agreed. For half my pay I put myself in his hands, committed to an unknown ship and an unknown destination. 'I booked your flight, by the way.' He grinned at me slyly. 'Did that soon as I heard you'd checked into the hotel.' He emptied the bottle into our glasses and when we had finished it, he got hold of Varsac and we had a meal together. There was more wine and cognac with the coffee. The talk turned to sex, interminable sordid stories of the Gulf. Varsac had been in Jibuti. He was very funny about the madame of a brothel who changed into a man. And Baldwick became morose. I mentioned the *Petros Jupiter* again, asking him whether he knew anything about the engineer he'd recruited, but he stared at me with such drunken hostility that I didn't persist. He knew I had been getting at something, but he was confused and he wasn't sure what. In the end I went to bed.

My room was close under the eaves. It was cold, the bed not aired and I couldn't sleep. The window rattled in the gusts and I kept thinking of that girl, the horror in her eyes, the way she'd spat in my face. I lay there, listening to the gusts, remembering that night off Sennen, the fog exploding into flames. And the Lloyd's agent trying to tell me I'd no proof. The girl, too. It's not his fault, she had said – 'She did it herself.' But they hadn't been there. They hadn't seen it. And Choffel. What would he say when I finally caught up with him, when I got hold of the murderous little bastard, my hands at his throat, the flesh yielding . . . ? The wind beat against the window, a cold draught on my face. God damn it! What sort of a monster had I become?

I was shivering then, my eyes wet with tears. God in Heaven! Why should I start on self-recrimination when I'd right on my side? It wasn't vengeance. It was justice. Somebody had to see to it that he never wrecked another vessel. And then I was thinking about why he'd done it. Greed! Stupid, senseless greed! But that wasn't peculiar to him. It was a curse affecting us all, the whole human race, harvesting the sea till there was nothing left but oceans and oceans of dead water, drilling for energy, tanking it round the world, feeding factories that poured toxic waste into the rivers, supplying farms with pesticides that poisoned the land, pumping heat and fumes into the life-giving atmosphere until it was a lethal hothouse. What was Choffel by comparison? A nothing, just a symbol, a symptom of human rapacity, and myself a Quixote tilting at the windmill of man's self-destructive urge.

It was an argument and a view of life that went round and round in my head as gusts rattled the door and the rafters crackled in the frost. And then I woke to complete stillness in a grey dawn that held everything in a grip of silence, the window panes frosted over and the rooftops opposite a glazed white. It was no longer freezing and by the time I was dressed there was a gleam of watery sunshine, the world outside beginning to thaw.

Baldwick was already there when I went into the bar-restaurant for breakfast, sitting at a table with a pot of coffee and a basketful of rolls in front of him. 'Take a seat.' He pulled out a chair for me, indicating the coffee. 'Help yourself.' He had his mouth full, chewing voraciously at a roll, his heavy cheeks glowing pink as though he had been for a brisk walk in the cold morning air, his big frame full of vigour. 'Paris is no go, thick as a pig's snout. If the fog don't lift you could be here another night.'

He had settled with the desk and had given Varsac the air tickets. All the time he was talking those little eyes of his were fixed on me intently. Something was worrying him, some sixth sense perhaps – 'Keep yer mouth shut.' He was suddenly leaning forward, his face close to mine and nothing in his eyes or his voice, nothing at all to indicate he had been drinking heavily the night before. 'Understand? Anyone starts talking they could find themselves in trouble. I'm telling you that 'cos I reck'n you're far too intelligent not to know you don't get double rates and a bonus for a run-of-the-bloody-mill voyage. Okay?'

I nodded, finding it difficult to meet the bright beady eyes barely a foot from mine.

'You still thinking about the *Petros Jupiter*? 'Cos if you are . . .'

I shook my head, reaching for the coffee and pouring myself a cup as I enquired why he had asked.

'Last night. You were asking questions about the engineer.'

'Was I?'

'You know bloody well you were. Did you think I was too drunk or something not to remember? How did you know I'd anything to do with the man?'

'You were in Sennen when the crew came ashore.' But the instant I'd said it I knew it was a mistake. He pounced on it immediately.

'Sennen? Who said I went to Sennen? Falmouth, I told you.'

I nodded, buttering myself a roll and not looking at him. 'I heard you'd been at Sennen earlier, that's all.'

'Who told you?'

'I don't know.' I gulped down some coffee. 'Everything was a bit mixed up at the time. A press photographer, I think.'

'I never was at Sennen. Understand?' His fist slammed down on the table, rattling the crockery. 'Forget it. Forget everything – okay? Just do the job you're paid for . . .' He looked up as Varsac joined us. The Frenchman's face was more cadaverous than ever, heavy pouches below the bloodshot eyes. 'Mornin', Albert,' Baldwick said brightly. 'You look as though you've been tangling with Madame all night.' He picked up the pot and poured him a coffee. 'You'll take it black, eh?' And as Varsac sat down heavily and buried his long nose in the coffee, he added, 'Bet yer if a nice plump Baluchi girl walked in now you couldn't do a thing aba't it.' And he let out a great guffaw as he slapped the wretched Varsac on the back.

His taxi arrived a few minutes later and as he got up from the table, he paused for a moment, staring at me. 'See you in Dubai,' he said. 'And no tricks, see?' He was smiling at me, but not with his eyes. For a moment he stood there, looking down at me. Finally he nodded as though satisfied, turning abruptly and going out to the waiting taxi.

Flights south were leaving on schedule, but Paris and all the north of France was fogged in. It looked as though we'd be kicking our heels in Nantes for some hours yet and I went in search of the papers. The only English ones I could find were the *Telegraph* and the *Financial Times* and I looked through them over a *fine à l'eau* in the bar. There was no news of the missing tankers in either of them, the front page of the *Telegraph* full of the trial of terrorists charged with the Piccadilly bomb outrage, and there had been a demonstration outside the Old Bailey in which shots had been fired at the police. It was in the *Financial Times* that I found a small paragraph tucked away on an inside page headed TANKER CLAIM REJECTED: 'Solicitors for a Lloyd's syndicate operated by Mr Michael Stewart have rejected a claim by the NSO Harben company of Schiedam in respect of the loss of the tanker *Petros Jupiter*. No reason has been given, but it is presumably based on their assessment of the evidence that will be given at the Enquiry due to begin on January 27. The amount of the claim is put at over £9 million for the hull alone. This is the largest marine insurance claim so far this year.'

Just before midday we were informed that it was unlikely we would get away until the following morning. A definite decision would be made after lunch. I got hold of a city plan and walked down to the riverside quays where the cargo ships lay. The sun was quite warm, the streets all dripping with melted snow. At the offices of the Réaux shipping company my request to speak to somebody who had actually known Choffel resulted in my being shown into a tiny waiting-room and left there for a long time. The walls were hung with the framed photographs of ships, most of them old and faded, and there was a table with copies of French shipping magazines. Finally, a young-ster, who spoke good schoolboy English, took me along the quay to a small grain carrier that had only just come in. There I was introduced to an elderly chief engineer who had been on the *Tarzan* in 1959.

He described Choffel as a quiet man who didn't say very much, just got on with the job. He had had very little French at that time, but was eager to learn because he wanted to live in France. I asked him why, but he just shrugged.

'Was he a good engineer?'

'*Mais oui – excellent.*' And then he said something that came as a complete surprise to me. He said, '*Henri Choffel, vous savez, il était anglais.*' English! That was something that hadn't occurred to me. But then suddenly things began to fall into place. The girl – it explained the lilt, that sense of familiarity, that vague likeness to Karen, the name even. Of course, Welsh! How would a French engineer know the difference – Welsh, English, it was all one to him.

But it didn't help me to an understanding of the man, and he couldn't tell me what ships he'd been on or where he came from. I asked him what sort of company Choffel had kept when they were in port, but apparently he had usually stayed on board, studying French and talking to the French members of the crew. He was on the *Tarzan* almost a year, and by the time he was promoted to another of the Réaux ships he was quite fluent. There was only one other worthwhile thing he told me. Choffel had had the word FORMID-ABLE and the date 1952 tattooed across his chest. The old man pronounced it, of course, in the French way, but it could just as easily have been English and the name of a ship.

Barre was out to lunch by the time I reached his office, but I arranged with his secretary for a telex to be sent to Pritchard advising that a search be made for the name of any Welshman serving as a conscript in the engine-room of HMS *Formidable* in 1952. It was a chance. Once Pritchard had the man's original name, he'd be able to find out what merchant ships he'd served in later and whether any of them had been wrecked shortly before he had joined the *Tarzan* under the name of Henri Choffel.

Back at the hotel, after a meal and a bottle of wine at a little restaurant by the river, I found Varsac waiting anxiously for me in reception with his bags packed. Paris was now clear and our flight would be leaving Nantes at 16.10. I got my key and was told there was a Mademoiselle Choffel wishing to speak with me. She was having a coffee in the bar.

I left Varsac to order a taxi, got the bags from my room and then went through into the bar-restaurant. She was sitting in a corner facing the door into the hotel and she got up with a nervous little smile as I went towards her. There were dark shadows under her eyes and her face was flushed. She held out her hand. 'I had to come. I want to apologize. I was upset. Terribly upset. I didn't know what I was saying, or doing. It was such a shock.' The words poured out of her as we shook hands, her clasp hot and moist.

'You should be in bed,' I said. 'You look as though you're running a temperature.'

'It doesn't matter.' She sat down abruptly, waving me to the seat on the opposite side of the table. 'I couldn't let you leave, like that. As if I had no under-standing, no sympathy.'

'You're Welsh, aren't you?' I asked.

'Half Welsh, yes. My mother was French.'

'From Vertou.'

Her eyes widened. 'So you've been making enquiries?'

'Of course.' And I added, 'My wife was Welsh. But not her name. Her name was Karen.'

'Yes, I know. I read about it. When I heard the news I read all the English papers I could get . . .' Her voice faded, floundering over the macabre memory of what had been printed in the English press.

'Karen was from Swansea. That's where we met. In the docks there.'

'It was nothing to do with my father,' she whispered urgently. 'Please. You've got to believe that. You must believe it, because it's true. It was an accident.'

'And he's a Welshman, you say?'

'He was born there, yes.'

'Where?'

'In the middle somewhere. I'm not sure.'

'What was his name then?'

It was on the tip of her tongue, but then she hesitated. 'Why do you ask?'

'A fellow Welshman . . .' I murmured, not looking at her now, knowing I had tried to trap her.

'You're not Welsh.' Her voice was suddenly harder, an undercurrent of impatience. 'The way you talk sounds like it sometimes, but if you were Welsh now—'

'It would make no difference.'

'If you were, you would have the imagination to see—'

'I have plenty of imagination,' I cut in angrily. 'Too much perhaps.'

She was staring at me now, her eyes wide and the same look of horror dawning. 'Please. Won't you try to understand. He's never had a chance. Ever since the *Stella Rosa*. You know about the *Stella Rosa*, I suppose?'

'Yes.'

'He was exonerated, you know.'

'The *Stella Rosa* was gun-running.'

'There was no other ship available. My mother was sick and he needed the money.'

'Honest engineers don't go gun-running,' I told her. 'Then, when the ship was wrecked, he blamed one of his engineer officers, a man named Aristides Speridion.'

She nodded slowly, her eyes dropping to her hands.

'What happened to Speridion? Has he told you?'

She didn't answer.

Varsac poked his head round the door to say the taxi had arrived. I waved him away. 'Tell it to wait,' I said. And then to the girl, 'You realize that when the *Petros Jupiter* went on to the rocks by Land's End he was in charge of the engine-room? And masquerading under the name of Aristides Speridion. He even had Speridion's passport.'

'I know.' The admission seemed dragged out of her, the words a whisper. She suddenly reached out, touched my hand. 'There's some explanation. I know there is. There must be. Can't you wait – until after the Enquiry? It's like a court of law, isn't it? The truth – the real truth – it'll all come out.' Her voice was urgent, desperate to believe that he would be vindicated, his innocence proved. 'He's such a kind man. You should have seen him when my mother was dying—'

'If there were a chance that the Enquiry would vindicate him, he'd surely have stayed. Instead—' But I left it at that. His action in fleeing the country made it all so obvious and I'd no quarrel with her. I began to get to my feet. She should have had the sense to face up to the situation. The man was guilty as hell and no good her pleading his innocence when the facts were all against it. 'I'm sorry,' I said. 'I've got to go now. The flight to Paris—'

'It's Dubai, isn't it? You're going to Dubai.'

I nodded.

'When you see my father . . .' She got slowly to her feet, tears in her eyes as she stood facing me. 'Give him my love, will you. Tell him I did my best. I tried to stop you.' She stood quite still, facing me, with her hands to her side, as though she were facing a firing squad. 'Please remember that when you find him.' And then, in a sudden violent outburst, 'I don't understand you. Will nothing satisfy the bitterness that's eating you up? Isn't there anything—' But then she stopped, her body stiffening as she turned away, gathering up her handbag and walking blindly out by the street door.

She left me with the bill for her coffee and a feeling of sadness that such a nice girl, so absolutely loyal, should have such a man as her father. Nothing she had said had made the slightest difference, his guilt so obvious that I thought she was probably convinced of it, too, as I went out to the waiting taxi. Varsac was already there with the door open. I handed my bags to the driver, saw to it that he put them both in the boot and then, as I was bending down to get in, the girl's voice behind me called out, '*Monsieur. Un moment.*' I turned to find her standing by the bonnet of the taxi with one of those flat little miniature cameras to her eye and at that moment the shutter blinked. It blinked again before I had time to move. 'Why did you do that?' I was reaching out for the camera, but she put it behind her, standing stiff and defiant. 'You touch me and I'll scream,' she said. 'You can't take my camera.'

'But why?' I said again.

She laughed, a snorting sound. 'So that my children will know what the murderer of their grandfather looked like. The police, too. Anything happens to my father and I'll give these pictures to the police.' She took a step back, the camera to her eye again as she took another snap. Then she turned, darting across the pavement into the hotel.

'*Dépêche-toi. Dépêche-toi. Nous allons louper l'avion.*' Varsac's voice sounded agitated.

I hesitated, but there was nothing I could do, so I got into the taxi and we drove out of Nantes across the Loire to the airport. And all the way there I was thinking about the photographs, her reason for taking them – 'When you meet my father—' Those were her words. 'Dubai,' she had said. 'You're going to Dubai.' So now I knew, Choffel was in Dubai. He would be waiting for me there, an engineer in the same ship.

Two hours later we were in Paris, at the Charles de Gaulle Airport, waiting for the flight to Dubai. In the end we didn't board until 20.30, and even then we were lucky in that there had been several cancellations, for this was the Thursday morning flight, delayed now by over thirty hours and every seat taken.

PART FOUR

THE DHOW

CHAPTER ONE

It was a six and a half hour flight from Paris to Dubai and nothing to do but sit there, thinking about my meeting with Choffel, what I was going to do. Up till then I hadn't given much thought to the practicalities. I had never owned a gun, never even fired one. I had no weapon with me of any sort, and though I had seen death out in the Hindu Kush when I was a kid, it was death through cold or disease or lack of food. Once, in Basra, I had watched from a hotel balcony as an armoured car and some riot police gunned down a handful of youths. That was before the Iraqi-Iranian war, a protest by Shia sect students and again I was only a spectator. I'd never killed anyone myself. Even the little Baluchi boy, whose doll-like features haunted me, had been thrown into the Creek by the others. I had taken no part in it.

Now, as the big jet whispered through the sky at 37,000 feet, my mind was on Dubai, and the thought that tomorrow, or the next day, or when we boarded the tanker, I could be confronted with Choffel caused my skin to prickle and perspiration to break out all over my body. I pictured his face when we met, how he would react, and the excitement of it shook me. So vivid was the picture my imagination produced that, sitting there, with the seat at full recline and a blanket round my waist, the lights dimmed and all the rest of the passengers fast asleep, the blood drummed in my ears, fantasies of killing flickering through my brain so that suddenly I had an overwhelming orgasmic sense of power. A knife. It would have to be a knife. One of those big silver-hilted, curved-bladed *kanjar* knives the Bedu wore tucked into the belts of their flowing robes. Getting hold of a knife like that wouldn't be difficult, not in Dubai, where Arab merchants along the waterfront sold anything from gold and opium to slave girls, and a pistol would be equally available. Still, a knife would be better. But then what did I do? And where would I find him? At one of the hotels in Dubai or holed up in some desert hideout? He could be in one of the neighbouring sheikdoms – Abu Dhabi or Sharjah, or at some Bedu house in the El Ain oasis.

And the tanker, where would that be berthed? The only place Baldwick had mentioned was Dubai. If it was in Port Rashid at the entrance to the Creek, then Choffel could already be on board. I pictured myself going up the gangway, being taken to my cabin, then joining the other officers in the mess-room and Henri Choffel standing there, his hand held out in greeting, not knowing who I was. What did I do then – wait until the end of the voyage? A full shipload of Gulf crude, that would mean Europe most likely – down Africa, round the Cape and up almost the full length of the Atlantic. Five weeks at least, presuming the evaporators were in good condition and the boiler didn't start cutting out, five weeks during which I would be meeting Choffel daily, in the mess-room at the evening pour-out, at mealtimes in the saloon.

The thought appalled me, remembering what had happened, thinking of Karen. Even now, with Balkaer and the Cornish cliffs far behind, I could still feel the soft smoothness of her skin, the touch of her as she lay in my arms – and just remembering the feel of her I was aroused. She had always had that ability, to rouse me instantly, by a touch, often just by a look, or the way she laughed. And then, just when we had come to Balkaer and she was doing a lot of heavy carrying, discovering she was pregnant. I could see her face. It was so clear in my mind it seemed framed in the perspex window against the star-bright night, her eyes alight with happiness and that big mouth of hers bubbling with excitement as she came out of the back room the doctor used as a surgery on his weekly visits to Sennen. 'I'm going to have a baby,' she'd cried and flung her arms round my neck, right there in front of the doctor's patients.

And then six months later she'd lost it. The pains had started at dusk, quite suddenly. One moment she was sitting in that junk chair of hers, the next she was writhing on the floor, screaming. It had been a black, windy night, rain driving in off the sea in sheets. The Kerrisons' telephone line was down and I had had to run all the way to the Cunnacks' farm, which was over the hill. God, what a night that had been! So much of it waiting, helpless, first for the doctor, then for the ambulance, with Karen clutching at us, her face screwed up in agony, her hair dank with sweat. And in the dawn, a wild wet dawn, carrying her up the hill to the ambulance.

By then she had miscarried and was quiet, sunk in a coma of exhaustion. She never told me what exactly went wrong, or what they did to her in the hospital in Penzance, only that she would never be able to have another child. It was then that she began to develop that deep emotional feeling for the wildlife around us, the birds in particular, and also for the book I was struggling to write.

I was thinking of her off and on all through that long night, and of Choffel, excitement, love and hatred all mixed up, until at last, exhausted and so utterly drained I could have slept for a week. The engine note changed and we began the long run down the diamond-studded sky to our destination. Soon there was movement in the body of the aircraft, then the lights were turned on full and the *défense de fumer* sign lit up. Blinds were raised and through the porthand windows the first pale orange glow of dawn showed the Gulf horizon in silhouette, and beyond it, just visible, the pale snow tops of the Iranian mountains. To starboard there was nothing, only the shadowy brown darkness of the desert stretching away in limitless monotony to the great wastes of the Rub al Khali – the Empty Quarter.

It was full daylight by the time we landed, but the sun not yet risen and the air still pleasantly cool as we crossed the tarmac to the terminal building. The Arabs who had looked so incongruous at Charles de Gaulle Airport in their flowing robes, with the black *agal* of the Bedu encircling their white *kayffiah* headgear, now blended into the desert sandscape and it was the Europeans in their crumpled suits who looked out of place. Varsac, who had hardly spoken during the flight, became suddenly talkative as we approached the immigration desk, and when he handed over his passport, I noticed his hand was trembling. The immigration officer glanced up from the passport, staring at him curiously. '*Vous êtes francais.*' It was a statement, the dark eyes in the dark face lighting up. He turned to me. '*Et vous, monsieur?*'

'English,' I said.

He took my passport and stamped it almost perfunctorily, talking all the time to Varsac in French. He was a Pakistani, proud of speaking French as well as English, and it seemed an age before he let us through with a flash of white teeth and a murmured 'Have a good time.'

'What were you worried about?' I asked.

Varsac shook his head, still nervous, his face longer and sadder-looking than ever. '*Rien.* I am afraid they might have some records, that is all.' He shrugged. 'You can nevair be sure, eh?'

'Records of what?' I asked him.

He hesitated, then said, 'It is in the Gulf, an old cargo sheep from Bombay to Khorramshahr. It is

August and we are lying with no engines, the sheep so hot the metal is blistering our hands. No morphia. Nothing.' There was a long pause. 'He is broken – crushed in the main drive. An engineer. Finally – I shoot him.'

I stared at him. 'You mean a man, you killed him?'

'He was my friend.' He gave a half-shrug. 'What else? And such a nice boy, from Indo-Chine.' He wouldn't say anything more, only that it was a long time ago and he had had to jump a big dhow bound for Muscat. The baggage appeared, and when we were through Customs we were met by a pock-marked Libyan in a smart new suit who drove us into town through dusty, crowded streets, to a hotel just back of the Creek.

It was five years since I'd been in Dubai, yet now it seemed but a few weeks, the smell of the place just the same, a compound of spices, charcoal fires, sweat, putrefaction and desert – the dust of ages everywhere, the dust of old mud stucco crumbling into decay, of desert sands swirling against the concrete breakwaters of high-rise blocks, the scuff of countless human feet. I removed my tie and put it in my pocket. The sun was already throwing deep shadows and it was getting hot.

Deeper into the town I saw how quickly oil had made its mark, the skyline altered and new buildings everywhere. The Persian wind-towers, those dainty filigree turrets that were the earliest form of air-conditioning, tunnelling the sea breezes down into the rooms below – they were all gone now. They had been such a feature of the place when I had first come here with my mother, and the business section of the Creek had been crowded then with great merchant houses, ornate stucco walls that kept the world at bay, the secret inner courtyards inviolate. Now banking houses and company offices paraded their wealth in a façade of marble and glass.

So much had changed since those faraway days before the oil-tide reached Dubai. But not the crowd. The crowd was still as thick, still as cosmopolitan, a constant flow of movement, with only the Bedu Arabs motionless in the cafés waiting for the metallic Tannoy voice on the minaret of the nearby mosque to call them to prayer. And the Creek itself, that was still the same, except that even more of the dhows had converted entirely to power, hardly a mast to be seen. But there were just as many of them rafted against the wharfs, a jumble of *sambuks, booms* and *jalibuts* loading tramp ship goods from all over the world for distribution through the Gulf, most of them still with the traditional thunderbox built out over the side like a small pulpit.

When we reached the hotel, the Libyan, whose name was Mustafa, gave us his card, which was gold-embossed with an address in one of the back alleys near the *suk*, also the name of a nearby store where we would be provided with lightweight trousers and sleeveless shirts. We would be at the hotel for at least two days, he said – until LB arrived. No, he didn't know the name of the tanker, or where it was berthed.

He was a travel agent. He knew nothing about ships. Anything we spent in the hotel would be paid for, food, drinks, everything, but if there was something special required we could contact him. The dark eyes stared at us coldly and I wondered what a Libyan was doing running a travel agency in Dubai. He left us with the information that two of our ship's officers were already billeted in the hotel and another would arrive tomorrow. Choffel was not among the names he mentioned.

After checking in, I went straight to the store. It was a cheap place, if anything could be called cheap in Dubai, the trousers and shirts poor quality cotton and not very well cut. But at least they were cool, for by the time I had had a shower the sun, beating on to the balcony of my room, was very hot. I went down to the desk again and had them check through the names of all the guests in their hotel. The place was a microcosm of modern Dubai, business men from Japan, Germany, France, Holland, Britain, anywhere that produced the machines and infrastructure the Gulf exchanged for its oil. There were even two Chinese and a little group from Byelorussia, all of them with briefcases brimful of specifications and optimism. There were oilmen, too, and air crews staying the night, as well as men like ourselves, officers from coasters in the Creek and ships in Port Rashid, all vocal testimony to the fact that Dubai remained the mercantile centre of the Gulf, the entrepôt for the United Arab Emirates.

But there was no Choffel, no Speridion, not even

anyone with a name that looked as though it might be Welsh. Something I did discover, however – there had been half a dozen guests booked in by Mustafa's agency the previous week and they had left three days ago, not in taxis, but in Land Rovers. Again, Choffel had not been one of them. Before that there was no record of any of Mustafa's clients having stayed at the hotel, though back in October he had booked accommodation and then cancelled it. The receptionist remembered that because the hotel had been fully booked and the last minute cancellation of four rooms had upset the management.

I walked down to the Creek then, turning left towards the bridge and found a place where I could sit in the sun with a coffee and a glass of water and watch the world go by. There was a coaster coming in from the Gulf flying the Iranian flag, lighters and launches and small boats bobbing in its wake, the whole waterborne concourse a pageant of movement with a big ocean-going dhow, a *boom* by the look of it, though it was hard to tell as it lay like a barge right in front of the coaster's bows, its engine presumably broken down. Noise and movement and colour, every type of dress, every coloured suit, the smell of dust and spices, and the bloated carcase of a goat floating slowly past with its legs stiff in the air like the legs of a chair. I finished my coffee and closed my eyes, dozing in the warmth of the sun. The unhurried tempo of the desert was all about me, men walking hand-in-hand or squatting motionless, the leisurely, endless haggling over price at every shop and stall in sight. Time stood still, the Muslim world of Arabia flowing round me, familiar and relaxing. It is an atmosphere in which fatalism thrives so that, dozing in the sun, I was able to forget my worries about the future. I was tired of course. But it was more than that. It was in my blood, the feeling that I was just a straw in the stream of life and everything the will of God. *Insh'Allah!* And so I didn't concern myself very much about the reaction of Baldwick and his friends if they were to discover I was visiting the Lloyd's agent and GODCO. My only problem, it seemed to me at the time, was which of them I should visit first, or whether to go at all. It was so much easier to sit there in the sun, but I did need to check those crew details with the oil company's marine superintendent.

In the end, after cashing a traveller's cheque at one of the banks, I went to the GODCO building first, largely because it was there in front of me, a towering new block dominating the downstream bend of the Creek. After the noisy, saffron-scented heat of the waterfront, the cloistered air-conditioning of the interior hit me like a refrigerator. The marine superintendent's offices were on the fifth floor with a view seaward to a litter of cranes, masts and funnels that was the Port Rashid skyline. Captain Roger Perrin, the name Saltley had given me, was the man in charge of the whole of the Company's fleet, and when I was finally shown into his office, he said curtly, 'Why didn't you phone? I'd have had everything ready for you then.' He was bearded, with pale cold eyes and a presence that I suspected had been carefully cultivated in the years he had been moving up the Company's marine ladder. He waved me to the chair opposite him where the hard light pouring through the plastic louvres of the venetian blinds shone straight on my face. 'Well, why are you here? What do the solicitor people want to know that I haven't already told them?' And he added, 'I'm responsible for Casualty Co-ordination, but I tell you now, in this Company we don't expect casualties. And in the case of these two tankers there's nothing to co-ordinate. They've just disappeared and your people know as much about it as I do. So why are you here?'

The only reason I could give him was the crew pictures, but when I asked to see them, he said, 'I sent a full set of the pictures to our London office. That was three days ago. You could have seen them there.'

'I had to go to France.'

'France?' The fact that I hadn't come straight out from London seemed to make a difference. He gave a little shrug. 'Well, I've no doubt you have your own lines of enquiry to follow.' He reached behind him to a bookcase where a potted plant stood like a rubbery green sentinel, picked up two files and passed them across the desk to me. I opened the one labelled *Aurora B*. There were copies of design drawings for the ship's hull and engines, detailed specifications, and, in an envelope marked PERSONNEL, a crew list, together with a full-face close-up of each individual. This was the only item of real interest and while he was telling me how the Indian airforce had mounted a search in the sea area west of Sri Lanka and the oil company's representatives had appealed through the local press and media for anybody who might have picked up a radio signal or voice message, I went slowly through the pictures. I had met so many odd characters in cargo runs around the Gulf that there was always a chance.

'Also we have checked the background of every officer – wives, girlfriends, sexual eccentricities, everything.' He had a flat, rather monotonous voice and my mind kept drifting away, wondering vaguely whether the Lloyd's agent would have heard from Pritchard yet. My contact was Adrian Gault. I had met him once, a little shrivelled man who was said to have his ear to the ground and spies in every merchant house on the waterfront. An old Gulf hand like that, surely to God he would know by now what dhow had picked Choffel up, where it had taken him. It was four or five days since the man had left the *Corsaire*, time enough for news to filter through, for rumour to get its tongue round the story and spread it through the cafés and among the Gulf Arabs cooking over fires on the decks of dhows.

' . . . no wreckage, only the dumped remains of ships' garbage and one oil slick that was traced to a Liberian cargo vessel.' He said it in an aggrieved tone, resentful of the trick fate had played on him. 'I always run a tight ship here at GODCO, maintenance, damage control, everything A1. Our record speaks for itself. Since I took over this office we've had a long run . . .'

'Of course. I understand.' I found myself embarrassed at his need of self-justification, concentrating on the pictures then, while he began talking about the absence of any radio signal. Not a single ham operator had responded to their appeal, and in the case of the *Howdo Stranger*, with the very latest in tank cleansing equipment . . .

I wasn't listening. There, suddenly, staring up at me, was a dark Semitic face I had seen before – in Khorramshahr, on a stretcher. The same birthmark like a burn blurring the full lips, the same look of intense hostility in the dark eyes, the womanish mouth set in a nervous smile. But it was the birthmark – not even the dark little beard he had grown could hide that. *Abol Hassan Sadeq, born Teheran, age 31, electrical engineer.*

I turned the picture round so that Captain Perrin could see it. 'Know anything about him?'

He stared at it a moment, then shook his head. 'You recognize him, do you?'

'Yes, but not the name. It wasn't Sadeq.' I couldn't recall the name they had given us. It had been six years ago. Summer, and so hot you couldn't touch the metal anywhere on the ship, the Shatt al Arab flat as a shield, the air like a steam bath. Students had rioted in Teheran, and in Abadan there had been an attempt to blow up two of the oil storage tanks. We should have sailed at dawn, but we were ordered to wait. And then the Shah's police had brought him on board, shortly after noon. We sent him straight down to the sick bay and sailed for Kuwait, where we handed him over to the authorities. His kidneys had been damaged, he had three ribs broken, multiple internal bruising and his front teeth badly broken.

'Interrogation?' Perrin asked.

'I suppose so.'

'He wasn't one of the students then.'

I shrugged. 'They said he was a terrorist.'

'A terrorist.' He said the word slowly as though testing out the sound of it. 'And that's the same man, on the *Aurora B*. Does that make any sense to you?'

'Only that a bomb would account for her total disappearance. But there'd still have to be a motive.' I searched through the file, found the man's dossier and flipped it across the desk to him. It simply listed the ships he had served on.

'We'll check them all, of course,' Perrin said. 'And the security people in Abu Dhabi, they may know something.' But he sounded doubtful. 'To blow up a tanker the size of the *Aurora B* . . .' He shook his head. 'It's got to be a hell of a big explosion to leave nothing behind, and no time for the radio operator to get off a Mayday – a suicidal explosion, in fact, for he'd have to be resigned to his own death. And it doesn't explain the loss of the other tanker.'

I was working through the pictures again, particularly those of the *Howdo Stranger* crew. There was nobody else I recognized. I hadn't expected there would be. It was only the purest chance that I had ever set eyes on Sadeq before. And if it hadn't been for the GODCO practice of taking crew pictures for each voyage . . . I was still trying to remember the name the Shah's police had given us when they had rolled him screaming off the stretcher on to the hot deck plates. It certainly hadn't been Sadeq.

We discussed it for a while, then I left, promising to look in the following day. After the cool interior of the oil building it seemed much hotter outside on the crowded waterfront. Noisier, too, and smellier. I crossed the Creek in a crowded launch to one of the older buildings just upstream of the warehouses. Gault's office was on the first floor. There was no air-conditioning and the windows were wide open to the sounds and smells of the wharfs with a view over the rafted dhows to the mosque behind the financial buildings on the other side. Gault was at the door to greet me, a thin, stooped man in khaki slacks and a short-sleeved shirt of virulent colour. He had a wide smile in a freckled, sun-wrinkled face, and his arms were freckled, too. 'Heard you'd arrived safely.'

'Did you think I wouldn't?' I asked him.

'Well, you never know, do you?' He stared at me, still smiling. 'Salt telexed yesterday. Last time we met you were mate of the old *Dragonera*. Then you left the Gulf.' He took me over to the window. 'There you are, nothing changed. The Gulf still the navel of the world and Dubai the little wrinkled belly-button that handles all the traffic. Well, why is he employing you?'

'He seems to think my knowledge of the Gulf—'

'There are at least two ships' captains on Forthright's staff who have a bloody sight more experience of the Gulf than you, so that's the first thing I want to know. Two tankers go missing down by Sri Lanka and you come out here, to Dubai – why?'

I began talking about Karachi then, but he cut me short. 'I read the papers. You're after Choffel and you're on to something. Something I don't know about.' He was staring at me, his eyes no longer smiling and his hand gripping my arm. 'Those tankers sailed from Mina Zayed loaded with Abu Dhabi crude. But still you come to Dubai. Why?'

'Baldwick,' I said.

'Ah!' He let go my arm and waved me to a leather pouf with an old mat thrown over it. 'Coffee or tea?'

'Tea,' I said and he clapped his hands. A small boy with a rag of a turban appeared at the door. He told him to bring tea for both of us and squatted cross-legged on the Persian carpet. 'That boy's the son of one our best *naukhadas*. He's here to learn the business. His father doesn't want him to grow up to be nothing but the skipper of a dhow. He thinks the dhows will all be gone by then. You agree?' I said I thought it likely, but I don't think he heard me. 'What's Baldwick got to do with those missing tankers?'

'Nothing as far as I know.'

'But he knows where Choffel is hiding up, is that it?'

I nodded.

'You'd better tell me about it then.'

By the time I had given him an account of my dealings with Baldwick the tea had arrived, hot, sweet and very refreshing in that noisy, shadowy room.

'Where's the tanker you're supposed to join?' he asked.

'I thought you might know.'

He laughed and shook his head. 'No idea.' And he had no information to give me on Baldwick's present activities. 'There's rumours of Russian ships skulking in the Straits of Hormuz. But it's just bazaar talk.' As a youngster he had served in India and he still referred to the *suk* as a bazaar. 'You know how it is. Since the Red Army moved into Afghanistan, the dhow Arabs see Russian ships in every hidey-hole in the Gulf. And the *khawrs* to the south of the Straits are a natural. You could lose a whole fleet in some of those inlets, except that it would be like putting them in a furnace. Hot as hell.' He laughed. 'But even if the Russians are playing hide and seek, that's not Len Baldwick's scene at all. Too risky. I've known the bastard on and off now for more than a dozen years – slave girls, boys, drugs, gold, bogus oil bonds, anything where he takes the rake-off and others the rap. Who owns this tanker of yours, do you know?'

I shook my head.

'So you're going into it blind.' He finished his tea and sat there for a moment thinking about it. 'Tell me, would you be taking that sort of a chance if it wasn't for the thought that Choffel might be on the same ship with you?'

'No.'

He nodded and got to his feet. 'Well, that's your business. Meanwhile, this came for you this morning.' He reached across his desk and handed me a telex. 'Pritchard.'

It was the answer to my request for background information on Welsh national servicemen in the engine-room of HMS *Formidable* in 1952. There had been two of them. Forthright's had then checked four sinkings in suspicious circumstances in 1959, also two in late '58. There followed details of the sinking in October 1958 of the French cargo vessel *Lavandou*, an ex-liberty ship, off the Caribbean island of Martinique. She had been abandoned in deep water, but the edge of a hurricane had drifted her into the shallows north-east of the island so that divers had been able to get down to her. They had found extensive damage to the sea water inlets to the condensers. Second engineer David Price, accused of sabotage by both captain and chief engineer, had by then disappeared, having taken passage on a vessel sailing for Dutch Guiana, which is now Surinam. The enquiry into the loss of the *Lavandou* found Price to blame. *Final clincher for us*, the telex concluded, *is that he was signed on to the Lavandou as engineer at the port of Cayenne in French Guiana in place of Henri Alexandre Choffel who fell into harbour and drowned after a night on the town. Company owning Lavandou registered in Cayenne. A David Morgan Price served HMS Formidable 1952. Thank you. Pritchard.*

That settled it. No good his daughter, or anybody else, trying to tell me he was innocent. Not now. Price, Choffel, Speridion – I wondered what he was calling himself now. None of the names, not even Price, was on the hotel guest list. I asked Gault about the dhow that had met up with the *Corsaire* in the Straits of Hormuz, but he knew nothing about it and wasn't really interested. 'Dhows gravitate to Dubai like wasps to a honey-pot. If you think he was brought in here, then you'd better try the carpet dealers, they know all the gossip. As far as I'm concerned, the *Petros Jupiter* is a UK problem. Choffel's no concern of mine . . .' He sat staring down at his coffee. 'Who do you think would employ a man like Baldwick to recruit ships' officers?' Another pause. 'And why?' he added, looking straight at me.

'I hoped you could tell me that,' I said.

'Well, I can't.' He hesitated, then leaned towards me and said, 'What are you going to do when you meet up with this man Price, or Choffel, or whatever he's calling himself now?'

I shook my head. 'I've got to find him first,' I muttered.

'So you're letting Baldwick recruit you.'

'Yes.'

'A ship you know nothing about. God, man! You don't know where she is, who owns her, what the purpose of the voyage is. You're going into it absolutely blind. But you could be right.' He nodded to himself. 'About Choffel, I mean. A man like that – it makes sense. There has to be something wrong about the set-up or they wouldn't be offering double rates and a bonus, and Baldwick wouldn't be mixed up in it. When's he get in to Dubai, do you know?'

'Mustafa said tomorrow.'

'Have you got his address here?'

I remembered then. 'A telephone number, that's all.'

He went to his desk and made a note of it. 'I'll

have somebody keep an eye on him then. And on this Libyan travel agent. Also, I'll make enquiries about the tanker you're joining. But that may not be easy, particularly if she's over the other side of the Gulf in an Iranian port. Well, that's it.' He held out his hand. 'Nothing much else I can do, except tell you to be careful. There's a lot of money washing around this port, a lot of peculiar people. It's much worse than it was when you were last here. So watch it.' He walked with me to the stairs. 'That boy who brought the tea. His name is Khalid. If my people pick up anything useful I'll send him to you.'

'You don't want me to come here?'

'No. From what you told me it could be dangerous. And if it's politics, not money, you've got yourself mixed up in, then my advice is take the next flight home. Your background makes you very vulnerable.' He smiled and patted my shoulder. '*Salaam alykoum.*'

I walked back to the hotel, changed into a pair of swimming trunks and had a light meal at a table by the pool. The courtyard, airless in the shadow of piled-up balconies, echoed to the murmur of voices, the occasional splash of a body diving. Afterwards I lay in a chair sipping an ice-cold sherbet and thinking about the *Aurora B*, what it would have been like on the bridge, on watch, when spontaneous combustion, or whatever it was, sent her to the bottom. The people I had contacted in the insurance world – underwriters, Lloyd's agents, marine solicitors, everyone – they had all emphasized that marine fraud was on the increase. Like ordinary crime, it was tax free, and as the stakes got bigger . . . I was thinking of Sadeq then, suddenly remembering the name the Shah's police had given him, a name he had confirmed to us as he lay in the *Dragonera*'s sick bay. It had been Qasim. So what was Qasim, a man they had claimed was a terrorist, doing on board the *Aurora B* under another name? Terrorists were trained in the handling of explosives, and instantly I was seeing the fireball holocaust that was so indelibly printed on my mind, knowing that if a bomb had been cleverly placed there was no way the radio operator would be able to put out a call for help.

Was the tanker we were joining intended to go the same way, delayed-action explosives attached to the hull? And us promised a bonus at the end of the voyage! But at least Baldwick was predictable. There was nothing political about him, or about Choffel, and fraud was almost certainly less dangerous. At least, that's what I tried to tell myself, but Adrian Gault's warning stayed in my mind. Here in Dubai anything seemed possible.

In the cool of the evening I took a stroll through the *suk*, looking in on several stall-holders I had known. Two of them were Pakistani. One, an Afridi, dealt in old silver jewellery – bangles, Bedu blanket pins, headpieces, anklets. The other, Azad Hussain, was a carpet merchant. It was he who told me about the dhow. It wasn't just a rumour, either. He had heard it from a *naukhada* who had recently brought him a consignment of Persian carpets. They had been smuggled across the border into the little Baluchistan port of Jiwani. There had been two other dhows there, one waiting to embark cattle fodder from an oasis inland, the other under charter to Baldwick and waiting to pick up a group of Pakistani seamen being flown from Karachi.

He couldn't tell me their destination. It's a question *naukhadas* are wary of asking each other in the Gulf and he had only mentioned the matter to Azad because he was wondering why an Englishman like Baldwick should be shipping Pakistanis out of a little border port like Jiwani. If it had been hashish now, trucked down from the tribal areas close under the Hindu Kush or the Karakoram ranges of the Himalayas . . . He didn't know the *naukhada*'s name or the name of the dhow, only that the seamen embarked numbered a dozen or so and the dhow had left immediately, heading west along the coast towards the Straits of Hormuz.

That night I went to bed early and for the first time, it seemed, since Karen's death I slept like a log, waking to bright sunlight and the call of the muezzin. Varsac was waiting for me when I went down, his eyes shifty, the pupils dilated and his long face wrestling with an ingratiating smile. He wanted a loan. 'Ees *très cher*, Dubai,' he murmured, his breath stale, his hand clutching at me. God knows what he wanted it for, but I had seen the ragged-turbaned little boy hovering in the entrance and I brushed Varsac off, telling him to stay in the hotel where everything was provided. The boy came running as he saw me. 'What is it, Khalid?'

'The sahib send you this.' He held a folded sheet

of paper out to me. 'You read it inside please, then nobody see.'

It was very brief: *Dhow chartered by B came in last night. Loading ship's stores. Khalid will take you to see it. Take care. You were followed yesterday. A.G.* I stuffed the note into my pocket and went out into the street again, Khalid clutching hold of my arm and telling me to go down the alley opposite the hotel and at the Creek I would find his uncle waiting for me with a small boat. I should hire it, but behave as though it were a sudden thought and argue about the money. He would cross by one of the ferry launches and meet me somewhere by the wharfs. Having given me my instructions he ran off in the direction of the mosque. I stood there for a moment as though savouring the warmth of the sunlight that slanted a narrow beam between two of the older dwellings. A casual glance at the Arabs hanging around the hotel narrowed it to two, and there was another inside the entrance who seemed to be watching me, a small man in spotless robes with a little pointed beard and a *khanjar* knife at his belt. I went back into the hotel, bought an English paper, and then sauntered across to the alley that led to the Creek.

I walked slowly, reading the paper as I went. An attack on the Government by the conservationist and fishing lobbies for failing to do anything about oil pollution in the North Sea had ousted the Iranian bombers as the lead story. At the waterfront I paused, standing with the paper held up to my face, but half turning so that I could see back up the alley. There was nobody there except a big fair-bearded man strolling with his hands in his pockets. His face was shaded by the pale khaki peak of his kepi-type cap.

Khalid's uncle proved to be a hook-nosed piratical-looking rascal with a headcloth pushed well back to reveal a thin untidy fringe of black hair that straggled down each cheek to join a neat little wisp of a beard. The boat was from a *boom* loading at one of the wharfs. It was little more than a cockleshell and crossing the Creek it bobbed and bounced to the wash of power boats, launches, ferries, runabouts and load-carriers. I lost sight of the man with the kepi cap and on the far side of the Creek, where we were out of the shadow of the high bank buildings and in the sun, it was hot and the smells stronger as we threaded our way through the dhows, through narrow guts between wooden walls that sun and salt had bleached to the colour of pale amber. He rowed me to what I think he said was a *baghla*. 'Khalid say is this one.'

It was a big dhow, one of the few that hadn't had its mast sawn off and was still capable of carrying sail. It had its upcurved bow thrust in against the wharf. Two men were unloading cardboard cartons of tinned goods from a trolley, carrying them across a narrow gang plank and passing them down into the hold. Khalid was there already, beckoning me to join him on the wharf. I clambered up and he grabbed hold of my hand and drew me back into the shadowed entrance to the warehouse. 'Sahib say you look, then you know what ship is and who is on her.'

It was a two-masted vessel with an exhaust pipe

sticking up for'ard of the poop and a little group squatting in a tight huddle round a *huqqah*, or water pipe, whose stem they passed from one to the other. Khalid pointed the *naukhada* out to me, a big man with a bushy beard and wild eyes peering out of an untidy mass of black hair. 'Mohammed bin Suleiman,' he whispered. 'Is not Dubai. Is from Ras al Khaimah.'

I stood there a while, taking in the details of the dhow, memorizing the faces squatting round the bubbling water pipe. Then Khalid was tugging at my arm, pulling me further back into the warehouse. The man in the kepi cap was coming along the wharf. I could see him clearly now, the sunlight providing his burly figure with a black shadow and glinting on the fair skin and the blond sun-bleached beard. He came abreast of the little group on the dhow's poop and stopped. I couldn't hear what he said, but it was in English with a strong accent and he indicated the warehouse. Then he was coming towards us and we shrank back into the dim interior, slipping behind a pile of mealie bags.

He stopped in the entrance, pushing his cap back and mopping his brow as he shouted for a man called Salima Aznat who was apparently in charge of the warehouse. He wore locally-made sandals with curved-up toe guards, dark blue trousers and a white short-sleeved shirt with sweat stains under the arms. '*Waar is het?*' he muttered to himself. '*Waar hebben zy het verstopt?*' It sounded like Swedish, or Dutch maybe. He turned, beckoning to the Arabs loading the dhow, then began moving slowly into the warehouse, peering at the labels on the larger wooden crates, checking the stencilling on the sides.

'Who is he?' I whispered as he was joined by the warehouseman and the two of them disappeared into the cavernous recesses of the building. But Khalid didn't know. 'Is at your hotel,' he said.

'One of Baldwick's people?'

He nodded. The sound of voices echoed from the far end and a moment later there was the slam of a crate and the rumble of a trolley being dragged towards us. The little group was coming back now, two or three cases on the trolley. They reached the entrance and paused, so that I saw the man very clearly, the bleached hair, the pale eyes, his bare arms like freckled gold in the sunlight. He was talking quickly, radiating a ponderous sense of nervous energy. A round, Dutch-looking face. Hals! I was remembering what Baldwick had said at Balkaer when he'd talked about pollution. It had to be Pieter Hals. And as the little group stood there for a moment in the sun I could see the letters stencilled on the wooden sides of the nearest case. RADIO EQUIPMENT – FRAGILE – HANDLE WITH CARE. The word FRAGILE was stencilled in red.

Back at the hotel I found that Pieter Hals had checked in that morning. I also enquired about Price, but nobody of that name had stayed in the hotel for the past month at any rate. I was convinced then that the dhow had taken him straight to the ship and that he was there on board. I didn't see Hals again that day, and though I met up with several people I had known before and had a word with Perrin on the phone, none of them could tell me anything about Baldwick's tanker people or where the vessel lay. I even took a taxi at considerable expense to Port Rashid, but every ship in the harbour was owned by old-established companies.

That evening, strolling along the waterfront just as dusk was falling, I saw bin Suleiman's dhow haul out into the crowded waterway and watched her crew hoist the lateen mainsail as she motored with a soft tonk-tonk round the down-town bend towards the open sea. From this I concluded that Baldwick's employers must have their tanker loading at Mina Zayed in the neighbouring sheikdom of Abu Dhabi, a supposition that was to prove hopelessly wrong.

That night I had dinner at the hotel, in the roof garden restaurant where Varsac and our two other ship's officers had got themselves a corner table with the sort of view over the dog-legged waterway that a sheikh's peregrine would have, poised high in the air before a stoop. The Creek was an ink-black smudge curving between dimly-lit buildings. The only brilliance seemed to be the flood-lit tracery of some sort of palace and Port Rashid with its cranes and ships and and an oil rig lying to its reflection, all brightly illuminated in the loading lights. Varsac hailed me as soon as I entered the room and when I paused at their table I found myself confronted by a ferrety little Glaswegian engineer with ginger hair and a grating accent. A cigarette burned unheeded on the plate beside him and in the middle of the table was an ashtray full of stubs.

'Ah'm Colin Fraser,' he said, holding out his hand. 'What's yur nem?'

'Trevor Rodin.'

'And yur job on boord?'

'Second mate.'

'Aye, weel, Ah'm an engineer mesel', so we'll not be seeing very much of each other now. Sit down, man, and have a drink.'

The other man, a big Canadian, pulled out a chair for me, smiling, but not saying anything. I sat down. There wasn't anything else I could do. Fraser turned out to be a casualty of the Iraqi-Iranian war. He had been in one of the cargo vessels stranded in the Shatt al Arab. It was Greek-owned and had been badly shelled. The end of it was her owners had abandoned her and he had been thrown on to the beach, an engineer with shrapnel wounds in the shoulder, no ship, no money, not even a fare-paid passage home. 'Bankrupt the bastards were.' The world was still in recession, the beach a cold place to be. 'Och, the stories Ah could tell yer. Ah bin on rigs, ferry boats, aye, on dhows, too, an' if it hadna bin for our mootual friend Len B . . .'

He was drinking whisky and was half cut already, his voice rambling on about the despicable nature of employers and how it was they who had kept him out of a job, a black against his name and the word passed from owner to owner, even out to this godforsaken end-of-the-earth dump. 'Ah couldna get a job oot here if I was to promise the effing agent a whole year's salary. It's me politics, see.' As far as I could gather he was well to the left of the Militant Tendency and back home in Glasgow had been a union troublemaker. 'Colin Fraser. Ye remember surely? It was all in the papers. I took three cargo ships doon the Clyde and anchored them roond the Polaris base so the nuclear subs couldna move in or oot.'

He also claimed to have been a member of the IRA for a short time. Stranded in Belfast when his ship couldn't unload because of a dock strike, he had been given a Kalashnikov and had gone gunning for the RUC in the Falls Road district with a bunch of teen-agers. 'Made bombs for them, too, in a hoose doon in Crossmaglen. But they didna pay me. Risking me life Ah was . . .' It was an aggrieved voice that went on and on, the Glasgow accent getting harder, the ferrety face more vicious. In the end I ignored him and talked to the Canadian who had been recruited by Hals as first mate. His name was Rod Selkirk. He had been a trapper and a sealer, had then met Farley Mowat, whose book *Never Cry Wolf* had affected him deeply, and after that meeting he had stopped killing animals for a living and had switched to coasters, trading into the ports of the Maritimes and the Gulf of St Law-rence. 'Guess I'm okay on navigation, but when it comes to figures . . .' He shrugged, his body as massive and solid as you would expect of a man who had spent most of his life in the hard North of Canada. His round, moonlike face broke into a smile, causing the puffed lids of the mongoloid eyes to crease into fat-crinkled almond slits. 'I'm an inshore navigator really, so reck'n I'll never make it any higher. I'd never pass the exams, not for my Master's ticket.'

'Where did you meet Pieter Hals?' I asked him.

'Shatt al Arab, same as Colin here. I was tramping, and they just about blew us out of the water. The Iranians. They couldn't reach the Iraqi shore, not to hit anything worthwhile, so they took it out on us. Just for the hell of it, I guess – a bit of target practice. Infidels don't count anyway, know what I mean?' The smile spread into a grin. He was a very likeable giant and he hardly drank at all, his voice very soft, very restful.

'What's Hals's job?' I asked.

'Captain.'

Hals had only been first mate when he'd hit the headlines and been sacked for the bomb threats he had made in the Niger. 'Is that why he's joined this Baldwick outfit?' I thought he might see it as his only chance for promotion after what he'd done, but the Canadian said No, it was pollution. 'He's got something in mind,' he murmured hesitantly. But when I questioned him about it, he said he didn't know. 'You ask Pieter. Mebbe he'll tell you, once we get aboard. Right now, he doesn't talk about it.' He was watching me uncertainly out of those slit eyes. 'Marine pollution mean anything to you?'

He hadn't read the papers, didn't know about Karen, and when I told him she'd blown a stranded tanker up to save the coast from pollution, he smiled and said, 'Then you and Pieter should get on. He blames it all on the industrial nations, says they'll pollute the world to keep their bloody machines going. You feel like that?'

'The transport of oil presents problems,' I said cautiously.

'That's for sure.' He nodded, expressing surprise that it was Baldwick who had recruited me, not Pieter Hals. 'I never met Baldwick,' he said, 'but from what I hear . . .' He gave an expressive shrug and left it at that.

'*Qu'est que c'est?*' Varsac was suddenly leaning forward. 'What ees it you 'ear?'

'Ah'll tell yu,' Fraser cut in, laughing maliciously. 'Ah'll tell yu what he hears aboot Len Baldwick, that he's a fat eunuch who's made a pile pimping for oil-rich Arabs. That's the worrd from the lads Ah was talking to last night. They say his fat fingers are poked up the arse of anybody who's got dirty business going in the Gulf, an' if yu think this little caper's got anything to do with saving the worrld from pollution yu're nuts. There's fraud in it somewhere, and I wouldna be surprised to find meself fixing bombs to the hull of this tanker somewhere off the coast of Africa.'

Varsac stared at him, his face longer and paler than ever. '*Monsieur Baldwick m'a dit—*'

'Och, the hell wi' it.' Fraser was laughing again, prodding Varsac with a nicotine-stained finger. 'Yu'd hardly expect him to dite yu wha' it's all aboot. He gets his cut, tha's all he cares. An' he's no sailing wi' the ship.'

The Frenchman's Adam's apple jerked convulsively. 'Not sailing? You know this? Ees true – certain?' He shook his head doubtfully. 'I don't believe. I don't believe you know anything about it. Or about him.'

'Not know aboot him!' Fraser was almost bouncing up and down in his seat. 'Sure Ah know aboot 'im. Ah worked for the man, didn't Ah? Ran a dhow for him. That's how Ah know aboot Len. Cold-hearted bastard! The Baluchi lassies, now. We'd pick 'em off a bench near Pasni. Virgins by the look of them. All bleedin' virgins. We'd take 'em across the Gulf and land them in the sand doons north-east of Sharjah. A Pakistani was behind it, some woman who gave their families a wee bit o' money and said they would be trained as nurses. Nurses, my arse! They were being sold as whoores, and it was the Pak woman and Len Baldwick made a killing in the trade, not me, Ah just ran the bleedin' dhow for them.' He called for a waiter, but nobody took any notice. 'Yu got any cigarettes?' He cocked his head at me, fiddling with an empty packet. 'It's clean oot, Ah am.'

Rumours of Baldwick's involvement in the trade had been circulating when I was last in the Gulf, but I had never before met anybody directly implicated. I sat there, staring at him, disgusted and appalled. This vicious little Glaswegian, and right beside him, the big friendly Canadian, looking as though he'd seen a devil peeping out from under a stone . . . They were like oil and water. They didn't mix. They didn't fit. And yet they'd been recruited for the same purpose. They'd be together, on the same ship, and so would I – some of us recruited by Baldwick, some by Hals.

I got to my feet. Fraser had found a waiter now

and was ordering cigarettes and more drinks. I excused myself, took the lift down to the street and walked quickly through the alleyway to the Creek. The air was pleasantly cool, the stars bright overhead, and I sat there by the water for a long time watching the traffic and wondering what it was going to be like isolated from the rest of the world and cooped up on board a ship with a man like Fraser. And Choffel. I wished to God I knew about Choffel, whether he was on the ship or not.

Next morning Baldwick had arrived. He was in the lobby when I went down, looking large and rumpled in a pale blue tropical suit. He had another Frenchman with him, an engineer he had picked up in Marseilles, and Mustafa was flapping around with the drivers of two Land Rovers drawn up outside the hotel. 'You get ready please,' he said to me. 'We leave in twenty minutes.'

'Where for?'

But he turned away.

'Where's the ship?' I demanded, grabbing hold of him.

He hesitated. 'Ask LB. He knows. Not me.'

I turned to Baldwick then, but he had heard my question and was staring at me, his eyes red-rimmed and angry. 'Just get your things.'

I hesitated. But the man was tired after the flight. He'd been drinking and I'd know soon enough. 'No, wait,' he said as I was moving away. And he asked me what the hell I'd been up to at the GODCO offices. 'And you went to see Gault. Why?'

'How do you know?' I asked.

'Think I wouldn't have somebody keep an eye on you.' He came lumbering towards me. 'You been talking?' His tone was menacing.

'I like to know what ship I'm sailing on, where it's berthed.'

'You been asking questions?'

'Look,' I said. 'Adrian Gault I've known on and off for years. Perrin, too. With time to kill I looked them up. Why not? And of course I asked them.'

'I told you to keep yer mouth shut.' He was glaring at me, and suddenly I couldn't help it, I had to know.

'Choffel,' I said. 'Will he be on the same ship as me?'

'Choffel?' He seemed surprised, repeating the name slowly, his voice reluctant, his eyes sharp. 'No.' He was frowning angrily, groping for the right reply. 'The only engineer on board at the moment is the Chief.' And to settle the matter he added quickly, 'His name's Price if you want to know.'

So I was right. That picture with Baldwick on the edge of it, at Sennen, when the crew came ashore. He had recruited him then, made all the arrangements for getting him to the Gulf. And now he was on board. He was there, waiting for me. I suppose I must have been staring open-mouthed. 'You don't concern yourself with Price. Understand?' He was glaring at me, conscious that the name had meant something to me, but not certain what. 'You're not an engineer. You've never met him before.' He was still glaring at me doubtfully and it was Varsac who came to my rescue. He had been talking very fast in French to the new arrival. Now they were both of them looking at Baldwick – the same question.

'*Le tankair. Où ça?*'

Baldwick turned his head slowly, like a bull wearily finding himself baited from another direction. 'We're keeping it as a surprise for you,' he growled. 'Where the hell d'you think it is? In the bloody water, of course.' His small eyes shifted to me, a quick glance, then he went off to get a shower.

We all had breakfast together, coffee and boiled eggs, with Baldwick's beady little eyes watching me as though I was some dangerous beast he had to keep an eye on. Afterwards, when I had packed and was coming away from reception after handing in my room key, Khalid suddenly appeared at my side. 'For you, Said.' He slipped me a blue envelope. 'Sahib say it arrive last night.' He was gone in a flash, scuttling out into the street, and I was left with an English air mail letter card in my hand. The writing was unfamiliar, a round, flowing hand, and the sender's name and address on the back came as a surprise. It was from Pamela Stewart.

I was thinking back to that lunch at Lloyd's, the Nelson Exhibition room. It was all so remote. And to have reached me now she must have sent the letter off the instant Gault had reported my arrival in Dubai. The Land Rovers had started up, Baldwick shouting to me, and I slipped it into my pocket, wondering why she should have written, why the urgency.

It was just after ten as we pulled away from the

hotel, Baldwick with the engineer officers in the first Land Rover, Mustafa with myself and the other deck officers in the second. There was no sign of Pieter Hals. I slit open the air mail letter and began reading it as we threaded our way through Dubai's crowded streets. It appeared to have been written in a hurry, the writing very difficult to read in places. *Dear Trevor Rodin*, it began. *Daddy doesn't know I'm writing, but I thought somebody should tell you how much we appreciate what you are doing and that our thoughts are with you.* It went on like that for almost half a page, then suddenly she abandoned the rather formal language, her mood changing. *I was a fool, leaving you like that. We should have gone on to a club and got drunk, or gone for a walk together, done whatever people do when the heart's too full for sensible words. Instead, I made a silly excuse and left you standing there under the Nelson picture. Please forgive me. I was upset. And my mind's been in a turmoil ever since.*

I stopped there, staring down at the round, orderly writing on the blue paper, aware suddenly that this wasn't an ordinary letter. 'God Almighty!' I breathed.

The Canadian was saying something. His hand gripped my arm. 'It's not Mina Zayed. Abu Dhabi is west of Dubai. We've turned east.'

I slipped the letter back into my pocket and looked out at the chaos of construction work through which we were driving. This was the outskirts of Dubai and he was right. We were on the coast road headed east towards Sharjah, and the *shamal* was starting to blow little streamers of sand across the tarmac road.

'Is it Mina Khalid, you reck'n?' I shook my head. I didn't think it was deep enough. 'Mebbe an SMB.' He turned to Mustafa. 'They got one of the big single mooring buoys for tanker loading along the coast here?' he asked.

The Libyan stared at him blankly.

'Well, where the hell are we going?'

But all Mustafa said was, 'You see. Very good accommodation. Sea view very fine.'

I was staring out of the sand-blown side window, memories of childhood flooding back. Nothing had changed, only the road and a few modern buildings. The country either side was just the same – a vast vista of sky and sand. We passed the remains of the little tin-roofed hospital where my mother had been a nurse. I could remember playing in the dunes there, pretending to be Sayid bin Maktun, the old sheikh of Dubai who had surprised a big raiding force from Abu Dhabi and slaughtered sixty of them at their camp in the desert. We played at pirates, too, using an old dugout canoe we had found washed up on a sand spit in the silted Sharjah estuary, and the little Baluch boy was our slave.

I sat there, staring out as the low dunescape dropped away to the gleaming mud flats of the *subqat* that stretched out to a distant glint of the sea. The wind was stronger here, blowing out of the north-west, and I could have cried for the memory of that little Baluch boy, so thin, so scared, so dead these many years. We skirted Sharjah, the *subqat* giving way to low coastal dunes, sand blowing again in long streamers from the wheels of the leading Land Rover. Occasionally we caught glimpses of the sea, a dark blue-green shot through with the white of breaking wavetops, and the cloudless sky pearl-coloured with the glare of the sun. A glimpse of the fort that had been a radio communications centre in the early days and we were driving fast along the coast towards Ras al Khaimah, the interior of the Land Rover hot and full of sand, the dunes shimmering.

We stopped only once, just beyond Umm al Qaiwain, for sandwiches and coffee served on the tail-board of the leading Land Rover. We didn't stay long, for though we were under the lee of a small dune sparsely covered with brittle dried-up furze, the wind blowing straight off the sea filled the air with a gritty dusting of fine sand. Less than an hour later we pulled into Ras al Khaimah, where the Jebel cliffs begin to form a red background. Here we were given quarters in a little fly-screened motel with cracked walls and temperamental plumbing. The skeletal ribs of a half-constructed dhow thrust pale wooden frame-ends against the blue sky.

What the hell were we doing at Ras al Khaimah? Mustafa and the Land Rovers had left as soon as our luggage had been off-loaded. And since Baldwick wouldn't talk about it, speculation was rife, particularly among the deck officers. Accustomed to think in terms of navigation, our guess was that the ship was across the other side of the Gulf in Iranian waters, or perhaps loading at one of the island tanker terminals, Abu Masa or Tumbs. The engineers didn't care so much. Fraser had got hold of a bottle of Scotch and the man from Marseilles, Jean Lebois, had brought some cognac with him. Baldwick and Varsac joined them and the four settled down to drink and play poker. I went for a walk.

The motel was set in what looked like a piece of waste ground left over from the construction boom, bits of plastic, broken bottles, rusting iron scattered everywhere, half buried in the sand, and all that was left of the attempt to improve the surroundings were the remains of bushes dead of heat and neglect. But where the sand was untouched, stretching in a long yellow vista into the sun, there was solitude and a strange beauty. The wind had dropped, the sea making little flopping sounds and long white lines as the wavelets fell upon the dark glint of wet sand. And inland, beyond the radio tower, red-brown slopes rose endlessly to the distant heights of the Jebel al Harim. I sat in the sand, watching the sun go down and reading Pamela Stewart's letter again.

The round, rather careful writing, the conventional phrasing – I could picture her face, the simple straight-forward plainness of the features, the directness of the gaze from those quiet eyes, the mobility of the over-large mouth. It was the only sexy thing about her, that large mouth. So why did I remember her so clearly? *I don't know where, or in what circumstances, you will read this, or even if it will reach you, but I wish I were able to do what you are doing. We should be able to find out the truth for ourselves, not ask somebody else to do it for us. There is that, which is a natural feeling I think, but there is also something else, something I'm not sure I understand, which is perhaps why I left you so abruptly with such a silly excuse.*

The sun was low now, the sky paling overhead, and the sails of a dhow stood black in silhouette against the pink of cloud shapes hanging over the Iranian shore. The energy packed into that strongly-shaped body, the sense of vitality, quiet and controlled – that, too, I remembered. *I've never faced this problem before . . .* That was how the letter ended – *I've never faced this problem before, so bear with me. I will be thinking of you, and praying that all goes well.* Nothing else, except her signature – *Pamela.*

I sat there for a long time with the letter in my hand, thinking about it as the sun's rim touched the sea and the whole desert shore blazed with fire, wondering if she had any idea what her words meant to me – that somebody, somewhere in the world, was thinking of me and believed, however temporarily, that she cared.

And then the sun was down, the cliffs behind me darkening and the dhow was feeling its way into the creek. I walked quickly back along the sands, hearing the tonk-tonk of its diesel in the fast-gathering dusk, and when I was back, at the point where the creek widened out into a large flat sheet of water, I found it lying at anchor right off the motel. I knew then that it was bin Suleiman's dhow, but nobody came ashore from it, so that I wasn't sure Pieter Hals was on board until we embarked the following morning.

The *shamal* was blowing again then and even in the shelter of the creek it took time to embark the six of us, the dhow's only tender being a small wooden boat. Baldwick came with us and there was a quantity of locally-grown produce to load. It took altogether six trips, so that it was almost eleven before the anchor was up and we were motoring seaward. The sky was a clear, bright blue and the sun shone warm on the red cliffs, the waters of the Gulf foaming white at their base. It was a wonderful day for a sail, but where would we end up? Rod Selkirk and I were standing together on the leeward side of the high poop, both of us watching the bearded figure of bin Suleiman motionless beside the helmsman, a loose end of his turban flying in the wind. The low sand spit slid away to port and the dhow thrust its curved beak into deeper water. Would he hold his course and head for Iran, or turn along the coast?

'I don't get it,' Selkirk said. 'Why all the secrecy?' He had spoken to Hals when he came forward, but had got nothing out of him.

We were plugging almost dead to windward, no sails set, the dhow beginning to slam as the bows thrust into the steepening waves. 'Sure looks like Iran,' he said, and at that moment bin Suleiman nodded to the helmsman. The long wooden arm of the tiller was thrust over and the dhow came slowly round on to a north-easterly heading. Shouts and the deck erupting into violent activity as the big lateen sail was hoisted up the mainmast. Soon both sails were set, the engine stopped, and we were creaming along, rolling heavily with the spray flying silver in the sun and a long vista of ochre-red cliffs opening up to starboard, the Straits of Hormuz not fifty miles away.

Pieter Hals came up from below. I think he had been checking the stores loaded at Dubai. He stood for a moment in the waist of the dhow staring out at the coast, towards the little port of Mina Saqr nestled right against the mountains. I had been there once, in the dhow that had taken me to Baluchistan. I moved across the deck to join Hals. 'Where are we going?' I asked him.

'One of the *khawrs*.' His voice sounded vague, his mind on something else.

The *khawrs* were rocky inlets. There were a lot of them cutting deep into the Musandam Peninsula on the south side of the Straits, none on the Iranian side. 'So our ship is not in Iran?'

'No.'

'Why is it anchored in one of the *khawrs*?'

He didn't answer, still staring at the coast. And when I repeated the question, he turned his head slowly, staring down at me vacantly, his mind still far away. His eyes were a light blue, crease-lines in the skin at the corners, and there were freckles under the sun-bleached beard. 'You're Rodin, are you?'

I nodded.

'Your wife,' he said. 'I read about that.' He held out his hand. 'Ja. She is an example to us all.' He stared at me. 'Tell me, did you know?'

'Know what?' But something in his eyes gave me the answer.

He waited.

'I was at a meeting,' I said. 'She did it on the spur of the moment. When she heard the result.'

'When she heard they weren't going to do anything to prevent the next oil spill.'

I nodded, wishing I hadn't spoken to him now, wanting to get away. 'She didn't realize the whole ship would be blown up,' I muttered quickly. 'She was not a very practical person.'

'No?' He smiled. 'Eminently practical, I should say. Ja. But not political. A pity that. Her death achieved nothing. She should have threatened, made terms, forced them to do something. A law of the sea to control pollution. Powers of arrest, and the death penalty, if necessary – with naval vessels and aircraft constantly on patrol in restricted waters with power to take immediate action, against any ship, of any nationality. Only that way will we stop the destruction of our marine environment. You agree?'

I nodded. It was what we had so often talked about.

'Is that why you're here?' He was frowning. 'You're not one of my boys. You're Len Baldwick's lot.'

'Does that make a difference?'

The blue eyes seemed to look right through me. 'You don't know, do you? So, why are you here?'

'Is Choffel one of your boys?' I asked him.

'Choffel?'

'The man who calls himself Price. David Price.'

'The chief engineer.'

'Somebody sent a dhow to pick him up from a French ship in the Straits.'

'Baldwick sent it.' He stood there, frowning. 'Choffel? Ah!' His hand slammed down on the wooden capping of the bulwarks. 'So that's it. That's who he is.' He seized hold of my arm, staring at me. 'Choffel! The *Petros Jupiter*. He was the engineer, ja?' He nodded, his lips under the pale beard spreading to the ghost of a smile. '*Goed! Zeer goed!*' And suddenly he was laughing. 'Different nationalities, different motives – it will bekom an interesting voyage, I think.' He was still laughing, a wild look in those pale blue eyes. I thought of him then as he had appeared in the press, holding the whole world at bay, a bomb in his hand and a loaded tanker under his feet. He was moving away from me, crossing the deck and climbing slowly up the steps to the poop that looked high enough and old enough to have Bligh himself pacing its deck. He seemed lost in his thoughts again, and I stood rooted to the spot, wondering just how mad or unpredictable he would prove to be. The captain of a tanker, whose whereabouts I still didn't know, officered by men of different nationalities, different motivations. An interesting voyage, he had said, laughing, and the cold pale eyes looking wild.

It was a long day, sailing on a close reach, the *shamal* virtually a westerly, deflected by the red volcanic mountains. A great dish of rice and goat meat was cooked in the waist over a charcoal fire and we

ate it squatting on the poop with the wooden pulpit-
like thunderbox on the windward side, the mountains
falling away and deep indents appearing in the coastline, so that the heat-hazed outline of its jagged cliffs
had the fluted look of a red-hot organ. I had never
been this close to the upthrust finger of the peninsula
that was the southern side of the Straits of Hormuz.
It looked hellish country, which doubtless explained
the nature of the people who inhabited it. The Shihuh
had a bad reputation.

And then, just as the sun was slanting so low that
the whole dragons'-toothed line of jagged cliffs turned
a bright blood-red, we turned and headed in towards
them. The great sail was dipped for'ard of the mast
and brought round on to the port side, the wind on
the starboard quarter and the dhow piling through a
sea so red it was like molten lava. It was a fantastic
sight, the sun going down and the world catching fire,
red rocks toppling in pinnacles above us and all of us
staring unbelievingly as we ran suddenly into black
shadow, the narrow gut opening out into a great basin
ringed with sheer rock cliffs, and the whole wild,
impossible place as red as the gates of hell, sculpted
into incredible, fluted shapes.

At the far end, clamped against the red cliffs, red
itself like a huge rock slab, a shape emerged that took
on the appearance of a ship, a long flat tank of a ship
with the superstructure at the far end of it painted the
same colour as the cliffs, so that the one blended into
the other, an optical illusion that gradually became a
reality as we furled our sails and motored towards it

in the fading light, the sound of our diesel echoing back from the darkening cliffs. It was hot as hell and a red flag with a hammer and sickle fluttered above the dim reddish outline of the tanker's funnel.

CHAPTER TWO

We had known, of course, the instant we turned into the *khawr* that this was where the ship lay; what came as a surprise was to find her jammed hard against the side of the inlet instead of anchored out in the open. The light was going fast, the shape of her merging into the towering background of rock, no colour now, the red darkening to black, and the gloom of the heat-stored cliffs hanging over us. She was a VLCC, about 100,000 tons by the look of her, the side-windows and portholes of her superstructure painted out so that she looked blind and derelict, like a ship that had been stranded there a long time. I think all of us felt a sense of eeriness as we bumped alongside, the hot reek of metal, the stink of oil and effluent that scummed the water round her, the silence disintegrating into a jabber of voices as we gave vocal expression to our feelings at this strange embarkation.

But it wasn't just the circumstances of the vessel. There was something else. At least there was as far as

I was concerned. I was conscious of it as soon as I had climbed aboard, so that I stood there, shocked into immobility till the heat of the deck coming up through the soles of my shoes forced me to move.

I have always been sensitive to atmosphere. I remember, when I was about ten, I went with a camel train to Buraimi and burst into tears at the sight of an abandoned village with the well full of stones. I had no idea at the time why it upset me so, but long afterwards I discovered that Wahabi raiders had thrown all the males of that village down the well before blocking it up. And it didn't have to be the destruction of a village, or of whole armies, as in the Khyber where that dreadful little triangle of flat land in the depths of the pass shrieks aloud of the thousands trapped and slaughtered. Standing on the deck of that tanker, with the cliffs leaning over me and the stars brightening, I could accept the fact of her extraordinary position, tucked in against the rock face, the mooring lines looped over natural pinnacles. The flag, too. Given that this was some sort of fraud, then the painting of the hull to match the ochre-red of the rock, the blanking out of all the windows, these became sensible, practical precautions, and the flag no more than a justification for the ship's concealment should the crew of an overflying aircraft be sharp enough to spot her. Everything, in fact, however strange, had a perfectly rational explanation – except the atmosphere.

An Arab was coming towards us along the flat steel promenade of the deck. He had a gaunt, pock-marked face and a nose like the beak of a ship. There was a suggestion of effeminacy in his voice as he greeted bin Suleiman, but beneath the old sports jacket I glimpsed the brass-bound leather of crossed braces and belt, the gleam of cartridge cases against the white of his flowing robes. This was a Bedu and equipped for fighting. 'Gom,' he said, in soft, guttural English, and he took us back along the deck to the steel ladder that reared up on the port side of the superstructure. I could hear the faint hum of a generator deep in the bowels of the ship as we climbed to the level of B deck, where he opened the door for us, standing back and motioning us to enter.

One moment I was standing on the grating, darkness closing in from the east, and to the west, behind the first outcrops of the Jebel al Harim, the last of the sunset glow still lingering in the sky, the next I had stepped inside, into the blacked-out accommodation area, everything darkened and the lights glowing dimly. Rod Selkirk's quarters were, as usual in this type of tanker, on the starboard side, mine the next cabin inboard, so that both mates were immediately below the captain's quarters on C deck. I had a wash and was stowing my gear when Rod poked his head round the door. 'Officers' saloon is just down the alley from me, and they got beer in the cold box – coming?'

'Pour one for me,' I said. 'I'll be right with you.'

'Sure. Be seeing you then.'

He closed the door and I stood there for a moment, looking vaguely round for the best place to stow my empty bags, conscious that his sudden need of company reflected my own mood, the sense of being alone and on the brink of a voyage whose end I didn't want to think about. The cabin was hot and airless, the two windows looking for'ard obscured by an ochre-coloured wash, the lights dim. I scratched at the window glass with my thumb nail, but the wash was on the outside. It annoyed me that I couldn't see out, the place seeming claustrophobic like a prison cell. I changed into my clean white shirt, combed my hair back, my face pale and ghostly in the damp-spotted mirror, then turned to the door, thinking of that beer.

It was then, when I was already out of the cabin and had switched off the light, that the windows were momentarily illuminated from the outside, a baleful glow that revealed a tiny diamond-gleam of white where a brush stroke had lifted clear of the glass. It was in the bottom right-hand corner of the further window, but it was gone before I could reach it, and when I crouched down, searching with my eye close to the glass, I had difficulty in locating it. Then suddenly there was light again and I was looking down on to the deck of the tanker, every detail of it picked out in the beam of a powerful torch directed for'ard at two figures standing in the bows. I saw them for an instant, then they were gone, the torch switched off, and it took a moment for my eye to adjust to the shadowy outline of the deck barely visible in the starlight. A man, carrying something that looked like a short-barrelled gun, came into my line of vision, walking quickly with a limp towards the fo'c'sle, and when he reached it the torch shone out again, directed downwards now, three figures, dark in silhouette, leaning forward, their heads bent as they peered into what was presumably a storage space or else the chain locker.

They were there for a moment, then there was again no light but the stars and I couldn't see them any more, only the dim shape of the fo'c'sle with the two anchor windlasses and the mooring line winch. Several minutes passed, my eye glued to the little peep-hole of clear glass, but the figures did not reappear, the steel of the deck an empty platform with the black silhouette of the cliffs hanging over it. Once I thought I saw the glow of a light from a hatchway, but my vision was becoming blurred and I couldn't be sure.

I straightened up, blinking my eyes in the dark of the cabin. It was an odd feeling to be an officer on a ship and not know who was on board or what they were up to. Those shadowy figures, and the man with the gun limping towards them – probably they were just checking the mooring lines, or inspecting the lie of the anchor chain, making certain that the ship was ready to haul off and get under way, but the sense of something sinister was very strong.

I went out then and shut the cabin door, standing uncertain in the dim-lit passage. There was a small baggage room opposite my door, an oil-skin store next to it, then the officers' washroom and the alleyway leading down the starboard side to the mess-room. I could hear the sound of voices. But still I hesitated, thinking about the men Baldwick had shipped in by dhow from Baluchistan. Had they brought the ship into the *khawr* and moored it against the cliffs, or had there been a different crew then? The crew's quarters would be on the deck below. I had only to go down there to learn if they were Pakistanis. I glanced at my watch. It was just after six-thirty. They'd probably be having their evening meal, in which case this was the moment to take a look round the ship. There'd be nobody in the wheelhouse now, or in the chart room, the radio shack too – somewhere up there on the navigating bridge there would be some indication of the ship's background, where she was from. And on the deck below, on the port side of C deck – the opposite side to the captain's quarters – would be the chief engineer's accommodation . . .

Perhaps it would all have been different if I'd gone up to the bridge then. But I thought it could wait, that just for a moment a beer was more important. And so I turned right, past the washroom, down the alleyway to the mess-room door, and there, sitting talking to Rod Selkirk and the others, was Choffel.

Behind him a single long table with its white cloth stood out in sharp contrast against the soft, almost dove-grey pastel shade of the walls. The chairs, upholstered in bright orange, gave the room an appearance of brightness, even though the lights were almost as dim as in my cabin. Nevertheless, I recognized him instantly, despite the dim lighting and the fact that his chin was now thickly stubbled, the beginnings of a beard. He was wearing navy blue trousers and a white, short-sleeved shirt with chief engineer's tabs on the shoulders. He looked older, the face more drawn than in the photographs I had seen, and he was talking with a sort of nervous intensity, his voice quick and lilting, no trace of a French accent.

He stopped at the sight of me and got to his feet, asking me if I would like a beer. They were all of them drinking beer, except Fraser, who had got hold of a bottle of whisky. For a moment I just stood there, staring at him. He looked so ordinary and I didn't know what to say. In the end I simply told him my name, watching his face to see the reaction, thinking that would be enough. But all he said was, 'David Price, Chief Engineer.' And he held out his hand so that I had to take it. 'Welcome aboard.' He turned then and emptied the remains of a can of beer into a glass, handing it to me and pulling up a chair, his dark eyes giving me no more than a casual glance.

My name meant nothing to him. Either he hadn't taken it in, or else he didn't realize what had happened to the *Petros Jupiter*. 'You're Welsh, are you?' I asked. 'Somebody told me the Chief was a Greek.'

He looked at me sharply. 'Who? Who told you that, man?' And when I shrugged and said I couldn't remember, he gave a quick little laugh. 'With a name like Price, of course I'm Welsh.'

I nodded. 'My wife was Welsh,' I said and sat down, knocking back half the beer he had given me, very conscious of his proximity, the dark eyes and the black wavy hair streaked with grey, the stubble thick on his jaw and throat.

'Your wife, where was she from then?' His voice displayed no more than polite interest and I knew he hadn't a clue who I was or why I was here, didn't even know how she had died.

'From Swansea,' I said. And I told him her maiden name had been Davies. 'Karen Davies.' I remembered the way she had looked, leaning against her bicycle and speaking her name to me for the first time. 'Karen,' I said again and his only comment was that it didn't sound very Welsh.

'Well, what about your own name?' I said. 'Price doesn't sound exactly Welsh.'

'No?' He laughed. 'Well, let me tell you then. Price is a bastardized form of ap-Rhys or Rees. Ap meant son of, you see. Like ap-Richard – Pritchard.'

I asked him then if he'd been born in Wales and he said, 'Yes.'

'Where?'

'I was born near Caio,' he said, 'In an old stone cottage about a mile from Ogofau, where my father worked.' And he added, 'That's hill-farming country, the real heart of Plaid Cymru where the old shires of Cardigan and Carmarthen met before they re-named them Dyfed. After me, you know.' And he smiled, a humorous little smile that creased the corners of his mouth and tucked a small hollow into each cheek. 'My father was a miner, you see. Started in the anthracite pits down in the valleys beyond Merthyr. It was there he got the silicosis that finally killed him.'

He got up and went over to the cold box, coming back with a fresh beer for each of us. And then he was talking about the Ogofau gold mine, how it was an open-cast mine in the days of the Romans, who had built a guard post at Pumpsaint and seven miles of sluices. He said there were historians who believed it was because of Ogofau that the Romans invaded Britain. 'All through the occupation they were exporting something like 400 tons of gold a year to Rome. That's what my father said.'

Sitting there, staring at that Welsh face, listening to that Welsh voice telling about his childhood and about going down into the mine with his father after it had closed in the thirties – it wasn't a bit as I had expected, this meeting between myself and the *Petros Jupiter*'s engineer. He was describing what his father had told him about working underground in a mine that had been producing gold for more than two thousand years – the rock face caving in as they struck one of the old shafts, the roar of the dammed-up water engulfing them, rising chest-high as they fled and stinking of two millennia of stagnation. And then one of the crew came in, a Pakistani who said something to him about the tiller flat, and he nodded. 'All right then,' he said, gulping down the rest of his beer and excusing himself. 'You Mates, you come off watch and that's that, but a Chief Engineer now . . .' And he smiled at us as he hurried out.

I stared after him unbelievingly. God knows how many ships he'd sent to the bottom, how many men he'd drowned, and he was so ordinary, so very Welsh, so pleasant even. I could see his daughter, standing there in that extraordinary house built into the cliffs above the Loire, her voice rising in anger as she defended him – such a kindly, generous, loving father. God Almighty!

Behind me I heard Varsac saying, 'I don't think he know anyzing. If he do, why don't he tell us.' And Lebois insisting that an officer who had been on board over a week must have learned something. 'But all he talks about is the Pays de Galles.'

The French, with their customary realism, had already accepted that it was either a scuttling job or a cargo fraud, Varsac insisting that we weren't loaded with oil at all, but ballasted down with sea water. 'You check, eh?' he told Rod. 'You're the Mate. You examine the tanks, then we know.' He wiped his lips with the back of his hand, leaning forward and smiling crookedly. 'If it is sea water, not oil, then we demand more pay, eh?'

Fraser suddenly erupted into the discussion: 'Don't be bloody stupid, man. Yu du that an' yu'll find yursel' left behind to fry on the rocks here.' He reached for the whisky bottle. 'Yu seen the guard they got patrolling the deck. Start pokin' yur nose into those tanks an' yu'll get a bullet in yur guts.' And he added as he refilled his glass, 'Yu ask me, we're sitting on a tanker-load of high explosives – bombs, shells, guns.' He stared at Varsac morosely. 'There's enough wars fur God's sake.'

I left them arguing over the nature of the voyage and went back to my cabin to peer through the tiny chink of clear glass at the deck below. I could see no movement at all, though the stars were brighter than ever and the deck clearly visible with the masts of the dhow like two slender sticks lifted above the port rail. I thought I could make out a figure standing in the shadow of the nearby derrick, but I couldn't be sure. Then a match flared, the glow of a cigarette, and shortly afterwards two Arabs came over the rail at the point where the dhow was moored alongside. The guard stepped out of the derrick's shadow, the three of them in a huddle for a moment, and then they were moving down the deck towards the bridge-housing all dressed in white robes and talking together so that I knew the guard was also an Arab.

I watched until they passed out of sight below, then I straightened up, wondering who set the guards, who was really in charge? Not Baldwick, he'd only just arrived. Not Hals either.

But Hals was the most likely source of information and I went along the alleyway to the lift. It wasn't working and when I tried to reach the exterior bridge ladder I found the door to it locked. It took a little searching to find the interior stairs. They were in a central well entered by a sliding fire door that was almost opposite my cabin.

The upper deck was very quiet. There was nobody about, the alleyway empty, the doors to the offices and day rooms of both captain and chief engineer closed. I tried the lift, but it wasn't working on this deck either. I don't think it was out of order. I think the current had been switched off. At any rate, the door leading to the deck and the external ladder was locked, the intention clearly to restrict the movement of officers and crew.

The lift being on the port side it was right next to the radio officer's quarters. I knocked, but there was no answer and the door was locked. He would be the key man if it were fraud and I wondered who he was. A door opposite opened on to stairs leading up to the navigating bridge. I hesitated, the companionway dark and no sound from the deck above. At the back of the wheelhouse there'd be the chart table, all the pilot books, the log, too, if I could find it. And there was the radio shack. Somewhere amongst the books, papers and charts I should be able to discover the identity of the ship and where she had come from.

I listened for a moment, then started up the stairs, treading cautiously. But nobody challenged me, and when I reached the top, I felt a breath of air on my face. I turned left into the wheelhouse. The sliding door to the port bridge wing was open and the windows were unobscured so that I could see the stars.

There was no other light, the chart table and the control console only dimly visible. But just to be there, in the wheelhouse, the night sky brilliant through the clear windows and the ship stretched out below me in the shadow of the cliffs – I stood there for a moment, feeling a wonderful sense of relief.

It was only then that I realized how tensed up I had become in the last few days. And now I felt suddenly at home, here with the ship's controls all about me. The two years at Balkaer slipped away. This was where I belonged, on the bridge of a ship, and even though she looked as if she'd been stranded against towering rocks, I was seeing her in my mind as she'd be when we were under way, the wide blunt bows ploughing through the waves, the deck moving underfoot, all the world at my command.

There were no lights here and it took a moment for my eyes to become accustomed to the starlit gloom. The long chart table unit formed the back of the wheelhouse, just behind the steering wheel and the gyro compass. There was a chart on it, but even in that dim light I could see that it was the plans of the Persian Gulf, which included large scale details of the Musandam Peninsula, and no indication of where the ship had come from. This was the only chart on the table, and the one ready to hand in the top drawer, the big Bay of Bengal chart, was no help either. It was the log book I needed, but when I went to switch on the chart table light to search the shelves, I found the bulb had been removed. I think all the bulbs in the wheelhouse had been removed.

However, the books were the usual collection to be found on the bridge of any ocean-going ship, most of them immediately recognizable by their shape – the Admiralty sailing directions, light lists, tidal and ocean current charts, nautical almanacs, and the lists of radio signals and navigational aid stations and beacons.

I turned my attention to the radio room then. This was on the starboard side, and groping my way to it I stumbled against a large crate. It was one of three, all of them stencil-marked RADIO EQUIPMENT. They had been dumped outside the entrance to the radio room which, even in the darkness, showed as a ragged gap boarded up with a plywood panel. Jagged strips of metal curling outwards indicated an explosion and the walls and deck were blackened by fire.

The sight of it came as a shock, my mind suddenly racing. Radio shacks didn't explode of their own accord. Somebody had caused it, somebody who had been determined to stop the ship from communicating with the outside world. The crates were obviously the ones Hals had loaded on to the dhow from the warehouse at Dubai. The larger one would be the single-sideband radio and the other two would contain the other replacements for instruments damaged in the explosion. Was that why I hadn't seen any sign of a radio officer? Had he been killed in the blast? I was remembering Gault's warning then, feeling suddenly exposed, the others all in the mess-room drinking, only myself up here on the bridge trying to find out where the ship had come from, what had happened to her.

The need to be out of the wheelhouse and in the open air, away from those grim marks of violence, made me turn away towards the door on the starboard side, sliding it open and stepping out into the night. The starboard bridge wing was so close to the cliffs I could almost touch them with my hand, the air stifling with the day's heat trapped in the rocks. The masts of the dhow lying just ahead of the port-side gangway were two black sticks against the dull gleam of the *khawr*, which stretched away, a broad curve like the blade of a *khanjar* knife in the starlight. Deep down below I could just hear the muffled hum of the generator. It was the only sound in the stillness of that starlit night, the ship like a ghostly sea monster

stranded in the shadow of the cliffs, and that atmosphere – so strong now that it almost shrieked aloud
to me.

Standing there on the extreme edge of the bridge
wing, I suddenly realized I was exposed to the view of
any hawk-eyed Arab standing guard on the deck
below. I turned back to the shelter of the wheelhouse.
No point in searching for that log book now. With the
radio room blasted by some sort of explosive device,
the log would either be destroyed or in safe keeping.
Hals might have it, but more likely it was in the hands
of the people who had hired him. In any case, it didn't
really matter now. The destruction of the ship's means
of communication could only mean one thing – piracy.
She had been seized from her owners, either whilst on
passage or else in some Middle Eastern port where the
harbour authorities were in such a state of chaos that
they were in no position to prevent the seizure of a
100,000-ton ship.

I had another look at the blackened fabric of the
radio room. There was absolutely no doubt, it had
been blasted by an explosion and that had been followed by fire. I wondered what had happened to the
poor wretched Sparks. Had he been there when the
explosion occurred? I didn't attempt to break into
the room, but at least there was no odour of putrefaction, only the faint smell of burnt rubber and paint. I
checked the crates again, wondering why they needed
to replace the radio equipment. For purposes of
entering a port to sell cargo or for delivering the ship
a small VHF set would be quite adequate.

Other questions flooded my mind. Why hadn't they organized the replacement crew in advance, instead of harbouring the ship against the cliffs here? Why the delay, running the risk of her being sighted by an Omani reconnaissance plane monitoring movements through the Straits or picked out from some routine surveillance satellite photograph? Surely speed in an operation like this was essential. I moved across to the port side to see if the radar room had also been damaged.

It was then that a shadow moved by the door to the port bridge wing. I saw it out of the corner of my eye, heard the click of metal slotting home as I spun round, and a voice, with a strong accent, said, 'Who are you?'

He was standing in silhouette against the stars. The deck guard presumably, for I could see the robes and the gun. 'Second mate,' I said. 'Just checking the bridge. No need for you to worry.' My voice sounded a little hoarse, the gun pointed at my stomach. It was some sort of machine pistol.

'Below plees. Nobody come here.'

'Whose orders?' I asked.

'Below. Below. You go below – quick!' His voice was high and nervous, the gun in his hand jerking, the white of his eyes staring.

'What's your name?'

He shook his head angrily. 'Go quick.'

'Who gave you orders to keep the ship's officers off the bridge?'

'You go – quick,' he repeated, and he jabbed the muzzle of his machine pistol hard into my ribs.

I couldn't see the man's face, it was in shadow, but I could sense his nervousness. 'Is Captain Hals allowed on the bridge?' I asked. I don't know whether he understood the question, but he didn't answer, jabbing the gun into me again, indicating that I should get moving.

I never saw what he looked like, for he didn't come down with me into the lower part of the ship, simply standing at the top of the bridge companion and motioning me below with the barrel of his pistol.

Back on C deck I went straight to the captain's office. The door was just past the central well of the stairs. There was no answer to my knock so I tried the handle. To my surprise it opened and the light was on inside. There was a desk with a typewriter on it, some papers, steel filing cabinets against the inboard bulkhead, two or three chairs. The papers proved to be invoices, and there was a radio instruction manual. The inner door leading to the day cabin was ajar and, though the light was on, there was nobody there. The decor was the same as in the officers' mess-room, the walls grey, the furnishings and curtains orange. It looked bright and cheerful, no indication at all of any violence.

The bedroom door, outboard on the far side, was not only shut but bolted from the inside. I called out and after a moment a sleepy voice answered. 'Ja. Who is it?' And when I told him, he asked, 'Is it already time for the night food?'

I glanced at my watch. 'It's almost twenty past seven,' I told him.

'Ja. It is almost time.'

I heard movement, then the door was unbolted and he emerged completely naked, his eyes barely open and his blond hair standing up in a tousled mop, so that if he'd had a straw in his mouth, he would have made a very good caricature of a stage yokel. 'What is it you want?' he asked, standing there with his mouth open in a yawn and scratching himself.

'The name of the ship,' I said. 'I want to know what's happened to her and why.'

He stopped scratching then, his mouth suddenly a tight line, his eyes watching me. 'So. You want to ask questions – now, before the voyage is begun. Why?' And when I told him I'd just come from the wheelhouse he smiled, nodding his head. 'Sit down.' He waved me to the settle and dived back into the bedroom. 'So you have seen our bombed-out radio room and come to the obvious conclusion, that there is an attempt at piracy and they make a balls of it, eh? But take my advice, Mr Rodin, do not leap to the conclusion that they are stupid people and incompetent. They learn their lesson very well.'

'What happened to the radio officer?' I asked.

'Dead, I think.'

'And the other officers, the crew?'

'One, per'aps two, killed, also several wounded.' There was the sound of water running and then he said, 'Better you don't ask about that.' And after a moment he emerged in white shorts and shirt, running a comb through his damp hair. 'You want to stay alive, you keep your mouth shut. These people are very tough.'

'Who?'

'You will see in good time, my friend. There are five of them and they mean business. So, if you don't like it, better you don't do anything quick, without proper thought. Understand?'

I nodded, conscious that his choice of words distanced himself from them. 'Where do you come into it?' I asked him.

He didn't even answer that, slipping the comb into the breast pocket of his shirt, watching me all the time out of those very blue eyes. Finally he said, 'Per'aps when we know each other better, then maybe we could talk freely. For the present, you are the second officer and I am your captain. That is all between us. Right?'

I got to my feet then. I couldn't force him to talk. But at least I knew he wasn't part of what had already happened. 'On the dhow,' I said, 'when we were coming up from Ras al Khaimah—' I hesitated, wondering how to put it. Since I didn't know what the operation was I couldn't be sure he was opposed to it. But I wanted him to know that, if there was any question of pollution, and he was opposing it, he could count on me. 'When you knew who I was, you talked about my wife. You said Karen should have been more political, that she should have threatened the authorities, demanded a law of the sea to control pollution. Those were your words. You meant them, didn't you?'

'Ja. Of course. But the *Petros Jupiter*, that was only a ten thousand ton spillage.'

'But is that the reason you're here, on this ship?'

'What reason?'

'Pollution,' I said. 'The same reason you risked your life in that tanker on the Niger.'

'Ah, you know about that.' He sat down and waved me back to my seat. 'I risked my job, too. After that nobody want to employ me, not even as an ordinary seaman.' He laughed. 'Then I got this job.'

'Through Baldwick?'

He shook his head. 'I was in Dubai and I hear some talk ...' He reached into a locker beside the table. 'You like a whisky?' He poured it neat, not waiting for me to answer. 'You know, the first bad slick I ever see, the first real pollution? It was in South Africa. I had just taken my mate's certificate and was on leave ...' His mother was apparently from Cape Town and he had been staying with relatives, some people called Waterman, who were English South African, not Afrikaner, and very involved in the environment. 'Victor was a marine biologist. Connie, too, but she had a baby to look after. You remember the *Wafra*?'

I shook my head.

'And before that the *Kazimah*?'

He drank some of his whisky and sat, looking down at the glass in his hand, his mind back in the past. It was the *Wafra* he talked about first. That was in 1969, he said, and he had been between ships, enjoying himself, wanting to see as much as he could of the country. He had arrived there in November, just two days before the *Kazimah* got herself impaled on the Robben rocks. 'Robben is an island out in Table Bay about seven miles from Cape Town.' He paused, still looking down at his glass, and when I asked him the cause of the stranding, he shrugged and said, 'The engine. Ja, it is always the engine. Almost every tanker gets into difficulties—' And then he was talking about the organization for the conservation of coastal birds that had been formed the previous year and how he had spent the best part of a month helping his cousin, Connie, who was a member of the organization, collect oil-soaked penguins and take them to the cleansing centre. There had been a lot of people working desperately hard at penguin recovery, but even so her husband reckoned around 10,000 died.

And, earlier that same year, the whole penguin population of Dyer Island, over to the west near Cape Agulhas, had been wiped out by another oil slick. 'Everything, every bloody tanker, all the oil for Europe and the West goes round the Cape. And I come back from two months wandering through the Kalahari, and over to the Skeleton Coast and Namibia, to find Connie Waterman exhausted with the effort of dealing with the *Wafra* disaster. It was the breeding season and they were literally evacuating the birds from Dyer Island to prevent them being hit again.' He paused then, lifting his head and looking directly at me. 'That is how I have become involved in environment.' And he added, a little smile moving the hairs of his beard, 'Per'aps it is true what my mother says, that I am half in love with Connie.' She had been only a few years older and he'd been tramping, no fixed abode, no attachment, seeing the world, taking life as it came. It was working with her, he said, handling the poor pitiful wrecks of birds, and all the time the terrible sense of inadequacy felt by Connie and the other men and women working so hard to save what they could, knowing that whatever they did, nothing would alter the fact that tomorrow or the next day, or the next, there would be another tanker in trouble, another oil slick, more pollution, more birds to treat – on and on and on till 'the bloody bastards who own and run the sheeps are made to realize what it means when oil is vented, either intentionally or accidentally. And—' He was very tense now, very worked up, the words spilling out of him with great force – 'it is not only the Cape. It is the coasts of Europe. My own country – the Nederlands, that is very vulnerable, also the UK, France, the whole of the English Channel . . .'

He stopped there, wiping his face with his handkerchief. 'But the politicians, the bureaucrats, they don't care. Nothing will be done, nothing at all until the industrial nations that demand all this oil are themselves threatened with pollution on a massive scale.' He was looking straight at me, his eyes wide and staring, his whole body radiating an extraordinary intensity. 'Then maybe they get tough, so the bastards can be arrested on the high seas. And if,' he went on, his teeth showing white through his beard, 'when the captain is arrested, he is thrown into the sea to float in his own filthy oil until he is half dead – like the birds, eh? – like the keel-haul updated – then, I tell you, man – then there will be no more oil slicks, no more venting at sea. But not till then. You understand?' He leaned forward, tapping my knee. 'You worry about the *Petros Jupiter*. What about the *Amoco Cadiz*? And the *Metula* down in the Magellan Straits – fifty thousand tons in an area where the cold makes biological breakdown of the tarry mousse much slower. Tanker after tanker. And the venting and the leaks – they go on all the time. How much oil do you think is spilled into the sea from bilges, engine-rooms and illicit tank cleaning operations? You will not believe me, but I tell you, it is one and a half million tons of oil. Ja.' He nodded, cracking his knuckles, an angry brightness in his eyes. 'There must be a stop put to it.' His mouth opened to emit a harsh barking laugh. 'Drown them in it. That is good justice. Do you agree?' He was deadly serious, his eyes very wide, almost staring, and fixed on mine as though conveying some unspoken message. 'So. We have another talk some time. But when we are at sea,' he added, glancing at his watch. 'Now we will go to eat.'

He got to his feet, padding barefoot back into the bedroom to put on some shoes, while I sat finishing my whisky and thinking about it. Almost everybody involved in the cleaning of oiled birds had probably wished at some time it was the men responsible for the slick they were trying to clean. Rough justice, but if those responsible for a spillage were forced to swim for it in their own filth . . . it was politically impossible, of course. Karen had talked about it. So had others at the Cornish cleansing station, the women mainly. But how many nations would agree to pass and enforce such a Draconian law?

It started me thinking about the ship again and Hals saying that nothing would be done until the industrial nations were faced with the threat of massive oil pollution. Was that his plan? An interesting voyage, he had said – different nationalities, different motives. 'What's our destination?' I asked him.

'You will be told soon.'

'Do you know it?' He didn't answer that, his foot on the chair, bending to tie the laces of a new pair of canvas deck shoes. 'What about the name of the ship?' I asked.

'They don't have a name for it yet.'

'But the original name?'

'It has been painted out.'

'Yes, but what was it?'

'You ask too many questions.' He came back into the day cabin, and at that moment the door of the office was swung open and a voice behind me said, 'Captain. I told you, no one is to go on the bridge.' It was a soft, sibilant voice, the English quite fluent. 'Is this the man?'

I swung round to see a slight, dark figure standing in the doorway. He was bearded, with thick, curly black hair, dressed in very pale khaki trousers and tunic, a chequered scarf at his throat and a pistol holstered in his leather belt. But it was the face, the dark eyes, the birthmark just visible beneath the beard . . . I jumped to my feet. 'Qasim!' The name was out before I could stop myself, before I had time to think what his presence meant.

I saw the sudden wariness in his eyes, the hesitation as he considered his reply. 'We have met before?' He sounded uncertain, his hand going, almost automatically it seemed, to the pistol in its holster.

'The *Shatt al Arab*,' I said, recovering myself. 'Remember? You were brought on board by the Shah's police and we took you to Kuwait.'

He thought back, frowning. 'Ah, yes, of course.' He nodded, his hand coming slowly away from the gun. 'I remember now.' He was smiling then, some of the tension going out of him. 'You were very good to me, all of you, on board that ship. And I had had a bad time of it, you know.'

'You made a good recovery I see.'

'Yes, I am fully recovered, thank you. But my name is Sadeq now. Abol Sadeq.' He came forward into the day cabin holding out his hand. 'I am sorry. I remember your face, of course. You were the second mate, I think. But I forget your name. Excuse me.' I told him my name and he nodded and shook my hand. 'Of course.' He was looking at me curiously. 'You have lost your wife. Mr Baldwick told me. I am sorry.' The dark eyes stared at me a moment. 'Are you the man who is in the wheelhouse just now?'

'Yes.'

'Why?'

'Why not, if I'm second mate?'

He laughed then. 'Of course. Why not. But why don't you stay with the others? You don't like to drink?

Or is it that you're curious?' He seemed to be trying to make up his mind about something. 'You don't answer.'

I shrugged. 'I've never been on a ship where the bridge was barred to the mates.'

'Well, now you are on such a ship. Until we sail.' He turned to Hals. 'Didn't you warn them?'

Hals shook his head. 'I left that to Baldwick.'

'But you are the captain and I told you . . .' He stopped there and gave a little shrug. 'It does not matter now. I have just been in the mess and I told them myself.' He turned back to me. 'There is a guard on the deck. He is an Arab, one of the Shihuh who inhabit this part. You could have been shot.' He nodded curtly, a gesture that seemed to dismiss the subject for he was suddenly smiling, his expression transformed into one of friendliness. 'I did not expect somebody on board to whom . . .' He hesitated. 'I think perhaps I owe you my life.'

'You don't owe me anything,' I said.

He shook his head, still with that friendly smile. 'If not my life, then my good health. I remember you sat by my bed. You gave me courage to stand the pain and now I must consider how to repay you.' He was frowning again as though faced with a sudden intractable problem, and he turned abruptly, walking quickly out through the office.

I waited till he was gone, then shut the door and faced Hals. 'You know who he is?' I asked.

'Ja. He is the boss. He directs this expedition.'

'But you don't know his background?'

'No. Only that he gives the orders. He has the money and the others do what he tells them.'

'Are they Iranians, too?'

'Ja, I think so.'

'Terrorists?'

'Per'aps.'

'Do you know what his politics are?'

'No. But when you meet him before, you talk with him then. You must know what he is.'

'I'm not sure,' I said. And I told him the circumstances in which we had met. 'All I know is what the Shah's police said, that he was a terrorist. That means he was either a Communist or a supporter of the Ayatollah Khomeini.'

'Don't he tell you which, when you are sitting beside his bed in the sick bay on board your ship?'

'I didn't ask him. The man was in desperate pain. I wasn't even sure he'd live till we reached Kuwait and got him to a doctor. You don't cross-examine a man when he is close to death and slipping in and out of a coma.'

'Okay, so you don't know any more about him than I do.' He gave a shrug, turning towards the door. 'We go and feed now.'

'There's something else,' I said.

'What?'

'This ship. You really mean you don't know its name?'

'Is that important?'

'It's the *Aurora B*,' I said.

CHAPTER THREE

By the time Hals and I entered the officers' mess-
room the big table at the after end had been laid
and there was a steward in attendance dressed in white
trousers and tunic. The chief engineer was back, sitting
beside Rod Selkirk with a beer in front of him, but
not talking now. Sadeq wasn't there, nor was Baldwick. The steward began sounding a gong as the
captain went straight to his place at the head of
the table. The others followed, and when we were
all seated, the steward brought in plates piled with
vegetables in a dark sauce. It was a Pakistani dish,
the vegetables cold, the sauce curry-powder hot. 'Jesus!
We got ter put oop wi' this rubbish!' Fraser's voice
expressed the instinctive disgust of those unaccus-
tomed to Eastern food.

I ate almost automatically, not talking, my mind
still stunned by the knowledge that this was the *Aurora
B*. Saltley wouldn't believe it. Not that I had any means
of contacting him, but if I had, I knew I'd find it

difficult to convince him – not only that the tanker was still afloat, but that within a few days of our meeting I was actually dining on board the *Aurora B*. It didn't seem possible. And opposite me, only one place further down the table, was the little Welshman who had sunk the *Petros Jupiter* and was now being employed . . . I glanced across at him, wondering – employed to do what?

A terrorist in charge of the voyage and an engineer who was an expert in sabotage! And what was I to do about it? Knowing what I did . . . I was still looking at the chief engineer as he turned his head. Our eyes met for an instant and it was as though some spark of telepathy passed between us. But then he had turned away, to the man on his left. It was Lebois and he was speaking to him in French.

He was like a chameleon, French one moment, Welsh the next, and his name was Price. Even Baldwick called him that, though he knew damn well his name had been Choffel for years now. 'Price!' he called as he came in with some letters in his hand. Presumably they had come up with us from Dubai in the dhow. 'A letter for you,' he said and handed it to him.

The curried vegetables were followed by a steak and some ugly-looking potatoes. The steak was deep frozen and tough, and for those who refused to face up to the potatoes there was sliced white bread that was already staling in the heat. The only thing that seemed to have maintained its freshness was the array of bottled sauces in the centre of the table. I hoped the dhow had loaded some provisions in Dubai, something more interesting than those shipped at Ras al Khaimah, otherwise I could see tempers getting very frayed. Varsac pushed his plate away, Lebois too. Clearly the French were not going to take to Pakistani cooking.

Somebody – Hals, I think – wondered jokingly how long scurvy took to develop. We were discussing this, and the length of time hunger-strikers had taken to die of starvation, when I was suddenly conscious of the Welshman staring at me, his steak untouched, the letter open in front of him and a small white square of pasteboard in his hand. It was a photograph. He glanced down at it quickly, then looked across at me again, his eyes wide, the shock of recognition dawning. I knew then that the letter must be from his daughter and the photograph in his hand one of those she had taken in Nantes as I was leaving for the airport. His mouth opened as though to say something, and in that moment he seemed to disintegrate, a nerve twitching at his face, his hand trembling so violently the photograph fell into his plate.

With a visible effort, he pulled himself together, but his face looked very white as he grabbed up the photo, still staring at me with an expression almost of horror, his hands fluttering as he tried to fold the letter and put it in his pocket. Then he got suddenly to his feet, muttering 'Excuse me' as he hurried out of the room.

'*Malade?*' Lebois asked. Varsac muttered something in reply, reaching across and scooping up the meat from the abandoned plate. A hand fell on my shoulder. I looked up to find Baldwick standing over me. 'Come outside a moment.' I followed him to the door. 'What did you say to him?' he demanded, his little eyes popping with anger.

'Nothing. It was the letter.'

'Well, leave him alone. Understand? He's chief engineer and they need him.' He leaned down, his heavy-jowled face close to mine. 'You can't blame him for wot your wife done to herself. That wot you had in mind?' And when I didn't say anything, he went on, speaking slowly as though to a child, 'Well, if it is, cut it out, d'you understand – or you'll get hurt.' And he added, still leaning over me, his face so close I could smell the whisky on his breath, 'This isn't any sort of a kindergarten outfit. You just remember that. Price is nothing to do with you.'

'His name's Choffel,' I said.

'Not on board here it isn't. He's David Price. That's wot you call him. Got it? And another thing—' He straightened up, jabbing his forefinger at my chest. 'Don't go letting on to the others wot he done to the *Petros Jupiter.* They got enough to think about without they start chewing that over in the long night watches.'

'And what's he going to do to this ship?' I asked him.

He tried to turn it into a joke then. 'Think you're going to have to swim for it?' He laughed and patted my shoulder. 'You'll be all right.'

'How do you know? You're going back in the dhow, aren't you?' And I added, 'What happened to the first crew?'

The question took him by surprise. 'The first crew?'

'The *Aurora B* was last heard of in the Arabian Sea, just a few hours after she cleared the Hormuz Straits.'

I thought he was going to hit me then. 'How do you know what ship this is?'

'Sadeq,' I said.

'Yes, he told me you had met before. Asked me why the hell I'd recruited you. But what's that got to do with the *Aurora B*?'

'He was on the *Aurora B*.' And I told him about the crew pictures Perrin had showed me. 'So what happened to the crew?'

'I should've dumped you,' he muttered. 'Soon as I knew you'd been talking to Perrin and Gault, I should have got rid of you.'

'Hals thinks there's probably one dead and two or three injured. What about the others?'

'None of my business,' he growled. 'And none of yours, see. You ask questions like that—' He shrugged his shoulders. 'Go on, get back to your meal and forget about it.' And he pushed me away from him, turning quickly and going through the fire doors into the alleyway beyond. I was alone then, very conscious of the fact that Baldwick himself was beginning to get scared. He didn't want to know about the crew of the *Aurora B*. He didn't dare think about it, because if somebody had been killed, it wasn't just piracy he was mixed up in; it was murder, too.

I went back to my place at the table, but by then

the others had almost finished their meal and I wasn't hungry. The questions they asked me made it clear they were under tension, all except Hals, who seemed relaxed and not in the least concerned about the nature of the voyage or where we were bound. I remember afterwards, when I was sitting with a whisky in my hand and a growing feeling of exhaustion, Rod Selkirk asked him how long the ship had been in the *khawr* and what sort of crew she had, and he said he didn't know, that, like ourselves, this was the first time he had been on board. And he added, glancing quickly at me, 'The crew is mainly Pakistani, but there are others also on board.' And he took the opportunity to warn us not to leave the area of our quarters. 'Which means, of course, we are confined to this deck and the one above – decks B and C. That is, until we sail.' And he added, 'There are guards to see that this order is obeyed, and they are armed. So you stay in your quarters please, all of you.'

They wanted to know the reason, of course, but all he said was, 'I don't know the reason no more than you. I don't know anything about this voyage, except that we are all being well paid for it. I will try and do something about the food, but it is not important. We are signed on for a single voyage, that is all.'

'Weel, here's to the end o' it then.' Fraser raised his glass, then saw mine was empty, sloshed some more whisky into it and went round the others, moving carefully as he topped up their glasses, whistling softly through his teeth. 'If we had a piano noo—' The tune he was whistling was Loch Lomond, and when he'd finished the round, he stood swaying in front of us and began to sing:

> '*Aboot a lassie Ah'll sing a song,*
> *Sing Rickety-tickety-tin;*
> *Aboot a lassie Ah'll sing a song,*
> *Who didna have her family long –*
> *Not only did she du them wrong,*
> *She did every one o' them in – them in,*
> *She did every one o' them in . . .*'

By the time she'd set her sister's hair on fire and danced around the funeral pyre— 'Playing a violin – olin', we were all of us laughing. The Ball of Kirriemuir followed and then he had switched to Eskimo Nell, verse after verse— 'Roond and roond went th' bluidy great wheel, In and oot . . .' The sweat was shining on his face, dark patches under his arms, and when I got up to go to my cabin he was suddenly between me and the door. 'Where yu think yu're goin'? Is it tha' yu don't like ma singin', or is it the song?' He was almost dancing with sudden rage. 'Yu a prude or somethin'?'

'I'm just tired,' I said, pushing past him. I must have done it clumsily for he lost his balance and came bouncing back at me, his arms flailing, mouthing obscenities. Somebody hauled him back, but I barely noticed. I wanted to be on my own and think things out. The fire doors closed behind me, their voices fading as I went along the alleyway to my cabin. Inside it was desperately hot, the air conditioner not working and no fans. I stripped off and had a cold shower.

There was no fresh water, only sea water, which was tepid and left me feeling hotter than ever and sticky with salt. I lay on my bunk, just a towel over my stomach, listening to the sounds of the ship – the deep-buried hum of the generator, the occasional footstep in the alleyway as somebody went to the heads opposite.

It must have been about half an hour later and I was still there on the bed, when there was a knock on the door. 'Mind if I come in?'

I sat up, suddenly very wide awake, for the door was opening and I could see his head in silhouette against the light outside, the stubble growth on his cheek shading the line of the jaw. 'What is it? What do you want?'

'A word with you. That's all.' He stood there, hesitating. 'You've got it all wrong, you see. I have to talk to you.'

I switched on the light and Choffel's face leapt into view. He came in and shut the door. 'I didn't know, you see ... about your wife, I mean.' His face was pale, his hands clasping and unclasping. 'Only just now – my daughter wrote to me ...' He shrugged. 'What can I say? I'm sorry, yes, but it's nothing to do with me. Nothing at all.' He moved closer, coming into the cabin, his voice urgent. 'You must understand that.'

I stared at him, wondering at the nerve of the man. I didn't say anything. What the hell did one say? Here he was, the man who had put the *Petros Jupiter* on the rocks – and by doing so he had been as much the cause of Karen's death as if he'd taken her out there and killed her with a blow torch. But what could I do – leap from my bed and throttle him with my bare hands?

'May I sit down please? It's a long story.' He pulled up a chair and a moment later he was sitting there, leaning forward, his dark eyes fixed on mine, and I thought, My God, this isn't at all how it should be, the little bastard sitting there and me still on my bunk. 'Get out!' I said hoarsely. 'Get out, d'you hear?'

But he shook his head. 'I have to tell you—' He held his hand up as though to restrain me. 'Gwyn has got it into her head you're planning to kill me, you see. She is being over dramatic, of course. But it is what she says in her letter, so I thought it best to have a word with you. If it is true, and you think I had something to do with what happened to the *Petros Jupiter*, then I understand how you must feel.' His hands finally clasped themselves together, locked so tight the knuckles showed white. 'First, I must explain that the *Petros Jupiter* was not at all a good ship. Not my choice, you understand. The skipper was all right, but a man who did everything by the book, no imagination at all. The deck officers were much the same, but I only saw them at meals. It was the chief engineer – he was the real trouble. He was an alcoholic. Whisky mostly, about a bottle and a half a day – never drunk, you understand, but always slightly fuddled, so that nothing ever got done and I was expected to cover for him all the time. I didn't know about that until we were the better part of a week out from Kuwait. He was a Greek and a cousin by marriage of the skipper.

I knew then why I had got the job. Nobody who knew the ship would touch it, and I'd been on the beach, you know, for a long time . . .'

He looked at me as though seeking sympathy, then gave a shrug. 'But even when I knew about him, it never occurred to me there would have been a whole voyage, more than one probably, when the oil filters hadn't been properly cleaned, almost no maintenance at all. You leave the oil filters dirty, you get lack of lubrication, you see – on the gears, both the primary and the secondary. The primary are double helical gears and the debris from them settles to the bottom and finishes up under the secondary reduction gear. In a seaway, rolling like we were that night, broadside-on to the waves, pieces of metal must have got sloshed up into the gears. We were all working flat out, you see, on the evaporator pipes. It had been like that all the voyage, the tubes just about worn out and always having to be patched up, so I didn't think about the gears. I didn't have time, the Chief mostly in his cabin, drinking, you know, and then, when we got steaming again . . .' He gave a shrug. 'I didn't do anything. I didn't put anything in the gears. It was the debris did it, the debris of bad maintenance. You understand? We were only a few miles off Land's End when the noise started. It was the secondary reduction gear, the one that drives the shaft. A hell of a noise. The teeth were being ripped off and they were going through the mesh of the gears. Nothing I could do. Nothing anybody could do. And it wasn't deliberate. Just negligence.'

He had been talking very fast, but he paused there, watching to see how I would react. 'That was how it happened.' He passed his tongue round his lips. 'My only fault was that I didn't check. I should have gone over everything in that engine-room. But I never had time. There was never any time, man – always something more urgent.'

He was lying, of course. It was all part of the game. 'What did they pay you?' I asked him.

'Pay me?' He was frowning, his eyes wide.

'For doing the job, then slipping away like that so that no one else could be blamed, only Speridion.' A professional scuttler, he would only have done it for a straight fee. A big one, too, for there was the skipper of the Breton fishing boat to pay and then the cost of flying out to Bahrain and fixing passage on the *Corsaire*.

He shook his head, his dark eyes staring at me and his hands clasping and unclasping. 'How can I convince you? I know how it must appear, but my only fault was I didn't check. I thought we'd make it. After we got through Biscay I thought that junk yard of machinery would see me through to the end of the voyage.' Again the little helpless shrug. 'I did think of going to the captain and insisting we put in for complete refit, but it was a Greek company, and you know what Greek shipowners are like when you suggest anything that cuts into their profits, and after the Cape . . . Well, there was nowhere after that, so I let it go.' And he added, his hands clasped very tight, 'Only once in my life—' But then he checked himself, shaking his head slowly from side to side, his eyes staring at me as though hypnotized. 'Can't you understand? When you've been without a job for a long time—' He paused, licking his lips again, then went on in a rush of words: 'You'll take anything then, any job that comes along. You don't ask questions. You just take it.'

'Under an assumed name.'

His mouth opened, then closed abruptly, and I could see him trying to think of an answer. 'There were reasons,' he murmured. 'Personal reasons.'

'So you called yourself Speridion. Aristides Speridion.'

'Yes.'

'And you had a passport – Speridion's passport.'

He knew what I was driving at. I could see it in his face. He didn't answer, his mouth tight shut.

'What happened to the real Speridion?'

He half shook his head, sitting there unable to say a word. 'My God!' I said, swinging my legs off the bunk. 'You come here, telling me I don't understand, but it's not only my wife you've killed—'

'No!' He had leapt to his feet. 'I took his papers, yes. But the ship was sinking and he was dead already, floating face down in the oily water that was flooding the engine-room.' And he said again, urgently, 'He was already dead, I tell you. He'd no use for the papers any more.'

'And Choffel?' I asked. 'Henri Choffel, who fell into the harbour at Cayenne just when you needed a job.' I, too, was on my feet then, tucking the towel around my waist. I pushed him back into the chair, standing over him as I said, 'That was 1958, wasn't it? Just after you'd sunk the French ship *Lavandou.*'

He was staring up at me, his mouth fallen open, a stunned look on his face. 'How do you know?' He seemed on the verge of tears, his voice almost pathetic as he said hoarsely, 'I was going to tell you – everything. About the *Lavandou* as well. I was just twenty-two, a very junior engineer and I needed money. My mother . . .' His voice seemed to break at the recollection. 'It all started from that. I said it was a long story, you remember. I didn't think you knew. It was so long ago, and ever since—' He unclasped his hands, reaching out and clutching hold of me. 'You're like all the rest. You're trying to damn me without a hearing. But I will be heard. I must be.' He was tugging at my arm. 'I've done nothing, nothing to be ashamed of – nothing to cause you any hurt. It's all in your imagination.'

Imagination! I was suddenly shaking with anger. How dare the murderous little swine try and pretend he was misunderstood and all he had ever done was the fault of other people. 'Get out of here!' My voice was trembling, anger taking hold, uncontrollable. 'Get out before I kill you.'

I shall always remember the look on his face at that moment. So sad, so pained, and the way he hung his head like a whipped cur as he pushed the chair away, stepping back and moving slowly away from me. And all the time his eyes on mine, a pleading look that seemed desperately trying to bridge the gap between us. As the door closed behind him I had the distinct impression that he was like a drowning man calling for help.

Mad, I thought. A psychiatric case. He must be. How else could he try and plead his innocence when the facts stared him in the face? It was a Jekyll and Hyde situation. Only a schizophrenic, temporarily throwing off the evil side of his nature and assuming the mantle of his innocent self, could so blatantly ignore the truth when confronted by it.

God, what a mess! I lay back on the bunk again, anger draining away, the sweat cold on my body. I switched off the light, feeling exhausted and rubbing myself with the towel. Time stood still, the darkness closed around me. It had the impenetrable blackness of a tomb. Maybe I dozed. I was very tired, a mental numbness. So much had happened. So much to think about, and my nerves taut. I remember a murmur of voices, the sound of drunken laughter outside the door, and Rod Selkirk's voice, a little slurred, singing an old voyageur song I had heard a long time ago when I shared a cabin with an ex-Hudson's Bay apprentice. A door slammed, cutting the sound abruptly off, and after that there was silence again, a stillness that seemed to stretch the nerves, holding sleep at bay.

Thinking about the *Aurora B* and what would happen to us all on board during the next few weeks, I had a dream and woke from it with the impression that Choffel had uttered a fearful muffled scream as he fell to his death down the shaft of an old mine. Had he been pushed – by me? I was drenched in sweat, the stagnant water closing over his head only dimly seen, a fading memory. The time was 01.25 and the faint murmur of the generator had grown to the steady hum of something more powerful – the auxiliary perhaps. I could feel it vibrating under me and some loose change I had put with my wallet on the dressing table was rattling spasmodically. I got up and put my eye to the little pinpoint of clear glass. There were men in the bows, dark shadows in the starlight, and there were others coming up through a hatchway to join them with their hands on top of their heads.

The crew! It was the crew, of course – the crew of the *Aurora B*. That's why nobody had been allowed on the bridge, why there was a guard on the deck. They had been imprisoned in the chain locker, and now they were bringing them up and hustling them across to the starb'd rail at gunpoint. But why? For exercise? For air? They were at the rail now, a dozen or more, still with their hands on their heads, and above them the cliffs towered black against the stars.

I stood back from the peephole, resting my eyes and thinking about that chain locker, what it would be like down there in day time with the sun blazing on the deck above, the stifling heat of it, and nowhere to lie but on the coiled, salt-damp rusty links of the anchor chain. A hell hole, and nothing I could do about it, not for the moment at any rate.

The ship shuddered slightly, the beat of an auxiliary growing, a faint clanking sound. I put my eye to the peephole again. Everything was the same, the prisoners against the rail, their guards, three of them, standing watchful with automatics in their hands, the bows, lit by the flicker of torches, like a stage set with the cliffs a towering backdrop. There were two men by the anchor winch now, bending over it, and another with a hose playing a jet of water on the open vent of the hawse hole. The beat of the auxiliary slowed, it was labouring and I saw the cliffs moving.

And then it happened and the sweat froze on my body as one of the crew turned suddenly, another with him, their hands coming away from their heads, both of them reaching for the rail. Another instant and they would have been over, for the attention of the guards had been momentarily distracted by the winch and its turning and the anchor chain coming in. The first was half over the rail when a guard fired from the hip. The clatter of the automatic came to me faint as a toy, a distant sound like the ripping of calico, and in the same instant the man straddling the rail became an animated doll, his body jerking this way and that until suddenly it toppled over, falling into the widening gap between the ship and the cliff.

A thin cry reached me, like the scream of a far-off seabird, and the other man had gone, too. Out of the corner of my eye I had seen him leap. He must have been a young man, for he had been quicker, just the one hand on the rail and vaulting over, and all three guards rushing to the ship's side, searching and pointing. More firing, and one of them running to the point of the bows, clambering up and standing there, braced against the flag post.

There was silence then, except for the clank of the

anchor chain, the rest of the prisoners standing as though petrified, their hands still on their heads. For a moment nobody moved. Then the man in the bows raised his automatic to his shoulder and began firing single shots. He fired half a dozen, then stopped.

I stood back, resting my eye again. Had the second prisoner got away? I wondered who he was, whether he had found any place to land. When I looked again the bows were well clear of the cliffs and I could see the dark shape of the heights above us climbing in jagged pinnacles towards the Jebel al Harim. I could imagine what it would be like climbing those bare rock hills in the heat of the day, no water and the sun burning the skin off his back, the oven heat of the rocks blistering his feet. I didn't think he had a hope in hell, and the only people he would meet up there would be the Shihuh who were supposed to be distinctly hostile to Christians trespassing in their barren fortress.

The time was now 01.34 and low down by the entrance to the *khawr* the stars were being blotted out one by one. It took them just on twenty minutes to inch the ship away from the cliffs so that she was lying to her anchor bows-on to the entrance. By then the whole sky was clouded over and it was almost impossible for me to see anything except when the figures in the bows were illuminated by the flickering light of hand torches as they secured the anchor chain.

I had another shower, towelled myself down and put on my clothes. By then the ship had fallen silent again, the engine noise reduced once more to the faint murmur of the generator, and no sign of anybody on the deck below. I couldn't see the bows now and no torches flickered there. A wind had got up, a line of white beginning to show where waves were breaking against the base of the cliffs. The *shamal* – that was why they had decided to haul off in the middle of the night. The holding here was probably not all that good. The anchor might well drag if they tried to haul off in the teeth of a gale, and if they had stayed put, they might be held pinned against the cliffs for several days. Now we could leave at first light.

It was past two now. Four hours to go before the first glimpse of dawn. I opened the door of my cabin and peered out into the alleyway. There was nobody there, the lights glimmering dully, the ship very still now and quite silent except for the faint background sound of the generator. I had no idea what I was going to do, I hadn't even thought about it. I just felt I had to do something. I couldn't just lie there, knowing what ship it was and that the crew were held in the chain locker.

My first thought was to contact one of the Pakistani seamen. It was information I needed. How many guards on duty, for instance, where were they posted, above all, how long before we left and what was our destination? I closed the door of my cabin and stood listening for a moment, alert for those tiny sounds that occur on a ship at anchor so that I could identify them and isolate them from any other sounds I might hear as I moved about the ship. Somewhere a slight hissing sound was just audible beneath the low-toned persistent generator hum. It came from the heads where the urinal flush seemed to be constantly running, and now that I was outside Rod Selkirk's cabin, I could hear the sound of his snoring, a regular snort followed by a whistle. Occasionally a pipe hammered softly. An airlock, probably. And sometimes I thought I could hear the soft thud of the waves slapping against the ship's sides.

Those were the only sounds I could identify. A torch; I'd need my torch. The quick flash of it in a man's face could save me if I suddenly ran into one of the guards. I went back into my cabin, and after getting the torch from the locker beside my bunk, I had a last quick look through the peephole. The line of white marking the base of the cliffs was further off now. The wind must be coming straight into the *khawr*, the tanker lying wind-rode, stern-on to the cliffs. The deck below was a long dark blur, only discernible as a blank in the sea of broken water that glimmered white around it. I could see no movement.

Back in the alleyway outside my cabin, I pushed through the fire doors and started down the stairs to A deck. It was a double flight and I paused on the landing. The deck below was lit by the same low wattage emergency lighting as the officers' deck. Nothing stirred. And there were no unusual sounds, the hum of the generator a little louder, that was all. I continued on down, through the sliding fire doors to the alley that ran transversely across the ship. I hesitated then, seeing the closed doors and trying to remember visits I had made in various ports to tankers of a similar size. This would be the boat deck and usually there were offices facing for'ard at this level.

I tried one of the doors. It was locked. They were all locked, except one, which, as soon as I opened it, I knew was occupied. I cupped my hand over my torch, moving softly past a desk littered with papers to an annexe where the body of a man lay huddled in a blanket, breathing softly, a regular sighing sound.

He didn't look like a Pakistani and the papers on the desk, accounts for food mainly, indicated that this was the chief steward's office. As on the upper deck, the lift was switched off. Bolder now, I walked quickly down the port and starb'd alleyways. Most of the doors were shut, but the few that had been left latched open showed them as cabins occupied by sleeping bodies.

I went back to the stairs then, down the final flight to the crew's sleeping quarters. There was a smell about this deck, a mixture of stale food and human bodies overlaid with the pungent scent of spices and the background stink of hot engine oil. It was a strange feeling, wandering those empty alleyways, knowing that all around me men were sleeping. Here and there I could hear the sound of their snores, muted behind closed doors, louder where the doors were open. There was one man with an extraordinary repertoire, the tone of his snores bass on the intake, almost treble when breathing out. I was at the for'ard end of the starb'd alleyway then and I could hear him quite clearly the whole length of the passage. I shone my torch on him, but he didn't stir, and though I was certain he was one of the Pakistani seamen, I didn't wake him. The ship was so quiet, everything so peaceful at this level, that I thought it worth trying to have a look outside the superstructure before taking the irrevocable step of making contact with one of the crew.

There were doors to the deck at each end of the transverse alleyway, but they were locked. I went back up the stairs, moving quickly now. At A deck again I paused. I had already tried the doors leading direct on to the external ladders at the after end of the port and starb'd alleyways, also those by the lift. All had been locked and it was only on the offchance that I tried the starb'd doors leading out on to the boat deck. To my surprise these were not locked. Presumably the cox'n, or whoever had been in charge of the foredeck anchor party, had left them open for the convenience of the crew if the wind increased during the night and there was a sudden emergency. I stepped out into the night, the air suddenly fresh and smelling of salt. Straight in front of me was the starb'd lifeboat, the wind thrumming at its canvas covers.

After the sleeping stillness of the crew's quarters the noise on the boat deck seemed shattering, the night full of the sound of breaking waves, the scream of the wind in the superstructure, and astern the continual uproar of seas foaming against the base of the cliff. It was very dark and not a light anywhere. I felt my way to the rail, standing there between the after davit and a life raft in the full force of the wind, waiting for my eyes to adjust themselves. The time was 02.19.

Gradually the vague outline of the ship emerged. With my head thrown back I could just make out the dark, shadowy shape of the funnel, and a little for'ard of it the mast poking its top above the side of the bridge housing. Looking aft everything was black, the cliffs and the mountains above blotting out any vestige of light filtering through the cloud. For'ard I could just see the gangway hoist and beyond it the shadowy outline of the hull stretched dark against the broken white of water far below. I thought for a moment I could see the outline of one of the jib crane masts and the manifold, but beyond that the ship disappeared into a void of darkness.

I waited there for a good five minutes, but I could see no movement. Finally, I faced into the wind, feeling my way along the side of the lifeboat to the rail at the for'ard end of the boat deck, following it as it turned across the ship until I found the gap where the midships ladder led down to the central catwalk. I went down it, and down another, shorter ladder to the vast open stretch of the upper deck, not daring to expose myself on the catwalk.

I had never been alone on the deck of a tanker before, always in company, and always either in daylight or in the blaze of the ship's deck lights. Now, in the wind and in complete darkness, with the sound of broken water all round me, it was like advancing into a primeval void, and even though the tanker was quite a modest one by modern standards, the night made it seem huge.

I was pulled up almost immediately by the sudden

emergence of a crouched shape. It turned out to be one of the mooring winches and the figure beyond it one of the 'dead men', its head the wheel that guided the hawser from fairlead to winch.

I stood for a moment looking about me, checking for some movement, but it was darker now and I couldn't see a thing. Already the dim shadow of the superstructure had disappeared, nothing visible anywhere except the nebulous outline of pipes running ahead of me and disappearing into the blackness. I felt very alone then, very naked and unarmed, the steel deck under my feet, the bulk of the winch and those pipes, nothing else visible and the knowledge that the deck went on and on until it reached the raised fo'c'sle where the captive crew had been brought up out of the chain locker and those two poor devils had gone over the side.

I moved on, walking slowly, feeling my way with each step. Even so, I found myself tripping over the small tank washing pipes called lavomatics that were stretched across the deck at regular intervals. There were inspection hatches for each tank and purge pipes to clear the gases, and at one point I barged into a slender, screw-capped sounding pipe that was about knee-high. The deck, in fact, was littered with obstacles for a man moving warily in complete darkness, and now there was a new sound. I thought for a moment it was somebody whistling and stopped abruptly, my heart in my mouth, but it was only the wind. A little further on the sound of it changed. It was like somebody moaning. All about me the wind sighed and moaned and the sea made rushing, slapping noises, and at each new sound I paused until I had identified it, convinced that somewhere along this endless dark expanse of steel plating an armed guard lurked, my eyes searching ahead along the line of the raised catwalk for the tell-tale glow of a cigarette.

A shape emerged, grew suddenly tall and I stopped again. I was in the centre of the ship, following the line of the pipes. The shape was away to the right, very straight and tall, motionless by the starb'd rail. I crouched down, moving slowly forward in the shadow of the pipes. There was another shape to my left now. I hesitated, my heart pounding, feeling suddenly boxed in.

I stayed like that for maybe a minute, the figures on either side of me frozen motionless like myself. Gradually it dawned on me that they were further away than I had imagined and much taller than any man could possibly be. The derricks – the jib cranes for handling pipe! I got slowly to my feet, trembling slightly and feeling a fool as I ducked under the manifold with its mass of pipes running transversely across the ship, big valves showing like crouched figures in the gloom as I negotiated the breaker that stops waves running the length of the deck. After that there were no more pipes, only the catwalk running fore and aft.

I must have veered left for I was suddenly confronted with a new sound, an intermittent thumping noise, as though somebody were regularly striking at the steel hull with a heavy wooden maul. The noise of the sea was louder here. I was almost at the port rail and my eyes, following the line of it aft, fastened on the dark outline of a thin shaft standing straight up like a spear against the pale blur of waves breaking in the *khawr* beyond. For a moment I stood there, not moving and wondering what it was. Then I remembered the dhow moored amidships with its two masts just showing above deck level. I went to the rail then and looked down, the dark shape of the Arab vessel just visible as it rose and fell, its wooden hull banging regularly at the ship's side.

A man coughed and I spun round. Nothing there, but then the cough was repeated, strident now and more like a squawk. A sudden flurry and I ducked as a vague shape took wing and disappeared into the night. I went on then, moving quickly, my hand on the rail, determined not to be scared of any more shadows. More roosting seabirds rose into the air and I jabbed my toe against a set of fairleads. There were inspection hatches at intervals, each hatch, and particularly the vents, appearing first as some lurking watcher. Then at last I was at the rise of the fo'c'sle deck with the foremast a slender shaft spearing the darkness above me.

A faint glimmer of light filtered through the cloud layer. I found the ladder to the fo'c'sle deck and felt my way through the litter of anchor and mooring machinery to the bows. Here for the first time I felt safe. I had traversed the whole length of the tanker from the bridge housing to the fo'c'sle unchallenged, and now, standing with my back to the bows, all the details of the ship stretching aft to the superstructure invisible in the darkness, I felt relaxed and secure.

This was nearly my undoing, for I started back along the catwalk. There were shelters at regular intervals, two between the fo'c'sle and the manifold, and four foam monitor platforms like gunhousings with ladders down to the deck. I was using my torch to peer inside the second of these firefighting platforms when a figure emerged coming towards me along the catwalk. I just had time to reach the deck and was crouched under the platform when he passed, hurrying to the fo'c'sle with something that looked like a toolbox in his hand.

He didn't re-emerge, though I stayed there several minutes watching the point where his figure had disappeared. Cautiously I moved to the ship's rail, not daring to go back on to the catwalk. I could see the derrick now and by keeping close to the rail I was able to bypass both the breaker and the manifold. I was moving quite quickly, all the sounds of the ship, even the quite different sounds of the dhow scraping against its side, identified and familiar. A seabird squawked and flapped past me like an owl. I could see the dhow's mainmast, and had just passed the portside derrick winch, when I heard the clink of metal against metal. It came from further aft, somewhere near the deeper darkness that must be the superstructure emerging out of the gloom.

I hesitated, but the sound was not repeated.

I moved away from the rail then, making diagonally across the deck towards the line of pipes running fore and aft down the centre of the ship. Moving carefully, my eyes searching ahead in the darkness, I stubbed my toe against what seemed to be some sort of a gauge. There was a sounding pipe near it and another of those access hatches to the tanks below. I could see the pipes now, and at that moment a figure seemed to rise up, a looming shadow barring my way. I dropped instantly to the deck, lying sprawled against the steel edge of the access hatch, my eyes wide, probing the darkness.

There was something there. The shape of one of the foam monitor platforms perhaps, or was it a small derrick? Something vertical. But nothing moved, no sound I didn't know. I rose slowly to my feet, and at that same moment the shape moved, growing larger.

No good dropping to the deck again. He must have seen me. I backed away, moving carefully, step by step, hoping to God I wouldn't stumble over another hatch. If I could back away far enough to merge into the darkness behind me ... The clink of metal on metal again, very close now, very clear, and the figure still seeming to move towards me.

I felt the sweat breaking out on my body, the wind cooling it instantly so that I was suddenly shivering with cold. That metallic sound – it could only be some weapon, a machine pistol like the guard in the wheelhouse had jabbed in my stomach. I wanted to run then, take the chance of bullets spraying in the hope of escaping into the darkness. But if I did that I'd be cornered, pinned up for'ard with no hope of making it back to my cabin.

My heel touched an obstruction. I felt behind me with my hand, not turning my head for fear of losing sight of the shape edging towards me. The winch – I was back at the derrick. I dropped slowly to the deck, crawling behind one of the winch drums and holding my breath.

Nothing moved, the figure motionless now, merging into the darkness. Had I been mistaken? Crouched there, I felt completely trapped. He had only to shine his torch . . .

'Who's there?'

The voice was barely audible, lost in the wind. The dhow thumped the side of the ship. A seabird flew screaming across the deck. Silence now, only the noise of the wind howling through pipes and derricks, making weird groans and whines against the background rushing of waves in the *khawr*, and the dhow going thump – thump.

Surely I must have imagined it?

I lifted my head above the big steel drum, staring towards the central line of pipes, seeing nothing but the vague shadow of the bridge-like outline of the firefighting platform, the foam gun like a giant's pistol. Above my head the derrick pointed a long thick finger at the clouds.

'Is there anybody there now?'

That voice again, in a lull and much clearer this time. So clear I thought I recognized it. But why would he be out here on the deck? And if it were Choffel, then he'd have a torch with him. He wouldn't go standing stock still on the deck asking plaintively if anyone was there.

I thought I saw him, not coming towards me, but moving away to the right, towards the rail. He must have been standing exactly between me and the fire monitor platform, otherwise I must have seen him for he wasn't more than ten paces away.

Then why hadn't he shone a torch? If he were armed . . . But perhaps I'd been mistaken. Perhaps he wasn't armed. Perhaps he thought I was one of the guards and then, when he'd got no reply and had seen no further sign of movement, he'd put it down to his own imagination. And the fact that he hadn't used his torch, that could be explained by a standing order not to show a light at night except in extreme emergency.

What was he doing here anyway?

Without thinking I moved forward, certain now that it must be Choffel. Curiosity, hate, determination to see what he was up to – God knows what it was that drew me after him, but I moved as though drawn by a magnet. The outline of the rail showed clear, and suddenly beyond it the dhow's mast. The figure had drifted away, lost from sight. I blinked my eyes, quickening my step, half cursed as my foot caught against another of the tank inspection hatches. A gap in the rail, and a few yards further aft the outline of a davit. I had reached the head of the gangway.

No sign of Choffel. I stepped on to the grating at the top. I couldn't see him, but I could feel the movement of somebody descending. The dark shape of the dhow was for'ard of the gangway so that it was obvious there must be a boat for communication between dhow and tanker.

What a moment to take him! A push, a quick push – nothing else. I could dimly see the water rushing past, small whitecaps hissing and breaking as the wind hit the sheer side of the tanker, flurries gusting down into the sea. Quickly, my hand on the rail, I began to descend. The gangway swayed, clinking against the side. I heard his voice hailing the dhow. An Arab answered and a figure appeared on the dhow's high poop, a hurricane lamp lighting his face as he held it high, and below, in the water, I saw a small wooden boat bobbing on a rope at the dhow's stern. 'O-ai, O-ai!' The sound of a human voice hurled on the wind, the words unidentifiable. More voices, the cries louder, then the light of another lamp swaying up from below.

I squatted down, sure he must see me now, crouching low and pressing my body against one of the gangway stanchions, desperately willing myself to be unseen, my guts involuntarily contracting. When he had shone that torch, screening it beneath his jacket, I had seen the thin jutting pencil line of what I was certain had been the barrel of a gun.

There was a lot of activity on the dhow now, men gathered in the waist and the boat being slowly hauled along the ship's side in the teeth of the wind and the breaking waves. Crouched there I had a crane's-eye view as one of the Arabs tucked his robes up round his waist and jumped into the boat. Then they floated it down, paying out rope steadily, till it reached the staging where Choffel stood at the bottom of the gangway.

Spray flew over him as he reached down to steady the boat. Now! Now, I thought, while his mind was on the boat, and I rose to my feet, and in that instant a beam stabbed the darkness from above, groping along the side of the ship till its light fell on the boat with the Arab kneeling in it, gripping tight to the last stanchion, and Choffel just about to step into it. They remained like that for an instant, frozen into immobility, as though caught by the flash of a camera, while from aft, from the wing of the bridge came a distant cry lost in the wind.

The men on the dhow began shouting – something, I don't know what. It was unintelligible. But they were beckoning and heaving on the rope. The man in the boat let go of the stanchion. Suddenly there was a gap opening up between the boat and the gangway and I saw Choffel's face in the light of the torch, very pale and twisted in the expression of some strong emotion, his mouth open.

Then he had turned and was pounding up the gangway towards me.

I had no time to get out of his way. He came straight at me, and when he saw me he didn't stop, merely flashed his torch on my face. 'You!' He clawed past me, and a moment later I saw him standing precariously balanced on the rail capping, watching for the sway of the dhow as it thumped the side. And then he jumped, a shadowy outline flying in the darkness, to finish up clasping his arms round the swaying mast and sliding down into the folds of the great furled sail.

No shouts from the bridge now, and everything dark again, the only light a hurricane lamp in the waist of the dhow. I felt rooted to the spot, standing there on the gangway peering down at the figures gathered on the dhow's deck, their big-nosed, Semitic faces staring upwards. Then suddenly he was among them, standing with his gun in his hand, his cap cocked rakishly on the side of his head – I remember that distinctly, the fact that he was wearing a cap, and at an angle – and his torch stabbing here and there as he issued orders to the dim-seen, long-robed figures gathered around him.

One of them disappeared below. The engineer, I guessed, and Choffel followed him. I started down the gangway, my mind in a whirl, descending it quickly, wondering whether he would make it out to sea, what he would do with the crew, where he would head for.

I was halfway down when the dhow's engine coughed behind me, then spluttered into life. And at that instant a torch flashed out from the deck above. Somebody shouted. I waved acknowledgment, pretending I understood and was trying to prevent the dhow's escape. I was at the bottom of the gangway now, standing helpless, wondering whether I could swim for it, knowing I'd be swept away, and remembering the look of panic on the man's face, the way his mouth had opened – 'You!' he had exclaimed, hurling himself past me. Only a man driven by fear and desperation would have made that incredible jump for the mast.

And now – now there was no way I could stop him. I should have reacted quicker. I should have taken him on the gangway, the moment he recognized me, when he was off-balance, held there for a second by the shock of seeing me.

A shot sounded, but not from above. It came from the dhow, the stern of it growing bigger. I couldn't believe my eyes. Instead of swinging out from the side of the tanker, it was falling back towards me. It cleared the gangway by inches, then the big hull closed in, grinding along the grating, slowly crushing it. Arab faces, pallid and jabbering with anger, peered down at me. Somewhere for'ard along the dhow's deck a voice screamed – 'Go! Go now!' There was the sound of a shot, very loud, the crack of a bullet and the beam of a torch stabbing the gloom.

The waist was abreast of me, and without thinking I seized hold of a rope, pulled myself up and over the bulwarks, and as I dropped to the deck, the Arab crew were clawing their way over the side, tumbling down on to the gangway grating to lie there in a heap, bin Suleiman among them, his eyes rolling in the light of a powerful spotlight directed from high up on the bridge wing as bullets sang through the rigging, ploughing into the woodwork, sending splinters flying.

'*Insh'Allah!*' I think it was the *naukhada*'s voice, but whether it was his ship or his own life he was committing into the hands of God I don't know, for Choffel was coming aft, running through the spatter of bullets. He had let go the for'ard mooring line and the dhow was sliding back, its hull grating against the gangway and along the ship's side. Then it was brought up short, still held on the stern mooring line so that it hung there for a moment, illumined by the spotlight, while the Arabs went scrambling up the gangway on to the tanker's deck. There was no sign of Choffel. Crouched there by the bulwarks, I had a vague impression of his having leapt for the steps leading up to the poop.

Slowly we began to swing away from the ship's side. The dhow was turning in the wind, swinging on the stern warp, and then in a rush we closed the tanker again, the wooden timbers on the far side crashing against the steel plates with a jar that went right through me. The deck lights were switched on, everything suddenly sharp-etched, the shattered remains of the dhow's boat drifting past and faces peering down from the rail high above. Sadeq was there. He had brushed the Arabs aside and was standing at the head of the gangway, his bearded face clear in the lights as he seized hold of a guard's machine pistol, rammed in another clip, and then, holding the gun close at his waist, swung it towards me, his movements deliberate, his expression coldly professional. There was nothing I could do, nowhere I could go, the muzzle pointing straight down at me, his hand on the trigger. Then he seemed to freeze into immobility, his eyes narrowing as he saw who it was he was about to kill. It must have been that, for after a moment's hesitation, he lifted the barrel of the gun, lifted it deliberately away

from me, aiming at the dhow's poop, his finger contracting, the muzzle jerking to the spit of bullets, and
the staccato chatter of it echoed by the sound of them
slamming into wood, splinters flying and a man
screaming.

I thought Choffel fired back, but it was just a single
shot followed by a sharp twanging sound as the stern
line parted. Then we were bumping along the tanker's
side, the hull moving past us faster and faster, and the
high wooden bulk of the poop between me and
the shots being fired. I heard the engine note change,
suddenly deepening, felt the throb of the screw as it
gripped the water and I got to my feet.

We were clear of the tanker's stern now and turning
into the wind, no longer falling back towards the cliffs,
but slowly turning into the seas, and the whole vast
bulk of the brightly lit tanker stretched out high above
us on the starb'd quarter. We turned till the superstructure was astern of us, and it was only then that I heard
a voice calling my name. It came like a gull crying in
the night, a voice of pain and fear and exasperation –
'Ro-o-d-in! Ro-o-d-in!' Then – 'Quick – hu-rry!'

I felt my way in the blackness over piles of rope to
the outline of the high poop deck, found the wooden
steps leading up to it and came out on to the top of
the dhow's great after castle to see the dim outline of a
figure sprawled across the helm. 'Take her, man! The
entrance. There's a launch, you see – inflatable – take
time to launch it though.' His voice came slowly, full
of coughs and gurgles, so that I knew there was blood
in his throat.

'You're hit,' I said. It was a bloody stupid remark.

'Take the helm,' he gurgled, slipping away from me in the dark and sliding to the deck.

The dhow yawed, the swept-up curve of the bow swinging away to port, the wind lifting the furled sail so that it flapped with a loud cracking noise. I looked up from the dark shape sprawled at my feet to see the lit tanker with the frowning cliffs behind it swinging across our stern. The movement quickened, the wind catching the bows, and I dived for the helm, throwing my weight against the long timber arm of it, forcing it over to port. I felt the pressure of the water on the rudder and slowly the bows steadied and began to swing back into the wind.

I waited until the tanker was directly astern of us, then I centred the helm, holding the dhow into the wind, hoping I was steering for the entrance. There was no chance of doing anything for Choffel or even finding out how badly he was injured. The dhow wasn't easy to steer. Like most straight-keeled vessels I had to anticipate her movements, countering each attempt of the head to pay off with a slight correction to the helm. She waddled and yawed like an old woman and once the wind got hold of her she was hard to control, very slow to respond and the engine labouring.

Ahead, I couldn't seem to see anything beyond the ship's stem, the lights of the tanker producing just enough of a glow to illuminate the waist with its muddle of ropes, pulleys, sleeping mats and cooking gear and the mast with the great roll of sail strapped to the curved wing of the spar. These were all very clearly picked out, the upswing of the prow, too. But beyond that there was nothing, just a stygian blackness.

I could hear Choffel groaning. Once I thought he cried out. But the dhow required all my concentration and when I did glance down I couldn't see him. That was when I remembered he was armed, but the dhow was paying off, the wind catching hold of the rolled-up sail and the bows falling off. Part of the sail had come loose, a fold of it billowing out in a dark bubble of canvas so that I thought I'd never get the bows back into the wind.

Away to port I could hear the sound of breaking waves, could just make out a line of white. Dark cliffs loomed, the line of white nearer, the sound of the waves louder. We were being set down on to the south shore of the *khawr* – or was it the land closing in as we neared the entrance? With the helm hard over, the bows slowly swung through the wind. I could feel it on my left side now, my eyes searching the darkness to starb'd, ears strained for the sound of breakers. I should have looked at that chart more closely, up there on the tanker's bridge when I had the chance. There was a box fixed to the poop deck just for'ard of the helm, a big wooden box with an old-fashioned brass-knobbed binnacle in it. But I didn't want to use my torch, and anyway I'd no idea where exactly the tanker had been moored in relation to the entrance, what the bearing would be. All I could remember was that the entrance was narrow and dog-legged, the bend being leftward going out.

The line of white was very close now, the cliffs visible as a darker darkness in the night. I put the helm over and the bows swung easily to starb'd. I glanced astern at the lights of the tanker. They were swinging across our starb'd quarter and already she looked quite small, the reddish glow of the cliffs behind her fading. I was being forced off course, but the line of broken water to port was still closing in and nothing visible to starb'd. I heard a cry and saw a figure standing clutching at the ornamental rail near the thunderbox on the port side, his arm pointing for'ard. I checked the helm, peering beyond the vague flapping bundle of the sail. A dark line showed high above the bows, the shape of low hills, and in that instant I heard waves breaking and dragged the helm across to starb'd.

There was no response.

The wind had strengthened. It was blowing half a gale and I knew we were nearing the entrance. But there was nothing I could do, the long arm of the helm right over and the dhow not responding, her head held in the grip of the wind and the engine labouring. I watched appalled as the looming outline of the land ahead grew darker and higher, the sound of the surf louder.

And then the engine note changed, a sudden surge of power and the bows were coming round. I caught a glimpse of a figure crouched, or more likely collapsed, over some sort of a control rod set into the deck. But it was only a glimpse, for we were turning to port and in the entrance now, the blackness of land on either side, the wind howling and waves breaking all round us.

It was like that for five, perhaps ten minutes. It seemed an age. Then suddenly the wind died away, the sea took on a regular pattern with only the occasional break of a wave. We were out of the *khawr*. We were out into the Persian Gulf and the dhow was bashing her way through the waves, rolling wildly, the engine racing and everything rattling and shaking as we steamed into the night with no land visible any more, just an empty void of darkness all around us.

PART FIVE

VIRGINS UNLIMITED

CHAPTER ONE

Dawn broke with ragged clouds streaming low overhead and a lumpy sea. It was a grey world, visibility growing reluctantly but, as the light increased, gaps appeared in the overcast, glimpses of clear sky showing a greenish tinge. The dhow wallowed sedately, rolling as her bows ploughed into the waves, and the beat of the engine was unhurried and regular. We were at least ten miles from the shore. I could see it on the starb'd quarter, low down to the south and west of the familiar Group Flash Two of the Didamar light, the dark line of it turning an arid brown as the sun rose.

We were out into the Hormuz Straits, into the main shipping lanes. There was a tanker quite close with its steaming lights still showing white, another hull-down, and a third coming up astern. I had the binnacle box open and was steering a full point east of north. Choffel, when I had hauled him off the engine speed control linkage, had muttered about the tanker's

launch being very fast, powered by a single big outboard. But I thought it more likely they would be
searching the inshore traffic zone, between the
Didamar and Tawakkul lights, not right out here
between the west and eastbound tanker lanes.

There was blood on the deck where Choffel had
lain after collapsing at the helm, blood on the carved
end of the helm itself. But he hadn't bled where he
had lain clutching the speed control lever, or in the
vicinity of the thunderbox where he had hauled himself
up by the rail to warn me we were driving on to the
north side of the entrance. And when I had got him
down to bin Suleiman's hovel of a cabin and laid
him out on a sleeping mat with a stinking salt-stiffened
blanket to cover him, I didn't think he had been
bleeding then.

A pity Sadeq hadn't killed him. Now it was up to
me. I yawned, my eyes heavy-lidded, my body sagging
with tiredness. I had had no sleep and I always found
the first twenty-four hours at sea a little trying.

I couldn't just pitch the man over the side. Or
could I? Fate had delivered him into my hands as
though of intent, so why didn't I do it – now, while I
was too tired to care whether he was a corpse or not?
If I didn't do it now, if I let him stay there, then I'd be
responsible for him. I'd have to feed him. I'd have to
do something about his wound. It was in his stomach,
he'd said. And I'd have to clean him up. My God!
acting as nurse and sick-bay attendant to the man who
had sent Karen to her death! If that was what I'd have
to do, then fate had played a dirty trick.

In the east the clouds were turning a flaming red, the sea catching fire as it had done that evening at Ras al Khaimah. It seemed a long time ago. A gap in the clouds took on the appearance of an open furnace, the ragged edges gleaming like red-hot clinkers. I saw a heraldic lion crouched in the cloud-gap. I blinked my eyes and it was a dragon breathing fire, its scales all crimson, and then the sun appeared, a bright red orb that slowly turned through vermilion and orange-yellow to a searing glare that changed the sea to a brilliant purple and the waves to glittering gold. Suddenly it was hot, the sun burning up the clouds, the fire-brown streak of the Musandam Peninsula lost in haze.

How far to Qisham, the big island on the north side of the Straits? I couldn't remember. And there was Larak, and inside of that Hormuz itself, both of them much smaller islands. I stood leaning on the helm, swaying with it as I tried to remember the chart, my eyes drooping, half-closed against the glare. Surely I was far enough out? Why not turn now, head eastwards into the sun? The Straits were like a horseshoe facing north. As long as I kept to the middle, steering clear of all the ships, and of the islands and reefs of Ras Musandam, following the curve of the Iranian coast, there was no reason why the dhow should attract the attention of sea or air patrols from either side, and at an estimated six to eight knots we should reach the border between Iran and Pakistan some time tomorrow night. Gwadar. If I could anchor off Gwadar. Must check the fuel. I didn't know whether we had enough to reach Gwadar. But that was the nearest place that had an air service to Karachi. Two days to Gwadar. And if we were short of fuel, then I'd have to sail the brute. Through slitted eyes I stared up at the great curved spar with the sun-bleached, heavily-patched sail bagged up round it. My head nodded and I caught myself, wondering whether one man could possibly set it alone. But my mind drifted away, abandoning any thought of how it could be done, unable to concentrate. I was thinking of Hals, and Sadeq – Baldwick, too. A kaleidoscope of faces and that little ginger-haired Glaswegian. Sadeq spraying bullets. Standing at the head of the gangway, very much the professional, a killer. I couldn't recall the expression on his face, only the fact that he was about to cut me down and didn't. I owe you my life, he had said, and now I couldn't recall his expression. Not even when he'd lifted the barrel and fired at Choffel. Hate, pleasure, anger – what the hell had he felt as the bullets slammed into the poop?

There comes a moment when tiredness so takes hold of the body that the only alternative to sleep is some form of physical activity. When I opened my eyes and found the sun's glare behind me and the dhow rolling along almost broadside to the waves, I knew that point had arrived. The sun was higher now, the time 08.23, and a big fully-loaded tanker was pushing a huge bow wave barely a mile away. I wondered how long I had been dreaming at the helm with the dhow headed west into the Persian Gulf. Not that it made much difference, with no chart and only the vaguest idea where we were. I hauled the tiller over, bringing the bows corkscrewing through the waves until the compass showed us headed east of north. There was a rusty iron gear lever set in the deck close by the engine control arm and after throttling right down, I put the lever into neutral. Lengths of frayed rope, looped through holes cut in the bulwarks either side of the tiller arm, enabled me to make the helm fast so that we were lying wind-rode with our bows headed east into the Hormuz Straits.

I went for'ard then, into the waist of the vessel, running my eye over the bundled sail as I relieved myself to leeward. Then I went round the ship, checking the gear. It was something I would have had to do sooner or later, but doing it then I knew it was a displacement activity, putting off the moment when I would have to go into the dark hole of the shelter under the poop and deal with Choffel.

The dhow was rolling heavily. With no cargo to steady her, she was riding high out of the water, heeled slightly to starb'd by the wind and wallowing with an unpredictable motion, so that I had to hold on all the time or be thrown across the deck. I was feeling slightly nauseous, dreading the thought of that dark hole as I made my way aft. The entrance to it was right by the steps leading to the poop, the door closed with a large wooden latch. I couldn't remember closing it, but perhaps it had banged to on a roll. I pulled it open and went in.

It was the smell that hit me. Predominantly it was the hot stink of diesel oil, but behind that was the smell of stale sweat, vomit and excrement. At the stern of the cabin two shuttered windows either side of the rudder post showed chinks of light. I had settled Choffel on a mat on the starb'd side. We had been heeled to starb'd then, as we were now, but sometime during the night, or perhaps in the dawn when I was off-course, he must have been rolled right across the ship, for I found his body precariously huddled on the port side. I could only just see it in the dim light from the doorway, the blanket I had wrapped him in flung into a heap at his feet and his hands pressed against the timbers of the deck in an effort to hold himself steady.

He looked so lifeless I thought for a moment he was dead. I was not so much glad as relieved, his stubble-dark features white against the bare boards, his eyes wide and staring and his body moving helplessly to the sudden shifts of the ship wallowing in the seaway. I started to back away, the smell and the diesel fumes too much for me. The engine noise was much louder here, and though it was only idling, the sound of it almost drowned the groans of the ship's timbers. They were very human groans, and seeing the man's head roll as the deck lifted to a wave, I had a sense of horror, as though this were a ghost come to haunt me.

Suddenly I felt very sick.

I turned, ducking my head for the doorway and some fresh air, and at that moment a voice behind me murmured, 'Is that you, Gwyn?' I hesitated, looking back. The dhow lifted to the surge of a wave, rolled to starb'd and, as it rolled, his body rolled with it, his groan echoing the groan of the timbers. 'Water!' He suddenly sat up with a shrill gasp that was like a scream suppressed. One hand was pressed against the boards to support him, the other clutched at his stomach. He was groaning as he called for water again. 'Where are you now? I can't see you.' His voice was a clotted whisper, his eyes staring. 'Water please.'

'I'll get you some.' It was the salt in the air. I was thirsty myself. The salt and the stench, and the movement of the boat.

There was a door I hadn't noticed before on the port side. It opened on to a store cupboard, oil cans and paint side by side with sacks of millet, some dried meat that was probably goat, dates and dried banana in plastic bags, a swab and buckets, bags of charcoal and several large plastic containers. These last were the dhow's water supply, but before I could do anything about it, my body broke out into a cold sweat and I had to make a dash for the starb'd bulwarks.

It was very seldom I was sick at sea. The wind carried the sickly smell of the injured man to my nostrils as I leaned out over the side retching dryly. It would have been better if I had had more to bring up. I dredged up some seawater in one of the buckets. We were on the edge of a slick and it smelt of oil, but I washed my face in it, then went back to that messy cubby-hole of a store. There were tin mugs, plates and big earthenware cooking pots on a shelf that sagged where the supports had come away from the ship's side. I had a drink myself, then refilled the mug and took it in to Choffel.

He drank eagerly, water running down his dark-stubbled chin, his eyes staring at me with a vacant look. It was only when he had drunk nearly the whole of a mugful that it occurred to me the water was probably contaminated and should have been boiled. In Karachi everybody boiled their water and I wondered where the containers had last been filled. 'Where am I? What's happened?' He was suddenly conscious, his eyes searching my face. His voice was stronger, too. 'It's dark in here. Would you pull the curtains please.'

'You're on a dhow,' I said.

The ship lurched and he nodded. 'The shots – Sadeq.' He nodded, again feeling at his stomach. 'I remember now.' He was quite lucid in this moment, his eyes, wide in the gloom, looking me straight in the face. 'You were going to kill me, is that right?'

'Do you want some more water?' I asked him, taking the empty mug.

He shook his head. 'You think Sadeq saved you the trouble.' He smiled, but it was more a grimace. 'I've shat my pants, haven't I? Fouled myself up.' And he added, 'This place stinks. If I had something to eat now . . .' The ship rolled and I had to steady him. 'I'm hungry, but I can't contain myself.' He gripped hold of my arm. 'It's my guts, is it?'

My fingers where I had held him were a sticky mess. I reached for the blanket, wiping my hand on the coarse cloth. I could clean him up, but if I got water anywhere near the wound it would probably bleed again. I started to get to my feet, but the clutch of his hand on my arm tightened convulsively. 'Don't go. I want to talk to you. There are things . . . Now, while I have the strength . . . I was going to escape, you see. I was going to Iran, then maybe cross the Afghan frontier and get myself to Russia. But you can't escape, can you – not from yourself, not from the past.'

His voice was low, the tone urgent. 'No,' he said, clutching hold of me tighter still as I made to rise. 'The *Lavandou*. You mentioned the *Lavandou*. My third ship. A boy. I was just a boy and my mother dying, you see. Cancer and overwork and too much worry. She'd had a hard life and there was no money. My father had just died, you know. His lungs. Working in the mines he was when just a boy. The anthracite mines down in the Valleys. He was underground. Years underground. A great chest he had, and muscles, huge muscles. But when we laid him to rest he was quite a puny little chap – not more than six or seven stone.' His voice had thickened and he spat into the mug, dark gobs of blood.

'Better not talk,' I said.

He shook his head urgently, still clutching me. 'I was saying – about the *Lavandou*. I was twenty-two years old . . . and desperate.' His fingers tightened. 'D'you know what it is to be desperate? I was an only child. And we'd no relatives, you see. We were alone in the world, nobody to care a bugger what happened to her. Just me. God! I can still see her lying there, the whiteness of her face, the thinness of it, and all drawn with pain.' His voice faltered as though overcome.

'They knew, of course. They knew all about how desperate I was. She needs to go into a clinic. Private, you see – not waiting for the National Health. And me at sea, unable to make sure she got proper attention. It's your duty, they said. And it was, too – my duty. Also, I loved her. So I agreed.'

He stared up at me, his eyes wide, his fingers digging into my arm. 'What would you have done?' His breath was coming in quick gasps. 'Tell me – just tell me. What would you have done, man?'

I shook my head, not wanting to listen, thinking of Karen as he said, 'The ship was insured, wasn't she? And nobody got hurt, did they?' His eyes had dimmed, his strength fading. I loosened his fingers and they gripped my hand, the cold feel of them communicating some deep Celtic emotion. 'Just that once, and it went wrong, didn't it – the Lloyd's people twigged what I'd done, and myself on the run, taking another man's name. God knows, I've paid. I've paid and paid. And Mother . . . I never saw her again. Not after that. She died and I never heard, not for a year. Not for over a year.' He spat blood again and I could see his eyes looking at me, seeking sympathy.

What do you do – what the hell do you do when a creature like that is dying and seeking sympathy? At any moment he'd start talking about the *Petros Jupiter*, making excuses, asking my forgiveness, and I didn't know what I could say to him. I thought he was dying, you see – his eyes grown dim and his voice very faint.

'We're wasting fuel,' I said, unhooking his fingers from my hand. I think he understood that for he didn't try and stop me, but as I got to my feet he said something – something about oil. I didn't get what it was, his voice faint and myself anxious to get out into the open again, relieved at no longer being held by the clutch of his hand.

Clouds had come up and the wind had freshened. Back on the poop I put the engine in gear and headed east into the Straits. We were broadside to the waves, the dhow rolling and corkscrewing, spray wetting the parched timbers of her waist as the breaking seas thumped her high wooden side. I was hungry now, wondering how long the *shamal* would blow. No chance of a hot meal until I could get the dhow to steer herself and for that I'd need almost a flat calm. But at least there were dates in the store.

I secured the helm with the tiller ropes and made a dash for it, coming up with a handful just as the bows swung with a jarring explosion of spray into the breaking top of a wave. I got her back on course, chewing at a date. It was dry and fibrous, without much sweetness, and so impregnated with fine sand that it gritted my teeth. They were about the worst dates I had ever eaten, but being a hard chew they helped pass the time and keep me awake.

Towards noon the wind began to slacken. It was dead aft now, for all through the forenoon hours I had been gradually altering course, following the tankers as they turned south through the last part of the Straits. Soon our speed was almost the same as the breeze, so that it was hot and humid, almost airless, the smell of diesel very strong. The clouds were all gone now, eaten up by the sun, the sky a hard blue and the sea sparkling in every direction, very clear, with the horizon so sharp it might have been inked in with a ruler. There were a lot of ships about and I knew I had to keep awake, but at times I dozed, my mind wandering and only brought back to the job on hand by the changed movement as the dhow shifted course.

I could still see the Omani shore, the mountains a brown smudge to the south-west. The wind died and haze gradually reduced visibility, the sun blazing down and the dhow rolling wildly. The sea became an oily swell, the silken rainbow surface of it ripped periodically by the silver flash of panicked fish. The heat ripened the stench from the lazarette beneath my feet. Twice I forced myself to go down there, but each time he was unconscious. I wanted to know what it was he had said about oil, for the exhaust was black and diesel fumes hung over the poop in a cloud. I began listening to the engine, hearing strange knocking sounds, but its beat never faltered.

Water and dates, that was all I had, and standing there, hour after hour, changing my course slowly from south to sou'sou'east and staring through slitted eyes at the bows rising and falling in the glare, the mast swinging against the blue of the sky, everything in movement, ceaselessly and without pause, I seemed to have no substance, existing in a daze that quite transported me, so that nothing was real. In this state I might easily have thrown him overboard. God knows there were fish enough to pick him clean in a flash, and skeletons make featureless ghosts to haunt a man.

I can't think why I didn't. I was in such a state of weary unreality that I could have had no qualms. I did go down there later, towards the end of the afternoon watch – I think with the conviction he was dead and I could rid myself of the source of the stench.

But he wasn't dead. And he wasn't unconscious either. He was sitting up, his back braced against the stern timbers and his eyes wide open. It just wasn't possible then. I couldn't pick him up and toss him overboard, not with his eyes staring at me like that. And as soon as he saw me he began to talk. But not sensibly. About things that had happened long, long ago – battles and the seeking after God, beautiful women and the terrible destruction of ancient castles.

He was delirious, of course, his mind in a trance. And yet he seemed to know me, to be talking to me. That's what made it impossible. I got some sea water and began cleaning him up. He was trembling. I don't know whether it was from cold or fever. Maybe it was fear. Maybe he'd known and that's why he was talking – you can't throw a man to the fishes when he's talking to you about things that are personal and take your mind back, for he was talking then about his home in Wales, how they had moved up into the old tin hills above a place called Farmers, a tumble-down longhouse where the livestock were bedded on the ground floor to keep the humans warm in the bedroom above. It was odd to hear him talking about Wales, here in the Straits with Arabia on one side of us, Persia on the other. 'But you wouldn't know about the *Mabinogion* now, would you?' he breathed.

I told him I did, that I had read it, but either he didn't hear me or he didn't take it in. His mind was far away on the hills of his youth. 'Carreg-y-Bwci,' he murmured. 'The Hobgoblin Stone. I've danced on it as a kid in the moonlight, a great cromlech on its side – and the Black Mountain visible thirty miles away. It never did me any harm,' he added in a whisper. Then his hand reached out towards me. 'Or am I wrong then? Was I cursed from that moment?' The dhow rolled, rolling him with it, and he clutched at his guts, screaming.

I steadied him and he stopped screaming, gulping air and holding on to me very tightly. I got his trousers open at the fly and in the light of my torch could see the neat hole the bullet had punched in his white belly. He wasn't bleeding now and it looked quite clean, only the skin round it bruised and bluish; but I didn't dare turn him over to see what was the other side, in the back where it must have come out.

I cleaned his trousers as best I could and all the time I was doing it he was rambling on about the *Mabinogion*, and I thought how strange; the only other person ever to talk to me about it was Karen. She'd got it from the travelling library, asking for it specially. And when she had read it she had insisted that I read it, too, the four branches of it containing some of the oldest stories of the Welsh bards. A strange book full of fighting men who were always away from home and wives that gave themselves to any valiant passerby, and everything, it seemed, happening three times over, all the trickery, the treachery, the blazing hopes that led to death. Some of its eleven stories had borne a strange resemblance to the tribal life in the hills where my mother's people had come from – the feuds, the hates, the courage and the cruelty. And this man talking of the country above Lampeter where Karen and I had stayed one night in a wretched little inn with hardly a word of English spoken to us.

It was just after we were married. I had been on leave from the Gulf and had borrowed her father's car to drive up to the Snowdonia National Park. Just short of Llanwrtyd Wells I had turned north to look at the Rhandirmwyn dam and we had come out of the wild forested country beyond by way of an old Roman road called the Sarn Helen. I could even remember that huge cromlech lying on its side, the sun shinning as we stopped the car and got out to stand on the top of the earth circle in which it lay, and the late spring snow was like a mantle across the rolling slopes of distant mountains to the south. And as I was zipping up his trousers, hoping he wouldn't mess them up again, I saw him in my mind's eye, a wild Welsh kid dancing on that stone in the full light of the moon. A demonstration of natural wickedness, or had he really been cursed? I was too tired to care, too tired to listen any longer to his ramblings. And the stench remained. I left him with some water and dates and got out, back into the hot sun and the brilliance of sea and sky.

By sundown the sea was oily calm, the dhow waddling over the shallow swells with only a slight roll. She would now hold her course for several minutes at a time, so that I was able to examine the rusty old diesel engine in its compartment below the lazarette. I found the fuel tank and a length of steel rod hung on a nail to act as a dipstick. The tank was barely a quarter full. It was quite a big tank, but I had no idea what the consumption was, so no means of calculating how far a quarter of a tank would take us.

The sunset was all purples and greens with clouds hanging on the sea's eastern rim. Those clouds would be over Pakistan and I wondered whether we'd make it as I stood there munching a date and watching the sun sink behind the jagged outline of the Omani mountains and the colour fade from the sky. To port, night had already fallen over Iran. The stars came out. I picked a planet and steered on that. Lighthouse flashes and the moving lights of passing ships, the dark confusion of the waves – soon I was so sleepy I was incapable of holding a course for more than a few minutes at a time.

Towards midnight a tanker overhauled us, outward-bound from the Gulf. I was steering south-east then, clear of the Straits now and heading into the Gulf of Oman. The tanker passed us quite close and there were others moving towards the Straits. Once a plane flew low overhead. Sometime around 02.00 I fell into a deep sleep.

I was jerked awake by a hand on my face. It was cold and clammy and I knew instantly that he'd come back to me out of the sea into which I'd thrown him. *No. I didn't do it. You must have fallen.* I could hear my voice, high-pitched and scared. And then he was saying, 'You've got to keep awake. I can't steer, you see. I've tried, but I can't – it hurts so.'

I could smell him then and I knew he was real, that I wasn't dreaming. I was sprawled on the deck and he was crouched over me. 'And the engine,' he breathed. 'It's old. It eats oil. I can hear the big ends knocking themselves to pieces. It needs oil, man.'

There were cans of oil held by a loop of wire to one of the frames of the engine compartment. The filler cap was missing and there was no dipstick. I poured in half a can and hoped for the best. The engine certainly sounded quieter. Back on the poop I found him collapsed again against the binnacle box and the dhow with its bows turned towards the north star. A tanker passed us quite close, her deck lights blazing, figures moving by the midship derricks which were hoisting lengths of pipe. How I envied the bastards – cabins to go to, fresh water showers, clean clothes and drinks, everything immaculate, and no smell. I couldn't make up my mind whether it was food I wanted most or some ice-cold beer. The cold beer probably. My mouth was parched with the salt, my eyes gritty with lack of sleep. Choffel lay motionless, a dark heap on the deck and the minutes passed like hours.

Strange how proximity alters one's view of a person, familiarity fostering acceptance. I didn't hate him now. He was there, a dark bundle curled up like a foetus on the deck, and I accepted him, a silent companion, part of the ship. The idea of killing him had become quite remote. It was my state of mind, of course. I was no longer rational, my body going through the motions of steering quite automatically, while my mind hovered in a trance, ranging back over my life, reality and fantasy all mixed up and Karen merging into Pamela. And that black-eyed girl with a cold cursing me in French and spitting in my face. *Guinevere*. How odd to name a girl *Guinevere*.

'That's my daughter,' he said.

I blinked my eyes. He was sitting up, staring at me. 'My daughter,' he said again. 'You were talking about my daughter.' There was a long silence. I could see her very clearly, the pale clear skin, the square strong features, the dark eyes and the dark hair. 'She tried to stop me. She didn't want me to go to sea again – ever.' He was suddenly talking about her, his voice quick and urgent. 'We have some caves behind our house. *Champignons! Parfait pour les champignons*, she said. So we grew mushrooms, and it worked, except we couldn't market them. Not profitably. She would keep us. That was her next idea. She was a typist. She did a course, you see – secretarial – after she left school. I can earn good money, she said. But a man can't be kept like that, not by his daughter. He's not a man if he can't stand on his own feet . . .' His voice faded, a despairing whisper that was thick with something he had to bring up. 'The *Petros Jupiter*,' he breathed. A fish rose, a circle of phosphorus on the dark water behind him. 'She was in tears she was so angry. They'll get at you, she said. They'll get at you, I know they will. And I laughed at her. I didn't believe it. I thought the *Petros Jupiter* was all right.' He choked, spitting something out on to the deck. 'And now I've got a bullet in my guts and I'll probably die. That's right, isn't it? You'll see to that and she'll say you murdered me. She'll kill you if you let me die. She's like that. She's so emotional, so possessive. The maternal instinct. It's very strong in some women. I remember when she was about seven – she was the only one, you see – and I was back from a year's tramping, a rusty old bucket of a wartime Liberty called *St Albans*, that was when she first began to take charge of me. There were things to mend – she'd just learned to sew, you see – and cooking ... living in France girls get interested in the cuisine very young. She'd mother anything that came her way, injured birds, stray puppies, hedgehogs, even reptiles. Then it was people and nursing. She's a born nurse, that's why she works in a clinic, and beautiful – like her mother, so beautiful. Her nature. You know what I mean – so very, very beautiful, so ...' His voice choked, a sobbing sound.

He was crying. I couldn't believe it, here on this stinking dhow, lying there with a bullet in his guts, and he was crying over his daughter. A beautiful nature – hell! A little spitfire.

'It was after the *Stella Rosa*. You know about the *Stella Rosa*, don't you?'

'Speridion.'

'Of course, you mentioned him.' He nodded, a slight movement of the head in the dark. 'Speridion had been paid to do it, only the thing went off prematurely, blew half his chest away. There was an Enquiry and when that was over I went home. She was still at school then, but she'd read the papers. She knew what it was all about, and she'd no illusions. You're a marked man, Papa. She never called me Dad or Daddy, always Papa. That was when she began to take charge, trying to mother me. Jenny wasn't a bit like that. Jenny was my wife's name. She was a very passive, quiet sort of person, so I don't know where my daughter got it from.' He stopped there, his voice grown weak; but his eyes were open, he was still conscious and I asked him about the *Aurora B.* 'Did you know it was the *Aurora B?*'

He didn't answer, but I knew he'd heard the question, for I could see the consciousness of it in his eyes, guessed in the wideness of their stare his knowledge of what my next question would be. Yes, he knew about the crew. He nodded slowly. He knew they were kept imprisoned in the chain locker. 'You couldn't help but know, not living on board as I was for over a week.' And then, when they'd called for power to the main anchor winch, he'd known they'd have to bring the prisoners up out of the chain locker and he had come on deck to see what happened to them. 'You saw it, too, did you?' His voice shook. And when I nodded, he said, 'That's when I decided I'd have to get away. I could see the dhow and I knew it was my last chance. In the morning it would be gone. That was when I made up my mind.' His voice dropped away. 'Always before I've stayed. I never believed it could happen – not again. And when it did—' He shook his head, murmuring – 'But not this time. Not with a cold-blooded bastard like Sadeq. And there was you. Your coming on board—' His voice died away completely.

'There are two ships,' I said. 'Did you know that?'

I thought he nodded.

'What happened to the other?'

He didn't answer.

'The seizing of *Aurora B*,' I said, catching hold of him and almost shaking him. 'That went wrong, didn't it? That was the first one, and it went wrong.'

He stared up at me, his eyes wide, not saying anything. 'And then they grabbed the second ship, the *Howdo Stranger*. Did you see her?'

'No.' He said it fiercely, an urgent whisper. 'I don't know anything about it. Nothing at all.'

'Are they going to meet up? Is that why they're getting the *Aurora B* officered and ready for sea?' His eyes had closed, his body limp. 'Where are they going to meet up? Where are they going to spill their oil? They're going to spill it on the coast of Europe. Isn't that the plan?' I was shaking him violently now, so violently that he screamed out with the pain of it like a shot rabbit.

'Please, for God's sake!' His voice was thick with blood and hardly audible.

'Where?' I shouted at him.

But he had fainted away, mumbling something about the salvage, which I didn't understand, his body collapsing in the grip of my hand. I cursed myself for having been too rough, the man in a coma now, his body shifting limply to the movement of the ship. I went back to the helm then, and though I called him several times, repeating my questions over and over again, he never answered. I passed the time watching the fish rise, pools of brightness in the dark, and our wake a fading lane of sparkling brilliance. We were well into the Gulf of Oman now, the fish more numerous than ever and the sea's phosphorescence quite spectacular. Sharks went under us leaving torpedo-like wakes and shoals of fish broke up like galaxies exploding. It was a fantastic pyrotechnic show of brilliant white lights forming below the surface of the sea and then bursting, constantly vanishing only to reappear, another patch of dark water suddenly illuminated.

Dawn came at last, a greying in the east, on the port bow. My second dawn at the dhow's helm and still nothing hot to eat, only dates and unboiled water. It came quickly, a magic burst of violent colour thrusting in flame over the horizon and then the sun like a great curved crimson wheel showing its hot iron rim and lifting fast, a visible movement.

I had parted company with the tanker traffic at the beginning of the dawn watch, steering a course just south of east that I hoped would close the coast in the region of the Pakistani-Iranian frontier. There were moments when I thought I could see it, a vague smudge like a brown crayon line away to port just for'ard of the thunderbox. But I couldn't be sure, my eyes playing me tricks and the sun's rapidly growing heat drawing moisture from the sea, the atmosphere thickening into a milky haze. Another eighteen hours! I went below and dipped the fuel tank. It was almost empty. Smears of dried blood marked the poop deck.

Choffel's eyes were closed, his head lolling. His features, his whole body seemed to have shrunk in the night, so that he was like a wax doll curled up there by the binnacle.

I secured the helm and went up into the thunderbox to squat there with my bottom hung out over a slat and bare to the waves, my head poked out above the wood surround, looking at the dhow and the injured man and the water creaming past. Afterwards I stripped off and sluiced myself down with buckets of sea water. And then I carried him back to the lazarette.

It was too hot for an injured man on the deck. That's what I told myself anyway, but the truth was I couldn't stand him there. He had begun mumbling to himself. *Jenny!* He kept on saying Jenny, so I knew he was talking to his wife. I didn't want to know the intimate details of their life together. I didn't want to be drawn closer to him through a knowledge of his own private hell. *Jenny, oh my darling – I can't help.* He choked over the words. *I've nothing left to give you.* And then he whispered, *The stomach again, is it? He said he'd bring more pills.* He nodded, playing the part. *Yes, the doctor's coming, darling. He'll be here any minute.* His eyes were closed, his voice quite clear, trembling with the intensity of recollection. *Doctor!* His eyes were suddenly open, staring at me, but without sight. *Have you brought them? For the pain. It's in the belly* . . . I put him down quickly and fled, back into the sunlight and the sanity of steering.

A few minutes later the engine gave its first tentative cough. I thought perhaps I was mistaken, for it went on as before giving out full power. But it coughed again, checking, then picking up. It picked up on the dip of the bows, so I knew it was now dependent on the last vestige of fuel being slopped back and forth in the bottom of the tank. I suppose we covered another two or three miles under increasingly uneven power, then suddenly all was quiet, only the splash and gurgle of water along the ship's side. The engine had finally died, the tiller going slack as we lost way.

The air was heavy and very still, only occasional cat's-paws ruffling the oily calm that stretched away on all sides until lost in the white glare of the heat haze. A sudden whisper of spray to starb'd and the whole surface of the sea took off, a thousand little skittering slivers of silver breaking the surface, and behind the shoal a dozen king mackerel arched their leaping bodies in pursuit, scattering prisms of rainbow colours in the splash of a myriad droplets. Again and again they leaped, the shoals skittering ahead of them in a panic of sparkling silver; then suddenly it was over, the oily surface of the sea undisturbed again, so undisturbed that the voracious demonstration of the hard piscatorial world below might never have been.

It was very humid, unseasonally so, since it was still the period of the north-east monsoon, and now that we were into the Arabian Sea we should have had the benefit of at least a breeze from that direction. The current, which was anticlockwise for another month, would have a westerly set and would thus be against us. I spent over an hour and all my energy unfurling and setting the heavy lateen sail. To do this I had to shin up the spar with a butcher's knife from the store and cut the rope tie-ers. The rest was relatively simple, just a matter of hard work, using the block and tackle already attached to the spar and another that acted as a sheet for the sail. With so little wind it hung over me in folds, flapping to the slow motion of the ship. But it did provide some shade on deck and in an instant I was wedged into the scuppers fast asleep.

I woke to the sound of water rushing past, opening my eyes to see the great curved sail bellied out and full of wind. Even as I watched, it began to shiver. I leaped to my feet, wide awake and diving up the steps to the tiller, hauling it over just in time to avoid being taken aback. The wind was north-west about force 3, still in the *shamal* quarter, so that I could only just lay my course. The coast was clearly visible now. The haze had gone, the day bright and clear, the sea sparkling, and the sun was almost overhead. I glanced at my watch. It was 13.05. I couldn't believe it. I had been asleep for something like four hours.

We were making, I suppose, about three knots and as the afternoon wore on the Iranian coast vanished from my sight. And since visibility was still good I thought it probable I was opposite Gwadar Bay which is on the frontier between Pakistan and Iran. It is a deep bay with salt flats and the bed of a river coming in from Baluchistan. Visualizing the chart I had so often had spread out before me on the chart table, I reckoned we were less than forty miles from Gwadar.

No shipping now to point the way, the sea empty to the horizon, except once when a sperm whale blew about half a mile away and shortly afterwards shot vertically out of the water like some huge submarine missile, leaping so high I could just see the flukes of its tail before it toppled with a gigantic splash back into the sea. At sunset I thought I could make out a line of cliffs low on the port bow. They were of a brilliant whiteness, wind-carved into fantastic towers and minarets so that it was like a mirage-distorted view of some incredible crystal city. Was that the Makran coast of Baluchistan?

Night came and I was still at the helm, the wind backing and getting stronger, the dhow thundering along at six knots or more. Suddenly it was dark. I had to start thinking then, about what I was going to do, how I was going to make it from dhow to shore. I had only a rough idea how far I had come, but at this rate, with the wind still backing and freshening, and the dhow empty of cargo, it looked as though I could be off Gwadar about one or two in the morning – presuming, of course, that the disappearance of the coast in the late afternoon really had been the bay and river flats that marked the frontier. I wondered how far off I would be able to see Gwadar at night. In daylight it was visible for miles, a great 500-ft high mass of hard rock sticking up out of the sea like an island. It was, in fact, a peninsula, shaped like a hammer-headed shark with its nose pointing south, the body of it a narrow sandspit with the port of Gwadar facing both ways, east and west, so that there

was safe anchorage in either monsoon – always provided a vessel could weather the rock and cliffs of the
peninsula's broad head.

My years at sea told me that the prudent thing to
do would be to lower the great lateen sail and let the
dhow drift through the night, hoisting again at dawn
when I could see where I was. But what if the wind
went on increasing? What if I couldn't hoist the bloody
thing? Seeing it there, bellied against the stars, I knew
it needed several men on the tackle to be sure of taming
the power of that sail. And I was tired. God! I was
tired.

Prudence can't compete with the lethargic urge to
leave things as they are, and so I went plunging on
into the night, relying on being able to pick up the
automatic light on top of the headland, ignoring
the nagging doubt in my mind that said it was probably out of order. If I hadn't been so tired; if I hadn't
had the urgent need to contact the authorities and get
a message out to the world about the *Aurora B*; if the
wind had only died – at least, not backed so much
into the south where it shouldn't have been at this
time of the year; if the light had been working or I
had taken into consideration that with the wind south
of west there might be an onshore set to the current . . .
If – if – if! Disasters are full of ifs, and I was a trained
deck officer with a master's certificate – I should have
known, even if I wasn't a sailing man. The sea never
forgives an error of judgment, and this was an error
due to tiredness. I was so goddam weary, and that

brute of a sail, bellied out to port like a black bat's wing against the stars.

It came at me when I was half asleep, the roar of breaking waves and a darkness looming over the bows, blotting out the stars. In an instant I was wide awake, my heart in my mouth and the adrenalin flowing as I hauled on the tiller rope, dragging the heavy steering bar over to port. Slowly, very slowly the dhow turned its high bow into the wind. I thought she'd never make it, that she'd fall off and go plunging away down-wind and into the cliffs, but she came up into the wind at last, and there she hung. She wouldn't go through it on to the other tack. And if she had, then I realized the lateen rig required the whole spar to be tipped up vertically and man-handled round the mast. An impossible task for one man with the wind blowing 5 or 6.

I didn't move fast enough. I can see that now. I should have secured the helm and hauled in on the sheet until the sail was set flat and as tight in as it would go. But even then I don't know that she'd have completed the tack. Not with just the one sail, and anyway I couldn't be in two places at once. The wind, close inshore, was so strong it was all I could do to manage the tiller, and when she wouldn't go through the wind, I just stayed there, my mind a blank, the sail flogging in giant whipcracks, the sea and the waves all contributing to the confusion of noise, and the dhow taken virtually aback, driving astern towards the surf breaking in a phosphorescent lather of light.

And while I crouched there, hauling on the tiller

which was already hard over, I watched appalled as the bows fell away to port, the lateen filling with a clap like thunder and the dhow lying over, driving virtually sideways into a maelstrom of broken water, and the cliffs above me looming taller and taller, half the stars in the sky blotted out and the movement of the deck under me suddenly very wild.

We struck at 02.27. I know that because I checked my watch, an action that was entirely automatic, as though I were in the wheelhouse of a proper ship with instruments to check and the log to fill in. We had hit a rock, not the cliffs. The cliffs I could vaguely see, a black mass looming above white waters. There was a thud and the rending sound of timbers breaking, and we hung there in a welter of broken waves with spray blowing over us and the dhow pounding and tearing itself to bits.

I had no idea where I was, whether it was the Gwadar Peninsula we had hit, or some other part of the coast. And there was nothing I could do. I was completely helpless, watching, dazed, as the prow swung away to port, everything happening in slow motion and with a terrible inevitability, timbers splintering amidships, a gap in the deck opening up and steadily widening as the vessel was literally torn apart. Years of neglect and blazing heat had rendered the planks and frames of her hull too brittle to stand the pounding and she gave up without any pretence of a struggle, the mainmast crashing down, the great sail like a winged banner streaming away to drown in the boiling seas. Then the for'ard half of the dhow broke entirely away. One moment it was there, a part of the ship, the next it was being swept into oblivion like a piece of driftwood. For a moment I could see it still, a dark shape against the white of broken water, and then suddenly it was gone.

I heard a cry and looking down from the poop I saw Choffel's body, flushed out from the lazarette by the wash of a wave and floundering in what little of the waist remained. I had my torch on and in the beam of it I saw his face white with his mouth open in some inarticulate cry, his hair plastered over his forehead and his arm raised as a wave engulfed him. I remember thinking then that the sea was doing my work for me, the next wave breaking over him and sweeping him away, and the same wave lifting the broken stern, tilting it forward and myself with it. There was a crash as we hit the rock, and a scraping sound, the mizzen falling close beside me and the remains of the dhow, with myself clinging to the wooden balustrade at the for'ard end of the poop, swept clear and into the backwash of broken water close under the cliff.

There was no sign of Choffel then. He was gone. And I was waist-deep in water, the deck gyrating wildly as it sank under me, weighed down by the engine, and then a wave broke over me, right over my head, and my mouth was suddenly full of water, darkness closing in. For a moment I didn't struggle. A sort of fatalism took charge, an *insh'Allah* mood that it was the will of God. Choffel had gone and that was that. I had done what I had intended to do and I didn't struggle. But then suddenly it came to me that that wasn't the end of it at all, and as I sank into the surge of the waves and quiet suffocation, Karen seemed to be calling to me. Not a siren song, but crying for all the life that would be destroyed by Sadeq or the twisted mind of Hals when those two tankers released their oil on the shores of Europe. I struggled then. I started fighting, threshing at the engulfing sea, forcing myself back to the buffeting, seething white of the surface, gulping air and trying desperately to swim.

CHAPTER TWO

The sun was burning holes in my head, my eyelids coloured blood and I was retching dribbles of salt water. I could hear the soft thump and suck of waves. I rolled over, my mouth open and drooling water, my throat aching with the salt of it, my fingers digging into sand. A small voice was calling, a high piping voice calling to me in Urdu – *Wake up, sahib. You wake up plees*. And there were hands on my shoulders, shaking me gently.

I opened my eyes. There were two of them, two small boys, half naked and dripping water, clutching at their sodden loin-cloths, their eyes round with the shock of finding me, their bodies burnt brown by the sun and the salt. Behind them was a boat drawn up on the sand, a small open boat, the wood bleached by the sun to a faded grey, the hull black with bitumen. Slowly I pushed myself up, my eyes slitted against the sand-glare. The wind had gone, the sea calm and blue with sparkling wavelets falling lazily on the sloping shore. Away to the left, beyond the boat, a very white building sprawled hull-down among some dunes. Behind the dunes I could see the brown tops of mud brick houses and in the far distance the vague outline of a headland. Two mules were grazing on the sparse grass of the dunes behind me. 'What's the name of that village?' I asked.

The dark little faces stared at me uncomprehendingly. I pointed towards the white building and the roofs beyond. 'Name? You tell me name of village.' They laughed, embarrassed. I switched to Urdu then, speaking slowly since these were Baluchi and I knew my accent would be strange to them.

'Coastguards,' they said, speaking almost in unison. 'Gwadar Coastguards.'

Gwadar! I sat with my head in my hands, feeling drained. So I had made it. And now there was a new battle to fight. I had to explain myself – on the telephone to Karachi – talk to officials, to the Lloyd's agent, to all the people who had to be alerted. And I was tired, so deadly tired. It wasn't just my body that was exhausted – it was my brain, my mind, my will. Vaguely I remembered swimming clear of the wreck, hanging on to a piece of the dhow's broken timbering and the seas breaking over me, rocking me into the oblivion of total exhaustion. A piece of timber, part of a mast by the look of it, lay half-submerged a little way along the dark sands, rolling gently back and forth in the wash of the small waves breaking.

A man appeared, a bearded, wrinkled face under a rag of a turban peering down at me. He was talking

to the boys, a quick high voice, but words I could
not follow and they were answering him, excitedly
gesturing at the sea. Finally they ran off and the old
man said, 'I send them for the Havildar.'

He knew there had been a dhow wrecked during
the night because bits of it had come ashore. He asked
me whose it was, where it had come from, how many
others had been on board – all the questions I knew
would be repeated again and again. I shook my head,
pretending I didn't understand. If I said I was alone
they wouldn't believe me. And if I told them about
Choffel . . . I thought of how it would be, trying to
explain to a village headman, or even some dumb
soldier of a coastguard, about the *Aurora B*, how we
had taken the dhow, cutting it free in a hail of
bullets . . . How could they possibly accept a story like
that? They'd think I was mad.

I must have passed out then, or else gone to sleep,
for the next thing I knew the wheel of a Land Rover
was close beside my head and there were voices. The
sun was hot and my clothes, dry now, were stiff with
salt. They lifted me up and put me in the back, a
soldier sitting with his arm round me so that I didn't
fall off the seat as we jolted along the foreshore to the
headquarters building, which was a square white
tower overlooking the sea. I was given a cup of sweet
black coffee in the adjutant's office, surrounded by
three or four officers, all staring at me curiously. It
was the adjutant who did most of the questioning,
and when I had explained the circumstances to the
increasingly sceptical huddle of dark-skinned faces, I

was taken in to see the colonel, a big, impressive man with a neat little moustache and an explosive voice. Through the open square of the window I found myself looking out on the brown cliffs of the Gwadar Peninsula. I was given another cup of coffee and had to repeat the whole story for his benefit.

I don't know whether he believed me or not. In spite of the coffee I was half asleep, not caring very much either way. I was telling them the truth. It would have been too much trouble to tell them anything else. But I didn't say much about Choffel, only that he'd been shot while we were trying to get away in the dhow. Nobody seemed to be concerned about him. His body hadn't been found and without a body they weren't interested.

The colonel asked me a number of questions, mostly about the nationality of the men on the tanker and where I thought they were taking it. Finally he picked up his hat and his swagger stick and called for his car. 'Follow me please,' he said and led me out into the neatly white-washed forecourt. 'I now have to take you to the Assistant Commissioner who will find it a difficult problem since you are landed on his lap, you see, with no passport, no identification, and the most unusual story. It is the lack of identity he will find most difficult. You say you have been ship's officer in Karachi. Do you know somebody in Karachi? Somebody to say who you are?'

I told him there were a lot of people who knew me – port officials, shipping agents, some of those who worked at the Sind Club and at the reception desk of the Metropole Hotel. Also personal friends. He nodded, beating a tattoo on his knee with his stick as he waited for his car. 'That will help perhaps.'

The car arrived, the coastguard flag flying on the bonnet, and as we drove out of the compound, he pointed to a long verandahed bungalow of a building just beyond an area of sand laid out with mud bricks baking in the sun – 'Afterwards, you want the hospital, it is there.'

'I'll be all right,' I said.

He looked at me doubtfully. 'We get the doctor to have a look at you. I don't like you to die with me when you have such an interesting story to tell.'

We passed one of those brilliantly colourful trucks, all tinsel and florid paintings, like an elaborately decorated chocolate box; conclusive proof to the wandering haziness of my mind that I really was in Pakistan. From fine-ground sand and a cloud of dust we moved on to tarmac. Glimpses of the sea, long black fishing boats anchored off, their raked masts dancing in the sun – this was the eastern side of the Gwadar Peninsula, the sea still a little wild, the shore white with surf. There was sand everywhere, the sun glaring down.

'We have a desalination plant, good water from the sea, all by solar.' The colonel's voice was far away, the driver's forage cap perched on his round black head becoming blurred and indistinct against the moving backcloth of open bazaar booths and mud-brick buildings. 'We see Ahmad Ali Rizivi now.' The car had stopped, the colonel was getting out. 'This is what you call the town hall. It is the house of the Assistant District Commissioner.'

We were in a dusty little open space, a sort of square. A janitor in long robes sat in the doorway. I was vaguely conscious of people as I followed the colonel up the steps and into the dark interior. A clerk sat on a high stool at an old-fashioned desk, another ushered us in to an inner office where a man rose from behind a plain wooden desk that might have been a table. He waved us to chairs hastily placed. It was cooler and there were framed maps and texts on the wall – texts from the Koran I presumed. And the inevitable picture of Jinna – Quaid-i-Azam, the man who had led Pakistan out of the Empire, out of India, to independence and partition. The pictures came and went, the voices a dark murmur as a hot wave of weariness broke over me, my head nodding.

Coffee came, the inevitable coffee, the colonel's hand shaking me, the Assistant District Commissioner gesturing to the cup, a bleak smile of hospitality. He wanted me to tell it again, the whole story. 'From the beginning please.' His dark eyes had no warmth. He didn't care that I was exhausted. He was thinking of me only as a problem washed up by the sea on to his territory, the survivor of a wreck with an improbable story that was going to cause him a lot of trouble. There was a clerk there to take notes.

'He is Lord of the Day,' the colonel said, nodding at Rizivi and smiling. 'He is the Master here. If he says off with his head, then off with his head it is.' He said it jokingly, but the smile did not extend to his eyes. It was a warning. Who was the Lord of the Night, I wondered, as I drank the hot sweet coffee, trying to marshal my thoughts so there would be some sort of coherence in what I had to tell him.

I have only the vaguest memory of what I said, or of the questions he asked. Afterwards there was a long pause while he and the colonel talked it over. They didn't seem to realize I understood Urdu, though it hardly made any difference since I was beyond caring whether they believed me or what they decided to do about me, my eyes closing, my mind drifting into sleep. But not before I had the impression that they were both agreed on one thing at least – to pass the problem to higher authority just as soon as they could. People came and went. The colonel was alone with me for a time. 'Mr Rizivi arrange air passage for you on the next flight.' The Assistant District Commissioner came back. He had spoken to Quetta on the R/T. 'You go to Karachi this afternoon. Already we are consulting with Oman to see if your story is true.'

I should have made the point then that the *Aurora B* would probably have sailed by the time arrangements had been made for a reconnaissance flight over the *khawr*, but my mind was concentrated entirely on the fact that I was being flown to Karachi. Nothing else mattered. We were in the car again and a few minutes later the colonel and his driver were thrusting me along a verandah crowded with the sick and their relatives to an office where an overworked doctor in a white coat was examining a man whose chest was covered in skin sores. He pushed him away as we entered, peering at me through thick-lensed glasses. 'You the survivor of the wrecked dhow?'

I nodded.

'They talk of nothing else.' He jerked his head at the crowded verandah. 'Everybody I see today. They all have a theory, you see, as to how it happened. How did it happen? You tell me.' He lifted my eyelids with a dark thumb, brown eyes peering at me closely. 'They say there is no *naukhada*, only a solitary English. Is you, eh?'

I nodded, feeling his hands running over my body. 'No fractures. Some bruising, nothing else.' He pulled open my shirt, a stethoscope to his ears, his voice running on. Finally he stood back, told me there was nothing wrong with me except lack of sleep and nervous exhaustion. He gave me some pills and made me take one of them with a glass of water right there in the stuffy confines of his little consulting room. After that I don't remember anything at all until I was in a Land Rover being driven out to the airfield, the wind and dust blowing, the land flat, a desert scene with passengers and officials standing in the glare of the sun, baggage lying around them on the ground.

The plane came in, a Fokker Friendship bright as a dragon-fly against the hard blue of the sky, the gravel airfield spouting long streamers of dust as its wheels touched down. The adjutant himself saw me on to the plane and remained beside it until the door of the fuselage was finally closed. We took off and from my window I had a good view of Gwadar as we climbed and banked, the hammer-headed peninsula with an area of water and green trees like an oasis on one corner of its barren top, and below it, in the sand, the glass-glinting square of the desalination plant, then the town, neat acres of brown, the white of the coast-guards' buildings, and the sea on either side with the fishing boats lying off or drawn up on the sand. And against it all I suddenly saw Choffel's face, his mouth wide open, the black hair plastered to his white fore-head and his arm raised as he sank from sight in the wash of a wave. Somewhere down there his body floated in the blue sea, pale skeleton bones beginning to show as the fish picked him clean.

I remember thinking about the eyes and that I should have done something to help him. His features were so appallingly vivid as I stared through the window at the line of the coast stretching away far below.

And then the wheels touched down and I opened my eyes to find we had landed in Karachi. One of the pilots came aft from the flight deck insisting that nobody moved until I had got off the plane. There was a car waiting for me and some men, including Peter Brown, the Lloyd's agent. No Customs, no Immi-gration. We drove straight out through the loose-shirted untidy mob that hung around the airport entrance, out on to the crowded Hyderabad–Karachi road, the questions beginning immediately. Sadeq – I had referred to a man called Sadeq. Who was he? What did he look like? But they knew already. They had had his description from the oil company's Marine Superintendent in Dubai. They nodded, both of them,

checking papers taken from a coloured leather briefcase with a cheap metal clasp. Peter Brown was sitting
in front with the driver, neatly dressed as always in a
tropical suit, his greying hair and somewhat patrician
features giving him an air of distinction. He was a
reserved man with an almost judicial manner. It was
the other two, sitting on either side of me in the back,
who asked the questions. The smaller of them was a
Sindhi, his features softer, his dark eyes sparkling with
intelligence. The other was a more stolid type with a
squarish face heavily pock-marked and horn-rimmed
glasses slightly tinted. Police, or perhaps Army – I
wasn't sure. 'He had another name.'

'Who?' I was thinking of Choffel.

'This Sadeq. A terrorist, you said.' The small man
was riffling through the clipful of papers resting on his
briefcase. 'Here – look now, this telex. It is from Mr
Perrin at the GODCO offices in Dubai.' He waved it
at me, holding it in thin dark fingers, his wrist as
slender as a girl's. 'He said – that's you, I'm quoting
from his telex you see . . . He said Sadeq was an Iranian
terrorist, that he had another name, but that he did
not know it, which may be true as it is several years
back during the Shah's regime.' He looked up. 'Now
you have met him again perhaps you recall his other
name.' He was peering at me sideways, waiting for an
answer, and there was something in his eyes – it is
difficult for eyes that are dark brown to appear cold,
but his were very cold as they stared at me unblink-
ingly. 'Think very carefully please.' The voice so soft,
the English so perfect, and in those eyes I read the

threat of nameless things that were rumoured of the security section of Martial Law prisons.

'Qasim,' I said, and he asked me to spell it, writing it down with a gaudy-coloured pen. Then both of them were asking questions, most of which I couldn't answer because I didn't know what offences Qasim had committed against the Shah's regime before the Khomeini revolution or what he was doing on board the *Aurora B* under the name Sadeq, why he had hi-jacked the ship, what the plan was. I didn't know anything about him, only his name and the fact that the dead Shah's police had said he was a terrorist. But they didn't accept that and the questioning went on and on. I was being grilled and once when I nodded off the little man slapped my face. I heard Brown protest, but it didn't make any difference, the questions continuing and becoming more and more searching. And then, suddenly, when we were into the outskirts of Karachi on the double track of the Shahrah-e-Faisal, they stopped. 'We will take you to the Metropole now so you can sleep. Meanwhile, we will try to discover some more about this man Choffel.' He leaned over to Peter Brown. 'Let us know please if you have any information about these ships from London.'

The Lloyd's agent nodded. 'Of course. And you will let me know the result of the Omani airforce reconnaissance.'

The little man pursed his lips, a smile that was almost feminine. 'You're finding this story difficult to swallow, are you?' Brown didn't answer and the man leaned forward. 'Do you believe him?' he asked.

Brown turned and looked at me. I could see the uncertainty in his eyes. 'If he isn't telling the truth, then he's lying. And I don't at the moment see any reason for him to lie.'

'A man has disappeared.' The cold dark eyes gave me a sideways glance. He took a newspaper cutting from the clip of papers. 'This is from the Karachi paper *Dawn*, a brief news item about a tanker being blown up on the English coast. It is dated ninth January. Karen Rodin. Was that your wife?'

I nodded.

'It also says that a French engineer, Henri Choffel, accused of sabotaging the tanker and causing it to run aground, is being hunted by Interpol.' Again the sly sideways glance. 'The man who is with you on this dhow – the man you say is shot when you were escaping from the *Aurora B* – his name also is Choffel . . . What is his first name, is it Henri?'

'Yes.' I was staring at him, fascinated, knowing what he was thinking and feeling myself suddenly on the edge of an abyss.

'And that is the same man – the man Interpol are looking for?'

I nodded.

'Alone on that dhow with you, and your wife blown up with the tanker he wrecked.' He smiled and after that he didn't say anything more, letting the silence produce its own impact. The abyss had become a void, my mind hovering on the edge of it, appalled at the inference he was drawing. The fact that I hadn't done it was irrelevant. It was what I had planned to do, the reason I was on the *Aurora B*. And this little man in Karachi had seen it immediately. If it was such an obvious conclusion . . . I was thinking how it would be when I was returned to the UK, how I could avoid people leaping to the same conclusion.

The car slowed. We were in Club Road now, drawing into the kerb where broad steps led up to the wide portico of the Metropole. We got out and the heat and the dust and noise of Karachi hit me. Through the stream of traffic, beyond the line of beat-up old taxi cars parked against the iron palings opposite, I glimpsed the tall trees of the shaded gardens of the Sind Club. A bath and a deck chair in the cool of the terrace, a long, ice-cold drink . . . 'Come please.' The big man took hold of my arm, shattering the memories of my *Dragonera* days as he almost frog-marched me up the steps into the hotel. The little man spoke to the receptionist. The name Ahmad Khan was mentioned and a key produced. 'You rest now, Mr Rodin.' He handed the key to his companion and shook my hand. 'We will talk again when I have more information. Also we have to decide what we do with you.' He gave me a cold little smile and the Metropole seemed suddenly a great deal more luxurious. 'Meanwhile Majeed will look after you.' He nodded in the direction of his companion who was talking now to an unshaven loosely-dressed little man who had been hovering in the background. 'Can I give you a lift?' he asked the Lloyd's agent.

Peter Brown shook his head. 'I'll see Rodin settled in first.'

'As you wish.' He left then and I watched him go with a sense of relief, his slim silhouette changing to powder blue as the glare of the street spotlighted his pale neat suit. 'What is he – Intelligence?' I asked.

Brown shrugged. 'Calls himself a Government Information Officer.'

'And the other?'

'Security, I presume.'

We took the lift to the second floor, tramping endless cement-floored corridors where bearers, sweepers and other hangers-on lounged in over-employed idleness. The Metropole occupies a whole block, a great square of buildings constructed round a central courtyard. The first floor is given over to offices, almost every room with a sign over it, the names of countless small businesses and agencies. I glanced at my watch. It was still going, the time 17.36. We stopped at a door and the policeman handed the key to the unshaven little man who had accompanied us. He in turn handed it to the bearer who was now in close attendance. The room was big and airy, with a ceiling fan turning slowly and the windows open and looking out on to the huge courtyard. Kites were coming in to roost on the trees and window ledges, big vulture-like birds, drab in the shadows cast by the setting sun. 'You will be very comfortable here.' The policeman waved his hands in a gesture that included the spartan beds and furniture, the big wardrobes and tatty square of carpet, a note of envy in his voice. The Metropole to him was probably the height of glamour.

He searched the drawers and the wardrobes,

checked the bathroom. Finally he left, indicating the unshaven one and saying, 'Hussain will keep watch over you. And if there is something more you have to tell us, he knows where to find me.'

'Is there?' Brown asked as the door closed behind him.

'Is there what?'

'Anything more you have to tell them.'

'No.'

'And it's true, is it – about the *Aurora B*?'

I nodded, wondering how I could get rid of him, wanting nothing except to get my head down now and sleep while I had the chance. It was more important to me even than food. He moved to the phone, which was on a table between the two beds. 'Mind if I ring the office?' He gave the switchboard a number and I went into the bathroom, where the plumbing was uncertain and the dark cement floor wet with water from a leaking pipe. When I had finished I found the unshaven Hussain established on a chair in the little entrance hall and Brown was standing by the window. 'I think I should warn you, a lot of people are going to find this story of yours a pretty tall one. You realize we've no record of a tanker ever having been hi-jacked. Certainly no VLCC has been hi-jacked before. That's straight, old-fashioned piracy. And you're saying it's not one, but two – two tankers boarded and taken without even a peep of any sort on the radio. It's almost inconceivable.'

'So you don't believe me?'

He shook his head, pacing up and down the

tattered piece of carpeting. 'I didn't say that. I just think it's something people will find difficult to accept. One, perhaps, but two—'

'The first one went wrong.'

'So you said. And you think a bomb was thrown into the radio room, a grenade, something like that?'

'I don't know what happened,' I said, sitting on the bed, wishing he would go away as I pulled off my shoes. 'I've told you what I saw, the radio shack blackened by fire and a hole ripped in the wall. I presume they met with resistance on the bridge, discovered the radio operator was going to send a Mayday and dealt with the situation the only way they knew.'

'And this happened, not in the Indian Ocean, but when the *Aurora B* was still in the Gulf?'

'Yes. When she was in the Straits probably.'

'So the radio contact with the owners, made when the ship was supposed to be somewhere off the coast of Kutch, was entirely spurious. That's what you're saying, isn't it? – that it never happened, or rather it was made from a quite different locality and was not the captain reporting to the owners, but the hi-jackers conning them.' He nodded to himself. 'Ingenious, and it's been done before. But usually with non-existent ships or cargoes, and not on this scale, not with oil involved and big tankers. Fraudulent insurance claims, we know a lot about those now, I've had instances myself. But always general cargo ships. Small ones, usually old and in poor condition. Four at least I can remember, all single-vessel owners, two of them had only just changed hands. They were all cargo frauds based on forged documents.' He began describing the intricacies of the frauds, bills of lading, packing lists, manufacturers' certificates in two cases, even EEC certificate of origin in one case, all forged.

'I'm tired,' I said irritably.

He didn't seem to hear me, going on to tell me a complicated story of trans-shipment of car engines from a small freighter at the height of the port's congestion when there were as many as eighty ships anchored off Karachi awaiting quay space. But then he stopped quite suddenly. 'Of course, yes, I was forgetting – you're tired.' He said it a little huffily. 'I was simply trying to show you that what you've been telling us is really very difficult to believe. These are not small ships and GODCO is certainly not a single-vessel owner. They are, both of them, VLCCs, well-maintained and part of a very efficiently operated fleet.' He was gazing out of the window at the darkening shadows. 'Maybe they picked on them for that reason.' He was talking to himself, not me. 'Being GODCO vessels, maybe they thought their disappearance would be accepted – something similar to the disappearance of those two big Scandinavians. They were in ballast and cleaning tanks with welders on board or something. An explosive situation. That's what I heard, anyway.'

'It's got nothing to do with it,' I said. 'This is quite different.'

'Yes, indeed. Quite different. And it doesn't sound

like fraud.' He had turned from the window and was staring at me. 'What do you reckon the purpose is?'

'How the hell do I know? I was only on board the ship a few hours.'

'And the cost of it,' he muttered. 'They'd need to have very substantial backers, particularly to escalate the operation to a second tanker at short notice.' He glanced at his watch. 'You want to rest and it's time I was getting back to the office. There'll be people at Lloyd's who'll be greatly cheered to know the *Aurora B* at any rate is still afloat. I'll telex them right away.'

'You'll be contacting Forthright's, will you?'

He nodded. 'They'll have a full account of it waiting for them in their office tomorrow morning. Mr Saltley can then take what action he thinks fit.' He lifted his head, looking at me down his long nose. 'If they locate this ship, the one you say is the *Aurora B*, then there'll be all sorts of problems. Maritime law isn't exactly designed to cope with this sort of thing. And you'll be in the thick of it, so much depending on your statement.' And he added, 'On the other hand, if she's sailed and the subsequent search fails to locate her . . .' He paused, watching me curiously. 'That's why I stayed on, to warn you. What happens if they don't believe you? If they think you're lying, then they'll want to know the reason and that may lead them to jump to conclusions.' He smiled, 'Could be awkward, that. But let's take things as they come, eh?' He clapped me on the shoulder. 'Have a good rest. I'll see you in the morning.'

Sleep came in a flash and I woke sweating to a

surge of sound, red lights flickering and a wild voice. My body, naked under the coarse sheets, felt battered and painful, my limbs aching. I had no idea where I was, staring wide-eyed at the big fan blades above my bed, revolving slowly to reflect a kaleidoscope of colours and that voice. I sat up. A woman was singing, a high Muslim chanting, and the surging sound was an Eastern band, the shriek of pipes and tam-tams beating.

I pulled back the sheet and stumbled to the window, conscious of the stiffness of my muscles, the ache of a deep bruise in the pelvis, staring down into the courtyard, which was a blaze of light, girls in richly coloured saris, tables piled with food and drink. A wedding? So much tinsel decoration, balloons and lanterns, and the men loutish and ill-at-ease in their bright suits. The singing stopped. The music changed to Western jazz played fast and the crowd mingling, men and women clinging uncertainly, dancing double time. A bird swirled up like a great bat, the lights red, yellow and green and somebody pointing so that I drew back quickly, conscious that I was standing there stark naked. But it was the bird they were pointing at.

A shadow moved beside me. 'You all right, sahib?' It was my watchdog.

I couldn't sleep for a long time after that, listening to the band and the high chatter of voices, the lights flickering on my closed eyes, and thinking about what was going to happen when they found the ship. Would they arrest her on the high seas? Who would do it – the British, the Americans, who? And what about me?

Nobody was going to thank me for handing them such a problem. I wondered what Sadeq would do when the Navy came on board, what explanation he would give. Would he still be flying the hammer and sickle? And Baldwick – I suddenly remembered Baldwick. Baldwick wouldn't be able to leave without the dhow. He'd still be on board. What would his explanation be, or would Sadeq dispose of him before he had a chance to talk? I could see Sadeq, as I had glimpsed him when I was crouched below the poop, the gun at his waist, the bearded face fixed in what was almost a grin as he sprayed bullets with cold professional accuracy and Baldwick thrown backwards, his big barrel of a stomach opened up and flayed red. Choffel – my mind was confused. It was Choffel whose stomach had been hit. And I was in Pakistan with information nobody was happy to hear ... except Pamela and those two sailing men, her father and Saltley. If I was in England now, not lying here in Karachi with a wedding thumping out jazz and Eastern music ...

I suppose I was in that limbo of half-coma that is the result of shock and exhaustion, my mind in confusion, a kaleidoscope of thoughts and imaginings all as strange as the lights and the music. Darkness came eventually, and sleep – a sleep so dead that when I finally opened my eyes the sun was high above the hotel roof and Hussain was shaking me. He was even more unshaven now and he kept repeating, 'Tiffin, tiffin, sahib.' It was almost ten o'clock and there was a tray on the small central table with boiled eggs, sliced white bread, butter, marmalade and a big pot of coffee.

My clothes had gone, but the notes and traveller's cheques that had been in my hip pocket were on the table beside me. Kites wheeled in a cloudless sky. I had a quick shower and breakfasted with a towel wrapped round my middle. A copy of *Dawn* lay on the table. *Founded by Quaid-i-Azam Mohammed Ali Jinnah*, it said – *Karachi, 21 Safar, 1400*. The lead story was about Iran, the conflict between the IRP and the left-wing Mujaheddin. I could find no mention of a dhow being wrecked off Gwadar or of anybody being washed ashore there. The bearer came with my clothes, laundered, ironed and reasonably dry. As soon as I was dressed I rang the office of Lloyd's agents down near the Customs House, but Peter Brown was out and the only other person I knew there, a Parsi, had no information to give me. I sat by the window then, reading the paper from cover to cover and watching the kites. Hussain refused absolutely to allow me out of the room and though I had a telephone call from Brown's office it was only to say he would contact me as soon as he had any information. I could have done with a drink, but the hotel was under strict Islamic laws and drier than the sands of Baluchistan.

Just after midday Ahmad Khan arrived, the jacket of his blue suit slung over his shoulder, his tie loosened. 'There is no ship,' he said in his rather high lilting voice. He was standing in the middle of the room, his dark eyes watching me closely. 'Muscat report their aircraft have overflown all the *khawrs* of the

Musandam Peninsula. There is no tanker there.' He paused to let that sink in. 'Also, Gwadar report no body being washed onto the coast.'

'Was there any sign of the man who jumped overboard?' I asked.

'No, nothing. And no sign of the ship.'

'I told you they would have sailed the morning after we escaped. Have they made a search along the tanker route?'

'Oman say they are doing it now. I have told my office to let me know here as soon as we receive a report.' He threw his jacket on to the nearest bed, picked up the phone and ordered coffee. 'You want any coffee?'

I shook my head. Just over two days at full speed, the ship could be nine hundred, a thousand miles from the Straits, clear of the Oman Gulf, and well out into the Indian Ocean – a hell of a lot of sea to search. 'What about other ships? Have they been alerted?'

'You ask Mr Brown that. I have no information.'

His coffee came, and when the waiter had gone he said, 'You don't wish to amend your statement at all?'

I shook my head. 'No, not at all.'

'Okay.' And after that he sat there drinking his coffee in silence. Time passed as I thought about the route the tanker would have taken, and wondered why he was here. It was just on twelve-thirty that the phone rang. It was Brown and after a moment he handed it to me. All shipping had been alerted the previous night. So far nothing had been reported. 'I've just been talking to the Consul. I'm afraid they're a bit sceptical.'

'Do you mean they don't believe me?'

'No, why should they? I don't think anyone's going to believe you unless the tanker actually materializes.'

'Do you?'

There was a moment's hesitation. 'I might if it wasn't for your story about Choffel. Let's wait, shall we? If the body turns up, or we get a sighting of that tanker . . .' His voice drifted away apologetically. 'Anyway, how are you feeling now – rested?'

'Yes, I'm all right.'

'Good, good.' There was a pause while he searched around for something else to say. 'Glad you're all right. Well, if I hear anything I'll give you a ring.' There was a click and he was gone.

The conversation left me feeling lonely and disconsolate. If he didn't believe me, the little Sindhi intelligence man sipping noisily at his coffee certainly would not. Hussain arranged for lunch to be brought up from the café below, a spiced rissole, chilli hot, with slices of white bread and some tinned fruit. Ahmad Khan hardly spoke and I was speculating what was going to happen to me when it was realized the tanker had vanished. Obviously, once outside the Gulf of Oman, it would be steering well clear of the shipping lanes. Clouds were building in the white glare above the rooftops and the kites were wheeling lower.

Suddenly the phone rang. It was Ahmad Khan's office. Muscat had reported both reconnaissance planes back at base. They had been in the air over $3\frac{1}{2}$ hours and had covered virtually the whole of the Gulf from the Straits right down to Ras al Had, south-east of Muscat, and had also flown 300 miles into the Arabian Sea. Of all the tankers they had sighted only five or six had approximated to the size of the *Aurora B*, and none of those had answered to the description I had given. Also, most of the ships sighted had been contacted by radio and none had reported seeing anything resembling the *Aurora B*. All the ships sighted had been in the normal shipping lanes. They had seen nothing outside these lanes and the search had now been called off. The same negative report had been made by seaborne helicopters searching the Musandam Peninsula and the foothills of the Jebel al Harim. That search had also been called off.

He put the phone down and picked up his jacket. 'I am instructed to escort you to the airport and see that you leave on the next flight to the UK. Please, you will now get ready.'

'Any reason?'

He hesitated, then gave a little shrug. 'I don't think it matters that you know. Your allegations have been discussed in the highest quarters. They are regarded as very sensitive. Accordingly your Consul has been informed that you are persona non grata in this country. You understand?'

I nodded. I felt suddenly as though I had some contagious disease, everybody distancing themselves from me. But at least I was being allowed to leave.

'You come now please.' Ahmad Khan had his jacket slung over his shoulder and was standing waiting for me. I had nothing, only the shirt and trousers in which I had arrived. 'I'll need a sweater, something warm. It's winter in London.'

But all he said was, 'That is for your Consul. Come please.' Hussain was standing with the door open. We went back down the cement corridors, the room bearer following us a little forlornly. We left him at the lift muttering to himself. A driver was waiting for us at the reception desk, a big, serious-looking man with a black moustache and a sort of turban, who led us out to an official car. We went first to the Abdullah Haroon Road Bazaar, where I had passport photos taken, and after that we drove out on the Khayaban-i-Iobal road to the British Consulate, which was close to the Clifton seaside resort. I had been there once before. It was up a long drive through a well-tended estate and gardens.

I asked to see the Consul himself, but he, too, was distancing himself from the whole affair. He wasn't available and I had to be content with a grey-haired, harassed-looking Pakistani, who issued me with temporary papers and then, by raiding some emergency stores, produced a pair of patched grey flannel trousers and a blue seaman's jersey, socks and a pair of boots.

It was in this peculiar rig that thirteen hours later I arrived at Heathrow. Ahmad Khan had stayed with me until I was actually on the plane. In fact, he saw me to my seat, accompanied by the senior steward. It was a PIA aircraft full of emigrants going to join relatives in Britain, a bedlam of a journey with the toilets awash and one or two children who had never seen a flush lavatory before in their lives. I don't know what the chief steward was told about me, but he and the stewardess kept a very careful watch over me with the result that I had excellent service, my every want attended to immediately.

Brown had not seen fit to see me off and I had been refused permission to telephone. However, I was told he had been informed of my time of departure and flight number, and I presumed he would have passed this on to Saltley so that he would know my ETA at Heathrow. But there was nobody there to meet me and no message. I was delayed only a few moments at Immigration and then I was through and just one of the great flood of humanity that washes through Heathrow Airport. There is nothing more depressing than to be on your own in one of the terminals, all of London before you and nobody expecting you, no plans. The time was 08.27 and it was Sunday. Also it was blowing hard from the north-west and raining, the temperature only a little above freezing – a typical late January day. I changed my salt-stiffened franc notes and Emirate currency, got myself a coffee and sat over it, smoking a duty-free cigarette and thinking over all that had happened since I had left for Nantes ten days ago. No good ringing Forthright's, the office would be closed and I hadn't Saltley's home number.

In the end I took the tube to Stepney Green and just over an hour later I was back in the same basement room, lying on the bed, smoking a cigarette with the legs of passers-by parading across the top of the grime-streaked window. I was looking at the typescript of my book again. 'You left it here,' Mrs Steinway had said to me when she brought it down from her room at the back of the ground floor. 'The girl found it lying on the floor underneath the bed after you'd gone.' From flipping idly through the pages I began to read, then I became engrossed, all our life together and Balkaer, Cornwall, the birds – it all flooded back, the bare little basement room filled with the surge of the Atlantic breaking against the cliffs, the cry of sea-birds and Karen's voice. There was a strange peacefulness in the words I had written, a sense of being close to the basics of life. In this moment, in retrospect, it seemed like a dream existence and I was near to tears as the simplicity and richness of our lives was unfolded, so vividly that I could hardly believe the words were my own. And at times I found myself thinking of Choffel, those bare hills and the simplicity of his boyhood, Cornish cliffs and Welsh hills, the same thread and at the end the two of us coming together on that dhow.

Next day I phoned Forthright's, but Saltley's secretary said he would be at the Law Courts all morning. He was expecting me, however, and she said I could see him in the late afternoon, around four if that was convenient. I was back in the world of marine solicitors, insurance and missing tankers.

CHAPTER THREE

'**Yes, but** what's the motive?' I was sitting facing Saltley across his desk and when I told him I didn't know, he said it was a pity I hadn't stayed on board instead of jumping on to the dhow just because I was determined to destroy Choffel. 'If you'd stayed, then you'd have discovered their destination, and sooner or later you would have had an opportunity to get a message out by radio.'

'Unlikely,' I said.

He shrugged. 'There are always opportunities.' And when I pointed out that at least he now knew the tanker was still afloat, which was more than he could have expected when he employed me, he said, 'I appreciate that, Rodin, but I've only got your word for it.'

'You don't believe me?' My voice trembled on the verge of anger.

'Oh, I believe you. You couldn't have made it up, not all the people and the astonishing sight of a tanker against cliffs at the head of that inlet. But the ship isn't there any longer. To get a claim for millions of dollars set aside we've got to be able to prove the *Aurora B* is still afloat.'

'And my word isn't good enough?'

'Not in law. Now if Choffel were still alive . . .' He was leaning on his desk, his hands locked together on top of the thick file his secretary had left with him. 'Is there anything else he told you that's relevant? Anything at all? You were two days on that dhow together.'

'He was wounded and a lot of the time he was unconscious, or nearly so.'

'Yes, of course.' But then he began to take me through every exchange of words I had had with the man. I found it very difficult to recall his exact words, particularly when he had been rambling on about his boyhood and his life up there in the bare Welsh hills, and all the time those dark eyes staring at me unblinking. Finally Saltley asked me why I thought he had seized the dhow. 'Surely it wasn't just to get away from you?'

'I don't know.'

'Were you really going to kill him?'

'Possibly. I can't be sure, can I?'

'You said his daughter had told him, in that letter of hers, that you were going to kill him. Is that right?'

'Yes, that's what he said.'

He was silent for a long time, thinking. 'If I put you in court, as a witness, they'd dig that out of you right away. They'd say you were mentally unhinged at the time, that you weren't responsible for your actions, and that you now don't know what is true and what is the product of your imagination.'

'They'll know soon enough,' I told him angrily. 'In a few weeks from now the *Aurora B* will appear in some port or other and Sadeq will carry out his mission. They'll know then all right.'

He nodded. 'And Choffel gave no hint to you at any time what that mission might be?'

'No.'

'Or the destination?'

'I tell you, no.'

'Did you ask him?'

'About the destination?'

'Yes. Did you specifically ask him what it was?'

'I think so,' I murmured, staring at him and trying to remember, feeling as though I were already in the witness box and he was cross-examining me. 'I think it was during that first night at sea. We were through the Straits then and into the Oman Gulf and he'd somehow dragged himself up to the poop to tell me the engine needed oil. He started talking then, about the ships he'd been in, the *Stella Rosa* and the engineer whose name he'd taken. I asked him about the *Aurora B* and the other ship, and what they were going to do with the oil, where they were going to spill it. It had to be something like that and I thought it was probably a European port, so I asked him where. I remember I kept on asking him where and shaking him, trying to get it out of him.'

'And did you?'

'No, I was too rough with him. He was screaming

with pain, his mind confused. He said something about salvage, at least that's what I thought he said. It didn't make sense unless he was harking back to the first ship he destroyed, the *Lavandou*, which was supposed to have sunk in deep water but drifted on to a reef instead.'

'Salvage.' Saltley repeated the word, staring past me into space. 'No, I agree. It doesn't make sense. Do you think he knew what the destination was?'

But I couldn't answer that, and though he kept on at me, probing in that soft voice, the blue eyes fixed on mine in that disconcerting stare, it wasn't any good. 'Oh well,' he said finally, 'we'll just have to accept that he hadn't been told the ship's destination.' He relaxed then, that crooked mouth of his breaking into a smile that made him suddenly human. 'Sorry. I've been pressing you rather hard.' He took his hands from the file and opened it, but without looking down, his mind elsewhere. Finally he said almost briskly, 'If we accept your story as correct, then there are certain assumptions that can be made. First, the *Aurora B* is afloat with a full cargo of oil. Second, since the Omani air search has failed to sight her, she has sailed from the inlet where she has been hiding and is at sea somewhere in the Indian Ocean. The Pakistan airforce also flew a search. Did you know that?'

I shook my head and he tapped the file. 'A report came in yesterday. Search abandoned, no sighting. Now we come to the main assumption.' He hesitated. 'Not so much an assumption as a pure guess, I'm afraid. The *Aurora B*, you think, is headed for a European port, which means she will pass south of the Cape and head up the Atlantic coast of Africa. We will say, for the purpose of our assumptions, that the *Howdo Stranger* is well ahead of her – has, in fact, passed the Cape into the Atlantic. Is that your reading of the situation?'

'It could be anywhere,' I said guardedly. The man was a lawyer and I wasn't going to commit myself.

He smiled. 'The first hi-jack was bungled. That's your theory, isn't it? The evidence being the damaged radio room and the crew imprisoned in the chain locker. Incidentally, there's no report of that man who jumped overboard being found, so we'll have to presume that he's dead. They then hi-jacked a second tanker and the operation is successful. They now have two tankers. One is despatched on its mission. The other is to follow when it is crewed-up with what one might call Baldwick's mercenaries. And since the second one has now sailed it seems obvious that the plan is for a joint operation. That means a rendez-vous. You agree?'

I nodded. 'That's what I was trying to get out of Choffel.'

'You said it was the destination you were trying to get out of him – the target in other words.'

'That and where the two ships were going to meet.'

'And he said something about salvage.'

'I think that's what he said. But he was confused and in pain. I can't be certain. I was very tired.'

'Of course.' There was a moment's silence, then he said, 'That's it then. They'll meet up somewhere and then they'll act in concert, the two of them together.' He leaned back and stretched his arms, yawning to relieve the tension of the half hour he had spent taking me step-by-step through my story. 'We don't know where they'll meet. We don't know the target or what the motive is. And unless the ships are sighted, or alternatively that man is found alive on the Musandam Peninsula, there's absolutely nothing to substantiate your quite extraordinary story – and I use the word there in its original and exact meaning.' He took a slip of paper from the open file and handed it to me. 'That was posted in the Room at Lloyd's yesterday. *The Times* and the *Telegraph* both carried it this morning on their foreign news pages.'

The slip was a copy of a Reuters report from Muscat referring to rumours emanating from Pakistan that a Russian tanker was concealed on the Omani coast south of the Hormuz Straits. It stated that the airforce, having carried out a thorough search of the coast and of the Arabian Sea adjacent to Oman, had proved the rumours to be quite unfounded.

'And this came in this morning.' He handed me another Reuters message datelined Karachi. This referred to me by name as the source of the rumour – *a shipwrecked Englishman Trevor Rodin has been repatriated, his story of a tanker concealed in an inlet on the Omani side of the Gulf having been proved incorrect. It is considered possible that Rodin may have had political motives and that his story was intended to damage the friendly relations existing between Pakistan and Oman, and also other countries.*

'I think you may find yourself the focus of a certain amount of official attention,' he added as I handed it back to him. 'The whole area is very sensitive.'

Saltley's warning proved only too accurate. The following day, when I returned from buying some clothes after opening an account at the local bank and paying in the cheque he had given me, Mrs Steinway informed me the police had been asking for me. 'Haven't done anything wrong, have you, luv?' She was a real Eastender, and though she said it jokingly, her eyes watched me suspiciously. 'Cos if you have, you don't stay here, you understand?'

They had asked when I would be back, so I was not surprised to have a visit from a plain clothes officer. I think he was Special Branch. He was quite young, one of those shut-faced men who seem to rise quickly in certain branches of the Establishment. He wasn't interested in what I could tell him about the hidden tanker or about Choffel, it was the political implications that concerned him, his questions based on the assumption that the whole story was a concoction of lies invented to cause trouble. He asked me what my political affiliations were, whether I was a communist. He had checked with the Passport Office that I was the holder of a British passport, but was I a British resident? Was there anybody who knew me well enough to vouch for me? He was a little more relaxed after I had told him I owned a cottage on the cliffs near Land's End and that my wife had died in the *Petros Jupiter* explosion. He remembered that and he treated me more like a human being. But he was still suspicious, taking notes of names and addresses and finally leaving with the words, 'We'll check it all out and I've no doubt we'll want to have another talk with you when we've completed our enquiries. Meanwhile, you will please notify the police if you change your address or plan to leave the country, and that includes shipping as an officer on board a UK ship. Is that understood?' And he gave me the address of the local police station and the number to ring. 'Just so we know where to find you.'

It was dark by the time he left, a cold, frosty night. I put on the anorak I had bought that morning and walked as far as the river. I was feeling isolated and very alone, quite separated from all the people hurrying by. Lights on the far bank were reflected on a flood tide and the sky overhead was clear and full of stars. I tried to tell myself that an individual is always alone, that the companionship of others is only an illusion, making loneliness more bearable. But it's difficult to convince yourself of that when loneliness really bites. And what about my relationship with Karen? I leaned on the frosted stonework of an old wharf, staring at the dark flowing water and wishing to God there was somebody I could talk to, somebody who knew what it was like to be alone, totally alone.

I was very depressed that evening, staring at the river shivering with cold and watching the tide mark. And then, when I went back to pick up the typescript so that I would have something to read over a meal, Mrs Steinway came out of her back room with the evening paper in her hand. 'I just been reading about you. It is you, isn't it?' she asked, pointing to a paragraph headed: *Missing Tanker Man Returned to UK*. It was the Reuters story datelined Karachi. 'No wonder you've got the law keeping tabs on you. Is it true about the tanker?'

I laughed and told her I seemed to be about the only one who thought so.

'They don't believe you, eh?' The bold eyes were watching me avidly. 'Well, can't say I blame them. It's a funny sort of story.' She smiled, the eyes twinkling, the heavy jowls wobbling with delight as she said, 'Never mind, luv. Maybe there's one as will. There's a young woman asked to see you.'

'Me?' I stared at her thinking she was having a bit of fun. 'Who? When?'

'Didn't give her name. I didn't ask her, see. You'd been gone about ten minutes and she said it was urgent, so I told her she could wait in your room. 'Course she may be a newspaper girl. But she didn't look it. I've had them before, see, when there was that Eddie Stock here and they mistook him for the fellow that did the Barking shotgun hold-up . . .'

But by then I had turned and was hurrying down the basement stairs. It had to be her. There was nobody else, no girl at any rate, that could have found out where I was. Unless Saltley had sent his secretary with a message. I don't know whether the eagerness I felt stemmed from my desperate need of company or from a sexual urge I could hardly control as I jumped down the last few stairs and flung open the door of my room.

She looked up at my entrance, the jut of her jaw

just as determined, but the squarish, almost plain face lit by a smile. There were other parts of her that jutted, for she was wearing slacks and a very close-fitting jersey-knit sweater. A fleece-lined suède coat lay across the bed and she had the typescript of my book in her hands. She got up and stood facing me a little awkwardly. 'I hope you don't mind.' She held up the dog-eared typescript. 'I couldn't resist.' She was unsure of herself. 'Salt was very stuffy about it at first – the address, I mean. But I got it out of him in the end. Such an incredible, marvellous story. I just had to see you.' She had a sort of glow, her eyes alight with excitement.

'You believe it then?'

'Of course.' She said it without the slightest hesitation. 'Salty said nobody could possibly have invented it. But then of course,' she added, 'we want to believe it, anyway Daddy, Mother, me, Virgins Unlimited . . . I told you about the syndicate, didn't I? The rude name they call it. The other syndicates, too.' She was nervous, talking very fast. 'You don't mind, do you?' She put the typescript carefully down beside her coat. 'I read a couple of chapters, that's all, but I've learned so much – about you and what you want out of life. I'd like to take it with me. It's so moving.'

'You like it?' I didn't know what else to say, standing there, gazing at her and remembering that letter I'd received at Ras al Khaimah.

'Oh, yes. What I've read so far. If I could borrow it . . . there's a publisher, a friend of ours, lives at Thorpe-le-Soken . . .' Her voice trailed away. 'I'm sorry. I'm being bossy. Daddy says I'm always trying to run other people's lives for them. It's not true, of course, but I'm afraid I sometimes give that impression. Do sit down please.' She looked quickly round the room and I could almost see her nose wrinkling at the bare bleakness of it. 'Did you get a letter from me?' She said it in an offhand way, busying herself with picking up her coat and hanging it on the hook of the door. 'Perhaps the bed will be more comfortable. That chair's an arse-breaker, I can tell you.' She plumped herself down on the far side of the bed. 'Well, did you?' She was watching me intently, her eyes bright. 'Yes, I see you did. But you never replied.'

I hesitated, my blood beginning to throb at the invitation I thought I could see in her eyes. 'Yes, the dhow brought it to me.' I sat down on the bed beside her and touched her hand. 'And I did reply to it. But if you believe my account of what happened you'll realize the reply is still on board that tanker.'

Her fingers moved against mine. 'I only know what Salty told me. Daddy and I were at his office late this afternoon. He gave us an outline, but very brief. Daddy was there to decide what action should be taken as a result of your report.' She gripped my hand. 'When I insisted Salty give me your address, and Daddy knew I intended seeing you, he said to give you his warmest thanks for risking your neck and achieving – well, achieving the impossible. Those were his words. And Salty thought the same, though of course he didn't say so. What he said was that he'd only given you what had been agreed, but that if your information resulted in any of the GODCO claims being set aside, then there would be a proper recompense.'

'I had my own motives,' I muttered.

'Yes, I know that. But it's just incredible what you did, and all in little more than a week.'

'Luck,' I said. 'I was following Choffel.'

She nodded. 'Tell me what you said, would you please.'

'To Saltley?' I half shook my head, remembering that long cross-examination and not wanting to go over it all again. But then I thought it might help for her to know, so I started to tell her about Baldwick coming to see me at Balkaer. But that wasn't what she wanted. It was the letter. 'What did you say – in that letter I never received. Please tell me what you said.'

I shook my head. It was one thing to write it in a letter, another to say the same words to her face. I took my hand away and got up. 'I don't really remember,' I muttered. 'I was touched. Deeply touched. I said that. Also, that I was lonely – a little afraid, too – and your letter was a great comfort . . . to know that somebody, somewhere, is concerned about whether you live or die, that makes a great difference.'

She reached out and touched my hand. 'Thank you. I didn't know how you'd feel. It was so—' She hesitated, blushing slightly and half smiling to herself. 'After I posted it – I felt a bit of a fool, getting carried away like that. But I couldn't help it. That was the way I felt.'

'It was nice of you,' I said. 'It meant a great deal

to me at that moment.' And I bent down and kissed her then – on the forehead, a very chaste kiss.

'Go on,' she said, and giggled because she hadn't intended it as an invitation. 'You started telling me about the man who came to your cottage. I interrupted, but please . . . I want to know everything that happened after I left you that day at Lloyd's.' She patted the coverlet beside her. 'You went off the following day by air for Nantes . . .'

I took it up from there, and now she listened intently, almost hanging on my words, so that halfway through, when I was telling her about my eerie night walk the length of the tanker's deck, I suddenly couldn't help myself – I said, 'I warn you, if you stay and listen to the whole thing I may find it very difficult to let you go.'

'I could always scream the house down.' She was suddenly laughing and her eyes looked quite beautiful. But then she said quickly, 'Go on, do – how did you and Choffel land up alone on that dhow together?'

But at that moment footsteps sounded on the stairs. There was a knock at the door. 'Can I come in?' It was Saltley. He checked in the doorway, smiling at the two of us sitting on the bed, his quick gaze taking in the details of the room. 'So this is where you've holed up.'

'Why have you come?' I was on my feet now, resenting the intrusion.

He unbuttoned his overcoat and seated himself on the chair. 'Have the police been to see you?' And when I told him about the Special Branch visit, he said, 'That was inevitable, and I warned you.' He was staring at me, the smile gone now and his eyes cold. 'Are you sure you didn't shoot Choffel?'

'Why do you ask? I told you how it was.'

And Pamela, suddenly very tense, asked, 'What's happened?'

He turned to her and said, 'It was just after you left. A girl came to see me, a dark-haired, determined, very emotional sort of person. A secretary at some clinic in France, she said, and in her early twenties. She had flown in from Nantes this morning and had been given my name and the address of the office by the Lloyd's agent.'

I sat down on the bed again, conscious of his eyes on my face. 'Choffel's daughter.'

He nodded, and my heart sank, remembering her words as I had left for the airport. 'She claims you killed him. Says she'll go to the police and accuse you of murder. Did you kill him?'

'No. I told you—'

He waved aside my protest. 'But you intended to kill him, didn't you? That's why you went to Colchester to check what other names he used, why you went to Nantes, why you got the Lloyd's agent to take you to see his daughter. You were tracking him down with the intention of killing him. Isn't that true?'

I didn't say anything. There was no point in denying it.

'So the girl's right.'

'But I didn't kill him.'

He shrugged. 'What does that matter? He's dead.

You had the opportunity and the intention.' He leaned forward and gripped my arm. 'Just so that you see it from her point of view. I'd like you to get yourself lost for a time. Sooner or later the man's body will turn up. They'll find a bullet in his guts and you'll be arrested.' And he added, 'I don't want you charged with murder before those tankers materialize.'

'And when they do?' I asked.

'We'll see. If they do, then part of your story will be corroborated and they'll probably believe the rest of it, too. At least, it's what I would expect.' He asked me to continue then with the account I had been giving Pamela. 'There's one or two things towards the end I'd like to hear again.' His reason was fairly obvious; if I was lying, then it was almost inevitable I'd slip up somewhere, small variations creeping in with each telling.

The first thing he picked me up on was Choffel's reference to the *Lavandou* and what had followed. 'His mother was ill. That's what you said in my office. She was dying, and it was to get her the necessary treatment that he agreed to scuttle the ship. Did he tell you he was only a youngster at the time, twenty-two or twenty-three?'

'Yes,' I said. 'Twenty-two he told me.'

'That's what his daughter said. Twenty-two and the only ship he ever sank. Did he say that to you?'

'No, not in those words.'

'But he implied it?'

I nodded, the scene coming back to me, the sound of the sea and the stinking lazarette, and the dhow wallowing. 'Only once, he said, or something like that. He was talking about the *Lavandou*, how the operation had gone wrong and Lloyd's had twigged it. I remember that because it was an odd way of putting it.'

'You didn't tell me that. Why not?'

'Well, it's what you'd expect him to say, isn't it?'

'You said that before, when you were trying to shake the destination out of him.'

'Not the destination,' I corrected him. 'I'd been asking him that, yes. But when I was shaking him, and shouting *Where?* at him, it was where the two tankers were going to meet I was asking him.'

'And he didn't know.'

'I'm not sure he even understood. His mind was wandering, not quite delirious, but bloody near it. I think he was probably referring back to one of the ships he'd wrecked. It might even have been the *Petros Jupiter.* There was a Dutch salvage outfit trying to get her off the Kettle's Bottom before he'd even come ashore.'

'And where do you think those tankers are going to meet up?'

'You asked me that before. I don't know.'

'Have you thought about it?'

'Not really. I've had other things—'

'Well, I have. So's Michael.' He turned to Pamela. 'We discussed it for quite a while after you'd left. We even got the charts sent up. If the destination is Europe—' He turned back to me. 'That's what you think, isn't it – that the target is somewhere in Europe?

If it is, then it's over twelve thousand miles from the Hormuz Straits to the Western Approaches of the English Channel. That's about forty days slow steaming or just over twenty-eight at full speed; and they could meet up at countless points along the west coast of Africa.' And he added, 'The only alternative would be the Cape, but I am not aware the Iranians have ever shown any interest in Black Africa. So I agree with you, if there is a target, then it's somewhere in Europe where several countries hold Iranian prisoners, the Germans and ourselves certainly.'

We discussed it for a while, then he left, taking Pamela with him. He had his car outside, and when he said he had arranged to meet her father for a drink at their club, she immediately got her coat. 'Can I take this?' She had picked up the typescript and was holding it gripped under her arm.

I nodded dumbly, standing there, watching, as the lawyer helped her on with her coat. 'I'm glad you didn't kill the man,' he said, looking at me over his shoulder and smiling. 'His daughter was quite positive the *Lavandou* was the only ship he wrecked.'

'She was bound to say that,' I told him angrily.

He nodded. 'Nevertheless, I found her very convincing. She said he had paid dearly for that one criminal action.'

That phrase of his struck a chord, and after they had left, when I was standing at the window, staring up at the street and thinking about the way she had accepted his offer of a lift, as though coming to see me had been just an interlude and her own world so much more congenial than this bare little room and the company of a man who might at any moment be charged with murder, it came back to me. Choffel had used almost identical words – *God knows I've paid*, he had said, and he'd repeated the word *paid*, spitting blood. Had he really become so desperate he'd taken jobs he knew were dubious and then, when a ship was sunk, had found himself picked on, a scapegoat though he'd had no part in the actual scuttling? Could any man be that stupid, or desperate, or plain unlucky? The *Olympic Ore*, the *Stella Rosa*, the *Petros Jupiter* – that was three I knew about, as well as the *Lavandou*, and he'd used three different names. It seemed incredible, and yet . . . why lie to me so urgently when he must have known he was dying?

I thought about that a lot as I sat alone over my evening meal in a crowded Chinese restaurant. Also about his daughter, how angry she had been, calling him an innocent man and spitting in my face because I didn't believe her. If she could more or less convince a cold-blooded solicitor like Saltley . . .

But my mind shied away from that, remembering the *Petros Jupiter* and that night in the fog when my whole world had gone up in flames. And suddenly I knew where I would lie up while waiting for those tankers to re-emerge. If they wanted to arrest me, that's where they'd have to do it, with the evidence of what he'd done there before their eyes.

I didn't tell the police. I didn't tell anyone. I left just as dawn was breaking, having paid my bill the night before, and was at Paddington in time to catch the inter-city express to Penzance. And when I arrived at Balkaer, there it was just as I had left it, the furniture and everything still in place, and no board up to say it was for sale. It was dark then and cold, hardly any wind and the sea in the cove below only a gentle murmur. I got the fire going, and after hanging the bedclothes round it to air, I walked back up to the Kerrisons' and had a meal with them. They had met me at Penzance and Jean had seemed so pleased to see me I could have wept.

That night I slept on the sofa in front of the fire, unwilling to face the damp cold of the empty bedroom upstairs. The glow of the peat was warm and friendly, and though memories crowded in – even the sofa on which I lay conjured a picture of Karen, her dark eyes bright with excitement as it was knocked down to us for next to nothing at the tail end of a farmhouse sale – they no longer depressed me. Balkaer still felt like home and I was glad I had come, glad I hadn't put it up for sale immediately, the key still with the Kerrisons.

There was no wind that night, the air very still and the wash of the sea in the cove below muted to a whisper. The place was snug and warm and homely, my mind at peace now. Choffel was dead. That chapter of my life was closed; it was the future that mattered now.

But in the morning, when I walked up to the headland and stood staring out across the quiet sea at the Longships light and the creaming wash of the Atlantic swell breaking on the inshore rocks, the wretched man's words came back to me – *you can't escape, can you, from either yourself or the past.* I knew then that the chapter of my life that had started out there in the fog that night was not closed, would never be closed.

This was the thought that stayed with me as I tramped the clifftop paths alone or went fishing off Sennen in Andy's boat. The weather was good for late January, cold with little wind and clear pale skies. It was on the fourth day, when I was fishing out beyond the Tribbens, that I felt Choffel's presence most. The swell was heavier then and the boat rocking; I suppose it was that which conjured up the memory of that dhow and what had happened. And his words . . . I found myself going over and over those rambling outbursts of his, the face pale under the stubble, the black curly hair, and the stench, the dark eyes staring. It all came back to me, everything he had said, and I began to wonder, And wondering, I began to think of his daughter – in England now and hating my guts for something I hadn't done.

The line tugged at my hand, but I didn't move, for I was suddenly facing the fact that if I were innocent of what she firmly believed I had done, then perhaps he was innocent, too. And I sat there, the boat rocking gently and the fish tugging at the line, as I stared out across the half-tide rocks south of the Tribbens to the surf swirling around the Kettle's Bottom and the single mast that was all that was left above water of the *Petros Jupiter. I've paid and paid.* And now the girl was accusing me of a murder I hadn't committed.

I pulled in the line, quickly, hand-over-hand. It was a crab of all things, a spider crab. I shook it loose and started the engine, threading my way back through the rocks to the jetty. It was lunchtime, the village deserted. I parked the boat and took the cliff path to Land's End, walking fast, hoping exertion would kill my doubts and calm my mind.

But it didn't. The doubts remained. In the late afternoon a bank of fog moved in from seaward. I just made it back to Sennen before it engulfed the coast. Everything was then so like that night Karen had blown herself up that I stood for a while staring seaward, the Seven Stones' diaphone bleating faintly and the double bang from the Longships loud enough to wake the dead. The wind was sou'westerly and I was suddenly imagining those two tankers thundering up the Atlantic to burst through the rolling bank of mist, and only myself to stop them – myself alone, just as Karen had been alone.

'Think about it,' Saltley had said. 'If we knew where they were meeting up . . .' And he had left it at that, taking the girl's arm and walking her down the street to where he had parked his low-slung Porsche.

And standing there, down by the lifeboat station, thinking about it, it was as though Karen were whispering to me out of the fog – *find them, find them, you must find them*. It was a distant foghorn, and there was another answering it. I needed an atlas, charts, the run of the pilot books for the coasts of Africa, dividers to work out distances and dates. Slow-steaming at eleven knots, that was 264 nautical miles a day. Forty days, Saltley had said, to Ushant and the English Channel. But the *Aurora B* would be steaming at full speed, say 400 a day, that would be thirty days, and she had left her hidey-hole by the Hormuz Straits nine days ago. Another twenty-one to go... I had turned automatically towards Andy's cottage above the lifeboat station, something nagging at my mind, but I didn't know what, conscious only that I had lost the better part of a week, and the distant foghorn drumming at my ears with its mournful sense of urgency.

It was Rose who answered the door. Andy wasn't there and they didn't have a world atlas. But she gave me a cup of tea and after leaving me for a while returned with the *Digest World Atlas* borrowed from a retired lighthouse keeper a few doors away, a man, she said, who had never been outside of British waters but liked to visualize where all the ships passing him had come from. I opened it first at the geo-physical maps of Africa. There were two of them right at the end of Section One, and on both coasts there were vast blanks between the names of ports and coastal towns. The east coast I knew. The seas were big in the monsoons, the currents tricky, and there was a lot of shipping. The Seychelles and Mauritius were too populated, too full of package tours, and the islands closer to Madagascar, like Aldabra and the Comores Archipelago, too likely to be overflown, the whole area liable to naval surveillance.

In any case, I thought the rendezvous would have been planned much nearer to the target, and if that were Europe then it must be somewhere on the west coast. I turned then to the main maps, which were on a larger scale of 197 miles to the inch, staring idly at the offshore colouring, where the green of the open Atlantic shaded to white as the continental shelf tilted upwards to the coastal shallows. I was beginning to feel sleepy, for we were in the kitchen with the top of the old-fashioned range red-hot, the atmosphere overwhelming after the cold and the fog outside. Rose poured me another cup of tea from the pot brewing on the hob. Tristan da Cunha, St Helena, Ascension – those were all too far away. But on the next page, the one for North and West Africa, there was Hierro, Gomera, Palma, all out-islands of the Canaries and on the direct route. The Selvagens, too, and the Desertas, and Porto Santo off Madeira. Of these, only the Selvagens, perhaps the Desertas, could be regarded as possibles, the others being too well populated.

The tea was strong and very sweet, and I sat there wrapped in the cosy warmth of that hot little kitchen, my head nodding as my mind groped for something I knew was there but could not find. Andy came back and I stayed on and had a meal with them. By the time I left, the fog had cleared and it was very close to freezing, the stars bright as diamonds overhead and the flash of the Longships and other lights further away, the glimmer of ships rounding Land's End, all seemingly magnified in the startling clarity.

Next morning I went up to the main road at first light and hitched a ride in a builder's van going to Penzance. From there I got the train to Falmouth. I needed charts now and a look at the Admiralty pilots for Africa, my mind still groping for that elusive thought that lurked somewhere in my subconscious, logic suggesting that it was more probably a rendez-vous well offshore, some fixed position clear of all shipping lanes.

The first vessel I tried when I got to the harbour was a general cargo ship, but she was on a regular run to the Maritimes, Halifax mainly, and had no use for African charts. The mate indicated a yacht berthed alongside one of the tugs at the inner end of the break-water. 'Round-the-worlder,' he said. 'Came in last night from the Cape Verdes. He'll have charts for that part of the African coast.' And he went back to the job I used to do, checking the cargo coming out of the hold.

The yacht was the *Ocean Brigand*. She flew a burgee with a black Maltese cross with a yellow crown on a white background and a red fly. Her ensign was blue and she had the letters RCC below her name on the stern. She was wood, her brightwork worn by salt and sun so that in places bare wood showed through the varnish, and her decks were a litter of ropes and sails and oilskins drying in the cold wind. The skipper, who was also the owner, was small and grey-haired with a smile that crinkled the wind-lines at the corners of his eyes. He had charts for most of the world, the pilots, too. 'A bit out of date, some of them,' he said. 'But they cost a fortune now.'

He sat me down at the chart table with a Bacardi and lime and left me to find what I wanted. 'Still some clearing up to do.' He smiled wearily. 'We had it a bit rugged off Finisterre and the Bay was mostly between seven and nine. Silly time of year really to return to England, but my wife hasn't been too good. Packed her off to hospital this morning.'

I had never been on a real ocean-going yacht before, the chart table so small, tucked in on the starb'd side opposite the galley, yet everything I'd ever needed in the way of navigation was there – except radar. He hadn't got radar, or Decca nav. And there was no gyro compass. But everything else, including VHF and single-sideband radio.

I went through all his charts that showed any part of Africa and in the end I was no better off than I had been with the lighthouse keeper's atlas. It had to be the last stretch, even as far north as the Bay of Biscay, but more likely somewhere in the neighbourhood of those Spanish and Portuguese islands off the coast of Spanish Sahara and Morocco. And of these the Desertas and the Selvagens, being without water and therefore more or less deserted, seemed most likely. But even then, with the pilot book open in front of me, I didn't see it. Like the chart, it referred to both groups of islands by their Portuguese names. There was no indication that there might be an anglicized version of the name Selvagen.

A pair of sea boots appeared in the companionway to my right and the owner leaned his head down, peering over my shoulder. 'Ah, I see you're reading up on the Madeira–Canaries passage, but I doubt whether your friends would have put into either the Desertas or the Selvagens. No water, no safe anchorage and both of them bloody inhospitable groups of islands by all accounts. Never been there myself, but our vice-commodore now, he went to the Selvagens I seem to remember – 1980, I think . . .' He went past me into the saloon, putting on a pair of half-spectacles and peering along a battened-in shelf of books. 'Here we are.' He handed me a carefully plastic-wrapped copy of the *Royal Cruising Club Journal*. 'There's a glimpse of what he calls the Salvage Islands. A little more descriptive than the Pilot.'

It was a short piece, barely two pages, but it was the title that caught and held my attention – *A Look at the Salvage Islands*. 'We sailed two days ago from Funchal . . .' Averaging probably no more than 100 miles a day, that was in line with the Pilot which gave the distance from the southern-most of the Desertas to Selvagem Grande as 135 miles. The names were the same, too, except for the *m* where it was singular – Selvagem Grande and Selvagem Pequena and, so that there should be no doubt whatsoever, he had written, 'I had always hoped to visit the Salvage (Salvagen) Islands.' He must have got the English name from somewhere and my guess was the Navy – at some time in the distant past British sailors had anglicized it and called them the Salvage Islands, just as they had called Ile d'Ouessant off the Brittany coast of France Ushant. And looking at the Atlantic Ocean Chart 2127 I saw that there the group were named the Salvagen Is – an *a* instead of an *e*.

Was that what Choffel had meant when he talked of salvage? Was it the Salvagen Islands he had been referring to?

There was Selvagem Grande and Selvagem Pequena, and an even smaller one called Fora. And I remembered that a mate I had served under had once described them to me as we were steaming between Gibraltar and Freetown – 'Spooky,' he had said of the smaller Selvagem. 'The most godforsaken spooky bit of a volcanic island I ever saw.' And reading the *Journal*, here was this yachtsman's daughter using almost the same words – 'Spooksville,' she had called it, and there had been the wrecked hulk of a supertanker hung on the rocks, her father claiming he had never seen a more dreadful place.

'They were on their way to the Caribbean,' the owner said. 'Just two of them on the leg south from Madeira to the Canaries.' He gave me another drink, chatting to me for a while. Then a doctor arrived and I left him to the sad business of finding out what was wrong with his wife. There had been just the two of them and it was the finish of their second circumnavigation.

I phoned Forthright's from the station, making it a personal call on reverse charges. Fortunately Saltley was in, but when I told him about the Salvage Islands, he said he and Stewart had already considered that possibility and had read the piece in the *RCC Journal*. In fact, they had chartered a small plane out of Madeira to make a recce of the islands and he had received the pilot's report that morning. The only tanker anywhere near the islands was the wreck stranded on the rocks of Selvagem Pequena. 'Pity you've no date for the rendezvous. It means somebody keeping watch out there.' He checked that I was at Balkaer and said he'd be in touch when he'd spoken to Michael Stewart again.

It was almost dark when I got back to the cottage and there was a note pinned to the door. It was in Jean's handwriting. Saltley had phoned and it was urgent. I trudged back up the hill and she handed me the message without a word. I was to take the next ferry out of Plymouth for Roscoff in Brittany and then make my way to Gibraltar via Tangier. 'At Gibraltar he says you can hide up on a yacht called *Prospero* which you'll find berthed in the marina.' And Jean added, 'It's important, Trevor.' Her hand was on my arm, her face, staring up at me, very serious. 'Jimmy will drive you there tonight.'

'What's happened,' I asked. 'What else did he say?'

'He didn't want you to take any chances. That's what he said. It's just possible there'll be a warrant issued for your arrest. And it was on the radio at lunchtime.'

'On the radio?' I stared at her.

'Yes, an interview with Guinevere Choffel. She gave the whole story, all the ships her father had sailed in, including the *Petros Jupiter* – but differently to what you told us. She made him out a poor, unfortunate man trying to earn a living at sea and always being taken advantage of. Then, right at the end, she accused you of murdering him. She gave your name and then said she'd be going to the police right after the pro-gramme. It was an extraordinary statement to come over the radio. They cut her off then, of course. But the interview was live, so nothing they could do about it.'

I was in their sitting-room, leaning against the door, and I reached into my pocket for a cigarette. I felt suddenly as though the world of black and white had been turned upside down, Choffel declared innocent and myself the villain now. I offered her the packet and she shook her head. 'Vengeance,' she said, a look of sadness that made her gipsy features suddenly older. 'That's Old Testament stuff.'

'I didn't kill him.' The match flared, the flame trembling slightly as I lit my cigarette.

'It was in your mind.'

She didn't need to remind me. I half closed my eyes, inhaling the stale duty-free nicotine, thinking of Choffel. She didn't have to start lecturing me, not now when I was being hounded out of the country. I wondered how he had felt, making up stories nobody believed. And then to seize that dhow just because I was on board the tanker, confronting him with his guilt. Did that make me responsible for the bullet in his guts?

'Would you like me to try and see her?'

'What the hell good would that do?'

She shrugged, shaking her head. 'I don't know.' There were tears in her eyes. 'I just thought it might be worth a try. If I could get her to come down here. If she saw where the *Petros Jupiter* had been wrecked, what a threat it had been to all our lives – if I told her, woman-to-woman, the sort of person Karen was, what she had done and why... Perhaps she'd understand then. Don't you think she would?' Her voice faltered and she turned away. 'I'll go and see what Jimmy's up to,' she said. 'You phone Plymouth and find out when the ferry leaves.'

In fact, there wasn't one until noon next day so I had a last night at Balkaer and took the early train from Penzance. I felt very lost after saying goodbye to the Kerrisons, feeling I would never see them again, or Balkaer, and that I was now a sort of pariah condemned like Choffel to roam the world under any name but my own, always looking over my shoulder, half afraid of my own shadow. Even when I had boarded the ferry, my temporary papers given no more than a cursory glance, I positioned myself at the rail so that I could see everyone who boarded the ship, until at last the gangway was pulled clear and we sailed.

It was the same when I got to France. There was no trouble on landing, yet I still glanced nervously over my shoulder at the sound of footsteps, watchful and suspicious of anybody going in the same direction as myself. It was all in my imagination, of course, and a psychiatrist would probably have said I was developing a persecution mania, but it was real enough to me at the time, that sense of being watched. And so was the stupidity of it, the sheer craziness of it all. It was like a nightmare what was happening. A man wrecks a ship, your wife kills herself trying to burn up the oil spill he's caused and you go after him – and from that simple, natural act, the whole thing blows up in your face, the man dead and his daughter accusing you of killing him. And nobody to prove you innocent.

Just as there had been nobody to prove him innocent. That thought was in my mind, too.

How quickly you can be brainwashed, by changing circumstances or by the behaviour of other human beings. How strangely vulnerable is the human mind when locked in on itself, alone with nobody to act as a sounding box, nobody to say you're right – right in thinking he'd sunk those ships, right to believe he was the cause of Karen's death, right to believe in retribution.

Alone, the nagging doubt remained. An eye for an eye? The Old Testament, Jean had said, and even she hadn't thought I was right, insisting that I do what Saltley said. The best friends a man could hope for and they had not only helped me run away, but had insisted I had no alternative. A lawyer, the media, two such good friends – and I hadn't killed him. The stupid little bitch had got it wrong, leaping to conclusions. I could have thrown her father overboard. I could have taken him back to the tanker. Instead, I had cleaned him up, given him water . . . I was going over and over it in my mind all the way to Tangier, and still that sense of unreality. I couldn't believe it, and at the same time that feeling of being watched, expecting some anonymous individual representing Interpol or some other Establishment organization to pick me up at any moment.

I reached Tangier and nobody stopped me. There was a levanter blowing through the Straits and it was rough crossing over to the Rock, Arabs and Gibraltar-ians all being sick amongst a heaped-up mass of baggage. Nobody bothered about me. There was no policeman waiting for me on the jetty at Gibraltar. I got a water taxi and went round to the marina, the top of the Rock shrouded in mist and a drizzle of rain starting to fall.

Prospero, when I found her, was about fifty feet long, broad-beamed with a broad stern and a sharp bow. She looked like a huge plastic and chrome dart with a metal mast against which the halyards flapped unceasingly in the wind, adding to the jingling metallic symphony of sound that rattled across the marina. Terylene ropes lay in tangled confusion, the cockpit floorboards up, the wheel linkage in pieces. A man in blue shorts and a blue sweater was working on what looked like a self-steering gear. He turned at my hail and came aft. 'You're Trevor Rodin, are you?' He had broad open features with a wide smile. 'I had a telex this morning to expect you. I'm Mark Stewart, Pamela's brother.'

He didn't need to tell me that. They were very alike. He took me below into the wood-trimmed saloon and poured me a drink. 'Boat's a bit of a mess at the moment, but with luck we'll get away by the end of the week.' They had originally been planning to make Malta in time for the Middle Sea Race, but his father hadn't been able to get away and Saltley, who usually navigated for them, was tied up on a case he felt he couldn't leave. 'So we're still here,' he said. 'Lucky really.' And he added, 'Pamela and the old

Salt will be here tomorrow. There's Toni Bartello, a Gibraltarian pal of mine, you and me. That's the lot. Anyway, going south we shouldn't get anything much above seven or eight, so it should be all right. Pam's not so good on the foredeck – not so good as a man, I mean – but she's bloody good on the helm, and she'll stay there just about for ever, no matter what's coming aboard.'

'Where are we going?' I asked.

'Didn't Salt brief you?'

I shook my head. No point in telling him I'd been offered the boat as a hide-out for a fortnight or so until somebody somewhere sighted those tankers.

He took me over to the chart table and from the top drawer produced Chart No. 4104, Lisbon to Freetown. He spread it out. 'There. That's where we're going.' He reached over, putting the tip of his forefinger on the Selvagen Islands.

We finished our drink then and he took me on a tour of the ship. But I didn't take much of it in. I was thinking of the Selvagens, the bleakness of that description I'd read, wondering what it would be like hanging round the islands in the depth of winter waiting for two tankers which might never appear.

PART SIX

THE BLACK TIDE

CHAPTER ONE

Gibraltar was a strange interlude, quite unreal in a sense, the Rock towering above us and most of those in the marina in holiday clothes and a holiday mood. The sun shone and it was quite warm by day, except in the wind which blew hard from the east. There was a lot to do, for the boat had been stripped of everything to get at the hydraulics, which ran the length of the hull and had sprung a leak, and there were stores to get, water and fuel to load. Each day I listened to the BBC news on the radio above the chart table, half expecting to hear my name and hoping to God I wouldn't.

I had asked Saltley, of course, as soon as he'd arrived on board. But as far as he knew no warrant had been issued for my arrest. 'I'm not at all sure the Choffel business comes within their jurisdiction.' We were down in the bare saloon then, his bags opened on the table as he changed into work clothes of jeans and T-shirt. Pamela was changing up for'ard and Mark had taken the taxi back into town. 'It's probably a question of where the killing took place.'

'He was shot on the dhow.'

'Yes, yes.' I think he was a little tired after his flight, his voice impatient. 'That's Arab territory. But the dhow was tied up alongside the tanker, and if it could be proved that the *Aurora B* was still a British ship, then they would have jurisdiction, the killing having occurred on British territory.' He zipped up his trousers and reached for the drink I had poured him. 'Personally I don't think she's a hope in hell of getting you arrested. So just relax and concentrate on the job in hand, which is finding that bloody tanker.'

'But if you thought that, why did you tell Jean Kerrison to get me on the next ferry to France?'

He looked at me over his drink, the lop-sided face and the china blue eyes suddenly looking a little crafty. 'I wasn't taking any chances, that's all. I wanted you here.' He raised his glass, smiling. 'Here's luck – to us both.' And he added, 'I'm not a criminal lawyer, but I do know something about the law as it applies inter-nationally. For that girl to have you arrested, she's either got to prove you killed her father on British territory or get whatever country it happened in – the Oman, say – to order your arrest, and since this yacht is British territory it then depends on whether we have an extradition treaty with the Oman.'

'But when she went to the police . . . Jean Kerrison heard a programme on the radio, an interview with her, which ended with her saying she was going straight to the police and a warrant would be issued for my arrest on a charge of murder. Did she go to the police?'

He shrugged. 'I've no idea.'

'But presuming she did, what would happen next? What action would the police take?'

'I think it would depend on the evidence she produced. I imagine it's pretty thin but, if she did convince them, then her statement would be sent on to the office of the Director of Public Prosecutions with whatever comments the police felt were warranted, together with the results of any enquiries they may have instituted. It would be up to the Public Prosecutor then.'

'And what happens when they discover I've fled the country?' I was remembering the Special Branch man's instructions to notify the nearest police station of any change of address. They would almost certainly trace me to Balkaer and question the Kerrisons. I was angry with him then, feeling he was using me. Fleeing the country was the most damning thing I could have done.

'They may notify Interpol,' he said. 'But by the time they've traced you to Gibraltar we'll almost certainly be at sea. Forget about it,' he added. 'If we find that tanker waiting for us out there by the Selvagens, then that part of your story will be confirmed. Once they believe that, they'll believe the rest.'

I had to accept that, since it was my only hope, but I should have stayed. I should have faced her accusations, reiterating the truth of what had happened. Instead, I had run away at the instigation of this ruthless bastard who was only interested in finding the missing tankers and saving his friend's skin. If I'd had any guts I'd have walked off the boat then and there and taken then next plane back to London. But I didn't. I stayed on board and each day I listened to the BBC news, waiting, always waiting to hear my name mentioned.

We sailed for the Selvagens on Saturday, February 6. It was just six days since the Kerrisons had driven me into Penzance to catch the Brittany ferry, seventeen days since the *Aurora B* had left her bolt-hole in the Musandam Peninsula. 'She'll be about halfway,' Saltley said. 'Just rounding the Cape probably.' We were standing at the chart table, the boat heeled over as we ploughed our way through the Straits, thrashing to windward with the bows slamming and sheets of spray hitting the mains'l with a noise like gunshot. 'That is, if she's steaming at full speed. Pity we've lost that levanter.' He smiled at me, looking more like a gnome than ever in his bulky oilskins. 'Hope you're a good sailor. It could be a hard beat.'

Only the previous day the wind had gone round to the south-west and now it was blowing force 5 to 6, a dead-noser, for it was south-west we needed to go. 'I had reckoned on reaching the islands in less than six days, which would make it Day Twenty-two of the *Aurora B*'s voyage. But if it's going to go on blowing from the south-west we'll be increasing our miles through the water considerably. It could make a difference of two or three days.'

We had the Rock and the African shore in sight all through the daylight hours. It was wind against current most of the time, with steep breaking waves and a movement more violent than I had ever previously experienced. It was impossible to stand without holding on to one of the hand grips all the time and in the cockpit we were all of us wearing our safety harnesses clipped to securing wires.

It was towards dusk, when the wind had eased slightly, that I took my first trick at the helm under Pamela's supervision, the others having got their heads down in preparation for the long hours of darkness when they would be standing lone watches. It was only then, with my hands gripping the wheel, that I began to appreciate the extraordinary power of an ocean-racer. Until then I had only seen them at a distance, but now, feeling that wind-driven power under my hands and vibrant throughout the ship, I experienced a feeling of intense excitement, a sense of overwhelming exhilaration as though I were a god riding the sea on a white-winged Pegasus. And when Pamela clapped me on the shoulder and said, 'You'll do, mate,' I felt a wave of pleasure as though I were a kid and had passed some sort of a test. She got up then, bracing herself with a hand on the bar-taut mainsheet. 'You're on your own now. I need a pee and there's the evening meal to get.'

She left me to my own devices then, so that for almost two hours the ship was mine, and as we powered to windward I found myself revelling in the extra thrust that came from slight adjustments of the wheel, the way I could slide her over the worst of the waves, and once in a while Pamela, keeping an eye on me from the galley, gave me a little smile of approval. With no make-up on, a dirty old woollen cap pulled down over her head and yellow oilskins she looked more like a ship's boy than the owner's daughter, and how she could cook with the boat pitching and slamming I couldn't imagine. When Toni Bartello finally relieved me and I went below I found I had no interest in food and had to get my head down or be sick.

The seasickness didn't last, but the sou'wester did. The wind seemed fixed in that quarter, staying there for almost a week, sometimes light, sometimes blowing a near-gale, and always we were beating.

It was a strange life, the five of us cooped up together, at such close quarters, and in some respects in such rugged conditions, that it was almost the equivalent of serving as a seaman in the Navy two centuries ago. Most of my working life had been spent at sea so that it was difficult for me to understand at first why anyone would do it for pleasure, particularly a girl. So little space and no privacy, the violence of the movement – and yet it worked, our lives ruled by the sea and the wind, and little time or energy to think who it was had left the bunk warm for me when I came below tired after a sail change or a long spell at the wheel with the salt of the wind-driven spray crusted on my face.

The sun shone most of the daylight hours and when the wind dropped and we had the engine on, all of us up in the cockpit with a drink in our hands, then it was different. We were relaxed, talking uninhibitedly about our lives, or speculating what we would find when the Selvagens appeared over the horizon. Would we find the *Howdo Stranger* sitting there, waiting? And if so, what would she be called now, what false name would they have painted on her bows and stern? We had a lot of fun inventing names for her, and for the *Aurora B*, laughing uproariously at simple jokes, like twinning them and calling them *Castor* and *Bollocks*. We laughed a lot at silly ordinary things, ate enormously and drank well. It was, in fact, a singularly happy ship, made more so I think by the presence of a girl who was a good cook, a good sailor and good company. There were times when I found it difficult to take my eyes off her, for it was getting warmer all the time and, ghosting along in light airs after Saltley had decided we needed to save our fuel, she was wearing very little at the midday pour-out.

We were drinking wine, not spirits, but it was strong Spanish stuff and I suppose my interest in her showed. It was on the eighth day, when the wind had at last gone round to the north-west, where it should have been all the time. I had the middle watch and when I took over from Mark he brewed us mugs of cocoa and joined me in the cockpit. 'Lovely night,' he said, staring up at the stars. He was silent for a long time after that, so I knew he had something on his mind. At last he came out with it. 'Look, Trevor – hope you don't mind, but I think I'd better tell you.' He paused there, not looking at me, his face in silhouette against the light of the compass. 'About Pam,' he went on awkwardly, burying his face in his mug and speaking very quietly. 'I know she admires you, thinks you're quite a guy, in fact. And you're not exactly – well, disinterested. I don't mind myself, your eyeing her I mean. But if I've noticed it, then Salt will have, too, and he is . . . well, in love with her, I suppose. It's generally recognized – in the family, I mean – that she'll marry him in the end. You see, he's been after her ever since she left finishing school – oh, before that . . . since ever almost – hanging round her like a bee round a honeypot.' He finished his cocoa and got up very abruptly. 'You don't mind my mentioning it, I hope, but if you could just keep your mind concentrated on the job in hand . . .'

He dived down the companionway then, leaving me alone at the wheel. The boy was embarrassed and I knew why. Saltley might be an older man with a lopsided face, but he'd been to the right schools, belonged to the right clubs. He had the right background, and above all, he was the man their father turned to when there was underwriting trouble. Also, and perhaps this rankled more than anything, they knew my own family background.

I didn't sleep much that night and in the morning Saltley asked me to take a noon sight myself and work out our position. It made me think he had put Mark up to it. But we were under spinnaker now, sailing on a broad reach at just over six knots, and with only another day to go before we raised the Selvagens it was obviously sensible to make use of my professional capabilities and get a check on his last fix.

I took the sights, and when I had finally got a

position, there was only a mile or two in it, Selvagem Grande bearing 234°, distant 83 miles. It was now twenty-six days since the *Aurora B* had sailed. Only two or three more days to go. It depended how much of a lift the strong Agulhas current had given her, what speed she was making. She could be a little faster than we reckoned, or slower. It was just conceivable the rendezvous had already taken place. But Saltley didn't think so. 'Things always take a little longer than people reckon.' But he was convinced the first tanker would be in position at least two days ahead of schedule, just in case, 'That means we could find the tanker already there. I don't think it will be, but it's just possible.' He gave me that lop-sided smile. 'We'll know tomorrow.' And he added. 'Wind's falling light. We may have to run the engine later.'

It was only now, as we neared our objective, that we began to face up to the fact that if we were right, then we were the only people who could alert the countries bordering the English Channel and the southern North Sea to the possibility of a major marine disaster. In putting it like that I am being a little unfair to Saltley. The thought would have been constantly in his mind, as it was in mine. But we hadn't talked about it. We hadn't brought it out into the open as something that could make the difference between life and death to a lot of people, perhaps destroy whole areas of vital marine habitat.

And that evening, sitting in the cockpit drinking our wine with the last of the sun's warmth slipping down to the horizon, I began to realize how far from the reality of this voyage the three younger members of the crew were. Pam and Mark, they both knew it could affect them financially, but at their age that was something they took in their stride. Sailing off like this to some unknown islands had been fun, a sort of treasure hunt, a game of hide-and-seek, something you did for kicks, and adventure. I had to spell it out to them. Even then I think they saw it in terms of something remote, like death and destruction on the television screen. Only when I described the scene in the *khawr* as the dhow slid away from the tanker, with Sadeq standing at the top of the gangway, a machine pistol at his hip spraying bullets down on to us, only then, when I told them about Choffel and the stinking wound in his guts, and how bloody vulnerable we could be out there alone by the Selvagens facing two big tankers that were in the hands of a bunch of terrorists, did they begin to think of it as a dangerous exercise that could end all our lives.

That night it was very quiet. We had changed from spinnaker to a light-weight genoa at dusk and the boat was ghosting along at about four knots in a flat calm sea. I handed over to Mark at midnight and my bunk was like a cradle rocking gently to the long Atlantic swell. I woke sometime in the small hours, a sliver of a moon appearing and disappearing in the doghouse windows, the murmur of voices from the cockpit.

I was in the starb'd pilot berth, everything very quiet and something about the acoustics of the hull made their voices carry into the saloon. I didn't mean to listen, but then I heard my name mentioned and

Mark saying, 'I hope to God he's right.' And Pam's voice answered him. 'What are you suggesting?'

'He could be lying,' the boy said.

'Trevor isn't a liar.'

'Look, suppose he did kill that French engineer . . .'

'He didn't. I know he didn't.'

'You don't know anything of the sort. And keep your voice down.'

'He can't hear us, not in the saloon. And even if he did kill the man, that doesn't mean he's wrong about the tankers.'

Her brother made an angry snorting sound. 'You've had the flags out for him ever since the old Salt sent him off in search of the *Aurora B*.'

'I think he's got a lot of guts, that's all. Getting himself on board that tanker, then getting away on the dhow with the man he was looking for. It's quite incredible.'

'Exactly. Salt thinks it's so incredible it must be true. He says nobody could have made it all up. The next thing is every word he's uttered is gospel, so that here we are, out in the Atlantic, everything hung on that one word *salvage*. And I'm not just thinking of the money. I'm thinking of Mum and Dad, and what's going to happen to them.'

'We've all of us got stop-loss reinsurance,' she said. 'Mine is for fifty thousand excess of thirty. Daddy's is a lot more I know. It probably won't save us, but it'll help.'

'I told you, I'm not thinking of the money.'

'What then?'

'If Trevor's lying . . . All right, Pam, let's say he's told us the truth, say it's all gospel truth, but we've got it wrong about where they're going to meet up and there's no tanker waiting at the Selvagens, how do we ever prove that the vessels we insured aren't lying at the bottom of the sea? We've got to show that they're afloat and in the hands of Gulf terrorists, otherwise that cleverly worded war zone exemption clause doesn't operate.'

'The tanker will be there. I'm sure it will.' There was a long pause, then she said, 'It's Daddy you're worried about, isn't it?' He didn't answer and after a while she said, 'You're thinking of suicide, is that it? D'you think he might – do you think he really might?'

'My God!' His voice sounded shocked. 'The way you put it into words. *You're thinking of suicide* – just like that, and your voice so bloody matter-of-fact.'

'You've been skating around it.' Her tone was sharp and pitched high. 'You know you have, ever since you brought up the question of what we'll find when we get to the island. If Trevor's wrong and our tanker doesn't turn up, if nothing happens to prove that the two of them are still afloat, then the money we lose – that's everything, the house, this boat, all Mother's jewellery, her clothes even – it will be nothing to the damage Daddy will suffer . . . all his friends, his whole world. At his age he can't start again. He'd never be able to at Lloyd's anyway. You can't make a come-back when everybody knows you cost your Names just about every penny they possess. Do you think I don't know this? I've been living with it for the last month or more, knowing that for him it'd be the end of the world. I don't think he'd want to go on living after that. But whether he'd go as far as to take his own life . . .'

'I'm sorry, Pam. I didn't realize.'

She seemed to ignore that, for she went on almost as though he hadn't spoken: 'And don't start hitting out at Trevor without stopping to think what it's like to see your wife burn herself up in an attempt to save some seagulls. Or at me either. I may have hung out some flags as you put it, but what have you done, or Salty, any of us? He found the tanker and though he wasn't doing it for us—' There was a crash and I heard her say, 'Bugger! That's my hat gone overboard.' There was a stamp of feet on deck, the sound of sails flapping. A few minutes later the girl's figure slipped past me as she went to her quarters up for'ard.

I woke to the smell of bacon frying, the sun already burning up the dawn clouds. A haze developed as the morning wore on, the sun very hot and Pamela dressed in shorts with a loose-tailed shirt reading a book on the foredeck in the shadow of the spinnaker. It wasn't until after lunch that we began to detect a smudge like a tiny cloud growing on the horizon. It was straight over the bows and couldn't be anything else but Selvagem Grande. It grew steadily in size, and though our eyes were constantly searching, there was no satellite smudge that could represent the tanker.

By 15.00 we could see the island quite clearly and had altered course to pass to the north of it. It was a sort of Table Mountain in miniature, the highest point

597 feet according to the Admiralty pilot, and cliffs rising sheer to 400 feet. These cliffs formed an unbroken line, heavily undercut and edged white by the breaking swell, their flat tops arid and desolate with a cap of black basalt sitting on the red sandstone like chocolate on a layer cake. No trees anywhere, no sign of vegetation, just the two layers of rock with a new light structure perched like a white pimple on the summit of one of the basalt *picos*.

The wind was backing into the north and for a time we were busy handling the spinnaker and setting a working genoa. It was blowing force 3 or 4 by the time we got everything stowed and by then we were close off the northern end of the island with no sign of any other vessel. There was still a chance that the tanker was hidden from us by the southern part of the island, but our hopes faded as we rounded Punto do Risco and began to run down the western side. There were plenty of shearwaters, which is the main reason the Portuguese government declared the island a nature reserve, but otherwise the place looked totally lifeless. There were some shacks by the landing place on the south-western side and a roped pathway climbed steeply to the lighthouse, but apart from that, the only sign of any human presence was the mass of Communist slogans painted on the rocks. This ugly display of giant graffiti had presumably been put there by fishermen who had been ardent supporters of the revolution.

Off the landing place we turned back on to our original course, heading for Selvagem Pequena ten miles away. This is quite a different sort of island, being little more than an above-water reef, but with the wind increasing we could soon make out the white of waves breaking on the horizon. By sunset the remains of the wrecked tanker were visible and we could see right across the island to where waves were breaking on the smaller reef island of Fora a mile or so to the west. From Fora a chain of above-water rocks six to twelve feet high extended several miles to the north. This was the Restinga do Ilheu de Fora, but there was no tanker waiting there, and with visibility now vastly improved, we could see there wasn't even a fishing vessel anywhere within a radius of a dozen miles of us. We were the only vessel afloat in the neighbourhood of the Selvagen Archipelago.

Once this had sunk in we felt suddenly very lonely. The islands had an atmosphere of their own. If there was any place at sea that could be described as unfriendly I felt this was it and I found myself remembering that word *spooky*. It was a strange word to use about a group of islands, but now that I was among them I knew it described their atmosphere exactly. They were spooky and I wondered how long Saltley would be willing to hang around them waiting for a tanker that might never turn up.

I voiced my misgivings that evening, not in front of the others, but to Saltley alone. We had had an excellent meal hove-to on the starb'd tack four miles to the east of Selvagem Pequena, the light on the main island just visible over the bows. I took him up on deck on some pretext or other and told him bluntly that I'd no real confidence in the conclusion we had reached. 'I'm not even sure Choffel used the word salvage. It sounded like it, that's all. If you remember, I made that quite clear.'

He nodded. 'Understood. But Mike and I didn't come to the same conclusion solely on the basis of what you had told me. We worked it out for ourselves. Unless they were going to operate independently, they'd want to rendezvous as near the target as possible.'

'It doesn't have to be an island,' I said. 'There's all the mainland coast, or better still a fixed position out at sea.'

He shook his head. 'The mainland would be too risky, but we did give a lot of thought to a sight-fixed rendezvous. It's what you or I would choose. But we're navigators. Terrorists tend to be urban creatures. They wouldn't trust a rendezvous that was arrived at by using a sextant and tables stuffed with figures. They'd want a fixed point they could see.' We were in the bows then and he had his hands in his pockets, balancing himself easily to the plunging movement of the ship. 'You picked on the Selvagens, so did we, and the more we thought about it, the more ideal they appeared. And now I've seen them—' He turned his head to port, staring westward to where the sound of the seas pounding Selvagem Pequena came to us as a continuous deep murmur. 'No ship's captain wants to tangle with that lot. They give this group a wide berth, and the silly idiot who ran his vessel on to the rocks there only goes to make the point that it's a bloody dangerous place.' He turned then, walking slowly back towards the empty cockpit lit by the faint glow of the lights below. 'Don't worry about it,' he said. 'Our friend will turn up. I'm sure of it.'

'Maybe,' I said. 'But probably not tomorrow or the next day or the next – just how long are you prepared to hang around here?'

'For three weeks if necessary,' he said. And when I asked him if we'd got enough food on board, he answered curtly, 'If we have to stay that long, it's water, not food, will be the problem.'

I thought it might be the humans, too, for the prospect of hanging around these godforsaken islands for three weeks appalled me. But, as his words indicated, we were committed now and no point in leaving until we were absolutely sure this wasn't the meeting place.

That night it came on to blow. Even though we were hove-to there was a lot of movement and the noise of the wind in the rigging and waves breaking made it difficult to sleep. Saltley seemed to be up and about most of the night checking our position against the light on Selvagem Grande and some time in the early hours, at the change of the watch I think, the ship was put about with a great crashing of gear and slatting of sails, feet pounding on the deck and somebody shouting to run her off as the jib sheet was caught up on the winch. All this I heard as in a dream, clinging to my bunk, not wishing to be roused from the half-sleep in which I lay. A cold wind came down through the open hatch and when, after running for some minutes, they turned about again, bows into the wind and hove-to, I distinctly heard Mark call out, 'The light's gone.' And a moment later – 'It's raining. I can't see a bloody thing.' As I fell back into slumber again, I was thinking of the red painted slogans on the rocks and the waves breaking over the Pequena and Fora reefs, hoping to God Saltley knew his stuff as an inshore navigator.

The next thing I knew the first grey light of a dismal dawn was filtering into the saloon. Toni Bartello was shaking me violently. 'We're reefing. Get up please.' And as I stirred he yelled in my ear – 'Oilskins and seaboots. There's a lot of water in the cockpit and it's raining like hell.'

It was a foul morning, the wind near gale force and poor visibility. I have seen plenty of rough seas, but it's one thing to observe them from high up in the closed-in comfort of a big ship's wheelhouse, quite another to face steep breaking waves virtually from sea level. Saltley told me to take the wheel while the rest of them, all except Pamela who was still fast asleep, reefed the main and then changed down to storm jib, and all the time the crash of seas bursting against the hull, spray flying across the deck and everything banging and slatting as the boat bucked and rolled and the wind came in blustering gusts.

'Where are the islands?' I yelled to Saltley as he half fell into the cockpit. We were hove-to again and nothing visible except a bleak circle of storm-tossed water and grey scudding clouds.

'Over there,' he yelled, putting on his harness and making a vague gesture towards the porthand shrouds.

All that day we only saw them once, but that once was enough to scare us badly, for we suddenly saw heavy breaking seas quite close on the starb'd bow and as we put about, I caught a glimpse of that wrecked tanker's superstructure, a dim ghost of a shape seen through a blur of rain and spray. After that Saltley took no chances and we ran south for a good hour before turning and heaving-to again.

Later the rain eased and the wind dropped, but we had been badly frightened and even when there were no more clouds and the stars paling to the brightness of the young moon, we still kept to two-man watches. Dawn broke with high peaks aflame in the east as the sun rose firing the edges of old storm clouds. No sign of the islands, no ship of any sort in sight, the sea gently heaving and empty to the horizon in every direction.

Fortunately we were able to get sun sights and fix our position. We were some twenty miles east southeast of Selvagem Pequena. We had already shaken out the reefs and now we set the light-weight genoa. The contrast was unbelievable, the ship slipping fast through the water, the sea almost flat calm and the decks dry, not a drop of spray coming aboard.

Saltley took the opportunity to check his camera. It was a good one with several lenses, including a 300 mm. telephoto lens. He also took from his brief-case some official GODCO pictures of both the *Howdo Stranger* and the *Aurora B*. He asked us to study them carefully so that if our tankers turned up, however brief the sighting, we'd still be able to identify them. Later he put them in the top drawer of the chart table so that if we needed to check any detail they'd be ready to hand.

It was the middle of the afternoon before we raised Selvagem Grande. We sailed all round it and then down to Pequena and Fora. No tanker, nothing, the wind falling very light, the sea almost a flat calm with ripples that caught the slanting sun in reflected dazzles of blinding light. It was quite hot and towards dusk a haze developed. This thickened during the evening till it was more a sea fog, so that we had another worrying night with no sign of the light on Selvagem Grande and no stars and the moon no more than a ghostly glimmer of opaque light.

In the end we turned eastward, sailing for three hours on a course of 90°, going about and sailing a reciprocal three hours on 270°. We did that twice during the course of the night and when dawn came there was still the same thick clammy mist and nothing visible.

We were making towards Selvagem Grande then and by the time breakfast was over and everything washed up and stowed, the sun was beginning to burn up the mist and just visible as a golden disc hung in a golden glow. Water dripped in rainbow drops from the gold-painted metal of the main boom and the only sound on deck was the tinkling gurgle of water slipping past the hull.

Shortly after 10.00 I handed the wheel over to

Pamela. Saltley was dozing in his bunk, which was the starb'd quarter berth aft of the chart table, and Toni and Mark were up in the bows servicing the snap-shackle end of the masthead spinnaker hoist which was showing signs of chafe. I paid a visit to the heads, had a shave and then began checking Saltley's DR position. I was just measuring off the distance run on each course during the night when Pamela called down to ask me how far off the island was supposed to be.

'According to the dead reckoning at ten o'clock approximately nine miles,' I said. 'Why – can you see it?'

'I think so.'

'Speed through the water?' I asked.

She checked the electric log and reported 4.7 knots. We had covered perhaps 2½ miles since the last log entry. 'I've lost it now,' she called down. 'The mist comes and goes.'

I dived up into the cockpit then, for if she really had seen the island it must be a lot closer than Saltley's dead reckoning indicated. The sun's pale disc was barely visible, the mist iridescent and so full of light it hurt the eyes. Visibility was little more than a mile. She pointed away to port. 'The bearing was about two-thirty.'

'The island should be on the starb'd bow,' I told her.

'I know.' She nodded, staring into the mist, her eyes narrowed, all her hair, including her eyebrows, sparkling with moisture. 'I just caught a glimpse of it, very pale and quite sheer.' But in a mist it is so easy to imagine you can see what you are expecting to see. 'I'm sure it was those sandstone cliffs.'

I stayed with her, conscious of her proximity, the female scent of her, finding the bluntness of her hands on the wheel, the intentness of her square determined face somehow attractive. She was such a very capable girl, so unemotional, quite the opposite of Karen. There had been an early morning watch when everybody was still asleep and she had joined me in the cockpit, sitting so close that every time the boat rolled I could feel the pressure of her body against mine. I had touched her then and she had let me, till without saying a word, but smiling quietly to herself, she had gone below to get breakfast. But that was two days ago, when we were hove-to in the gale.

'There!' She pointed and I saw the mist had thinned. Something glimmered on the edge of visibility. The boat lifted on a swell and I lost it behind the port shrouds. 'Gone again,' she breathed. It was as though we were sailing along the edge of a cloud, a lost world, all blinding white, sea and air merged together and fleeting glimpses of blue overhead. Then I saw it myself, like a pale cliff rising out of the opaque miasma which was the horizon.

Her brown hands shifted on the wheel, the boat turning to put that pale glimmer of a cliff close on the port bow, our sight of it unobstructed by the sails. I was standing now, my eyes narrowed against the sunglare, the mist coming and going and nothing visible any longer but a glimmering void. 'What do you think?' she asked. 'I'm steering two-forty. Shall I hold on that or get back to two-seventy?'

I hesitated. Had we really seen the cliffs of Selvagem Grande, or had it been a trick of the mist in the confusing glow of the sun's hidden light? I brushed the moisture from my eyelashes, watching for the horizon to appear again. 'I'll hold on then,' she said. 'I'm certain it was the cliffs.'

I nodded, imagining I saw something again. But when I shifted my gaze I could see the same vague shape on the edge of visibility wherever I looked. A trick of the light. I closed my eyes, resting them against the glare, and when I opened them I could see a horizon emerging and there, over the bows, was that cliff, shining palely in that opaque world of mist and sun. 'Something there,' I murmured, reaching for the binoculars, and she nodded, standing herself now and steering with her bare foot on the wheel, her hair hanging loose and all bright with moisture like an autumn web. Swirls of mist and a little breeze cat's-pawing the surface of the sea. The binoculars were useless, making the mist worse. Then the veil was drawn back, drifting astern of us, and suddenly we were in hazy sunshine, with the horizon hardening to a line and those cliffs emerging again and sprouting a funnel.

No doubt about it now, it was a ship hull-down ahead of us. I shouted to Saltley, my voice echoing Pamela's, and the others came tumbling up on deck. The breeze was picking up and we were moving through the water at a good five knots. Nobody spoke, all of us staring intently, willing it to be the ship we were looking for. The minutes passed slowly, the hull gradually lifting above the horizon until at last we knew it was a tanker. What is more, she was hove-to; either that or she was anchored, for the bearing didn't change.

The time was 11.17. The date February 19. Day thirty since the *Aurora B* had sailed. Saltley turned to Pamela. 'I think I'd like you sunbathing on the fore-deck. A bikini if you would, Pam, and a towel so that you can wave as we go close under their stern. I'll be down below taking pictures through the hatch.'

Mark took the helm and Saltley briefed him very precisely. What he wanted was clear photographic evidence of the name and port of registry painted on the tanker's stern. We would then sail up the vessel's port side and he would take shots of the name on the bows.

By the time Pamela came on deck again, stripped almost to the bare flesh and bronzed like a young Amazon, the mist was a dirty smudge astern of us, the sun shining out of a clear blue sky. There was more wind now, the boat close-hauled and slipping fast through the water, the air getting warmer. The tanker was lying with her bows pointing north. She was about three miles away, and beyond her, to the north-west, we could just see the black basalt tops of Selvagem Grande lifting above the horizon.

Through the glasses it was already possible to see that the superstructure, which had looked almost white glimmering at us through the mist, was in fact painted emerald green, the funnel white with a bright red band and two golden stars. The hull was black and as soon as all the details of the vessel were clearly visible Saltley was checking them against the photographs laid out on the cockpit seats. It was difficult to be sure about her tonnage, but everything else matched, except the colour. The *Howdo Stranger* had been painted in the GODCO colours of blue hull with a blue funnel above a sand-yellow superstructure.

There was little doubt in my mind, or in Saltley's. Every little detail of the deck layout matched, and as we closed with her, making to pass close under her stern, I knew she was about the same tonnage. 'Don't forget,' Saltley said to Mark as he dived below. 'Get right under her stern, then gybe.'

We came down on her very fast, the black hull growing, until it towered above us, massive as an iron breakwater. High up on the bridge wing there was a little knot of men watching us. I counted seven, a motley group with only one of them in any sort of uniform. Pamela was lying stretched out on the foredeck. Two men in overalls appeared on the upper deck just below the lifeboat, one of them pointing as Pamela sat up and turned her head. Then she got languidly to her feet. They waved and we waved back, the group on the bridge watching us. I saw the flash of binoculars and then we lost them as we passed under the massive steel wall of her stern. And there close above us was the name, *Shah Mohammed – Basra* picked out in white and startlingly clear against the black of the hull.

A man leaning over the stern rail was joined by others, all of them waving. The yacht yawed, swinging round. 'Duck!' Saltley shouted. The boom came over with a crash, the sail slatting, everything in a tangle, and down below Saltley crouching out of sight, the camera with its telescopic lens directed at the ship's name, the shutter clicking. Even with the naked eye we could see the second O of the original name just showing as a faint raised shadow in the gap between *Shah* and *Mohammed*.

Everything was very quiet, no sound of engines as we sorted out the deck, coming round on to the port tack and sailing up the side of the tanker. In repainting the hull they appeared to have used only one coat, for here and there glimpses of the old blue showed through the black, and when we reached the bows, there it was again, the shadow of the O just visible in the middle of *Shah Mohammed*, which was again painted white so that it stood out with great clarity.

Saltley passed up an aerosol foghorn and Mark gave three blasts as we sheered away, back on to our original course. The tanker remained silent, the same little knot of watchers now transferred to the port bridge wing. Through the glasses I could see one of them gesticulating. Then, when we were almost a mile away, the *Shah Mohammed* suddenly emitted two deep long-drawn-out belches from its siren as though expressing relief at our departure.

The question now was, did we head for the nearest port with the evidence we had or wait for the *Aurora B* to show up? I wanted to get away now. I hadn't liked the look of the little group on the bridge wing. All the original crew must be locked up in her somewhere and the sooner she was arrested the more chance there was that they'd be got out alive. But Saltley was adamant that we must wait. 'Who do you suppose is going to arrest her?'

'Surely the Navy—'

'In international waters? Didn't you see the flag she was flying, the colours they'd painted her in? Black, white and green, with red and two stars on the hoist, those are the Iraqi colours. I think *Lloyd's List* will show the *Shah Mohammed* to be properly registered as an Iraqi vessel. They're sure to have made it legal, to that extent, and if they have, then the Navy couldn't possibly act without government authority, and you can just imagine the British government authorizing the seizure of a ship belonging to Iraq. It could upset the Arab world, spark off a major international row.'

I thought his twisted legal mind was splitting straws. 'And if we wait,' I said, 'until we have evidence of the two ships meeting – what difference will that make?'

He shrugged. 'Not a lot, I admit. But two ships meeting at a lonely group of islands does suggest a purpose. At least it's something I can argue.'

'But you've got the proof already,' Mark insisted. 'That's the *Howdo Stranger* out there. No doubt of it. Repainted. Renamed. But it's still the same ship, the one Dad insured and the owners claim has disappeared. It's there. And you've got photographs to prove it.'

'Given time and a court of law.' Saltley nodded. 'Yes, I think we probably could prove it. But I've got to persuade top-level civil servants at the Foreign Office to advise the Secretary of State he's justified in authorizing what amounts to a flagrant breach of international law. I've got to convince them there's no risk to them or to the country, that what they find on board will prove absolutely the hostile and deadly nature of the operation.' He was standing in the hatch and he leaned forward, his hands on the teak decking. 'If you can tell me what that operation is . . .' He paused, his eyes staring at me, very blue under the dark peaked cap. 'But you don't know, do you? You don't know what it's all about and you never thought to question Choffel about it.' His eyes shifted to the stationary tanker. 'So we wait for the *Aurora B*. Agreed?' He stared at us for a moment, then, when nobody answered him, he turned abruptly and went down into the saloon.

A moment later he was back with glasses and a bottle of gin, a conciliatory gesture, for I don't think he liked it any more than I did. We drank in moody silence, none of us doubting now that the *Aurora B* would appear in due course, but all wondering how long it would be before we were released from our lonely vigil.

The rest of the day proved fine and bright. We lay hove-to off the western coast of Selvagem Grande till nightfall, then shifted our station two miles to the north with the light bearing 145°. There was no sign of the tanker. I was certain she was still there, lying hove-to without lights. Saltley was certain, too, but when the moon rose and still no sign of her, he had the sail hoisted and we back-tracked towards the position where we had originally found her.

I didn't like it and I said so. I was certain our metal mast would show up as a clear blip on their radar screen. After a while we turned south-west towards Selvagem Pequena, reducing sail until we were moving at little more than three knots. We heard the swell breaking on the rocks before we could see the island, and then suddenly there was our tanker lying just to the south of Fora.

We turned then, heading north, back towards Selvagem Grande. 'I think she's seen us.' Mark was watching through the glasses. 'She's under way and heading towards us.'

We hoisted the genoa again and seemed to hold our own for a while, then she came up on us very fast, steaming at full ahead and pushing a mountain of water ahead of her broad deep-laden bows. We altered course to starb'd as though making for the landing place on Selvagem Grande. The tanker also altered course, so that the bows were less than a cable's length away as she steamed up abreast of us. A searchlight stabbed the night from high up on her superstructure, flooding the water round us until it picked up the white of our sails and fixed on us, blindingly, as the long black hull went thumping past. The stink of diesel fumes enveloped us seconds before we were picked up by the massive bow wave and flung sideways into the suck and break of such a massive bulk being driven through the water at about fifteen knots.

For a moment all hell seemed to break loose. Toni

Bartello was flung against me so that I ended up half-bent over one of the sheet winches with a sharp pain in the lower part of my rib cage. Pamela was on her knees clinging to the guardrail and down below the crash of crockery and other loose objects flying about the saloon was almost as loud as the slatting of sails and boom. And all the time the searchlight remained fixed on us.

Then suddenly we were out of the wash, everything preternaturally quiet. Blackness closed over us as the searchlight went out. It took a little while for my eyes to become accustomed to the darkness. Somebody said, 'She had her nav lights on.' I could see the broad back of her now, the stern light showing white and the Iraqi flag picked out by the steaming light on her after-mast. Moonlight gradually revealed the surface of the sea. Was this her final departure? Had the *Aurora B* arrived in the darkness? We searched the horizon, but no sign of another tanker, and shortly after 03.00 we lost sight of the *Shah Mohammed* behind the dark outline of Selvagem Grande.

When dawn broke the sea was empty and no vessel in sight.

We were north of the island ourselves then, all of us very tired and arguing wearily about what we should do. In the end, we turned downwind with the intention of checking that the tanker hadn't returned to her old position south of Fora. Shortly after noon I heard Toni Bartello wake Saltley to tell him he had sighted the smaller islands and a tanker lying to the south of them.

We were all up then, putting about and changing sail so that we lay hove-to with the tanker just in sight like a sheer rock on the edge of visibility. We kept it in sight all afternoon, lying drowsily on deck, stripped to the waist and warm in the sun.

Towards evening the wind began to back, the air thickening till we could no longer see the tanker. A small boat came out from under the lee of Pequena, its bows lifted and moving fast. It was an inflatable with three men in it. We could hear the sound of its outboard clear and strident above the growing rumble of the reef surf as it made straight towards us. Only when it was a few yards off did the man at the wheel cut the engine and swing it broadside to us. One of the three stood up, clasping the top of the windshield to steady himself. 'Who is Captain here?' His face was narrow with a high-bridged nose and a little black moustache, and his accent was similar to Sadeq's.

Saltley stepped into the cockpit, leaning forward and gripping hold of the guardrail. 'I'm the captain,' he said. 'Who are you?'

'What you do here please?' the man enquired.

'Are you Portuguese?'

The man hesitated, then shook his head.

'You're from that tanker?'

'Yes.'

'The *Shah Mohammed*?'

Again the hesitation. 'I ask you what you do here?' he repeated. 'Why you wait in these islands?'

'We're waiting for another yacht to join us. And you – why are you waiting here?'

'How long before the yacht arrive?'

'A day, two days – I don't know.'

'And when it arrive, where you go then?'

'The Cape Verde Islands, then across the Atlantic to the Caribbean. Are you the captain of the *Shah Mohammed*?'

'No.'

'Well, tell your captain he came too close last night. I shall, of course, make a report. You tell him.'

'Please? I don't understand.' But obviously he did, for he said something to the man at the wheel and the engine burst into raucous life.

'What are you waiting here for?' Saltley yelled to him.

The man waved a hand to the driver and the engine quietened to a murmur. 'We wait here for instructions. We have new owners. They have re-sold our cargo so we wait to know where we go.' He leaned his weight on the inflated side of the boat. 'You in Selvagen Islands before this?' And when Saltley shook his head, the man added, 'Very bad place for small ships, Portoogese fishermen no good. Understand? They come aboard in the night, kill people and throw them to the sharks. Okay?'

'Do you mean they're pirates?' Saltley smiled at him. 'You understand the word piracy?'

The man nodded. 'Yes, pirates. That is right. These very perilous islands. You go now. Meet friends at Cape Verde. Okay?' Without waiting for a reply he tapped the driver on the shoulder. The motor roared, the bows lifted and they did a skid turn, heading back towards Pequena.

'What did he mean by pirates?'

Saltley looked round at Mark. 'A warning probably. Depends whether I satisfied him we were going transatlantic.'

That night, just in case, we had two of us on watch all the time. The wind continued to back until it was sou'westerly with a thin cloud layer. Towards dawn the clouds thickened and it began to drizzle. Visibility was down to little more than a mile and no sign of the tanker. After feeling our way cautiously south and west for nearly two hours we suddenly saw broken water creaming round the base of a single rock. This proved to be Ilheus do Norte, the northernmost of the chain of rocks running up from Fora. We turned due south, picked up Selvagem Pequena, skirting the island to the east in thickening visibility.

We wasted more than two hours searching to the south'ard before turning north-east and heading for Selvagem Grande. We were running then in heavy rain and we were tired, so that when we did sight the vague outline of a ship on our starb'd quarter it took us a little time to realize it wasn't the *Shah Mohammed*. It was coming up on us quite slowly and at an oblique angle, its shape lost for a moment in a downpour, then reappearing, closer and much clearer. Its hull was black, the superstructure a pale green and the white funnel had a red band and two stars; the same colours as the *Shah Mohammed*, but there was a difference in the layout, the stern deck longer, the davits further aft and the derricks were a different shape. I recognized her then. 'It's the *Aurora B*.' I said, and Saltley nodded, standing in the hatch with the GODCO photographs in his hand.

She was called the *Ghazan Khan* now, the name painted white on the bow and standing out very clearly against the black of the hull. She passed us quite close, steaming at about eight knots, the grating platform at the top of the lifted gangway plainly visible, the memory of Sadeq standing there firing down at us suddenly vivid in my mind. We altered course to cross her wake and again the name *Ghazan Khan* was painted on her stern and the port of registry was Basra.

Day Thirty-two and the time 14.47. 'Well, that's that,' Saltley said. 'All we need now is a picture of the two of them together.'

We got this just over an hour later, the two tankers lying within a cable's length of each other a mile or so to the east of Selvagem Grande. We went in close enough for Saltley's telescopic lens to record the white-painted names on the two fat sterns, then veered off to take shots of the two of them in profile. We didn't go in close, for the *Ghazan Khan* had her gangway down and the *Shah Mohammed*'s high speed inflatable was alongside. They could, of course, be going over the plans for their operation, but it did occur to me they might also be considering what to do about us. We went about and headed south-east for Tenerife, sailing close-hauled into a confused and lumpy sea.

The wind was still backing and as darkness fell Saltley made a near-fatal decision, ordering Pam to take the wheel and put her about, while the rest of us eased the sheets and got her going at her maximum speed downwind. It was certainly much more comfortable, and though the island of Madeira was further than the Canaries, if the wind continued to back and held in the south all next day it would be a lot quicker, and he needed to get to a telephone as soon as possible.

The course took us to the west of Selvagem Grande and as we picked up the faint glimmer of the light through a mist of rain, I wished Stewart had fitted his yacht with radar. Presuming the tankers had now left for their final destination, I would like to have known what course they were steering. Saltley joined me at the chart table and we discussed it for a while, all the various possibilities, while the aroma of onions assailed us from the galley as Pamela fried up a corned beef hash.

I had the first watch, taking over from Mark as soon as I had finished my evening meal. The course was just west of north, the rain dying away to intermittent showers and the wind almost dead aft so that we were running goose-winged with the main to port and the genoa boomed out to starb'd. Alone at the wheel I was suddenly very conscious of the fact that I was the odd man out. The other four were all part of the yacht, part of the owner's life, moving in a world entirely different from mine. Through the hatch I could see them sitting over their coffee and glasses of Spanish brandy, talking excitedly. And well they might, for they had the proof they needed.

But what about me? What had I got out of the

voyage? I was back to the uncertainty of that wild accusation, to fear of arrest, perhaps trial and conviction. All very well for Saltley to say that, once the tankers had reappeared, the nature of their operation known, then confirmation of the statements I had made would include acceptance of my version of what had happened to Choffel. But there was no certainty of it and already I was feeling that sense of withdrawal from the others that is inevitable when an individual knows he is destined to take a different path. Brooding over it, sitting at the helm of that swaying, rolling yacht with the wind at my back and the waves hissing past, everything black, except for that lit saloon and Pamela, with her arms bare to the elbows and the polo-necked sweater tight across her breasts, talking animatedly – I felt like an outcast. I felt as though I were already consigned to oblivion, a non-person whom the others couldn't see.

Ridiculous, of course! Just a part of that accident of birth that had plagued me all my life, drawn to the Middle East yet not a part of it, neither a Christian nor a Moslem, just a lone, lost individual with no real roots. I was thinking of Karen then, my one real lifeline – apart from my poor mother. If only Karen were alive still. If only none of it had happened and we were still together, at Balkaer. In the darkness I could see the fire and her sitting in that old chair, the picture superimposed on and obliterating the lit saloon below. But her face . . . I couldn't see her face, the features blurred and indistinct, memory fading.

And it was then, with my mind far away, that I

heard a sound above the hiss of the waves and the surge of the bows, a low murmur like an approaching squall.

The sound came from astern and I looked over my shoulder. There was a lot of wind in the sails and it was raining again, but the sound coming to me on a sudden gust was a deep pulsing murmur. A ship's engines. I yelled to Saltley and the others. 'On deck!' I yelled, for in a sudden panic of intuition I knew what it meant. 'For your lives!' And as they came tumbling up I saw it in the darkness, a shadow coming up astern of us, and I reached forward, pressing the self-starter and slamming the engine into gear. And as I yelled to them to get the boom off the genoa, I felt the first lift of the mass of water being driven towards us.

Everything happened in a rush then. Saltley seized the wheel, and as the boom came off the genoa, he did something I would never have done – he put the yacht about, screaming at me to tag on the genoa sheet. Mark and Toni were back in the cockpit, the winch squealing as the big foresail was sheeted home, the yacht heeling right over and gathering speed as she powered to windward, riding on the tanker's bow wave, spray flying in solid sheets as the black hull thundered past our stern, smothering us with the surge of her passage. We were driving down the side of the tanker's hull then, back-winded and trying to claw our way clear, the tip of our mast almost touching the black plates as we yawed. And then we were into the wake, everything in sudden appalling turmoil, the boat swamped with water. It swept clean across us.

Somebody slammed the hatch, trying to close the dog-house doors as he was flung into the guardrails with a cry of pain. I grabbed him, then lost him as I was swept aft, my feet half over the stern before I could seize hold of anything.

I was like that for a moment and then we were clear, Saltley still gripping the wheel like a drowned limpet, the rest of us distributed all over the cockpit area. 'Did you see a light?' Mark shouted in my ears. 'Somebody flashing a light – up by the stern. I swear it was.' His hair was plastered to his skull, his face dripping water. 'Looked like Morse. A lot of flashes, then daa-daa ... That's M isn't it?' Pamela's voice called up from below that there was a foot of water in the saloon. 'Or T. It could be a T repeated.' I lost the rest, listening to something else.

Saltley heard it, too, the deep rumble of an engine borne on the wind and dead ahead of us. 'Ease sheets!' he screamed and spun the wheel as the bows of the second tanker emerged like a half-tide rock out of the darkness ahead. The yacht turned away to starb'd, but too slowly, the wall of water taking us on the port bow, slamming us over, then lifting us and sweeping us from end to end. We took it green, a sea breaking over my chest and flinging me against Saltley. Somebody was gripping hold of my ankles as I was swept to starb'd, and then the rumbling giant was sliding past our starb'd quarter and the sails were drawing, pulling us away from that sliding wall of steel. The wake hit us as the tanker passed, but not as badly as before. Suddenly all was quiet and we were free to pick ourselves up, the boat slipping smoothly through the water and the sound of those engines fading into the night like a bad dream.

We were lucky. None of us had been wearing safety harness, and though we were all suffering from bruises and cuts and were in a state of shock, nobody had been washed overboard and no bones had been broken.

It was only after we were back on course, everything sorted out on deck and beginning to clear up below, that I remembered the light Mark had seen flashing from the stern of that first tanker. But he couldn't tell whether it had been the flash of a torch or a cabin light being switched on and off, the flashes seen through the circle of a porthole. It could even have been somebody accidentally triggering off the safety light on a lifebuoy.

One thing we were in no doubt about, the two ships coming up on us like that had been deliberate, an attempt to run us down. It couldn't be anything else, for they had been steaming west of north and on that course there was nothing after Madeira anywhere in the north Atlantic until they reached Greenland.

We finished the bottle of brandy, deadening the shock of such a near disaster, then went into two-man watches for the rest of the night. And in the morning, with the wind beginning to veer into the west and the sky clearing to light cirrus, we could see the Desertas lifting above the horizon and clouds hanging over the high mountains of Madeira.

All day the islands became clearer and by nightfall Funchal was just visible as a sparkling of lights climbing the steep slopes behind the port. The wind was in the west then and falling light, a quiet sea with a long swell that glinted in the moonlight. I had the dawn watch and it was beautiful, the colours changing from blue-green to pink to orange-flame, the bare cliffs of the Desertas standing brick-red on our starb'd quarter as the sun lifted its great scarlet rim over the eastern horizon.

This I knew would be the last day on board. Ahead of me Madeira lifted its mountainous bulk into an azure sky and Funchal was clearly visible, its hotels and houses speckled white against the green slopes behind. I could just see the grey top of the breakwater with its fort and a line of naval ships steaming towards it. Just a few hours now and I would be back to reality, to the world as it really was for a man without a ship. It was such a lovely morning, everything sparkling and the scent of flowers borne on the wind, which was now north of west so that we were close-hauled.

I began thinking about the book then. Perhaps if I wrote it all down, just as it had happened . . . But I didn't know the end, of course, my mind switching to Balkaer, to that morning when it all started with the first of the oiled-up bodies coming ashore, and I began to play with words, planning the way it would open. Twelfth Night and the black rags of razorbacks washing back and forth down there in the cove in the slop of the waves . . .

'Morning, Trevor.' It was Pamela, smiling brightly as she came up into the cockpit. She stood there for a moment, breathing deeply as she took in the scene, her hair almost gold as it blew in the wind, catching the sunlight. She looked very statuesque, very young and fresh. 'Isn't it lovely!' She sat down on the lee side, leaning back and staring into space, not saying anything, her hands clasped tight together. I sensed a tension building up and wondered what it was, resenting the intrusion, words still building in my mind.

Ripples stirred the surface of the sea, a flash of silver as a fish jumped. 'Something I've got to tell you.' She blurted the words out in a tight little voice. 'I admire you – what you've done this last month, the sort of man you are, your love of birds, all the things you wrote. I think you are a quite exceptional . . .'

'Forget it,' I said. I knew what she was trying to say.

'No. It's not as easy as that.' She leaned forward on the lift of the boat and put her hand over mine on the wheel. 'I don't regret that letter, you see. It's just that I don't know.' She shook her head. 'I don't understand myself really, but I think what it was – I was reaching out for a new dimension. That's what you represented to me, something different, something I'd never really come across before. Are you a vegetarian?'

'I've eaten everything I've been given, haven't I?' I said it lightly, trying to laugh her out of the tense seriousness of her mood.

'But in Cornwall, you were vegetarian, weren't you?'

'Karen was. I conformed. I had to. We'd no money to buy meat, and we grew our own vegetables.'

'Yes, of course. I've still got the typescript, by the way. But what I was trying to say – I was like somebody who's been carnivorous all her life and is suddenly faced with the idea of becoming a vegetarian. It's so totally different. That's what I meant by new dimension. Do you understand?'

I nodded, not sure whether I did or not. No man likes to be faced with an attractive girl making a statement of rejection, and certainly not in the dawn with the sun coming up and the sea and the sky and the land ahead all bright with the hopes of a new day. 'Forget it,' I said again. 'You've no cause to reproach yourself. I'll keep the letter under my pillow.'

'Don't be silly.'

'And when I'm feeling particularly low . . .' Saltley's head appeared in the hatch and she took her hand away.

'Thank you,' she breathed. 'I knew you'd understand.' And she jumped to her feet. 'Two eggs for the helm?' she asked brightly. 'Our last breakfast and everything so lovely. Two eggs and four rashers.' She nodded and disappeared below to the galley. Saltley stared at me a moment, then his head disappeared and I was alone again, my thoughts no longer on the book, but on Karen and what I had lost. The future looked somehow bleaker, the feeling of separation from the others more intense.

CHAPTER TWO

It was shortly after noon when we turned the end of Funchal breakwater, lowering sail as we motored to a berth alongside a Portuguese tug. I had been to Madeira only once before, tramping in an old Liberty ship, and then the long dusty breakwater had been almost empty. Now it was crowded, for there was some sort of NATO exercise on with warships of half a dozen nations lying alongside and US off-duty sailors already at baseball practice among the cranes and stacked containers.

Saltley didn't wait for Customs and Immigration. At the end of the jetty, beyond a complex huddle of masts and radar, with Canadian and Dutch flags fluttering in the breeze, there was a missile destroyer flying the White Ensign. Neatly dressed in his shore-going rig of reefer, blue trousers and peaked cap, he crossed the tug and was lost immediately among the stevedores working two Panamanian-registered cargo ships. He had a long walk, for the tug to which we had moored was only about a third of the way along the jetty, just astern of a Portuguese submarine and only a few yards beyond the fort, its stone wall rising sheer out of the rock on which it was built.

Nobody seemed interested in our arrival and we sat on deck in the sunshine, drinking beer and watching the kaleidoscope of tourist colour across the harbour, where crowded streets climbed steeply up from the waterfront with slender ribbons of roads disappearing in hairpin bends a thousand feet above houses smothered in bougainvillaea. I could see the twin towers of Monte and the Crater's cobbled way dropping sheer into the town, and to the west the massed array of big hotels culminated in a promontory with Reid's red roofs and hanging gardens dropping to the sea.

It was the medical officer who arrived first, just after we had finished a very late lunch. He was still in the saloon improving his English over a Scotch when Saltley returned. He had contacted Lloyd's and reported the two GODCO tankers still afloat, but under different names. Fortified by Navy hospitality, he had then waited for Lloyd's to contact the authorities and check with their Intelligence Services for any listing of the *Shah Mohammed* and the *Ghazan Khan*. It had been almost an hour before he had the information he wanted. Both tankers had recently been acquired by an Iraqi company with offices in Tripoli and both had been registered in Iraq on January 16, port of registry Basra. As far as could be ascertained from a quick check Lloyd's had no information as to their present whereabouts, possible destination, or nature of cargo, if any. 'And the authorities show no inclination to get Britain involved,' Saltley added as Pamela sat him down to a plate of tinned ham and egg mayonnaise.

It was late afternoon before we were cleared and by then the destroyer's Captain was on board with a Rear-Admiral Blaize, who was in charge of the NATO exercise, a small man with rimless glasses, his face egg-shaped and very smooth so that he had a cold hostile look until he laughed, which he did quite often. Saltley's suggestion that the tankers be stopped and searched if they entered the English Channel had been rejected. 'The Navy is not empowered,' the Admiral said, 'to take that sort of action on the high seas in peacetime. I can tell you this, however. In view of the fact that Mr Rodin is on board here with you, and the public interest that was aroused by certain statements he made before leaving the country, MoD are passing the information you've given on to the Foreign Secretary, copy to the Department of Trade. I imagine the Marine Division of the DoT will be keeping watch on the situation through HM Coastguards. Oh, and a personal request from the Second Sea Lord. I think you said he's a sailing friend of yours.'

'I've met him several times,' Saltley said.

'He asked me to say he thinks it important you return to London as soon as possible and bring Rodin with you. I'm having one of my officers check now and make provisional reservations on the first flight out, whether it's to Gatwick, Heathrow or Manchester. That all right with you?'

Saltley nodded and the Admiral relaxed, leaning back against the pilot berth. 'Now perhaps I can have the whole story first hand.' His eyes fastened on me. 'I think perhaps if you would run over very briefly your side of it, the events that led to all of you setting off for a doubtful rendezvous in the Selvagen Islands.' He laughed. 'Wish they'd given me authority to mount a search. It would have been good practice for the motley crowd I'm commanding at the moment.' He laughed again, then stopped abruptly, sipping his pink gin and waiting for me to begin.

It was the first of a number of times I would be called upon to repeat my story in the next few days. And when Saltley had finished describing the meeting of the tankers and how they had nearly run us down in the dark, the Admiral said, 'I think what I would do in the circumstances is keep a very close watch on them after they enter the Channel and alert other nations of our suspicions. As soon as they enter territorial waters, then it's up to the nation concerned to take whatever action is considered appropriate.'

'Will you be advising the MoD to that effect?' Saltley asked.

'I'll be making a report, certainly.'

'That wasn't what I asked, Admiral.' Saltley was leaning across the table, his voice urgent. 'At twenty knots the Western Approaches are only three days' steaming from where we last saw them, just west of Selvagem Grande. This time tomorrow they could be into the Channel. They could be into Le Havre, Southampton, Portsmouth even, by first light the following morning. That's how urgent it is.' And he added, 'If it were Brest now . . .'

There was a tap on the doghouse roof and a naval lieutenant peered down through the hatch to say there was only one seat vacant on the first plane out in the morning, which was a TAP scheduled flight via Lisbon. He had booked that and also a seat on a tourist charter plane to Gatwick later in the day.

'No flights tonight?' Saltley asked.

'None, sir. The next flight out is the one to Lisbon.' And he went on to tell us that the captain of the Portuguese tug had to meet a freighter coming in and required us to shift our berth immediately.

We did this as soon as the Admiral had left, moving our warps to the submarine, which now had a queue of Portuguese sightseers entering by the for'ard hatch and coming out at the stern, some of the bulkier ladies severely testing the serious demeanour of the sailors detailed to assist them. As soon as we were tied up, Saltley and I packed our bags and we all went ashore to the Casino Park, the big circular concrete and glass hotel built on the high ground overlooking the old town and the harbour. Our first priority was hot baths, and having booked two rooms and checked that there was no way we could reach London any quicker, Saltley got on the phone to Michael Stewart while Pamela bathed in his room and the rest of us shared my bathroom and shower.

I came down to find the night outside the

glassed-in reception area very still and studded with stars. I ordered a glass of sercial and stood at the window sipping the fortified wine and looking up to the floodlit castle and all the myriad lights twinkling on the slopes high above. Pamela joined me and we took our drinks outside, strolling through the lawned gardens to the stone parapet overlooking the harbour. The water below us was oily calm, the lights of the ships along the jetty reflected in the flat black surface.

We stood there for a time, talking quietly, both of us strangely relaxed and at ease. But then, as we finished our drinks and began to walk slowly back, Pamela suddenly said, 'I think I should warn you, about Salt. He's quite ruthless, you know. He'll use you. He's good at his job, you see.' She looked up at me, smiling a little hesitantly. 'Some day I'll probably marry him, so I do know the sort of man he is, how single-minded he can be. Right now he has only one interest, and it's not the same as yours. He's not really concerned with the damage those tankers could do, except incidentally as a potential insurance claim. He just wants to prove their true identity. That lets my father's syndicates out and chalks up another success for him. Do you understand?' She had stopped by a rose bed, her blunt fingers toying with a dark red bloom as she leaned down to smell it. 'Where there's fraud involved he's like a bloodhound. He'll follow the scent quite regardless of anybody else.'

'Yes, but anything I say can only support his case.'

She nodded, her eyes large and luminous in the dim light. 'I expect you're right, but we won't be alone again after this and I felt I should warn you. On board you've seen perhaps his nicest side. But on the job, remember he's a real professional and determined to be accepted as the best there is. Anyway, good luck when you reach London.' She smiled abruptly, then went on into the hotel to join the others who were now standing at the bar.

Later we took a taxi to Gavinas, a fish restaurant built out over the sea beyond the old whaling station to the west of Funchal. We had fish soup, I remember, *espada*, which is the black scabbard fish peculiar to Madeira, the light *vinho verde* to drink and fresh strawberries to finish with. It was a strange meal, for it was part celebration, part farewell, and sitting over our coffee and Malmsey we were all of us a little subdued, Saltley and myself faced now with the problem of convincing the authorities, the other three with a voyage of some 800 miles ahead of them. And all the time the flop and suck of the waves around the concrete piers below us.

We left shortly after ten and the last we saw of the depleted crew was three faces calling farewell from the dark interior of the taxi as it drove them on from the Casino Park to the harbour. 'Think they'll be all right?' Saltley murmured. 'Mark's taken the boat from Plymouth to the Hamble and once across the Channel, but Madeira to Gib . . .' He stared dubiously at the taxi's rear lights as it swung into the Avenida do Infante. 'And Pamela, too,' he muttered. 'Mike would never forgive me if anything happened to them.'

'They'll be all right,' I said.

'He's only nineteen, you know.' The taxi disappeared down the hill and he turned abruptly into the hotel. 'Well, let's have a drink. I expect you're right.'

It was over that drink that he suddenly said to me, 'You may find there's some delay when you get to Gatwick. If there is, don't worry. These next few days could be very hectic, so any little problem you encounter may take a while to resolve.'

His words could only mean one thing. 'You heard something – when you were on the destroyer.'

He didn't answer and I was remembering what Pamela had said about him. 'They'll arrest me, is that what you mean?'

'No, I don't think so. But since we won't be together on the flight home I thought it only fair to warn you.' Which meant, of course, he wouldn't lift a finger to help me unless it suited him and he thought I could be useful. 'The deadline is very tight,' he murmured half to himself. 'If they are in the Western Approaches tomorrow evening, then I've got to get planes up and the ships located by the following morning.'

'They may not be bound for the Channel.'

'Where do you think they're headed for – the States?' He gave me a lop-sided smile and shrugged. 'The Americans would have them boxed in and boarded before they were within miles of the eastern seaboard, and they know it. They'll be in the Channel tomorrow night, I'm certain they will.'

We went to our rooms shortly afterwards and in the morning he was gone. The moment of reality had arrived. I was on my own again, and though I was prepared for it, it still came as a shock after living for several weeks in the close company of others. But then the coach arrived and for a while my thoughts were diverted by the long coastal drive to Santa Cruz and the airport with its views of the Desertas and the lighthouse standing white and lonely on the eastern tip of Madeira.

We were flying against the sun so that it was dark by the time we were over the Channel. The man next to me was sleeping peacefully to the background hum of the engines, everybody in the plane very quiet, even the stewardesses no longer rushing about. All during the flight I had been thinking over what Saltley had said the previous night, and now, over the English Channel, with a strange feeling in my guts that those tankers were somewhere down below me, I found my mind made up. If they were going to detain me at the airport – and I was certain Saltley knew something that he hadn't passed on to me – then I had nothing to lose. I tore a page out of the inflight magazine *Highlife* and scribbled on a blank space: *Please request press or other media representatives Gatwick to meet Trevor Rodin on arrival – 2 Iraqi tankers*, Shah Mohammed *and* Ghazan Khan, *expected English Channel imminent. Terrorists on board. Target not yet known. URGENT URGENT URGENT. Rodin.* I reached up and rang for the stewardess.

She was tall and slightly flushed, her hair beginning to come adrift and a faint smell of perspiration as she leaned over the recumbent figure next to me and asked whether she could get me anything. I handed her the slip of paper and when she had read it, she continued to stare at it, her hands trembling slightly. 'It's all right,' I said. 'I'm quite sane.'

Her eyes darted me a quick look, then she hurried away and I saw her conferring with the senior stewardess beside the pantry, both of them staring in my direction. After a moment the older girl nodded and slipped through the door to the flight deck. I sat back then, feeling suddenly relaxed. It was done now. I had committed myself, and even if the captain didn't radio ahead, the girls would almost certainly talk.

After a few minutes the head stewardess came down the aisle to me. 'Mr Rodin?' I nodded. 'Would you come with me, sir. The Captain would like a word with you.'

He met me in the pantry area, a tall, thin, worried-looking man with stress lines running down from the nose and greying hair. The door to the flight deck was firmly closed. 'I read something about you, some weeks back. Right?' He didn't wait for a reply. 'I cannot, I'm afraid, communicate with the media. That's a matter for the airport authority. If they see fit, they'll contact them.'

'But you'll tell them about the tankers, won't you?' I asked.

'I'll tell them, yes. But it will be for you to convince them after we've landed. Okay?' He half turned towards the door to the flight deck, then checked. 'You mean what you've written here, do you?' He held the torn scrap from *Highlife* under my nose. 'Terrorists. Are you sure?'

'Quite sure,' I said.

'You escaped in a dhow. I remember now.' Grey, worried eyes stared at me for a moment. 'But that was in the Gulf. How do you know these tankers will be in the Channel now?'

I told him how we had sailed out to the Selvagen Islands, had seen them rendezvous there and then been nearly run down in a deliberate attempt to obliterate us. 'The way you say it—' He was watching me very closely. 'I don't know.' He shook his head. 'Why are you on your own? What happened to the marine solicitor?' And when I told him Saltley had taken the early flight via Lisbon, there was a sudden wariness in his eyes and I was conscious of a tenseness building in him. He glanced at the stewardess. 'Get Dick, will you. He's my navigator,' he said, and began talking about air speed, winds and our ETA at Gatwick, his voice suddenly matter-of-fact.

The navigator was a big man and as soon as he had shut the flight deck door, the captain turned to me and in a quiet, slightly strained voice said, 'Mind if we check you over?'

'For weapons, do you mean?'

'Just in case.' He nodded to the navigator and the two of them pressed forward, forcing me to the back of the pantry, where the captain ran his hands under my arms and between my legs, the muscles of his neck corded into tense knots and the navigator standing off, his fists clenched ready.

'Is that necessary?' I asked as he straightened up, letting out his breath, his body relaxing.

'We have to be careful.' His eyes still had that wary look. 'You know about the controllers' strike at Lisbon, I suppose?'

I stared at him, a feeling of shock running through me. 'Strike? I don't know anything about a strike.' I was thinking of Saltley marooned in Lisbon and myself alone with nobody to confirm my story.

'You could have heard about it at the airport. The staff were full of it.'

'I heard nothing. I didn't ask.'

His mouth was shut in a tight line, the jaw muscles visible as he watched me. 'No – well, probably you didn't know then. They walked out during the morning, a manning schedule we were told. But we'll be landing soon. I've no time to check with Lisbon. They could take an hour or more to make sure whether your man is stranded there or not.'

'So you'll do nothing?' I suppose my own fears, the strain in my voice, something communicated itself to him, for the wary look was back in his eyes.

'I'll report to Gatwick, of course. I've said that already.'

'And the media?'

He hesitated. 'I'll have a word with the PR man, if he's still there. He likes to know when there's a—' He checked himself. I thought perhaps he had been going to say 'when there's a nut on board'. 'When anything unusual is happening. That satisfy you?'

I didn't know whether he believed me or not, but I

knew it was the best I could hope from him. I nodded and he let me out of the pantry then, requesting me in a neutral, official voice to return to my seat. I was conscious of the two of them and the chief stewardess watching me as I pushed past the queue for the toilets and went back down the aisle. By the time I was in my seat again the officers had disappeared, the door to the flight deck was closed and the stewardesses were seeing to last minute requests as they had a final clear up. The man next to me was still sleeping, the engines whispering very quietly now as we lost height. Everything was normal again.

The only thing that wasn't normal was my state of mind. I could think of nothing but the fact that Saltley wouldn't be around when we landed in England. I would be on my own, the only person available to the authorities who had seen those tankers rendezvous in the Selvagens. Would they believe me without Saltley's physical presence to confirm it? A voice on the telephone from Lisbon wasn't the same at all. Would they believe anything I said? I was thinking of the captain, the wariness, the tenseness, the way he had summoned the heaviest of his crew, the search for arms. Would Forthright's help, or Lloyd's – would their Intelligence Services have discovered anything to corroborate my story?

The seat belt sign came on, the flaps slid out from the wings and I heard the rumble of the undercarriage going down. I felt suddenly sick, a void in my stomach and my skin breaking out in a sweat. It was nerves, the tension of waiting, wondering what was going to happen. And then we were down with the runway lights flashing by and I braced myself, breathing deeply, telling myself I had nothing to be afraid of, that the truth was the truth, something I couldn't be shaken on, so that eventually they must believe me.

The plane came to a halt and a chill wind blew in as the fuselage door was thrown back. We filed out past the chief stewardess, who said her usual piece, hoping I'd had a good flight, and I saw her eyes widen in confusion as she realized who it was. And when I boarded the bus one of the airport staff got in with me and kept his eyes on me all the way to the arrivals area.

The time was just after 19.30 GMT when I joined the queue at the UK passport desk. It moved quickly so that in a moment I was handing my temporary papers to the immigration officer. He glanced at them and then at me, his glasses reflecting the glint of the lights, his eyes faintly curious. 'What happened to your passport, sir?'

'I lost it.'

'Where?'

'I left it on board a tanker in the Persian Gulf.'

He looked down at some papers on the desk beside him. 'And this is your correct name – Trevor McAlistair Rodin?' He turned and nodded to a man over by the wall. 'This gentleman will look after you now.' The man came quickly forward, positioning himself at my elbow. He took my papers and said, 'This way please.'

He led me through into the Customs hall, where

he arranged for my baggage to be cleared and brought to me. 'Am I under arrest?' I asked, not sure whether he was airport police or CID.

'Just a few questions, that's all at this stage.' We went upstairs and into one of the airport offices, and when he had sat me down at the desk facing him, I asked to see his credentials. He was a detective-inspector of the Surrey police force. I started to tell him about the tankers then, but he stopped me almost immediately. 'I'm afraid that's nothing to do with me. I'm told the information you gave the captain of your aircraft about tankers and terrorists has already been passed to the proper authority. My concern is a much earlier statement you made, about how you escaped in some native craft in the Persian Gulf with a French engineer named Choffel. I'd be glad if you'd now go through that again, so that I can prepare a statement for you to sign.'

I tried to argue with him, but he was insistent, and he gave me the usual caution about the possibility of evidence being used against me. And when I told him about the statement I had already made in London a month ago, he said, 'That's the Metropolitan area, Special Branch by the sound of it.' He was an ordinary-looking man, quite human. 'I have my orders, that's all.'

'Who from?'

'The Chief Constable.'

'But not because of what I said about those tankers. It's because Choffel's daughter has accused me of killing her father, isn't it?'

'She made a statement, yes.'

'But there's no warrant for my arrest.'

He smiled then. 'Nobody has told me to do anything more than get a statement from you, all right?'

'And it'll go to the Chief Constable?'

He nodded. 'He'll then pass it on to the office of the Director of Public Prosecutions or not as he thinks fit. That's why I had to caution you.' He pulled his chair into the desk and got his pen out. 'Now, shall we get started? I don't imagine you want to be all night over it any more than I do.'

There was nothing for it then but to go over the whole story from the beginning, and it took time, for he was summarizing it as we went along and writing it all out in longhand. By 08.30 I had only got as far as my arrival on the tanker and the discovery that it was the *Aurora B*. He rang down to somebody for sandwiches and coffee to be sent up from the cafeteria, and it was while we were eating them, and I was describing how Sadeq had stood at the top of the gangway firing down on to the deck of the dhow, that the door opened and I turned to find myself looking up at the shut face and hard eyes of the man who had visited me in my Stepney basement.

He handed a piece of paper to the detective. 'Orders from on high.'

'Whose?'

'Dunno. I'm to deliver him to the Min of Def – Navy.' He turned to me. 'You slipped out of the country without informing us. Why?' I started to explain, but then I thought what the hell – I had been talking for an hour and a half and I had had enough. 'If you haven't bothered to find out why I'm back here in England, then there's no point in my wasting your time or mine.'

He didn't like that. But there wasn't much he could do about it, his orders being simply to escort me, and the local inspector waiting to get his statement completed. It took another half hour of concentrated work to get it into a form acceptable to me so that it was almost ten before I had signed it. By then two journalists had tracked me down, and though the Special Branch man tried to hustle me out of the terminal, I had time to give them the gist of the story. We reached the police car, the reporters still asking questions as I was bundled in and the door slammed. Shut-face got in beside me, and as we drove out of the airport, he said, 'Christ! You got a fertile imagination. Last time it was a tanker hiding up in the Gulf and an Iranian revolutionary firing a machine pistol, now it's two tankers and a whole bunch of terrorists, and they're steaming into the Channel to commit mayhem somewhere in Europe.'

'You don't believe me?'

He looked at me, his face deadpan, not a flicker of reaction in his eyes. 'I don't know enough about you, do I?' He was staring at me for a moment, then suddenly he smiled and I caught a glimpse of the face his wife and children knew. 'Cheer up. Presumably somebody does or our branch wouldn't have been asked to pick you up.' The smile vanished, his face closed up again, and I thought perhaps he didn't have a family. 'Lucky the local CID were taking an interest in you or you might have gone to ground in another East End basement.' And he added, his voice harder, more official, 'You can rest assured we'll keep tabs on you from now on until we know whether those tankers are real or you're just a bloody little liar with an outsized capacity for invention.'

There wasn't much to be said after that and I closed my eyes, my mind wandering sleepily in the warmth of the car. Somebody at the Admiralty wanted a first-hand account of our meeting with those tankers. The Second Sea Lord – a friend of yours, the admiral at Funchal had said to Saltley – and Saltley wasn't here. Was it the Second Sea Lord who wanted to see me? Whoever it was, I'd have to go over it all again, and tomorrow that statement I had signed would be on the Chief Constable's desk, and he'd pass it on. Any official would. It was such a very strange story. He'd leave it to the Director of Public Prosecutions. And if those tankers blew themselves up ... There'd be nobody then to prove I hadn't killed Choffel. They'd all be dead and no eye-witness to what Sadeq had done.

That feeling of emptiness returned, sweat on my skin and the certainty that this shut-faced man's reaction would then be the reaction of all officialdom – myself branded a liar and a killer. How many years would that mean? 'Why the hell!' I whispered to myself. Why the hell had I ever agreed to return to England? In Tangier it would have been so easy to disappear – new papers, another name. Even from

Funchal. I needn't have caught that charter flight. I could have waited and caught the next flight to Lisbon. No. The controllers were on strike there. I was thinking of Saltley again, wondering where he was now, and would he back me, could I rely on him as a witness for the defence if those tankers were totally destroyed?

It was past eleven when we reached Whitehall, turning right opposite Downing Street. 'The main doors are closed after eight-thirty in the evening,' my escort said as we stopped at the Richmond Terrace entrance of the Ministry of Defence building. Inside he motioned me to wait while he went to the desk to find out who wanted me. The Custody Guard picked up the phone immediately and after a brief conversation nodded to me and said, 'Won't keep you a moment, sir. 2LS's Naval Assistant is coming right down.'

My escort insisted on waiting, but the knowledge that two such senior men had returned to their offices in order to see me gave me a sudden surge of confidence. That it was the Second Sea Lord himself who was waiting for me was confirmed when a very slim, slightly stooped man with sharp, quite penetrating grey eyes arrived, and after introducing himself as Lt Cdr Wright, said, 'This way, sir. Admiral Fitzowen's waiting to see you.' The *sir* helped a lot and I seemed to be walking on air as I followed him quickly down the echoing corridors.

The Admiral was a big, round-faced man in a grey suit which seemed to match the walls of his office. He jumped up from behind his desk to greet me. 'Saltley told me you could give me all the details. I was talking to him on the phone to Lisbon this morning.'

'He's still there, is he?' I asked.

But he didn't think so. 'Told me he'd get a train or something into Spain and fly on from there. Should be here some time tomorrow. Now about those tankers.' He waved me to a seat.

'Are they in the Channel?'

'Don't know yet, not for sure. PREMAR UN – that's the French admiral at Cherbourg – his office has informed us that two tankers were picked up on their radar surveillance at Ushant some forty miles offshore steaming north. They had altered course to the eastward just before moving out of range of the Ushant scanner. It was dark by the time we got their report and the weather's not good, but by now there should be a Nimrod over the search area and the French have one of their Navy ships out looking for them.' He began asking me questions then, mostly about the shape and layout of the vessels. He had pictures of the GODCO tankers on his desk. 'So Saltley's right, these are the missing tankers.'

I told him about the O of *Howdo Stranger* still showing faintly in the gap between *Shah* and *Mohammed*. 'Salt made the same point. Says his photographs will prove it.' He leaned towards me. 'So what's their intention?' And when I told him I didn't know, he said, 'What's your supposition? You must have thought about it. Some time in the early hours we're going to have their exact position. If they are in the Channel I must know what their most likely course of action will be. You were on the *Aurora B*. That's what it says here—' He waved a foolscap sheet at me. 'When you were in England, before Saltley got you away in that yacht, you made what sounded at the time like some very wild allegations. All right . . .' He raised his hand as I started to interrupt him. 'I'll accept them all for the moment as being true. But if you were on the *Aurora B*, then you must have picked up something, some indication of their intentions.'

'I had a talk with the captain,' I said.

'And this man Sadeq.'

'Very briefly, about our previous meeting.' I gave him the gist of it and I could see he was disappointed.

'And the Englishman who recruited you – Baldwick. Didn't he know anything about the objective?'

I shook my head. 'I don't think so.'

'Tell me about your conversation with the captain then.' He glanced at his notes. 'Pieter Hals. Dutch, I take it.'

It was the better part of an hour of hard talking before he was finally convinced I could tell him nothing that would indicate the purpose for which the tankers had been seized. At one point, tired of going over it all again, I said, 'Why don't you board them then? As soon as you know where they are—'

'We've no authority to board.'

'Oh, for God's sake!' I didn't care whether he was a Sea Lord or what, I was too damned tired of it. 'Two pirated ships and the Navy can't board them. I don't believe it. Who's responsible for what goes on in the Channel?'

'Flag Officer, Plymouth. But I'm afraid CIN-CHAN's powers are very limited. He certainly hasn't any powers of arrest. Unlike the French.' He gave a shrug, smiling wryly as he went on, 'Remember the *Amoco Cadiz* and what the spillage from that wreck did to the Brittany coast? After that they instituted traffic lanes off Ushant. Later they insisted on all tankers and ships with dangerous cargoes reporting in and staying in a third lane at least twenty-four miles off the coast until they're in their correct eastbound lane, which is on the French side as they move up-Channel. And they have ships to enforce their regulations. Very typically the British operate a voluntary system – MAREP, Marine Reporting.' And he added, the wry smile breaking out again, 'I'm told it works – but not, of course, for the sort of situation you and Saltley are envisaging.'

I brought up the question of boarding again, right at the end of our meeting, and the Admiral said, 'Even the French don't claim the right of arrest beyond the twelve-mile limit. If those tankers came up the English side, there's nothing the French can do about it.'

'But if they're on the English side,' I said, 'they'd be steaming east in the westbound lane. Surely then—'

He shook his head. 'All we can do then is fly off the Coastguard plane, take photographs and in due course report their behaviour to their country of registry and press for action.'

I was sitting back, feeling drained and oddly

appalled at the Navy's apparent helplessness. All the years when I had grown up thinking of the Navy as an all-powerful presence and now, right on Britain's own doorstep, to be told they were powerless to act. 'There must be somebody,' I murmured. 'Some minister who can order their arrest.'

'Both Saltley and yourself have confirmed they're registered at Basra and flying the Iraqi flag. Not even the Foreign Secretary could order those ships to be boarded.'

'The Prime Minister then,' I said uneasily. 'Surely the Prime Minister—'

'The PM would need absolute proof.' He shrugged and got to his feet. 'I'm afraid what you've told me, and what Saltley has said to me on the phone, isn't proof.'

'So you'll just sit back and wait until they've half wrecked some European port.'

'If they do come up-Channel, then we'll monitor their movements and alert other countries as necessary.' The door had opened behind me and he nodded. 'In which case, we'll doubtless see each other again.' He didn't shake hands. Just that curt, dismissive nod and he had turned away towards the window.

Back along the echoing corridors then to find Shutface still waiting. A room had been booked for me at a hotel in the Strand and when he left me there with my bags he warned me not to try disappearing again. 'We'll have our eye on you this time.'

In the morning, when I went out of the hotel, I found this was literally true. A plain clothes man fell into step beside me. 'Will you be going far, sir?' And when I said I thought I'd walk as far as Charing Cross and buy a paper, he said, 'I'd rather you stayed in the hotel, sir. You can get a paper there.'

I had never been under surveillance before. I suppose very few people have. I found it an unnerving experience. Slightly eerie in a way, a man you've never met before watching your every movement – as though you've been judged guilty and condemned without trial. I bought several papers and searched right through them – nothing. I could find no mention of anything I had told those two journalists at Gatwick, no reference anywhere to the possibility of pirated tankers steaming up the English Channel.

It could simply mean they had filed their stories too late, but these were London editions and it was barely ten o'clock when I had spoken to them. Hadn't they believed me? I had a sudden picture of them going off to one of the airport bars, laughing about it over a drink. Was that what had happened? And yet their questions had been specific, their manner interested, and they had made notes, all of which seemed to indicate they took it seriously.

I didn't know what to think. I just sat there in the foyer, feeling depressed and a little lost. There was nothing I could do now, nothing at all, except wait upon others. If they didn't believe me, then sooner or later the Director of Public Prosecutions would make up his mind and maybe a warrant would be issued for my arrest. Meanwhile . . . meanwhile it seemed as though I was some sort of non-person, a dead soul waiting where the souls of the dead wait upon the future.

And then suddenly the Special Branch man was at my elbow. There was a car at the door and I was to leave for Dover immediately. I thought for a moment I was being deported, but he said it was nothing to do with the police. 'Department of Trade – the Minister himself I believe, and you're to be rushed there as quickly as possible.' He hustled me out to a police car drawn up at the kerb with its blue light flashing and two uniformed officers in front. 'And don't try slipping across to the other side.' He smiled at me, a human touch as he tossed my bags in after me. 'You'll be met at the other end.' He slammed the door and the car swung quickly out into the traffic, turning right against the lights into the Waterloo Bridge approach.

It had all happened so quickly that I had had no time to question him further. I had presumed he was coming with me. Instead, I was alone in the back, looking at the short-haired necks and caps of the men in front as we shot round the Elephant & Castle and into the Old Kent Road. There was a break in the traffic then and I asked why I was being taken to Dover. But they didn't know. Their instructions were to get me to Langdon Battery as quickly as possible. They didn't know why, and when I asked what Langdon Battery was, the man sitting beside the driver turned to me and held up a slip of paper. 'CNIS Operations Centre, Langdon Battery. That's all it says, sir. And a Dover patrol car will meet us at the last roundabout before the docks. Okay?'

The siren was switched on and we blazed our way through the traffic by New Cross Station. In moments, it seemed, we were crossing Blackheath, heading through the Bexley area to the M2. The morning was grey and windtorn, distant glimpses of Medway towns against the wide skies of the Thames estuary and my spirits lifting, a mood almost of elation. But all the men in front could tell me was that their instructions had come from the office of the Under-Secretary, Marine Division, at the Department of Trade in High Holborn. They knew nothing about any tankers. I leaned back, watching the forestry on either side flash by, certain that the ships must have been sighted. Why else this sudden call for my presence at an operations centre near Dover?

Half an hour later we were past Canterbury and at 11.22 we slowed at a second roundabout just outside Dover with the A2 dipping sharply between gorse scrub hills to the harbour. A local police car was waiting where the A258 to Deal branched off to the left and we followed it as it swung into the round-about, turning right on to a narrow road leading directly to the square stone bulk of Dover Castle. To the left I had fleeting glimpses of the Straits, the sea grey-green and flecked with white, ships steaming steadily westward. A shaft of sunlight picked out the coast of France, while to the east a rainstorm black-ened the seascape. Just short of the Castle we swung left, doubling back and dipping sharply to a narrow bridge over the A2 and a view of the docks with a hydrofoil just leaving by the eastern entrance in a flurry of spray.

The road, signposted to St Margaret's, climbed sharply up rough downland slopes round a hairpin bend, and in a moment we were turning through a narrow gateway into MoD property with tall radio masts looming above a hill-top to our left.

Langdon Battery proved to be a decaying gun emplacement of First World War vintage, the concrete redoubt just showing above a flat gravel area where a dozen or more cars were parked. But at the eastern end the emplacement was dominated by a strange, very modernistic building, a sort of Star Wars version of an airport control tower. We stopped alongside a white curved concrete section and an officer from the local police car opened the door for me. 'What is this place?' I asked him.

'HM Coastguards,' he said. 'CNIS – Channel Navigation Information Service. They monitor the traffic passing through the Straits.'

We went in through double glass doors. There was a desk and a receptionist drinking coffee out of a Government issue cup. My escort gave her my name and she picked up a microphone. 'Captain Evans please . . . Mr Rodin has just arrived, sir.' She nodded and smiled at me. 'Captain Evans will be right down.'

Opposite reception was a semicircular enclave with display boards outlining the work of the Operations Centre – a map of the Straits showing the east–west traffic lanes and the limits of the radar surveillance, diagrams showing the volume of traffic and marked drop in collisions resulting from traffic separation, radar surveillance and the reporting in by masters carrying noxious and dangerous cargoes, pictures of the Coastguards' traffic patrol aircraft and of the Operations Room with its radar screens and computer console. 'Mr Rodin?'

I turned to find a short, broad man with a lively face and a mane of greying hair. 'David Evans,' he said. 'I'm the Regional Controller.' And as he led me up the stairs to the left of the reception desk, he added, 'The SoS should be here shortly – Secretary of State for Trade, that is. He's flying down from Scotland.'

'The tankers have been sighted then?'

'Oh yes, there's a Nimrod shadowing them.' The first floor area was constructed like a control tower. 'The Operations Room,' he said. 'That's the Lookout facing seaward and the inner sanctum, that curtained-off area in the rear, is the Radar Room. We've three surveillance screens, there, also computer input VDUs – not only can we see what's going on, we can get almost instant course and speed, and in the case of collision situations, the expected time to impact. The last position we had for those two tankers was bearing 205° from Beachy Head, distance fourteen miles. The Navy has sent *Tigris*, one of the Amazon class frigates, to intercept and escort them up-Channel.'

'They're past Spithead and the Solent then?'

He checked on the stairs leading up to the deck above. 'You were thinking of Southampton, were you?' I nodded.

'You really thought they were going to damage one of the Channel ports?'

I didn't say anything. He was a Welshman, with a Celtic quickness of mind, but I could see he hadn't grasped the implications, was dubious about the whole thing.

'They're rogues, of course.' He laughed. 'That's our term for ships that don't obey the COLREGS. They didn't report in to the French when they were off Ushant, nor to us, and now they're on our side of the Channel, steaming east in the westbound lane. That makes them rogues several times over, but then they're under the Iraqi flag, I gather.' He said it as though it was some sort of flag-of-convenience. 'Well, come on up and meet our boss, Gordon Basildon-Smith. He's responsible for the Department of Trade's Marine Division. We've got a sort of subsidiary Ops Room up here.'

It was a semicircular room, almost a gallery, for on one side glass panels gave a view down into the Lookout below. There were several chairs and a desk with a communications console manned by a young auxiliary coastguard woman. A group of men stood talking by a window that faced west with a view of the harbour and the solid mass of Dover Castle. One of them was the man who had addressed that meeting in Penzance the night Karen had destroyed the *Petros Jupiter*. 'Good, you're just in time,' he said, as Captain Evans introduced me. He seemed to have no inkling that he was in any way connected with her death. 'I want the whole story, everything that happened, everything you saw in those islands. But make it short. My Minister will be here any minute now.'

He wanted to be sure they really were the missing tankers, listening intently and not interrupting until I told him about the pictures Saltley had taken and how the old name was still just visible on the stern of the *Shah Mohammed*. 'Yes, yes, it was in the report we had from Admiral Blaize. Unfortunately we don't have the pictures yet. But Captain Evans here has flown off his Coastguard patrol plane with instructions to go in close—' He turned to the Regional Controller. 'That's right, isn't it, David? He has taken off?'

Evans nodded. 'Yes, sir. Took off—' He glanced at his watch. 'Three minutes ago.'

There was a sudden flurry of movement as a voice announced the arrival of the Secretary of State for Trade. In an instant I was almost alone and when I looked down through the glass panels I saw a tall, dark man with thinning hair and prominent ears being introduced to the watch officers and the auxiliaries. He said a few words to each, moving and smiling like an actor playing a part, then he was climbing the stairs to the upper deck and I heard him say in a clear, silvery voice, 'The French have been alerted, of course?' And Captain Evans replied, 'We're co-operating very closely with them, sir. In fact, it was PREMAR UN who originally alerted us – that was when they passed Ushant and failed to report in.' He introduced us, but the Minister's mind was on the problem he now faced. 'What about other countries – the Belgians, the Dutch?' Evans said he couldn't answer that and a

Navy officer present asked if he should check with Flag Officer, Plymouth. 'I'm sure it's been done, sir. As C-in-C Channel he's bound to have given his opposite number in all NATO countries the information Admiral Blaize passed to us from Funchal.'

'Check, would you,' the Minister said.

A woman's voice announced over the PA system that the tankers had now been picked up on the Dungeness scanner. Course 042°. Speed 18.3 knots. 'And the Germans,' the Minister said. 'Make certain the Germans have been notified. They have at least two Kurdish groups in custody.' He turned to Basildon-Smith. 'What do you think, Gordon – leave it as it is or inform the PM?'

Basildon-Smith hesitated. 'If we bring the PM into it, then we need to be clear as to what advice we're going to offer.' And, in the pause that followed, Evans's Welsh voice said quietly, 'What about the journalists, sir? They've been pressing me all morning for a statement.'

'Yes, Gordon told me.' The Minister's voice was sharper and he passed a hand over his eyes. 'How many?'

'There must be twenty or more now.'

He turned to me, his dark eyes hostile. 'You should have kept your mouth shut. What was the idea?' He stared at me, and I suddenly remembered he had been a barrister before going into politics. 'Trying to pressure us, is that it? Or trying to divert attention from your own problems. You're accused of killing a Frenchman. That right?' And when I didn't answer, he smiled and nodded, turning to Evans. 'Where are they?'

'In the Conference Room, sir.'

'Ah, that nice, circular, very expensive room of yours with the pretty view of the Straits.' He moved to the desk and sat down, his eyes fastening on me again as he took a slip of paper from his pocket. 'We'll assume for the moment that your statement is correct in so far as those tankers are concerned. To that extent your story is confirmed by this marine solicitor—' He glanced down at his aide-memoire. 'Saltley. Any news of him?' There was silence and he nodded. 'We must take it then that he's still stuck in Lisbon. Pity! A trained, logical, and unemotional—' He was looking at me again – 'witness would have been very helpful to me. However . . .' He shrugged. And then, working from his single-sheet brief, he began to cross-examine me. Was I sure about the identity of the second tanker? What were conditions like when we had sighted it? 'You must have been tired then. Are you sure it was the *Aurora B*?' And then he was asking me about the night when the two of them had tried to run us down. 'That's what makes your story less than entirely convincing.' And he added, 'My difficulty, you see, is that there are three witnesses at sea and unobtainable, and this man Saltley still lost apparently somewhere between here and Lisbon.'

I pointed out, of course, that Saltley had been present when Admiral Blaize had come on board the *Prospero* in Funchal, but all he said was, 'Yes, but again it's secondhand. Still . . .' He fired a few more questions at me, chiefly about the men who had visited us in the inflatable off Selvagem Pequena, then got up and stood for a moment at the window staring out to the harbour at an odd-looking craft with a slab-fronted superstructure and a pile of giant fenders balanced on the stern. 'All right.' He turned, smiling, his manner suddenly changed. 'Let's deal with the media. And you,' he said to me, 'you'll come too and back up what I say.'

'And the PM, sir?' Basildon-Smith asked.

'We'll leave that till we've seen these buggers through the Straits.'

The Conference Room was big and circular, with combined desks and seats custom-built on a curve to fit its shape. Venetian blinds covered the windows. The place was full of people and there were television cameras. In the sudden silence of our entry the lash of a rainstorm was a reminder of the room's exposed position high up over the Dover Straits.

The Minister was smiling now, looking very assured as he addressed them briefly, giving a quick résumé of the situation and concluding with the words, 'I would ask you all to bear in mind that these vessels are registered in Iraq, flying the Iraqi flag. We do not *know* they are planning mischief. All we know, as fact, is that they failed to report in to the French at Ushant and that they are now steaming east in the westbound traffic lane to the great danger of other vessels.'

'And avoiding arrest by keeping well away from the French coast,' a voice said.

'Yes, that is a perfectly valid point. As you know,

we still do not have powers of arrest, not even in our own waters. Much as we should like these powers—'

'Why don't you bring in a bill then?' somebody asked him.

'Because we've not had an experience like the French. There's been no equivalent of the *Amoco Cadiz* disaster on the English coast.' Inevitably he was asked whether the Prime Minister had been informed, but instead of answering the question, he turned to me and I heard him say, 'Most of you will recall the name Trevor Rodin in connection with a missing tanker, the *Aurora B*, and some of you may have seen a Reuters report issued this morning containing statements made by him yesterday evening after he had flown in from Madeira. Because those statements will have to be borne in mind when we come to the point of deciding what action we take, if any, I thought it right that you should hear what he has to say from his own lips.'

He nodded towards me, smiling as those near me moved aside so that I stood isolated and exposed. 'May I suggest, Mr Rodin, that you start by giving the gist of the information you gave the Second Sea Lord last night, then if there are any questions . . .' He stepped back and I was left with the whole room staring at me. *Go on. Tell us what you said. Do what the Minister says.* Urged by their voices I cleared my throat, cursing the man for his cleverness in switching their attention to me and getting himself off the hook. Then, as I began speaking, I suddenly found confidence, the words pouring out of me. I could feel their attention becoming riveted, their notebooks out, scribbling furiously, and the faint whirr of cameras turning.

I told them everything, from the moment we had reached the Selvagen Islands, and then, in answer to questions, I went back over what had happened in the Gulf, the extraordinary sight of the *Aurora B* moored against those ochre-red cliffs. It was such a wonderful opportunity to present my case and I had just started to tell them of my escape and what had happened on the dhow, when somebody said there was a report in from the pilot of the Coastguard patrol plane. I lost them then, everybody crowding round the DoT press officer. I had been talking for nearly twenty minutes and I think their attention had begun to wander long before the report came in that confirmed the shadow of the old name showing on the *Shah Mohammed*.

I walked out, past some officers and a spiral staircase leading down to the bowels of the old fort, to a glassed-in passageway. The rainstorm had moved off into the North Sea and a shaft of watery sunlight was beamed on the waves breaking against the harbour walls. I thought I could see the atomic power station at Dungeness and I wondered how much of what I had said would find its way into print, or would it all be submerged in the threat posed by Sadeq and his two tankers? Something was going to happen, out there beyond the wild break of the seas, but what? Down below the horizon, beyond the black louring clouds of that rainstorm, the ports of northern Europe lay exposed and vulnerable. I should have said that. I should have talked about pollution and Pieter Hals, not concentrated so much on my own troubles. If Karen had been there, she would have seen to it that I concerned myself more with the threat to life, the sheer filth and destruction of oil slicks.

I was still standing there, trying to figure out how long it would be before those tankers came into sight, when one of the BBC's TV news team asked if they could do an interview. 'Nothing's going to happen for some time, so it seems a good opportunity.'

It was a good opportunity for me, too. They filmed it outside with the Lookout and the Straits in the background and I was able to channel it so that for part of the time I was talking about the problems of pollution and what men like Hals stood for.

'That's the first we've heard of Hals being on board. You've claimed all along they're terrorists. Why would Captain Hals join them?'

I couldn't answer that. 'Perhaps he was desperate and needed a job,' I said. 'Or he could have been thinking that a really catastrophic disaster in one of the major European ports would force governments to legislate against irresponsible tanker owners.'

'Europort, for instance. Is that what you're saying – that they'll go for Europort?'

'Perhaps.' I was remembering Hals's actual words when he had said nothing would be done – nothing until the nations that demand oil are themselves threatened with pollution on a massive scale. There was almost a quarter of a million tons of oil in those tankers. The Maas, the Noord Zee Canal, the Elbe – they were all prime targets.

I had an audience now of several journalists and was still talking about Hals when somebody called to us that the Flag Officer, Plymouth, was on the phone to the Minister requesting instructions now that a Navy frigate was in close company with one of the tankers and had identified it as the *Aurora B*. There was a rush for the Conference Room and I was left standing there with only a watchful policeman for company.

I was glad to be on my own for a moment, but shortly afterwards the Minister came out with Basildon-Smith and they were driven off in an official car – to the Castle, the police officer said, adding that it was past one and sandwiches and coffee were available from the canteen. Several journalists and most of the TV men drove off in their cars, heading for the hotel bars at St Margaret's. Clearly nothing was going to happen for some time. It began to rain again.

I went back into the Operations Centre and had a snack, standing looking out the windows of the Conference Room. Time passed slowly. I had a second cup of coffee and lit a cigarette, rain lashing at the windows. Later I strolled along the glassed-in passageway to the Lookout. There were one or two reporters there and the watch officer was letting them take it in turns to look through the big binoculars. Nobody took any notice of me until Captain Evans came in to check the latest position of the tankers. He also checked the latest weather position, then turned to me and said, 'Care to see them on the radar?' I think he was tired of explaining things to landlubbers, glad to talk to a seaman.

He took me through the heavy light-proof curtains at the back. 'Mind the step.' It was dark after the day-bright Lookout, the only light the faint glow from a computer console and the three radar screens. It was the left hand screen that was linked to the Dungeness scanner and the circling sweep showed two very distinct, very bright, elongated blips to the south and east of Dungeness. 'What's the course and speed now?' Evans asked.

'Just a minute, sir. They've just altered to clear the Varne.' The watch officer leaned over, fed in three bearings on the central monitoring screen and at the touch of a button the computer came up with the answer: 'O-six-O degrees now, sir. Speed unchanged at just over eighteen.'

'Looks like the Sandettié light vessel and the deep-water channel.' Evans was speaking to himself rather than to me. 'Outside the French twelve-mile limit all the way.' He looked round at me. 'Should be able to see them any minute now.' And he added, 'That friend of yours, Saltley – he'll be arriving at Dover airport in about an hour. Apparently he's chartered a small Spanish plane.' He turned quickly and went out through the curtains. 'Try calling them on Channel 16,' he told the woman auxiliary manning the radio. 'By name.'

'Which one, sir? The *Ghazan Khan* or the—'

'No, not the Iraqi names. Try and call up Captain Hals on the *Aurora B*. See what happens.'

It was while she was trying unsuccessfully to do this that the watch officer in the Lookout reported one of the tankers was visible. The Secretary of State came back from lunching with the Governor of Dover Castle and those not working in the Lookout were hustled out.

Another squall swept in and for a while rain obliterated the Straits so that all we could see was the blurred outline of the harbour. Saltley arrived in the middle of it. I was on the upper deck then, looking down through the glass panels, and I could see him standing by the state-of-readiness boards in front of the big map, talking urgently to the Minister and Basildon-Smith, his arms beginning to wave about. He was there about ten minutes, then the three of them moved out of sight into the Radar Room. Shortly afterwards he came hurrying up to the gallery, gave me a quick nod of greeting and asked the auxiliary to get him the Admiralty. 'If the DoT won't do anything, maybe the Navy will.' He looked tired and strained, the bulging eyes red-rimmed, his hair still wet and ruffled by the wind. He wanted the tankers arrested or at least stopped and searched to discover the identity of the people running them and whether they had prisoners on board.

The squall passed and suddenly there they were, plainly visible to the naked eye, with the frigate in close attendance. They were almost due south of us, about seven miles away, their black hulls merged with the rain clouds over the French coast, but the two superstructures showing like distant cliffs in a stormy shaft of sunlight.

Saltley failed to get Admiral Fitzowen and after a long talk with somebody else at the Admiralty, he put in a call to Stewart. 'I've a damned good mind to contact the Prime Minister myself,' he said as he joined me by the window. 'Two pirated ships sailing under false names with a naval escort and we do nothing. It's bloody silly.' I don't know whether it was anger or tiredness, but there was a slight hesitancy in his speech that I had never noticed before. In all the time I had been with him in the close confines of the *Prospero* I had never seen him so upset. 'There's thirty or forty million involved in the hulls alone, more on the cargoes. I told the Minister and all he says is that underwriting is a risk business and nobody but a fool becomes a Member of Lloyd's without being prepared to lose his shirt. But this isn't any ordinary risk. A bunch of terrorists – you can't counter claim against them in the courts, there's no legal redress. The bloody man should act – on his own responsibility. That's what we have Ministers for. Instead, he's like a little boy on the pier watching some pretty ships go by.'

The bearing of the tankers was very slowly changing. Both VHF and R/T channels were filling the air with irate comments from ships finding themselves heading straight for a bows-on collision, the CNIS watch officer continually issuing warnings for westbound traffic to keep to the inshore side of the land and maintain a sharp radar watch in the rain-storms.

They were all in the Lookout now, the Minister, Basildon-Smith and Captain Evans, with Saltley hovering in the background and everybody watching to see whether the tankers would hold on for the Sandettié light vessel and the deepwater channel or turn north. A journalist beside me muttered something to the effect that if they ran amok in Ekofisk or any of the bigger North Sea oilfields there could be catastrophic pollution.

It was at this point that I was suddenly called to the Lookout and as I entered the big semicircular glassed-in room I heard the Minister ask what the state of readiness of the Pollution Control Unit was. His voice was sharp and tense, and when Evans replied that he'd spoken to Admiral Denleigh just before lunch and the whole MPCU organization was alerted, but no dispersant stock piles had yet been moved, he said, 'Yes, yes, of course. You already told me. No point in starting to shift vast quantities of chemical sprays until we have a better idea of where they'll be needed.'

'They may not be needed at all, sir,' Evans said.

The Minister nodded, but his expression, as he turned away, indicated that he hadn't much hope of that. 'I should have been speaking at a big party rally in Aberdeen this afternoon.' His voice was high and petulant. 'On oil and the environment.' He was glaring at the Head of his Marine Division as though he were to blame for bringing him south, maybe losing precious votes. But then he saw me. 'Ah, Mr Rodin – this man Hals. He's not answering. We've tried repeatedly, VHF and R/T. Somebody's got to get through to him.'

His eyes were fixed on mine. 'You've met him. You've talked to him. I'm sending you out there. See if you can get through to him.'

'But—' I was thinking of the dhow, the way I'd left the ship. 'How?' I asked. 'How do you mean – get through to him?'

'*Tigris* is sending a helicopter for you. It's already been flown off so it should be here any minute. Now about this story of somebody flashing a light from one of the tankers. Saltley here says you and a young man on this yacht both thought it was some sort of signal. Morse code. Is that right?'

'I didn't see it myself,' I said, and started to tell him about the circumstances. But he brushed that aside. 'The letter M, that's what Saltley here has just told me. Is that right?'

'Several quick flashes, then two longs,' I said. 'We were in the tanker's wake then—'

'Two longs, that's M in Morse, is it?'

'Or two Ts. But we were being flung about—'

'You think it could have been part of a name.' He turned to Saltley again. 'One of the crew held prisoner on board signalling with a torch or a light switch, trying to give you the destination.' He moved forward so that he was standing by the radar monitor, his eyes fastening on me again. 'What do you say, Rodin? You stated quite categorically that in the case of the *Aurora B*, members of the crew were being held prisoner. Was this an attempt, do you think, to communicate and give you the target these terrorists are aiming at?'

'It's a possibility,' I said.

'No more than a possibility?' He nodded slowly. 'And the only one to see it was this boy. In a panic, was he? You'd nearly been run down.'

'Excited,' I told him. 'We all were, but nothing wrong with his ability to observe accurately.'

He smiled thinly. 'Then it's a pity he wasn't able to decipher more of the message – if it was a message. There's an M in several of our estuary names, the Thames, the Humber—'

'And the Maas,' Evans said sharply. 'Ports like Amsterdam, Hamburg, Bremen, and Rotterdam, there's two Ts there.' He pointed to the plot marked up on the large scale chart laid out on the flat surround below the Lookout windows. 'If it's our coast they're headed for, they'll have to turn soon or they'll be blocked by the Fairy and North Hinder banks.'

'Suppose the target were the North Sea oilfields?'

Evans shook his head. 'Those tankers are already loaded. They'd have no excuse.'

The chop-chop-chop of a helicopter came faintly through the glass windows. I turned to Saltley. 'Is this your idea?' I was remembering Pamela's warning that evening in Funchal. 'Did you put it into his head?' I could see myself being lowered by winch on to the deck of the *Aurora B*. 'Well, I'm not going,' I said, watching, appalled, as the helicopter emerged out of the rain, sidling towards us across the wind.

'Don't be a fool,' he said. 'All we want is for them to see you, on the bridge of the *Tigris*. A loud hailer. It's more personal than a voice on the air.'

I think the Minister must have sensed my

reluctance, for he came over and took me by the arm. 'Nothing to be worried about. All we want is for you to talk to him, make him see reason. And if you can't do that, then try and get the destination out of him. In any terrorist situation, it's getting through, making contact – that's the important thing.'

'Hals isn't a terrorist,' I said.

He nodded. 'So I gather. You and he – you talk the same language. You're both concerned about pollution. He won't talk to us here, but he may to you, when he sees you right alongside him. Commander Fellowes has his instructions. Make contact with him, that's all I ask. Find out what the target is.' He nodded to the naval liaison officer, who took hold of my other arm and before I could do anything about it I was being hurried down the stairs and out to the car park. The noise of the helicopter was very loud. It came low over the top of the Lookout and I watched, feeling as though I was on the brink of another world, as it settled like a large mosquito in a gap between the gorse bushes. The pilot signalled to us and we ducked under the rotor blades. The door slid open and I was barely inside before it took off, not bothering to climb, but making straight out over the Dover cliffs, heading for the *Tigris*.

Five minutes later we landed on the pad at the frigate's stern and I was taken straight to the bridge where the captain was waiting for me. 'Fellowes,' he said, shaking me by the hand. 'We're going close alongside now. Hope you can get some sense out of them. They're an odd-looking crowd.'

The bridge was built on a curve, not unlike the Lookout, but the changed view from the windows was quite dramatic. From the shore-based Operations Centre the tankers had been no more than distant silhouettes low down on the horizon. Now, suddenly, I was seeing them in close-up, huge hunks of steel-plating low in the water, the *Aurora B* looming larger and larger as the relatively tiny frigate closed her at almost thirty knots. 'We'll come down to their speed when we're abreast of the superstructure, then the idea is for you to go out on to the open deck and talk direct.' He handed me a loud hailer. 'Just press the trigger when you want to speak. Don't shout or you'll deafen yourself. It's a pretty loud one, that.' He turned his head, listening as the ship's name was called on VHF. It was the Dover Coastguards wanting to know whether contact had yet been made with the *Aurora B*. He reached for a mike and answered direct: '*Tigris* to Coastguard. Helicopter and passenger have just arrived. We're all set here. Am closing now. Over.'

We were coming in from the west at an oblique angle, the bulk of the *Aurora B* gradually blotting out the shape of the other tanker, which was about a mile to the east. The Dover cliffs showed as a dirty white smudge on our port side and there were several ships in the westbound lane, foam at their bows as the waves broke over them. Closer at hand, two small drifters danced on the skyline, and almost dead ahead of us, I could see the ungainly lanterned shape of a light vessel.

'The Sandettié,' Cdr Fellowes said. 'We'll be in the deepwater channel in ten to fifteen minutes.' Behind him the radio suddenly poured out a torrent of French. It was the fishery protection vessel now shadowing the tankers from the eastbound lane. We could just see it past the *Aurora B*'s stern steaming north-east ahead of a large ore carrier. 'Ready?' Fellowes asked me, and I nodded, though I didn't feel at all ready. What the hell was I going to say to Hals?

I was still thinking about that, the loud hailer gripped in my hand, as he led me out on to the starb'd side deck below the tall square needle of the radar mast. The *Tigris* was turning now, her speed slowing as we ranged alongside the tanker's superstructure. I could see the length of its deck, all the pipes and inspection hatches that I had stumbled over in the night, the long line of the catwalk. And right above me now the wheelhouse with faces I recognized framed in its big windows. Sadeq was there and the Canadian, Rod Selkirk, and two men I didn't know, both of them dark and bearded. And then Hals appeared, his pale hair and beard framed in the glass of the bridge wing door. I raised the loud hailer to my lips. *Captain Hals*. I had my finger locked tight round the trigger and even my breathing came out in great audible puffs. *This is Rodin. Trevor Rodin. I was with you in the Gulf, that* khawr – *remember? It's Rodin*, I repeated. *Please come out on to the bridge wing. I want to talk to you.*

I thought he was going to. I saw the uncertainty on his face, could almost read his intention in the expression of his eyes. We were that close, it seemed. *I must speak to you, Pieter. About pollution.* He moved then. I'm certain of it, reaching out to slide open the door. But then Sadeq was beside him, and one of the others. A moment later they were gone, all three of them, the glass panel empty.

'Ask for his destination,' Fellowes said. 'That's what CINCHAN wants and he's got the SoS breathing down his neck. Try again.'

But it was no use. I kept on calling over the loud hailer, but there was no response. And no faces at the window, the bridge appearing blind now as the tanker ploughed on. 'Well, that's that, I guess.' Fellowes turned away, walking quickly back to his wheelhouse. I remained there, the wind on my face, sensing the heel of the ship as the *Tigris* pulled away from the tanker, dropping back until the light vessel became visible beyond the blunt rounded stern. It was so close now that the name SANDETTIÉ stood out very clear on its hull. We were in the deepwater channel.

It was then, just as I was turning to follow the captain back into the shelter of the frigate's bridge, that something happened, up there on the tanker's high superstructure. The door to the bridge wing was suddenly slid back, four men stumbling out in a cloud of thick billowing smoke. And the tanker was turning. I could see the bows shifting away from us, very slowly. She was turning to starb'd, towards the Sandettié bank, towards the other tanker. And her speed was increasing. She was drawing ahead, her stern turning towards us so that I could no longer see what was happening, the bridge wing empty, no sign of anybody, only the smoke hanging in a haze behind the super-structure. I dived back into the frigate's wheelhouse and as I came through the door I heard Fellowes' voice calling: '*Tigris* to Coastguard. Something odd going on. The *Aurora B* is shifting course. She's turning to starb'd. Also she's on fire. There's smoke pouring out of the wheelhouse area. Looks as though she intends to close the other tanker. Over.'

'Any change of speed?' It was Evans's voice.

'Yes, she's increased at least a knot. Her bows are pointing diagonally across the channel now. And she's still turning . . .'

'*Aurora B. Aurora B.*' It was Evans again, his voice a little higher. 'You're standing into danger. *Ghazan Khan.* This is Dover Coastguard. We have you on our radar. You are approaching collision course. I repeat – collision course. You are standing into danger.'

Silence then. A deathly hush on the frigate's bridge and the tanker still turning. And just below the clouds, circling ponderously, was the Nimrod, the pilot quietly confirming that from where he was, right above the tankers, collision appeared inevitable. Then, suddenly, a new voice: '*Tigris.* This is the Secretary of State for Trade. I want you to stop that tanker, put a shot across the bows. Acknowledge.'

'I can't, sir,' Fellowes replied. 'Not at the moment. She's stern-on to us and the other ship's right ahead of her in the line of fire.' And almost in the same breath he was dictating a signal to CINCHAN and ordering gun crews closed up. The loudspeaker crackled into life again, a different voice calmly reporting: 'On collision course now.' It was the watch officer on surveillance duty in the Radar Room fourteen miles away. 'Two minutes forty-seven seconds to impact.'

'My God!' It was the Minister again. '*Tigris*.' His voice was suddenly firm and decisive. 'That rogue tanker. Open fire immediately. On the stern. Take the rudder off, the propeller too.'

'Is that an order, sir?' And as the Minister said, 'Yes, yes, an order,' a voice I recognized as Saltley's said, 'If that Navy ship opens fire, I have to tell you it could be argued later that you were responsible for the subsequent collision.'

There was a short silence. Fellowes was handed a signal, gun crews were reporting and the frigate was gathering speed, turning to starb'd. I could see the bows of the *Aurora B*, now barely half a mile from the long low shape of the ship she was going to ram, and in that moment I had a clear mental picture of the wheelhouse and Hals standing there in the smoke and flame steering his ship to total destruction. It was deliberate. It had to be. Like Karen – immolation, death, it didn't matter, the object a disaster that would shake Europe into action. And in the silence the Minister's voice shouting, 'Open fire, man. Hurry! There's barely a minute to go.'

I heard Fellowes give the order, and in that same moment a new voice erupted on the air: 'Rodin! Are you there? Can you hear me?' It was Pieter Hals. 'It's fixed now. Nothing they can do.' There was a crash, a spurt of flame from the for'ard gun turret and instantaneously a matching eruption from the tanker's stern. It was low down on the waterline, a single shot, and the whole blunt end of the *Aurora B* instantly disintegrated into a tangle of steel, like a sardine can ripped open at one end. The ship staggered at the impact, smoke and flames and the debris of torn-out steering gear and bollards splashing the sea. But it made no difference. The gaping hole, and the sea rushing in – it didn't alter her course, it didn't stop her progress through the water. With her steering entrails hanging out of her stern she went ploughing on, and in the sudden silence Hals screaming, 'It's fixed, I tell you. Nothing you can do about it. Seconds now . . .' There was a noise like ripping calico, the sound of a great gasp of air – 'Go-o-d!'

I heard it, but somehow I didn't take it in, the moment of Pieter Hals's death. My gaze, my whole consciousness was fixed on the *Aurora B*'s bows. They were turning now, turning back to her original course – but too slowly. Steadily, relentlessly they were closing the gap that separated them from the other tanker. There was no further order to fire, nothing *Tigris* could do, the oil-filled bulk of the tanker ploughing on and everybody holding their breath waiting for the moment of impact.

It came, strangely, without any sound, a crumpling of the bows, a curling up and ripping open of steel plates below the *Howdo Stranger*'s superstructure, all in slow time. And it went on and on, for the collision was at an oblique angle and the *Aurora B* went slicing up the whole long side of the other tanker, ripping her open from end to end, and the sound of that disembowelment came to us as a low grinding and crunching that went on and on, endlessly.

It stopped in the end, after what seemed a great while, the two black-hulled leviathans finally coming to rest with barely two or three cables of open water between them, water that became dark and filthy, almost black, with the crude oil bubbling out of them, the waves all flattened by the weight of it. No fire. No smoke. Just the oil bubbling up from under the sea like a volcano erupting.

The Nimrod made a slow pass over the scene, the pilot reporting – 'From where I'm sitting it looks as though both tankers are aground on the Sandettié. One has her port side completely shattered. She was going astern at the moment of collision so she really got herself carved up. She still has her engines at full astern. I can see the prop churning up the seabed, a lot of brown mud and sand mixing with the oil pouring out of her tanks. The other tanker – the rogue – she's got her bows stove in, of course, and it looks as though she's holed on the starb'd side right back as far as the pipe derricks. A lot of oil coming out of her, too . . .'

And Pieter Hals dead. I was quite certain he was dead. That sound had been the chatter of automatics. 'Looks like the Kent coast is going to get the brunt of it,' Fellowes said quietly. The forecast was for the westerly winds to back south-easterly and increase to gale force in the southern North Sea. And since oil slicks move at roughly one-thirtieth of the wind speed he reckoned the first of the oil would come ashore right below the Langdon Battery Operations Centre at about noon the next day.

It was two days later, after dark, that I finally arrived back at Balkaer, stumbling down the cliff path in the starlight, the squat shape of the cottage showing black against the pale glimmer of the sea. There'd be a fire to welcome me, Jean had said when I'd phoned her from London, and now I could see the smoke of it drifting lazily up. I could hear the beat of the waves in the cove, the sound of them surging along the cliffs. Suddenly I felt as though I had never been away, everything so familiar. I would lift the latch and Karen would come running . . .

The key was there in the door and it wasn't locked. I lifted the latch and pushed it open. The bright glow of the fire lit the interior, shadows flickering on the walls, and I was thinking of her as I closed the door, shutting out the sound of the sea in the cove. And then I turned, and my heart stood still.

She was sitting in the chair. In her own chair. Sitting there by the fire, her hands in her lap, her head turned towards me and her face in shadow. She was watching me. I could feel her eyes on me and my knees were like water.

'Karen!'

I heard myself breathe her name, and the figure rose from the chair, her firelit shadow climbing from wall to ceiling, so big it filled the room.

She spoke then, and it wasn't Karen, it wasn't her voice.

'I'm so sorry,' she said. 'I'm afraid I startled you.' The voice was liquid, a soft lilt that was Welsh like Karen's, but a different intonation. 'Jean Kerrison—' she pronounced it Jarne. 'They're out this evening, at St Ives. So she gave me the key, said I could wait for you here.'

'Why?' I had recognized her now and my voice was hostile, thinking of the miles of beaches black with oil, all those ships, men working round the clock – the *Petros Jupiter* all over again, and now Choffel's daughter, here at Balkaer. Had they found his body? Was that it? Was he still alive? 'Why?' I said again. 'Why have you come here?'

She gave a shrug. 'To say I am sorry, I suppose.' She had turned away so that the fire's glow was on her face and I could see the determined line of the jaw, the broad brow beneath the jet black hair. 'Did Jarne tell you she came to see me? In London. Almost a month ago, it was. She came to my hotel.'

'Jean – to London!' I was still staring at her.

'She want to tell me about the ship my father is in, the *Petros Jupiter*, and how you were out in a boat searching for your wife in a fog when she destroyed it. She want to tell me also what kind of man you are, so that I would know, you see, that you were not the man to kill my father.' I had moved towards the fire and the flames lit her face as she looked at me, her expression strangely serene. 'She is very fond of you, I think.' And she added, 'You are a lucky man to have

463

people like Jarne and Jim Kerrison who will do so much for you. She almost convince me, you see.'

'So you still think I killed him?'

'It's true then. You don't know.' She half shook her head, sitting down again and smiling gently to herself. 'I don't believe it when she tell me you don't know.'

I stared at her, feeling suddenly very tired. 'What is all this? Why are you here?'

'I tell you, to say I am sorry. I didn't believe you, but now I know.' And then she blurted it out: 'I have withdrawn everything – everything I say about you. I should have done that after Jarne saw me, but instead I went back to France. I do not say anything, not then. But now... There is a full statement from the Pakistani crew. Everything you say about how my father is shot and wounded is confirmed. It was that man Sadeq.' She hesitated, and there were tears in her eyes. Then she said, her voice almost choked with emotion, 'So now I am here. To apologize to you, and to ask you something...' Again the hesitation. 'A favour.' There was a long silence. At length she said, 'Will you tell me what happened please, on the *Aurora B*, when you meet my father, and later, particularly later, when you are together on the dhow.'

I had slumped into my usual chair, unable to think of anything at that moment but the fact that I was cleared. Free! Free of everything now, except the past. Just as he had said, no one can escape that.

'Please,' she said. 'I want to know.'

'It's all in my statement.'

'I know it is. I have read it. But that is not the same, is it now? I would like you to tell me yourself.'

Go through it all again! I shook my head.

'Please,' she pleaded. And suddenly she was out of the chair, squatting on the rush matting at my feet. 'Don't you understand? What I did to you, the accusations, the anger, the hate – yes, hate – was because I loved him. He was such a gentle, kindly man, and with my mother dead, he was all I had. He brought me up, and whatever he did wrong was done out of love for my mother. Try to understand, will you – and forgive.' Silence then and the firelight flickering on her face, her eyes staring at me very wide. 'What did you talk about, on that dhow? What did he say? He must have said much. All that time together, two days. Two whole days.'

I nodded slowly, the memory of him in that stinking cubby-hole under the poop coming back. And now, looking down on her, crouched there at my own fireside, I understood her need. She was his daughter. She had a right to know. So in the end I told her everything, even admitting to her that when I'd joined him on the dhow it had been with the intention of killing him.

She didn't comment on that. She didn't interrupt me once, and as I talked, her face so intent, her dark eyes seeming to hang on my words, it was like talking to Karen again.

THE BIG FOOTPRINTS

Dedicated to the memory of

BILLY

who was my publisher for over thirty years, a
friend whose enthusiasm was a constant source
of encouragement; that the last book of mine he
was to read should have been this story of Africa
is strangely appropriate and the best tribute I can
offer him.

September 1976

CONTENTS

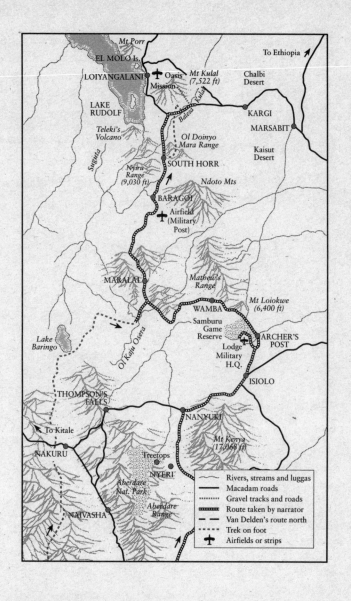

Mt Porr

EL MOLO Is.

LOIYANGALANI

Oasis Mission

To Ethiopia

Mt Kulal
(7,522 ft)

Chalbi Desert

KARGI

MARSABIT

LAKE RUDOLF

Teleki's Volcano

Ol Doinyo Mara Range

Kaisut Desert

Nyiru Range
(9,030 ft)

SOUTH HORR

Ndoto Mts

BARAGOI

Airfield (Military Post)

MARALAL

Mathew's Range

Mt Loiokwe
(6,400 ft)

WAMBA

Samburu Game Reserve

ARCHER'S POST

Lake Baringo

Lodge Military H.Q.

ISIOLO

THOMPSON'S FALLS

NANYUKI

To Kitale

Mt Kenya
(17,068 ft)

NAKURU

Treetops

NYERI

Aberdare Nat. Park

NAIVASHA

Aberdare Range

Rivers, streams and luggas
Macadam roads
Gravel tracks and roads
Route taken by narrator
Van Delden's route north
Trek on foot
Airfields or strips

PART ONE

THE WILDLIFE CONFERENCE

CHAPTER ONE

It was raining, a solid tropical downpour, and the beer was warm. The supply trucks had brought it up with the food from Nairobi over the bomb-scarred gravel road I had glimpsed from the plane as we landed. We were rationed to one can each, the froth and the sweetness cloying, and the water unfit to drink. I looked at my watch. It was after ten and the night black, no chance that he would arrive now.

I lit a cigarette, perched on the crumbling parapet of what had once been a veranda, staring through the rain at the big half-circle of rooms lit by hurricane lamps and candles. The shattered glass of the sliding windows showed walls pock-marked by bullets. Some of the conference delegates were already preparing for bed, shadows in silhouette stripping off their clothes and climbing into the two-tier bunks. Others, like myself, out on the battered verandas, talking quietly, voices subdued by the atmosphere of the place.

The night was very still, no breeze, only the sound

of the rain falling vertically and somewhere the hum of a generator. The organizers had rigged lights in the dining-room and kitchens, but these had been switched off now, the power concentrated on spotlights beamed on the waterhole as though to remind us what the gathering was all about. The big circular pool showed pale and flat through the rain, but nothing moved, not even a bird. Perhaps there really were no animals left.

I finished my beer and the mood of depression settled deeper on me. I thought of all the tourists who had sat here on this veranda, lolling with ice-cold drinks, watching for elephants and rhinos, and all the small fry that had come like shadows out of the night to drink at the floodlit waterhole. It must have been quite a place then, the Lodge so carefully planned and the waterhole like a stage set. Now the lawn was a jungle growth, the swimming pool cracked and empty, the buildings battered and fallen into decay. It would make a good opening shot, but that was all, and a wildlife conference without wildlife . . . I stared at my cigarette, listening to the rain. It would be a dead duck, and the only reason I had accepted the assignment, the man I had come here to meet – Cornelius van Delden, who knew the northern frontier – not arrived yet.

The voices on the next veranda were louder now: *I tell you, it's pointless. The tourists won't come back, and without tourism . . .*

You agree with Kirby-Smith then?

About culling? Yes, if it's properly organized.

And somebody else, strident and angry: *Killing, you mean. Call it by its proper name, for God's sake. Shoot anything that moves, make way for cattle. And you call that culling.*

A heavy rasping Bostonian voice cut in. *Major Kirby-Smith is a businessman, that's all. So let's be practical, gentlemen. Call him what you like, but he's efficient and he's got the Government behind him. So I have to tell you this, the Foundation I represent accepts that this pilot scheme is the best deal we're . . .*

A figure appeared out of the night, dripping wet, his safari hat shielding his camera. 'Fabulous!' It was Ken's current word when he had something good. He had been playing around with his Leica taking stills. 'It's the rain and the hurricane lamps, all those bunks, and the bullet holes, reflections in pools of water.' He came in under the shelter of the veranda, shaking himself like a dog and smiling his satisfaction. 'It was in black and white, of course, but tomorrow, shooting in 7252 colour – could be difficult. The light, I mean.' He went through into the room behind me, enthusing again about the pictures he had taken, wiping his camera before he bothered to strip off and towel himself down. 'Our room mates are on their way.' His voice was muffled as he rubbed at the dark mass of hair. 'Two CBS men.'

'How do you know?'

'Karanja told me. They're coming by truck. He was posting an attendance list on the noticeboard.'

'Was van Delden on it?'

He shook his head, towelling vigorously. 'There was a Delden representing some American magazine. But the initial was M. There was no Cornelius van Delden.'

So he wasn't coming after all. The one man who really knew the NFD, the man whose father had opened the route across the Chalbi Desert to Lake Rudolf and published a book of his travels in Afrikaans.

'Have you roughed anything out yet?'

'No.' And I stayed there, staring out at the rain, thinking about the script, convinced it wouldn't be any good and the whole thing a waste of time now that Cornelius van Delden wasn't coming.

In the end I went inside and mulled over the agenda and the old tourist maps they had given us, sitting at the broken-legged camp table with the hurricane lamp at my elbow. Tsavo, Serengeti, Arusha, Ngorongoro and its crater, all those national parks and game reserves that had once been household names, and in the North – Meru, Samburu, Marsabit. And further north still, up by Lake Rudolf on the Ethiopian border, the least known, most remote of all – Ileret. At dinner they had been talking about Ileret and unconfirmed reports of game moving up the Rift Valley to the waters of Lake Rudolf. The only real haven left, they had said. But none of them had known Ileret. To them it was the edge of the unknown, all desert country and lava fields, and across the BP map, glazed to protect its surface against the sweat of tourists' hands, some official had banged his rubber stamp, the single word FORBIDDEN staring at me in violet ink.

The map didn't mark Porr, or the islands, only Loiyangalani and Mt Kulal – Oasis Fishing Camp, it said. There would be no fishing camp now, and I didn't need to measure the mileage. I knew how far it was, a hell of a long way, and the whole area forbidden territory. I reached for my bag, for the map and the translation of that old book – but what was the point of reading the typescript again? I knew the passages by heart, the map clear in my mind, and who else could take me there in present circumstances? *I am retired now, but if they ask me I will come.* Well, they had asked him and he wasn't here and the Conference opening in the morning.

I leaned back, staring at the wall opposite, where a gecko flicked its tongue, feet and tail spread flat like a little jewelled brooch – the only sign of life. Ken turned in his bunk, complaining about the light, and I told him to go to hell. I was feeling angry and frustrated, the rain drumming on the roof, gushing from the broken guttering, the persistent sound of it filling the room and a trickle of water seeping in at one corner where the plaster was cracked and stained. It glistened wet in the lamplight and I was thinking of the last time I had seen the kindly, ineffective man who had helped to bring me up. Almost a year ago now, and his hand quite steady as he gave me Pieter van Delden's book and the translator's typescript of it headed JOURNEY THROUGH THE CHALBI TO LAKE RUDOLF. Tucked into the typescript I had found the map drawn on heavy parchment paper. Two days later he had been found dead in that same dingy little basement office in Doughty Street.

The gecko moved, darting its long tongue at some insect, and I remembered his words, the sense of failure – *There's nothing else of any value for you here.* Those words had stayed in my mind. Had there been a note of censure in his voice? I couldn't remember now. Probably not. He had been too mild a man, and at the time I had regarded his words as a sort of epitaph to his mismanagement of Southly Tait. When he had taken over from my father it had been quite a thriving little publishing house specializing in travel. Inflation and a changing world had killed it – and him. Or was it my fault, not his? If I had gone into the business, as they had both hoped . . .

I pushed back my chair and got to my feet. It had been a long twenty-four hours, the night flight to Nairobi, the interminable wait on the cratered tarmac at Wilson Airport – odd how habit had retained that very English name – and now the rain, the bloody everlasting rain, and this damnable dreary battered place. I should have brought some Scotch. I could hear the clink of glasses next door, the sound of voices mellowed by drink. A bottle of Scotch would have cushioned my mind against the morbid thought of his inadequacy and my own selfish determination to go my own way. Ken Stewart was asleep now. I could hear his breathing, soft as a child's, and I envied him living for the moment, for the instant exposure of his next shot, his total involvement in camera angles.

I started to undress then, wondering whether I could have breathed some life into the business. The memory of his body laid out in that funeral parlour had haunted me ever since. The rain, my own loneliness, the dreary atmosphere of this Lodge – he had been lonely, too, after my aunt's death, and I had been too busy writing scripts, launching my own company, to help him cope with a rundown business and an alien world. And now here I was in Africa trying to make use of the only thing he had left me – a map that he had asked me to return, knowing he was going to die.

Footsteps sounded on the veranda outside. I was half undressed and I turned to find a soldier holding an umbrella and two men coming in out of the rain. Their plastic macs dripped water on the tiled floor as they introduced themselves. They were both TV men, the taller of the two, Erd Lindstrom, fair-haired, blue-eyed, the other, Abe Finkel, slim, dark and intensely Jewish. 'You're representing the BBC, are you?'

'On assignment only.'

'An independent, eh?' He stared at me, then gave a quick shrug. 'Well, I guess it has its advantages.' But I knew what he was thinking as they dumped their equipment and stripped off their plastics. 'Has anybody given you a forecast? How long is this rain gonna last? It's supposed to be the dry season.'

'The little rains didn't materialize, so they think this may be it and the weather out of step again.'

'So we film it all against a backdrop of rain. And we were told there was a drought. That's why we

trucked up. Thought we might get some shots of elephant carcasses, something to give a visual point to
all the talk, and the rain caught us as we climbed up
out of the Rift. You been out at all since the rain
started?'

'No.'

'Hear that, Erd? They've been stuck in this dump
since the rain started.' His voice was in time with the
rain, a flat continuous monotone. 'At least we got
shots of the truck up to its axles, but I'm sure glad
we don't have to market this one. That Karanja says
nobody's seen anything since they arrived, not even
the elephant who used to go the rounds of the garbage
cans each morning at breakfast time. You seen
anything?'

'Nothing.'

Ken rolled over, blinking his eyes. 'I got a quick
shot at a warthog, tail up and going like a little train.
But the light was bad and we're using 7252 – Ekta-
chrome Commercial. If this rain continues we'd do
better with EF 7241. You got any of that?'

It was Lindstrom who answered. 'No, we're on
Kodak 7242, and it's negative, not reversal.' They
were equipped with a Bolex and a Bach-Auricon.
They also had the remains of a bottle of rye, so that
by the time I finally climbed into my bunk I was
happily insulated against morbid thoughts.

The opening day of what was officially designated
the East African Federation's Conference on Wildlife
Resources dawned humid and heavy, the air reeking
of wet earth. It had stopped raining, but that was

about all, the clouds hanging over the Lodge like a damp blanket, moist and menacing. Breakfast was a soup-kitchen affair, tin mugs and platters on the verandas because the dining-room roof had leaked during the night and all the tables were wet. The room toilets and showers didn't work, of course, and the area around the tin-roofed conference latrines was soon a quagmire of reddish mud. There were several women delegates and Ken made the most of their ablutions until he was distracted by the appearance of Karanja in a neat grey suit, an ingratiating grin on his face and his big ears standing out like sails. He was holding a loudhailer as though it were a bazooka.

'Guess the Minister hasn't made it,' Abe Finkel said.

Karanja reached the centre of what had once been the lawn, turned to face the half-circle of rooms and put the loudhailer to his lips. 'Conference delegates and newspeople please I have to express the regret of our Minister, but due to circumstances of so unusual weather . . .' The Conference, due to open at ten with a speech of welcome to the delegates by Mr Kimani, Minister for Lands and Resources, was postponed until his aircraft could get through. It was not an auspicious start.

'Pity we can't take off for the Serengeti on our own.'

I pointed to the agenda. 'That's scheduled for tomorrow. Also a view of the cattle reserve in the Crater.'

'It'll be scrubbed,' Abe said. 'The only thing of real interest . . .'

A figure squelched on to the veranda. I didn't realize it was a young woman, not immediately, for she was tall and broad-shouldered, dressed like a hardened safari hunter in faded khaki trousers, bush jacket and worn calf-length boots, a floppy hat on her head with an ostrich feather stuck in it. 'Any of you men Colin Tait?' Her voice came deep from the throat, slightly husky.

I got up. 'Yes, I'm Colin Tait.'

She stared at me, a long, hard, searching look. 'I'd like a word with you.' And she turned abruptly and stepped down into the trampled grass, standing there, waiting. 'I'm Mary Delden,' she said as I joined her. 'Shall we go down towards the waterhole? I can't talk to you here.' She began walking then and she didn't say anything more until we had gone beyond the Lodge buildings, past what had been the VIP suite with its veranda directly facing on to the water. The long stalks of the drought-sered grass were wet with the rain, my trousers soaked by the time we stopped out of earshot. 'You wrote to Cornelius van Delden.'

'You're related, are you?'

She nodded. 'My father.' She had a dark, very unusual face, rather long with a wide, thin-lipped mouth and a determined jaw; but it was the nose that was the dominant feature, strong and aquiline. Her eyes, as she faced me, were large and of a deep aquamarine colour, the whites made whiter by the darkness of her skin. 'I dropped the "van" when I went to

America. There were political undertones and as a journalist Mary Delden seemed a more appropriate name.' She smiled and the smile lit up her whole face, softening the virility of it. 'Anyway, my mother was Italian, not South African.' Then abruptly she said, 'What did you want to see him about? You didn't say in your letter, only that you had a copy of *Reis deur Chalbi* and it contains new information about . . .'

'I was expecting to meet him here.'

'You don't want to tell me, is that it?' She said it lightly, still smiling, but the jut of the jaw, the frosty look in her eyes betrayed a certain hostility. 'Let's walk on.'

I hesitated, reminding her that the Conference was due to open as soon as the Minister arrived. She gave a derisive laugh. 'Nothing is going to happen today and the Conference won't start until tomorrow.'

'Did Karanja tell you that?'

'Of course not. But you've looked at your agenda. Tomorrow we were all going off in the supply trucks to have a look at the Serengeti and the Ngorongoro. The organizers in America insisted on that. Can you imagine what the mood of the Conference would be if the delegates were allowed to see the plains empty, the migrating herds all dead, no predators, not even a vulture, and the Crater full of cattle?' Her voice had risen sharply. 'They've been bloody lucky with the weather.'

'How do you mean?'

She looked at me as though I were a fool. 'It was never intended we should see the Serengeti. They'd have found some reason for the Minister to be delayed. Or the trucks would all have broken down. They'd have explained it in some way. Now they have the weather, a perfect excuse. Have you ever been to East Africa before?' she asked.

'No.'

She nodded as though it confirmed the impression she had already formed. And then she began questioning me, not about the reason for my seeking a meeting with her father, but about my background. Clearly she wanted to know what sort of person I was and I sensed that she was trying to make up her mind about something. Finally she stopped. We were at the far side of the waterhole. 'I don't know,' she said uncertainly. 'We've got time enough, all morning, but . . .' Her mouth tightened. 'I think you'd better tell me what it's all about.'

'I'm sorry,' I said.

'You're not doubting I'm Cornelius van Delden's daughter?'

I shook my head, wondering when she had seen him.

'Then why won't you tell me? Why the secrecy? Is it something in his past, something that happened up there at Marsabit?' She was staring at me, her eyes puzzled. 'No, of course not. That book was written long before. So what makes you think he'd risk his life to take you into the NFD?'

Something swept over my head, the whisper of wings planing, and a stork landed by the water, disturbing a pair of guinea fowl. It was the first sign of life I had seen. 'How did you know about my letter? Did you see your father before coming on here?' And when she didn't answer, I said, 'Is he still in the Seychelles? That's where he wrote from. It's his home, isn't it?'

'Yes, it's his home now. An old planter's house on La Digue that belonged to my mother's family.'

'But you've seen him, haven't you?' She must have. How else would she know about my letter. 'In his reply to me he said if they asked him, he'd come. I was expecting to meet him . . .'

'Do you really think they'd let him address a conference like this?' she demanded. 'Oh, yes, they asked him. They had to. With an international reputation like his . . . But he has too many enemies here. They'll never forgive him for saying that African cattle are an affront to God, that man should learn from animals how to keep the laws of nature and not plague the world with the product of his loins. Have you read his book *Man's Rage against Nature*?'

'No,' I said. 'But I've heard about it.'

'Then how could you think they'd allow him here, when all they're interested in is grabbing more land for the tribesmen's cattle. Kit Kimani is a hard-liner as far as animals are concerned, absolutely blinkered. I don't know where Karanja stands now – he was with us in the old days at Marsabit – but human greed is what dictates policy and the political pressures of a population explosion which has been going on now . . .' She gave a little shrug as though she thought it a waste of time explaining the problems of Africa to somebody who had never been there before. Then, speaking more slowly and in a quieter tone, 'When he landed at Nairobi Airport his passport was taken from him. A South African, they said. That was their excuse, though they knew damn well he hadn't been in South Africa since he was a child, and for the past three years he'd been living in the Seychelles.'

'So he did come.'

'Four days ago. He thought he might be able to influence the Government, not Kimani, but some of the others. He knows most of them.'

'You saw him in Nairobi then? Is he still there?'

'No, of course not. The security police kept him at the airport until the following night when a flight for the Far East came in. It refuels at Mahé in the Seychelles.'

So he had gone back and that was that. No chance now of discovering whether he had ever been to the top of Porr, of trying to persuade him to take me up into that forbidden area.

'Do you speak Afrikaans?' she asked.

I shook my head, still thinking about the documentary I had dreamed of, a new discovery that might have made my name and perhaps a lot of money.

'But you've read *Reis deur Chalbi na die Rudolfmeer*. That's what you inferred in your letter. A map, you said. There was no map in Pieter van Delden's book. Did you invent that?'

I shook my head.

'And it was never published in English, only in

Afrikaans – at Pietermaritzberg in 1908. So how could you have read it?'

I didn't know what to say, so I kept my mouth shut.

'I think I'm beginning to understand.' She was smiling, but not with her eyes. 'There's an English translation, unpublished. Now, what could there possibly be in that translation that is not in the original?' And then suddenly she switched to something else. 'You made a TV film on sea pollution. It was you, wasn't it?'

I nodded. It was the only one of my films to make the American market.

'I saw it. A very good production. But no heart.'

'It was a documentary on giant tankers and the problems of oil spillage,' I said, not following her train of thought. 'How can a subject like that engage the emotions?' Except fear, of course. It had frightened the life out of me when I was making it.

'Technological problems. You dealt with those all right. But you didn't follow on to show what happened to the seabirds and the dolphins and the seals.' She had suddenly become very tense. 'But now you're here . . . Why do you want to go into the Northern Frontier District?'

'If I could have talked with your father . . .'

'Why should he take you?' She was staring at me and again I had the impression that she was trying to make up her mind about something. 'You're not concerned about Marsabit and what happened to the elephants there. Why didn't you approach Alex Kirby-

Smith who has some influence with this new régime?' She paused, her extraordinary eyes fixed on me. 'It's the book, isn't it – something in the translation?'

'It's time we went back,' I said. 'The Minister will be arriving—'

'Kimani isn't going to arrive till the evening and the Conference won't start before tomorrow.' Her mood suddenly changed. 'I'm sorry, I shouldn't have said that about your tanker film. Few people care about the sufferings of animals. It's just that I was brought up . . .' She hesitated, the expression of her face gradually changing, a softer, almost appealing look. 'Won't you tell me what it is – this information you have?' There was a softness in her voice, too, and her hand touched my arm. 'I can contact him, you know.'

'How?'

But she only smiled. She was tall, about my own height, and her eyes, staring into mine, had a warmth I hadn't guessed at. 'Please tell me.' She was suddenly very feminine, all the hardness gone. I couldn't believe a girl could change so completely. Maybe it was the Italian blood in her, but I found her change of mood disturbing and I looked away from her, at the water-hole and the stork standing motionless, the bush running away into an endless vista of Africa, the Lodge remote and nobody near. We were alone and my own blood was responding to her warmth and the touch of her hand on my arm.

'Please,' she said again, and I shook my head, not trusting myself to speak for there was a tightness in my throat. She gave my arm a gentle squeeze, smiling at me with her eyes, her lips parted, conscious of the effect she was having. 'You must tell me,' she said. 'I can't decide unless you tell me.'

And because I thought it was just the story she was after, I said something about her taking after her mother, and that seemed to change her mood again, for she let go of my arm. 'I wouldn't know. She died when I was still a child.' There was a harshness in her voice as she said that. Her lips had tightened, the eyes gone hard again. 'So you're not going to tell me.'

'No,' I said. 'But if you know where I can contact your father . . .' I hesitated. 'I'm not having this hashed up for an American magazine.'

She laughed. 'You think I'd do that?' She turned, walking slowly away from me, and the stork rose, a slow flapping of wings as it beat its way across the waterhole, but she didn't look up, her eyes on the ground, deep in thought. Somewhere a dove was droning its somewhat do-doo-do call and I could hear the guinea fowl chattering, but nothing else, the heat pressing down and the clouds hanging in the sky with the promise of more rain.

When I looked at her again she had stopped and was bending down; she was watching a beetle rolling a ball of earth much larger than itself out of a hollow. 'That's a female dung beetle,' she murmured. 'The eggs are inside that ball.' Her gaze wandered along the edge of the waterhole, searching. 'Some animal has been here, otherwise there wouldn't be any dung to hatch the grubs.' She moved along the verge until she found what she was looking for, a turd the size of a football glistening with the rain. 'Phlump,' she said, and laughed. 'Elephants have always been phlumps in my childish vocabulary.' She stood contemplating the enormous stool with a frown. Then abruptly she turned and faced me. 'Can I trust you?' It wasn't a question that required an answer. She was speaking her thoughts aloud. 'I think perhaps . . . But I don't even know what it is that makes you want to go to Rudolf . . . It is Lake Rudolf, isn't it?'

I nodded. 'Lake Rudolf and a hill called Porr. Perhaps Kulal.'

'Kulal.' She said it slowly, rolling the name out as though there were some magic in it. 'I've always wanted to go to Kulal. Tembo is one of the very few men who really knows that strange volcanic mass . . . Will you promise—' But then she hesitated, shaking her head and smiling. 'No, that's no good. I'll have to trust you. Anyway, it's only for two days. On Thursday Alex addresses the Conference, then they'll face it out in front of the cameras and everybody will know.' She glanced down at the shoes I was wearing, gave a little shrug, then turned and began walking into the bush. 'It's not far,' she said over her shoulder. 'Half an hour or so, that's all.' And after that she didn't talk, walking with an easy swinging stride.

I didn't talk either, for we were almost immediately into an area of shallow swamp and it was as much as I could do not to lose my shoes. Once, waiting for me, she pointed to some tracks. 'Warthogs. If nothing else survives, the warthog will.' And she went striding on, brushing past a thicket of thorn and climbing a path through rock outcrops that had probably once been a game trail. And at the top she paused and nodded towards a line of green snaking across a burned-up plain. 'Down there,' she said. 'In the lugga.'

'You mean . . .' I hesitated, feeling bewildered, and she nodded, smiling. 'He's a very determined man. When he sets his hand to something . . .' She paused, then said, 'He went with the other passengers out to the aircraft, but he didn't board it. He just walked underneath it and out into the night, and nobody stopped him. By morning he was into the Ngong Hills, near an old camp where he had friends.' She was staring at me, and the expression on her face was very intense. 'It's dangerous for him. You realize that? They might kill him if they knew he was here.'

'But if he speaks at the Conference . . .' It didn't make sense. 'You said he was determined to speak.'

'At the Conference it will be different. He'll have the protection then of the delegates and people like us who report for the media. But out here—' She was looking at me hard. 'Out here he's alone and vulnerable. You understand?'

'I shan't tell anyone,' I assured her.

She nodded. 'No. I wouldn't take you there if I thought that.' She walked on again then, down into the plain where the acacia trees raised umbrellas of dark foliage.

Ten minutes later we were into the green belt, on the soft sand of a long-dried stream bed. There was a trickle of water flowing now, pools of it in the sand hollows, and over everything the glimmering, glowing green of growth renewed by rain. A goliath heron, standing like a sentinel, rose at our approach, its wings labouring at the air, and in a clearing beyond the red earth there was the bright flash of what she thought was a malachite kingfisher. The banks of sand were marked by the feet of birds. It was hot and very humid. It was also very quiet, only the soft drone of doves and the insistent bubbling of a coucal. 'The water-bottle bird,' she said, and at that moment a figure stepped out from a thicket, dressed in nothing but khaki shorts. His body glistened black and his face under the grizzled greyness of a thick cap of hair was old and wizened. He had a rifle in his hand and he kept it pointed at me, while he talked to the girl in Swahili.

'He says Tembo is following the track of a kudu up the lugga. He doesn't know when he'll be back.' She stood talking to the old man a moment, then he nodded, smiling, and disappeared back into the trees. We went across a smooth flat expanse of golden sand. 'I'm glad that old rascal is with him. His name is Mukunga.'

'A Masai?' I asked. I knew it was all Masai country here.

'No, no. He's of the Kamba people – the Wakamba. He came in last night after a thirty-six-hour trek.'

'How did he know your father was back?'

'I told you, he went into the Ngong Hills. The old

camp there was a poacher's hide-out. Most of his boys were ex-poachers and he knew some of them would have gone back to their old trade. So the word went out and now he's got three of them with him.'

'I thought he hated poachers,' I said.

'Oh, for God's sake! What do you expect? Mukunga's a hunter. They were all hunters. Killing for the pot, for survival, that's very different from killing for profit – that's what he and Alex fell out over. And at Marsabit – only one man ever tried it at Marsabit . . .' Her voice had dropped and I thought she gave a sigh, but I couldn't be sure. She was walking a little in front of me, her eyes on the ground. 'Tembo. That's what they called him. Tembo and ndovu, it's the same, it means elephant. And they're right. Over the years he's become more and more like a phlump. Sometimes I wonder . . .' She paused, half turning her head. 'I suppose you think it odd that I call him Tembo, but with my mother dead I spent most of my early life in bush camps looked after by men like Mukunga. They called him Bwana Mkubwa, the Big Chief, when addressing him formally, but among themselves he was always simply Tembo. I just got into the habit.' She gave a little laugh. 'I think when you meet him—' She turned her head at the croaking of a crow, watching it settle on the dead branch of a tree. 'We must be nearly there now.' She had slowed her pace and was peering at the bank. 'He's moving his camp each day, just in case.' There was a chattering sound, a bright flash of brilliant blue. 'Damned starlings,' she said. 'A camp, a carcass, anything at all and they tell you where it is.' She was climbing the bank, pushing her way through the undergrowth. I followed her and suddenly something hard was pressed into the small of my back and a voice said in English, 'No move.' I stood frozen, my skin crawling and the sweat dripping between my shoulder blades.

'It's you, Mtome, is it?' She came back, smiling and her hand held out. The pressure of the gun barrel on my back eased and I turned to find a tall, thin, very black man standing close behind me. The lobes of his ears hung slackly, pierced for ornaments he was not wearing. He was dressed in a sweat-stained shirt and khaki trousers held up by a big leather ammunition belt. He grinned in embarrassment, crinkling a deep scar on the left side of his face and revealing the broken stumps of two front teeth. 'Tembo not back?' she asked.

'No, Missamari. Back soon.' He glanced at the cheap watch on his wrist. 'Tembo gone one hour. You want something?'

'Tea would be nice. Have you got some tea?'

He nodded, smiling broadly now. 'Plenty tea, plenty sugar. Not got milk. Tembo gone milk a buffalo.' And he chuckled quietly at his own joke as he pushed ahead of us into a little clearing where there was a small tent and the blackened remains of a fire. Two guns lay cradled in the fork of a tree and pieces of meat hung drying in the branches. A starling perched close by, chattering and displaying the white band between chestnut belly and blue throat.

Mtome squatted before the embers of the fire, blowing them into a glow while the two of us sprawled on the damp ground. The fat, sleep-inducing drone of doves gave to the heavy humidity the effect of a sound-track and the distant call of the water-bottle bird added urgency to my interest in the blackened pot Mtome had placed on the fire. He was talking all the time to Mary Delden in a quick, clicking tongue.

'Mtome says he was cooking for some soldiers on the edge of the Rift Valley and a security patrol came in. That's how he heard Tembo was back.' Her voice was soft, almost drowsy. 'It must be all of sixteen years ago since that man was brought in from a northern safari. He'd been half killed by a buff in the Samburu country close under the Mathew's Range.' And she added, 'He's the best cook we ever had. He's also a very good shot.'

I remembered the Mathew's Range from studying the map. It was above the South Horr track leading to Lake Rudolf. 'Does he know the lake?' I asked.

'Of course. He's a Turkana. He was born up there and he's been back to Lake Rudolf many times with my father. Kulal, too. He knows all that country.'

'Yet you've never been there.'

'No. I was too young. We had a permanent camp on the Olduvai and I was always left there when the safari was a long one. Later, when my father began to specialize in the NFD, the camp was moved up near Isiolo, close under Lolokwe, but by then it was time for me to go to school in Nairobi.'

It was a strange life for a girl and I couldn't help

25

comparing her upbringing with my own. And now here I was sitting with her beside a fire on the edge of a dried-up stream bed, four thousand feet up and less than two hundred miles from the equator, waiting for her father, for Cornelius van Delden, the legendary figure who had been dubbed Jumbo van Delden by the popular press. I was wondering what he was really like, this man who belonged to a bygone world of tourist safaris and game parks, who had nursed wounded elephants, lived with them in the wild, and had now walked blithely into the territory of this new black régime, camping here regardless of its security forces. I wished Ken were with me. I hadn't even a camera, no means of recording the scene, and I sat there watching Mtome as the pot boiled and he threw in the tea, thinking of the script I could write if Cornelius van Delden really did make his appearance at the Conference.

She was talking to Mtome again. 'Is that Turkana you're talking?' I asked.

'No. A mixture of Samburu and Swahili. I was asking him about the scar on his cheek, which is new since I last saw him. He says he was a camel man with the Army and got shot up in the battle for Kitale.'

But it wasn't his war experience that interested me. It was the fact that he had been born near Lake Rudolf. 'Ask him whether he has ever climbed a mountain called Porr.' And I spelt it out for her, explaining that it was on the east shore of Lake Rudolf and looked like a pyramid.

She sat up, hugging her knees. 'I remember now.

It's mentioned in Pieter van Delden's book.' Mtome handed her a tin mug and she put it down quickly. 'Is that why you want to go to Rudolf, to climb Porr?'

I hesitated. But there was no point in being secretive about it now that she had brought me here to meet her father. 'It seems there was some sort of city there. Not a city as we understand it, more a huddle of rock dwellings on top of a pyramidical hill.' A mug of tea was thrust into my hand and it was so hot I nearly dropped it. 'Pieter van Delden thought it must be Porr. But he never got to the top.'

'Then how did he know about the rock dwellings?'

'It was on the pottery he found. Broken vases, cooking pots more likely, all very primitive, and this motif of rock structures on top of a pyramid, it was repeated again and again on the shards he pieced together.'

'That's not in his book.'

'No.' I hesitated, wondering how much to tell her, and at that moment a voice behind me said, 'Who's this, Mary?' It was a gentle voice, very deep, almost a rumble, and I turned to find him standing quite still, beside the tree with guns in it. He was watching me intently out of eyes that were pale like moonstones under the thick white brows.

'I'm Colin Tait,' I said, scrambling to my feet.

He didn't say anything and nor did I after that. I was too surprised at the size of the man and his appearance, the extraordinary sense of power that emanated from him. I knew from photographs in his elephant book that he was a striking figure, but none of them had been close-ups so that I wasn't prepared for the huge hatchet face that seemed all nose in a thicket of beard and long white hair. It took me back to my childhood and an illustrated Bible that had a picture of John the Baptist preaching in the desert.

'Colin wrote to you,' his daughter said.

He inclined his head very slightly, not taking his eyes off me. 'Why did you bring him here? I made it perfectly clear to you—'

'He wouldn't tell me what it was about and as there was nothing happening at the Lodge—' She gave a little shrug of her shoulders. 'After you've had your say at the Conference it would be very difficult to arrange a meeting.'

His hand went up to his beard, fingering it. 'The Conference hasn't opened then?'

'No. It's just as you expected. Kimani has been delayed.'

He nodded. 'So he's not going to give them a chance of seeing the Serengeti. Pity I couldn't talk to Maina or Ngugi in Nairobi. If I could have talked to them, or spoken on radio—' He stood stroking his beard and staring at me, deep in thought. 'You're a TV man, Mr Tait. I think that's what you said in your letter. I take it you have cameras with you?'

'Back at the Lodge, yes.'

'Would it interest you to film the Serengeti instead of the opening of the Conference?' He pulled a pipe from the pocket of his faded bush jacket and came forward, squatting down beside me and starting to fill it from a roll pouch made of what looked like leopard skin. 'Since you're here . . .' He was watching me, the cold stare of those pale eyes disconcerting.

Mtome was filling a mug from the blackened pot and I didn't say anything, thinking of the security forces out searching for him and how very alone he must feel. He took a long time filling his pipe. His hands were unusually large, strong and heavily veined, and all the time he never took his eyes from my face. Finally he said, 'Apparently Mary trusts you, so I suppose I must. But to make sure, I'm offering you the chance of pictures nobody else will get.' He put his pipe in his mouth, smiling at me, but the smile never touched his eyes. Have you got the guts to take a chance and risk getting shot?'

'I've never faced that sort of choice before.'

He gave a laugh that was more like a bark. 'At least that's an honest answer.' He reached for the mug Mtome was holding out to him and drank it off scalding hot. 'That's better.' He set it down and began lighting his pipe, looking across at his daughter, not at me. 'I went about two miles up the lugga, then struck out across country. Hard going and the air heavy.'

'Did you find the kudu?' she asked.

'I found the carcass, or what was left of it. The noose that strangled it was still hanging from a sapling and there were the remains of a fire. Somebody else trying to live off the land. Did you see any signs of life?'

'The tracks of a warthog, also elephant droppings, about two days old.'

He nodded. 'That elephant will die. They're all doomed, those that haven't got out. But the warthogs, they have survival quality. Giraffe, too, I think. I caught a glimpse of two adults and a young one, but I couldn't get near them. What's left of the game in this area knows it's being hunted. Everything's very shy now. Have you seen Mukunga yet?' And when she told him how he had emerged out of the trees, he smiled and nodded. 'Mukunga was at our old camp on the Olduvai when Alex began his slaughter. That's how I know what happened down there on the edge of the Serengeti. It was over a year ago, just before the start of the migration. Has Alex arrived?'

'No. Karanja says he'll be coming in with Kimani.'

'I ought to have a talk with that boy.'

'Karanja? It wouldn't do any good.'

'No, I suppose not. He'll be changed now, like everything else. He always did enjoy the limelight. Remember when he went in after that lion? Crazy show-off little bastard.' There was a note of affection in his voice, the words almost an endearment. 'You see him now as a public relations man,' he said, looking at me, 'but when he was with me he finished up as a better shot than any of us.' He shook his head and I sensed a nostalgic yearning for days that were gone. Then, turning to his daughter again, he said, 'So you haven't seen Alex yet. When you do, ask him what happened on the Olduvai a year ago. Mukunga says he must have slaughtered at least fifty thousand zebra there and as many wildebeest.'

'It was wartime and he had the Army to feed.'

He nodded. 'And that freezer plant I told you about. If the Ugandans had been smarter they would have known there'd be a war once that big freezer was completed. Why else would the Government have lent a commercial operator the cash to build such a huge plant? The Serengeti herds were doomed from that moment. No other way he could fill it.' He was looking at me again. 'The end of that killing was only eight months ago, so the evidence of it will still be there.'

'But that was the Army. It wasn't Alex. Mukunga told me that.'

He brushed her comment aside, an almost angry movement of his hand as he leaned forward, his pale eyes fixed on me. 'That interest you? An ossuary of wildlife, a charnel house of anything up to a quarter of a million beasts.'

I nodded uncertainly, not knowing exactly what he expected of me. 'My assignment is the Conference,' I murmured. 'Anyway, I don't see how I can possibly get there.' I wasn't sure how far it was, but I knew it was a lot more than a day's journey on foot.

He smiled. 'That's why I asked you whether you'd got the guts.'

'Tembo, you must be mad.' His daughter was leaning forward, her chin on her knees and a bright gleam in her eyes. 'The only transport in this area—'

'The first question I'll be asked at the Conference is what proof I have. How do I answer that if I've not seen it with my own eyes? Karanja could tell them.'

'Why should he?'

'Because he has a feeling for animals. But he won't, not now, when he has his feet on the rungs of a different ladder. Remember how good he was with the elephant calves?' He turned to me. 'At Marsabit he looked after my elephants for me, and elephant calves are difficult to rear. Not as bad as rhino, of course. Once when we were in the South Horr Valley—'

She laughed, tapping him on the arm. 'You're up to your old tricks – changing the subject. I want to know how you're going to get hold of a truck.'

'And I want to find out what this young man knows about Lake Rudolf that I don't. Now leave it at that, Mary.' He turned back to me. 'You realize there's nobody knows that area better than I do?'

'I realize that, sir.'

He nodded, frowning and sucking his pipe. 'I thought I'd been everywhere my father had been.' And then he was looking at me again. 'Your letter suggested it was something to do with his book. You've read *Reis deur Chalbi na die Rudolfmeer*?'

'Not in the original, only in translation.' And I told him about Southly Tait and how the typescript had come into my possession. 'I think it had been on my uncle's conscience, that he'd done nothing about the book. It seems he found it among a whole pile of abandoned manuscripts when he took over after the death of my parents. He only kept it, he said, because of the map, and the fact that the book itself was annotated with marginal inserts and footnotes, also several handwritten sheets stuck in with passepartout.'

'In my father's writing?'

'I presume so. It was all in Afrikaans, anyway. I've checked through the translation. The loose sheet insertions are certainly included, also the footnotes, so I imagine the margin insertions are also in the English text.'

'And you brought it with you?'

'Yes, and the map. Xerox copies, of course.'

'I always felt there should have been a map in the book, but probably there was no engraver in Pietermaritzberg then, or else they had no means of making a block. Does it mark his route?' And when I described it to him as best I could, he said rather tersely, 'It's all in the text. If you know the country you can follow it without a map.'

'But not the location of the rock drawings,' I said. 'Or the old sites where he found the broken pieces of pottery.'

'Rock drawings?' He stared at me. 'There's nothing about pottery or rock drawings in the book.' He took his pipe out of his mouth, regarded it for a moment, then put it back in his mouth again and shook his head slowly. 'Not my field, I'm afraid, and anyway, this is hardly the moment—'

'But the drawings,' his daughter said. 'An early culture, perhaps the earliest.' And she passed on to him what I had told her about the motif on the broken shards.

He listened to her, nodding absently. 'I heard something about it. Leakey, I think. Young Richard Leakey – another of his theories. And there was a much earlier expedition, middle 1800s – before Teleki.' He turned to me. 'Anything is possible up there, but you must realize I have other things on my mind.' He wasn't an archaeologist. A very early city dwelling meant nothing to him compared to the slaughter of the wildebeest in the Serengeti or even the sprung noose marking the death of a single kudu.

'Porr I know, of course,' he said slowly, as though making an effort to relieve my disappointment. 'From Loiyangalani and the El Molo islands it stands up out of the flat curve of the lake's east shore like a pyramid in the desert. And if the wind gives you the chance of getting over to South Island, then the similarity to an Egyptian pyramid is even more marked. A lot higher, of course – over three thousand feet. It's a trick of the light, I think, for it's only when you get near it you appreciate its height.'

'Have you ever climbed it?'

He shook his head. 'No. I've trekked all round it, along the lakeside and by the inland route. But there wouldn't be any life up there on that battered red-rock mass. Somebody has described it as one of nature's most dilapidated monuments, a once-solid mountain shaken to pieces. Hillaby, I think.' He gave Mtome his empty mug to refill and said, 'I find it strange that this information should have been written into the book only when he was seeking English publication. Is there no letter of explanation?'

'I suppose there must have been originally,' I said.

'But as it was handed to me there was just the original book, the map and the translation. I did make some attempt to find a letter, but there was such an accumulation of dusty piles of rubbish in that basement office . . .'

'Very strange,' he murmured. 'He was an Afrikaner and strongly anti-British. He lived by the Bible and his gun, a great hunter and as bigoted as hell. It's hard to believe he would seek English publication and that he would then include details he had not revealed in the Afrikaans original.'

'Didn't he ever talk to you about it?'

He shook his head. 'Not that I recall. But then he died just before my eighteenth birthday. He was suffering from malaria and was badly injured by an elephant he failed to bring down with his first shot.' He looked at me. 'You say the additional material was handwritten and in Afrikaans? And the original from which the translation was made is in your possession? I'd like to see that sometime. Does the writing look at all feminine?' And when I told him it was large and angular, he nodded. 'My mother's probably. He didn't leave her much to live on and English publication wouldn't have worried her, she was half German, half Belgian.' He smiled. 'I'm a bit of mongrel, you see.' And he didn't say anything after that, sitting there, drinking his tea, apparently deep in thought.

It was Mary who asked me about the map. 'Is the writing the same as in the notes?'

But I couldn't answer that because the lettering was all in capitals.

'And the translation, when was that done – in your father's time?'

'No. Much later. My uncle commissioned it in 1971. You remember Richard Leakey's discovery of a skull up by the Ethiopian border that put the origins of man about a million and a half years earlier than his parents' discoveries at Olduvai? It was a very controversial find, a lot of publicity, and Leakey aired a number of theories. One of them was that Lake Rudolf was the cradle of civilization. According to him, it was there, and not on the Nile, that pottery was first made. In fact, he claimed that Nilotic pottery should be renamed Rudolfic.' I turned to Cornelius van Delden. 'Leakey also found shards at his dig on Lake Rudolf and provisionally dated them pre-Nilotic. That was what decided my uncle to commission a translation of the book.'

'But he never published it – why?'

'I did find some correspondence that had a bearing on that. It seems almost two years elapsed before the typescript of the English version was finally delivered. I suspect the fee was so small the translator wasn't greatly interested in the work.'

'So it was never published.'

'No.'

'Just as well perhaps.' He said it so quietly that I wasn't sure he intended me to hear. And he added quickly, 'No chance now of anyone looking at what he found. It's closed, all that area.' He put down his mug and glanced at his watch. 'Time you were leaving, if you're to get back for lunch. We can't feed you here. One warthog is all I've been able to bag so far.' He indicated the strips of meat hanging in the fire's smoke. 'Bush pig and posho, that's not very good eating.' He smiled and got to his feet. 'Maybe when all this is over and things are normal again . . .' He gave that harsh bark of a laugh and shrugged his shoulders. 'When I'm back on La Digue, send it to me. Better still, come and see me. No animals there, but the birds are interesting.'

He looked quickly round the camp, nodded to Mtome and led the way down into the lugga. 'Now, about tonight . . .' And as he walked with us across the sandbanks of that rain-washed river bed, he gave us instructions where to wait for the truck. His daughter did her best to find out how he was going to get hold of the vehicle, but all he would say was, 'There's no problem there. It's returning it may be a little more difficult.' And he added, 'I plan to be at Lake Ndolo just about dawn.'

He saw us up to the point where we had entered the stream bed, the rock hill just visible at the edge of the plain, shimmering in the sweltering heat. 'Remember, if you're seen leaving the Lodge area, or challenged by one of the soldiers, then don't come. And a convincing explanation of your absence must be given to those who share your rooms.' He glanced up at the sky. 'Better bring waterproofs. The rain won't hold off much longer.' He patted his daughter on the shoulder. 'Don't take any chances, Toto.'

'Ndio, Tembo.' She was laughing, I think with excitement.

He turned then with a wave of his hand. 'See you about two in the morning then.' And he went ambling off up the lugga, his head swinging this way and that, alert and watchful. He didn't look back.

We went on then and I said, 'He's like a caged lion. He even looks like a lion.'

She smiled, shaking her head. 'No, not like a lion. Like an elephant. If you get to know him you'll notice he behaves like an elephant, too. He never forgets, never forgives and nothing ever stops him.' And she added, 'He's a very large man in every respect, and very exhausting, which is why I make sure there's a lot of ocean between us.'

CHAPTER TWO

The rain started again shortly after lunch, a heavy downpour as though a tap had been turned on. About an hour later a wind sprang up and the tap was turned off. Suddenly the sun was shining and everything steamed in the heat. I was lying on my bunk, but I couldn't sleep, the sound of voices a continuous murmur as delegates talked and argued, moving from one group to another, renewing old contacts, making new ones. Ken said it had been like that all morning, nobody minding very much that the Conference had not opened. I could see them now, out in the bright sunlight, endlessly talking; the newsmen, too, huddled together or moving from group to group trying for statements from those who were internationally known.

Shortly after four a light plane flew low over the Lodge, and half an hour later the Minister was being photographed with the Conference chairman, Sir Edmund Willoughby-Blair. Kimani looked very slight beside the big blond chairman, but what he lacked in height he made up in energy, his movements quick and full of vitality, his broad, rather flat features alive and full of smiles.

It was on this scene that the sunlight faded, snuffed out by an electrical storm that crashed round us for an hour or more. It was night before the rain finally stopped and we sloshed through mud to our evening meal – tinned stew, rice and over-cooked vegetables, tea from an urn and a can of beer beside each place. Soldiers moved around the tables, clearing the plates away, their faces glistening black in the light from the naked bulbs, and I watched Mary Delden talking animatedly to a group of men at a nearby table. No sign of nervous tension in that strong brown aquiline face and she didn't even glance in my direction.

A Frenchman at a table by the veranda suddenly called out, 'Regardez! Un éléphant,' and the dining room erupted, everyone trooping out into the night. The spots had not yet been switched on, but a young half moon and some stars showed through ragged clouds and for a moment everybody glimpsed a grey bulk standing motionless on the far side of the waterhole. A cloud shadow passed across it, and when the moon emerged again it was gone. Karanja was calling for the spotlights to be switched on, but it was too late. A big American with a Boston accent standing right beside me exclaimed excitedly, 'An elephant! I saw it with my own eyes.' And he added to the group about him, 'That just goes to prove what I been saying. Things aren't as bad as that guy Winthrop would have us believe.'

'Moonshine,' somebody said, and there was laughter, everybody happier now they had actually seen something.

A hand touched my arm and I turned. It was Mary Delden. 'Twelve-thirty,' she said. 'Okay? And bring a hand camera, nothing heavy.'

I nodded and she continued on past me, heading for her room.

The rest of that evening I spent on the veranda, dozing in the only chair with the Beaulieu news camera in its case beside me. It hadn't been difficult to convince Ken that we should split up in an endeavour to make good the lost excursion to the Serengeti; he would cover the opening of the Conference, using the Bolex electric H16, while I tried for some dawn shots under the guidance of somebody who knew the country. I think he guessed it was Mary Delden, but he wasn't the sort to ask questions.

The spotlights were switched off again at nine and an hour later the Lodge was silent, only a few lamps still glimmering in the dark, the moon cloud-covered, no wind and everything very still. I must have fallen asleep, for the next thing I knew there was a figure beside me and Mary Delden was whispering, 'Time to go. Are you ready?' She had a Retina camera slung over her shoulder, a waterproof draped over it and the pockets of her bush jacket bulging with film.

I nodded and got to my feet, picking up the Beaulieu and my plastic waterproof. She was already moving quietly out into the trampled grass, a dark shadow heading down towards the waterhole. I followed, keeping close behind her, feeling my way in the dark and thinking of that elephant. And if there was an elephant around, why not other beasts – rhino or lion? Wasn't this the time they came down to drink?

A branch broke under my foot. She reached back and took my arm. 'Quiet now,' she whispered. 'There's a patrol stationed on the road a mile south of the Lodge.' And she walked on, still holding my arm.

The moon was still hidden by cloud, only a faint luminosity lingering. We skirted the waterhole, leaving it to our left, and struck out into fairly open country. The going was firm, the hard gravelly soil sparsely covered with a coarse growth of stiff little bushes about knee height. Trees loomed up, dark shadows whose shapes seemed imbued with life.

'How do you think he's going to get hold of one of those Army trucks?' I whispered.

'I don't know.'

'Why didn't he tell you when you asked him this morning?'

'I'm a female, that's why. He's never heard of Women's Lib.'

'But he should have told you. You've a right to know what you're letting yourself in for.'

'He doesn't trust women.' She said it flatly, but there was an undertone of bitterness in her voice as she added, 'We've never been very close, and anyway he never tells anybody what he's going to do. He's a man who acts as though there was nobody else in the world—' She suddenly froze, her grip on my arm tightening. She was staring past me, at the dark shadow of a tree that became two trees, one of them moving. Or was it a trick of the light?

She moved on quickly, then stopped at the sound of wood striking wood and a thin squeal that might have been fear or pain, or the cry of some nocturnal bird. It wasn't repeated. Instead, there was a soft gravelly sound as though something heavy was being dragged along the ground.

'He should have put it out of its misery.' She was standing very still, staring after the fading sound. 'He knew what they'd done.'

'What was it?' I asked.

'Elephant. The same one.' The moon was coming clear of the cloud now and I saw her face, tight-lipped and angry. 'Bastards!' she murmured. And after that she was silent until at last we topped a rise in clear moonlight and saw the road winding down to the lugga. Nothing stirred, the open plain an opaque emptiness bounded by rock outcrops. She stopped then, watching the road. 'I think we're clear of the patrol. Karanja said it was at the top of the slope leading down to the lugga.'

We began the descent and halfway down to the lugga something chuckled away to our left. There was a mewing sound, then a soft whoop. I thought it was a night bird, but she had quickened her pace. 'They know,' she said. 'They always know.' The

whoops faded into the distance, lost behind an outcrop. 'I don't like hyena,' she murmured, staring
towards the black tree shadows where the road forded
the lugga, her head cocked, listening. But there was
no sound now and nothing moved. Dark clouds were
spreading towards us from the west, blacking out all
the plain, and in a moment the moon had gone and
we were engulfed in darkness. It began to rain as we
reached the road and walked down it to the ford
where we found a fallen tree growing out into the
lugga and sat there waiting.

'Half an hour to go,' I said, looking at my watch.

'He'll be ahead of schedule. He always is.'

There was the whisper of a breeze here, but apart
from the stirring of the leaves and the sound of the
rain there was nothing, only silence. I could just see
the outline of her features in silhouette and beyond
her the pale line of the road climbing to the skyline.
She was sitting very still, not tense, but alert, and I
sensed an undercurrent of excitement in her. We were
alone in the African bush, just the two of us, waiting,
and I had time then to consider what I had let myself
in for. The man was persona non grata, virtually on
the run, and stealing an Army truck . . . 'How far is
it to this lake he spoke of?' My voice sounded over-
loud in the silence.

'Lake Lgarya? Three or four hours. I'm not sure.'

'And how long shall we be there?'

'Long enough for you to get your pictures.'

I hadn't been thinking of that, but when I asked
her what she thought would happen when we got

back, she didn't answer. The silence was oppressive. Nothing in my whole life had prepared me for this and she sat there, remote and outwardly calm, as though this was just an ordinary safari. 'Those guns,' I said. 'Where did he get them from?'

'I've no idea.'

'He couldn't have brought them with him from the Seychelles.'

'Keep quiet, can't you, and listen.'

Silence again and the need to talk so urgent I had to keep a tight hold of myself. I could feel my heart thudding. I was scared, and I didn't know how to conceal it from her. Something flickered past my face. 'It's all right,' she said. 'Only a bat.' And I realized I had leapt to my feet. 'You drive a car, don't you?' She sounded faintly amused. 'When you're driving, you're like the zebra grazing alongside lions after a kill, you close your eyes to accidents, never admitting you could get killed, too. So stop worrying. You're far safer sitting here in the rain than driving a car along a motorway. Anyway, there isn't much left to be scared of in this area.' She turned her head, looking directly at me. 'Do you understand what he's trying to do?'

'I think so.'

'I wonder if you do.' She paused and then said, 'Have you talked to the delegates?'

'Some of them.'

'Then you'll have realized they're hopelessly divided. They're here at the invitation of the East African Federation. The state of the Lodge, the commissariat, everything, is a reminder that there has been a war here in Africa and many of them are more concerned with the practicalities of the moment than with what effect their actions will have for the future. In wildlife, as in everything else, there is the political element, and unless he can jolt them into concerted action . . . Are you any good with a camera?'

'I'm not a professional like Ken.'

She nodded. 'I'm not a professional either, but so long as our pictures are good enough to show the world what's been happening out here . . .' She paused, listening again. The rain had almost stopped, the wind increasing and the rustle of the leaves louder. 'The mere threat of world revulsion may be sufficient to swing some of them. Otherwise, I'm afraid they may go along with this idea of a pilot conservation scheme. You haven't met Alex Kirby-Smith yet.'

'I was told he hadn't arrived.'

'He flew in with the Minister. He's seen some of the delegates already, those they know they can rely on. Today he'll be trying to convince others privately.' And she added, 'He always had quite a different attitude to animals. Even as a child I sensed that. He's a commercial operator. He has the same attitude to animals as a tree-feller has to a forest. They're a natural resource, a crop.'

'You know him then?'

She laughed abruptly. 'Of course I know him. He and Tembo were partners. They ran a safari business together. They were both hunters then, operating under licence, fulfilling quotas. For Tembo it was a way of life. It brought him into close contact with the country and the animals. That's all he cared about. With Uncle Alex – I called him Uncle in those days—' She laughed again, a quick nervous laugh that was almost a girlish giggle – 'With him it was different. It was business. He began to build up an organization. He undertook scientific research for the Government, advising on numbers of lion, elephants, whatever it was to be culled. Then he'd go in with refrigerator trucks, the lot. He had all the back-up facilities so that even the hide and the bones, every morsel of the animals he culled was put to some use. It was all very scientific and he was so bloody persuasive.'

'And that was when your father and he parted?'

'No. It was before that. When I was about nine. It was shortly after my mother was killed and I remember I cried and cried.'

'You liked him then?'

'Yes. Much more than – my father. Uncle Alex was a great charmer. Still is. And for a little girl—' She sighed. 'Tembo, you see, has no graces. He's a tough, driving, hard-bitten man, and absolutely uncompromising.'

'And on Thursday he's going to confront Kirby-Smith—'

'Listen!'

For a moment I couldn't hear it. Then, faint above the wind in the trees, I heard the sound of an engine. The skyline up the road became limned in the light and a moment later the truck's headlights appeared over the rise. We went out on to the road, the lights blinding us until they were dipped. The engine slowed, the truck braking to a halt right beside us, and both the men in the cab were black. The African at the wheel sat staring at us and I didn't recognize him at first, his face ashen under the dark skin, sweat on his forehead and the whites of his eyes gleaming wildly. It was Karanja.

I thought at first something had gone wrong and he had come out to fetch us back to the Lodge. Then I saw that the other African was Mukunga and he had a rifle in his hands. A voice from the back of the truck said, 'All right, Karanja. You can ride in the back now.' And Cornelius van Delden climbed out over the tailboard.

'No trouble with the patrol?' his daughter asked.

He gave that barking laugh of his. 'They weren't there. The rain – I thought they wouldn't be. But I had Karanja drive just in case.' He turned to me. 'You ride in the back. Mukunga!'

'Ndio, Bwana.'

'You go in the back with Karanja. Keep an eye on him.'

Karanja was out of the driving seat, standing hesitantly on the road beside me, all the jauntiness he had displayed at the Lodge gone. 'Mr van Delden.' His voice was high and nervous. 'I think it better I walk back now. You are clear of any soldiers and—'

'You always called me Tembo. Remember?'

'Yes, Tembo. But I shall be missed. And how can I explain to the Minister—'

'Of course you'll be missed.' Van Delden's voice was harsh. 'Why do you think I brought you along with me?' He put his hand on the man's shoulder. 'You've got about ten hours in which to think up a good excuse for driving off with the truck. Besides, I want you to see what your people have done in the Serengeti. You, who were so good with animals. Think of Lucy, and the little toto you named Labda because you weren't sure she'd live. A big cow elephant now, but more likely she'll be dead with a bullet in her guts. That's if she's lucky. Now jump in the back and let's get going.'

For a moment I thought Karanja would make a dash for it. I was standing right beside him and I could see the whites of his eyes as he looked wildly round. He was breathing quickly and I think near to panic. Mukunga sensed it, too, and slipped the safety catch of his rifle. But van Delden's hand was still on Karanja's shoulder. 'Come on, man. Make the best of it.' He spoke quietly, as though gentling an animal, and somehow it seemed to get through to him, the tension relaxing, his body sagging in its grey suit. 'Okay, Tembo.' And he turned and climbed docilely into the back of the truck.

'Give me your camera,' van Delden said to me. 'It's going to be a rough ride.'

I don't know what it was like in front, but it was certainly rough in the back. Van Delden took it slowly through the lugga, but as soon as we had climbed the further slope he put his foot down. The truck was an open one and it was empty, nothing in the back but an old tarpaulin, black with oil and soaking wet. We tried folding it so that we had a cushion to lean against. This made it just bearable so long as we were on hard gravel, but the road worsened as we drove south into what had been Tanzania. The fighting had been heavy here the previous year and there were soft patches, badly rutted, the truck slithering wildly and no weight on the back wheels. In the end there was nothing for it but to stand, gripping the handbar at the back of the cab. I could see where we were going then and brace myself as we skidded and jolted across the rutted sections, but it was hard on the legs, and my eyes streamed. 'I am coming here one time,' Mukunga shouted at me. 'Very bad. Plenty lorries and much dust.'

'With Major Kirby-Smith?'

'No. That is Mtome. Me with Askari, hunting.'

'With the Army?'

'Ndio.' He nodded. 'Very bad.'

'What were you hunting – buffalo?'

'Hapana.' He shook his grizzled head, his teeth white in a grin. 'No, me hunt men. Me track, Askari shoot.'

I glanced at Karanja on the other side of me. No wonder he'd decided against making a dash for it. 'What were you doing during the war?' I asked him.

'Same as I am doing now, public relations.' He said it quietly so that Mukunga couldn't hear and I knew he was ashamed. Then the rain started again.

After that we didn't talk. The going got rougher and it was all we could do to hang on. Once van

Delden slowed, leaning his head out of the broken window and calling back, 'You all right, Tait?' I gritted my teeth and said I was, but when I asked how much further, he shouted, 'Not sure. Thirty, maybe forty miles. We'll be turning right on to a minor track soon. Better hang on then.' And he built up speed again, the headlights slashing the night and showing outcrops of red rock, great laval heaps of it. We crossed another lugga and he took it too fast, throwing us off our feet and nearly breaking an axle, the wheels thumping against the mudguards. Eyes blazed at us in the darkness, Mukunga's hand on my arm, his voice shouting, 'Fisi.' I had a glimpse of the hyena's grey ungainly body shambling clear of us as we thundered past, then we were over a rise and braking sharply as a bomb crater rushed towards us. I could see the dull gleam of water in it as the truck carved its way through low scrub on the verge, rocking wildly.

We slowed for a while, the rain teeming down and more craters. A burned-out scout car, some lorries, gaping holes, then we were clear of the battlefield, driving fast again. My hat was rammed down on my head, but the rain poured in under the collar of my waterproof. I was wet to the skin and cold. Mukunga did not seem to mind it, standing beside me, the sodden khaki shirt clinging to his hard frame, water streaming from his tough monkey-like face. Karanja, on the other hand, was shivering with cold, his cheap suit shapeless, his teeth chattering. He was looking at me, looking at my waterproof, and I knew what he was thinking. Then suddenly he let go of the handbar and dived for the tarpaulin. The wheel bucked, spinning, and he was flung against the side, where he lay for a moment as though stunned.

Mukunga suddenly thumped on the cab roof, called out something in Swahili as we slowed, and then the truck swerved, a sharp turn to the right on to a barely defined track, water in ruts gleaming pale in the headlights. The wheel spun as we slithered through mud to the burned-up grass of the flat land bordering the track. We headed across-country then, the wheels hammering at unseen holes. 'Serengeti,' Mukunga shouted to me. 'Njia nzuri sasa – road good now.'

I looked round and thought for a moment Karanja had been thrown out. There was no sign of him, only the bundle of tarpaulin heaped against the side. He had wrapped it round himself so completely he was cocooned in it. Rock outcrops loomed ahead like islands in a flat lake. The first glimmer of dawn showed behind low cloud. The rain died, visibility improving. We skirted the rock outcrops and they were like pictures I had seen of kopjes in the South African veldt, and as the light strengthened and I could see further and further ahead, the plain we were on seemed endless. The clouds thinned. Ragged gaps appeared. A glimpse of the morning star low down in the west and then the sky began to take fire, the clouds all aflame and constantly changing shape, so that we seemed to be headed into a cauldron of molten lava. Even the plain was red, the wetness of uncropped grass reflecting the volcanic flaming of the sunrise and everything beginning to steam.

It was then that we came to the first of the bones. They were scattered over an area of three or four hectares, a litter of skulls, rib cages and leg bones, all picked clean and gleaming in the blood red dawn. I thumped on the cab roof and van Delden slowed, leaning out of the window to tell me he expected larger concentrations of bones near the lake. But as he started to drive on again, I shouted to him that I wanted to film now, while the light was this startling, flaming red.

He slowed, stopping beside a clean-picked carcass, and I jumped out, calling for my camera. 'It's colour,' I told him. 'In this light it will look fantastic.' I was excited, my mind already scripting the words, beginning to grasp what could be made of this.

I had him back the truck, explaining that, as soon as I signalled I was ready, I wanted him to drive up to the carcass, then get out and bend over it. 'Pick up one of the bones,' I said, 'and I'll zoom in on you.'

He did it just as I suggested, and seeing him get out of the cab, the plain behind him all misted pink and his strong features picked out in a ruddy glow, even his beard tinged in red, I knew I had a subject that would make every viewer sit up electrified. But when he reached the bones, instead of bending down and picking one up, he turned suddenly, his back to the camera, and called out, 'Karanja. Come here.'

I nearly took my finger off the trigger, but then I thought I'd never have the light so good again and

I kept the camera rolling, gradually zooming in as Karanja clambered out of the back of the truck and walked towards van Delden, who now bent down, picking up a long shin bone, holding it out for the African to see.

I moved in then, walking quickly forward, keeping them in focus and circling until I could close in on their faces. Mukunga was in frame, too, his rifle lying across his shoulder, the wizened face very clear in the growing brilliance of the light. And then, as I zoomed in for a real close-up, Karanja seemed to notice me for the first time. His mouth gaped, a look of intense shock, and suddenly he covered his face in his hands. Then he bolted, running like a hunted animal back to the truck.

Van Delden turned and looked at me, still holding the bone and staring straight into camera. 'You realize what you've done?' He was smiling, and on that strange reflective smile the camera ran out of film and stopped.

'What do you mean?' I asked.

'Print that picture and it's as good as a death warrant.'

Mary Delden moved in front of me, her Retina held to her eye for a close-up of her father looking straight into the sunrise. I heard the click of the shutter and she said, 'You did it purposely.'

He nodded. 'Of course. Now he's been filmed here your pictures are safe. His life depends on your cameras not being seized.' He turned to me again. 'Have you finished now?'

I nodded, still thinking of Karanja running scared with his hands over his face.

'Then let's get on to the lake area. We haven't much time and I want pictures of my own to show the full extent of the slaughter.'

We drove on then, and as the sun rose we turned on to a track running west. A few miles further on trees appeared to the south of us, marking the edge of the Serengeti plain. All this time we were passing scattered areas of bones half-hidden in the dried-up grasses and Karanja sat on the floorboards as though in a trance, a dazed expression on his face, which was almost grey. He wouldn't stand up and hold on to the handbar, preferring to be bounced around in the bottom of the truck. It seemed he dared not look at the animal graveyards through which we were driving.

We crossed a track running south and almost immediately the wheels were crunching bone and from my vantage point in the back the plain ahead was marked with circular concentrations of rib-cages like great mushroom rings. It was as though an army had fought its last battle here, falling as it stood, regiment by regiment.

The sun was already climbing up the sky, all colour gone, and when we finally stopped we were in the middle of the battlefield, the weathered bones of dead regiments of wildebeest all round us. It was such an incredible sight that we just stood there for a moment, staring at it. Then Mary Delden turned to her father. 'Who did it? Not Alex. When he culls he does it properly, putting bone, hide, everything to use.'

'This was wartime. The last big battle was fought up there on the edge of the plains and with their lines of communication cut—' Van Delden shook his head. 'Good thing the Grzimeks can't see this.' It was the Grzimeks, father and son, who had pioneered this one time national park, had written a book I remembered – *Serengeti Shall Not Die*. 'Mukunga warned me, but I wouldn't have believed it possible – such an orgy of killing.' He was climbing up on to the roof of the cab. He had an old Polaroid camera and as he waited for the first picture to be developed, she said accusingly, 'You're going to show these pictures to the delegates and let them think it was Alex.'

'He had a contract to supply the Army out of the Serengeti.'

'But not like this, not killing everything.'

'It got out of hand, that's all. The troops saw how it was done and the lust for killing took over.' He took another picture, then turned to her. 'That's his business, isn't it – killing? And now he's going north, a new contract, to feed the starving Samburu. War or drought, it's business, and there's that big freezer plant. He's got to fill it with something.'

She was silent after that and I slipped another magazine on my camera, changing the lens, and took some panoramic shots, followed by some close-ups of discarded bones that had been piled in a heap.

Talking to van Delden afterwards I gathered that in their migration the wildebeest subdivided themselves into herds of anything up to two or three hundred beasts. Sometimes the concentrations were smaller, sometimes larger, but round every concentration of these remains we found the tyremarks of vehicles that had ringed them in, enclosing them while the men in the trucks had gunned them down. I was endeavouring to film a particularly clear group of tracks to show how the animals had been panicked into a mass when Mary Delden called to me. The urgency in her voice made me turn, and then I saw it, a grey shape, almost a skeleton, covered by mangy fur.

It was a hyena, all belly and hindquarters, and it was moving towards me, the eyes gleaming and a slavering froth on the jaw. It seemed half dead from starvation, it was coming towards me so slowly, and I swung the camera, shouting at it and backing away. 'Run, you fool!' she screamed. I ran then and the wretched animal, which had checked at my shouts, loped after me, moving suddenly with surprising speed.

A rifle cracked. Another shot and van Delden called, 'All right, Tait.' I stood there for a moment, feeling shaken and my legs trembling, then I took a close-up of the emaciated hyena lying dead on its side, and another of van Delden with the rifle to his shoulder. And afterwards, as we wandered through the neighbouring boneyards, we came upon several hyenas slinking among the skeletal remains, their powerful jaws crunching up bone in a desperate attempt to obtain sustenance to exist for one more day. It was a depressing, heartbreaking sight, and the Serengeti plain, emerald bright now in the sun, a smiling landscape dotted with rock outcrops. Except for these last few scavenging hyenas there was not a sign of life, not even a bird, the sky empty, a blue glare with the fluffy white of clouds piled up on hills too far away to see.

'Got all you want?' van Delden asked.

I nodded, staring down at the bones spread out in the grass at my feet.

'What you've seen here,' he said, 'is the work of man at his most destructive. The effects of this slaughter will have been rippling out for the past six months, upsetting the fine balance of nature from the jungle to the sea and as far north as the deserts of Ethiopia and Somaliland.' His pale eyes were fixed on me, almost glaring. 'Get that into your script. You've got the film. Use it. The migration here was at times about a million strong – zebras, wildebeest, finally the gazelles, Grants and Tommies. Tell people what it means to kill out great herds like that. Make them see how it affects all living things. Lions, hyenas, jackals, the bat-eared foxes, wild dog, too – they all lived off these beasts. Vultures, even eagles, right down to the ants that exist to clean up the last remains. Tell them.' He checked himself then. 'Karanja!'

Karanja was sitting in the shade of the truck, his head bowed between his knees. He lifted his head slowly. 'Yes, Tembo?'

'Have you thought out what you're going to say to the Minister?'

For a moment I thought he had lost himself in a mood of complete dejection. But then he got to his feet and came towards us, smiling and with something of his old jauntiness. 'If Mr Tait agree, and Miss Mary, perhaps I say I take the truck to find them, fearing for their safety.'

Van Delden did not say anything, busy with his Polaroid, and Karanja turned to me. 'You must say, Mr Tait, that you and Miss Mary go to get pictures of the dawn, some animals maybe, and then you get lost. Okay?'

I nodded. 'So long as they don't take our cameras.'

'No. I see to that.'

'And what about our films?' It would be so easy for him to have the film seized on some pretext.

'Your film will be safe.' But he said it without conviction, his eyes shifting.

Mary Delden was crouched by a litter of rib cages and, still with her eyes to the viewfinder of her camera, she said to her father, 'To be on the safe side I'll hand you some of my films.' She straightened up and produced two cassettes from the pocket of her bush jacket.

'No need.' Van Delden was waiting for the development indicator. 'If this comes out all right your camera and films should be safe.' He released the developing button and opened the camera. 'Clear enough I think.' And he tore out the film and held it up for us to see. It was a clearly identifiable picture of Karanja as he stood talking to me, and behind him was the truck and Mary Delden crouched with her camera before a heap of bones. 'Tomorrow I shall be showing the delegates the pictures I have taken this morning. Whether I include this one or not will depend entirely on you.' He leaned forward, his face close to Karanja's, tapping him on the chest with his finger. 'Just see that neither Mr Tait nor Miss Mary are in any way harassed for being so stupid as to lose their way. Got it?'

Karanja nodded, his eyes rolling, his tongue licking his lips. 'I see they are okay, Tembo.'

It was blackmail and I couldn't help feeling sorry for the man, routed out of bed at gunpoint and forced to commandeer one of the Army supply trucks, his position, his whole future threatened. I looked round at the endless plain, at the bones gleaming white in the hot sun, and a husky voice at my elbow said, 'Now perhaps you understand what this Conference is all about – how those who have lived with animals feel.' And then, with a sudden warmth that took me by surprise, she put her hand on my arm and added, 'Anything I can do to help, when you come to write your script . . .' She left it at that, her gaze wandering over the plain again, and then she turned quickly away. 'It's getting late,' she said to her father in a tight, controlled voice.

'Yes. Well, we'll just go as far as the lake. Now we're here and have the use of the truck.'

We drove on then, down the track that headed south towards the trees, and in ten minutes we had left the plain and were into an area of scrub and acacias. Here we saw our first vultures scavenging at the sodden hide of what appeared to be a recent kill. And then suddenly we were on the edge of the lake and there were flamingoes standing in the shallows, a splash of orange, and water birds swimming around unaffected by the slaughter on the plains.

We stopped then, and on the far side, on the slope above the lake, I saw a line of buildings. Van Delden got out and stood for a moment looking at them through his binoculars. 'When I knew this place it had only just been built. Later a lot of people who made their names filming animals in the wild for television used it as their base.' He mentioned several of them, names I had vaguely heard of. 'It was partly tented, the best positioned camp for anybody studying the migration. But the man who ran it gave it up in the end – the Tanzanians made it impossible for him. Now . . . See for yourself. It's just a ruin.' He handed me up the glasses and I saw that the buildings were roofless shells, the woodwork crumbling. Two had been gutted by fire, and behind the largest, which had the remains of a veranda, a long neck stood up like a thick pole camouflaged in black and yellow, the small head nibbling at the leaves of a tree.

'There's a giraffe,' I said.

'Several if you look carefully. And a waterbuck down in the reeds to the right.' His voice was very quiet, his eyes blinking, tears running down his cheeks. 'It was always a good place for game. The Olduvai river is only just over there.' I couldn't believe it, this hard old man weeping for the past, not bothering to hide his emotion as he nodded towards the trees sloping away to the left. 'That's where we had our first base camp. All the animals moving between the Ngorongoro Crater and the Serengeti watered in the Olduvai. There were a lot of lion, and cheetah. And on the edge of the plain behind us, in the evening, when the migration was moving through, the trees would be thick with vultures, maribous, eagles – all the scavengers and predators perched there, waiting for the next dawn to pounce on the afterbirth of the night's calving and the remains of the baby wildebeests killed in darkness. I used to sit out on that lodge veranda with the sun rising, hartebeest, zebra and wildebeest grazing within yards of me.' He shook his head and sighed, and I thought he was sighing for the animals that were no longer there.

'Things were different then.' He glanced at his daughter, blinking his eyes, then reached up for the glasses and climbed quickly back into the cab as though to hide his momentary weakness. And when she suggested driving as far as the lodge to get a picture of the giraffe, he said, 'No. We haven't time.' He said it gruffly and I guessed he didn't want her to know how the sight of the place had affected him.

'At least let me get a picture of the lodge. You and Mother had your wedding reception in the dining-hall there, didn't you?'

'Yes.'

'I've never seen it. I'd like a picture.'

'No.' His voice sounded oddly abrupt. 'The tank's barely a quarter full.' He started the engine and then after a moment's hesitation she climbed in again and we drove fast up the winding track, back on to the plain. The going was harder now, the land drying in the sun, and by ten-thirty we were back on the gravel highway. He stopped there and called back to Karanja: 'Do you think the Army will send a patrol out looking for you?'

Karanja hesitated, standing there beside me, a worried frown on his face. 'Is possible.' He shook his head, leaning down over the side of the truck. 'I don't think they have the petrol. They fill up at the Nairobi barracks, you see, and only enough for supplies to the Lodge, so they cannot waste it looking for me.'

'Good. Then I'll stop just short of the lugga and you can drive on from there.'

After that it was all we could do to hang on, for the ruts were hardening and he was driving fast. We saw two tiny little antelope that Mukunga said were dik-dik, also an emaciated jackal, nothing else, only birds, none of them big – no vultures, no eagles, the skies above us empty and low cloud drifting in. From bright sunlight the day grew overcast, and shortly before noon, we slowed by an outcrop of red rock coming to rest at the top of a rise. Ahead of us the road dipped down to the green of trees. Nothing stirred, the air heavy and very still, a sort of brooding quiet. Van Delden got out. 'All right, Karanja. You drive them to the Lodge now. And you, Tait – you get into the front with Mary. And remember, you've been lost in the bush all night.' He smiled at me as I dropped into the roadway beside him. 'You look tired enough so I think you'll get away with it.'

Karanja climbed slowly into the driving seat, his broad flat face tense. I didn't like it. He looked scared. And as I squeezed in beside Mary Delden he was saying, 'What I do if the Army arrests them?'

'See your Minister,' van Delden snapped. 'And stick to your story.' And he added, 'Remember, I've got a picture of you down there on the Serengeti and if anything happens to them, if their film is seized, then I'll produce that picture tomorrow. You understand?'

'Yes, Tembo.'

'D'you know what time Kirby-Smith is due to address the Conference?'

'No.' He shook his head. 'It will be in the morning, I think.'

'Well, find out the exact time and pass it on to Miss Mary. She knows how to contact me.' He looked across at her, his big head framed in the window, his white hair blowing in a sudden gust of wind. 'See you tomorrow,' he said and stood back, telling Karanja to drive on. The last I saw of him he was loping off into the bush, Mukunga behind him carrying his rifle.

'Will he really come to the Conference tomorrow?' I asked.

'Oh, sure,' she replied. 'It's Alex Kirby-Smith he's gunning for.'

'Why?'

She shook her head. We were across the lugga

and grinding up the slope beyond. 'Something that happened between them. That's all.'

'When they were partners?'

But all she said was, 'A long time ago.' She was sitting very stiff and straight, her teeth clamped down on her lower lip, staring straight ahead. She was like that for perhaps a minute and then she added, as though explanation were necessary, 'Their attitude to animals is so entirely different, you see. And now . . . I don't know . . .' Another long pause, then she turned to me, smiling. 'Well, you've met the great Cornelius van Delden, so what do you think of him?'

I didn't know how to answer her, conscious of the soft pressure of her body against me and her large eyes glinting with laughter. 'I've never met anybody like him before,' I murmured hesitantly, searching for some word to encapsulate his strange, wild personality. But all I could say was, 'He's larger than lifesize.'

She nodded, laughing. 'You can say that again. He's always been larger than life.' The laughter died and she said slowly, 'He's a very wild man, always has been, and he'll take chances . . .' She hesitated, then shook her head. 'I don't know any man . . . I've never met any man – his equal. Once he's made up his mind, nothing will shift him, no argument, no threat, nothing. He sets his mind to something and that's that, whatever the danger to himself or others.' She turned to Karanja. 'How do you think Tembo was looking?'

He glanced at her, his eyes staring. 'Very strong,' he said. 'Very strong and like a pig's head. He does not think what he is doing to others.' He knew what she had been saying and the echo of her words sounded a note of warning. My mouth was suddenly dry, for I knew I had got myself mixed up in something that wouldn't just end with him delivering a speech to the delegates. I sat there, thinking about it, and she was silent now, staring straight ahead again.

'This man Kirby-Smith,' I said, trying to distract my thoughts. 'You must have known him well. What's he like?'

'I was only a child.'

'But you've met him since.'

'Once or twice.'

'Then what's he like?'

She didn't answer, only shook her head, and at that moment we rounded a bend in the road and a soldier was flagging us down, his rifle at the ready. He wore a cap rather like a kepi with the insignia of a rhinoceros sewn on to the front. 'An ex-game scout,' she whispered as Karanja greeted him, smiling with obvious relief. 'They seem to know each other, which may help.' But the man still insisted on calling his corporal, who came out of the little shelter of boughs they had built for themselves, grasping a submachine gun.

The talk went on and on. Finally, the corporal nodded, shouted some instruction to his men and climbed into the back with the soldier. We drove on then and Karanja said, 'He will take us to his captain. Those are his orders.'

'Did they send out a patrol to search for you?'

'No. But they know you and Mr Tait are missing.'

'So they will not be surprised that you went out looking for us.'

'Perhaps. But I am not Army, and to take an Army vehicle . . .' He gave a quick shrug, his voice uneasy. 'And there is my Minister . . . He will be very angry because I'm not here this morning. And tomorrow, when Tembo . . .' He shook his head, looking worried and the sweat shining on his face. 'Miss Mary.'

'Yes?'

The Lodge was coming into view, the sprawl of buildings brown against brown clouds, the waterhole a pale circle gleaming dully. A hand banged on the cab roof, the corporal shouting instructions in a nervous, excited voice.

'Ndio,' Karanja called back.

'What was that about?' I asked, the nervous tension mounting, my hands gripped tight around the camera.

'He wants him to drive straight to the guard post.'

'Can't he drop us off first?' I was thinking of the film in my camera, the two reels in the camera case at my feet. But all she said was, 'It would only make them suspicious.'

And then Karanja was speaking, very fast, his voice high and uncontrolled: 'Please. You see Tembo tonight. You tell him it is not possible he come to the Conference. He think he has protection of delegates and newspeople. But I cannot guarantee. I know my Minister. Mr Kimani is political man and very ambitious.'

'He daren't have him arrested there, before all the delegates.'

'No. No, he cannot do that. But when your father is gone, then he will instruct the Army to act. He will not have the alternative. Please, Miss Mary, you must believe that. Mr Kimani is a hard man and such action . . . coming to the Conference, speaking to the delegates.' He shook his head. 'Is most extremely crazy please. Mr Kimani then has his hand forced and he will act. He has not any alternative. You understand?'

'I understand,' she said. 'But do you? He'll still have those pictures and he'll use them.' I was surprised at the hardness in her voice. 'I think you'd better talk to your Minister.'

We were already turning into the Lodge driveway, now overgrown and rutted, the welcome board on its timber arch half rotted away, its lettering unreadable.

'He will be stopped,' Karanja said obstinately. 'They do not let him reach the Lodge. His pictures will be taken. You tell him please.'

A hand banged on the tin of the cab roof and we swung left. I was looking at Mary Delden, her lips shut and drops of perspiration clinging to the tiny hairs on her upper lip. Her features were tightset, the nostrils below the bony curve of her nose flared slightly. Pressed close together as we were I could feel her tension. The truck stopped and in a tight voice she said, 'You can't arrest him. Not with all these delegates here. You tell Mr Kimani that.' The corporal jumped down and disappeared into an outbuilding. 'Do you understand, Karanja?'

He didn't say anything, his hands gripping the wheel so tight the knuckles looked almost white.

'Karanja, do you understand?' She spoke in a fierce whisper as though he were a child who had closed its mind to reason.

He shook his head slowly, sweat shining on his face and a look of hopelessness. 'He will be stopped. Not arrested, but taken to the airport under guard. I cannot prevent that.'

The corporal came out with an officer, a big man, very black, with three pips on his shoulder and a walk that had a sort of swagger to it. He went straight to the far side of the truck and began talking to Karanja. I couldn't understand what was said, but it was obvious that he was subjecting him to an angry cross-examination, and his manner was truculent. The talk went on and on while we sat in the heat of the cab. Finally, Mary Delden leaned across and spoke to the captain in Swahili, her voice angry, almost petulant. Then abruptly she turned to me. 'Open the door and let's get out. I'm tired and I want a wash.' She picked up her camera, slipping the strap over her head. 'Also I'm bloody hungry.' The corporal moved to prevent us and she turned on the officer and said in English, 'You've no right to keep me here. If you do I shall go straight to the Minister and demand that he gets the American Consul on the R/T.' She reached past me, thrusting the door open. 'Now, get out, Colin, and push that corporal out of the way. I'm not going to sit here and roast.'

I didn't have to push him. The captain barked an order and the corporal stood back. I got out then, and she followed me. 'Come on. A wash and lunch, then some sleep.' She didn't speak to Karanja or the officer, she just walked straight off towards the main building and I followed her. 'You think he understood you?' I asked as we entered the dark cool cavern of what had once been Reception.

'Of course. He understands English perfectly. Not speaking it is a matter of principle.' The delegates were already at lunch. We could hear the roar of their voices, the clatter of plates coming from the dining-room. 'Better get all your film into safe hands. Not your cameraman's. Somebody else. And if we're interrogated separately, then we went as far as the lugga, fell asleep for a time and finally made it out to the road, when Karanja picked us up just before midday.' A flicker of a smile and then she left me, walking with long easy strides towards her room down near the empty shell of the swimming pool.

CHAPTER THREE

That night I saw Alex Kirby-Smith for the first time. He was seated a few tables away, talking to a group of Americans, a tall, heavily-built man packed with a great deal of energy. His face as he talked was very alive, eyes creased by years of sun glare and a sharp aquiline nose that gave him a predatory look. His hair was long and fair, and it was swept back across his head as though blown flat by a wind. There was no mistaking him in that gathering. Even if I hadn't known it, I think I would have guessed he was a hunter, something in the sharpness of his eyes, the hard, bright gleam as he talked. His hands were in constant motion, emphasizing his words, and one of those hands was gloved. It was the left hand and the brown glove was so incongruous in the sultry heat of the dining-room, that my eyes were riveted. It was some moments before the explanation dawned on me. It was an artificial hand.

The men with him at the table were all Americans

and he seemed to be trying to convince them of something, leaning forward, his elbows on the table, a cigarette gripped in his right hand, talking energetically. But I couldn't hear what he said because Abe Finkel insisted on giving me his version of what had happened at the Conference. He was a good mimic and his account of the various speeches would have been very entertaining if my mind had not been on other things.

The Kirby-Smith table began to break up. He was still talking as he pushed his chair back and got to his feet. He was very tall, a striking figure in immaculate bush jacket with a red silk scarf at his throat, his heavy, clean shaven face almost boyish with enthusiasm. And he moved with extraordinary lightness as though constantly poised on the balls of his feet. 'It will be a hard trip,' I heard him say. 'But I think it might be arranged if you really want . . .'

'Don't you think that's great?' Abe Finkel said, tapping me on the arm. 'Coming from old Willoughby-Blair. Wildlife is part of the pattern of total life and animals as important to man as man is to animals. Isn't that a laugh?' And he sighed and shook his head at me. 'You miss the first day and you don't even listen when I'm giving you the benefit of my brilliant observational faculties. I don't believe you got lost.'

'Nor do I,' said Ken, grinning at me. 'You spend a night out with the only good-looking girl in the place . . .'

'It was raining, my friends.' Abe smiled. 'Girls

don't like having it off in the African bush in the rain, and even if there aren't any lions or rhinos there's still snakes and spiders—' He pretended for a moment he was lying out in the rain with soldier ants crawling over him, wriggling his body, his voice husky and complaining. 'That a puff adder you got there?'

'Go to hell,' I said, watching Kirby-Smith as he moved from table to table, talking to delegates.

'Not funny, eh?'

'No.'

I had a clearer view of him, only two tables away, and there was something about his face – the tight hard mouth, the sharp thin nose, and the eyes alive, almost sparkling. She was right about the charm. He was one of those men with an attractive smile that can be turned on at will and though he was about fifty now he still had the engaging air of a much younger man. I wondered how he had lost the hand. A hunter with only one hand . . .

'You didn't get lost.'

'What?' I turned to find Abe Finkel leaning close to me, no glint of humour now in his eyes. 'What do you mean?'

'You heard me. It's a load of crap, you and the girl getting lost. You went out on a job and you got something nobody else has got, right?'

'What makes you say that?'

'Do you think we don't check our equipment cases? You slipped three mags into the film carrier while we were at lunch. And what about Karanja? The story is he went out looking for you and got bogged down, that's why he wasn't in Conference this morning to introduce Kit Kimani. But this afternoon he was interrogating you and finally made off with the film from your camera. Why?'

'A precaution, I suppose. I don't know. He said he did it on the orders of his Minister.'

'Sure, but why? What did he think you might have got in the can?'

'I don't know.'

'You don't know! Jeez, you're a poor liar. And putting the exposed mags in our case. Erd found them there right after lunch, while you were still feeding, and I slipped them into my pocket just in case.' He stared at me, smiling. 'Well, you going to share your dark secret?'

He was much too sharp and I didn't say anything, only shook my head.

'I might hang on to them.'

I didn't know whether he meant it or not, his eyes watching me full of devilment. 'I don't think you'll do that,' I murmured.

'No? You think a hardened old pro like me has any kindness for new boys, and a limey at that?' He was still smiling, his tone light-hearted, but the dark eyes watching me showed he was serious. 'I want to know what you've been up to. Or would you prefer I asked the Delden girl?'

'You'll know tomorrow,' I said, and got to my feet. I was feeling tired now and I wanted some sleep.

'Tomorrow – where?'

'At the Conference. When Kirby-Smith speaks.'

And I added, 'You may want to do a deal then, so keep that film safe.' His eyes were alight with curiosity, his face shining in the naked glow of the lights, but he didn't ask any more questions, and I knew he wouldn't talk, not with the prospect of a deal. The film was safe with him and I left them and went to my room.

Ken came in as I was stripping off my clothes. 'You really got something, Colin?' He was frowning, his expression intent and puzzled. And when I didn't answer, he said, 'Karanja took off in that truck shortly after midnight. I got that from one of the guards. I was up at dawn this morning. I was worried about you.'

'You needn't have been.' I poured some water into the canvas wash-basin and began sluicing my face.

'There was a woman journalist wandering about, enquiring about Mary Delden. They share the same room and she was scared something had happened to her.' He paused, waiting, while I dried my face on the towel. 'Cornelius van Delden,' he murmured. 'I know something about him now and there's a rumour going around that he's in the country and the Army looking for him.'

'Who told you that?' I threw the towel down and turned to face him. 'Have you been asking questions?'

He shrugged. 'Not only me, but Abe and several others. We're all consumed with curiosity. And you out with that Delden girl. The same name.'

'Why the hell start asking questions?' I demanded angrily. 'I told you not to worry if I was late back.'

'No need to get excited. I'm the only one who knew you were anxious to contact Cornelius van Delden and I kept quiet about that.'

'Mary Delden is his daughter.' I reached for my pyjamas. 'That's all I'm going to tell you at the moment.' I was thinking of that camp site down in the lugga and how we had bunks and supplies trucked in, Army guards acting as servants; two entirely different worlds, and tomorrow he would walk into this Lodge – into a trap by the sound of it. 'These rumours. What exactly are they saying?' I asked.

'You've seen him, haven't you?' He was standing with his back to the window and at that moment the spots by the waterhole were switched on. His glasses glinted in the light. 'All right. If you don't want to talk . . .'

'What are they saying?'

'That he hates Kirby-Smith's guts. That it's Burton and Speke all over again and somehow he'll manage to address the Conference.'

'Burton and Speke?'

'It was Abe Finkel used that phrase. I don't know anything about it. All in the African books, he said. I'm not well read like Abe.'

I had a vague recollection of some Victorian drama. The source of the Nile – that was it. A duel of words and Speke supposed to have committed suicide. And if the Lodge was buzzing with rumours that van Delden would make an appearance . . . . 'Who've you been talking to?'

'Just the delegates and the media.'

'What about Kirby-Smith? Have you been talking to him?'

'No, but Abe has.'

'What did he say?'

'Merely that Cornelius van Delden was a crank and persona non grata with the present Government. He's quite certain they'll see to it he doesn't appear at the Conference.'

So the trap was set and tomorrow it would be sprung. A man with a beard like that, so recognizable, couldn't possibly slip into the Lodge unseen. The whole area was closely guarded now, patrols out and sentries posted. I could see them moving down by the waterhole. I ripped a page out of my pad, scribbled a note and gave it to Ken. 'Take that to Mary Delden, will you? Tell her what you've just told me.'

He hesitated as though about to ask more questions. But then he nodded. 'Okay, I'll tell her.' It was only after he had disappeared into the night that I realized I was still standing quite naked. I slipped into my pyjamas then and climbed into the bunk to lie awake for a time wondering how van Delden thought he could possibly get into the Conference. I was picturing him and Mukunga fighting it out with the Government guards, the sound of rifle fire echoing through the Conference room, and it was on this fantasy that I fell asleep, too dead tired to care what happened.

I heard an elephant trumpeting, high like a squeal, and shouts, and then I was awake, or thought I was, and there were voices whispering in the room.

Abe talking softly, no light and shadows moving in the dark. A door closed and there was silence. I thought I must have dreamed about the elephant, that it was only the others coming to bed, and I rolled over and went to sleep again. The next thing I knew it was dawn and I wanted to relieve myself. At night we had been using the room toilet, flushing it out with a bucket of water in the morning. I climbed sleepily down from my bunk and crossed to the bathroom. The door was shut and when I tried the handle it wouldn't budge. Abe's voice behind me said, 'Do it outside. The door's locked.'

'Why?'

'He's sleeping in the bath.'

'Who?'

'For Christ's sake! Who do you think? Go back to bed. It's not six yet.' And he pulled the blanket over his head.

I went outside and peed over the edge of the veranda, staring out at the silent Lodge. The mournful note of the mourning dove called down by the waterhole and a stork stood like a sentinel on top of the main building. Dawn was just beginning to break and the air full of the murmur of insects and the hoarse croaking of frogs. Nobody was about, everything was still, almost breathless, and van Delden asleep in our bathroom. He must have arrived in the early hours, which explained why there had been no light anywhere when I had woken to the whisper of voices.

I climbed back into my bunk, but couldn't sleep, thinking about the script and what the climax would be, whether I was qualified to write it. I knew nothing about animals, nothing about Africa. I was London born and bred and all the things I had done so far had been in the UK, except for that one tanker film, and then the crew had all been British. I looked across at Abe Finkel, rolled up tight again in his blanket, at the litter of equipment under Lindstrom's bunk. They were in on it now, and though they had admitted they knew little more than I did about wildlife, they were so much older, so much more experienced.

Ken stirred in the bunk below me. 'You awake, Colin?'

'Yes.'

'Think we could get a picture of him sleeping in the bath? There's a window at the back.'

'Is there enough light?'

'The sun's just rising and the window faces east.'

Abe sat up. 'You want to get yourselves shot? He's got a Colt strapped to his waist and a guy like that sleeps with one eye open.' He swung his legs out of his bunk and slipped to the floor. 'We'll set it up before we go to breakfast.'

'He may not agree,' Ken said.

'Oh, he'll agree. Didn't you hear what he said last night? We keep him here under wraps till Kirby-Smith starts talking and we'll get all the pictures we want. A guy like that, taking the risks he has, needs all the publicity he can get.' He went outside to relieve himself and then he began to dress. 'Our real problem is how to get the stuff out. I'm going to have a word with the pilot of that plane. I know where he bunks.'

He looked at me as he pulled on his boots. 'How much are you prepared to contribute by way of incentive money?'

'I'm on a tight budget,' I murmured.

'Aren't we all.' He shrugged. 'Never mind, leave it to me. We can settle up later.' And he went out, carrying his shaving things as though he were going to the wash house.

He was gone about half an hour and by the time he returned we were all of us up and getting dressed. 'He's flying the Minister out this afternoon, leaving about four, and he'll take our films with him.'

'How much?' I asked.

'He's one of their mercenaries and he doesn't take risks for nothing. I gave him a cheque on a Swiss bank account for a thousand Swiss francs to be countersigned by the American Consul on delivery. That okay by you? Your people have no representation.'

I didn't know. I was out of my depth, uneasily aware I hadn't the facilities for this sort of thing. And then Mary Delden appeared on the veranda, looking fresh and neat. 'Can I come in?' Her husky voice sounded nervous, her eyes darting around the room as she entered. 'Is everything all right?' she asked me, and I realized she wasn't sure of the others.

It was Abe who answered her. 'You might have warned us, Mary. Arriving like that in the middle of the night and your boyfriend dead to the world – I might have screamed my head off.' He was smiling, his dark face alive with the humour of it. 'Had me scared.'

'I'm sorry.' She was smiling herself now, an expression of relief. 'Where is he?'

Abe nodded towards the closed door of the bathroom. She went over to it and knocked. 'It's Mary. You all right?'

The bolt clicked back and he opened the door, fully clothed, his bulk filling the gap and his eyes taking in the occupants of the room, a swift appraisal. They fastened on Abe Finkel. 'Was it you I talked to last night? Good. And you've arranged for the pictures to be flown out.'

'We'll need your co-operation.'

'Yes, of course. I heard everything you said. What about the tape recording?'

'That's taken care of. The cassettes will go out with the pictures.'

'Excellent.' He turned to Mary. 'No change in the arrangements, I hope.'

She shook her head. 'Do you have to do it this way, in front of everybody?'

'How else?'

'They'll say it's because – you hate him.'

He shrugged. 'What does that matter, so long as I stop him.' And he added, 'So he starts speaking at ten-thirty?'

'About then. The Conference opens at ten as yesterday and there's one delegate to speak first, an ex-Senator from Boston named Franklin. Karanja thinks Alex will talk for about half an hour, then after that there will be a discussion, with the Minister winding up just before lunch. In the afternoon we'll be taken to have a look at the area designated for the pilot scheme. Mr Kimani will be promising us shots of rhinoceros, antelope, possibly lion, too.'

'He's got it all fixed, has he?'

'Army scouts will be upwind and the game will be driven.'

He gave a harsh laugh. 'They've been collecting the poor brutes in bomas for several weeks now. It's one of the things I shall be telling at the Conference.' He looked at Ken and then at Lindstrom. 'You're the cameramen, are you? Well, after I've had my say, see that you've got plenty of film in your cameras. You'll get a shot of an elephant then and it will be something much more startling than anything Mr Kimani can offer you.'

'Was that what we heard last night?' Abe asked. 'There was a lot of squealing and shouting from the barrack area. That's why we were awake when you arrived.'

The big lion-like head nodded. 'That was an elephant. The one you told me about, Mary.'

'And you drove it into the Lodge area, in that condition?' The words trembled in the morning air, a note of anger and her face outraged. 'How could you?'

'They posted guards so I had to distract them.' And seeing the look of distaste on his daughter's face, he added, 'It's doomed anyway. You know that very well, so don't be sentimental about it.'

But she had turned her head to the window. 'Karanja,' she said. 'I think he's coming here.'

Through the window we could see him strutting across from the main building. 'You'll come and fetch me, will you?' van Delden said to me. 'As soon as he gets on his feet.'

I nodded and he disappeared into the bathroom, bolting the door behind him.

Karanja made straight for our veranda. 'Good morning, Miss Delden. Mr Tait, everybody. I hope they do not wake you last night driving those elephants away.' He seemed to have recovered some of his cheerful self-confidence.

'Was there more than one?'

'Oh, yes. They come for the garbage, you know.' He hesitated, glancing uneasily at the two Americans, and then turning to Mary Delden. 'I speak to you privately please. And you, Mr Tait.'

He took us over towards the swimming pool, and when we were out of earshot, he said, 'You tell him please he is not to come here. It is not good for him. The officer in charge has guards posted all round the Lodge. After breakfast there will be more soldiers and there is no chance he will be able to slip past them, no chance at all.'

'And how do you expect me to tell him?' she asked.

'I think you have some signal arranged. Please tell him. That is all I have to say. Except that my Minister is most anxious he does not make a fool of himself, not here in front of all the delegates.'

'I can imagine.' She was smiling sourly. 'The Army

arresting him and the news camera rolling. That would really put Kimani on the spot.'

'Please, Miss Mary. No cameras will be recording. It will happen away from the Lodge. You understand? He will gain nothing.'

She nodded. 'I understand. But you know him. Once he's set his mind to a thing . . .'

'That is why I ask you, as personal favour please. You must convince him is no good.'

'You go and tell him. His camp is down in the lugga.' And she told him exactly where. 'I couldn't get through the guards, and anyway I have to be at the Conference.'

He hesitated, then shook his head, smiling craftily. 'I think he has left his camp now, otherwise you don't tell me where it is.' And then, assuming the mantle of authority, he said sternly, 'You will do as I say please. For his own good. To avoid trouble.' And he turned and walked quickly away. He had done what he had been told to do and I had the feeling that his confidence was a thin shell and that underneath he was scared.

'What will they do to him?' I asked as I followed her to the main building.

'He'll be all right,' she said. 'He's a Kikuyu, and so's Kimani.'

'Tribal loyalty?'

She nodded. 'They'll both of them blame the Army and Kimani's a clever little man. If that doesn't work—' She gave a shrug. 'Well, I guess Africa isn't all that different from Washington or London when it comes to politicians. Their main preoccupation is the same – the pecking order, and survival.' She stopped there, glancing back at the waterhole, sniffing the air. 'What a wonderful world it would be without politics. I always think of the Garden of Eden as a place devoid of politics. Even here, where we are supposed to be fighting for the survival of wildlife, it's all politics, each delegate with his own bloody axe to grind, his own image to project. Cornelius, he's the same – and Alex. They each have their own viewpoint and they're blind to anybody else's, a mental curtain ... Oh well, you coming to breakfast now? I'm ravenous.' She smiled and there was a sudden air of forced gaiety about her. 'A full belly is the best sedative.'

'I haven't shaved yet.'

'Okay. I'll see you at the Conference then.'

I watched her walk away, wondering what she was really feeling, brought up in a safari camp run by her father and Kirby-Smith, and now the two of them at each other's throats and about to come face to face. I was thinking of my own background, so orderly, so commonplace – and hers so explosive. Had she known what her father would do when she accepted the assignment? Had she realized it would be a confrontation and herself emotionally torn between the two of them? For that's what she seemed to imply – the two of them ruthlessly projecting themselves.

I went back to the room and got my washing case. Abe Finkel was there, neat and shaved, sitting on the veranda.

'Ken and Erd are feeding now. We'll go later. Can't risk a guard finding him here before the balloon goes up, hm?' His curly black hair gleamed and his eyes were alive like coals, a real professional newsman, knowing he'd got a break and keyed up to a pitch of excitement. 'The pilot is in room 71. He'll wait for us there.'

Right up until ten o'clock there were never less than two of us in the room or on the veranda. But the only guards we saw were out beyond the waterhole, where they had more sentinels posted and a detachment patrolling back and forth. It never seemed to occur to them that Cornelius van Delden might already be in the Lodge area.

Just before ten o'clock we all of us went over to the dining-room. The tables were stashed now, the chairs set out in rows, the room half full already. We found seats at the outer edge of a row and Ken set the Bolex up on its tripod. I had the Beaulieu with me just in case, but my main concern was the recording and I wondered whether I was near enough to the line of chairs and the lectern facing us. But once Sir Edmund Willoughby-Blair was on his feet and I had a playback of his opening words I knew it was all right. His brief résumé of the views expressed by the delegates the previous day was given in a clear strong voice. Concluding, he said, 'I think we all recognize the problems facing the Government of the East African Federation. Our concern is the future of wildlife in this area, but anyone who listened to the Minister's speech yesterday and still does not accept that these problems must have a bearing on the animals who at one time occupied so great a part of the Federation's land area is not being realistic.'

The Minister nodded and smiled. He was sitting next to the Chairman in a neat, rather too bright, blue suit, the gleam of a gold ring against the dark hand resting on his knee.

'The problems, as I see them and as they have emerged in Conference, are threefold: First, the after-effects of an exhausting and protracted war. Second, the aspirations of a people on the move, natural aspirations of land tenure in an area of a very high birthrate where population pressures have been increased by a flood of refugees. Whole tribes have been forced to move or expand their territories. Third, the resettlement of nomadic people from the drought-stricken areas of the north and the consequent switch from a pastoral way of life to the more efficient land use of husbandry. Those, gentlemen, are the three basic factors that confront us, and no amount of dedicated, even emotional argument will make them go away. Now today, the last full day of the Conference, we shall be concentrating on the practicalities, with a visit this afternoon to an area which I am told still has a concentration of big game that can, the Minister thinks, be preserved. In other words, a game reserve, or park, that is politically possible.'

He glanced down at the neat blue figure beside him. 'But we must not forget that Mr Kimani still has to sell the idea to his Government colleagues and to the Army.' He turned to his audience again, speaking slowly and emphatically to give weight to his words. 'I would ask you, therefore, not to make it impossible for him by passing resolutions this evening, at our final meeting, that he cannot possibly support. I say this again, and most urgently, we have to think in terms of practicalities, of what is possible, given the circumstances. And to assist in this I have limited this morning's proceedings to two speakers, both practical men. One of them – Alex Kirby-Smith – has lived in the country all his life, is one of the world's scientific authorities on the management of game, both in the wild and in reserves, and what is more important, because of his services during the recent war, he is acceptable to the present Government of the Federation.'

During this part of his speech, the Chairman had been looking across at Kirby-Smith seated by the veranda, where the glare of the sun was like a spotlight on the large, tanned faced, emphasizing the sharpness of the nose, the keenness of those sun-creased eyes. There was applause from a little group sitting near him and he smiled his acknowledgement, a glint of gold teeth in the sunlight, the red scarf at his neck a casual splash of colour against the khaki of his bush jacket.

'But first,' Sir Edmund went on, 'I'm going to call on George L. Franklin of the Boston Foundation, a practical man in a different sphere – the world of finance. We have to face the fact that any wildlife programme requires money, for administration, management, protection. It cannot be self-supporting as in the old days when tourists came in their thousands. Those days are gone, perhaps for good. So, subsidies will be required. So now I call on George Franklin.'

Franklin spoke for just over twenty minutes in that flat grating accent I had heard several times before. I think he was probably an accountant. Certainly there was no sentiment in his speech. He gave a breakdown of costs, facts and figures based on the old parks and up-dated to current rates of pay for wardens, scouts, roads, transport, and all the complex set-up for efficient management of an area of about two hundred square miles. And he concluded by stating that the foundation he represented was prepared to support such a project to the extent of twenty per cent of the cost for a minimum period of five years.

I glanced at my watch. The time was just ten twenty-five and Franklin was now answering questions. Cameramen were moving unobtrusively towards Kirby-Smith, positioning themselves for the pictures they wanted as he moved to the lectern. Karanja was unrolling a map on the wall. Ken tapped me on the arm. 'D'you want a shot of him as he starts speaking?' he whispered.

I shook my head, watching Abe Finkel as he moved quietly to the door. He was against the light then, in silhouette against the shattered windows, Erd Lindstrom beside him, and both of them had cameras. Mary Delden was already out on the veranda. She, too, had her camera, and from there she could see our room and keep an eye on the speaker. 'You stay here,' I told Ken. The light was too tricky for me to handle it. 'I want a close-up of Kirby-Smith's face as he sees van Delden enter.' I left the tape recorder running, picked up the Beaulieu and headed for the door, the voice of Sir Edmund Willoughby-Blair following me as he thanked the speaker for his frank and detailed assessment and the generosity of his Foundation.

'Not yet,' Abe said, gripping my arm. He was watching the Chairman. Erd Lindstrom was halfway to our room. 'I've sent him to warn the old man. We'll signal him when the moment is right.'

The Chairman was already calling on the next speaker and Kirby-Smith was on his feet, the cameras round him rolling and clicking. It was his moment and he made the most of it, even to the point of answering questions as mikes were thrust at him by men bored with the proceedings and in need of something more exciting, more colourful. 'You ever ridden a wild elephant, Mr Smith?'

'No, only rhinoceros.' They didn't care that it was just a joke. They lapped it up. And he was cheerful, almost debonair, the charm switched on. He moved on to the lectern, the cameramen following him. 'There's a rumour you're going north. Is that for the Government?'

'It's in my speech.'

He was at the lectern now, facing his audience, smiling, his good-looking features alive and vital, brimming over with confidence and Abe raised his hands. I saw Lindstrom acknowledge the signal and I watched the room, waiting. Kirby-Smith was talking now, about the war and the part wildlife had been forced to play. 'An army on the march takes what it can. It feeds off the land, and in Africa that means game. I know there are people here who think this inexcusable, but to expect men to starve so that elephant or rhino, or gazelle, will survive is to ignore your own nature. There's not one of you, not a single one of you here, however dedicated to the preservation of wildlife, who, put to the test, would starve himself to death when he had the means to kill. Even those of you who think it all right to kill for the pot, in other words subsist off the land, abhor the behaviour of men like Stanley and Teleki, moving through with a vast retinue of porters and killing to keep their men supplied with meat. But they did it to save their expeditions from foundering, as I did it during the recent war to feed an army.'

He paused, looking over the sea of faces, assessing the impact of his argument. 'Some of you, I know, do not condone my part in it. But what would you have? I will tell you how an army marching on its stomach would have done it . . .' Abe moved, raising his camera, and I turned, distracted from the speech, to see black guards running and Lindstrom walking backwards, his camera aimed at the leonine figure of Cornelius van Delden striding in battered sandals and dirty shorts towards us. Grey hair showed like a mat in the torn neck of his ragged shirt and there was a revolver strapped to his waist.

Heads turned, distracted by the shouts. The name Cornelius van Delden ran round the room. The newsmen, crouched in front of Kirby-Smith, cameras pointing, took their fingers off the trigger, leapt to their feet and ran. In a moment the room was in an uproar, delegates crowding to the windows and out on to the veranda. I made a circling gesture to Ken and he panned over the scene outside, the camera closing in on van Delden, over the emptying Conference room, and then he moved in on Kirby-Smith standing speechless and forgotten, on the Minister sitting dazed, and the Chairman banging an ashtray on the desk, and I switched off my tape recorder and pushed my way out on to the veranda.

The little backwards-moving procession reached the veranda, backed up against the craning delegates and halted. 'How did you get here? . . . We heard you had been deported . . . Mr van Delden, will you be speaking?' And a very Germanic voice: 'You will make a stadement please. Ve vant to know vether is true there is nodding of vild animal from 'ere to ze coast.' And somebody else, a Scandinavian by his looks – 'Ja, we like a statement now.'

The guards had halted, uncertain, black faces and khaki uniforms a crowded background to the bearded head of van Delden, and there was nothing they could do. They were faced by a battery of cameras and a solid phalanx of delegates.

'Gentlemen!' Sir Edmund's voice was no longer soft and persuasive. It boomed out like a sergeant-major's. 'Gentlemen, your attention please. Will you now go back to your seats. We are listening to a very important speech. Now, please – immediately.'

Slowly the scene dissolved as delegates began to

resume their seats, but many of them hung around after they had made way for the Chairman, doubtless to see how he would greet this man come out of the bush like some prophet of old. They were not disappointed. Sir Edmund had a great sense of occasion. 'Cornelius van Delden.' His face beamed, his hand outstretched. 'I remember you, back in '73 when half the scientists in the world, myself included, gathered at Lake Rudolf for that eclipse of the sun. Come along in. You were invited, of course, but I gather you were held up.' And he turned, his arm round van Delden's shoulders, his bland froglike face beaming at the cameras as he said, 'You know, we met before that, when I was serving in the KARs – the Mau-Mau troubles.'

It wasn't the most tactful thing to say, bearing in mind that the Minister was a Kikuyu, but perhaps he meant it that way, for he must have known how van Delden had been treated at the airport, the search for him that had been mounted. But I don't think Kimani took it in. He had remained seated, his face blank, lower lips sagging and the whites of his eyes showing as though he had seen a ghost.

'The minister I believe you know. And Alex, of course.' And still standing with his arm on van Delden's shoulder, as though afraid if he dropped it he would be out of camera, he faced the room, his voice booming: 'Gentlemen! I am sure you will all wish me to welcome the arrival at this Conference of a man who needs no introduction to you, at least as regards his reputation – Cornelius van Delden. He has unfortunately been delayed, circumstances beyond his control, but now that he is here, I know you will wish me to suggest that he gives us the benefit of his long experience – after Alex has finished speaking, that is.'

There was applause as he waved van Delden to a seat and then resumed his own. The Minister was conferring urgently with Karanja, but the room gradually settled and Kirby-Smith took up the threads of his speech, not as smoothly as before and not with quite the same control of his audience. Cornelius van Delden was too striking a figure, and the delegates were still craning to look at him. But Kirby-Smith was a good speaker and as soon as he came to his projected trip into the North he had their attention.

'I gather there has been a good deal of talk amongst Conference members about Ileret as a possible alternative to the pilot scheme offered by the Government and I believe most of you know already that I am leaving for the North very shortly to review the game situation on the shores of Lake Rudolf. Federation military aircraft overflying the region have reported considerable concentrations of game—' He turned to the map on the wall behind him. 'Particularly in the Horr Valley area.' He indicated the gap between the Nyiru and Ol Doinya Mara ranges below the southern end of the lake. 'Also, on the slopes of Kulal. In fact, there appear to be above average concentrations of game all the way up the east side of Rudolf.' He came back to the lectern then, not to look at his notes, but because it was the most dominant position, standing there between the Chairman and the Minister.

'Ileret is close to the Ethiopian border. It is now part of the Military Zone and as you will have noticed from your maps all the area you will probably remember better as the Northern Frontier District is designated forbidden territory. I have to tell you that this is not only because the Army regards it as vital to the defence of the Federation's northern flank, but there has, as you well know, been a prolonged drought in that area. It is a pastoral region occupied by nomadic tribes, mainly the Rendile and Samburu. Their herds have been almost wiped out, even their goats and camels have suffered terrible losses. These tribes face starvation and though rain is now expected in the area, this can have no immediate impact. A few days' rain may save the last of their cattle from extinction; it cannot create new herds on which the people can live. The Government – and I am sure you will agree with this on humanitarian grounds – has accepted that this is an area calling for urgent relief. As Sir Edmund has told you, the preservation of wildlife is not something that can be considered in isolation. The people of the country have parallel claims. This, gentlemen, is a disaster area and the concentrations of game reported to be moving into it could destroy the last vestiges of vegetation thus finally annihilating the Rendile and Samburu.'

The Minister nodded energetically, but a voice from the back called out, 'It's their cattle and goats, not the game, that's destroying their environment.'

'In the circumstances,' Kirby-Smith went on smoothly, 'you will appreciate that Ileret as a game reserve is not politically possible at the moment. But – and here I have some hopes for the future – the Government has asked me to undertake an expedition into the area. The objects of this will be twofold: to examine the situation on the ground and to take immediate action to relieve the threat of starvation.' He held up his hand as several voices were raised in protest. 'Before you express your quite understandable reaction, please remember this; here in the comparative comfort of this Lodge you are being fed on tinned rations that the Federation Government, with limited resources, has had to import. The general population, however, has to live off the land. In the north, there is almost nothing left for them to live off, except game moving into their area.'

'What game?' It was the same voice from the back.

'I'm talking about elephants mainly. There's other game, of course—'

'Have you any idea how many elephants are left?' And another delegate said, 'Can't be many. They've been under pressure for years, the forest burned up for charcoal, trees giving place to shambas and new villages, the herds of cattle multiplying even faster than the population, war, unrestricted poaching, finally drought. And now you want to—'

'Order. Order please, gentlemen.' Sir Edmund Willoughby-Blair banged with the glass ashtray he was using as a gavel and nodded to Kirby-Smith.

'As I was saying,' he continued, 'I fully understand your reaction, but when people are dying, as they are in the north, they will seek any remedy. If it is left to them to take advantage of this extraordinary north-ward migration there will be wholesale slaughter and much of it will be wasted, the flesh left to rot. I have equipment and men trained for the task in hand. Nothing will be wasted. It will be a scientific cropping of a natural resource and only a proportion of the animals will get killed, sufficient to meet the needs of the moment and tide the people over until their herds begin to increase again. I repeat, it will be scientifically done, the animals cleanly shot, the meat fully used. The result, I hope, will be a resumption of normal life for these tribes and viable units of wildlife preserved – by which I mean that the numbers of each species will be reduced to a level the country can reasonably support. Much of it is near-desert and for the animals, as well as for the people, it is essential that a balance be maintained between the available or potential vegetation and the population it has to support. The result of this operation – ' here he turned to the Minister again – 'when completed and a proper balance struck, will I believe be the re-establishment of Ileret as a game reserve. If this proves possible in the circumstances then prevailing I personally shall feel I have contributed both to this new country of the Federation and also to the cause which is most dear to the hearts of all of us here, the preservation of wildlife in East Africa.'

He sat down then and in the silence that followed the Minister rose quickly to confirm that the Government would consider sympathetically the case of Ileret as soon as the present disaster situation had been dealt with.

'I would like to put a question to Mr Kimani.' It was Cornelius van Delden, his voice surprisingly gentle, quite different from his appearance, which contrasted so startlingly with the immaculate khaki of the previous speaker.

The Chairman nodded. 'I was about to call on you to give your views on an area you were associated with for so long.'

Van Delden was standing now, his head thrust forward. 'It is some years since I last visited Lake Rudolf. I cannot, therefore, comment on the situation as reported by Major Kirby-Smith. I can only say I'm relieved to know there is still some game left in East Africa. Here, as you have seen for yourselves—'

'There are many places like Lake Rudolf,' the Minister snapped. 'Even here, near to the largest battle we fought . . . delegates will have the opportunity of seeing for themselves this afternoon.'

Van Delden nodded, turning and facing the body of the room, a big bear of a man in silhouette against the glare from outside. 'Yes,' he said. 'I've no doubt you'll be shown some animals, but they will not be from anywhere near here. If any of you newsmen care to forgo your lunch and can arrange to be taken to the area ahead of time, you'll be able to take pictures of the animals before they are released from their bomas.'

Kimani leapt to his feet. 'That is not true.'

Van Delden shrugged. 'Then take them. Straight

from here. Before you can give Karanja or anyone else instructions to let the beasts go.' He smiled, fixing Kimani with his hard pale eyes, staring him down, and it was obvious the Minister was at a loss. Kirby-Smith came to his rescue. 'Next, I suppose you'll accuse me of trapping them for the Government.' The expression of amused surprise on his face produced a ripple of laughter. 'It's well known, I'm afraid, among the older hands here that van Delden and I never hit it off. He's accused me of all manner of things since we broke up our partnership some fifteen years ago.'

'Are you saying you didn't do the capturing? You gave no instructions?'

'Of course I didn't.'

'But you don't deny the animals have been trapped?'

'This is ridiculous. You've only just arrived in the country—'

'It's what my scouts say. There's hardly anything left in this area larger than a warthog. The animals on show this afternoon will have been trucked in. And there won't be any elephants, not one, because full-grown elephants are too big to truck.' He turned to the Minister again. 'Your intention is obvious – clear the land of anything that competes with agriculture and cattle. So perhaps you would tell us now exactly what instructions you, or your Government, have given Kirby-Smith on this expedition to Lake Rudolf. Is it extermination?'

'No.' Kimani banged his hand on the table, his eyes almost bursting from his head. 'Of course it is not extermination. I have instructed Mr Kirby-Smith personally and my instructions are exactly what he has told the Conference.'

'Then another question. Did you personally instruct on the cropping to be done in the Serengeti during what is now I believe called the War of Federation?'

'No. The government then was military.'

'It was the Army that instructed me,' Kirby-Smith said quietly. 'Why?'

But van Delden ignored him, still facing Kimani. 'But now that you are Minister of Lands and Resources, you can't be totally ignorant of what happened.' He turned to the room, facing the delegates. 'Major Kirby-Smith had the job of feeding the Army. Just as he now has the job of feeding the nomads in the Northern Region. Scientifically. It will all be done scientifically, he says. Do you know what the word scientifically means to him? It means extermination.'

'Nonsense.' Kirby-Smith's face was flushed, the smile and the charm gone. 'You've accused me of all sorts of things. I've already said that. All of them without foundation. But to accuse me of exterminating wildlife, this is the most—'

'Then ask Kimani why he arrives so late that the opening of the Conference is delayed a day and the visit to the Serengeti cancelled. If delegates had gone to the Serengeti . . .'

'I take you tomorrow,' Kimani said quickly, still on his feet. 'Any delegate or newsman who wishes—'

'To Lake Lgarya?'

The man stood there, his mouth still open. Then he looked at Kirby-Smith and promptly sat down.

'No,' van Delden said. 'Nobody will be taken there, for if any of you saw it there would be such an outcry—'

'You know nothing about it.' Kirby-Smith was no longer looking at the delegates. He had eyes only for van Delden, the two of them facing each other across the room. 'Of course, animals were killed—'

'All the wildebeest, all the zebra, all the gazelles, the whole lot wiped out in a senseless orgy of killing.'

'You exaggerate, Cornelius. You were in the Seychelles. You've no idea of what the war was like here. All the area south of here was a battlefield. The troops had to be fed—'

'A million animals slaughtered.' Van Delden's harsh voice rattled round the room. 'Wholesale, indiscriminate slaughter. Killing for killing's sake.'

Kimani leapt to his feet again, ignoring the room to face van Delden as he shouted, 'It is a lie. It was economic killing. Sufficient for the Army, no more.' And he added, his voice high and very loud, 'I know why you make these accusations. You are disappointed that the authorities do not let you stay, and since you refused to accept the air passage for return to your home, you have been hiding somewhere, so you know nothing about it.'

'I have seen it,' Cornelius van Delden stared round at the delegates. 'I have seen what you will never be allowed to see – the graveyard of a million splendid beasts, trucks encircling droves of terrified animals, guns mowing them down as they milled in helpless masses, packed so close their bones lie heaped on top of one another.'

'You lie,' Kimani screamed. 'I will have you arrested as the agent of the South African whites determined to destroy my country.'

'I lie, do I?' Van Delden pulled a bundle of prints from his pocket and moving quickly along the rows of chairs distributed them to the delegates. 'Pass them round please. A man can lie, but not the camera. These were taken yesterday morning, using a Polaroid. They're not as clear as the human eye. They do not convey the vastness, the totality of this destruction of what used to be known as the Serengeti migration. You look at them. Just look at these pictures. That's what happens when there are no game laws and men are allowed to let their lust for killing run away with them. Extermination,' he thundered. 'And you sit there and let this man fool you into thinking it will be just a token culling. He has a contract and a freezer plant and you are condemning the last remaining herds of elephants to total extinction.'

There was a stunned silence as delegates passed the pictures from hand to hand. One of them got up and asked Kimani if they could be taken to Lake Lgarya tomorrow 'to see for ourselves', and the Minister shouted, 'No. It is a dam' lie. A trick.'

There was a ground swell of talking, the cameras panning from delegate to delegate, and I saw Karanja watching Kimani and smiling quietly as though enjoying his Minister's discomfiture. Kirby-Smith stood up again, said something about conditions being different now. 'In the Serengeti it was war.' But nobody was listening, the delegates all talking among themselves. Sir Edmund banged the ashtray. 'Order please, gentlemen. I suggest we adjourn now. Conference will open again after a quarter of an hour, in I trust a calmer atmosphere.'

Chairs scraped. The newsmen closed round van Delden, grabbing at the pictures, thrusting them into his hand and taking close-ups of them as he held them. Pandemonium reigned and Mary Delden at my elbow said in a trembling voice, 'He shouldn't have done it. Twisting it like so that they blame Alex . . .' She stopped there as Kimani thrust his way out on to the veranda, waving wildly at the guards leaning on their rifles. 'Oh God! They've got him cornered now.'

'Where's Karanja?' I thought Karanja might be able to help.

The corners of her mouth turned down. 'He's no help. He's scared stiff, poor devil.'

'No,' I said. 'He's enjoying it.'

But she didn't hear me, drawing herself up, as though bracing herself. 'I'll go and have a word with Alex. There's nobody else can stop them.' And she walked quickly across the room, pushing her way through the crowd until she was standing at Kirby-Smith's elbow. He was talking to Sir Edmund and I saw him turn and bend his head to listen to her above the din of voices. It made me realize how tall he was, for she was my height, yet her eyes only level with his chin.

Ken grabbed hold of my arm. 'Can you get me some more film? I'm nearly out, and if you want good coverage when they grab him . . .' but it was too late already. Kimani had the captain with him now. He was shouting orders and guards were running to him from their positions around the Lodge. A shot cracked out, a flat whiplash of sound that silenced everybody for an instant. I thought for a moment it was some trigger-happy soldier, but there were shouts now from beyond the circle of buildings. 'Ndovu, ndovu.' Another shot, followed by a squeal, and a grey shape swayed into view from behind the last of the rooms. It crashed against the VIP veranda, scattering tiles and moving forward again, dragging one leg, its trunk raised. It stopped at the sight of us all gathered outside the dining-hall, the trunk waving as it searched for our scent, its great ears spread like sails.

Suddenly I saw its eyes, small and sunken in great hollows behind the uplifted tusks. They were big tusks and the body behind the grey skull was all bone. I had just time to realize that the wretched beast was almost starved to the point of death when it trumpeted, the trumpet note ending in a squeal of fear, and then it was coming towards us again, its head and trunk swinging from side to side as though it did not know which way to turn.

That somebody wasn't trampled was due to Kirby-Smith's presence of mind. While we stood rooted to the spot, too surprised to move, he ran forward, grabbed a rifle from one of the guards, then, moving out ahead of us into the path of the elephant, he raised the gun to his shoulder, balancing it loosely on his gloved hand, waited a moment and then fired. The grey mass of bone came on without a check, then suddenly sagged at the knees, pitching forward, head lowered, tusks digging into the ground, scoring great furrows in the turf as it came to a stop and slowly keeled over on its side.

There was a great yell from the soldiers and in an instant they had fallen on it, knives appearing like magic in their hands, others using their bayonets as they hacked in a frenzy at the carcass, grabbing the meat they had been starved of for so long. The tall captain was in there too and it was Kirby-Smith who finally forced them to some semblance of order, shouting for men who had once been game scouts and arranging for the orderly dismembering of the carcass. Then he called to the delegates, gathering them about him and pointing to the left hind leg, which had a length of thick wire embedded in the flesh. The whole foot was rotten, all swollen up and thick with flies, the smell of putrefaction hanging on the air. 'That's what happens in Africa when the disposal of big game is left to men without rifles, men who are hungry for meat and have no feeling for the animals they prey upon.'

I looked round for van Delden, wondering what his reply to this would be. But he was nowhere to be seen. 'In the old days,' Kirby-Smith went on, 'this would be the work of poachers. But now there is no such thing as poaching. Anybody can kill . . .' He hesitated, then went on quickly, 'This is a wily old bull, who knows about humans and is not afraid to visit the waterhole here. Last night he was going over the garbage bins. He's probably the same beast the tourists used to photograph. But he put his foot into a wire noose attached to a log, an old poacher's trick, and a slow, painful death. Much better to deal with the problem cleanly with a rifle.'

I saw Mary Delden standing irresolute, her eyes searching the crowd, and I went over to her. 'Where is he?'

She shook her head, frowning, her mouth set in a thin line and tears in her eyes.

'What's the matter?' I asked.

She stared at me. 'Don't you understand?'

'What?'

'Christ!' she breathed. 'I told him about it. I told him there was an elephant around the waterhole, dragging a great log. Don't you remember? The dung beetle, the droppings. The rain had obliterated the marks, but in the night the squeal we heard, the dragging sound. He used it to get into the Lodge and now he's used it to get out, the boys driving it here, a sacrificial offering and the diversion he needed. Christ Almighty! The callousness of it!'

I understood then. Not just how he had planned to get away, but how everybody, however much they were committed to the preservation of wildlife, still made use of animals for their own ends – van Delden to make his escape, Kirby-Smith to support his business, Kimani to increase his political standing, and the delegates, committed and dedicated men who had come from the ends of the earth, all here because animals were a part of the position they held in life.

'While they're all bathing their heads in gore,' she said hoarsely, 'and disputing the rights of man and beast to live perpetually in a state of war, let's raid the kitchens and grab some beer. I want to get drunk. I want to get so drunk I don't have to think any more.' She grabbed hold of my arm and turned in a stumbling run, crying silently in a blind rage against humanity.

PART TWO

THE SOUTH HORR GAP

CHAPTER ONE

It was Sunday before we finally got back to Nairobi and like the rest, I was utterly exhausted, for the Conference had been extended a day with disastrous results. Realizing that the visit to the site of the proposed game reserve would be an anti-climax after the events of the morning, Kimani had insisted on personally conducting the delegates over the nearest battlefield, which was the one we had driven through on our way to the Serengeti. There he had lectured us in the pouring rain on the problems of an army fighting without lines of communication to any port and entirely dependent on the country for its food.

It had rained all that night and it was still raining on the Friday morning when we were huddled into wet hides for our promised view of wildlife in the reserve area. The animals had looked wet and bewildered, but by then the discomfort of our existence was such that nobody seemed much concerned about how we were able to see such a representative selection. Predictably the Conference voted later that day in favour of the pilot scheme.

We had left that same evening, everybody glad to get away from the leaking misery of the Lodge. But by then the roads were almost impassable and it had taken us almost two days to reach Nairobi, trucks bogged axle-deep, floods in the Rift Valley and our food exhausted. The rain had not let up until our vehicles were struggling into the outskirts of Nairobi and by then I was so thankful to tumble into a dry bed that left to myself I should have gone home with the rest. Even here there was muddle and uncertainty. Flight schedules had been posted at Reception, all of them subject to confirmation, and on the Monday the place seethed with rumours of cancellations and delays.

We had been booked into the Norfolk Hotel, which was not the most convenient for finding out what was going on. It was away from the centre of town, nicely secluded in its own grounds, which probably was why it was the only hotel still open to visitors, all the others having been taken over by the Government either as offices or army barracks. But the war had left its mark, a bomb crater gaping full of water in the middle of the central lawn, the glass of the surrounding windows all shattered and the phones in every room ripped out. With no taxis available, the only means of communication were the phones in Reception, and for these the newsmen had queued half the night only to find themselves cut off as soon as they tried to transmit copy that was considered in any way detrimental to the régime. All mention of Cornelius van Delden and the pictures he had taken in the Serengeti was banned.

The mood on that Monday morning was angry, particularly among the delegates. They were no longer guests of the Federation, meals were at black market rates and prices of accommodation exorbitant. And with the first flight cancellation a rumour circulated that we would be billed for the extra night we had spent at the Lodge. For the media this was acceptable as being part of the pattern of a disorganized country in the aftermath of war. Men like Abe Finkel were accustomed to it, but for the delegates, conscious that their expenses had to be found from funds raised by voluntary subscriptions, it came as a shock. And there was no certainty how long they would have to wait. Only the Americans were sure of getting away that night. They had chartered a plane. For the rest of us it was a day of uncertainty, of waiting.

I spent most of it working on my script. I wanted to get it all down in outline while it was still vivid in my mind. Ken and I had been allocated one of the chalet rooms. Originally it had big sliding glass windows opening on to the lawn, but now the glass was all gone and when darkness came the night pressed in on us, insects battering against the naked light bulb and an orchestra of sound, cicadas in the grass and frogs in the bomb crater. The first draft of the script finished, I joined Ken in the entrance foyer, which was crowded with delegates and their baggage.

'Is Abe back yet?' I asked. He had set out to walk into the city centre immediately after breakfast.

He shook his head. 'Erd's getting worried he'll miss his plane.' And he added, 'There's a rumour that we may get away tonight. A flight's due in from Tokyo around 2 a.m. and there may be seats.'

My eyes searched the crowd. Now that I'd licked my script into some sort of shape there were questions I wanted answered.

'If you're looking for Mary Delden, I haven't seen her either.'

'Was she here for lunch?'

'I didn't see her. But she may have had sandwiches in her room, same as you did.'

The woman who had shared her room at the Lodge was talking to Franklin and I pushed my way through the crowd. But she hadn't seen Mary either. 'We were booked in together, room 109, but I never saw her after we'd had dinner together on the terrace. I don't know what the hell she's up to, but she didn't sleep in the hotel last night.'

'Have you asked at the desk?'

'They say she checked out about nine-thirty this morning, paid her bill and took her baggage. And it was an Army truck came for her.' She stared at me, her eyes bright with curiosity. 'I sure would like to know what she's up to.'

I went in search of Erd Lindstrom then, but his only concern was for Abe. 'I don't trust that pilot. He's one of their boys, a mercenary, and now he's got his money . . .'

'You think they may have arrested him?'

'I don't know. Abe's pretty fly, but anything's possible in this crazy country.'

There was a movement in the crowd, a surge towards the baggage piled by the door. Over their heads I saw a coach drawing up in the roadway outside. It was painted camouflage green and brown, the windows empty of glass. 'Your transport's here.'

He nodded uncertainly. 'Looks like it.'

The Americans were trooping out now and Karanja was there. 'Please you take your place in Government bus for airport all people on flight to New York. You show receipted bills for hotel before boarding please.'

'What are you going to do?' I asked.

'Last Abe said to me was not to worry and get on the flight. So—' He shrugged and moved into the tail of the crowd, collecting his grip and his camera equipment as he reached the door. 'He's done this on me before. Something's cropped up, I guess. His gear's still in the room and I've left him the small camera with all the unexposed film. Tell him, will you. And I hope he doesn't get held up too long. The same goes for you. This is no place to have authority breathing down your neck.' He was frowning as he turned and followed the others out to the coach. And after that they just sat waiting with the doors closed, Karanja leaning against the side of the bus with a sheet of paper in his hand and two soldiers standing guard.

There was tension in the warm night air and it crossed my mind that if Abe had been arrested, Mary

Delden might be in trouble, too. After what had happened they might arrest all of us. I was wishing I could take Abe's place on the flight – New York, anywhere, so long as there was an end to this uncertainty of waiting. 'Sont-ils certains de trouver un avion à l'aéroport?' It was the *Paris Match* correspondent voicing all our thoughts and Karanja was talking to Erd now, questioning him. 'S'ils ne veulent pas que nous écrivons ce que s'est passé . . .' Marcel Ricaud left it at that, his words hanging in the air and an icy chill running through the group left standing on the terrace, every one of us conscious of our vulnerability. We had been given a glimpse of the ugly side of war. We had been told things that the Government did not want known, witnesses to their failure to prevent van Delden speaking his mind, and so long as we were here the world outside could be kept in ignorance.

'What's the hold-up, Mr Karanja?' It was Sir Edmund, his voice bland and reassuring.

Karanja didn't answer. He was still talking to Erd Lindstrom through one of the glassless windows.

'Mr Karanja.' The tone of command had its effect. Karanja turned. 'I asked what the hold-up was.'

'An American is not present.' And Karanja called out, 'Anybody know where is Mr Finkel representing CBS please?' His eyes rolled white in the lights and then fastened on me. He came over. 'You were with Mr Finkel at the Lodge. Where is he now?' His head was thrust forward, his manner slightly truculent, and I could smell the beer on his breath.

'I've no idea,' I said. 'And there's Miss Delden. She's missing too.'

'Miss Mary I know about. Is Finkel I am looking for.'

'Where is she?' I demanded. 'What have your people done with her? Is she under arrest?'

'No, is not under arrest.' He looked surprised, almost offended.

'Then what's happened? Where is she?'

'She didn't tell you?' He hesitated, then said, 'Is gone with Major Kirby-Smith.'

I stared at him. 'With Kirby-Smith? Are you sure?'

He nodded. 'Miss Mary okay, now you tell me—'

'But why?' I couldn't believe it. 'Why should she go with Kirby-Smith of all people?'

'Miss Mary good journalist, that's why. Now you tell me where is this man Finkel. All Americans present, only Mr Finkel missing. You tell me where he is please.'

'I don't know.'

'Then find him. He is not in his room and the bus cannot leave till he is found.'

'But he's been gone since before lunch.'

'I think,' Sir Edmund cut in, 'you had best let the coach go while you telephone the authorities. The Ministry will probably know where he is.'

'Is too late for the Ministry now.'

'Then phone the security police. Tell them to pick him up. He's probably in one of the bars. You might even try the old Muthaiga Club. But get those Americans away to their plane, now, before I ring Mr Kimani myself.'

I don't know whether it was Kimani's name or simply the long habit of obedience, but Karanja went back to the coach without argument and gave orders to the driver to proceed to the airport. The rest of us watched in silence as the coach drove off. I think, like me, they were all feeling a sense of abandonment as it disappeared down the heavily treed road, for the Americans had been by far the largest group at the Conference. There was a general movement towards Karanja who was suddenly engulfed, a sea of anxious faces deluging him with questions about flights and departure times, and all he could say to pacify them was, 'I will telephone.'

It was Sir Edmund who rescued him, taking him by the arm and leading him through the flap of the reception desk into the manager's office behind. When they emerged again Karanja was smiling. 'Everything arranged now,' he announced. 'You all leave by Government bus for the airport at twenty-three hundred.' And Sir Edmund added, 'I'm told there are two flights coming through the night, one of them, a jumbo, is half empty, so there will be seats for all of you.' The jumbo was bound for London via Naples, the other, a 707, for Frankfurt.

'Let's go and have a drink,' Ken said. Everybody was moving towards the bar at the end of the terrace, a sense of relief showing in their faces, in the suddenly increased volume of conversation.

'You go ahead,' I told him.

'Still worrying about her?'

I shook my head, feeling confused and not certain why it mattered to me that she had gone off with Kirby-Smith. A good journalist, Karanja had said. But it had to be something more than that. 'I'll join you in a minute.' And I went back through the foyer, climbing the stairs to room 109. But it was just as the woman had said, one bed still unmade, the other not slept in, nothing of hers left there, the wardrobe, the drawers, everything bare, including the bathroom. I stood there for a moment thinking about where she would be now, remembering the last time I had seen her, at the Lodge, lushed up on beer, her face puffed and shining with sweat, her dark eyes reflecting the violence of her feelings. She had looked older then, and I remembered how she had said, 'He's always been like that – ruthless, egotistical, always disappearing into the bush. I never had a proper father.' The tears had been streaming down her face. 'How can I love a man like that? I hate him.' And she had turned suddenly and left me, staggering blindly out into the rain, the beer not strong enough to drown the tide of her emotions.

And now she was with Kirby-Smith who was everything her father was not, a commercial hunter. Where would she be now, at his house in Karen? Abe had said he had one of the old settler's houses out on Miotoni Road. Or would she be camped somewhere on the road to the north?

I closed the door and went back down the stairs, wondering why I had bothered to check her room. It didn't matter to me what she was doing. Tomorrow I would be back in London, the whole episode nothing but material for a script. And yet . . .

I was still thinking about her, about the extraordinary love-hate relationship she had for her father, when I reached my room. But I didn't stay there. I went out on to the lawn where the night was like velvet, all diamond-studded, and the older building, beyond the crater, a white blur in the starlight. I could see the balcony of Abe's room, but there was no light there, the whole building dark. So he hadn't returned and again I had that sense of uneasiness, the feeling that Africa hadn't finished with me yet.

A light beamed out from one of the chalet rooms, a man standing there, dark in silhouette. It was a moment before I registered the light was in my own room. The figure moved, stepping through the glassless windows out on to the lawn. 'That you, Colin?' It was Abe's voice. And he added, coming towards me, 'Ken said you were somewhere around.' His tone was quiet and relaxed, no trace of tension in it.

'Where the hell have you been?' He didn't seem to realize the trouble his absence had caused. 'Karanja was going to hold the coach for you, but then Sir Edmund—'

'It doesn't matter.'

'You should be on your way out to the airport with the others. Where have you been?'

'Checking on your film for one thing.' He took hold of my arm. 'Come on, we'll go back to your room. We can talk there. And I've got myself a bottle of the real stuff. Maybe that'll quieten your nerves.' I started to protest that there was nothing wrong with my nerves, but his grip on my arm tightened. 'Wait till I tell you what I've arranged.'

'The thing you've got to arrange is transport out to the airport,' I told him, my mind still on the problem of getting safely clear of Africa. 'That charter plane is waiting there and if you don't get moving—'

'I'm not leaving with the others.'

'What do you mean?'

'I'm staying on here. And so are you – if you want to. Now come on back to your room and I'll fix you up with something better than local firewater.'

He wouldn't answer any of my questions until I was seated on my bed with a tooth glass half full of neat whisky. 'Where did you get this?' I asked him. 'It's Bourbon, isn't it?'

'Right. A present from the American Consul.' He lit a cigarette and flopped into the only chair, leaning back, his eyes half closed. 'It's been a long day,' he murmured, sipping at his drink. 'That was the first thing I did, checked at the Consulate to see the pilot had delivered your film safely. He had, and the Consul had countersigned my cheque.' He stared out into the night, rubbing his hand over his eyes. He looked tired. 'They picked me up as I came out of the building.'

'Who did? The Police?'

'Police, Army – I don't know. They weren't in uniform, just dark trousers and white open-necked shirts. They didn't ask me what I'd been doing at the

Consulate, they just hustled me into an old Peugeot, gave me a thorough going over in the back of the car and when they didn't find what they were after they drove me into town. I thought I'd land up in some goddam prison or maybe an Army barracks. They wouldn't talk. They wouldn't answer any of my questions. And they weren't interested in my press pass or the fact that I was an American TV man. And when I insisted on their taking me to the Ministry, the guy sitting beside me in the back just gave me a broad smile and said, "You'll be well cared for, Mr Finkel." I figured that was a threat and I was in real trouble, but instead of landing up in jail, I found myself on Ngong Road on the first floor of a fancy black market restaurant that turned out to be the old Nairobi Club. The windows were open on to a balcony and Kimani was sitting there in the sunshine with a drink in his hand, the pilot opposite him and another African, a man named Gerhenji or something like that, a director of the new Federation Bank.' He knocked back the rest of his drink and reached for the bottle. 'Are you ready for another?'

I shook my head. 'What did they want?'

'The film, of course. Kimani's no fool and he'd figured out what you'd got and how you'd got it. And by then, of course, I knew it was political dynamite. The Federation is pressing hard for full diplomatic recognition from the States. They want an American Embassy here, not just a Consulate. That's why they agreed to the Wildlife Conference. So in the end I did a deal with him.' He smiled at me. 'It was the least I could do after an excellent lunch and those gorillas waiting for me downstairs.'

I was thinking of that night drive through the rain, the incredible blazing dawn in the boneyard of the Serengeti. 'What sort of a deal?' I asked bleakly.

'You want to get to Lake Rudolf, don't you?'

'If I could have persuaded van Delden to take me, yes. Where is he? Did they tell you?'

'They don't know. At least, that's what Kimani said, and I think he'd have told me if they'd picked him up. He said he thought he was probably working his way down to the coast and would get out that way, back to the Seychelles. Now, do you still want to go to Rudolf, or don't you?'

I shook my head, feeling Africa closing round me, scared of what he might have arranged. 'Didn't they offer you money?'

'Oh yes. That's why the bank director was there. I have the impression Kimani's position isn't all that secure. What he had in mind was a straight cash deal through the bank's representative in Zurich.'

'Then why didn't you take it?'

'It wasn't my film, and knowing you wanted to get up north . . .'

'There are two planes coming through tonight,' I said. 'All I want is to be on one of them, out of here.'

He laughed and I knew by the sound of it he had had too much. 'So now van Delden's gone and the girl, too, you've lost your nerve.' He thrust the bottle in my hand.

It was half empty. 'You know about Mary Delden then. Did Kimani tell you?'

He nodded. 'Clever girl, tagging along with Kirby-Smith.'

'How do you mean?' The bottle rattled against the glass as I poured.

'She knows where there's a good story – drought, starvation, a culling operation. And Kimani wants it told. Saviour of the starving multitude. That's political stuff in the Third World. So I guess does Kirby-Smith, provided it justifies him.'

I slammed the bottle down. 'So that's it. You're afraid you're missing out on a story. You trade my film of van Delden in the Serengeti for the chance of meeting up with Kirby-Smith and getting something for your own network.'

He shook his head. 'I had no choice. Just think for a moment how that film of yours could be intercut with the shots of van Delden's intervention at the Conference. Actual pictures of him standing on the Serengeti plain viewing the carnage. It could be damning for a man in Kimani's position, knowing the President was bent on full American recognition. Anyway, that's my reading of the situation, and it fits in with Kimani's willingness to do a deal. He wants the world to know they have a problem up there in the north. So you get your trip to Rudolf. That's what you wanted, isn't it?'

He was twisting it, trying to make it appear he had done me a favour. 'You're not interested in Lake Rudolf,' I said.

'No, but you are. Would you care to tell me?'

'No.'

'Okay, but you have a reason.' He reached for the bottle, pouring himself another drink as he said, 'So do I. Not a spec – specific reason and I'm not after a story. It's not that at all.' He put the bottle carefully down on the floor. 'I'm a New Yorker, right? I was born and brought up in the Bronx, on the Grand Concourse. I'm a denizen of the concretest jungle in the world, and though I've been to a hell of a lot of countries, it's been mostly cities, or with mobs of people around – camps, mines, oilfields, anywhere there's a news story to cover. Driving out to that Lodge, the feel of Africa, the immensity, the solitude, and yesterday, coming back, we saw a lion – a wild lion on the prowl for food.' His voice had become a little slurred. 'It was so thin and emaciated the ribs stuck out like a wicker basket and it stood there looking at us from the other side of the flood water where we'd bogged down. I'd never seen a lion in the wild before, only well-fed beasts in cages. So I figured just once in my life I'd cut loose, do something I wanted – not for money, not as an assignment, just for kicks. D'you understand?' He shook his head, 'No, of course you don't. You're too young to have started worrying about what you've made of your life. But I'm close on fifty now, and seeing van Delden, his absolute commitment, his complete disregard of self – and the extraordinary impression he made . . .'

He paused there, staring down at his empty glass, his eyes half-closed and a strangely sad look on his face. 'Most of us, we live our lives, not believing in anything very much. But men like van Delden, they walk through life with God at their side, sure in the knowledge that they are here for a purpose.' He put his hands up over his face, leaning forward as though in prayer. 'Jesus! I envy them, now, when it's too late. I'm just a spectator. That's all I've ever been, all I wanted to be. Not involved, not committed. A spectator.' He spat the word out, contemptuous and sneering. 'I've read a lot. Biographies mainly. A substitute for the real thing.' He let his hands fall, staring at me with his dark eyes. 'D'you know why van Delden went to the Seychelles?'

'He retired,' I said. 'His wife's family had a house there . . .'

'Balls! He's not the sort of man to retire of his own accord. He was run out of Kenya – deported.'

I didn't know whether to believe him or not. 'How do you know?' I asked.

'*The Nation*. After I left Kimani I had a look through the back numbers. It was about a year before the war. A man named Enderby disappeared up near Marsabit in territory van Delden had acquired as a sanctuary. He was a white hunter collecting for zoos and safari parks and specializing in baby elephants. The mortality rate was appalling. But he didn't care, nor did the Government. Like the tourist traffic, it brought in foreign currency. Only van Delden cared, and when Enderby started moving in on his territory, he warned him – not privately, but in front of the African game warden at a meeting in the warden's office in Marsabit. He told him he didn't care whether he had a Government permit or not, if he started using guns and thunderflashes on his land he'd shoot him.' Abe nodded. 'I talked to the reporter who interviewed that game warden. He's still working for *The Nation* and he told me the warden was quite certain van Delden had meant what he said. He also told me it was common knowledge Enderby was involved in the ivory trade, and Marsabit was known for its big tuskers.'

'You think van Delden shot him then?' I was remembering that wild old man in the blazing Serengeti dawn, the cold anger in his pale eyes.

Abe shrugged. 'A man like that, with his moral standards and his love of elephants – it wouldn't seem like murder now, would it?'

'What about the reporter you spoke to, what did he think?'

'Served the bastard right, that was his comment. He said everybody knew van Delden killed the man.'

'Then why wasn't he put on trial?'

'No body, no witnesses, and anyway, they didn't dare. Think what he'd have made of it with some of the most prominent people in the country making fortunes out of ivory.' He sloshed some more whisky into his glass. 'Where do you reckon he is now?'

I shook my head, wondering whether there was any truth in it. And Abe's voice adding, 'He's always been an elephant man, and with their reconnaissance boys reporting herds of elephant moving north through the Mathew's Range and the Ndoto . . .' He was staring at me, his eyes glassy bright. 'There's a military post at Marsabit on the highway north into Ethiopia and they report elephant for the first time in over a year. Not much fodder for them there now I'm told and the springs where the Rendile once watered their cattle all dried up, but I've a feeling . . .' He shook his head, laughing at himself, a sound that reminded me of the giggle of a hyena. 'It's just the way I'm made, I guess, but Marsabit was van Delden's stamping ground.'

'You think he's trekking north, not heading for the coast?'

He shrugged. 'How the hell do I know? It's just a feeling. What would you do in his place, knowing elephants the way he does? At *The Nation* they had the old 1965 survey maps. To the north of Rudolf there's the Molo River, all swamp and thick bush. Marsabit Mountain is over 4000 feet high, and to the west, overlooking the lake, there's Kulal, over 7000; two oases of virtual rain forest before the long desert march to the Molo and survival.' And he added, 'The Tsavo now – Tsavo East and Tsavo West. Before the Africans started fighting each other, those were the two largest parks, and some of the best elephant country left. Now I'm told they're almost empty of game. What the Tanzanian army didn't kill, the Africans bordering these parks finished off. But not the elephants surely. Rhinos, yes and buffalo, but I don't reckon elephants would just passively stay there to be slaughtered. Do you?' He stared at me as though expecting me to say they would, his eyes gleaming belligerently. 'All I ever read about elephants . . . And game wardens. I've talked to some of them, interviews . . . It all adds up to this – elephants live so long, always in family groups – they have the percip . . . they have the intelligence to differentiate between areas of safety and areas of danger. You understand? So, a family group may have safe area knowledge going back two hundred years or more. Could be, even as far south as Tsavo, some wandering bull passed the word about van Delden's sanctuary. Too fanciful? Maybe. I don't know. So many hunters' stories, legends . . . difficult to tell what's fact and what's fiction.' He downed his drink and got carefully to his feet, scooping up the almost empty bottle as he rose. 'Well, I'm off to bed now. There'll be a truck here to pick us up about eight in the morning, and I've got Karanja acting as guide. If you want to go north—'

'You've got Karanja?'

'That's right. And I didn't ask for him. The Minister simply said Karanja would fix it and he'd send him with us.'

'From what you told me I'd have thought his Public Relations man is the last person he'd let you have.'

'Maybe he wants to get rid of him. I don't know. Could be Karanja's not his man. If you'd seen as much of politics as I have . . .' He held the bottle up to the light, squinting at it and shaking his head sadly. 'Don't reckon politics out here is much different from what it is back in New York. Just as rough, just as crooked, probably more so. Anyway, if you want to get to Lake Rudolf . . .'

'Marsabit is a long way east of Rudolf,' I said.

He turned, the door half open. 'Marsabit, Kulal, Rudolf – it's all one to me. So long as I meet up with some elephants.'

'The Army will have killed them by the time we get there.' I was thinking of what they had done in the Serengeti.

'I don't think so. They're not professional hunters like Kirby-Smith. And Marsabit is the most northerly outpost, less than a dozen men.' He was standing there, swaying slightly, a sardonic smile on his face. 'You think I've been talking a lot of crap, don't you? That I'm just a newshound on to another story. But you're wrong there.' He shook his head. 'It's not van Delden, or Kirby-Smith, I'm interested in. It's elephants . . . and Africa. The thought of all that space, the goddam frightful emptiness of it.' He focused his eyes on me, holding on to the door. 'You can come with me or not, just as you please. I don't care. Like the elephants, I'm following some strange compulsive urge of my own.' And he added, 'I don't expect you to understand. I don't understand myself.' He nodded, smiling. 'For once in my life I'm going to see what I want to see, film what I want to film. Goo'night.'

He staggered out, closing the door behind him, and I was suddenly alone, alone and feeling scared. I was sorry then that he had taken the bottle. I could have done with another drink, remembering what I had read of Lake Rudolf in that faded typescript, the desiccated lava landscape, the volcanic cones and the hot winds whistling down from Kulal. Was it worth risking my life chasing an archaeological will-o'-the-wisp in that God-forsaken country? And Abe Finkel – trading my Serengeti film for the sight of a few herds of elephant – God damn the man!

I moved to the chair he had vacated, sitting staring into the velvet darkness, my mind numb and the frogs croaking in the crater. Some strange compulsive urge, he had called it. Was I expected to share the problems of a man approaching fifty? I thought of London, trying to balance the life I knew against his offer of the unknown, the opportunity like a yawning void, a journey into space. Forbidden territory! I got the map out of my case and switched the light on, staring at it, trying to visualize what it meant, physically. I was hot and tired, exhausted after a day's work on my script, and I couldn't get van Delden out of my mind. Had he really killed that ivory hunter, or had Abe Finkel's imagination run away with him? An elephant man, and so sure they were being doomed to extinction. I remembered his words, the way he had faced the delegates, and then arranging for that poor beast to be driven into the Lodge area as into an arena so that he could slip away. And the tears standing in his daughter's eyes, her anger, her blazing anger at the callousness of it.

I was still sitting there, the map draped over my knees, when Ken came in to tell me the bus had arrived. I didn't say anything, thinking of the aircraft

flying through the night, back to England and nor-
mality, knowing I wouldn't be on it.

'You'd better get moving, we're on the first flight.'
And I heard myself say, 'I'm not coming. I'm staying
here.' And I told him about the opportunity to visit
Lake Rudolf, trying to keep my voice casual as I
arranged what he should take and what he should
leave for me – the Beaulieu, all the spare film and
what cash we had left. It wasn't easy to convince him
that I really meant it, but in the end he said, 'Okay,
if that's what you want. But rather you than me.'
And he began gathering up his things. It only took a
moment, and then he was at the door, lingering there
as though he half expected me to change my mind.
'What shall I tell John?'

I had almost forgotten about John Crabtree and
the BBC. I handed him the scribbled pages of the
script. 'Have that typed and give it to him, together
with the film. He'll have to make what he can of it.'

'And you'll be back – when?'

'How the hell do I know? Tell him I'm working
on something else, outside of our assignment. I'll see
him as soon as I reach London.'

Ken nodded, standing there loaded with gear,
waiting. 'I'll tell him,' he said finally. He wished me
luck and then he was gone, the door shut and the
room suddenly bleak and empty. I was alone again
with Pieter van Delden's book and the old map, the
frogs booming and my mind reaching out to the
north, imagination running riot, my thoughts chaotic.

I must have gone to sleep, there in the chair, for

the next thing I knew I was shivering, a damp wind blowing into the room and the time almost one-thirty in the morning. I undressed slowly and crawled into bed, asleep almost as soon as my head touched the pillow.

Dawn woke me, the harsh cry of birds, and I lay watching the almost instant blaze of the sun, the shade lines darkening. None of the softness here of the English countryside, the birdsong, everything harsher, the grass coarse and the sun's heat not a life-giving warmth, but something to be afraid of. I looked at my watch. It was almost seven o'clock. If he had been on the first plane Ken would be landing at Heathrow inside of an hour, and I was still in Africa, committed to something for which my life had not equipped me. But at this hour of the day there was a freshness in the air, a sparkle, and suddenly I didn't care. Rudolf, the northern frontier, a new world . . . I threw off the bedclothes, stripped and showered, the tingle of my body matching the change of mood. And then Abe came in, looking bright as a bird and full of energy.

'You're still here, then.' He was dressed in khaki shorts and bush shirt, and he had all his gear with him. He smiled. 'Just thought I'd check on my way to breakfast. I'll be out on the terrace.'

I nodded, wrapping my towel round me. 'I'll join you as soon as I've shaved. Order for me, will you? Has the truck arrived?'

'Not yet. But Karanja's here.'

'You think they're really going to give us a truck?'

'If they don't, then your film remains at the Consulate.' He turned to go, but then paused. 'There's news of van Delden, by the way. A Land-Rover has been hijacked from a military post at Narok.'

'How do they know it's van Delden?'

'You better ask Karanja. He's joining us for breakfast. Eggs and bacon do you? It may be the last decent meal we get for some time.'

Ten minutes later I dumped my kit in the foyer and went out into the bright sunlight of the terrace. It was almost empty now the Conference delegates had gone, a few Africans drinking coffee and Abe sitting at a table shaded by a thatched arbour. He was the only white man there and Karanja was sitting opposite him, dressed in a faded blue shirt and khaki trousers, a map spread out on the table between them. 'Jambo,' he said as I took the chair beside him. 'You have good breakfast now, then we go.'

'What's this about van Delden taking a Land-Rover?' I asked.

'The information come to Army Headquarters yesterday. There is a Land-Rover missing at Narok. Somebody steal it in the night.'

'You don't know it was van Delden then?'

He grinned, a white flash of teeth. 'You meet him. Nobody take a Land-Rover from the Army, only Tembo do a thing like that.'

'And where's Narok?'

'That's the point,' Abe said. 'Narok is almost due west of here, about sixty miles.' He swung the map round so I could see, his finger pointing. 'The scale is about thirty-six miles to the inch, so that puts him almost a hundred miles north of the Lodge.' From Narok a gravel road ran north to Nakuru with a main road to Thomson's Falls and Nanyuki to link up with the highway north to Marsabit.

'He's not making for the coast, then?'

'No, not if it's van Delden.'

Our breakfast arrived – bacon and eggs, toast, butter, marmalade, coffee, yellow slices of paw-paw and half a lime, sugar if we wanted it. 'No balance of payments problem here,' Abe said, and Karanja grinned: 'All black market for the rich men who run the rackets.'

'And that doesn't include you?'

He shook his woolly head. 'I am only here when I have guests of the Government. You are guests of the Government this morning, Mr Kimani's orders.'

Abe bowed his acknowledgement. 'Most generous of him. And even more generous to spare you to accompany us.'

Karanja laughed. 'Mr Kimani has his reasons.'

Abe's eyebrows lifted, but he didn't say anything, and Karanja went on, 'Those pictures at the Conference, some people think I engineer the whole thing.'

'Is that what Kimani thinks?'

'I don't know. Maybe. But is good excuse sending me with you.' And he suddenly burst out laughing for no reason that I could see except perhaps to cover embarrassment. 'He don't want me here in Nairobi.'

I think Abe had the same feeling as myself, that Karanja was in a very excitable state, his nerves on edge, for he quickly changed the subject. 'That Land-Rover, how much gas was in it, do you know?'

'Nobody tell me.' He was no longer laughing, his voice sulky.

'Could he get gas at Nakuru?'

'For petrol he must have a permit.'

'What about the black market?'

'Maybe.'

'At Nakuru?'

Karanja shook his head. 'At Nakuru, the police watch for that Land-Rover. At all towns, and there are Army patrols on the highway. I think he keeps to the small roads.' His finger traced a thin red line on the survey map running north from Narok to link with a network of tracks west of Nakuru. 'Maybe some farmer sell him petrol to get to Baringo. But after Lake Baringo . . .' He shook his head.

'What about us?' I asked. 'Where do we fill up?'

'At Samburu. That is Northern Army Head-quarters now.' He turned the map over, indicating a green patch just north of Isiolo. It was marked Samburu Game Reserve.

'And beyond Samburu?' Abe asked.

Karanja shook his head. 'I don't know. Maybe they have some soldiers at Maralal or Baragoi. Is more probable Baragoi. You see Horr Valley between the mountains – there.' He jabbed with his knife. 'Is only way for trucks coming south from Ethiopia, that track and the highway through Marsabit. And where there are soldiers is petrol.' He nodded emphatically. 'We ask at Samburu.'

I stared down at the map. Lake Baringo was at 3300 feet with mountains towering all round it and only a single track running north, soon petering out into a broken red thread in the vast emptiness of the Rift Valley as it sloped down to Lake Rudolf. If he made it to Baringo, then he would have no alternative but to take the track eastwards into the mountains, and if he were heading for Marsabit, that meant swinging north through Maralal, Baragoi and the Horr Valley. 'Have you read von Höhlen's account of Teleki's expedition to Lake Rudolf?' I asked Abe.

He shook his head.

'Well, I have, and unless he can find enough petrol I don't see how he can make it, not to Marsabit, through the mountains and across the desert.'

'Okay, so you've read about it. But he's lived there remember. It's his country.' He pushed his plate away and reached for the coffee. 'What do you say, Karanja? You know the area.'

'If he don't have fuel for the Land-Rover . . .' Karanja paused, his forehead creased in thought. 'Very bad now for foot safari. Very bad drought, no water in Balesa Kulal.' He pointed to a thin blue line on the map at the foot of the mountain's eastern slope. 'And if Kalama waterhole also dry . . .' He shrugged. 'Maybe there is some rain now.' But he said it without conviction. 'Maybe Samburu don't eat all their camels. With camels it is not more than two, three days from Horr Valley to Marsabit.'

'And there's water in the Horr Valley?' Abe asked.

'Yes, at South Horr. Always water at South Horr.'

He looked up as a soldier came to our table. They talked for a moment, and then he said, 'The bus is here.' He produced an envelope from his pocket and handed it to me. 'You sign please and I leave it for Mr Kimani at the desk.'

It was a typewritten letter authorizing the American Consul to hand over to the Minister of Lands the package containing my film, provided we had been transported to Lake Rudolf and returned safely to Nairobi. I looked across at Abe, but he was lighting a cigarette, avoiding my gaze. Outside on the road I could see a minibus drawn up in the shade, its dusty body still showing the zebra stripes of tourist days, but faded now and streaked with rust. Karanja was holding out a pen for me. 'If you don't sign, then maybe Mr Kimani think I engineer that too.' And again he burst into laughter that was high pitched and without any humour.

I was still reluctant, but all the delegates had gone now, the time for refusal past. I took the pen and signed it, and Karanja went off with it to the reception desk. 'I thought for a moment you were going to back-pedal.' Abe was smiling. I think with relief.

'What would have happened if I had?'

He shrugged. 'I guess we'd have been in trouble, both of us. Kimani's taking a bit of a risk as it is. The area we're going into is an Army responsibility.'

I nodded, feeling the sun hot on my back, a flutter of nerves in my stomach. 'I'd better get my things then and check out.' Nothing else I could do now, and he smiled and said, 'See you in the bus.'

In the foyer I found Karanja at the desk chatting up the pretty little African receptionist, and when I asked her for my bill, he said it was all settled. 'You and Mr Finkel are the guests of the Government now. I show you what we do for our people, how the Government is helping them. Also very interesting country. Not many white men go where we are going and you get better films, very much better film, with shots of the lake and El Molo people.' He said something to the girl, his teeth shining in a broad smile, and then he picked up my suitcase, leaving me to carry my camera, and we went out to the minibus.

Abe was already sitting in front beside the driver, two guns and a water bag beside him, cartons of ammunition at his feet. 'We'll take it in turns,' he said as I climbed past him. The body of the vehicle was a jumble of camping gear, sacks and cardboard boxes, with jerricans ranged along each side and two soldiers sitting on the heap of stores, clutching their rifles, their heads almost touching the roof. Karanja joined me on the transverse seat, sliding the door to behind him. 'Is more comfortable the minibus,' he said, but without much conviction, and I was thinking a Land-Rover would have been better.

We drove out through the centre of Nairobi and took the road north-east to Thika, climbing steadily into old settler country of citrus fruit, jacaranda everywhere and the Cape chestnut trees in flower. There were plantation houses set well back in the shade of the trees, but they looked tired and neglected, their verandas peeling paint, the gardens over-grown and littered with huts and rubbish, African children every-where. The road was almost empty of traffic, its macadam surface pitted with holes loosely filled with gravel that rattled against the chassis.

Beyond Thika we began to catch glimpses of Mt Kenya, its summit like a great medieval fortress, black rock against the crystal of perpetual snow and the hard blue sky. We were into more open country then, the Aberdares closing in to our left, and just before midday we passed the turning to Nyeri. There was a signpost there that still said Treetops, but when Abe asked Karanja whether there was any game left around this old tourist haunt, he said he didn't know. 'The Outspan Hotel, where tourists stop for lunch, is now administration office for resettlement of Aber-dare mountain region.'

'And Treetops is abandoned?'

'Not abandoned. Is camp for hunters working with the Ministry.'

'Your Ministry, eh?'

Karanja nodded.

Abe turned to me. 'I was at Treetops once.' His eyes gleamed behind his glasses. 'I had been attending the UNCTAD meeting here in Nairobi, a United Nations conference to work out how the rich nations could best assist in the development of the Third World. Very boring, and after it was over I decided to take a break and get a glimpse of this wildlife people talked about. You ever been to Treetops?' He didn't wait for me to answer, but went on talking in that fast monotone of his that was sometimes hard to follow because it came in one continuous flow. 'There was a white hunter with a rifle to meet our bus from the Outspan and we covered the last five hundred yards on foot with warnings not to talk and if we met a dangerous animal to slip into one of the hides provided. Good tourist stuff! I guess I was in one of my cynical moods. And then suddenly there was this rhinoceros less than two hundred yards away with a horn on him like a spike about two feet long, sniffing the air, his little ears cocked, and peering myopically in our direction.'

He grinned. 'I wasn't so sure about the tourist stuff then, but we made it to the stairs without him charging us and then we were back to the flush lavatory world we all knew. Treetops was no longer the original glorified hide in a tree, it was a comfortable hotel built on piles with a circular pool of muddy water in front of it and salt thrown down to attract the game. But nothing came, the rhino had disappeared and we had to be content with filming the baboons scampering about on the roof like clowns in a circus. At dusk some buffalo appeared, looking about as wild as a herd of black cattle; two of them had a wallow and that was just about the highlight. I was bored as hell.'

'You got nothing out of Treetops then.' I was wondering if that was the point of the story.

'Oh, but I did,' he murmured. 'That was the extraordinary thing. I got something so beautiful . . .' He hesitated, staring at the road ahead, the long slope of the mountain, then turning to me again and asking whether I was a balletomane. He shook his head at my reply. 'Then I'm not sure you'll understand, but I'm quite close to Lincoln Center – I live on West End and I see a lot of ballet. I love it. I really do.' He shook his head, smiling. 'It's difficult to explain if you don't appreciate the beauty of movement. We were still at dinner when somebody said, "There's an elephant out there." The long dining table emptied in a flash and there was this elephant, grey-white in the floodlights, surrounded by buffaloes. She just stood there, moving the tip of her trunk delicately over the ground until she finally fastened on the particular bit of salt she fancied. I'm sure it was a young female, she was so feminine, so dainty in all her movements and the buffaloes stood glowering at her, disputing the ground. She shook her head at them, fanning her ears and taking a few tentative steps as though about to charge. Then she wheeled abruptly and tripped off-stage like a ballerina who finds herself crowded by a bunch of yokels.'

He twisted further round, gripping my arm. 'You know, Colin, she was just about the prettiest thing I ever saw. No, that's not the word. I guess you can't describe an animal that big as pretty, but she was beautiful – so light on her feet, so graceful.' He shook his head, laughing at himself, then reached into the pocket of his bush jacket and brought out his wallet. 'I've always wondered whether I'd see her again and when I got this assignment—' He produced the faded photograph and passed it to me. 'I was shooting in black and white, of course, and that size I guess it doesn't look all that much. But the big blow-up I've got at home is really something. I shot three reels of her, so I had plenty to choose from.'

It showed an elephant limned in light and ghostly white, the ears spread out like the wings of a butterfly, the trunk curled up, and it appeared to be dancing, one foot raised, the body twisted slightly as though caught in the moment of pirouetting, and to the left of the picture was a rhino pawing the ground in a scuff of dust, the head lowered so that the long horn was like a spear. It was a fantastic shot, every detail clear and the whole picture so perfectly balanced it was like an artist's impression.

'Nice, isn't it?' he said. 'You know, I'm really proud of that picture. Compensation for all the dreary stuff I've shot in years of travelling around for the media.' He leaned over, his finger pointing at the animal's left ear. 'See that hole there. In the blow-up you can see it very clearly. It's a great tear shaped like a duck on the wing. That's how they recognize elephants. It's like a tag.'

'What caused it?'

'The horn of a rhino probably. That's what I'm told anyway. And she'll carry that mark to the end of her days.'

'And you shot three reels in that one brief sighting?'

'Oh, no. I was up watching her half the night. She came back, you see. About midnight. There were rhinos then as well as buffs. And one of the rhinos began snorting and mock charging her. It was always the same place, the same bit of salt, and she'd just stand her ground, flapping her ears and laughing at him. In the end she'd shrug and stroll away as though she wasn't really interested, make a slow, stately circuit of the waterhole and come back to the same spot. Then the whole ridiculous pantomime would start up again, the rhino snorting and Sally—' He looked at me, a solemn, sad look in his eyes. 'That's what I called her – Sally. My wife's name, you see. She was in the Corps de Ballet when I met her, such a beautiful balance, and so dainty.' He was silent for a moment, the smile gone. Then he gave a quick little shrug. 'Well, anyway, this elephant, she'd flap her ears at the rhino, standing tall and stately – just like Sally – her front legs close together so that she was slender and neat and statuesque. Yeah, that's the word – statuesque. Then she'd drift off silently for another circuit of the waterhole, moving like a shadow in and out of the trees until she'd disappeared. And after a while, suddenly, she'd be standing there like a ghost again, absolutely still, waiting to make her entrance.' He reached out and took the photograph from me, replacing it in his wallet. 'All that patience, all that quiet determination over a little bit of salt, it was a lesson in animal behaviour and in deportment. The rhino, too, all that snorting and pawing and mock charging, it wasn't real aggression. He wasn't spoiling for a fight. He was just saying, "For Christ's sake give me a little more room." And though Sally could have picked him up in her trunk, all two tons of him, and slammed his body on the ground and knelt on it, all she did again and again was take a wander round the pool.'

He had turned away and was looking out of the window towards the mountains, where wisps of smoke showed blue against the dark of forest green. 'That's what Treetops meant to me – the tolerance and beauty of big game animals. Also,' he added in a whisper, 'it gave me the urge to spend a few moments of my life in the company of elephants.' He nodded towards the fires and the gashes where the trees had been felled. 'There's going to be soil erosion there.' He twisted round and faced Karanja. 'Why doesn't your Ministry stop it? As well as soil erosion you'll have a drop in rainfall. Don't you ever think about the future? Or is that all our civilization has taught you – rape the land, grab what you can and to hell with tomorrow?' He stared at the puzzled Karanja, then looked at me, that sardonic little smile lifting the corners of his lips. 'A long time ago now,' he said, 'since your Queen heard of her succession up there in that Treetops lookout. A lot has happened, the world gone sourer on the human race and everything more complicated.' He said it sadly, then lit a cigarette and relapsed into silence.

We were just north of the equator then, close under the western slopes of Mt Kenya. A white cloud had formed over its top and our talk was desultory, the heat increasing. At Nanyuki the broad main street was almost deserted, its shops all boarded up. We stopped outside one of them. Faded lettering announced it as The Settlers' Stores. 'Maybe he have some beer,' Karanja said. 'Is the only place till we get to Samburu.' He remembered it as an Indian shop where safaris stocked up with wine and liquor, fresh vegetables and tinned goods, but it had been Africanized long ago and now the shelves were largely bare, only local produce sold, sacks of maize flour they called posho, melons over-ripe and crawling with flies, root vegetables I had never seen before. The beer was warm and flat from an old plastic container. We bought oranges and on Karanja's advice a bagful of local cigarettes, then we drove on.

I had changed places with Abe, but it was hotter in front and no more comfortable as we climbed into open country on the northern slopes of the mountain. 'Much resettlement here,' Karanja said, indicating the dried-up vista of grassland below us. It was dotted with groups of huts and patches of abandoned cultivation. 'After the settlers go the land is given to the Meru people and the Samburu.' But there was no sign of life there, no people, no cattle, no game.

'Where are they now?' I asked, and I had to shout above the noise of the labouring engine and the rattle of gravel against the mudguards.

He looked unhappy and shrugged his shoulders. 'Drought very bad.'

We came to the high point of the road and suddenly we were on the brink of the northern frontier region, a burned brown plain reaching out to desert in which towering buttes of pale red rock stood like castles shattered by wind and sand. The survey map showed that we were at 6390 feet, the road snaking down from the shoulder of Mt Kenya and running out into an infinity of sand and rock. Dust devils whirled and there was no horizon, the deadness of the country losing itself in haze, land and sky the same opaque sun-blistered white, and away to our left the blurred shape of mountains rising like ghosts on the edge of visibility. It was appalling, breathtaking. Abe leaned forward, his voice in my ear. 'The promised land!' He turned to Karanja. 'You reckon elephants can cross that and reach the mountains?'

'Oh, yes.' He nodded. 'Is not desert like the Chalbi. You look, you see trees, plenty of dry scrub, and they know where water is.'

We coasted down into the oven heat of lower altitude, swinging north where the road from Meru came in, everything shimmering now, acacias lifting their flat tops above a glazed heat mirror, thorn trees standing on their heads, wisps of brittle scrub floating in the water mirage and butte tops trembling in the distance. The little township of Isiolo appeared as a glint of corrugated iron winking in the sun. The road passed it by and the macadam stopped abruptly. We were on to gravel then, the noise deafening and dust streaming out behind us, and that was where we saw our first sign of animal life, two giraffe standing by a thorn tree, their necks leaning sideways and a quizzical expression on their faces as they stared at us absolutely motionless.

It was the driver who saw them and he braked, shouting excitedly and pointing. The soldiers in the back reached for their rifles. The giraffe were barely a hundred yards away, but by the time we had stopped they were already on the move, galloping off with that stiff, yet graceful gait that enables them to keep their heads at a constant elevation. 'They are reticulated giraffe,' Karanja said as though he were courier to a group of tourists. 'Is a species belonging to the north here.'

'It's good to see something that's survived,' Abe said sourly, his eyes on the two soldiers whose disappointment showed in their faces as we drove on.

'Very difficult to shoot giraffe,' Karanja said, as though he shared the soldiers' disappointment.

I was looking at the country now with a new interest, but we saw nothing else, only some ostrich, and ten miles further on we forked left on to a track that led to some round thatched huts that had once been the entrance to the Samburu Game Reserve. Now it was a military post. Karanja showed his pass and we were waved on, past some scout cars with their crews asleep in the shade of the armour, the track running out into open savannah country, a sort of plateau of sered grass bordered by a fine stand of acacia, dark umbrellas against a burning sky, mountains blue in the distance. The track had been pulverized to a fine grey dust and in the distance the dull green shapes of Army tents floated above the shimmering grass, a windsock hanging limp and the dust of a plane that had just landed lying like a pall of smoke over the improvised runway. Nothing stirred, the sun blazing down, the heat intense. 'You want to swim?'

'In the river?' I could see it marked on the map.

'No, not in the river. At Buffalo Springs.' He directed the driver at an intersection. 'Very good water, very clear. No crocodiles.' And he laughed.

'What about game?' Abe asked. 'Any game left?'

'I don't know,' he said uncertainly. 'I think only Army now.'

'How long since you've been here?'

'Four years, maybe five.'

'And what was here then, when it was a game reserve?'

'Herds of eland, zebra, buffalo, also gazelle and oryx. There were bustards here in the grass, and lion, always some elephant down in the doum palm by the river.' And then, brightening, he said, 'Here is Buffalo Springs. You swim now.'

The driver slowed. Two Army trucks were parked in the shade of some twisted trees. There were shouts and the sound of laughter, and when we stopped we saw the glistening black of naked bodies crowding a small rock pool. 'Is very nice the water, very cool.' Karanja's voice sounded uncertain, and when neither of us responded, he said abruptly, 'Okay. We go straight to lodge now.' And he spoke sharply to the driver.

The lodge had been sited close beside the river. It still possessed something of its original charm, but now that the Army had taken over, all but the largest trees had been cut down to make way for vehicles and a sprawl of tents and latrines. At the guard tent we dropped off our two soldiers and a corporal directed us to a stretch of the river bank where four large container trucks were parked. The river was very low, the trees on the further bank drooping in the heat and the head of a crocodile showing green in the sluggish water.

I climbed stiffly out and Abe followed me. 'Those look like refrigerator trucks,' he said. The grey slabs of their sides were painted with the Federation flag, an elephant on a bright background, and underneath in bold lettering were the words: K-S Game Control Coy. A Land-Rover drove into the parking area, stirring the dust.

'We're staying the night, are we?' I asked Karanja.

He shook his head. 'We are civilians, not Army. We cannot camp here.'

'Then what have we come for?' Abe asked, the heat giving an edge to his voice.

'Is necessary we have military permit, also petrol. And I have business to see about, a matter of communications.'

'Okay, and while you're doing that, you might enquire if Major Kirby-Smith is here. Looks like he's made this his base.' He walked over to the nearest truck and stood staring up at it. 'Game cropping must be quite a profitable operation,' he murmured. 'Those things aren't cheap.'

The truck was much bigger than any of the Army vehicles and it looked fairly new, the design on its side brighter than the tattered flag that had flown over the Wildlife Conference. Flip-flops sounded in the dust behind us and an Irish voice said, 'Don't say we got tourists now.'

It was the driver of the Land-Rover, a rather shabby little man with sandy hair and a rag of torn silk knotted round his throat. He held a battered briefcase in his hand and his bare toes were grey with dirt. 'That your minibus? I haven't seen one of those in years.'

There was a sudden gleam of interest in Abe's eyes as he looked at him. 'You must be the pilot of that plane we saw landing.'

The other nodded. 'How do you like our new flag? Pretty, isn't it?'

'A golden elephant with ivory tusks?' Abe gave a sour laugh. 'Very appropriate.'

'Would you be a conservationist then?'

'Television,' Abe said.

'Well, if you're looking for shots of the drought I can tell you this, there's plenty of material for you north of here, the carcasses of dead cattle thick round every dried-up waterhole.' His leathery face cracked in a grin. 'But that's no reason why we should die of thirst, too. Come and have a drink. My name's Pat Murphy.'

We introduced ourselves and Abe said, 'You fly reconnaissance, do you?'

'Right. Bill Maddox and me, we take it in turns to watch over the northern frontier.'

'And report on any unauthorized movements.'

'Our reports cover everything – tribes, animals, the state of the waterholes.' He stared at us narrowly, a nerve fluttering the corners of his eyelids. 'They're confidential, of course. You here on a story, or just for background shots?'

'Right at this moment I'm looking for Kirby-Smith.'

'Then you're out of luck. He's not here.'

'These are his refrigerator trucks.'

'He left this morning. They'll follow when he gives the word. Now do you want that drink, because I certainly do and we got a truckload of beer in yesterday.'

We left the driver in charge of our gear and followed the pilot along the river bank. At the entrance to the lodge Karanja went off to find the adjutant and Pat Murphy took us through into the old tourist bar. It was now the officers' mess. There were several Africans there, very spruce in clean shirts and neatly creased trousers. He back-slapped his way through them and gave his order to the barman. 'Did you come up through Nanyuki and Isiolo, or by way of Baringo?'

Abe did not say anything and when I started to answer his hand gripped my arm, silencing me, a bright gleam in his eyes.

Murphy had turned back to the bar. He settled for the drinks, then handed us our beer. 'Don't reckon you'd make it through Baringo.' He laughed. 'An old minibus like that, it's hardly the vehicle for the Baringo track.'

The beer was ice-cold from the fridge and as we

drank Abe said innocently, 'You flew out that way this morning, did you? See anything interesting?'

Murphy hesitated, gulping the rest of his beer down and watching us. 'Television, you said. We haven't had any television people up here before so you must have been at that Wildlife Conference.' He put his glass down and lit a cigarette. 'There was an old-timer, Cornelius van Delden, gate-crashed the Conference. That's what I heard. Care to fill me in on the details?'

Abe told him briefly what had happened.

'And now he's disappeared. Pinched an Army Land-Rover and took off into the blue.' Murphy hesitated. 'Is it Kirby-Smith or van Delden you're interested in?'

'Elephants,' Abe said and the Irishman laughed.

'Sure and you'll find them, too. But you're here on a story and that means van Delden.' He finished his beer and ordered three more. 'I have been flying bush a long time now. Safaris, oil prospectors, Government officials – I met most people. Not many of them left now. White people, I mean.'

'So you know van Delden?'

Murphy nodded. 'Sure I know the old devil. I was the one who flew him down from Marsabit after the Enderby affair. You heard about that?'

'Come to the point,' Abe said. 'You saw the Land-Rover, did you?'

Murphy smiled, 'I spotted a Land-Rover, yes.'

'On the track from Baringo?'

'Could be.' And he added, 'Yesterday Bill flew

Alex up to look at the South Horr Gap. So today I make my recce to the west along the edge of the Suguta.'

'And that's where you saw it?'

'Right.'

'Abandoned?'

'Hard to say. Could be just parked.' He had dropped his voice so that the African officers couldn't hear. 'My report doesn't go in till the morning if that helps and I owe van Delden something.'

'Could you show us the position on the map?'

He nodded and reached for his briefcase.

CHAPTER TWO

We were away from the Samburu Lodge by late afternoon and camped that night under Lolokwe, a great bald sugarloaf mountain that stood up out of the plain just north of the cut-off to Maralal. The sheer sides of it were red in the sunset as we pitched our tent, Karanja showing us how the tubular framing fixed in to the canvas fly while the driver got to work with a panga gathering wood. Starlings watched us with inquisitive eyes, their metallic plumage iridescent in the slanting light, and colonies of weaver birds darted noisily in and out of nests clustered like small coconuts in the wait-a-bit thorns. The fire was roaring and the tea made by the time we had our bedding laid out under the rotten canvas.

The dusk was brief, darkness rushing in, Lolokwe a black mass against the stars and only the crackle of the blazing fire. Everything was suddenly very still, no sound of birds now. 'Something I've always dreamed of,' Abe murmured, his voice a whisper in the night. 'Does it worry you, camping out like this in the middle of Africa?'

'No,' I said. 'No, of course not.' But there was a tautness running through me, an awareness of the senses I had never felt before, my ears alert for sound, my eyes straining to pierce the darkness beyond the fire.

A faint breeze was coming off the mountain and Karanja sniffed the air, his face glistening black in the lurid light of the flames. 'I think it rain tonight. Is why we sleep under cover.' And he added, 'You watch for scorpions in the sand here. Scorpions very bad.'

'What about snakes?' I asked.

He grinned. 'Snakes very bad, too, and we don't have snake kit. But here scorpions more bad than snakes.'

The evening meal was posho and tinned stew, and while we were eating it, squatting round the fire, I told Abe about Pieter van Delden's book and the reasons for my wanting to go to Lake Rudolf.

'It seems,' he said, 'there is a certain dichotomy of purpose. Yours is practical. You want to confirm an archaeological discovery and capture it on film. I just want to absorb the quiet immensity of Africa and see how elephants solve the problem of survival in the hostile world of man.' He lit a cigarette. 'But for tomorrow I think we're both agreed, aren't we? We go take a look at that Land-Rover.'

'I suppose so.' I said it reluctantly, thinking of Lake Rudolf. I had a chance now to get to Lake

Rudolf and I did not want to be side-tracked. 'The pilot didn't say it was abandoned.'

'He flew low over it and saw nobody.'

'That doesn't mean it's van Delden's vehicle.'

'All the more reason why we should take a look at it.' He was sitting hunched up, his hands clasped round his knees, and in the firelight I could see the glint of curiosity in his eyes. A newsman on the scent of a story, I thought. And then he looked at me, smiling quietly, and said, 'Have you thought about what we're doing here, really thought about it? We have moved back many centuries to a time when man was a part of the animal world. There are no garages here in the desert, and if we run out of gas, then we are as alone and vulnerable as those early men you've been telling me about who fired pottery on the shores of Lake Rudolf and marked it with the design of a pyramid topped by dwelling places. We are primitives now, huddled round a fire for protection, and for the future I can only think of the Arab word Inshallah. If it is God's will, then we shall find van Delden, and if van Delden is with us, then he is your best guide to Lake Rudolf. And for me — ' He hesitated, staring into the fire. 'He can teach me about elephants and how to live in harmony with this country where death and life are all one, an inevitable process that fascinates me because I've never felt it to be that way before.'

'And if we don't find van Delden?'

'Then there's Kirby-Smith at South Horr. If we get a chance to see him at work I guess we'll both of us have a better understanding of Genesis and how the tree of knowledge made all creatures afraid of man.' He turned and looked at me, smiling again. 'This, my friend, is a journey back in time, and if I die as a result, then I shall die with some understanding, my body disintegrating to merge with the dust of the desert where it will give life . . .'

'For God's sake!' I said. 'You're not going to die.'

'Of course not. But if I did — ' He shrugged, still smiling, and now his smile was melancholy in the firelight. 'I've never wanted to lie under the weight of a marble tomb in acres of headstones or have my carcass despatched to the crematorium because there's no room in the graveyards of our over population. Better my rotting flesh keep a jackal going for another day or contribute to the soaring flight of a vulture, my bones cleaned by ants — '

'What are you – a poet manqué?'

He laughed and shook his head. 'I never learned to write that well.' He stared into the fire a moment, then added quietly, 'All my reading has been in search of knowledge, an attempt to understand. Perhaps here – outside of books, outside of the experience of others – perhaps here, in this solitude, I may discover the meaning of life, the meaning of God even.' He shook his head again, smiling and getting abruptly to his feet. 'I'm sorry, I talk too much. I'm going to bed now.' And I was left with the feeling he was upset at having let his tongue run away with him, revealing a melancholic disposition normally concealed from everybody but himself.

I sat on by the fire for a while, smoking a last cigarette and listening to the stillness. And when I followed him to bed, I lay under the fly staring up at the bulk of Lolokwe unable to sleep. Some time in the night it began to rain and I woke to the sound of it on the canvas and the drip, drip, drip on the sand beside my camp bed. I remembered stories then of lions sheltering in safari tents and I lay curled up like a foetus, my ears straining for the slightest sound beyond the patter of the rain.

I woke with the dawn and birds were calling. Looking out from under the torn canvas I saw the rump of a small bird whiter-than-white against the black of a thorn and far in the distance an eagle nailed like a cross against the sky. The rain had gone, the sky was clear and in the still-grey light the desert browns had a freshness of colour. Drongos, looking like jet black flycatchers, flitted from bush to bush in the dry burned scrub and I lay there watching the light grow fast until the sun came up and the bare steep walls of Lolokwe turned blood-red. The driver threw off his blanket, putting sticks on the fire, blowing life into the embers, and Abe came strolling into sight between the thorns, slim and wiry looking in khaki bush gear, his head bent, his eyes on the ground. I thought he was following the track of some animal, but when I called to him to ask him what it was, he shook his head. 'Only birds,' he said. 'The sand's so soft after the rain the imprint of their feet is everywhere.' He came over to me smiling. 'You lazy bastard, you've missed the best of the day.'

We broke camp and were away as soon as we had had tea, and by eight-thirty we had passed the turning to Wamba and were on the road to Maralal, driving towards the mountains. It was a dirt road, the going sticky in places, and soon we were climbing in thick bush. Once, when we stopped to relieve ourselves, we saw a pigmy falcon perched like a small brown sentinel on the branch of a tree. The mountains were closing in on us then and shortly afterwards we came across some old elephant droppings. It was wild country, and just below Kisima lake a track came in from the left and Abe told the driver to take it.

'Is not the way to Maralal,' Karanja said.

'No, but we take it all the same.'

'Maralal straight on,' Karanja insisted.

'I know Maralal is straight on.' Abe had the map open on his knees. 'But I want to have a look at the escarpment running down into the valley of the Suguta.'

'We look over the Suguta Valley from viewpoint beyond Maralal. You see river bed, geysers, volcanoes, everything you want from viewpoint.'

The argument went on for several minutes while we sat there motionless, the engine throbbing and the heat trapped in the valley. I took no part in it, watching a bateleur, which I could now recognize by its distinctive cross-like shape against the blue sky. It was planing on the air currents high up where the grey crags thrust clear of the dense bush that clothed the slopes of the mountains to our right. In the end Abe had to tell him about the Land-Rover. Karanja was suddenly silent. He was sitting with me on the front seat and there was sweat on his face, his body tense. 'Is no good,' he murmured. 'They send patrol —'

'The pilot doesn't file his report till this morning.' Abe leaned forward, gripping Karanja's shoulder. 'Are you going to let them pick him up? You worked with him. You were one of his game scouts. You can't just drive on, now that I've told you.'

'Is Major Kirby-Smith you go to see. That is what you say to me and what I tell Captain Ngaru. Our permit is for Baragoi. Also,' he added desperately, 'we don't have enough petrol.'

'We have eight jerricans in the back.'

'They are water.'

'Four of them are water, four of them gas, so tell the driver to turn left.'

'Let's go on,' I said. 'It only means trouble if we do find him.'

'And suppose it isn't van Delden? Suppose it's some poor devil —'

'It's van Delden all right.' It had to be, no patrols out on the Baringo track and nobody but the Army allowed in the area.

'Okay then, it's van Delden. And how do you expect to find your way in the lava wastes round Lake Rudolf without him to guide you? It's what you wanted, isn't it, for him to take you there?'

I shook my head, knowing he had made up his mind and unable to argue with him in the suffocating heat. All I could say was, 'I'd rather drive on.' I had a deep, instinctive feeling of unease, and it wasn't only because of that strange old man; it was Abe, too. But I couldn't put my feelings into words and with a sense of inevitability I heard him say, 'Okay, Karanja, we turn left here.'

Something in the way he said it, the quiet certainty in his voice, seemed to settle the matter. Karanja spoke quickly to the driver in Swahili and we turned on to the track that led back in a south-westerly direction into the Ol Keju Osera valley. It was thick bush all the way, the road steep in places and sticky with the night's rain, and half an hour later we had a puncture. It was hardly surprising, the tyres were almost bald, and while we were helping the driver change the wheel Karanja took the shot-gun and went in search of game. He had heard the cackling call of guinea fowl.

'What happens if we do find van Delden?' I said. 'There'll be a patrol out after him now. Karanja's scared of him, and so am I in a way.'

We were pulling the spare wheel out of the back and Abe said, 'Trouble with you is you think too much. Try taking things as they come. And don't worry about Karanja. A few hours in van Delden's company and I guess he'd be the way he was before ambition and the importance of being a press officer to a Minister got hold of him.' And then he went on to tell me why the pilot hadn't reported the sighting of the Land-Rover immediately. A dozen or more years back he had taken off from Loiyangalani airstrip after flying some tourists in for the fishing on Lake Rudolf and had been caught in a hurricane blast of wind from Mt Kulal. 'There's an island in the lake there, South Island, and he crash-landed on the lava slopes and smashed his leg up. Van Delden happened to be at the Mission and he went out at once, paddling across eight miles of water on one of the El Molo log rafts they use for fishing. The wind started up again in the morning and blew for the better part of a week, so if van Delden hadn't paddled out immediately Murphy would have been done for.' And he added, 'I got it out of him while you were on the terrace looking at that hippo. That's why he gave us time to get down here ahead of the patrol.'

We had the spare wheel on and were tightening the nuts when two shots sounded in the distance. A few minutes later Karanja emerged from the bush, grinning and holding up a brace of helmeted guinea fowl. They were plump-looking birds, their dark bodies speckled with white spots, their heads strangely capped with a bony grey horn. He was very pleased with himself as he tossed the birds into the back. 'You want we brew some tea, Paul?' The driver nodded, his white shirt dark with sweat, beads of perspiration on his forehead. 'Okay, we have brew-up now, then we go find this Land-Rover.'

Out here alone in the bush it was somehow comforting to see how quickly they got a fire going. In no time at all the water was boiling and the driver was stirring in tea and sugar. He sat back on his haunches and suddenly his eyes widened. 'Ndovu!'

At first I couldn't see them, the bush hazed with heat, the light blinding. Karanja pointed. 'See them?

Elephants, beyond that big tree.' The excitement in his voice vibrated in the air.

I saw the tree, a big euphorbia on a rounded shoulder of the hills, and suddenly a grey shape moved, and then another. I don't know how many there were. I only caught glimpses of them as they glided quietly across a gap in the bush. 'Cows,' Karanja said. 'They have totos with them.' They passed across the dirt road, up by the furthest bend, grey ghosts moving north along the contour line, and suddenly they were gone, merged into the shimmering grey-green foliage of the hillside. Abe stood staring after them. 'Did you see, Colin? A whole herd of them. Kirby-Smith was right. There are elephants up here.'

Karanja handed him a mug of tea and he sat down abruptly. 'Meat on the hoof,' he muttered and a cold chill ran through me, the same sort of chill I had felt the day my uncle had taken his life. There had been other times, too. Over-sensitivity, that's what the doctor had said when I had played truant from school because I wouldn't share a desk with another boy. The over-sensitivity of a boy who has lost his natural parents, but I had known something dreadful was going to happen, and a few days later he was found at the bottom of the cliffs. That was when we lived at Peacehaven and I had been on an easy pitch on those same cliffs the week before, prising fossils out of the chalk.

'There ought to be some way we could communicate,' Abe said. 'Some language. Then we could warn them. But I guess elephant pidgin requires a deeper rumbling than I can manage on an empty stomach.' His hands were clasped round his mug, his head bent as though reading the future in the tea leaves floating on the oily surface. 'I wonder if van Delden can make himself understood? He's lived with them so long . . .' He sipped his drink, his eyes fastening on me, the pupils slightly enlarged by his glasses. 'All I know about elephants is what I've read since that visit to Treetops. They communicate by rumbling. But how much they communicate . . .' He took the plate Karanja passed him, cold baked beans and some slices of bread, and put it on the ground beside him. 'Nobody knows how much they can say to each other, any more than we understand the language of dolphins and whales. For instance, this concentration of game up around Lake Rudolf. You heard what Kirby-Smith said, and he particularly referred to pilots having sighted elephants. I asked Murphy about that, but he doesn't fly to Rudolf. His job is keeping watch on tracks and waterholes. It's daytime flying, anyway, and the only place he's seen elephants is up around South Horr.'

He reached for his plate, spooning beans into his mouth and gazing up at the slopes where the elephants had disappeared. 'Now if I knew their language I'd go after that bunch and warn them. The way they were headed they'll finish up inside of those refrigerator trucks.' He looked across at me, that sardonic little smile at the corners of his mouth. 'A hardboiled media man and here I am, squatting beside a dirt track in the middle of nowhere, worrying about a herd of cows and expecting something to happen.' His gaze switched back to the heat-hazed mountainside. 'It's almost noon. The hottest part of the day. Those elephants should have been under the shade of the trees, fanning their ears to keep themselves cool. Do you realize an elephant can lower its body temperature by as much as sixteen degrees just by flapping its ears?'

'Then I wish I had ears as big as that.' His words had made me uneasy again.

The driver rocked with laughter. 'Him got big ears.' He pointed at Karanja, leaning forward, still laughing, his teeth white. 'You flap now, Karanja. Make cool.'

'Time we got going,' I said.

'No hurry,' Abe leaned back, his eyes half-closed. 'We've been driving since first light.'

'We can't just sit here on the offchance he'll pass this way.' I reached for the map. 'We're about fifteen miles from where Pat Murphy saw the Land-Rover abandoned and there's another track running direct to Maralal.'

'Sure there's another track, but not suitable for vehicles and van Delden needs transport. He's a long way from Marsabit, and a Land-Rover out of gas is about as much use to him as a load of scrap.' He sat up suddenly. 'I don't think you quite understand the sort of man he is. He'll have seen that aircraft circling and the patrol when it comes will take the road.'

I stared at him. 'He can't jump an Army patrol.'

He shrugged, leaning back and closing his eyes again. Karanja moved uneasily, searching the bush as a dove went clattering through the branches above us. Away to the south the cackling of guinea fowl came faintly on the still air. The heat was heavy after the night's rain and I felt drowsy, lying back and staring up at the white drifts of cloud hanging over the mountains. 'I think we go back now,' Karanja said. He was getting agitated. 'When the patrol come they want to know what we are doing on this road.'

'It will be several hours yet before a patrol gets here.' Abe shifted on to one elbow, listening as a bird whistled urgently in the bush behind us. A moment later it took flight, a metallic flash of blue. 'Starling,' Karanja said. 'Something disturb him.' The guinea fowl had ceased their cackling, everything was still and quiet as though the bush held its breath, waiting. And then suddenly van Delden was there, coming soundlessly out of the undergrowth behind us. Mukunga was with him and they both had rifles. Mtome and a very erect, very good-looking man I hadn't seen before appeared on the opposite side of the track. All of them had old khaki knapsacks, bandoliers stuffed with ammunition, blankets rolled and slung round their shoulders.

'Karanja.'

'Ndio, Bwana.' He had leapt to his feet, his eyes staring.

'You come to find me?'

Karanja nodded, speechless.

'How did you know where I was?'

'The pilot,' Abe said.

Van Delden stood there for a moment, looking down at us. Then he came and sat beside me, placing his rifle carefully on the ground. 'I was expecting a patrol.'

'The pilot doesn't have to file his report till the morning,' Abe said. 'He stuck to his routine.'

'Didn't he have orders to look out for a Land-Rover?'

'He said he owed you something. His name's Murphy.'

'Pat Murphy? Yes, I remember.' He nodded. 'So we've a little time yet before a patrol comes.' He said something to Karanja, who moved quickly to the fire. 'And you came looking for me. Why?'

Abe shrugged. 'Not sure really. But we have a permit to go as far as Lake Rudolf. Thought you might need a lift.'

Van Delden shook his head. 'A vehicle, that's all I need.' He looked from one to the other of us, his pale eyes watchful. 'While tea is brewing maybe you'll tell me how you got hold of an old safari bus and a permit to enter the military zone.' He gave an order to Mukunga and his three Africans squatted down by the fire watching us. 'And Karanja. What's Karanja doing here?'

'He's on loan to us as a guide.'

He laughed, that same harsh bark. 'You have a way of getting what you want, don't you, Mr Finkel. So what are you going to film now?'

'That depends on you,' Abe said. 'If we give you a lift —'

'No.'

Abe gave a shrug. 'I guess you don't understand what television can do for you.' He hesitated, then changed the subject. 'I take it you're headed for Marsabit.' Van Delden didn't reply. His eyes had shifted to the slopes above us and Abe said, 'You saw those elephants?'

'They winded us.'

'Is this their territory, or are they on the move with a definite purpose?'

Van Delden shrugged. 'D'you know anything about the migration of elephants?'

'A little.'

'Their normal range, for instance?'

'Scientific records suggest the limit is about eighty miles.'

'Records – scientific records —' His emphasis on the word scientific was contemptuous. 'The only official records are for park conditions. Elephants are quick to learn the limits of their protected area.'

'And when it's no longer a protected area, what then?'

Van Delden shook his head. 'Who knows? There were no so-called scientists recording data when the Cape elephants were wiped out by my father's forebears, or when British hunters eliminated the vast herds of southern Africa, shooting them for their ivory and for the fun of killing. Who's to say that some of those elephants didn't trek north, away from the slaughter area, north into Matabeleland, across the Zambesi? For all any scientist can tell you, man, those elephants you saw up there' – he nodded towards the green-brown slopes – 'may be the distant descendants of elephants that came out of Cape Province more than a century and a half ago.'

'So they go north, an inherited instinct. Is that what you're saying?'

Van Delden shook his head. 'I've lived too long with elephants to be certain of anything. Like man, they're individuals, and, living almost as long, they are inpredictable, each according to his experience, some charging on sight, others fairly tolerant. At Marsabit they had a very restricted range. Just the mountain and its forest area and the grass of the slopes which they shared with the Rendile. They came down into the grasslands at night when the cattle weren't grazing. But there were others that came and went, bulls mainly, trekking from the Tana river, even from this area here. That was what the Boran said. But a scientist wouldn't accept that. He'd need to bug the beast with a bleep transistor and follow it in an aircraft before he'd believe anything a tribesman told him.'

Karanja handed him a mug of tea and he sat there, sipping at it noisily and frowning. 'You've got your cameras with you?' Abe nodded. 'And you're planning to film Alex Kirby-Smith with his gang of scientific exterminators.'

'That wasn't the object,' I protested.

But he was looking at Abe. 'How did you get Kimani to agree to that?' And when Abe had explained his eyes fastened angrily on me. 'So you traded the film you got with me for the chance of an archaeological find.' His voice was hard and unforgiving, the stare of those pale eyes almost baleful. 'Mary was right. She said you had no feeling for animals.' He turned to Abe again. 'Where's Kirby-Smith now?'

'At Baragoi.'

He nodded as though he had expected that. 'He'll take them as they come out of the South Horr Gap into the near-desert country beyond.' And then he was looking at me again. 'You'll need a cold heart and a strong stomach, boy. There'll be totos of all ages, from new-born up to a dozen years, all with their mothers, and all led by an old matriarch, a complete family unit, anything from five to fifty strong. He'll bunch them by buzzing them with an aircraft, or maybe he'll use trucks and Land-Rovers to drive them on to his sharp shooters. The matriarch will be shot first, fifty, maybe sixty years of life cut down in a flash, the whole group wiped out in minutes, every cow, every calf.' He turned back to Abe. 'That way there's no survivor to pass the knowledge of fear and pain and death on to others coming through the mountains, no warning to the next unsuspecting family. Something for your captive TV audience to gloat over.' He slung his empty mug at Karanja and got to his feet. 'I'm taking your vehicle.'

'Does it occur to you,' Abe said quietly, 'that the

captive audience may feel the way you do, that the sight of such wholesale slaughter will sicken . . .'

'There won't be any slaughter if I can help it.' He spoke quickly to Mtome, who began getting our bags out of the minibus. 'And if you were able to film it, do you think you'd be allowed to take that film out of the country?'

'Maybe not. But with your help we could smuggle it out.' Abe got to his feet.

'Stay where you are.' He was moving towards the minibus. 'Dima.' He motioned the tall African into the back. Mtome followed him, Mukunga standing beside the door, his rifle cradled in his arm.

'You're making a mistake,' Abe said. 'We come along with you now, we could film it all from your point of view. A great story. I could really make something of it.'

'You'd make a lot of money. That's what you mean, isn't it? Like Alex, you're not thinking of the elephants, only of money.'

'You're wrong. That's not why I'm here.' Abe moved towards him. 'What about it, van Delden? I'm offering you a world audience, the chance to make them understand the nature of elephants and what's happening to them in Africa.'

But he shook his head. 'What I have to do . . . I don't want anybody else involved.' He had the door open and reached inside. 'But you have your cameras.' He dumped the cases on the ground beside our bags.

I scrambled to my feet. 'You can't just leave us

here. We only turned down this track because we knew you were in trouble.'

'Relax,' Abe said. 'He's not going to take us and the patrol will be here in a few hours.'

Van Delden was moving round to the driver's seat and Karanja started forward, a tense, urgent look on his face. I thought for a moment he was going to try something desperate. So did Mukunga, but he was too late. Karanja was already on the far side of the vehicle talking urgently to van Delden. He seemed to be pleading with him. Then van Delden did a strange thing. He put his arm across Karanja's shoulder, a gesture of affection almost.

They were like that for a moment, Karanja staring up at the other with a rapt expression, then he was nodding and van Delden got into the driving seat. He nosed the minibus into the bush, backed and turned it. 'Karanja.' He leaned out of the window speaking quickly in Swahili. Karanja nodded, sweat on his face and his eyes wide. Mukunga climbed in and the bus moved off, a thick cloud of dust hanging in the air as it disappeared round the bend where the elephants had crossed the road.

I turned to Karanja. 'What were you telling him?'

He shook his head, his eyes still on the dust cloud. 'Is nothing.'

'What was it?' I insisted.

'I offered to go with him.' He turned away then, adding angrily, 'But he don't want me.'

'There was something else,' Abe said. 'Something

about Kirby-Smith. I distinctly heard him mention the Major's name.'

'Is a message, that's all.'

'What was the message?'

Karanja hesitated, then he shrugged. 'I am to tell him if he kills elephants his men will die.'

'Did he mean it?'

Karanja nodded unhappily. 'He always mean what he say.'

Abe looked at me, his dark eyes sombre. 'There's a line: *Now he is treading that dark road...*' He shook his head, the corners of his mouth turned down. 'It isn't just a civilian outfit he's up against. Kirby-Smith has the support of the Army and in every African unit there'll be men who've been hunters or trackers all their lives.' He turned to Karanja. 'You going to pass that message on to Major Kirby-Smith?'

'Yes. I tell him.' His eyes rolled, the whites showing. 'You know I have to explain how we lose our vehicle and everything in it.'

We went on talking about van Delden for a while, but gradually the heat overcame us and we lay there waiting as the sun slid down the brazen sky and the shadows lengthened. There was no wind, nothing stirring, no sound except the sleepy murmuring of doves. I was dozing when the patrol arrived.

They came in a truck, the driver slamming on his brakes at the sight of us, soldiers tumbling out of the dust cloud, deploying with their guns at the ready. They looked tough, battle-trained men, their camouflage-green merging into the bush. Karanja called to them, stepping out into the road and walking towards the stationary truck where a corporal stood waiting. He talked to him for a moment, then orders were shouted, the soldiers climbing back into the truck and it came on to stop beside us. 'You get in now,' Karanja said. 'When we find the Land-Rover I talk with the corporal about transport.'

'That Land-Rover would do us fine,' I said.

But Karanja shook his head. 'Is Army vehicle.'

We slung our gear into the back of the truck and clambered up, the soldiers making room for us. 'Looks like our only hope is Kirby-Smith,' Abe said doubtfully. The black faces around us were covered in dust, watchful and unsmiling. About three miles down the road we rounded a rock outcrop and ran slap into a barricade of thorn, the truck slamming to a halt, enveloping us in dust. It was the ideal place for an ambush, the road blocked and rocks all round. Under a wild fig we found the blackened embers of a fire, the stripped remains of a dik-dak carcass lying on the ground beside it. The thorn barrier took some time to clear so that it was dark when we reached the Land-Rover, the embers of another, larger fire, some blankets thick with dust and two empty jerricans lying on the ground.

It was cooler now, the soldiers more friendly as a fire was lit and food prepared, the empty tank of the Land-Rover filled with petrol. Over the meal Karanja talked to the corporal, trying to persuade him to let us go on to Baragoi in the Land-Rover. I don't know whether it was the military permit or the need to radio a report of van Delden's movements that finally decided him, but shortly after eight we got into the Land-Rover and started back up the track, the corporal driving us.

It was a clear moonlit night and he drove fast. At Maralal he stopped at the old safari lodge, now a military post, to radio his report back to headquarters. The town itself was off the main road, but all round the junction leading to it rough shelters sprawled over the grass, a great concentration of tribesmen driven into the mountains in search of food and water. Beyond Maralal the road climbed steeply through a forest of trees and it became quite cold. 'Soon we come to viewpoint,' Karanja said. 'Maybe we stop there.'

The trees were a black arch in the headlights, their branches blotched with some growth that was pale like lichen. And then they ceased and we were out on to the top, in a blurred brown scrub of moorland. Far away to our right the shadow of the Mathew's Range stood against the sky and to our left the land dropped steeply down into the Rift and the valley of the Suguta. The moon was clouded now and we did not stop, driving on and on through desolate country, the dirt road gradually losing height as we wound our way down towards Baragoi. I slept fitfully, my head lolling as the Land-Rover bucked and jolted over the uneven surface, and then suddenly we were there, driving slowly down a street of grey dirt flanked by dukas, the village shops that had been built by Asians long ago. It was a dilapidated miserable place, the wood and daub buildings falling into ruin and sleeping bodies lying in the dust.

The military post was a huddle of tents and trucks on the edge of a landing field east of Baragoi. We stopped at the guard tent and while the corporal and Karanja explained themselves, Abe and I stretched our legs. The night was clear again, the moon set, and all around us, at every point of the compass, the jagged outline of mountains reared up like cut-outs against the stars. Abe nodded towards the north, where the Horr Valley showed as a black V. 'I wonder if he made it through the gap there?'

I thought he probably had, but dawn would find him exposed on the semi-desert land beyond, and right beside us was a Cessna. It was the only plane on the field, and if it were serviceable, one quick sweep northwards would be enough, the dust stream of the minibus visible for miles. 'How far do you reckon he'll have got by sunrise?'

Abe glanced at his watch. 'Five hours from now, and he's about six hours ahead of us – that's eleven hours' motoring from Baragoi.' He shook his head. He'll have run out of gas long before then.'

'So he won't make Marsabit?'

'Not a hope.' He looked at me, a sidelong glance. 'Was he ever going there?'

'Where then?'

He shrugged, and I felt a sudden prickle of uneasiness. We were on the threshold now of country that van Delden knew better than anyone else. Karanja returned to say that Major Kirby-Smith was now camped about five miles beyond South Horr and the question of transport would have to wait until the morning.

We spent the rest of that night in the Land-Rover and woke in the dawn to the sound of voices and the movement of men as the camp came alive. I had never been in a military post before and my chief recollection of it is the open latrines, with African soldiers squatting and jabbering, dung-brown beetles crawling in human excrement, and the wood smoke smell of cook fires hanging in the still air. There must have been over a hundred Africans there including hangers-on, and when the officer in command saw us shortly after seven he had already been in contact with Kirby-Smith's outfit and established that a vehicle had crossed the lugga near their camp about ten-thirty the previous evening. Captain Kioko was still interrogating us through Karanja when an orderly came in to say that Major Kirby-Smith was on his way to Baragoi.

He arrived about half an hour later. I was sitting in the shade of one of the trucks re-reading von Höblen's account of the Teleki expedition's first sighting of Lake Rudolf when the open Land-Rover roared into the camp. There were two of them in it, the wind-screen folded flat and both of them wearing goggles. He stopped by the Cessna to have a word with the pilot, who was working on the engine, then he drove on to the command tent. Karanja was waiting for him there and when they had ducked inside the flap I returned to my book. We were so near to Lake Rudolf now that reading about it gave me the illusion I had leapt the intervening miles of desert and lava and was already there.

I was reading again the passage that begins: '*Almost at our last gasp, we hastened towards the slightly rippled sheet of water* ... when a shadow came into my line of vision and a husky voice said, 'So it is you. Where is he, do you know?'

I looked up, recognizing her voice, and for a moment I was too surprised to say anything. She was wearing the same faded safari jacket, the bush hat pulled down over her eyes. The book slipped from my hands as I scrambled to my feet, pleasure at seeing her again overcoming the sense of shock that she really was with Kirby-Smith. 'I didn't realize it was you – in that Land-Rover.'

'Where was he going?' she demanded, her face set, and no sign of greeting. 'Was it Marsabit?'

'He didn't say.'

'He must have told you something when he took your vehicle. What was it, a minibus? That's what we were told over the radio.'

I nodded, conscious of the tightness of her lips, the strained look in her eyes.

'Was there enough petrol on board for him to reach Marsabit?'

'No, I don't think so.'

'Just as well,' she murmured. 'Marsabit is no place for him now. Alex says there's hardly anything left of his sanctuary. It's been agronomized, most of the forest cut down to make way for shambas.' She was staring at me, her eyes wide. 'Why the hell didn't he make for the coast?'

'Perhaps if you'd been with him —'

'It wouldn't have made any difference.' She bent quickly down, picking up my book and glancing at the title. 'Still thinking about Lake Rudolf?'

I laughed. 'Not far now but it seems the last part is the most difficult. I need transport.'

'I'll talk to Alex. Maybe he can help. You shouldn't have let him get away with your minibus.'

'We had no alternative.'

She nodded. 'No, of course not. Did he say anything about Kulal?'

I shook my head.

'Some years back he tried very hard to have the rain forest on top of the mountain made into a game reserve. He was very friendly with John Mallinson at the Mission there. Do you think he was making for Kulal?'

'No.'

She was silent for a moment, her head turned to the north. 'So he's somewhere out there, waiting.' And she added almost in a whisper, 'God! If only he'd got out while he had the chance.'

I had a feeling then that it wasn't her father she was worrying about, and the question that had been at the back of my mind from the moment I had seen her burst from my lips. I asked her why she had gone off with a man whose business was to kill the animals that had been her father's whole life. 'I don't understand,' I said. 'I searched the hotel . . .'

'You don't understand?' Her eyes blazed suddenly in the sunlight. 'You saw what he did to that elephant. You were there. You saw Mukunga and Mtome drive it, with the snare still round its leg and the foot so rotten it was almost falling off ... Anyway, it's none of your business what I do.' And she added fiercely, 'At least Alex kills cleanly.'

These words, the way she defended him ... I stood there, staring at her dumbly, knowing now that it wasn't just for the story she was here. It was something else and I didn't want to think about it, remembering what she had said about his charm. And at that moment the Cessna's engine burst into life. I could see the pilot sitting at his controls running through his checks. 'Is that an Army plane?' I asked, glad of the excuse to break the awkward silence between us.

'No, it's ours – part of the outfit.'

'And it's being sent up to look for him?'

She nodded.

'Can't you do something?' I was thinking of the tough, wild African soldiers I had seen in the camp here and what would happen when the pilot reported seeing the minibus.

But all she said was, 'If he'd seen what I've seen these last two days ... the effect of this drought. As soon as you're clear of the mountains, all to the north ...' The Cessna was moving now and a stream of dust enveloped us as it turned and began taxi-ing out to the end of the dirt runway. 'There's been no rain up there, no rain at all. Every well, every waterhole is dry.' And she added, as though to justify her acquiescence in the search, 'If we don't find him, that's something he'll discover for himself. There's no water out there.'

'He has four jerricans full.'

'They won't last him long in that heat.' She turned to face me again. 'How many are with him now?'

'Three,' I said.

'Mukunga and Mtome. Who else?'

'A man called Dima.'

She nodded. 'Another ex-poacher. A Boran. All his best shots, except Karanja.'

The plane's engine note increased. It had reached the runway end and we watched in silence as it moved towards us, rapidly growing larger. The wheels lifted clear of the ground and it banked slightly, roaring low over our heads as it turned northwards. In a moment it was no more than a speck flying towards the mountains that formed the South Horr Gap. 'You should have stopped it,' I murmured.

She shook her head, still staring after the plane. 'Alex is afraid he'll try and do something stupid.'

'And when that plane finds him and they send the Army in – what happens then?'

She turned on me angrily. 'Do you suppose I haven't thought about that? But he's got to be stopped, somehow. He could have made for the coast. Instead he came up here, and I think Alex is right.'

It was incredible, his own daughter. 'You really want him caught.'

She gave a little shrug. 'Somebody's got to make

him see reason, and the sooner they get him out of here — '

'You don't care what happens to him, do you?' I think I wanted to hurt her then. 'You're not worrying about your father, only about Kirby-Smith.'

'How dare you!' she breathed. 'You know nothing about him, or about me. Nothing about either of them.'

I could see Karanja waiting in the sun outside the command hut and I told her the message he had been given. 'So you'd better make up your mind whose side you're on.'

She was staring at me, an appalled look in her eyes. 'So Alex was right.'

'If Kirby-Smith starts killing elephants . . .' I hesitated, but what the hell? How else could I get through to her, through the thick skin of her apparent hero-worship of the man she was camped with? 'When that recce plane gets back,' I said, 'you'd better arrange it so that you can talk to him. Talk to them both, or somebody's going to get killed.'

She stood there for a moment, still with that shocked look in her eyes. I think she was near to tears, her lips trembling, her nostrils flared. But then she turned abruptly and walked away, back towards the open Land-Rover. I watched her go, feeling wretched, her figure tall and graceful in the blazing sun and knowing the things I had said were better unsaid. I was still worrying about that when Abe appeared round the back of the truck. 'What did your girlfriend have to say?'

'Nothing,' I snapped, angry at the glint of laughter in his eyes.

Kirby-Smith had come out of the command tent. The captain was with him and they were talking to Karanja. 'She must have said something,' Abe murmured. 'You were talking with her long enough.'

'She said the plane that just took off belongs to Kirby-Smith and is flying a search.'

He nodded. 'That was to be expected.' He was looking at me curiously as he went on, 'But they won't find him, that's for sure. He's too old a hand, and the zebra stripes on that vehicle are designed for sunlight and shade. 'Did she tell you why she'd gone off with Kirby-Smith?'

I shook my head, not wanting to talk about it.

'She could be half in love with him.' That sardonic smile and the dark eyes laughing at me behind the glasses. 'You want some advice?'

'No.'

He laughed. 'I'll give it to you anyway. Lay her if you can, but don't get involved. She's a man-eater and you're too young for a girl who's half Italian and thoroughly Africanized.' He patted my shoulder and turned away as Kirby-Smith came towards us, his face hard and his jaw set, the muscles tight behind the cheekbones.

'Is it true what Karanja says about my men being at risk when we start culling?' He was looking at Abe. 'Is that what he said?'

Abe nodded. 'Karanja was to give you the message.'

'Do you think he meant it? Or was it just an empty threat?'

'No, he meant it.'

'Then we'll have to find him. A man like that at large, he's dangerous.' His shoulders straightened, his face loosening in that boyish smile. 'Well, it shouldn't take long.' He turned to the captain. 'Once he's located it'll be up to your boys. But no bloodshed. Get him surrounded so that he gives himself up.'

Abe started to protest, but Kirby-Smith shook his head. 'They're bush trained. They know their job. Now about your transport problem. You want to join me in my camp at South Horr, Karanja tells me.' He paused, his eyes on Abe's face as though trying to gauge his motives. 'I don't object to TV coverage of the way I operate, so long as it isn't slanted. We can talk about that later, but it'll be on my terms. Understood?'

'Naturally,' Abe said.

His gaze switched to me. 'And you?'

I nodded.

'Okay then. Get your gear into my Land-Rover. I'll be leaving just as soon as an Army plane arrives and I've had a word with the pilot.'

About half an hour later we heard the sound of it diving down out of the sun, and then it was coming in from the south-east, a twin-engined monoplane with its undercarriage down. It landed in a cloud of dust and when the pilot got out I saw it was a stranger. I had hoped it would be Murphy.

Kirby-Smith did not wait to see the plane take off

and we were halfway to Baragoi when it passed over us heading north. It was a windy hair-raising drive, the wheels skidding on gravel, half-floating in patches of sand, nobody speaking. Karanja had dropped his role of courier. Beside us in the back his flat broad-nosed features had a solemn, dejected look. Doubtless the captain had given him hell for turning on to the Baringo track and making van Delden a present of his vehicle, and I was quite certain Kirby-Smith had made him responsible for every foot of film we shot at his camp.

There were mountains either side of us now, the country thickening as we entered the restricted gap of the Horr Valley. We were between the Nyiru and Ol Doinya Mara ranges then, towering pinnacles of jagged rock glimpsed through the branches of trees, and shortly after ten we ran into the dusty little village of South Horr. Mary turned to Abe. 'This is the last village. North of here there's nothing, just desert till you get to Ethiopia.' It was the first time she had spoken and by making the observation direct to Abe she made it clear she was still angry with me and not prepared to recognize my presence.

The village, which was little more than a single street, was packed with tribesmen, some of them armed with slender spears, their ear lobes hanging in loops, and many of their women had necks, arms and ankles encased in rings of copper wire. They pressed so close around us that the Land-Rover was reduced to a crawl, the ring of dark faces thrust close, hands reaching out to pluck at us and their speech importunate. Some of the younger men with elaborate hair-styles shook their spears at us, older men thrust cowrie shells into our hands.

'It's all right,' Kirby-Smith said over his shoulder. He was talking to them all the time in their own language. 'They want food, that's all.' An old man, one of the elders, barred our way and we stopped while Kirby-Smith talked with him, everybody, even the young men, listening, silent. These were young warriors – the moran, Kirby-Smith called them – and they stood out like peacocks, slender, arrogant, almost naked, except for those with red blankets they wore like capes, and besides their spears, many of them carried a neck rest in the other hand so that they could lie down without disturbing the ochre plastering of their hair. Their elaborate hairstyles varied, some wearing it twisted in tiny plaits, long and swept back over the head, some in a fringe in front and falling halfway down the back, others in a bun or in two long pigtails, and all of them decked out with neck-laces and headbands of seeds or shells.

Finally a way was opened for us and we drove on, and a moment later we were clear of the village, back in the emptiness of the valley. 'It's this damned drought,' Kirby-Smith said. 'They'd never beg like that normally. That old man was telling me again how they'd lost all their cattle and their camels. They've trekked in from the desert on foot, depending on their moran for food, and those showy young men have just about killed everything that moves, except for the big game. That's the effect of hunger. They're an indolent lot normally.' He laughed, a surprisingly high sound. 'All the same, you don't want to tangle with them. They're a bit like the Masai, very proud, and they can be tricky.'

The track snaked between thickets of bush, the trees mainly euphorbia and acacia, some leathery leaved evergreens and wild olives, all laced with the parasitic growth of rope-thick lianas. The air was hot and aromatic, and there were sunbirds, flickering darts of colour. About five miles out of South Horr we dropped to a lugga where half-naked women were filling large earthenware pots and old kerosene tins. Clouds of insects that looked like mosquitoes hung over the muddy stream. The Land-Rover ground up the further slope, and after a few hundred yards, we turned to the right into a stand of giant acacia, where half a dozen tents were scattered round a clearing. Smoke drifted up from an open fire.

This was the base camp, a site, Kirby-Smith said, much favoured by safaris in the old days. 'And by elephants,' he added, indicating the trunks of the acacias, which all had polished bosses where the animals had rubbed themselves. He handed us over to a tall, very proud-looking African with a brightly coloured kikoi wrapped round his loins. 'Eddie is boss-boy here. He'll look after you. The others are all out preparing the airstrip. Don't let the girls bother you.' He nodded to a little huddle of women squatting at the edge of the clearing. 'See you later.' And he and Mary Delden drove off, leaving us standing there beside our bags.

Abe looked at me, smiling. 'If I've got my geography right, we're now within about thirty miles of your precious lake. And we're still in thick bush, trees all round us and a stream of fresh water close at hand.'

'That thirty miles could be as far as the moon if the road is blocked and we've no transport.' I wasn't prepared to let him read the typescript of Pieter van Delden's book, but I got volume II of Teleki's expedition out of my grip and handed it to him. 'I've marked the passages. Read it and perhaps you'll understand.'

Karanja called to us. 'You like tea now?' He indicated some canvas chairs grouped around a table under the fly of a tent. 'You sit there and I bring you tea.' He came with three tin mugs as we were moving our gear into the shade of the tent. 'That boy is Masai. I don't like Masai. They are very stupid people.'

It was during the day we spent alone in that camp, with nothing to do but read and sit talking about the lake to the north, the lava waste that surrounded it, and about van Delden, that I first began to be really scared about how it would end, a sense of premonition that I tried to pretend was due to the heat and the strangeness of the place. Karanja had cut himself an arbour of shade under a bush and sat there like an animal in its lair, motionless, with his eyes staring at nothing, his face expressionless. The women had gone, driven off by their menfolk, and only the Masai made his presence felt, moving gracefully and doing little, sometimes standing, still as an ebony carving, watching us. The trees towered breathless, their leaves shimmering in the sun's glare, and occasionally, just occasionally, I caught the flicker of a bird. It was hot as an oven with the door open, releasing scents I had never experienced before. It was a heady, overpowering atmosphere and I would not have been surprised if some strange beast out of the past had presented itself before us or an early ape-figure masquerading as man.

Once Abe looked up from von Höhlen's book and said, 'That typescript of yours, does it deal with Kulal in detail?'

'Yes, but he was attacked by the men of the rain forest, the Wandrobo. He never got to the top.'

'Our friend von Höhlen says it presents "*a terrible chaos of yawning chasms and ravines, with perpendicular brownish-black precipices, the general character and trend of which*" – he's not exactly my favourite travel writer – "*which led us to suppose this to be a continuation of the same fissure as that in which our progress had been arrested during our march along the western face of Mt Nyiro.*" That, I take it, is the dark fang of a mountain hanging over us now. If so, he says, then this fissure must extend for some forty miles.' He let the book fall on his lap, staring at me sleepily. 'Sounds pretty rough going. How do you propose getting to the top of it?'

'There'll be a track of some sort. Mary mentioned a Mission.'

'Okay, so you get to the top, and it's forest something like we're in now. How the hell do you figure on making an archaeological discovery buried under five or six thousand years of decayed tropical vegetation?'

I shook my head. I hadn't really thought about it. I had been relying on van Delden. But when I told him this he laughed. 'Van Delden has other fish to fry and his own safety to consider. He's not going to waste his time searching for pieces of pottery and the remains of an ancient civilization.' He picked up the book again. 'Better give some thought to what you plan to do, now you're within striking distance of the lake. And save your film.' A bird began a monotonous piping whistle from across the clearing as though calling for rain. Wet-wet-wet, it cried, trailing a long tail from one acacia to the next, where it sat on a branch watching us, its black wings folded, its tail hanging down and a large horned beak, bright red with an ivory tip.

I leaned back and closed my eyes, thinking about what he had said, wondering whether to show him the typescript. And still that feeling that it wasn't just Rudolf that was very close, but something more personal, more frightening. It would have been easy to convince myself that it was no more than the strangeness of my surroundings if I had not experienced this feeling before. Through my closed lids the sun shone red on my eyes, sweat on my chest and that bird, which I later learned was a Van der Decken's hornbill, piping away, the murmur of insects, everything drowsy in the midday heat. I knew Abe was right. Van Delden wasn't interested in archaeological remains. I could almost wish that they'd find him and ship him out.

But I knew they wouldn't, and as I dozed off I saw his face as he had stood looking at the remains of that wooden lodge at the edge of the Serengeti, tears in his eyes.

Dusk had fallen before Kirby-Smith returned, the Land-Rover leading in two trucks full of Africans, its headlights cutting a swathe through the trees. They had shot a duiker, and while the carcass of the little antelope was roasting over the fire, we sat drinking warm beer with a pressure lamp hissing behind us and the night full of stars. The plane had been unable to make contact by radio, but the pilot had dropped a message over the nearly completed runway. No sign of the minibus. He had swept an area from the Suguta up as far as Loiyangalani and east across the slopes of Mt Kulal. 'From here to the lake, it's all open country,' Kirby-Smith said. 'Desert and lava, a few isolated trees. Nowhere he could hide a vehicle except at Loiyangalani among the doum palms. But Jeff says he flew low over the oasis several times. If the vehicle had been there I think he would have seen it. So it must be Kulal.'

'The oasis or Kulal, what does it matter?' Mary said in a tight controlled voice. 'He's well clear of your operation.'

Kirby-Smith hesitated, his cigarette glowing in the dark. 'I'd still like to know,' he said quietly. 'I've a radio call — '

'Leave him alone, can't you.' She got suddenly to her feet, paused a moment as though about to say something more, then turned abruptly and went to her tent.

Kirby-Smith sighed. 'She's like her mother,' he murmured. 'Very emotional, and her mood changing from moment to moment.'

'You knew her mother well?' Abe asked.

'Of course.' He said it tersely, resisting any intrusion into that part of his life, and switched the conversation back to Kulal. 'He may have made it into the great gorge on the eastern side. If he's attempted to reach the top, then there's only one track and it goes past the Mission.'

The radio contact was for 20.30 hours, but when he had spoken with Northern Army headquarters he came back shaking his head. 'Their plane had no better luck than mine. Maddox flew from Loiyangalani across Kulal and halfway to Marsabit. Not a sign of him. No tracks visible, nothing.' He sat down again and picked up his beer. 'So that settles it, he's in the gorge on the eastern side of Kulal. Even Cornelius wouldn't risk foot-slogging it through the Chalbi in a drought.'

But later, when Abe had joined me under the fly of the tent we had been allocated, he said, 'If you were van Delden, what would you do – in a hijacked vehicle short of gas?'

I had turned in immediately after we had fed and was lying precariously balanced on the seat cushions of one of the trucks watching a satellite move steadily through the stardust of the Milky Way, enjoying the solitude and thinking of Lake Rudolf, the acacias like a cathedral arch above me and the fire glowing in the night.

'Are you awake?'

'Yes.'

He was standing over me rubbing at his teeth thoughtfully with the end of a green sliver cut from the bush the Samburus use to get the brilliant whiteness of their teeth. The toothbrush bush, Mary had called it. 'Well, what would you do?' he repeated.

I shook my head. I didn't want to think about van Delden. I just wanted to lie there, pursuing my fantasy of an archaeological find that would be the talk of the academic world.

'Kirby-Smith starts culling tomorrow.' He had stayed up talking to him and now, as he prepared for bed, he was determined to pass on the information he had gleaned. A born newsman, I thought, as he said, 'So this is where the action is. If I were van Delden, I know what I'd do. I wouldn't risk that vehicle out in open country. I'd drive it into the bush here and hide up within striking distance of the culling area.'

'Too many tribesmen around,' I murmured sleepily.

'Yes, but all of them close by the stream.' He wrapped himself in a blanket and lay down on the truck seat they had given him.

'What happened to that hand of his? I bet you asked him.'

'Sure I did.'

'Well, how did it happen?'

'Snake bite.' He smiled at me and I wasn't certain whether he was serious. 'He was playing around with a mamba. It was when he was a kid and he thought he could handle it like Ionides. So you watch out for yourself.' And then he suddenly asked me, 'How much film have you got?'

'Not sure. Seven or eight mags. Why?'

'Take my advice. Don't be carried away with the excitement of the kill. Save your film for when van Delden comes on the scene.'

'You think he'll carry out his threat?'

'I don't know. But if he does, you'll regret every foot you've wasted.'

'Kirby-Smith expects us to film the culling. So does Karanja.'

'So long as you've got a mag on your camera and they can hear it running, they won't know whether you're taking pictures or not. I've got about the same number as you, so maybe we'd better take it in turns. You want to save some for Rudolf – if you ever get there.' He reached out, rummaging in his grip. 'You taken your anti-malarial tablet?'

'I took it last Sunday. You only have to take them once a week.'

'I'm told it's safer to take the daily dose.' Something moved in the bush behind me. There was a snort, and then all hell broke loose, the crash of branches, the padded thud of rushing feet and a body like a tank hurtling past me. It was so close I felt the wind of it, smelled the musky smell of it, and then I saw it wheeling in the firelight, head lowered as it charged one of the tents, its long horn ripping the canvas, tossing it in shreds over its back. Suddenly the camp erupted, yells and shouts as the Africans tumbled out of sleep, and Kirby-Smith was there, a gun in his hand. But by then the rhinoceros had disappeared, leaving the wreckage of the tent scattered on the ground.

Karanja appeared, looking scared. Somewhere a man was screaming, a thin sound like an injured rabbit. 'Lord Jesus Christ!' Karanja sniffed the air, the white of his eyes gleaming in the starlight. 'I never know that only once before.'

'When was that?' Mary was suddenly there and her voice was shaky.

But Karanja shook his head. 'Long time back,' he muttered and went to join Kirby-Smith by the remains of the ripped-up tent. Flames leapt as branches were dragged on to the fire, black bodies in silhouette. The screaming died away. 'There's a breeze coming from behind us, off the mountain,' Mary said as we moved to follow Karanja. 'The camp was downwind of the beast, so it wasn't us that panicked that rhino.'

Kirby-Smith was straightening up, a hypodermic in his hands. 'Flattened,' he said. 'Not much I can do for the poor bastard.' He was staring past us at the dark shape of the mountain, black against the rising moon. 'One of my best trackers, too.' He looked at Abe, his face set. 'Did you hear anything? You were close to where it came out of the bush.'

Abe shook his head, and I said, 'There was a crashing in the undergrowth, and then suddenly it was going past me like — '

'But before that. Did you hear anybody shout, any sound of voices in the bush?'

'No, nothing.'

He turned to the ring of black faces crowding round us, questioning his men in Swahili. But they shook their heads, jabbering excitedly, their voices high in anger or fear – I wasn't certain which. In the end he posted sentries and went back to his tent. The camp gradually settled down again, but it was a long time before I got to sleep, and when I did I seemed to be woken almost immediately by the voice of the nearest sentry talking to his relief. The two Africans were sharp and clear in a shaft of moonlight. It was almost five and I lay awake until dawn began to steal over the mountains to the accompaniment of the chatter of some vervet monkeys and a rising chorus of birds. It was the dawn of a terrible day.

CHAPTER THREE

The dawn was cool, a freshness in the air, the mountains dark above the trees. I wanted to sleep now, but the camp had already come alive, full of the sound of African voices. Abe appeared, shaved and dressed, handing me a mug of tea. 'Better get moving. We'll be off in a few minutes.'

Two crows eyed me from a branch as I sat drinking my tea on the cushions to which I had clung during the night. 'It's barely light,' I muttered. 'Do we have to start this early?'

'Elephants are sensible beasts. When the sun's up they move into deep shade.'

'You got some sleep, did you?'

'Now and then, when you weren't snoring.' He cocked his head, listening. 'Sounds like the Army,' he said, and I heard the drone of an engine coming from the direction of South Horr. 'They're sending a patrol out with trackers.'

'What for?'

'What do you think? Rhinos don't normally charge into a camp like that.'

The truck's note changed as it ground through the lugga and Kirby-Smith came into my line of vision, neat in freshly-laundered slacks and a bush shirt, all khaki except for the bright splash of silk at his neck. Two Africans were with him, both with rifles.

'There was a man injured, wasn't there?' The whole episode was vague, like a dream.

'He's dead. Died almost immediately.'

I remembered the hypodermic, the look of anger in Kirby-Smith's face. The truck bumped its way into the camp and came to a stop, spilling soldiers. A sergeant jumped out of the cab, went up to Kirby-Smith, saluting. Heads lifted to a roar of sound and a plane swept low over the tops of the acacias heading north.

'Get dressed,' Abe said, 'or you'll be left behind.'

The tea was thick and sweet. I gulped it down and reached for my clothes. 'What's the plane for?'

'Spotter. The pilot is Kirby-Smith's partner. Name of Jeff Saunders.'

Karanja appeared with two plates as I was pulling on my trousers. 'Ten minutes,' he said. 'Okay? You take good pictures today.' Two eggs each, some sausages and a hunk of bread. I ate quickly, then went out into the bush rather than use the Africans' latrine. Squatting, with my trousers down, I thought of the night and that rhinoceros, feeling vulnerable despite the movement in the camp. Engines were being started up and through the leaves of a toothbrush bush I saw the patrol move off towards the mountains behind us, a tracker leading them. By the time I had finished men were climbing into the vehicles. There were four trucks, all 15-cwt J4s, open-sided with wire mesh guards over the radiators and handbars at the back of the cab. Kirby-Smith led the convoy out in his Land-Rover, Mary beside him and two Africans in the back.

We were in the last truck, and as we pulled out, the sergeant was posting guards round the camp. Karanja, standing beside me, gripping the handbar, pointed to a mound of freshly dug earth, the grave of the man who had been killed in the night. 'One time that man serve with me as game scout. Tembo van Delden very hard man.'

'What do you mean?'

But all he said was, 'He is a Turkana same as Mtome. Abdoul and Mtome, the best trackers Tembo ever had.' He shook his head. 'Very hard man,' he said again as we turned on to the main track and roared north into the choking dust of the convoy. The mountains fell away from us on either side, dim in that cold early light, and the thick bush dwindled, the only colour the flame of a shrub that was bright as a rose against the arid brown patches of sand. We crossed a deep-sided lugga, clinging tightly as the truck nosed down into the dry gravel bed, lifting its metal snout to the further side, gears grinding and the engine roaring.

It was then we saw our first manyatta, a complete village of pigmy huts like up-ended wicker baskets.

But no humans there. It was deserted, the boma surrounding it a withered tracery of thorn, thinned out
by wind and sand so that it looked like dannert wire.
The sand increased, the mountains dwindling away to
nothing behind us, lost in the thorn scrub, and ahead,
over the lip of the horizon, a lump began to take
shape. A rock, a mountain? It was hard to tell in that
pale light with nothing to measure it by, only the
stunted trees, the stiff dried scrub.

'Kulal,' Karanja said. 'Kulal is where upepo is
born. Upepo is the great wind that sweeps the lake.'

'Have you been there?' I asked.

But he shook his head. 'Only Marsabit. Kulal is
very much bigger than Marsabit Mountain.'

The dust cloud ahead of us thinned as the convoy
turned off the track, driving fast over open scrub to
where the Cessna stood parked beside a tent, a windsock hanging limp like an elephant's trunk. We came
to a halt, the four trucks in line as though paraded
for inspection, the drivers leaving their engines running and hurrying to the Land-Rover. The pilot was
talking to Kirby-Smith, a younger man, black-haired
with glasses and a pale blue shirt, his arm pointing
back across the lugga as he leaned over the lowered
windscreen. He made a circling movement, nodding,
and then he hurried off to his plane.

From where we stood in the back of our truck we
could see the flat expanse of the makeshift airstrip,
scrub and boulders piled along the line of its single
runway, and beyond it the thicker bush that marked
the line of the lugga, acacias with flattened tops, and

further still the greener growth spilling from the low arms of the mountains, the Horr Valley a sharp gash between cedar-dark slopes and the sky beginning to take on colour, the first rose tints of the rising sun. The Cessna's engine burst into life, streaming dust as it turned, the drivers running back from their briefing, everybody in a hurry and no time wasted.

The Land-Rover moved off, turning and coming alongside us. 'Well, this is what you came for,' Kirby-Smith yelled, his mouth stretched in a tight hard grin, goggles pushed up on his forehead, his left hand glinting silver in the sun, a metal split grip instead of the glove and the junction with the flesh of his forearm plainly visible now that he was in a short-sleeved shirt. 'Watch your cameras and keep your heads down. I don't want anybody hurt and you haven't done this before. Okay?' He snapped the goggles down, gave a signal for the trucks to follow him, and roared off down towards the lugga, driving one-handed and trailing a cloud of dust.

'You see something now,' Karanja shouted in my ear. His teeth were white in his black face, his eyes shining. Suddenly I caught his mood and found myself in the grip of a wild appalling excitement, my blood singing as the dust and wind flowed past me. I called something to Abe, but he paid no attention, his eyes on the plane, which was climbing steeply from the strip towards the mountains.

A track had been cut diagonally across the lugga and we took it at speed, wheels thumping the mudguards, and then we were into scrub, bashing our way through the thorn bushes, branches whipping across us and the dust choking. The plane was ahead of us now, circling and diving into a green patch of trees, its wings brushing their tops as it banked. The bush thickened until we were jinking between trees in second gear. And then we were in a clearing and Kirby-Smith was out of the Land-Rover, the lead truck stopped and men with rifles running to take up their positions. The second truck peeled off to the left. The one ahead of us turned right and we followed it. The stout stems of a toothbrush bush reared up over the radiator and I ducked to the crash of branches and the strong scent of its shredded leaves and pulped stems. When I looked again we were on our own and driving slower, the man riding beside the driver standing now, holding something in his hand. A glint of silver and the plane passed over us, leaving behind the roar of its engines. A short sharp bang like a backfire was followed by a squeal and then a trumpeting sound. And suddenly I saw them, grey humps through the bushes, huddled close, and the driver slammed on the brakes as one of the humps swung round, changing in an instant to a menacing spread of ears, the trunk swinging forward.

I saw the small eyes glaring, heard the thin squeal of rage as it charged, charged like lightning, and without hesitation. The driver had the truck in reverse. We were crashing backwards through the bushes, and the man beside him was swinging his arm in a wild forward movement. Something sailed through the air, the elephant looming large, dust rising from its feet. There was a flash, the crack of an explosion and the elephant stopped, bewildered. The driver stood on the horn. Karanja was yelling, we were all yelling and the man who had thrown the thunderflash was pounding on the door panel. The truck was stationary now, the engine ticking over, and the great beast shook its head and turned, moving off to rejoin the others. The driver took his hand off the horn and said something to the man beside him, who nodded.

'They say it is the leader.' Karanja's voice trembled with excitement. 'They're all cows, cows and totos. You see, they begin to move now.'

We sat there, waiting, listening to the others shouting and banging on the sides of their trucks. Then we were off again, swinging back on our tracks, moving slowly and glimpsing the grey shapes through the leafy screen of the bushes. We were riding the edge of the herd, ready to halt them if they broke our way. But they kept straight on, moving like ghosts, silently and fast in an attempt to get away from the smell and din of the trucks' engines behind them. And all the time the plane kept circling overhead. Suddenly we were on the edge of the clearing and my ribs rammed against the handbar as we stopped with a jerk, the engine killed. The elephants had stopped, too. I said something. I don't know what, and the driver hissed at me. 'Please. No talk.'

I counted five fully grown elephants, two with very small calves under their bellies. There were seven youngsters in all, some of them half grown. A total of twelve. The largest elephant was in the rear of the herd and she paused as though unhappy about the clearing, not sure which way to go. She turned and faced us, her ears spread wide, her trunk raised like a periscope, feeling the air. The sun was over the mountains, shining full on her, and I knew it was the one that had charged us. The trunk moved to and fro, testing and probing. There was a small breeze stirring the leaves above my head.

The whole herd had faced about, the cows' trunks waving, all of them undecided. There was no sound from the trucks now, but that breeze must have carried the taint of petrol fumes for the leader suddenly shook her head, turning and slapping one of the babies with her trunk, nudging it back under its mother. She laid her trunk for a moment across the other's neck as though to comfort her, then moved round into the lead and the whole herd started for the far side of the clearing, moving fast.

That was when Kirby-Smith shot her. The sharp sound of his gun was merged with the thunk of the heavy bullet smashing hide and bone. I saw the great beast check, watched the head sag, the ears folding back, and before she had fallen there were shots slamming in from all around the clearing. Three adults were down, another threshing wildly, then the little ones were falling in a cacophony of shots and squeals and trumpeted roars of pain.

In less than two minutes it was over, and all was quiet, only the great mounds of inanimate elephants lying like giant boulders in the slanting sunlight and the hunters coming out into the open, moving slackly like men who have drunk too much, their rifles across their shoulders and still smouldering with the kill.

The truck's engine sparked into life. We were moving out into the open and when we stopped Kirby-Smith was looking up at us, the goggles pushed up on his forehead, his eyes sparkling bright, his teeth showing between his lips. 'Now you know about culling – short and sweet, not a lingering death like that poor beast at the Lodge.'

He didn't have to give his men orders. They knew their business and they were already out of the trucks, axes in their hands, chopping away at the heads of the five adults, cutting off the tusks. The hunters exchanged rifles for knives, ripping into the hide, exposing the still warm flesh. Kirby-Smith was back at the Land-Rover with the long antenna of an aerial up, the mike close to his lips. The cook-boy was scattering diesel from an old jerrican on to a pile of branches and in an instant a fire blazed at the edge of the clearing.

I had climbed out of the truck and was leaning against it, the excitement drained out of me, my mouth dry and my legs trembling. Abe was already crouched in front of the fallen leader, his camera levelled as the two Africans pulled one of the tusks from the axed socket. It came out, red at the root, and they stood it on its tip, laughing and talking as they measured it with their eyes, passing it from hand to hand to test its weight. Abe straightened up and was standing quite still surveying the scene, arms limp and the camera hanging at his side. He called to me and beckoned. They were working to loosen the other tusk now and I went over and joined him, gazing down at the great head lying still, the limp trunk with the gaping hole below the glazed orb of the eye, surprised to see that the lid had lashes of fine hair.

'Guns are like power saws,' he said, speaking slowly. 'I once filmed a redwood being felled. Four hundred years old, they said. Four hundred years to grow and it was cut down in minutes. Have you reckoned up the years of animal growth lying dead around us?'

I shook my head, staring fascinated as the second tusk was worked back and forth to loosen it from its socket. It gave suddenly and the two men tugging at it fell on their backs laughing.

'Twelve elephants. Could be a total of 250–300 years cut down in less than that number of seconds. That's progress for you, the march of civilized man. Enough meat to keep a hundred humans alive for another week. Maybe more, I don't know, but — ' He gave a shrug. 'So little gain for so much destroyed.' He turned and looked at me, his glasses glinting in the sun. 'You didn't take any pictures.'

'No.'

'Your blood was up and you were yelling. Did you know you were yelling?'

I didn't answer, remembering the exhilaration of the hunt, feeling ashamed. He smiled, patting my arm. 'It's the Saxon blood, I guess. You're a barbarian at heart.'

'And you?' I asked. 'Didn't you feel any excitement?'

'No. We're an older, more sensitive race. City dwellers with a long history. I felt as though it were myself out there, as though I were this poor beast trying to lead my people away from the guns and persecution.'

A voice behind us said, 'We'll start with this one. How old would you say she is?' It was Kirby-Smith, and Mary was beside him, notebook open in her hand, her dark face streaked with dust and sweat, the mark of goggles still around her eyes.

'I don't know,' she said. 'But she was the leader, so she'll be on her last set.'

'I wonder how far they've come. They're not in very good shape.' Kirby-Smith bent down, tugging at the rubbery lip in an attempt to get the mouth open. The two Africans came to help, pulling the trunk clear and prising the jaw open with their axe handles. 'New molars coming forward, but the eight in use well worn.' His head was almost inside the gaping cavity of the mouth. 'Say forty years approximate. List her as SH.1. I'll have one of the molars extracted for microscopic analysis.' He gave an order to the two Africans, still feeling around the inside of the jaw. He straightened up, wiping his hand on his trousers. 'A cross-section of the root gives us the age,' he said, looking at us. 'The layers of dentine can be counted, rather like rings on the stump of a tree. There's a study being made now of the age at which cow elephants become herd matriarchs. This one I think is younger than average. She may have just taken over as leader, possibly breaking away from a larger group, or perhaps the old leader was killed. It's an interesting field for study.' And he moved off to the next adult, lying collapsed on its side, a gaunt grey mound.

'All done in the interests of science,' Abe murmured. But I was looking at Mary Delden, standing notebook in hand and watching as Kirby-Smith worked to prise open the jaws, the gaping tusk wounds oozing blood. She hadn't said a word to me, hadn't even looked at me.

'For your information,' Abe said, grasping my arm, 'an elephant has six teeth on each of the upper and lower jaws, only two in use at any time, and these are replaced by new molars moving forward from the back of the jaw. In the full span of its life it goes through a total of six sets of teeth. You're not listening.'

'Six sets,' I said, staring at her neat straight back and thinking of her father, wondering whether some tribesman would inform him of the death of these elephants. 'Can't see how it helps to know their age.' Could van Delden really carry out his threat – would he dare, against an organization as effective as this?

'Science, my friend. A lot of elephants have been killed over the years to prove this method of ageing them. We mustn't belittle the sacred cow of science.'

Karanja called to us, coming from the fire with mugs in his hands, and I was suddenly conscious of my thirst. Work stopped, the place like a factory pausing for its tea-break, and, as we stood around drinking, the first of the meat trucks came in from our South Horr camp, the back of it full of Samburu tribesmen. They rushed at the carcasses and had to be driven off at gunpoint. Guards were then posted and each man allowed to cut about a kilo from the flesh of one of the smaller elephants. More trucks were coming in, one of them so crowded with tribesmen they were clinging to the back of it like a swarm of bees. Others were beginning to arrive on foot and soon the clearing was a mass of half-naked Africans, all with long sheath knives of bright honed steel, their hide-covered handles worn with use. In an instant it seemed three of the carcasses had been stripped to the bone.

Kirby-Smith had obviously experienced this sort of thing before. He was out there, standing guard with his men on the other carcasses. He had a shotgun in his hand and when the first wild rush was spent he picked on a young warrior, red with ochre and splashed with blood, who was cutting out a huge chunk. He shouted at him, and when the man ignored his order, he raised his gun and fired into the ground at his feet. The moran screamed with pain, falling back and scrabbling at his legs which were blasted more by sand than shot. The whole ant-like mass of Africans was suddenly frozen into stillness. He called the elders out then, and with their co-operation some semblance of order was established, so that each man got his share, and those who were willing to work for more helped load the trucks.

It was the sort of scene cameramen dreamed

about, nomadic tribesmen, hunters with guns, and elephants being hacked to pieces, blood everywhere. Close-ups of men, half-naked, armed with spears and knives, dark skins stretched over staring rib cages, faces drawn and shrivelled looking, of dead elephants, of tusks and meat, of Kirby-Smith, the great white hunter, firing at a warrior with his red cloak flung back, his sleek ochred hair coming loose in coils like snakes and his knife flashing. Africa in Drought. I even had the title. But I had no build-up shots of cattle dead around the waterholes, of the Samburu abandoning their manyattas and the scene in isolation would make no sense. But I knew I was only making excuses. I had missed the opportunity.

And then Abe said, 'So you're taking my advice and saving your film. Funny thing,' he added, 'when it's an interview, just one guy and perhaps deadly dull, you've got a full unit every time. But get a subject like this, when you could throw the works at it, and you're lucky if you've got a single camera that's working, let alone a crew.' He watched as the first trucks moved off, loaded with meat and trailing a cloud of flies. 'I guess we'll have to make a show of filming this evening.'

Flies hung thick over the other trucks, crawling on the carcasses. There was a smell of urine and a fainter, sweeter smell, the sun already high and blazing down into the clearing, the blue sky turning white with heat. 'This evening?' I murmured.

'This evening there'll be another drive. There's a herd stalled in thick bush up on the slopes there and

Kirby-Smith suggested we stay with the hunters this time, show the world how neat and clean he does it. We got to earn our keep.'

A second truck went grinding past. The loading was almost complete, the carcasses stripped to skeletal remains that gleamed white and red in the sun. The Samburu were beginning to drift away, clasping their bloody packages of meat wrapped in leaves. 'The parable of the fishes, African style. You'll get hardened to it, and so will I, until it becomes just an operation – monotonous.' The two last trucks pulled out and work stopped, the hunters drifting towards the fire, the cook-boy pouring out mugs of tea from a huge blackened kettle, and the men drank, their arms and bodies caked with dried blood, the smell of it sour on the shimmering windless air.

A Land-Rover had brought in Kirby-Smith's partner from the airstrip and the two of them were deep in consultation. Mary was sitting alone under the shade of a thorn bush, the branches above her hung with the nests of weaver birds. I had just made up my mind to go over and talk to her when the driver of the last truck returned on foot. He was bogged down in the lugga and we all piled into one of the hunting vehicles.

The track through the lugga was now so badly churned and rutted that it was almost impassable. Trying to avoid the deep ruts of other vehicles, he had hit a soft patch of sand and was bellied down axle deep. It took the better part of an hour to dig the vehicle clear, then winch it out backwards, and they still had to get it across empty and then walk the meat across by hand and re-load it on the far side. It was almost two-thirty by the time we were back at the clearing and being issued with elephant steaks, fire blackened on the outside, raw inside. I was ravenously hungry, but by then I had had my fill of bloody bundles of meat crawling with flies and my stomach rebelled.

Mary was talking to Karanja and I saw her glance in my direction. She was holding a steak in her hand, tearing at it with her white teeth. She came over. 'You're a carnivore, remember.' She was smiling, a dribble of fat on her chin and her fingers clasping the charred steak were streaked red. 'Eat up or you'll run out of energy by the end of the day.' Her eyes, shaded by the safari hat, were gazing towards the distant mountains. 'You didn't film any of it this morning.'

'No.'

'Why not?'

'I didn't know what to expect.'

'The light may not be too good this evening.'

'It can't be helped.'

'And that scene with the Samburu streaming in, hacking at the carcasses. You won't get a repeat of that.'

'Christ! A sickening sight like that. Do you think I want to see that again?'

She laughed. 'You're all strung up still. But you'll get used to it, and it's what the public wants, isn't it? Plenty of blood, plenty of violence.'

'I don't make that sort of film.'

'Of course. I forgot. You like it to be remote, discursive, and only long shots of sea creatures dying of pollution.'

'Elephants aren't the same as fish,' I said. 'They're mammals, and no viewer wants to see—'

'Dolphins are mammals, too. And whales.' Her eyes glowed brightly, her face still flushed. 'But here, it's different. Africa isn't remote like the sea. You're in the thick of it. That's the difference, isn't it?'

'Maybe.' And I added angrily, 'You're in no position to read me a lecture. What the hell are you doing here?'

Her gaze went back to the mountain and she was silent for a long time. We were both of us silent, eating slowly. 'God knows,' she breathed. 'Something I've asked myself.' And she added, 'Hunting is in my blood, I guess.'

'Elephant cows with young,' I said. 'Is that what you call hunting?'

She sighed. 'Perhaps not. But it's all I'll get.' And then, her voice suddenly practical, 'Have you got enough film? Alex asked me to find out. He's always refused permission for cameramen to tag along. But now you're here, he's very anxious to have a proper record made of his culling methods. There'll be a truck going into Nairobi tomorrow. With a good supply of film you wouldn't have to be so careful of it.'

'There's no film to be had to Nairobi,' I said. 'At least, that's what Karanja told us.'

'The truck will be carrying ivory. If you're trading in ivory you can get anything in Nairobi.' She looked at me questioningly. 'Well?'

'I'll have a word with Abe,' I murmured.

'Surely you're old enough to make up your own mind. There'll be no charge to you. He asked me to make that clear.' She hesitated, then she said, 'Alex is English, remember. It's the BBC he's interested in, a BBC 2 programme.' She shrugged. 'Talk it over with Mr Finkel if you must, but let me know as soon as we get back to camp. I'll need a note of the make of film you require. Okay?'

When I told Abe of the offer, he smiled and shook his head. 'Strings,' he said. 'He gets the film and pays for it, and then he has a say in what you shoot.' He sighed, 'I came here for the ride, to see a little more of Africa, and what happens? – I'm being pressured back into the business. I don't want to make a film for Alex Kirby-Smith. I don't want to be professionally involved. If I film anything it's the solitude and the beauty I want to film, not bloody massacres, however well-intentioned.'

'You took pictures of the tusks being cut out.'

'Yes, ivory. I may need that.' He stared at me, his brown eyes sad. 'You do what you like, Colin. It's a question of motivation. I know what I'm doing here. But do you?' And he added, 'Better give it some thought. For all the chance you'll have of getting to Rudolf it might just as well be a thousand miles away.'

The fire was already being put out. Orders were shouted and within minutes we were embarked and headed towards the mountains. We were the lead vehicle this time, the Land-Rover close behind us, the back of it piled with tusks and Kirby-Smith pointing

the way by signalling with that gleaming metal hand
of his as he navigated by compass. Whenever we were
halted by a patch of bush so dense that we could not
bash our way through, everybody would be out with
pangas cutting and slashing.

·It was almost five by the time we reached the edge
of a dried-up stream bed. The Land-Rover went on
ahead, feeling its way up the middle of the lugga, over
banks of sand and round the gravel beds full of rocks
and boulders, until finally the lugga broadened out in
a wide curve towards the mountains, which were sharp
now against the western sun. It was then I used my
camera for the first time, filming as Kirby-Smith stood
on the seat of the Land-Rover briefing his hunters.
Seen through the viewfinder, it was like a picture I had
seen of Rommel in that desert war so many years ago,
his face burned and creased with the sun, his goggles
snapped over the brim of his safari cap. But this was
a man briefing African hunters, equipped with .458
magazine rifles which they carried carelessly slung over
their shoulders, not German Panzer troops, and he
was speaking Swahili.

A final gesture of the hand and then my camera
was swinging as the Africans ran to their trucks and
back again to Kirby-Smith, sitting now with the aerial
up talking into the mike. 'So you're going to play
along.' How long Abe had been at my side I don't
know.

'What else?' I asked, and he smiled and shrugged.
'The light's going to be tricky. Some cloud forming

and it'll soon be dusk. If I were you I'd open up a stop.'

'I know what I'm doing,' I told him, my words half-drowned in the roar of the Cessna as it passed over. It was so low I was able to trigger off a quick shot of it, its wheels almost brushing the trees on the opposite bank, its nose up as it began to climb. The engine note faded, to be replaced by the sound of the J4s as they fanned out, grinding and slashing through the bush.

'Four cows and about three calves,' Kirby-Smith's voice was close beside me, high and sharp. 'And Jeff says there's a young bull tagging along.' He gripped my arm, his hand tight on my bare flesh. 'Keep close to me and you'll be able to film the action as though you were seeing it over the sights of my rifle. I always fire the first shot. That's the signal – when I drop the leader. Got it?'

I nodded and he let go of me, moving quickly to the Land-Rover and backing it into a thicket of evergreens. Then he came back to the lip of the bank, carrying his rifle, a pair of binoculars slung round his neck. The rifle was a Rigby .416 with telescopic sights. He dropped to the ground, snapped the split grip that was his left hand on to the stock, settling himself comfortably on his elbows and slowly raising the gun to his shoulder. It was steady as a rock in the grip of that metal hand. He checked for wind, adjusting the sights, then his face became set in concentration as he swung the barrel across the broad open sweep of the lugga.

He must have heard the hum of my camera as I took a close-up, for he turned on me almost irritably and said, 'You can do the personal shots tomorrow. For the moment just keep your mind and your camera on what's going to happen down there in the open curve of the stream bed. You missed a great opportunity this morning. I'm told you didn't take any film at all. In my outfit everybody has to pull his weight.' He signalled to the others to get down under cover, then settled himself deeper into the hard sandy ground, took several deep breaths and relaxed.

The plane swung against the clouds piling up over the mountains, a glint of wings in the slanting sun as it dived. The sound of its engine came to us faintly, and we could hear the trucks still grinding up the slopes as they manoeuvred into position for the drive. 'About ten minutes,' Kirby-Smith said and motioned Karanja to move further back. 'But it could be sooner – you never know. Elephants move fast when they've a mind to.' He turned to Mary. 'Take the time from the first thunderflash. And then again from my shot to the last beast down. You've got the stop watch?'

She nodded, lying prone beside me. We were all of us lying stretched out on the ground, and after that nobody spoke, the only sound the monotonous call of a dove somewhere behind us. I checked my film. More than a hundred feet to go, almost three minutes' shooting. It should be plenty and I glanced at my watch. Five twenty-seven and the shadows lengthening every moment. The sun was only just above the trees, a bank of cloud below it to the west. If it went into the cloud . . . I was trying to decide what the setting should be if I lost the sun and then the first thunderflash went off. The sound of it was insubstantial, a distant bang. The birds heard it, the grey-headed social weavers setting up a squeaky chatter in a tree behind us that was festooned with their nests. A starling was chattering and whistling on the ground nearby. But the dove was suddenly silent. Far away across the lugga we heard the note of the trucks' engines change as they revved up. There was a faint breeze blowing towards us from the mountains, carrying the sound of shouts and the Cessna was diving, closer this time. The drive had begun.

'Wind's right and the light's still good.' Kirby-Smith's voice was quiet and controlled, no tension at all. 'Just relax,' he whispered, 'and concentrate on the centre of the bend. See that sandbank with the shadow of a tree across it? I shall take the leader about there. The whole bunch will be out in the open then.'

I saw the spot and checked the focus, the camera cradled on my arm. I glanced at Abe, his camera showing above Mary's shoulder as he lay stretched out beside her, and I wondered whether he was going to film the kill after all. Five twenty-nine and the lower edge of the sun almost lipping the clouds. But the trucks were coming fast, the sound of their engines growing, and when next the plane dived it was less than a mile away. Another thunderflash, followed by squeals, and the sound of trumpeting and of men yelling and beating on the sides of their trucks, the engines coming nearer.

'Very soon now,' Kirby-Smith breathed, his eyes fixed on the far side of the lugga, the heavy rifle pushed slightly forward, his good hand on the butt close by the breech. It was a big strong capable hand, the back of it sun-mottled and the hairs on his bare arms bleached almost white. A truck appeared on the far bank and stopped abruptly, the two men in it sitting motionless, watching. The plane came back, flying low, its engine drowning the noise of the other trucks, and suddenly a grey shape appeared far up the lugga, moving fast. Out of the tail of my eye I saw Kirby-Smith raise the rifle, snugging it into his shoulder. The grey shape paused on the lip of the bank, trunk raised, scenting the open space of the lugga. All was quiet, even the birds, a breathless hush. Then the elephant started down the bank, moving slowly now, and behind it the backs of others, ears spread, trunks waving.

It was at that moment that somebody fired. It wasn't Kirby-Smith. The shot came from up the lugga. There was a piercing squeal and the leader wheeled so fast I could hardly follow her as she plunged back up the bank. I saw the others turn, all trumpeting and squealing, and then Kirby-Smith fired, the crash of his rifle so loud my ears sang with the noise of it. But the leader did not check and in an instant the grey shapes had vanished from sight. More shots, the roar of engines starting up, and suddenly a burst of flame from far up the lugga. It was there for a moment, a great blossom of fire, and then it died to be replaced by a pall of smoke, rising and drifting, thick and heavy in the breeze.

'Christ!' Kirby-Smith had dropped his rifle, the binoculars gripped in one hand, levelled at the smoke. 'It's one of the trucks.' He leapt up, seizing his rifle and running for the Land-Rover. I squeezed the trigger of my camera, taking a wild sweeping shot as I jumped to my feet and followed him, the others piling in beside me as he started the engine, and we went bucketing down the bank and roared off up the lugga towards the dense pall of smoke still billowing over the bush ahead.

It was the far flank truck and as we rounded the bend we could see it out in the open on a sandbank in the lugga, a blackened hulk half-hidden in an oily cloud. All four tyres were alight and burning furiously, and when we reached it the heat was so intense we could not get near. Nothing we could do anyway. No water, no fire extinguisher. We just stood there helpless and watched it burn.

We couldn't even drag the bodies out. There were two of them in the front. We caught a glimpse of their charred remains as the smoke from the burning tyres rolled over them. 'Why didn't they jump clear?' Mary's voice was taut above the crackle of the flames. 'Surely to God they could have jumped.' And Kirby-Smith, close beside her, said, 'Wario could have been trapped by the steering wheel.' He was tight-lipped and frowning. 'But Jilo – he was a youngster, very quick, nothing to stop him jumping clear.'

And Abe's voice, whispering in my ear, 'Unless he was dead before the petrol tank caught fire.'

I turned, saw the look in his eyes and was suddenly appalled. 'For Christ's sake,' I breathed.

'There were shots, several shots.' And he added, still speaking so low the others could not hear, 'I started life as a newspaper reporter. Seen a lot of accidents and in cases of fire I never saw anybody burn to death without at least some evidence they had tried to get out. And this was an open truck.' He nodded at Kirby-Smith, watching him. 'Karanja warned him. And he's a hunter. He'll soon work it out.'

Mary was staring, her eyes wide, her face pale under the brown skin. Abruptly she turned away, sickened at the sight. The stench of burning rubber hung on the air, and with it the smell of hot metal and blistering paint, the sizzling stink of roasting flesh. Nobody said anything more, even the Africans were silent. I didn't know what to think, unwilling to accept Abe's observations, shutting my mind to the implication.

Gradually we all drifted away. Nothing we could do except leave the truck to burn itself out. The elephants were gone, the hunt over, and nobody wanted to talk about it, all of us, white and black, locked in on ourselves, silent. Surely to God it must have been an accident.

A voice spoke sharply in Swahili. It was Kirby-Smith ordering the men back to their vehicles. The sun had set, the short African dusk closing in on the lugga. Only Abe remained by the burning truck taking stills with a tiny miniature camera. Then he, too, turned away. But he did not join me. He went over to where Mary sat alone on a boulder, her head bowed as though in prayer, her face devoid of any expression. He sat on the sand beside her, not saying anything, just sitting there as though sensing that she had a need for the silent companionship of another human being.

I wished then that I had his emotional perception. Kirby-Smith was against the Land-Rover with the aerial up and the microphone in his hand, his African driver, with Karanja, squatting on the ground nearby. One by one the engines of the three remaining trucks started up, the sound of them gradually fading as they headed back to camp. Nobody else but ourselves now in the open curve of the lugga, the dusk deepening and the first stars showing, everything silent.

I was standing on my own, feeling isolated in the utter stillness. There was no sound, not even the call of a bird. Nothing moved, only wisps of smoke from the still-smouldering tyres, and my thoughts in turmoil as I tried to come to terms with the possibility that somewhere, out there in the gathering darkness . . . But my mind shuddered away from the prospect.

And then I heard Kirby-Smith's voice: 'Could be just the heat friction of a bullet passing through the tank.' He and his driver were moving slowly towards me, a powerful torch beamed on the ground and Abe was with them. 'Or maybe he was using tracer. Did you notice what sort of rifles his Africans had?'

'I know nothing about guns.' Abe's voice was a

disembodied whisper in the night. 'But he had a double-barrelled rifle. I remember that.'

'A Rigby .470, that's what he always used. He must have had it stashed away somewhere.' Silence for a moment, two figures bending down, searching the ground, and then Kirby-Smith straightened up and switched off the torch. 'Looking for a spent bullet in the gravel here, it's hopeless.' He was staring off into the darkness beyond the truck. 'An old Lee Enfield firing tracer, that's my guess.'

'Where the hell would they get tracer bullets?' Abe asked.

'Same place as the rifles. From the old battle areas. A lot of the game I've seen killed in the last year was shot with .303 and there's still plenty of ammunition lying around if you know where to look.'

They were moving off towards the Land-Rover and Abe said, 'You saw the driver's skull?'

'Of course.'

They came back with a pick, shovel and crowbar and we set about digging a grave. We dug it out on the top of the bank, working in the light of the Land-Rover's headlights, and by the time we had finished the truck was no longer even smouldering, the metal just cool enough for us to drag the remains of the two Africans out. It was a messy, unpleasant job, a roasted smell still clinging to the shrivelled tatters of flesh, the bones brittle from the heat. Karanja pointed to the driver's head, which had a hole drilled in the blackened bone just above the remains of the right ear, another larger hole on the other side. 'This man shot dead.'

His voice was high and excited, trembling in the hot, stinking air.

'His gun must have gone off by itself,' Mary said quickly. 'The heat . . .' But she stopped then, knowing it wasn't that, for Kirby-Smith's torch was beamed on the rifle still clipped to its bracket.

Nobody said anything after that and we laid the bodies on a groundsheet and carried them to the grave in silence. When we had shovelled back the earth and built a small cairn of boulders over the mound, Kirby-Smith drove us back to camp. He drove fast, crashing through the bush, swerving between the trees, tearing over the uneven ground, as though in fighting the wheel one-handed his powerful body found an outlet for the anger that showed in his face.

That night the tension in the camp was something almost tangible. Presumably Kirby-Smith had told his driver not to talk, but in a close-knit group of men it is impossible to conceal a thing like that entirely. It was in the air, a feeling of menace. And the patrol was back. They had found the tracks of humans mixed with those of the rhinoceros and further back the remains of a camp. Kirby-Smith's tracker and two of the patrol, who were also expert trackers, were agreed that the camp had been used the previous night. They had followed fresh tracks northwards in the direction of the morning cull, but had lost them where the intruders had waded through the waters of the stream. They had failed to pick up any tracks on the further bank, but the information they brought back had convinced every African in the camp that the rhinoceros had been cleverly manoeuvred into charging our tents, and that somebody, ivory poachers probably, with a vested interest in preventing an official cull of their source of supply, had been responsible for firing on the truck.

All this we heard from Karanja as we sat by the fire eating a mess of posho and elephant meat. And something else. The patrol had also backtracked the intruders on the approach to the site of their night camp. Again they had lost the track in the stream, but the approach had been made from the east, down the slopes of the Mara range. 'Many years ago,' Karanja said, 'when I first work for Tembo and he is Game Warden of this area, we capture a very bad poacher who is hiding in a secret hole in the rocks up there on the Mara.'

The cook-boy was issuing cans of beer, one to each man, and the patrol sergeant threw another branch on the fire. The flames rose, flickering on the black faces, everybody huddled in groups, talking, their voices hushed. And close beside me, Abe said, 'Do you think he's up there, holed up in the same place?'

'Maybe.' Karanja hesitated. 'Maybe he is somewhere else now, but is good place to hide. When we capture that poacher, if we do not have an informer with us to know the place, we never find it.' And he added, 'Also, there is only two ways to approach. We can climb up, or we can climb down, and if we don't surprise him we are all dead. He was bad man and he had a gun with him.'

'And what happens in the morning?' Abe asked. 'Is the patrol going out again?'

Karanja nodded. 'They will leave at dawn.'

'Which direction?'

'Up on to the Mara.'

'To search the other side of the stream for tracks.'

Karanja shrugged, his eyes shifting in the firelight, his hands gripped tight around his can of beer.

'Do you think they'll find any tracks?'

'Maybe.'

There was something in Karanja's manner that worried me. He seemed nervous and very tense, unwilling to continue the conversation. Abe snapped the ring-opener of his can, threw it into the fire and drank. 'Anybody else know of this hide-out?' It was said innocently enough, but I saw he was watching him out of the corner of his eyes.

Karanja didn't answer, and when Abe repeated the question, he shook his head. 'I sleep now.' He started to get to his feet, but Abe pulled him back, his hand on his arm, holding him.

'I have told you what I know,' Karanja said.

'Why?' Abe asked. 'Why did you tell us about this hide-out?'

Karanja shook his head again, the whites of his eyes gleaming in the flickering firelight. 'Maybe you, or Mr Tait, go with the patrol.'

'You told Major Kirby-Smith about it.'

'No, not Major Kirby-Smith.'

'The patrol sergeant then.'

Karanja was silent. Then suddenly he said, 'There

is a man in the patrol who is with the police when we bring that poacher in. He knows we caught him up in the Mara, but he don't know where.'

'So you told them.'

Karanja hesitated, then nodded slowly. 'What can I do? If I don't co-operate—' He spread his hands in a gesture of helplessness, then caught hold of Abe's arm. 'Why did he do it? Is crazy, to shoot men because they are killing elephants.'

'You're certain it was van Delden then?'

'Who else? Who else but Tembo van Delden do a crazy thing like that?' And he added, 'Once before, when we were at Marsabit—' He was suddenly silent, shaking his head. 'But now it is different. Now, if he's taken by the Army . . .' He was staring at Abe and his eyes in the twilight seemed to be pleading.

'You don't want his death on your conscience, is that it?'

Karanja hesitated, then nodded, a reluctant, barely perceptible movement of the head. 'If you were with the patrol – a newsman representing CBS – then I think they are more careful.' And after a moment he said hopefully, 'Then it is all right? I can fix it?' And he sat there, staring urgently at Abe, who didn't say anything for a long time, sitting hunched over his beer, sipping at it occasionally, lost in thought.

Finally he seemed to make up his mind. 'I have a better idea.' He finished his drink and got to his feet, dragging Karanja with him. 'We'll take a walk, see where the night guards are posted.' He turned to me. 'You stay here. I'll tell you what's in my mind later.'

And, still gripping the unwilling Karanja by the arm, he led him out of the circle of the firelight. I watched them until they were no more than shadows against the bright gleam of pressure lamps hung outside the tents.

I leaned back and closed my eyes. The night was full of sound, the crackle of the fire, the whisper of voices, the incessant, strident cacophony of cicadas. Somewhere an owl was hooting, the first I had heard, a mournful, monotonous sound, and down by the lugga a nightjar was over-riding the croak of frogs with a shrill churring. I thought how wonderful it would be, camped here under the mountains, if this were just a photographic safari, no killings, no sense of something hanging over me. There was a shout, the click of a rifle bolt and I opened my eyes, staring into the night. Abe and Karanja had been challenged by one of the guards. I could see a torch shining on their faces and I lay back again, watching a satellite, bright as a planet, moving steadily across the velvet sky.

Out of the tail of my eye I saw a figure move, flop down beside me, and Mary's voice said, 'What does Abe Finkel think?'

'About what?' I sat up, leaning on one elbow. The fire was dying and I could not see the expression in her eyes.

'About what happened, who did it. God, you're slow. What else?' The husky voice trembled on the night air and I felt sorry for her. She knew there was only one man who could have done it and silence was the only answer I could give her. 'You think I should have gone with him, don't you? You think I'm to blame. But it wouldn't have made any difference. He never listened to me.' Her hands were clasped tight together, the fingers locked. 'Well, say something, can't you?'

'What is there to say? You're here, and that's all there is to it.'

'You don't understand, do you?'

'No, I don't,' I said. 'If you'd have been with your father, if you'd gone with him—'

'He's not my father.'

I stared at her, shocked as much by the tone of her voice, the emotional violence of it, as by the denial. 'But when we were at the Lodge . . .'

'He gave me a name, brought me up – but he's not my father. Surely you must have guessed.' And when I shook my head, she said, 'Alex is my father. Now do you understand?' She seemed to expect some comment, but when I didn't say anything, she said angrily, 'Well, don't just sit there staring at me. He's my natural father and I don't know what to do. A situation like this – I need help.' She was staring at me, her eyes unnaturally bright. 'Well, Christ! Can't you say something?' And then she laughed, a trembling note near to hysteria. 'No, of course. Keep your mouth shut, don't get involved. Don't even bloody well think about it.' Her eyes shifted to the forest. 'All very well for you. But that man out there – you don't know him like I do.'

She was silent for a moment, and then, in a quiet voice tinged with bitterness: 'I thought – at that Conference – I really thought a confrontation would get it out of his system. I thought if they argued it out, the two of them, in public before all those delegates – that would be the end of it. I thought he'd be satisfied then, feel he'd done all he could. But I was wrong. Instead, it seemed to fuel again all the old resentment, all the basic fundamental differences. The two of them, they're like two sides of the same coin, both of them obsessed with the rightness of what they're doing.' The rush of words ceased abruptly, her voice trembling into silence. 'But not this,' she breathed, her nerves strung taut and a note of hopelessness. 'Nothing can justify this.' She was silent for a while, her fingers moving, clasping and unclasping. Then suddenly she rounded on me and said, 'You've got to stop it – somehow.'

'Me?' I stared at her, wondering what the hell she expected me to do about it.

'You and that American,' she said, her eyes staring at me, large and wild in the dimming firelight. 'You've got to do something. You're the only man here who can come between them.'

I sat there, silent, not knowing what to say. There was no comfort I could give her. And then Abe came out of the shadows, Karanja beside him, both of them subdued. 'The guards are on their toes,' he said. 'We were challenged twice.' He glanced at Mary, then sat himself on the far side of her. 'I think you could help.' He stared at her, then hesitatingly, 'That is, if you're willing. Karanja here knows of an old poacher's hide-out—'

'I know about that,' she said quickly. 'The patrol leaves at first light.'

He nodded. 'Then it's a question of whether you're prepared to let your father be cornered up there without warning him.'

'It doesn't worry you that he's killed two men?'

He smiled and shook his head. 'I've seen too much bloodshed, too many people killed . . .' He gave a little shrug. 'Too many of us in the world anyway.'

She turned to Karanja, speaking to him rapidly in his own tongue. And when he had answered her questions, she said, 'He may not be there, of course.'

Abe nodded. 'Then we come back. But if he is . . .' He paused, facing her. 'You realize they'll shoot him.'

'I was hoping,' she said, 'that I could persuade you . . .' She glanced at me. 'That's why I came to talk to you.' Kirby-Smith called to her and she said she was coming. 'He wants to dictate some notes.'

'Will you create a diversion for us so that we can slip away unnoticed?'

She nodded slowly. 'I – suppose so. Yes, of course. It's what I wanted – for him to be warned. But on one condition, that you make him realize it's useless to interfere. More troops will be arriving in the morning. He won't stop the culling and if he tries to attack the outfit again, then there'll only be one end to it. They'll track him down and kill him. Tell him that please, if you find him, and make him promise to head for the coast. It's his only hope.'

Quickly they arranged the details between them. Just after midnight Mary would approach one of the guards, tell him she had an upset stomach and go into the bushes. She would stay there long enough for them to become anxious, then she would scream and start to run. After the rhinoceros episode of the night before it would be sufficient to reduce the whole camp to instant turmoil. She got up. 'That's settled then.' She hesitated, suddenly bending down to Abe and kissing him on the forehead. 'You're a very strange man. Thank you.' And she turned and went quickly to the tent where Kirby-Smith sat at a table, his face lit by the bright light of a pressure lamp clouded with insects.

'Well?' Abe had shifted his position. He was close beside me now. 'What are you going to do – come with us or stay and film tomorrow's cull?'

I stared at him, thinking what it would be like climbing up through the forest in the dark, up the densely covered slopes of the Mara. A night march like that, God knows what we would meet – elephant, rhino, and Kirby-Smith had said there were lions. And if we made it, if we found the poacher's hideout and van Delden there . . . What then? Would he do what Mary asked? 'You really think you'll find him?'

He shrugged. 'It's worth a try.'

'So you'll go, tonight?'

He nodded. 'Karanja says there's a track goes up from the South Horr side of the stream.'

'And he'll guide you?'

'He thinks he can remember it.'

I looked across at Karanja, sitting cross-legged, his hands clasping his knees, his face sombre. I didn't understand why the man was prepared to risk his life, his whole career, and when I asked him he simply said, 'I must.' His eyes shifted, staring at me, a helpless look. 'If I don't then I am Judas.' And he added, his voice soft in the night, 'Many years and I almost forget how I love that man.'

I thought of van Delden, trying to understand what there was in him that could engender such a bond of loyalty and affection. But it was outside of my experience, something beyond my comprehension. And Abe – what made him take such a chance for a man he hardly knew? 'Why are you doing it?' I asked. But he only smiled that infuriating little secret smile of his. 'Do not ask,' he murmured. 'Such knowledge is not for us.'

'What do you mean by that?'

'Only that I don't know. You should read your Horace. He puts things very well. Probably better in Latin, but I was never taught Latin or Greek at school. I hadn't that sort of education.' His eyes stared past me into the ember glow of the fire. 'If we find van Delden I don't think he'll do what Mary asks. He'll be warned, that's all, and shift his base. In which case I'll see something I've never seen before, a man in total defence of another species. To film that, so the viewer sees it all through his eyes – the elephants, the trucks gathering for the drive, the hunters waiting for the kill, the long barrel of the rifle, the sights coming up on to their target, and the target not an elephant, but a man, and then the truck a blaze of fire . . . But that was today.' He smiled and shook his head, 'I missed a great opportunity today.'

'You'd have filmed it?'

'Sure I would. I won't get a chance like that again. Next time it will be different.'

'There won't be a next time,' I said. 'Or if he tries it, then the Army will get him.'

'Oh, I don't know. I guess he knows this country better than the Army.' He laughed. 'Anyway. I want to be with him when they start culling again. I don't want to be with the hunters. I'm on the side of the elephants, you see.'

'You'll be in real trouble then,' I was really concerned about him. I couldn't help it. I'd grown fond of Abe and to go off into the Mara seeking the company of a man who had put himself in such a terrible position seemed dangerous in the extreme. But when I tried to explain this to him he only laughed. 'I may not find him anyway.'

'No, but the patrol sergeant will know you were trying to warn him.'

'So?' He looked at me, a strange expression in his eyes. 'Does it matter?' And he added, 'I don't mind all that much what happens to me, not now.' His gaze had wandered back to the fire, and after a while he said, 'I know what you're thinking, that van Delden has killed two men. But that's not the point.' He paused for a moment, then he was looking at me and smiling again. 'That shocks you, I suppose? But it shouldn't, not when you consider it in the context of all the senseless killings that go on in the world. You see, he believes passionately in what he is doing. To him it is justified.' He stretched out his hand and gripped my knee. 'I guess you're too new at this game to grasp what it is we've got here. This man is no ordinary man. He's something unique. He has so identified himself with the elephants that they are in a sense his own people.'

'He didn't need to kill those men,' I said obstinately.

'Didn't he? How else was he to stop the slaughter? How else protect them from extermination?'

'He'd only to turn the leader.'

'That was today, but what about tomorrow and the next day and the next, the refrigerator trucks standing by, that freezer plant empty, and the word running like wildfire through South Horr to Baragoi and Maralal – all those tribesmen waiting to get their hands on the meat! One man against a bunch of professional hunters backed up by the Army.' He was staring off into the fire again. 'It's a damned odd story, the oddest story I've ever come across.'

It was stupid of me, but I thought then it was the story, not the elephants or van Delden's safety, that was driving him to this crazy idea of a night journey up the Mara. But when I put my thoughts into words, he turned on me angrily. 'You fool! How can you understand my motives when I don't understand them myself? All I know is I'm going. There's nothing for me here. Kirby-Smith can't give me what I'm seeking here in Africa. But this man van Delden, I think he can.' He got to his feet. 'I'm going to get some sleep now. Whether you come or not – that's up to you.'

PART THREE

THE LAST REFUGE

CHAPTER ONE

The moon was well up, but its light barely penetrated the leaf canopy. Evergreens and patches of thick impenetrable bush, the boles of tall trees, twisted ropes of lianas, and my heart pounding as we climbed, following the beam of Karanja's torch. We had been climbing for two hours without a break. I could hear Abe's breath coming in gasps, occasionally he stumbled. We were neither of us fit, but he kept going and I followed him, the camera and my grip becoming heavier, my shoulders aching. I no longer thought about the possibility of coming face to face with some nocturnal animal or even why I was here and not sleeping down at the camp. We had left in a scrambling chaos of men shouting, but whenever we paused to listen, half expecting the sound of pursuit, we heard nothing, only the rustlings of the night, the occasional clatter of tree fruit falling or a nut.

We came at last to a stream, the same little river the road forded below South Horr. Now it was

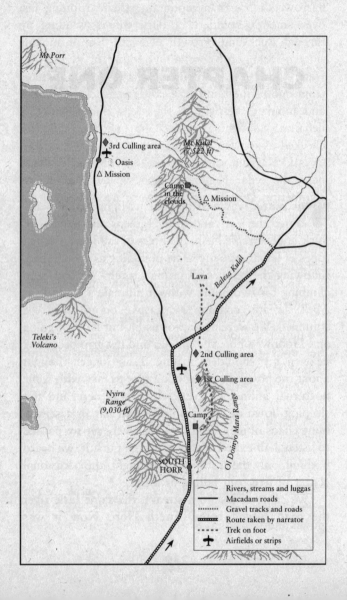

narrower, more of a mountain stream running fast over smooth boulders, a dark tunnel winding up through thick undergrowth. We waded up it, moving slowly, feeling for footholes, moonlight glinting on water and on the barrel of the rifle Karanja had taken from one of the hunters, everything black in shadow and monkeys restless in the trees, sharp barks of defiance. Something moved on the bank and we checked as it went crashing away through a thicket. 'Nyati,' Karanja said. 'Buffalo.' There was less bush now, the cedar beginning, and we left the stream, clambering straight up. We were no longer in the foothills. We were on the Mara itself. Exhausted, we reached the trail again. It was wider here and damp under the trees, the firm-packed earth marked with the footprints of elephants.

Abe flopped to the ground. 'How much further?' he gasped.

'I carry your bag now,' Karanja suggested.

But Abe shook his head. 'You keep your hands free in case we meet something. All I want to know is how far from here?'

'An hour, two hours. Is long time since I am here.'

'You haven't forgotten, have you? You know where it is?'

'Ndio.'

'And this trail leads to the hideout?'

But all Karanja said was, 'We go now. Maybe patrol wait for dawn, maybe is behind us.' He reached down and picked up Abe's bag, and then we were on our feet again, following the trail as it climbed up through the cedar forest, clinging to the face of the mountain, winding round outcrops, the ground falling away below us.

It was not all cedar. There were patches of green-leaved trees and shrubs, but these were now like clearings in the forest, the broken stems sticking up out of a trampled litter of branches, and only the largest trees left standing. For the first time I was seeing the role elephants play in the natural order of African ecology, but stumbling over broken branches with my feet slipping on the soft mush of elephant turds, and coming suddenly out into the first of these clearings, I was surprised to see the effect of such big animals browsing on forest growth.

Karanja had stopped. 'Many elephants come this way,' he said, looking cautiously about him.

'How long ago?' Abe asked.

He picked up one of the droppings and sniffed at it. 'That is old. But this—' He put his foot on a smaller, softer ball. 'This dung ball is fresh.'

'How fresh?'

He bent down to smell it, then shook his head. 'Maybe tonight. Maybe last night. I am not like Mukunga. Mukunga could say to an hour how old this is.' He straightened up, staring across the clearing again. 'Many elephants,' he said again, his voice sounding uneasy. And then abruptly: 'We go quickly now please. Is not far.'

We went on then, across the broken litter of branches into the forest again, our eyes searching ahead in the gloom, expecting any moment to see the dim shape of an elephant loom up through the trees. More areas of green-leaved devastation, and then we were under a wall of rock and Karanja had checked. The moon was low in the west, the light of it shining full on the mountains, jagged peaks pale against the stars and just ahead of us another clearing thick with a tangle of torn-off branches and trampled bushes. I saw leaves moving, heard the snap of a stem, a low rumbling sound, and Karanja was backing away, searching the cliff face. 'Ndovu,' he whispered. 'Is best we climb into the rock.' There was a crevice and as we scrambled up the rumbling was nearer. There was a thin squeal and the crash of branches, then silence.

We waited, crouched in the gulley, listening. More rumblings, nearer now, and then suddenly a grey shape moved below us. Tusks glinted pale in the moonlight, a trunk lifted high, sniffing the air. The elephants had stopped and I realized it was a cow for she had two calves following close behind her, one half grown, but the other so tiny it looked no bigger than a Shetland pony. It had a branch gripped in its miniature trunk and was trying to manoeuvre the leaves into its mouth, a puzzled, concentrated look on its small face. The cow turned, her ears spread in alarm, her stomach rumbling. She was so close I could see the way the top edge of her ears folded back, a sort of rubbery fringe, the bony outline of the huge head and the deep creases in her waving trunk.

The baby had caught the note of alarm now. It

dropped the branch and vanished from my sight. She was guiding it under her belly with her foot and the older one was pushing past her. There was a shrill squeal as the trunk came down, slapping it into position against her gaunt flank. They stood like that for a moment, mother and child together and her trunk raised again, the prehensile tip of it feeling the air as though sensing our presence so close among the rocks, while behind her the rest of the family group came into view. They were cows with two or three half-grown calves bunched close around them as they stood filling the trail, alarmed and restless, their trunks moving from side to side, their feet scuffing the ground.

Karanja gave a short sharp whistle and stood up, clutching a sapling growing out of the crevice. Silence then and the grey tide of heads and hunched backs flowing past us. In an instant the trail below us was clear and not a sound anywhere. 'Did you see it?' Abe breathed, his voice trembling on a note of surprise and wonder. 'When she stopped right below us, her ears spread?'

'See what?' I asked, still thinking of that baby elephant, the only tiny one in the group, the impression they had given of a family fleeing through the night, and wondering how far they had come, where they were going.

'I guess it was just a trick of the light,' he murmured. But as we scrambled down on to the empty trail I heard him ask Karanja how far we were from the Aberdares, and Karanja answered shortly, 'A long way.' He was moving out ahead of us, rifle gripped in his hands, head thrust forward peering down the trail.

We passed the rock face and came in sight of the clearing again, Abe beside me saying, 'She had two calves, and that little one, it couldn't have been more than a few months old. Did you see it?' He seemed to have an urgent need to talk, not caring that there might be more elephants ahead of us. 'A baby calf like that, could it come all that way? And they were heading north. Do you reckon they were the same elephants we saw from the Baringo track?' And when I didn't answer him, my eyes fixed nervously on the far side of the clearing, he said, 'Van Delden seemed to think it was some sort of inherited instinct. But north from here it's desert. Hey, Karanja!' And he caught him up. 'All those tracks we've seen, they're all heading north, isn't that right?'

'Yes, all going north.'

'So where do they go?'

'The major thinks Ethiopia, the Omo River maybe.' We had come into the clearing and he was walking slowly, his eyes searching the forest on the far side. It was difficult to see ahead, for there was more bush here. Close beside us was a tree festooned with strips of torn bark like pale streamers in the moonlight.

'They can't cross the desert. They looked shagged out already, and they've got calves with them. Those calves—'

Karanja silenced him with a sharp hiss. He had

stopped and was staring intently ahead. We stood in a bunch, listening, but there was no sound, everything very still, the air breathless in the moonlight and the trail running ahead of us, across the clearing into the dark of the cedars. And then we saw it, on the far side of the clearing, a dim shape coming towards us. No time to get back to the gulley and the bush thick on either side.

Karanja dropped Abe's bag, gripping his rifle. I heard the click of the bolt as he cocked it. The elephant heard it, too, its ears suddenly spread wide, the trunk curling upwards. It was out in the open now and I could see it quite clearly. It had stopped and was feeling the air, its trunk moving snakelike above its head.

Whether the elephant winded us or whether it actually saw us, I don't know, but its left eye was glinting in the moonlight and I had a sudden feeling it was focused on me personally. My heart was thudding, my mouth dry, and as though he sensed what was in my mind Karanja hissed. 'Stay still! Even if he charge, don't move.' He took a few steps forward and stopped, the rifle gripped in his hands ready. The elephant was less than a hundred yards away.

I think it saw Karanja move, for it suddenly curled its trunk and let out a wild trumpeting that echoed and re-echoed from the rock walls above us. Silence then and the grey bulk coming towards us, slowly, almost hesitantly, so that I was reminded of that elephant at the Lodge, weak from starvation. It stopped again, its front feet on a log, its head up and its ears spread wide. It looked enormous in the moonlight, my gaze so concentrated upon it that I had the distinct impression that it filled the clearing. 'Is bluffing,' Karanja whispered. But his voice trembled and I didn't believe him. The beast was swinging its right forefoot back and forth, scattering leaves and broken bits of branch, its body rocking from side to side and its trunk coiling and uncoiling.

'I've read about this,' Abe whispered. 'I never thought I'd see it.' He sounded excited rather than scared, and then the elephant tucked its trunk up under its tusks and charged. It was a slow, lumbering movement, yet it covered the ground all too quickly, and incredibly there was scarcely a sound.

I thought Karanja would fire then, and I stood rooted to the spot, expecting any moment the sound of the shot. But instead he jumped on to a fallen log and just stood there, the rifle high above his head, both arms raised, facing the elephant. And when it was barely ten yards from him, the huge bony head, with the ears spread like sails, seeming to fill the sky and the tusks pointing straight at us, it suddenly skidded to a halt, shaking its head furiously and scattering brushwood with its flailing trunk. Then for a moment it was still, its trunk uncurled and hanging down, its head lifted until it seemed as though it were standing on tiptoe to look at something behind us. Again that shattering trumpet sound, and then it seemed to grow smaller, the skin of its flanks hanging in folds and its bones showing, its ears folding back, the trunk hanging down again. It shook its head as though disgusted at its failure to make us give ground, turning slowly and shambling off, head and tail up, going downhill and making scarcely a sound.

Karanja let out his breath in an audible sigh of relief, and I knew he hadn't been as sure of himself as he had pretended. 'Long time since I see elephant behave like that. Tembo call it—' he frowned, laughing nervously. 'I don't remember what he call it.'

'Good for you.' Abe was laughing and clapping him on the back. 'But how did you know we weren't going to be trampled to death?'

Karanja shrugged, pleased with himself now and beaming all over his face. 'Is a bull,' he said, 'and not certain of himself. You see him swing his foot and sway, and then trumpeting and making to stand big. Not often bulls make real charge. Cows yes, specially when they have young. Not bulls.'

'It is what they call a threat display then?'

'Ndio.' Karanja nodded eagerly. 'Threat display.'

'Let's get on,' I said, annoyed that Abe could stand there, quietly discussing the behaviour of the beast, while my legs were still trembling and weak from the shock of that charge. He seemed entirely unaffected, as though what he had seen at Treetops God knows how many years ago had convinced him all animals were innocent of any real hostility. I picked up his bag and went on across the clearing, wanting to get off that trail as quickly as possible, my mind still full of the memory of that great bulk skidding to a halt and the big domed head and the great ears blotting out the stars.

Behind me I heard Karanja say, 'Is the word Tembo van Delden use – threat display. Where you learn it, eh?'

'Something I read.'

'In a book?'

'Yeah. In a book.'

Karanja shook his head. 'Is difficult for me. I don't have enough books – no books like that.' The cedars closed over our heads and we moved cautiously, the trail climbing steeply up through the forest. A lot of elephants had come that way, the trail marked by their great footprints, their droppings everywhere and a debris of leaves and discarded saplings. Once we disturbed a bird that went flapping past us silent as an owl. 'Mountain eagle,' Karanja said. 'Mountain eagle very common on Marsabit.' We were passing under a towering crag, almost a cliff, the face of it showing above the trees. 'We go up into the rocks soon.' We were on the level here, the going easier. I had got my second wind and I began thinking about the future, remembering the map and all the miles of semi-desert surrounding this range of mountains. The canopy thinned and I saw Abe's face looking down, his thin shoulders bowed and his breath coming in quick shallow gasps. 'You all right?' I asked him.

'Fine,' he said, and managed a smile. 'Not as young as you, that's all, and CBS never gave us time off for physical training.'

We were round the base of the cliff, the rock curving away to a dark cleft and there was the sound of water. It came from the thin trickle of a stream

falling over green-slimed rocks to a pool edged with
ferns that elephants had trampled, the marks of their
feet everywhere and lumps of dung. We waded into
the pool, drinking the water as it came fresh down the
rocks. It was clear and beautifully cool, and when we
had finished drinking we splashed our faces, cleaning
off the dried salt crust of our sweat.

Karanja drank only sparingly, then began searching the ground with his torch.

'Any sign of them?' Abe asked.

He shook his head and straightened up. 'Too many
elephants.'

'How far now?'

'Not far.'

'And you still think he's holed up on the mountain
here?' Abe's voice sounded doubtful. 'It's a hell of a
way to the lugga where he stopped the cull.'

'Eight miles maybe. Is nothing.' Karanja was
beside us, the rifle slung, his hands reaching for a grip
on the slimy rocks. 'We go up now.' He began to
climb, feeling for footholds. The rocks formed a slip-
pery staircase that went up at an angle of about forty-
five degrees. Burdened with cameras and our bags, it
took us a long time to gain the top where it flattened
out after about two hundred feet to a series of shallow
rock pools in a steep-sided gulley. It was almost dark,
the moon hidden by a black pinnacle of rock, the
gulley narrowing to a cleft and the thin whisper of
water falling. All round us were the shapes of fallen
rocks, everything dark and no breath of wind.

Karanja, probing with his torch, suddenly bent

down. 'Angalia!' He was pointing, and though he had spoken quietly the whisper of his voice came back to us from the surrounding cliffs, an eerie echo in the gloom. It was difficult to make out what he was exclaiming over. 'That stone – is dislodged. See the mark of his heel. There – is a toe.' It required a good deal of imagination to interpret those faint marks in the gravel, but Karanja seemed satisfied. 'One man wearing boots, another with bare feet. Now we know he has been here.'

I stared round the jumble of fallen rocks, remembering how Mtome had materialized out of the bush the first time I had visited van Delden. Just over a week ago. It seemed an age, and Mtome had moved so silently. 'Where?' I whispered, the hairs crawling on the back of my neck at the thought of a shot crashing into us from the shadows. 'Where's the hideout?'

Karanja shook his head. 'Is difficult,' he breathed, staring off into the darkness. High above us a pinnacle of rock gleamed white against the stars and the moon-pale sky. But the cleft was a black abyss, shut in and full of the whisper of water as it fell down some hidden rock face. 'Is higher, I think. When we capture the poacher we approach it from above.'

'That's quite a climb,' Abe said, staring up to where the V of the cleft showed on the skyline high above us.

Karanja nodded.

'But you brought him out this way.'

'Ndio.' He hesitated, then said, 'You stay here

please.' And he left us, moving deeper into the cleft, his shadowy outline merging into the rocks until suddenly I couldn't see him any more. A moment later he called softly, the murmur of his voice whispering among the rocks, giving his name and ours too. I think he spoke in two different languages for he repeated the names. After that there was a long silence.

'He's not there,' Abe said wearily.

'Well, if he's not there,' I said, 'there's no point in our whispering like a bunch of conspirators.' The place was getting on my nerves and only one way to settle it. 'Mr van Delden!' I shouted, and the cliffs were still repeating Delden as I announced who we were and why we had come. 'There's a patrol coming to get you in the morning. We came to warn you. Mary asked us to.' The echo of my words died away, then silence, only the sound of water. There was no reply.

'Pity,' Abe murmured, disappointment in his voice. 'If we could have gone with him—' A boulder moved in the stream bed behind us and I turned, my eyes straining into darkness. But nothing moved. A hand gripped my arm and Karanja said, 'You make too much noise. Is dangerous if patrol is close behind us.'

'What's it matter?' I said. 'He's not here.'

'For you, no. Is no matter. But for me . . .' The uncertainty in his voice, the shifting movement of his eyes in that dim light made me realize how much he had risked leading us up here. Abe realized it, too.

'I'm sorry,' he said. 'You were hoping to join him, weren't you?'

Karanja nodded.

'And now?'

There was a long silence. Then Karanja said, 'Now I must try to find him.' And he added in a whisper, 'Is nothing else for me to do.'

'Where do you reckon he is then?'

He hesitated. 'I think maybe he is waiting for tomorrow's hunt, out in the desert towards Kulal.'

'That's quite a way.' Abe sounded doubtful. 'Perhaps if we rest here, get some sleep—'

Karanja shook his head. 'Is necessary I go fast. In the morning there is more Army, more patrols. Is impossible for you.'

Abe put his camera down beside his grip and sat himself on the rocks. 'Okay, so you leave us here and go on alone. Is that it?'

He nodded, standing there, hesitant, staring up at the black V of the cleft. 'Is what I must do.' He said it reluctantly, unwilling to accept that van Delden had left and he had committed himself to no purpose. Then he turned to us again. 'You will be safe here. In the morning, when the patrol come, tell the sergeant please I go back to Nairobi.'

'Will he believe that?' I asked.

'Maybe.' He sounded doubtful. 'But tell him please.' And then he said, 'I go now. Goodbye, Mr Finkel. Happy to have met you.'

'I could say that I insisted on your guiding us here,' Abe murmured.

'Is no good, not after I lose the minibus.'

'That was my fault.'

But he shook his head. 'They do not believe that.' He gripped Abe's hand, then mine, and a moment later he was gone. The flicker of his torch showed for an instant as he searched for the first footholds leading down over the lip of the watercourse, then it disappeared and we were alone. 'Poor devil!' Abe murmured. 'All those years with van Delden...' He shook his head. 'And if he finds him, what then? What's the future for a man who abandons the position he has reached in the hierarchy of this new régime in Africa?'

His words reminded me of that night journey to the Serengeti, how scared Karanja had been. And now he was on his own, trying to make his way alone across a desert in search of the man who had been a sort of god to him long ago in another age. 'Why do you think he's doing it?' I asked. 'Burning his boats like that. It doesn't make sense.'

Abe laughed. 'You always want to know why.'

'Don't you?' I asked irritably. 'You're a reporter. You must be curious.'

'Oh sure. But logic and emotion...' He smiled and shook his head. 'Man is a crazy, mixed-up creature and I have long since given up trying to rationalize his behaviour. D'you think he'll make it?' he asked. 'On his own, and no water.'

'How the hell do I know?'

'You've read up on this country. You should have some idea. Have you brought that book with you?'

'Yes.'

'I'd like to have another look at it when it's light.'

'You'll wait here for the patrol then?'

'What else?'

'We'll be sent back under escort to Nairobi.'

'Probably.'

I sat there, feeling angry with myself. If I had stayed down there in the camp I could have been filming this morning. Something I could have sold and like a bloody fool . . .

'Mr Finkel.' The voice, coming to us out of the darkness, was so quiet it was barely audible above the thin sound of water. 'You're alone now, is that right?' A shadow moved, coming towards us. 'Cornelius van Delden,' it said.

The outline of his head was in silhouette against the stars, the beard and the long flowing hair showing white, the barrels of his rifle gleaming dully. He called softly into the darkness, giving instructions. 'Now we must go out by a different route, and that will take longer.' He glanced at his watch. 'I was intending to leave at three and it's already past that.' He hesitated and Abe got to his feet, facing him.

'Where were you planning to go?'

'There's a family of elephants must be kept moving or they'll be caught in the culling area. We ran into them at dusk browsing on some wild fig on the north shoulder of the Mara.'

'And we met another bunch on the way up here,' Abe said. 'But there's nothing you can do about it now. You've killed two Africans and the Army is sending more troops.'

But all van Delden said was, 'Where did you meet this new lot?'

'Coming past the first outcrop about half a mile back.'

'How many?'

'We didn't count.'

'We've sighted thirty-seven so far. Three family groups with a few odd bulls tagging along. All going north. Were yours going north?'

Abe nodded. 'And the tracks we've seen, they're all going north, too. But this is no time for you to be worrying about elephants. Your only hope is to get out of here.' And he added, his voice suddenly urgent, 'Make for the coast. That's the message Mary sent you.'

Van Delden shook his head. 'I've no intention of leaving now. Those elephants need me and I want to know where they're going. If I can keep them moving, get them clear of the culling area by dawn and then follow them . . .' He turned away abruptly, calling softly to Mukunga. And when the man appeared like a shadow at his side, fully equipped with a rifle and bandolier, he spoke to him softly in his own language. The word *simba* was repeated several times, Mukunga nodding, a gleam of white teeth in the darkness. Then he had gone, disappearing down the rocks we had climbed, silent as a cat and moving fast. 'Mukunga imitates a lion very well,' van Delden said. 'Bulls don't mind so much. But cows accompanied by their calves will keep away from lions. He'll get them moving, and he'll do it better on his own.'

'And suppose he meets the patrol?' Abe's voice was suddenly angry. 'Risking your own life, that's one thing, but sending a man out—'

'I know what I'm doing,' van Delden said sharply. 'It's you who are risking lives, coming here . . . why? Why did you come?'

'I told you, Mary asked us—'

'She's a fool, sending two men up here who know nothing about Africa. And Karanja, why did he come?'

'God knows, since you let him believe you weren't here. But he said something about remembering the love he had for you, and because he'd told the patrol sergeant about this poacher's hide-out—'

'Said that, did he?' van Delden laughed softly to himself, adding harshly, 'Silly bugger. He's Kimani's man now.' He called to Mtome. 'We'll get moving now, if you're ready. I'm afraid you'll find it pretty hard going. And we're out of grub. Have you got any food with you?'

Abe shook his head. 'But you'll take us with you, will you?' There was a note of surprise in his voice.

'I can't very well leave you to tell the patrol Karanja was right. They're bound to have a good tracker with them.' He started to move, but then hesitated, turning again to Abe. 'About those elephants you ran into. They were cows, I take it?'

'I guess so. They had some young with them. But

there was a lone bull following behind, a big gaunt-looking fellow.' And Abe told him how Karanja had stood his ground when the bull charged.

'Damn fool thing.' There was a grudging respect in his voice. 'You could have been killed, all of you.'

'I don't think so,' Abe murmured. 'He seemed to know what he was doing, and the bull wasn't sure of himself.'

'You were lucky, that's all. At Marsabit, when I was there, you could do a thing like that and not much danger. The elephants were safe and they knew it. But here, after all that's happened—' He shook his head. 'Here all the elephants are driven by a desperate urge to get away from man. I've been charged three times already. You were damned lucky.' He paused and then, as though merely voicing his thoughts: 'A bull, you say. There were bulls hanging around the family group we saw at dusk, another with the herd we stopped them culling.' He seemed about to say something more, but then he turned. 'Wait here.' He went back into the rocks calling softly to Mtome again and issuing orders.

I looked at Abe. 'You going with him?'

He nodded, and I caught a gleam of excitement in his eyes. 'It's what I came for.'

'But what if he attacks Kirby-Smith's outfit again . . .' I was thinking of that elephant at the Lodge. He could use us, as I suspected he was using Karanja. 'You realize it was deliberate. He deliberately waited until Karanja had left on his own.'

'Sure. What else do you expect after you'd shot your mouth off like that?'

'How do you mean?'

'You shouted it all round this gulley, that the patrol was on its way, and he knew at once there was only one man who could have told them about this poacher's hideout.'

'So I'm to blame – is that what you're saying? It's my fault if Karanja gets killed.'

'It doesn't matter.' He had sat down again, leaning back gazing up at the stars. 'Heading north,' he murmured. 'The only migration I've read about was between the Tana River and what used to be Tanzania. That was years ago when there were big herds. But whether it was just the bulls – bulls range wider than cows . . .' He seemed lost then in contemplation of an enigma that had no bearing on our situation.

'You don't seem to care that you're risking your life.' The echo of my words sounded high and uneasy.

He smiled at me. 'Scared?'

'Yes, but you're not. That's what I don't understand.'

'No, that's right. I don't care very much.' He turned slowly towards me, leaning on one elbow. 'You can still go down that watercourse, back the way we came until you meet up with the patrol. So maybe I ought to tell you. My wife died, just over a year ago. It was a long, slow, painful end, and we were very close. After that – well, I guess, my view of life changed. You've never been in love, have you?'

'Of course I have.'

'But not with one woman, over many years.' His voice trailed off into silence.

'Haven't you any children?' I asked.

'No. And if we had, I don't know that it would have made any difference. They'd have been grown up by now. That's how long we were together.' He leaned back again. 'Well, there you are – that's as near as I can get to explaining why I'm here, why I'll go on with van Delden. You do what you like.'

But then van Delden reappeared, Mtome beside him, and I no longer had any choice. 'Time we left.' He picked up Abe's bag, feeling the weight of it. 'What's in it, film?'

Abe nodded. 'Some clothes, too.'

'Shirt, spare trousers, socks, towel, pullover, that's all you'll need.'

'My camera is no good without films.'

'We're travelling light.'

'I guess that settles it then,' Abe murmured, still sitting there on the rock and his voice obstinate. 'I'm not leaving without my camera.'

Van Delden stared at him a moment, then pushed my bag with his foot. 'More film?' And when I told him what was in it, he added, 'All right then. One camera and one bag with as much film as you think you can carry.' He was turning away, but then he paused. 'Didn't that Austrian Count hunt elephant on the shores of Lake Rudolf? When was that? I can't remember.'

'March, 1888,' I said.

'Just cows, or were there bulls, too?'

'Bulls and cows.'

He nodded. 'Interesting, providing he knew the difference. It's a long time since I read von Höhnel's account of that expedition. If it isn't too heavy bring it along. And the map, too.' He went back into the rocks then, leaving Mtome standing over us while we packed everything into the one bag.

'Which camera?' Abe asked me. 'I've never used a Beaulieu before, but I think it's lighter so maybe we should take that.'

'Whichever you like.' I think he was being kind, knowing the Beaulieu belonged to me personally, but at that moment I didn't care. I was in a gloomy mood now, convinced that we would never have the opportunity of filming anything. How could we, in the company of a man waging a sort of guerrilla war? We would be lucky if we got away with our lives. And yet he had agreed to our taking a camera. First Kirby-Smith, now van Delden – it was extraordinary how publicity-conscious these men were. Each seemed to have a need for their activities to be recorded.

We left Abe's Bolex, and a bag with our discarded clothing, hidden under some stones in a crevice. Then we went up into the rocks, to a niche above the poacher's cave where van Delden and Dima were busy obliterating all sign of footprints. And when they had swept the ground clean with a leafy branch, we left, clambering up a rock face that brought us out above the thin trickle of the waterfall. The time by my wristwatch was just after three-thirty and the moon was lost behind the mountains across the valley.

It was all rock, the cliffs and peaks black above us, and we travelled fast, only the stars to light us, stumbling for footholds in the dark. The bag I was carrying became a leaden weight dragging at my shoulders. Once van Delden dropped back. 'Want one of my men to carry it for you?' But I shook my head. They were already burdened with packs, blanket cloaks, water bottles, ammunition belts and rifles.

'I'll be all right,' I said, knowing that if we were going to make a film I would just have to get used to it. Abe, with only the camera to carry, was finding the going difficult enough.

Shortly after that we began to descend and soon we were clear of rock and into the cedars again, following some sort of a game trail. It was very dark, the descent steep as we dropped down on to the northern shoulder of the range. Here van Delden left us, taking Mtome with him. He gave no explanation, merely saying, 'Dima will look after you now. He knows where to go.' The forest swallowed them and we were alone with Dima, who said urgently, 'We go quick now. In little time is day.'

'Where are we going?' I asked him.

But he walked on, not answering, and Abe, beside me, said, 'The question is, where's van Delden gone?'

'To join Mukunga, I imagine.'

But he seemed doubtful. 'If it was that, why didn't he go with him at the start?'

Dima hissed at us to be quiet and we stumbled on through the dark in silence. Gradually the forest thinned, gave way to a mixed growth that dwindled into bush as the first glimmer of light showed in the east. It was over half an hour since van Delden had left us and as the ground became easier Dima increased the pace. For a while I was barely conscious of the improving visibility, then dawn came in a rush and we could see the whole sweep of the Nyiru range rearing peaks of bare rock on the far side of the Horr Valley. Ahead of us the land sloped to the desert brown of sand and gravel, and far ahead, where the horizon merged with the milk-pale sky, I thought I could see the top of Kulal.

We came off the shoulder of the mountain into dry scrub country dotted with thorn and acacia, and here we saw a zebra the moran had failed to kill. It was a Grévy's zebra, the type peculiar to this arid northern territory. It had a large head and neck, and the stripes were closer. It stood watching us curiously until we came within its flight range, then it cantered off, pausing occasionally to look back at us. There was a sparkle in the air now and a freshness I had not felt since arriving in Africa.

We crossed a lugga fringed with trees and shrubs, their leaves dropping from lack of moisture. Probably the same lugga we had been in the night before, but further east. Dima had lengthened his stride, the going good over hard sandy gravel, and no sound except a few bird calls. We passed the thorn skeleton of an old manyatta and I wondered what van Delden was up to and whether Mukunga would get those elephants past the culling area in time. Kirby-Smith would be leaving camp now and soon the plane would be in the air. 'We should be able to see the plane when it takes off,' I said.

Abe turned, looking back at me. 'If we can see it, then the pilot will be able to see us.' His face looked drawn and tired, dark shadows under his eyes.

'Maybe that's what van Delden wants.'

He gave me a wan smile. 'Maybe.' And we pushed on, silent again, walking in a pale, cool light that was the interregnum between night and day. But it was brightening all the time and then suddenly the sun pushed a great shield of burnished red up into the eastern sky, and instantly the land flared with colour. From the flat sepia of desert gravel it turned to a dried blood hue in which everything glistened with light, scrub and thorn and skittering birds all brilliant with the great red glow of heat to come. It was fantastic, breathtaking, and all because I was seeing it on foot, not riding in the dust cloud of a line of trucks. And it was in that fantastic sunrise flare that I saw the neck of a giraffe stuck up like a post and peering at us over a wait-a-bit thorn. I wanted to stop then, enjoy this moment of startling beauty, but Dima hurried on.

The giraffe moved, became four, thin long necks and sloping bodies shining in panels of rich dark red separated by variegated lines of white as though a wide-meshed net had been flung over them. They stood in a bunch watching us, then trotted off with a rolling, camel-like gait that changed for a moment into a supremely graceful gallop that disturbed a family of ostrich. 'Reticulata,' Abe breathed as though making a mental note. He paused for a moment to stare after them, then trudged wearily on, his shoulders bent.

We were climbing now, the land sloping gently upward, the heat increasing rapidly. Blood pounding in my ears and both of us tired, walking on and on in a daze, gravel and sand glaring in the sun and dust devils beginning to form. And then, from the top of a rise, we had our first sight of the lava that lay ahead, a great wall of it like a railway embankment, black in shadow with not a tree or a shrub, nothing growing. Beyond it, bright in the sunlight, were what appeared to be slag heaps and old mining tips. 'Is where we go,' Dima said, pointing to the formidable embankment of lava. 'We find spring there.'

'It'll be dry,' Abe told him, and the African nodded. 'Dry.' He paused, his face glistening black and frowning as he stared northward. 'One day it rain again.' He said it hopefully, but without conviction. 'After rain desert very good.'

The humped back of Kulal lay on the horizon like a stranded whale and in the clarity of that early light the green of forest showed a glint of emerald below the pink-white cloud suspended over the summit.

It was while we were still standing there, staring at the desolation ahead, that, faint on the morning stillness, came the sound of a shot. It came from our left, a sharp thin sound, followed by another and another. And then a wisp of smoke curled up as though somebody far to the west of us had lit a bonfire. I looked at Abe. 'What is it, another truck?' Surely to God the man wouldn't have tried the same thing twice.

'Not a truck,' Abe said quietly. 'The plane, I think.'

Dima seized hold of the bag, wrenching it from me. 'We go quick.' He said it urgently, shouldering the bag and breaking into a long loping stride.

'It has – to be – the plane,' Abe grunted. 'Those elephant . . .' But he was trotting now and had no breath for talk. I took the camera from him and as we went down the northward slope, first Kulal and then the lava ridge dropped from view, our horizon closing in. Ten minutes later we encountered the first of the lava, an area of crumbled, perforated rock that forced us to a walk, picking our way and balancing precariously on shifting lumps of volcanic magma. More gravel interspersed with lava incursions, then the gravel became isolated patches and soon we were into nothing but lava, an incredible brown waste, all rounded boulders, through which we moved laboriously, the embankment black in shadow and rising up ahead of us like a slice of the industrial revolution painted by a madman.

Never in my life had I seen such a country, a hellish misery of moonscape rubble that looked as though great slabs of chocolate had been put through a mincer, then flung with wild abandon by giant hands across the face of the earth. And the embankment, when we finally reached it, was a crumbling wall of shattered metallic rock, so shot through with holes that it had the appearance of a fire-blackened row of office blocks badly shelled and falling into ruin. We moved slowly along the petrified base of it, feeling our way like crabs along the edge of a reef, and though we were in shadow the heat was overpowering. Twice Abe fell and it was only the fact that he had his hands free that saved him; the second time he grazed a knee, tearing a hole in his trousers. We were half an hour covering less than a mile, the shadows hardening as the sun struck with growing fierceness on the lava field to produce a blinding glare that hurt the eyes. Dima was well ahead of us then. I stumbled, just saving myself, and when I looked up again he had vanished. Far away to our left a stunted thorn tree stood on its head, the first mirage of the day's heat. He was nowhere to be seen and I had a sudden crazy feeling that the lava had swallowed him up. Then he was there again, beckoning us on, and he no longer had the bag in his hand, only his rifle.

It was a great cleft in the lava cliff and he was waiting for us at the entrance. 'Stay now till Tembo come.' The cleft was deep, a dark gash in the fault line, and at the back of it brown grit like a very coarse sand overlaid the crumbled rock. It was cool by comparison with the temperature outside. Abe flung himself down, his thin chest heaving, his mouth open, panting with exhaustion.

'Where's the water?' I asked Dima.

'Dry now. All dry.' He pointed to where he had dug with his hands in the grit. The hollow was cool to my touch, but bone dry.

'So what do we do now? Where do we get water?'

'Sleep now,' he said.

I felt the dryness of my lips with my tongue, staring at the waterbottle at his belt. But when I asked him to give us some, he shook his head. 'No drink. When Tembo come—'

'We want a drink now.'

'No drink,' he repeated obstinately. I stared at the bottle thirstily, knowing it was no good. He had his orders and that could only mean van Delden knew bloody well there wasn't any water between here and Rudolf.

'How far to the lake?'

He shrugged. 'For this man—' He nodded to Abe, who was lying back, his eyes closed. 'Too far, I think.'

I sat down and leaned my back against the rough metallic surface of the rock. A wave of tiredness swept over me. And if I was tired . . . 'You all right?' I asked Abe. There was no reply and I saw he had fallen asleep, his mouth open and his tongue showing dark and rough. I closed my eyes and in an instant I, too, was asleep.

I woke to the moan of wind and a gritting sifting of sand in the cleft. Dima was squatting in the entrance, his rifle wrapped in his cloak and his eyes slitted. Beyond him the lava glare was subdued, nothing visible, a sepia haze of windblown sand. The moaning died, the glare increasing as the sand subsided until the walls of the cleft framed an eye-searing glimpse of heat-hazed rubble. No shade now, the sun striking down almost vertically and my body parched. I glanced at my watch, surprised to find that it was already past eleven. I had slept almost two hours.

The moaning started up again, but distant now like a faraway roar of an express train. 'That damned wind,' Abe murmured.

'How long has it been going on?' I asked.

'About an hour, I guess. It comes and goes.'

I nodded, seeing his cracked lips, feeling dehydrated myself. God, the sun was hot!

'What's happened to van Delden?'

He shook his head, a minuscule movement as though even that was too much of an effort. I leaned back against the rock, trying to visualize what it would be like driving wild elephants into the teeth of a sandstorm, remembering von Höhnel's description of hurricane winds roaring down off Kulal. If only it would rain. I closed my eyes against the glare, hearing the murmur of his voice as he said, 'In two hours we'll have shade again.'

'You think he'll come?'

Abe didn't answer and when I looked at him again he had his towel over his head to keep off the sun. Through narrowed eyes I looked out across the field of lava to where the wind was spiralling sand high into the air. 'This evening,' I said, 'when it's cooler and no wind, we'll have to try and make it to Sirima. There's a waterhole there.'

'How far?'

But it wasn't a question of distance. I tried to explain the sort of terrain we would have to cross, but I couldn't remember how long Teleki had taken. Four hours, a whole day? I couldn't remember and I hadn't the energy to get the book out and look it up. 'There's a moon,' I murmured. 'A night's march—'

'Forget it,' he said. 'It'll be dry like this place.'

'There's always the lake.'

'Forget it, I tell you.' His voice had risen to a sharper pitch. 'No elephants can live in this sort of country and I am not going where there are no elephants.'

'There were elephants on Lake Rudolf when Teleki was there, lots of them.'

'Bugger Teleki,' he snapped. 'You're always quoting Teleki. It's nearly a hundred years ago. The climate has changed. Everything has changed. And if van Delden doesn't come I'm going back.'

I looked at Dima. 'Are there elephants on the shores of Lake Rudolf?' I asked him.

He shook his head, frowning, and I didn't know whether it was because he didn't understand or whether he was saying there were no elephants. 'We'll decide when it gets cooler,' I muttered.

'Do what you like,' Abe said petulantly and hid his head in his towel again as another moaning holocaust of wind drove sand into the cleft.

I must have dozed off, for when I opened my eyes again it was with a jerk and the instant knowledge that Dima was gone from his watchdog post. I forced myself up and went to the entrance. No wind and the sun directly overhead. The reflected glare of the lava was worse than any studio's arc lights. It was eye-blinding and for a moment I could see nothing except sand moving a long way off and carrying with it the faint murmur of the wind. No sign of Kulal. It was hidden in a sepia haze. I shaded my eyes, straining south to where something shimmered in the heat. Bushes, trees – or were they moving? I wasn't sure. They merged and became one, separated into three, no five, all blurred, and then they started to run.

It took me a moment to realize they were ostrich, longer to work out that something had disturbed them. They were at least a mile and a half away, out beyond the lava where the first of the scrub showed as a wavering reedlike fringe. A man appeared, clear and sharp, and the shape of him was instantly shattered by the heat, a sand devil twisting up at the very spot where I had seen him.

'What is it?'

I turned to find Abe coming out into the entrance and when I looked again the sand devil was gone and there were two men, not one. 'Van Delden,' I said. 'At least, I think it is. Dima has gone to meet him.' I had seen Dima now, standing motionless at the far end of the lava wall, the dark of his body merged with the rock. A brown haze of airborne sand was flowing to the west of us and the sun bore down like a furnace.

'I wonder what he's done with those elephants,' Abe murmured.

The figures moved in slow motion, crawling across the shimmering edge of visibility towards Dima and the lava wall. A breeze touched my face, the sand haze moving closer, the sound of it rising, and we went back into the torrid sun-trapped heat of the cleft, wrapping our towels round our faces. But this time it did not reach us, and when we went out into the entrance again I could see them quite clearly. Dima hurrying back ahead of them.

He was panting when he reached us, sweat glistening on his forehead. 'Tembo say you go in.' And he pushed us back into the cleft. A few minutes later van Delden arrived, Mtome close behind him. They flopped down, both of them exhausted, and I was shocked to see how deep the lines of van Delden's face showed under his beard. 'What happened?' I asked.

He didn't answer for a moment, wiping his face on the sleeve of his bush jacket. Then he leaned back against the rock and closed his eyes, a pair of binoculars still slung round his neck, his rifle propped up beside him. 'There was a guard on the plane, of course, and the damned fool had sat himself in the cockpit. Gone to sleep there and he didn't get out until he heard the Land-Rover coming in from the South Horr camp. It was Alex's partner, Jeff Saunders, and he had four soldiers with him.' His voice was thick, almost a croak. 'Didn't give us much time. We hit the plane and ran. We had to backtrack as far as the stream and wade up it. Only way I could be sure of shaking them off. A hell of a trek.'

'Why wait for the guard to get out?' Abe asked.

Van Delden's eyes flicked open. 'He might have been killed, that's why. The poor devil wasn't there because he liked it. He was a soldier, not a hunter.'

Abe shook his head, smiling at such a fine distinction. 'Where's Mukunga?' he asked.

'Still on the shoulder of the Mara with those elephants.'

'Will they be all right?'

'I think so. With no plane it will take time to locate them. Too late to set up a proper cull. And if they do catch up with them it'll be dangerous stalking. Those elephants had Mukunga making lion noises at them all night. They'll be thoroughly roused and in an angry mood.' He closed his eyes again, breathing deeply, his belly moving in and out in a controlled exercise of the diaphragm.

'There's no water here,' Abe said.

'No. I hardly expected there would be.'

'So what do we do now?'

'Wait for Mukunga. He knows where to join us.'

'Yes, but what then? Where do we go from here?'

'Sirima, the lake, Balesa Kulal – wherever those elephants are going.' He looked across at me. 'Have you got that book? I'd like to check what von Höhnel says about the elephants they shot on the shores of Lake Rudolf. It was the east shore, wasn't it?'

'Yes, but when they discovered the lake, they were approaching it from the Nyiru range, not from where we are now.' I got the book out of the bag and handed it to him. 'If I remember rightly they found two herds of elephants just south of the lake, then nothing till they were north of Mt Longondoti.'

He nodded. 'Elephants would never move into the lava country under Kulal.'

'Then how would they get up to the Longondoti area?'

'They could have come south along the lake shore from Abyssinia. But if they were going north, like the ones we've been following, then they've either got to cross Kulal or else follow the bed of the Balesa Kulal up the east side of the mountain. There's usually water there under the surface, but I don't think there'll be any now, not after the drought.' He had opened the book and I watched him as he pulled a pair of steel-rimmed half glasses from his haversack, marvelling at the man's stamina. He had been on the go most of the night and half the day and he still had the energy to check on von Höhnel's book.

The wind sound rose, sand driving against the lava edges of the cleft and we lay curled up, our heads covered. This time it kept on blowing for a long time and even when the sound of it finally subsided I remained where I was, locked tight inside myself, wondering what the night would bring, where we would be tomorrow. I didn't dare think further ahead than that, committed now to the company of this old man and his strange obsession. Once, when I pushed the towel away from my face, I saw him still propped up against the rock, but his eyes were closed, book and glasses lying on the ground beside him. The others were asleep, too, and I dozed off to memories of Battersea Park in summertime and the shade of trees.

Surfacing at last, I found the sun had shifted, striking obliquely across the cleft, so that we were in shadow. Van Delden had the book in his hands again and was making notes. He looked across at me over his glasses. 'You were right,' he said. 'Two herds of elephant just south of the lake on the edge of the lava country. After that, nothing till Longondoti, and then it was a young bull he encountered.' He searched back through the pages. 'That was March 17. Five days later Teleki refrained from shooting a herd of – "*six females with five little ones of different ages ... the Count brought down a rhinoceros and we heard lions roaring in the night.*" That's on the shore of Alia Bay. Later the same day Teleki bags five elephants. He was firing so furiously he ran out of ammunition and had to send to camp for more. Two herds were involved, one of six cows with young, the other five full grown bulls. As you said, bulls and cows, and both on the shore and in the water.' He leaned back. 'I can't remember ever hearing before of elephants browsing on seaweed.'

I had shifted my position, for I found it difficult to follow him, tiredness accentuating his peculiar accent. 'There was a bull browsing on weed,' I murmured. 'It smashed the canoe they'd carried up from the coast.'

'He doesn't say it was a bull, and he doesn't say it was eating the stuff.' He looked down at the book again. 'He just says it was "*quietly rooting up sea-weed.*" – he means lakeweed, of course. Later—' He searched the next few pages. 'Later he meets up with "*a great many elephants – first two, then four gigantic beasts with huge tusks; then a herd of twelve bulls, four of which were very old; then three young bulls, with tusks reaching to the ground; and lastly, a herd of fourteen animals bigger than any we had yet met with.*" And the only comment he makes at a sight like that is to tot up the value of the ivory!' He gave that strange laugh of his, half bark, half grunt, then turned the page and said: 'Ah, this is what I was looking for: Wednesday March 28 – "*During the afternoon a herd of female elephants with young ones went down into the lake near the camp, and remained for a long time standing still with water up to their bellies, rooting up seaweed with their trunks, from which they shook the water before eating it.*" ' He closed the book with a snap. 'The man's too dull a writer to have made it up.' And he added wearily, 'But there's no weed in this part of the lake and Alia Bay is almost a hundred miles to the north beyond Mt Longondoti and Jarigole.'

'There's Loiyangalani,' I said. 'That's marked on the map as an oasis.'

He nodded. 'There's always water there. It comes down from Mt Kulal, down the great gorge. There's a track runs from the Horr Valley to Loiyangalani built by the missionaries. But even if it has survived the war, and hasn't been destroyed by earth tremors, it's still no good to elephants. They wouldn't like it. Goes through the most Godforsaken country, nothing but lava and old volcanic vents.' He stared out into the blinding glare. 'No, my guess is they're going to pass Kulal to the east. They'll make for the dry bed of the Balesa Kulal and if they can't find water there, then the only hope is to try and drive them towards the track that leads up the shoulder of Kulal, past the mission and into the forest.' He shook his head. 'Not easy, but we'll have to try it. Alex can't cull there, too far and the forest too thick. At least, it used to be thick. I don't know what it's like now.'

'It's still green on top,' I said. 'You can see it.'

He was silent for a while, then he looked at his watch. 'Nearly two. Better try and sleep now. We'll have food and water in three hours' time, start moving again at five-thirty. See if we can find Mukunga before it's dark.' He put his glasses away, laid the book on top of our bag and, stretching himself out, was instantly asleep.

I sat there for a while, thinking about what he had said and gradually resigning myself to the certainty that I would never get to the great rock pyramid of Porr. So near. I picked up von Höhnel's book, unfolding the flimsy map at the end with their route marked in red and the dates of each camp. The closest they had come to where we were now holed up was March 5 and it was March 13 before they had been skirting the lake under Mt Porr. I folded the map up again and threw the book down in disgust. A big expedition with a herd of cattle for food and it had taken them over a week to cover less than fifty miles.

I lay down then and the next thing I knew there were voices and Mukunga was there, squatting beside van Delden, talking urgently. The words ndovu and askari were repeated several times. 'What's happened?' I asked. Van Delden shook his head impatiently and they went on talking. Finally Mukunga moistened his mouth from his waterbottle, curled up and went to sleep. Abe stirred and asked for water. 'Lie still,' van Delden said, 'and you won't need it.'

'Mukunga's had water.'

'He's been on the run, that's why. The patrol that was sent out after you picked up the elephant tracks and if they hadn't been diverted by their desire for meat they'd have got him. They shot a full grown calf and are camped beside the carcase.'

We left at the time he had said, having had a sip of water. The wind had died, the sun low in the west. Behind us Mt Kulal was a great reddening sprawl, the forest on its top showing green, the cloudcap gone. Everything was very clear in that evening light. There was a family of ostrich waiting for us as we came off the last of the lava into scrub. Ten minutes later we came upon the tracks of a vehicle.

The sun was setting in a red glow behind us, colour flooding the desolate landscape, lighting up the face of the lava embankment away to our left so that it was brilliant with purples and greens and sulphurous streaks of yellow. Faint on the evening stillness came the sound of an engine revving. Van Delden said something to Mukunga and he went on ahead, loping up a rise topped by the ragged shape of a thorn. When we reached the thorn tree he was far down the further slope, running for the cover of a thorn thicket, and in the plain beyond a Land-Rover was raising a cloud of dust and a group of elephants was milling round in confusion.

There was no doubt what the Land-Rover was doing, as it turned, then turned again. It was trying to head the elephants off by driving back and forth across their line of march. Van Delden had halted, standing with his head thrust forward, staring angrily. 'Too late,' he muttered. 'Another hour and they—' He stopped there, his body rigid. 'Who's that?' A figure had emerged from the thicket, a man no bigger than a speck in the immensity of the rolling gravel plain. But even at that distance I could see that he was an African, and he carried a rifle in his hand. He was running – running towards the elephants. 'Who is it?' van Delden said again and raised his binoculars to his eyes.

I turned to Abe, a sudden thought in my mind. He had the camera to his face and was looking through the eyepiece. 'Can you see?' I asked him, but he shook his head.

'Can't be one of the hunters,' van Delden murmured. 'They'd never risk their lives on foot, not with all those elephants, and they're thoroughly roused now.'

The Land-Rover had turned again, the sound of it over-laid by squeals and trumpeting. Then suddenly there was only the sound of the Land-Rover. The elephants had closed up in a tight bunch, several calves in the centre so that they were completely lost from view in the packed mass of grey backs and widespread ears. They were all facing the Land-Rover, and behind them the African was approaching them, trotting now and moving out to the flank.

The grip was suddenly wrenched from my hand and Abe zipped it open, burrowing around to produce the telescopic lens. 'Light's not good, but worth a try.' He was tense with excitement, his hands trembling as he changed the lenses. And at that moment the shot came, the sound of it clear in the sudden stillness, the silent, frightened herd standing like sculptured figures, motionless. Mukunga was only halfway to the thicket, standing now, his rifle still slung across his shoulder, staring at the tight-packed elephants and the Land-Rover's dust stream. It could only be the unknown African who had fired, but I couldn't see him. It was as though the desert had swallowed him up. There was not a tree, not even any scrub in which he could have hidden himself.

Another shot, and then another, and suddenly the Land-Rover was swerving, half out of control.

The elephants had all swung round, trunks weaving, seeking the new source of danger. No trumpeting now, everything silent, even the Land-Rover stopped. I saw him then, lying prone, the rifle out in front of him, his body merged into the sunset red of the desert gravel. In that stillness we could just hear the Land-Rover's engine ticking over. The elephants heard it, too, and it distracted them from the lone figure lying so close to them. They turned, and suddenly one of them moved out ahead of the herd trumpeting loudly. The next instant the dust was flying from its feet and it was charging with its head up and its trunk curled below its tusks. I heard the soft whirr of the camera and then it was lost in the revving of the Land-Rover's engine as it began to move, heading in our direction, but slowly, jerkily, its wheels spinning and throwing up streamers of red dust. The elephant was gaining on it fast, and it wasn't a mock charge. It was the real thing. 'What the hell's wrong?' I breathed, and Abe close beside me answered through clenched teeth, 'They've got a flat.'

The Land-Rover stopped, I think to engage 4-wheel drive, and he still had the camera turning when the elephant reached it, lowering its head and ramming its tusks into the rear of the vehicle. It pushed forward perhaps twenty yards, head down and flanks heaving, the man in the passenger seat struggling to turn round, a rifle in his hand. The elephant lifted its head, tearing its tusks free, slamming them into it again and trumpeting in a fury of rage. Then it got a grip and was lifting the Land-Rover up off its back wheels, heaving and growling at it. For a moment I thought it would toss the whole thing over on to its nose, but the man with the gun at last managed to turn into a kneeling position and the crack of the shot seemed to stop everything dead, the animal standing there and the Land-Rover still upended, engine roaring and the rear wheels spinning. Then the ears folded slowly back, the head and shoulders sagged, and as the elephant sank to its knees, the wheels got a grip and with a rending of metal the Land-Rover jerked forward.

The driver must have seen us now for the vehicle was heading straight up the rise towards us, grinding slowly in 4-wheel drive and bumping over loose stones, riding on the rim of a flat rear wheel. Through the haze of its dust I could see the dead elephant lying motionless like a great grey rock, and beyond it, the rest of the herd, half hidden in their own dust cloud, milled around, the sound of their squealing and growl-

ing coming to us as a distant, confused din, like the
roar of a panicking crowd.

The Land-Rover topped the rise and in the last of
the sun I saw Mary driving, and Kirby-Smith, beside
her, had his hand on the wheel, trying to turn it away
from us. Then it stopped, the engine gently ticking
over, everything silent, even the elephants quiet.
Nobody said anything, Kirby-Smith sitting there, his
face caked in dust and sweat, and van Delden standing
with his head thrust forward, staring.

'Leave your rifle and get out.' Van Delden started
to move slowly forward. Mary and Kirby-Smith still
sitting there watching him as though stunned. Her face
was drained of blood and white under the tan. She
pushed her goggles up, glancing at the man beside her,
eyes wide and scared-looking. Her lips moved and in
answer to the whisper of her words he shook his head,
climbing slowly out and standing there, facing van
Delden, his gun left on the seat behind him.

Slowly he pulled off his goggles, staring at van
Delden, the white of his teeth showing in a smile, a
conscious effort to appear casual. 'You might have
killed us.'

'Maybe I will next time,' van Delden said quietly.
'But it wasn't any of my men fired those shots.'

'Who was it then?'

Van Delden shrugged. He had reached the Land-
Rover, his eyes on Mary sitting there behind the wheel.
'After all I've taught you!' His voice was thick and
angry. 'Get out of there.'

She shook her head, staring at him dumbly.

I thought for a moment he was going to tear her bodily out of the driving seat. 'Get out,' he said again, and it was obvious from the tone of his voice that he couldn't bear the sight of her sitting there in Kirby-Smith's Land-Rover. 'Stop playing the fool with this man.'

Her mouth opened, her eyes suddenly wide and appalled. 'You think that? You think because my mother—'

'Shut up!'

The harshness of his voice was like a slap on the face, and she shrank back, her hands clenched on the steering wheel, her body rigid, the two of them staring at each other. Then he turned to Kirby-Smith. 'I brought her up to respect life.' He moved a few paces forward then till they stood face to face. 'Now I'm warning you, Alex,' he said, speaking slowly, 'I'll do anything, anything at all . . .'

'You've done quite enough already.' Kirby-Smith's voice was high and angry. 'Yesterday it was a truck and two men dead. This morning you shoot up my plane. That can't go on.'

'Why not? Do you think I'll give up?' And then he leaned his great head forward, his voice gentler, almost reasonable. 'Even you must have realized there is something strange about this movement of elephants northward. You must have noticed their condition. I've seen two of them dying on their feet. And though they're exhausted, they don't stop. Even you and your hunters don't turn them back. They keep on coming, in family groups that are small and unbalanced.

Haven't you noticed? Cows and bulls all mixed up. They've lost most of the very old and the very young. Only a few calves left. It's a pitiable sight. I've been following them now for three days, observing them. They're all converging here, so that I have the feeling this is some sort of gateway to a place they know about. Is that your observation? You've had planes flying. You must know far more about their movements than I do.' He paused, staring at Kirby-Smith. 'Well? Am I right? Are these the last sad remnants coming together in their effort to find a place of safety?'

Kirby-Smith hesitated, and I got the impression he was trying to work out in his mind how best to meet this long outburst. 'They certainly seem to be converging—'

'Little groups from all over this part of Africa. All that's left.'

'I wouldn't say that.' And he added quickly trying hard to maintain a casual reasonable air. 'Really, you know, it's quite impossible to be sure of the exact distribution and numbers of the elephant population. There may be more left than you think.'

Van Delden nodded, fingering his beard. 'It's a nice, comforting thought. I'd like to think you're right. But I've lived in the company of elephants long enough to sense when something unusual is happening, and I tell you, Alex, what you're witnessing here is a quite extraordinary migration. It may be this is the last time these great animals will move over the face of Africa in large numbers for them to make a pattern.' And he added, still speaking quietly and with great intensity, 'They were nearly wiped out once before. It took the fall of the Roman Empire to save them that time – because the trade routes that took the ivory to the East were cut. Almost as though the country closed in to protect its own. But this time—'

'I think you exaggerate.'

'I hope I do. But when the last of the bisons stood before the hunters, they didn't know it was the last.'

'I assure you I have no intention of shooting them all. I made that clear at the Conference. I've always stuck to my quota—'

'Your quota!' Van Delden gave that harsh laugh. 'You'll do what Kimani tells you and if I know that little man it's ivory he's interested in. Like you, he's a business man, and when there's no more ivory, no more elephants, then you'll start in on any other profitable species that hasn't been wiped out, until one day you'll be down to a quota for warthogs.' He stared at him for a moment, then said quietly, 'You've a long walk ahead of you, so better get going.'

It took a moment for Kirby-Smith to realize what he meant. Then his gaze shifted to the Land-Rover. I could see him measuring the distance, considering the time it would take him to jump in and get clear. Van Delden saw it, too. 'Just stay where you are, Alex. I need a vehicle, so I'm borrowing yours. And I'm taking Mary with me.'

'That's for her to decide.' His eyes were still on the Land-Rover. 'Taking my Land-Rover won't get you far,' he said. 'As for the culling, you can't stop me. I've got a Government contract and the support of the Army. You can't take on the Army.'

'Up here I can do anything.' Van Delden said it slowly in a tone of absolute conviction. 'I know this country. You don't.' He turned then, calling to Dima to get the wheel changed, and then he reached into the Land-Rover, picked up the discarded rifle, emptying it of ammunition and throwing it into the back. He came back then to face Kirby-Smith again, saying quietly, almost conversationally, 'I've nothing to lose, you know. Nothing at all. I don't set great store by my life in the Seychelles. I only went there when they kicked me out of Africa because it was handy, not because I liked it. But you . . . you've always managed your life so much more cleverly than I have. You've got plenty to lose, haven't you? Everything you've built up over the years.'

Kirby-Smith gave a little shrug, and after that they didn't say anything, the two of them standing facing each other while Dima got the jack out of the back of the Land-Rover and slid it under the rear axle. The sun had set and down in the darkening plain the elephants had gone. Nothing stirred and no sign of the African who had fired those shots.

'Give Dima a hand, will you,' van Delden said to me, not shifting his gaze from Kirby-Smith, and I got to work on jacking up the vehicle, glad of something to do. Mary was still sitting there, a lost, frozen look on her face. But in the end she got out and helped me to get the spare wheel down. I think she felt in need of something to occupy her mind.

Dima had obviously done this many times before. It didn't take us long to get the wheel off, darkness already closing in as I hefted it up on to the bracket at the rear. Its rim was badly dented, the outer case cut to shreds. Behind me I heard Kirby-Smith talking to Abe, trying to persuade him to get van Delden to see sense. 'More troops arrived in camp this morning and the Army now has two patrols out. They've already found the minibus and it's only a matter of time—'

'You could stop the cull,' Abe said mildly.

'You saw what he did yesterday. Two men killed.'

'I'm just a newsman.'

'You saw it. You're a witness.'

'They were shot, yes. I saw that. But I didn't see who shot them.'

'I shot them,' van Delden growled.

Kirby-Smith started to say something, then checked himself, turning to Abe again. 'Tomorrow the Army are sending up another plane. He hasn't a hope—'

'Oh, sure,' Abe said. 'He hasn't a hope, as you say. But he'll do it, just the same.'

'Then stop him. You heard what he just said. You're a witness to that.'

Abe shook his head, smiling. 'I didn't hear anything. You see, Major, I don't go along with what you're doing, so don't expect me to hold your hand.'

We were tightening the wheel nuts and Mary was standing close beside me, just standing there, watching them, her eyes staring, the pale oval of her face devoid of expression, her body tense. I could guess what she was feeling, all hell let loose inside her in a conflicting tide of loyalties and emotions. From the rear of the Land-Rover came the scrape of metal as Dima pulled the jack clear. Kirby-Smith heard it, too. 'Be sensible, Cornelius. All this part of the Federation is under Brigadier Osman and his Army Brigade.' He was making a conscious effort again to appear reasonable. 'The old days are gone. They're gone for good. Taking my Land-Rover—' He hesitated, then said, 'Tell you what I'll do. I shouldn't, but for old times' sake I'll tank up with fuel and drive you through to Marsabit. From there you should have a chance of reaching the coast.'

'And what about the elephants?' Van Delden laughed. 'No. You want a deal, you know my terms.'

'I told you, I'm under contract. I can't break that.'

'You mean you don't want to. That's understandable, since I hear you worked very hard to get it.' He thrust his great white-maned head forward. 'But it's a contract you can't fulfil. You tell them that.' He stood like that for a moment with his head thrust out, and then he said, 'I don't give a damn about my life. I've told you that. Or yours either. All I care about now is to see that enough of those elephants get through to wherever it is they're going. Then they'll be able to rest up, recover, breed, begin the long slow cycle all over again, building up their numbers. That's what important, all I care about.'

Kirby-Smith shook his head. 'Your trouble is you've lived on your own too long. It's not what you want. Not any more.' His voice had risen, the need for self-justification very evident as he said, 'It's what the people want now. The people and the Government of this new Federation . . .'

But van Delden had turned his back on him. 'Dima.' He jerked his head towards the driving seat, and as the African slid behind the wheel and started the engine, he came over to Mary and said, 'Get in the back.'

She shook her head, her eyes unnaturally bright. 'I'm not coming.'

'Get in.'

'I'm not coming, I tell you.' Her hands clenched tight on the clips that secured the bonnet, and when he reached out and took hold of her arm, she flung him off. 'I'm not. I'm not.' Her voice was high, on the edge of hysteria. 'I wish to God I'd never asked them to warn you.'

To my surprise he turned to me. 'Get her in the back and keep her there.' His voice was surprisingly gentle. He looked at Abe. 'I take it you're coming with us.'

'Sure I'm coming with you.'

'Then get in. It'll be difficult to see their tracks soon.'

The first stars were already showing in the night sky. I tried to take hold of Mary's arm, but she drew back from me, half turning towards her father, staring at him as he stood there. The others were already clambering into the Land-Rover and I thought I was going to have trouble, but then she suddenly turned and walked to the back of it with her head up and her face set, climbing in and seating herself close to the tailboard. As I joined her I heard Kirby-Smith say, 'What about my gun? I'm not leaving without my gun.'

Van Delden looked at him. 'Your gun. Of course.' He reached into the back, picked it up by the barrel, then standing back, he swung it up and brought the stock crashing down against the hub of the spare wheel. He handed it to him then without a word and got into the seat beside Dima.

I didn't hear what Kirby-Smith said, his words lost in the revving of the engines and the slam of the gears as we began to move. The lights came on and for a second he was outlined in the red glow of the tail lights, a solitary figure standing with the broken rifle in his hand. Then he was gone, lost in darkness and the dust thrown up by our wheels. 'He didn't have to do that,' Mary breathed, her voice barely audible and a shiver running through her. 'He'll never forgive that.'

No point in reminding her there were evidently things van Delden could never forgive. The man's pride had been injured, and I pictured him in the morning limping wearily into camp with that broken rifle. To lose face in front of his African hunters, in front of the Army, too – she was right, he'd never forgive van Delden for that. I reached out and took her hand. It was hot to the touch and I could feel her trembling. She let it rest there for a moment, her hand in mine quite passive, then suddenly her fingers tightened, gripping hold of me as though she was desperate for somebody to cling to. She stayed like that, tense and rigid, as we went roaring down the slope and into the flat land below. Then gradually her fingers relaxed their grip and she let go my hand.

The gravel plain was a narrow strip barely half a mile wide. Black outcrops of lava loomed away to our left. The Southern Cross showed faintly above the outline of the mountains to our right. We turned eastward, lurching and bucketing as Dima swerved to avoid patches of wind-bared rock. And then we had slowed, searching the sand with our headlights dipped for the tracks left by the elephants.

CHAPTER TWO

It seemed a long time before we finally found those tracks. We had been casting back and forth over a wide area, driving slowly with Mukunga and van Delden standing up in the front of the Land-Rover. It was Dima who spotted the broken branch on the small acacia and after that Mukunga went ahead on foot, tracking them by the light of our headlights. It was slow work and the moon was just rising when we sighted them, dark shapes all motionless in silhouette. Dima cut the engine and switched off our lights. Darkness enveloped us, the moon like the half of an orange on the hard black line of the horizon.

Abe leaned forward. 'Where do you think they're going?' And when van Delden didn't answer, he added, 'They can't survive in this waterless desert.'

'Don't talk. Just watch.'

We sat there in silence as the moon lifted clear of the horizon, its flattened orb changing from dull orange to white, its brilliance lighting the desert, resolving the shapes of the elephants. We could see several half-grown calves huddled against their mothers, and ahead, a little to the left of them, a group composed entirely of adults moving restlessly. 'Bulls.' Van Delden had the binoculars to his eyes. 'Strange to see half a dozen bulls herding with cows and their young.' There was no wind, the air completely still. Faint rumblings made a ghostly sound in the stillness. Gradually their ears were laid back against their massive shoulders and the trunks stopped testing the air, first one of the bulls, then another, turned their backs on us, and in a moment the whole herd was on the move, and we were following them, driving slowly through a pale white desiccated landscape with the moon hanging over the bonnet of the Land-Rover like a great lantern in the sky. Far ahead of us the elephants lumbered towards it as though drawn by its light.

Suddenly the Land-Rover stopped, van Delden reaching for his binoculars again, staring fixedly at the pale distant shapes. One of the elephants had paused, its trunk nuzzling something on the ground, pushing at it with a forefoot. 'Toto,' Mukunga muttered and van Delden nodded. All the elephants had stopped now, the cows bunching to present a solid front as they faced towards us, their ears spread, their trunks moving. They were about two hundred yards away, and I thought for a moment they were going to charge, they looked so menacing. The bulls, too, were restless, milling around, an impression of confusion and hostility.

'Have they winded us?' Abe asked, but van Delden shook his head. 'It's the Land-Rover they don't like. That means they've already had experience of being hunted from vehicles.'

Two of the cows detached themselves from the bunched family group, moving slowly back to join the distracted mother. She had got the calf to its feet and it was standing there, head drooped, ears flat against its shoulders, the little trunk hanging straight down. The three elephants were close around it now, their trunks moving over its body as though to give it confidence, urging it forward. 'Can't be more than a few months old.' Van Delden sounded surprised. 'That's the only toto we've seen. In fact, we've seen very few calves and most of those have been nearly full grown.'

'Is that because of the drought?' Abe asked.

'That and the fact that calves are vulnerable to predators and man.'

'And this is the only baby elephant you've seen. Strange that hers should have survived.'

'She's probably the matriarch of this group. That might explain it.' He shook his head. 'Doesn't look as though it will last much longer though.'

We had lost sight of it now, all three elephants close around it and moving slowly to rejoin the others. It was the signal for the whole group to begin moving again, but as Dima reached to start the engine van Delden held up his hand. The mother had stopped again, and a moment later I caught a glimpse of the calf between her front legs and there was a bigger calf beside her, pressing against her flanks. She pushed the baby away, and Mary said in an appalled voice, 'She's no milk.' The calf tottered to one of the other cows, pushed between her forelegs, attempting to suckle, then wobbled to one side and collapsed on the pale sand. Again the three elephants gathered round it, the older calf hovering in a restless, distracted manner, and the whole herd watching uneasily. This time the little calf did not rise and even at that distance I could see the emotional disturbance affecting the whole herd, their distress obvious from their movements, some of them coming back to stand over the small bundle lying collapsed on the ground, moving their trunks over its body, the others either milling around or just standing distractedly, shifting their feet and swinging their heads.

Abe found a pair of binoculars in the back and he had them glued to his eyes, leaning forward intently. Once I heard him mutter something about it being the same one, but he was only talking to himself and after that he was silent. We were there the best part of an hour while the little group round the fallen calf gradually broke up, leaving just the mother and two other cows trying to nudge it to its feet or lift it with their tusks. 'Once in Marsabit,' van Delden said, 'one of my cows was wandering around three or four days carrying a dead calf in her tusks. But I don't think they'll be long now.'

It was the bulls who moved first and I realized they had not the same close-knit family association. As soon as they had disappeared over the horizon the cows became very agitated, finally beginning to move off uncertainly, and looking back every now and then, sometimes half turning as though still unwilling to leave. Then the two remaining cows followed and only the mother was left, scuffing irresolutely at the ground, the older calf close against her as she continued to move her trunk over the body of her baby as though to fix it in her memory. Finally she abandoned it, turning and moving hesitantly after the others, rumbling and growling her distress, occasionally laying her trunk across the older calf's head and back. Abe let the binoculars fall. 'She's very gaunt, quite different – she must be half-starved.'

Van Delden nodded. 'They're none of them in good shape. Looks like they've come a long way, travelling fast.'

'It's the same herd we saw last night,' Abe was still staring after the retreating elephants. 'They've come a very long way.' He shook his head, his eyes strangely bright behind his glasses. Dima started the engine and beside me Mary's voice, high and urgent, cried, 'You can't leave it – not like that.'

'Why not?' van Delden asked. 'It's not our job to interfere with nature, or have you forgotten?'

'But suppose it's still alive? You can't—'

'If you've got bitten by the silly sentimentality of the cities, forget it. As long as you're with me—'

'I didn't ask to come with you.'

He nodded. 'Nor you did. But you're here, so don't argue.' And he told Dima to get moving again while she sat there staring sullenly at the back of his head. 'You could have shot it,' she murmured. 'If it had been Alex . . .' But Abe turned on her angrily, almost shouting: 'Isn't it enough, just to have watched it? No need for a post mortem.'

The body of the calf was already merging into the moonwhite landscape, the mother moving after the rest of the herd, the half-grown youngster still beside her. But her movements were slow and she kept on turning her head and looking back as though still expecting the calf to get to its feet and follow her. Finally she stopped beside a stunted acacia and began tearing at a branch. We stopped, too, Abe picking up the glasses again and watching her intently as she wrenched the branch off and then went all the way back to lay it over the inert bundle lying in the sand. She remained there for some time, her head bent and her trunk constantly moving over it, then suddenly she turned and went lumbering off after the others already disappearing over a ridge dotted with a few thorns. Her feet made no sound and though she seemed to be moving slowly she covered the ground at surprising speed. We waited until she had disappeared, then followed, and when we sighted her again she was back with the rest of her group and they were bunched together with the bulls out ahead and moving quickly.

Gradually the moon shifted its position. From being over the bonnet it swung slowly to our right until it was above Abe's head. The elephants had changed direction. They were headed north now, and away to our left Kulal loomed, a pale cloud-capped sprawl.

I leaned across Mary, calling to van Delden, 'They're making for the Balesa Kulal, aren't they?'

'Probably. The river bed isn't far now.'

'Hey, but that's a dry watercourse.' Abe seized my arm. 'Didn't you say it was dry? Somebody said it was dry.'

The Land-Rover slid to a halt. The elephants were standing in a huddle, so close they seemed to be in conference. I grabbed the binoculars lying by Abe's feet thinking another calf was in trouble.

'How much water do they need? I read somewhere it's thirty gallons a day. Right?'

'That's about the normal intake for a full-grown adult,' van Delden said.

'Hell! There must be twenty, thirty elephants there.' He turned to me. 'Are they clear enough to count? How many are there?'

Through the glasses I could see them quite clearly, all standing in a line as though they had come to some sort of fence. 'I make it seventeen,' I said, 'but it's difficult to be certain. There are several big calves and they're keeping very close to their mothers.'

'That's almost five hundred gallons a day. A lot of water, and in country as dry as this only a man like Aaron—'

Van Delden told him to be quiet. The elephants were moving again and he signalled Dima to drive on. But we were too close now and at the sound of the engine starting up several elephants whirled about, ears spread as though about to charge, and the mother who had lost her calf moved out in front, swinging her trunk and throwing sand in the air. Van Delden leaned forward quickly and switched off the ignition. In the sudden silence we could hear them, a low rumble of sound. They stood there watching us for perhaps a minute, but with the light breeze off the mountain blowing towards us, the Land-Rover still and no sound, they gradually relaxed, finally losing interest and going off after the others. Occasionally one of them looked back.

'Would she have charged us if we'd gone closer?' Abe asked as we got moving again.

Van Delden nodded. 'Probably. She's very distressed. The others certainly would. They're just about at the end of their tether, but cows in defence of their calves wouldn't hesitate.'

We could just see them now, heading north-east, and a few minutes later we discovered what it was that had stopped them. It was a track that still showed the faint treadmarks of vehicles, its edges bordered by stones. Van Delden said it led through the Chalbi Desert to Kargi and on to Marsabit. 'In two or three miles they'll come to a crossroads. There's a well just to the west of it.'

'They can't draw water from a well,' Abe murmured.

'It will be dry anyway.'

'Can they make it across the Chalbi?'

'The bulls might. But not the cows with their young.'

Sitting there, being driven through the stark beauty of that moonlit night, the desert flowing white to the pale horizon and Mt Kulal towering high above us, I had a sense of unreality as though it were all a dream, the death of that little calf, the distress of its mother and her family group, the whole macabre scene vivid in my mind, and yet everything strangely remote. And the elephants out ahead of us, dim ghostly shapes moving steadily towards a hostile, waterless desert. Looking at that dry, desiccated scene, knowing that worse lay ahead of us if the herd tried to cross the Chalbi, I was suddenly very conscious of the dryness of my mouth. There was only a single jerrican in the back of the Land-Rover, presumably petrol, and nothing that looked as though it contained food. It was twenty-four hours now since we had fed. 'How far to the well?' I asked, hoping he was wrong and there would be water in it. Mary laughed, her teeth white in the oval of her face. 'Haven't you ever been thirsty before?'

I shook my head, not answering her. We had left the track and there was scrub now, occasional thorn trees. We were heading across country in a more northerly direction, our speed gradually increasing, patches of soft sand, the scrub thicker and more trees. Then suddenly we had stopped, the engine switched off. In the stillness we could hear the elephants rumbling to each other. We were closer than we had been before, but they ignored us, standing shoulder to shoulder in a ring.

They had found the well.

They remained like that, in a tight huddle, for several minutes. Two of the younger calves showed signs of exhaustion. One was sitting all alone on its haunches with its ears drooping like a dejected bloodhound. The other kept moving in on its mother, searching for a teat and being constantly thrust back by her trunk or a foot. And there were one or two almost fully grown who had just stood waiting patiently, occasionally scuffing at the ground or feeling it with their trunks.

It was the cows that broke away first, drawn by the plaintive sounds of their young. They spread out uncertainly, searching the ground with their trunks and digging into it with slicing movements of their front legs, the toenails acting like a spade. One cow went on digging with her forefeet until she must have been down three or four feet. Two younger females came to help her, using the tightly curled tips of their trunks to scoop the loose sand out. But though they could smell water, they could not reach it.

The bulls began milling around, their trunks waving, their bellies rumbling. They were unsure of themselves and in a testy mood, the larger animals turning on the others if they got in their way. Finally one of them moved off. Others began to follow him, their backs towards us, a baggy-trousered shambling walk, the cows watching, some still digging at the soft sand. They took no notice of us, rumbling amongst themselves and then, with much squealing and growling the few young were marshalled and led away, out of the dry bed of the Balesa Kulal towards the great volcanic heap that towered above us in the moonlight.

Van Delden leaned back, lighting his pipe, the smell of his tobacco strong in the dry air. 'There's a gorge,' he said, 'runs right back, almost splitting the mountain in two. Looks like they're making for that.'

'Any water?' Abe asked.

'No. Not in a drought like this. Least I don't think so. But there's shade and enough green stuff for them to browse on.' He sat there for a while, smoking and not saying anything while the elephants disappeared from view over a rise that seemed to be a part of a long shoulder running up towards Kulal. 'Well, we know where they're headed now, so no point in wasting good meat.' He gave an order to Dima and we turned back on our tracks. We drove back until we reached the fallen heap of the baby elephant. I don't know whether it was actually dead, but it made no movement as Mtome plunged his knife into it and began carving out chunks of flesh. Blood was darkening the sand as I joined Dima in the Land-Rover to go in search of wood for a fire.

It was a strange, eerie meal, squatting there beside the carcass of the little elephant, the desert white in the moonlight and flames flickering from thorn tree branches hacked off with a panga that was part of the Land-Rover's equipment. At first Abe refused to touch the blackened meat, but when Mary said, 'For God's sake, be practical,' and began feeding him bits of her own steak, he overcame his revulsion, she watched to make certain of it, then asked me, 'What happened to Karanja? Where is he? And when I told her how he had left us the previous night, she nodded. 'So it was Karanja.' She turned to van Delden. 'It was Karanja who fired on us, wasn't it?'

He was squatting on his hunkers between Mukunga and Dima, gnawing at a rib bone. 'Could be,' he said, working round the bone with his teeth.

'But why? I don't understand why.'

He looked at her, holding the bone like a corn-cob, 'Because he's back in a different world now, and in his way he's fond of elephants.'

Abe shook his head. 'If it was Karanja, then why did he disappear like that? He must have seen you standing there.'

'He knows I don't trust him.'

'But he wanted to join you.'

'Maybe.' He tossed the bone away and reached into the embers for a piece of meat. 'He's an ex-Mission boy, you know. Clever as a vervet.'

'And handsome,' Mary whispered to me with an odd look on her face.

'After all the years I've known him I wouldn't like to say what goes on in his head. He's cunning and he never does anything without a reason. He's a bit of a showman, too.'

'But a shot like that,' Abe murmured. 'Hitting the tyre on a moving vehicle. He wouldn't have risked that with Mary driving.'

'He didn't know it was Mary, and there was no risk. He's a first-class shot. You know, when he left the Mission to join the Game Department he wasn't

good for anything but office work. Most of my boys
made fun of him, so he set out to become a better
shot than any of them. I've seen him go into a thicket
after a wounded lioness, no hesitation and grinning
all over his face. Bravado, you'd say, but not quite
that. He knew what he was doing, how sudden it
would be. You see, a lioness doesn't growl a warning
like a lion, the growl is instantaneous with the spring.
I had a touch of malaria at the time, so I didn't dare
risk it myself, too shaky. I let him have my .470 and
he dropped the animal dead, right at his feet, with a
single shot.' He wiped his hands on his beard. 'So
long as he's got an audience ... He must have an
audience.' He turned to Mtome. 'Chai. Brew up some
chai, and then we'll get going.' And he added, 'We'll
drop Dima off to keep track of those elephants, then
drive up on to the mountain. I've a feeling that's
where they're headed. There's always water on Kulal.'

There was a goatskin waterbag I hadn't noticed
before, a chargul hung on the side of the Land-Rover.
Mtome produced a blackened tin from the back and
in no time at all we were passing round an enamel
mug of hot tea.

The moon was high in the sky when we finally
left the white-boned carcass with a pile of red meat
bloodying the back of the Land-Rover. We crossed
the track again and stopped at the well, dropping the
bucket on its frayed rope into the hole. There was no
splash, no drop of water in it when we wound it up
on the cumbersome wooden roller. Dima left us here,
filling his waterbottle from the chargul and taking

some of the meat with him. 'Kambi ya mawingo,' van Delden said as he got into the driving seat, and Dima, slinging his rifle over his shoulder, waved a hand in acknowledgement as he set off after the elephants.

Van Delden sat there for a moment, watching until the lone figure had disappeared from sight. Then he started the engine. 'Kambi ya mawingo – that means the camp in the clouds. If we can get through to it, we'll stop the night there. I want to take a look into the western gorge.' We moved off then, heading westward up the track that climbed the long shoulder of the mountain, and I sat there, feeling the hot air rushing past, thinking that at least I was going to get part of what I wanted. I was going up on to the great volcanic mountain that Pieter van Delden had written about with such awe.

It was a rough ride, and it got rougher as we climbed, the surface deteriorating until we were grinding up in low gear round hairpin bends flanked by crumbling banks of earth, the disused track falling away in places to the moonwhite desert far below. High up on the shoulder, we rounded a bend and, suddenly, we were out on the lip of the world, looking down into a yawning chasm with the pale glimmer of cliffs and buttresses rising sheer on the far side. Ahead of us, the great bulk of the mountain filled the sky, half obscured by cloud, the gorge running back into it and lost in shadow.

We stopped there, all of us getting out to stand on a flat rock platform that seemed to hang in space. The bottom of the gorge was a good two thousand

feet below and deep in moonshadow. Van Delden was
scanning it through his glasses, Mukunga lying flat
on the rock, his woolly head over the edge, peering
down. 'Fantastic!' Abe murmured, sucking in his
breath at the sight of the world falling away into
darkness below us. 'Just fantastic! It must have been
one hell of an earthquake to split the mountain open
like this.' He was staring down into the depths and
he added sadly, 'No way they could climb up out of
that. No way at all.'

'The Wandrobo had a way,' van Delden said.

'You've been into that gorge, have you?'

'Once, but not right to the end.'

'Then how do you know?'

'Jack Mallinson. He was the missionary here and
he said the people of the forest used to come and go
between this gorge and the one leading down to the
lake.'

Abe shook his head. 'Mountain people maybe. But
not elephants. They'll be trapped down there.' The
way he said it conjured a picture in my mind of elephants backed up against sheer buttresses of rock and
the ring of hunters closing in.

Van Delden let his glasses fall, looking at him curiously. 'Nothing we can do about that.'

'And tomorrow, when Alex goes in after them –
where will you be?' Mary's voice was a hoarse whisper,
barely audible. 'And there's Karanja. Karanja never
liked Alex, and if he's down there —'

'You think he'd shoot him?'

She hesitated, staring at him. 'There was that man

Enderby.' She said it slowly, almost reluctantly. 'There was only you and Karanja at Marsabit when it happened. I know that now, so it was either — '

'You know nothing about it. You weren't there.' He had gripped hold of her arm, silencing her. They stood like that for a moment, facing each other. Then he let go of her, leaning down and tapping Mukunga on the shoulder. 'See anything?'

'Hapana, tembo. Is too dark.' He got to his feet.

Van Delden nodded, turning back to the track. 'We'll get moving then.'

'They won't have a chance,' Abe murmured.

'Dima will tell us what happens.'

Abe was silent then and my gaze shifted to the mountain, remembering the older van Delden, who had climbed Kulal, alone and on foot, all those years ago. But not from this direction. He had gone up from Lake Rudolf, spending six days exploring the mountain, finally driven down by starvation and the damp chill of the clouds. He'd found no traces of any civilization, only the small black people who lived in the rain forest, the Wandrobo, and they had proved hostile. Now, looking up at the huge mass of the mountain, I felt it was hopeless, like searching for a needle in a slag heap. What possible chance was there of my stumbling on some vestige of the culture that had prompted a design on pottery that might be five, ten thousand years old? This was all part of the Rift Valley, shattered by volcanic upheavals; so much could have happened in that time.

The engine of the Land-Rover started up and I

turned to find van Delden already at the wheel. 'Hurry up. We need some sleep and we've still got quite a way to go.'

The two Africans were getting into the back. Mary lingered a moment, gazing down into the gorge, her face pale in the moonlight. Then she turned abruptly and I followed her. Only Abe remained, a slight, lone figure standing on the lip of the gorge.

'Mr Finkel.'

He turned as though in a dream. 'I'm not coming,' he said. 'I'm going back.' He spoke slowly, hesitantly, and I could see by the look on his face he was appalled at his own decision. 'That gorge is nothing but a great rock trap. If somebody doesn't shift them out —'

'Don't be a fool, man,' van Delden said sharply. 'You go down into that gorge, you won't shift them out – more likely you'll get trampled to death.'

'I can at least try.' It was crazy, and he knew it. To go back down the track and into that gorge, no gun, no food, and nobody with him. It would be the first time he had been on his own in Africa.

Van Delden shrugged. 'Please yourself.'

It was then that I started to climb out. I didn't want to, but I couldn't just leave him to go off on his own. Mary caught hold of my arm. 'Don't be silly,' she hissed. But it was van Delden who stopped me, leaning out of the driving seat and speaking quietly. 'You scare them out of that gorge and tomorrow Alex will be able to run circles round them with his trucks. And if Alex doesn't kill them, then the heat will. It's hot like a furnace down there in the heat of the day.

Now, for God's sake, man, get in. Those elephants need time to recover themselves. Dima will tell us where they are when we pick him up in the morning.'

There was a long silence, Abe standing there, irresolute, a small figure dwarfed by the immense bulk of the mountain behind him. Slowly he turned his head, looking back down into the gorge. 'What is it?' Mary whispered. 'Why is he so concerned?' But I couldn't tell her. I wasn't sure myself. It could be the ghost of his dead wife he saw trapped down there. Anything seemed possible in that weird light, and when van Delden turned to me and said sharply, 'Go and get him,' I shook my head. He revved the engine then, and the sound of it shattering the stillness seemed to break Abe's reverie. He looked round, his shoulders sagging, and as though still in a dream came slowly off the rock and got into the Land-Rover without a word.

There were only a few more bends, then the track straightened out and we were approaching the Mission. Mary, close beside me, whispered, 'All my life I've wanted to come up here, but he wouldn't let me.'

'Why not?'

She shrugged and the movement of her body so close against me was disturbing. 'I was fifteen then.' She gave a little giggle. 'Perhaps he didn't trust me. It was a two-day journey from Marsabit to Kulal. It meant camping out in the desert. He sent me to school at Nairobi instead.'

We had come out on an open stretch of grassland, the clouds low and casting a dark shadow ahead. There was no wind and nothing stirred as we turned off the track, driving out on to the shoulder of the mountain where a rock outcrop stood black against the moon like a ruined castle. Below it was a waterhole that had once been used by the Mission cattle. It was fed by a pipe and there was still a steady trickle of water running out of it, but there were no cattle now. Instead, the ground was marked by the feet of elephants, the dry sered grass trampled bare and the waterhole itself a muddy wallow. 'So there is water here,' Abe said, and van Delden nodded.

'It's the forest and the proximity of the lake,' he said. 'At this height the combination of the two tends to produce cloud.'

'You knew that, and yet you let them go into that gorge when they could have come straight up the track.' Abe was staring at him accusingly. 'You could have herded them on to the track and up to the water here.'

'Maybe.' But he sounded doubtful. 'Those elephants weren't in a mood to be driven. And I didn't know what we'd find here.'

'But you said there's always water on Kulal.'

Van Delden turned on him angrily. 'Look, man, a lot has happened in this part of Africa during the last few years and Mallinson's been gone a long time. What they did to Marsabit they could have done here. As soon as I left Marsabit the bloody missionary there let the Rendile and Samburu move into the forest. Dima was there about a year ago and he says the whole mountain was bare, nothing but shambas, the lake we called Paradise dried up, most of the waterholes too.

And not an elephant to be seen.' He turned to Mukunga, who was bent down, studying the ground round the pipe. 'Any totos, Mukunga?'

'Ndio. Ndovu na watoto yao walikuwa hapa.'

'He says cows with calves have been here.' Van Delden sounded puzzled. 'I never saw any cows here before. Either they're staging through on their way north, or else some of my elephants have moved in from Marsabit.'

'I thought you said they couldn't cross the Chalbi.'

'Not now they couldn't. But once in a while it rains. They could have crossed then.'

Mtome had started to fill the goatskin bag from the pure clear water running out of the pipe and I was thinking of all those tribesmen we had seen, their cattle and their camels dead. 'Why didn't the tribes move up here?' I asked him.

'They're desert people and Kulal is cold and damp. Most of them are afraid of the mountains anyway.'

'But the Mission had cattle.'

'The Mission was closed at the start of the African war.' Mtome had finished filling the waterbag and van Delden went over to the pipe, drinking from it in his cupped hands, then sluicing it over his face and neck, and Abe, standing beside him and waiting his turn, said, 'Would you recognize your elephants if you saw them now?'

'Of course.'

'After more than two years? It's at least two years since you had to leave.'

'Nearer three. But I'd still know them. And they'd know me.'

'I'm told you can talk to them.'

Van Delden straightened up smiling. 'You don't want to believe all you hear, Mr Finkel. I can imitate some of their rumblings, but the vocabulary, if you can call it that, is limited. I wouldn't be able to enquire of a cow how she's got here, for instance.' He turned back to the Land-Rover. 'Leave it at that, shall we? We'll know soon enough.'

Abe followed him, his voice persistent. 'And if they were yours, how would you know? By earmarkings, or have you some other method?'

'Sometimes by the way they move, the tone of their rumblings, squeals and growls. But earmarks are the most reliable method.'

'Those could have changed in three years.'

'More rents and tears, yes. But the old marks still remain.'

We were all back in the Land-Rover then and he had started the engine. Abe leaned forward, his voice urgent. 'So if there was a big, very recognizable tear, you don't reckon it would have changed?'

'No, I don't.' Van Delden glanced back at him, a gleam of interest in his eyes. 'You've seen one of those elephants we were following before, is that it?'

Abe hesitated, then nodded reluctantly.

'Where?' van Delden asked him.

'At Treetops. It was a long time ago.'

Van Delden looked at him a moment, then smiled. 'So that's why you didn't want to eat from that calf.

It was the mother, was it?' And as he let in the clutch, heading back to the track, he said, 'That rent won't have changed much. Point her out to me if we come across her again.'

The Mission was set on a rise above the track. The sprawl of wooden single-storey buildings had a dramatic appearance in the changing light, the moon coming and going as outlying veils of the cloudcap shifted. There was foliage growing through the roofs, no paint anywhere and the veranda of one building almost completely collapsed. Where the track bent round to the right, towards some store-sheds, van Delden stopped to sit gazing at what was obviously a staff cottage. It had been a pretty place at one time, but now the roof was sagging and all one end of it had collapsed inwards. 'Elephant,' he murmured. Then turning to Abe, he said, 'That was Jack Mallinson's place. He, and the man before him, were very conscious of the ecological importance of the forest. If the forest were cut down, then there would be no cloud over Kulal, no rain, just wind erosion, the sort of thing that's happened at Marsabit, at Meru and the Aberdares, all over the country. That's why the water is piped, so the cattle had no excuse to invade the forest. It was quite a job for a Mission to undertake, out on a limb here with supplies a major problem.'

'And there weren't any elephants here then?' Abe asked.

'The odd bull, that's all Jack and I ever saw. I used to come regularly at one time to check on the greater kudu. It's a good place for kudus. But this mountain isn't like Marsabit. The altitude there is much lower and no storms.'

He turned his head away, staring at the black impenetrable shadow ahead of us. 'Now we go into the forest. It's about six miles and if elephants have taken up permanent residence it may be slow going with a lot of tree shifting.' He flicked the headlights to high beam and put the Land-Rover in 4-wheel drive as we ploughed left through the remains of a gate and down a vague track surfaced with the soft mould of forest humus, the moon suddenly obscured by the leaf canopy that had closed over us.

At first it was easy going, but in less than a mile we were bashing our way through a close thicket of reed-like stems. 'Like driving through corn,' Abe said as we crouched low to avoid the springing stems and flying debris. Twice Mtome got out to hack a way through with the panga, but after we had ploughed through the swamp of a stream bed, the track climbed again and we were slipping and sliding on mud-covered boulders. It was like that for perhaps another mile, our progress slow but steady, then quite suddenly we were into an area of forest that had obviously been browsed over by elephants. Their droppings were everywhere and as we laboured up the track, mud to our knees, clearing the fallen trees ahead of the Land-Rover, we became covered with mud and dung slime. Fortunately it was all fairly small timber we had to shift, but by the time we were through the area and back on to almost clear track again, I was feeling utterly exhausted. Mary, who had been working just as hard as any of us, simply went to sleep.

Shortly after that we joined another track, turning left and climbing steadily along what seemed to be the crest of the mountain. The trees were taller now, the going firmer, less mud and no boulders, only elephant turds that sometimes looked like small boulders in the headlights. We stayed in 4-wheel drive, but moving fast, for there were no trees across the track, just the brash of stripped and broken branches. It was very dark here in this high forest, dark and dank and no sign of the moon. We were into the cloud now and the contrast between this and the dry desert country far below was such that I had a feeling of intense anticipation. I don't know what I expected, but my tiredness was gone as I leaned forward, straining to see beyond the headlights, feeling that if I watched closely some marvellous revelation would leap into view.

I think perhaps I was a little light-headed. The only thing of note we saw was one of the sacred trees. It was a giant of tremendous girth and van Delden, pointing it out to us, said that the people of the forest believed that if ever those trees were destroyed it would be the end of the world. 'It's a taboo that Jack Mallinson always respected. The Wandrobo would never survive the destruction of the forest.'

'Have you ever met them?' I asked him, thinking that if I were to find the needle of that old civilization it could only be through the people whose home it was.

But he shook his head. 'Jack knew them, of course. He was always walking the forest alone. He loved it. Occasionally one of the few safaris that made it to the top of Kulal would report food or clothing missing, but they never caught sight of the thieves. The Wandrobo know their forest and they move like shadows in the mist. They're a very secretive — '

The brakes slammed on, throwing us forward. And then we were roaring backwards, two grey shapes in the headlights, their heads up and their trunks tucked underneath their tusks as they charged us. They were gaining, the two of them shoulder to shoulder and filling the track. I could see their feet moving, but there was no sound, no trumpeting, only the noise of the engine. Rotting undergrowth cracked under our wheels and suddenly we were flung to the floor as the back of the Land-Rover smacked into the bole of a tree. We stopped dead, the engine stalled. Van Delden switched the lights off, everything black and no sound.

I didn't know what was going to happen and I just lay there, not daring to move. And then they trumpeted. The sound of it was startling in the stillness and very close, the most terrifying sound I thought I had ever heard. The lights came on and over my shoulder I could see the pair of them standing on the track with their trunks curled upwards and the eyes in their great domed heads glinting as they stared into the headlights. The starter whined, the engine came to life and then we were driving straight at them, the horn blaring and van Delden swinging the wheel over as we hit the track. I had a glimpse of the two heads towering over us, the bright ivory of their tusks and their trunks writhing, then we were past them and driving furiously along the track.

Nobody spoke as we sorted ourselves out. I could still see the black outline of Mukunga in the front, still with his rifle gripped ready in his hands. Van Delden turned his head and laughed. 'All right in the back? You all right, Toto?'

'I'm okay, Tembo. We're all okay.' She was laughing, too, as she gripped my arm and said, 'You're trembling like a leaf. Wait till the engine doesn't start and they're leaning over you, ramming their tusks into the bodywork.' Her grip was hard, her eyes glinting with excitement, and close beside me Abe's voice asked, 'What were they, bulls or cows?'

'Cows,' van Delden said.

'From Marsabit? Could you recognize them?'

'In that light and with them charging us?' He laughed. 'Not a chance.' And he added, 'Cows don't usually charge like that, without any warning at all. Wonder where it was they got such a bellyful of man that it changed their nature.' He was driving slower and both he and Mukunga were peering cautiously ahead. Once he stopped and switched off the engine, but there was no sound, the forest wrapped in its shroud of mist.

A little further on the trees fell away and we were into a clearing that was like a meadow climbing steeply up to the left of the track. Shadows moved in the mist and we stopped again. Beside us a pool of water had been trampled into mud and above it the grass of the slope was beaten flat. 'Kambi ya mawingo,' van Delden said. 'But no good to us. It's already occupied.' Vague shapes loomed beyond the headlights, their outlines blurred by the light drizzle that was falling. 'We'll have to camp on the open slopes.' The engine roared again and we shot across the clearing and into the dark tunnel of the trees on the far side, elephants moving like shadows and the track littered with broken branches so that we were crashing through a sea of half dead foliage.

Gradually the debris thinned until finally the track was almost clear, the forest normal again and only the football-sized heaps of dung indicating that it had been used by elephants. The trees were smaller now and thinning out. Suddenly we were at the end of the track, a deep trench running across it. Van Delden backed the Land-Rover into the undergrowth and switched off. Darkness enveloped us and a great stillness, only the faint sound of moisture dripping from the leaves. 'What now?' Abe asked and there was a tenseness in his voice.

Van Delden got out. 'We go on foot now. A few hundred yards, that's all. Put on all the clothes you've got. It will be a cold night.'

It was a relief to get into our sweaters, for we were already chilled by the drive. Mary wrapped herself in a blanket he found for her under the front seat and then we skirted the trench, climbing through a tracery of thin-stemmed growth. It was, as he had said, about two hundred yards, and suddenly we were out in the open and there was grass beneath our feet. The cloud cover was thinner here, the moon's light filtering through. Just clear of the forest we cut branches and lit a fire, huddling close to it, grateful for the warmth and drinking scalding hot tea from a single tin mug passed from hand to hand. Incredibly it was still only just after midnight. We seemed to have been travelling for hours.

But tiredness did not seem to have dampened Abe's curiosity. 'How long can the forest support that number of elephants?' he asked.

Van Delden shook his head. 'To answer that requires a proper count, and we don't know how much of the forage is suitable. Not all of it, I suspect. Like I told you, Kulal has never been a natural habitat for elephants.'

'It's a staging post on their way north, is that what you're saying?'

'Possibly.' Van Delden took out his pipe and began to fill it. 'That's what I need to know.'

'And if they're just passing through, then they must have a way up and a way down. Isn't that right?'

'It's logical. But animals are directed by instinct, not logic.'

'Are you sure? Would instinct alone be directing them north? It's a time of crisis for them and you said yourself they could be heading north because of some deep-seated knowledge. That's not instinct. That's something passed on from generation to generation. Or maybe it's imprinted in their genes.'

'It's all speculation.' A match flared, the hook-nosed bearded face momentarily lit as he put it to his pipe. The tobacco smoke was comfortingly normal in the strangeness of that place. 'There was an elephant at Marsabit – Ahmen. The biggest tusker anyone had ever seen. He was under the protection of Jomo Kenyatta. The one elephant whose ivory was safe. That was before the war, when Kenya was still a separate country. He was reckoned to be more than seventy years old when he died. That's a lot longer than most of them live. The average is about fifty years. But even fifty years, you go back three generations and you're back before the South African war, before Rhodes and the main drive of the English settlers.' He was silent for a moment, drawing on his pipe. Then he said, 'They can communicate, that I know. But what they can communicate is a different matter. The knowledge of safe territory is very abstract information compared with danger warnings, behavioural instructions, food satisfaction.'

Abe nodded, taking out a packet of cigarettes and staring at it thoughtfully. It was his last packet and there were only three left. He put it away, sniffing the smoke from van Delden's pipe. 'How many conversational sounds have you identified?' he asked.

'About forty.'

'And they're all concerned with ordinary everyday things like food and behaviour?'

'Those I have identified, yes.'

'What about extra-sensory perception?'

'I'm not an animal psychiatrist.'

'Meaning you don't believe in it?'

'I stick to what I know, that's all. Things like

telepathy . . .' He was staring into the fire, fingering his beard. 'I just don't know. Anybody who's lived close to animals has observed patterns of behaviour they can't explain.'

'So you've no idea why they're moving north, why there's this concentration of them up here?'

He puffed out a stream of smoke and shook his head. 'Any observation I made now would only be guesswork. It could be that roaming bulls remember Marsabit as a safe area, nothing more complicated than that. But to switch to Kulal would mean they also know that Marsabit can no longer support them.' He shook his head, silent then and gazing thoughtfully into the fire. 'Inherited memory, a built-in survival instinct. I don't know what makes them head north, but that's what they're doing. And if there's a way up out of that gorge—' He tapped his pipe and got to his feet. 'We'll see what Dima has to tell us in the morning.' He said something about having used a lot of fuel on the way up, but by then I was so drowsy I could no longer keep my eyes open. Mary was already asleep, curled up in her blanket, and in the glow of the embers Mukunga lay on his back with his mouth open, snoring gently.

I stretched out on the grass, already half asleep, firelight flickering on my eyelids as Mtome added more branches. The sound of voices came to me as a vague murmur, but I was lost to the world and no longer heard what they said.

Maybe I dreamed. But I don't think so. I was too tired to dream. I woke with a piercing scream still ringing in my ears. My heart was pounding in my throat and I was shivering. The fire was glowing faintly, but there was no warmth in it. A breeze was stirring in the trees behind and it was cold, a damp chill. I knew instantly where I was, who the bodies stretched out around me. Nobody else had stirred. No sound anywhere now and stars showing through a ragged gap in the clouds above. Something moved in the shadow of the trees. The light from the moon momentarily increased and I thought I saw a figure standing erect and covered in hair. I sat up, fear clutching at me, my mind leaping from the Wandrobo to yetis and all the stories I had read of wild primitives found on mountains. Again that piercing cry, a scream of rage and fear that made the hair crawl on my neck. The figure had vanished.

I sat there, shivering and staring at the forest. But the gap in the clouds had closed and all was dark again. 'Baboon.' The voice so close beside me was quietly reassuring. In the glow of the embers I could just see his bearded face, one eye open and his teeth showing in a smile. 'I should have warned you.'

'It looked so big,' I murmured.

'Yes, they're very big up here. They live in the gorge.'

'I thought we'd left the gorge miles away.'

'Kulal is full of gorges.' The eye closed and I lay down again.

The next thing I knew dawn had broken and Mtome was trying to rekindle the fire with wet branches cut from the undergrowth close by. It was a grey dawn shrouded in mist, the grass beaded with moisture and falling away from us in a smooth down-land sweep that vanished into a veil of cloud. I lay there clinging to the last vestiges of sleep, too cold to move. Somewhere the sun was shining, our opaque world beginning to glimmer with a strange iridescence.

Mary came out of the bushes looking like a squaw with the blanket draped round her shoulders and her black hair hanging damp and straight. 'There's a breeze,' she said.

I could feel it on my face then. Flames flickered in the piled-up branches and overhead the mist swirled, the sun's iridescent glow coming and going. Away to our right a phantom pile of rock appeared in the sky. It was there for a moment, a disembodied peak hanging in space, then it was swallowed up again in the slow gyration of the clouds. Van Delden sat up, beard and hair glistening with moisture. 'What's the time?'

'Gone eight.' The mist had lifted and she was standing looking out across the grassy slopes to where they ended abruptly at a fringe of small rock outcrops. 'I want to see the lake,' she said. 'We'd be able to see it from here, wouldn't we?'

'If the cloud shifts,' van Delden said.

'It's shifting now and it's only thin stuff. The sun will soon burn it off.'

'Maybe, but Kulal is unpredictable, and it's the gorge I came to see.'

Abe sat up abruptly. 'You think those elephants could have made it across into this gorge?'

'It leads down to the lake and if we get a

breeze—' Van Delden glanced up at the thin layer of mist covering the sun. 'Dima will be at the Mission now, but he can wait. We'll breakfast here and see if it lifts.'

I got up then and went into the bushes. Abe followed me. 'I didn't sleep much, did you?' His face looked thin and drawn.

'The baboon woke me.'

'What baboon? I didn't hear any baboon.'

'You were dead to the world. It practically screamed in your ear.'

He laughed. 'I guess I did get some sleep then. But I didn't feel as though I did. I was worrying about those elephants, and about Karanja. You think it was Karanja fired those shots?'

'Van Delden seems to think so.' A pale shaft of sunlight came through the branches. 'Dima may be able to tell us something.' And I went quickly out into the open again. It was warmer now, patches of blue sky and the mist blowing in the wind. The others were all standing by the fire, gazing down the grass slopes to where they ran out over the lip of a gorge. More and more of those grass slopes were slowly unveiled, the gash of the gorge smoking with mist, pinnacles of rock appearing and disappearing. Then suddenly the veil of humidity was swept aside and far below us Lake Rudolf emerged, a great expanse of water running north and south, bright in sunlight. There was an island, brown and bare, all lava, and the far shore just visible as a line of cliffs. The lake itself was pale blue and flecked with white.

'The Jade Sea,' Mary murmured. 'But it's blue not green.'

It was like that for a moment, an astounding, unbelievable revelation. Then the mist closed in again and it was gone, the glimpse so brief I could scarcely believe that what I had seen was real, clouds swirling over the sun.

'How far below us?' Her voice was still entranced.

'About six thousand feet,' he said.

'Kulal is higher than that.'

'The peak lies north-east of us, the other side of the gorge. We're a good bit lower here.'

'And the gorge runs down to Loiyangalani?'

'It's the water from that gorge that makes it an oasis.'

She turned, staring rapt at the mist rolling along the lip of it. 'I'm going to have a look.'

He nodded absently, fingering his pipe. The brew tin was boiling and Mtome, sitting cross-legged in front of the fire like a black priest at some primitive rite, threw in a handful of tea. Baby elephant steaks sizzled on their sticks, the embers blazing momentarily as the mist came down again so that Mary became a ghostly figure walking into an opaque void. 'Last night,' van Delden murmured, sucking at his empty pipe and looking sideways at Abe, 'I was thinking. No elephant droppings on the track up the mountain. Did you notice any droppings?'

'Not till we got to the Mission.' A sudden gleam of interest showed on Abe's face. 'You mean there is a way up out of that eastern gorge?'

'A lot of elephants have been through the forest here and they didn't come up the Mission road.' He nodded. 'Yes, that's what I was thinking. This must be the route they're taking, all of them.' He stared into the fire a moment, then slapped his hand against his side, turning to Abe again, the great head thrust forward, the pale eyes gleaming. 'If that's the case, then elephants have a built-in survival sense, that draws on the experience of previous generations. Exactly what you were talking about last night. I've never seen elephants on the shores of Lake Rudolf. There haven't been any there in my lifetime. But, according to von Höhnel, Teleki was shooting at them in the water there and they were feeding on the lakeweed. How could animals far to the south of here know there was weed in that lake, or even that Rudolf existed?'

'They couldn't,' Abe said. 'It's either intuition or inherited memory.'

'Or else the sounds they make are capable of expressing more than I had thought. Some wandering bull . . .' Mtome handed him the tin mug full of tea and he passed it on to Abe. 'A form of telepathy?' He shook his head. 'That's getting close to your extra-sensory perception.'

'I guess we have to accept,' Abe said slowly, blowing on the tea, 'that there are some forms of communication unknown to us. Or perhaps forgotten by us in our civilized materialism.'

Van Delden grunted sceptically, his eyes shifting towards the gorge. The mist had closed right down on us, no sign of Mary, nothing but the damp green of the coarse grass. He called to Mukunga, who was dragging some more branches towards the fire and he dropped them and hurried off into the mist. I followed him, hoping the mist would lift again. I don't think I would have risked it on my own, but I wanted to see down into that gorge. Behind me I heard Abe say, 'Birds and migration, elvers, the young salmon – I guess we don't know so very much after all.' But when I glanced back over my shoulder the two of them had been swallowed up and only the glow of the embers showed dull red through the thick cloud blanket that enveloped the mountain. From somewhere far away there came a faint cry. It fell away into echoing cries smothered by distance and humidity. 'Nyani,' Mukunga said, the wizened face grinning at me. But he moved faster after that so that I was almost trotting. The grass ended, rock emerging, and he stopped abruptly, the ground falling away in a series of ledges and outcrops. The cry of the baboons was louder now, echoing up from below.

'Where is she?'

He raised his hand, listening, and then Mary's voice, away to the left: 'Is that you, Colin?'

She appeared suddenly, her figure taking on substance as she climbed up out of a fold in the gorge edge. 'Phlumps,' she said, her eyes sparkling, her face fresh with exertion and the moisture in the air, 'I'm sure I saw phlumps, then the bloody cloud clamped down.'

A breeze touched my face, the opaque void at my feet shifting, the greyness glimmering. She pushed her damp hair back from her face. 'They were on a sort of island, a mile, maybe two miles down the gorge. It was there for a moment only, floating in the mist and bright green in a shaft of sunlight. They were on the slopes, just grey lumps like rocks. But I saw them move – I'm sure they moved.'

'Then there must be a way down.' Or did this gorge link with the one we had seen last night? 'Are you sure they were elephants, not baboons?'

'Don't be silly. I was brought up with them and I'm long-sighted.' Her face was suddenly clouded. 'Do you think they were the ones we were following? If it's all one great gorge, the mountain slashed in two—' I knew what she was thinking, that if the elephants could get through then so could the hunters. She lifted her head. 'Look! The sun.' And she turned to me, laughter lighting her face. 'Now, at this moment, all I care about is that the world is beautiful. This mist, this gorge, everything—' She hesitated, looking at the mist flowing now like a river down the gorge. 'Strange,' she murmured. 'Back down where we've come from it's all heat, sand and lava, the harshness of life – reality. And up here—' She turned to me again, smiling. 'Let's forget about reality, shall we? Just enjoy this moment.'

I nodded, not sure what she expected, conscious of the mist flowing past us, brightening as the washed-out orb of the sun scintillated on a myriad airborne droplets, feeling my blood respond to the vitality that emanated from her. 'Look!' She was pointing up the gorge and I turned to see the peak I had glimpsed earlier floating again, disembodied, high against a pastel blue sky. But this time it did not disappear.

The wind was strong now. I could feel the weight of it against my body, could see it blowing her dark hair back from her face. A shaft of sunlight swept across the grass, the slopes spreading further and further, a downward sweep of incredible, brilliant green. Mukunga moved, craning forward. He said something and then went scrambling down the rocks, sure-footed as a goat, to stand on a final outcrop, peering down.

'He thinks he saw somebody.'

'A man?'

'He's not sure. Maybe a baboon.' She had turned away from me, staring down the gorge, watching as the sun burned the clouds up and the wind tore them into fragments. 'There!' Her island had appeared, a jagged pinnacle of rock and grass swimming in a white sea of cotton wool. 'See them?' She was pointing. 'Pity we didn't bring the glasses.'

Grey shapes dotted the emerging slopes, but whether elephants or rocks I could not be sure. I was too busy searching the summit, where exposed rock topped the whole green pyramid like a castle or small walled city. But it was too far away to make out whether there were any vestiges of human habitation. The gorge was opening out further and further, the clouds breaking up into isolated wisps, the glimmer of the distant lake beginning to show through. Mukunga called to us, scrambling back up the rocks. 'What's he say?' I asked.

She shook her head. 'I couldn't hear.'

Behind us van Delden's voice said, 'So there are elephants down there.' He had his glasses to his eyes and was chewing on a piece of meat. 'Half a dozen at least, one or two half grown. What's Mukunga up to?'

'I think he's seen something,' she said.

'Better get some grub,' he told her. 'Time we were moving.'

The baboons were quiet now. No sound except the blowing of the wind, and the lake becoming clearer, a gleaming sheet of bright water on the edge of visibility. I could feel the sun now, grateful for the warmth of it. 'Can I have a look through the glasses?'

He handed them to me, but though I searched every rock on the top of that tooth of worn volcanic debris I could see nothing that belonged to man. Two young elephants, bulls I think, were flexing their muscles, bodies straining to the thrust of head and tusk, locking in mock battle, and close beside them a cow suckled a half grown calf. It was all very peaceful, a relief to watch after what I had seen near South Horr, and behind me I heard Mukunga talking quickly, explaining something in his own tongue. 'He thinks he saw two men climbing up out of the gorge.' And van Delden added, 'Could be Wandrobo, or perhaps Samburu. The Samburu used to graze their cattle on the lower slopes.' He turned to Mukunga, questioning him. The word nyani passed between them, and in the end he shrugged. 'It could have been baboons. He's not certain. There was a lot of foliage and he only caught a glimpse.' He turned to Mary. 'Your tea will be getting stewed.'

She nodded, staring down the gorge. But the wind was dying as fast as it had risen, clouds like wreaths of smoke eddying around the green sloped pinnacle, the elephants lost to view. We started back then, the sun already half obscured and the top of Kulal disappearing in a bank of cloud. 'It was down there in that gorge,' I said to van Delden, 'that your father made some of his pottery finds.'

'Where exactly?' But I could tell by the tone of his voice he wasn't really interested.

'I can show you on the map,' I said. 'It gives the position of all his finds.' He didn't say anything and I asked him whether he could talk to the Wandrobo if they had been Wandrobo down there in the gorge.

'I think Dima could. He's a Boran and familiar with the people of this area. But I certainly can't, nor can Mukunga.' He strode ahead then, calling to Mtome, and Mary said quietly, 'Pottery doesn't interest him and he hated his father.'

'Then why did he ask me to lug the typescript and the map with me?'

She shrugged. 'Perhaps he thought it could tell him something about Kulal, or Lake Rudolf – something he doesn't know.'

'Such as?'

'Elephants,' she said, grinning at me. 'Or water. Some spring he doesn't know about, and elephants do.'

We reached the fire just as the mist drove down

over us again, thicker than ever, and I sat there drinking tea and chewing on a great hunk of meat, wondering why I hadn't the guts to walk off into the mist. There must be a way down into the gorge, and if I could meet up with the people of the forest who knew the mountain . . . I pictured myself being taken by little dark men to a peak of rock, the mist lifting like a veil to reveal some strange primeval stone wall, the sort of wall the Incas built. But it was just fantasy. I was daydreaming, knowing very well I would never survive without van Delden and his Africans. And so, when they started packing up and moving along the edge of the forest, back towards the Land-Rover, I went with them, carrying the bag with the film and the typescript in it.

'Why didn't you go and see what you could find in the gorge?' there was laughter in her eyes, a glint of mockery. She guessed what I had been thinking.

'How did you know?'

'What else could you be thinking about with such a lost, dreamy look on your face? Well, why didn't you?'

'Because I don't have that sort of nerve,' I said angrily.

'Suppose I got hold of a rifle?'

'And came with me?'

She nodded, her eyes bright and I didn't know whether she was serious or just fooling. 'I'm a pretty good shot. At least I used to be.'

But we were into the forest now, slithering down the muddy game trail in single file. Through the small-stemmed trees I could see the trench. It was deeper than I had realized, a vertical-sided gash with a water pipe still visible at the bottom, the same pipe that served the Mission. Beyond it the bonnet of the Land-Rover gleamed wet behind its screen of leaves. We piled into it and got going, but we were hardly out on to the track when the engine coughed and died. The fuel gauge showed the tank empty and I asked van Delden what the reading had been when he had taken it over.

'More than half full, say ten gallons. He's sure to have had an extra tank fitted in place of the tool box.'

We could hardly have used that much, and while Mtome unclipped the spare jerrican, I jumped out and crawled underneath, cleaning the mud off the tank with my bare hands. There was some rusting, but it was a dent in the side welding at the base of the tank that produced a reek of petrol on my fingers. 'We snagged it on a branch or a piece of rock,' I called up.

'I was afraid of that,' van Delden said. 'We were using too much on the way up.' And he added, 'More likely one of those bullets ricocheted.'

We found some electrical tape in a toolbox in the back and bound it up as best we could. But I didn't think it would last and the spare jerrican was barely two-thirds full, so we had only about three gallons. At kambi ya mawingo we had to wait for a big tusked bull to finish showering himself at the spring. The sun was shining then, the grass slope glistening with moisture, steaming in the heat, and there were yellow swallow-tailed butterflies sunning themselves on the broken bushes close beside us.

It was very quiet as we sat watching the elephant syphoning the water up with his trunk and squirting it over his head and back, everything done in slow motion and time standing still. 'Look! A turaco,' Mary whispered. It was staring down at us from the branch of a tree, its body bright green with a splash of red on its wing, the black head cocked. Below it a sunbird flashed a brilliant emerald, its curved beak darting. It was a place of extraordinary peace. But then the bull began to move, ambling silently up the slope, and we drove into the dark of tall timber beyond the spring.

Where the track forked, and we came off the spine of the mountain, it was all downhill and we made it to the Mission in about half an hour, thrashing our way through the debris of broken branches without any hold-up. There was no sign of Dima, the Mission deserted and nobody answering the blare of our horn. 'Have a look at that tank,' van Delden said, and he and his two Africans started up the slope to the Mission buildings.

The tape hung in tatters and I could smell the leak before I had even touched it with my finger. Mukunga was hallooing up the slope and above me Abe said, 'Maybe he went up to that clearing.' I called to Mary to pass me a rag and the remains of the tape, and I was still lying there under the chassis, cleaning the mud off the fuel tank, when I thought I heard the sound of something far away. Mukunga had stopped calling, everything quiet again except for a distant bee-like drone. 'Can you hear anything?' I asked.

There was silence, then Mary said, 'Sounds like an engine.'

'Coming up the road?'

'No. No, it seems to be above us.'

I finished the taping and when I crawled out from under the Land-Rover, I could hear it quite clearly, the drone of an engine high up on the mountain. 'Must be a plane,' Abe said. Van Delden had heard it too. He was standing by the broken veranda staring up at the sky. 'There!' Mary was pointing and I saw it then, coming low over the forested slopes, its wings tilted slightly as it banked and headed straight for us, the sound of it growing until the roar of it was sweeping over us. It was so low I felt the rush of it through the air, saw the Federation markings and the face of the pilot looking down at us.

It was a twin-engined monoplane and as it zoomed over the Mission buildings, it tipped over on to one wing, sliding round in a tight turn. 'Was that Murphy?' Abe was staring up, shading his eyes with his hands. 'It was an Army plane and I thought . . .' His words were drowned in the noise of it passing low over the Mission. It climbed steadily above the forest, dwindling until it was a bright metallic speck glinting in the sun. 'I'm sure it was Murphy.'

And then van Delden was back. 'Mary, and you, Mr Finkel – quick get out. I'm leaving you here, all three of you.' He turned to me. 'How's that leak?' And when I told him, he said, 'It doesn't matter. It's all downhill now and what's left in the tank wouldn't get me back up again.'

The plane was coming back, drifting down with its nose almost at the point of stall, its engines throttled right back. And as it glided over us something white fluttered down from the open cockpit window and I saw Pat Murphy wave to us. Then he boosted the engines and went zooming up, turning and heading away down the line of the gorge. What he had dropped was his handkerchief, and tied into one corner of it was a message: *K-S plus Army support moving Kulal E gorge. Advice proceed Marsabit fastest. Radio-ing report abandoned Land-Rover Kulal Mission. Good luck, Pat. (Destroy)*

Van Delden read it out to us, then put a match to it. 'I'll come with you,' Abe said. He knew – we all knew – he was going down into the gorge. But he shook his head. Mtome was already unloading the remains of the meat, Mukunga checking the rifles and ammunition. 'You'll stay here, the three of you. I don't know what's happened to Dima, but when he turns up tell him to wait for me here.' He was already moving round to the driver's seat. 'Get that meat cooked right away, then take it into the forest with you and hide up. They're bound to send a patrol.'

'What are you going to do?' Mary was still sitting in the back of the Land-Rover, and the tone of her voice, the frozen look on her face, the way she sat, bolt upright, her body tense, her hands clenched – I knew what she was thinking. 'Please,' she said. 'Go back into the forest. Go back, before it's too late.'

He stood there, looking at her a moment, his big head hunched into the massive shoulders, the grey hairs of his chest showing in the gap of his half-buttoned bush jacket. 'I've never run away from anything in my life.'

'But you can't do anything.' The words came desperately, as though trying to break the barrier of his obstinacy with the strength of her own emotions. 'Please. For my sake.'

He shook his head, a slow, angry movement. 'When he stops killing elephants, then I'll go. Not before.'

'I'll come with you. I'll talk to him.'

Again he shook his head. Then, in a surprisingly gentle voice, he said, 'Nothing you can do. We are all of us born the way we are.' He smiled, the smile creasing his eyes, lightening the hard lines of his face. 'You stay and wait for me here. I'll be back by nightfall. Now get out, there's a good girl.'

'I'm coming with you.'

'No.' He reached out, gripping hold of her arm, his voice harder now: 'I'm in a hurry.'

She shook her head dumbly, her eyes wide, her body straining back from the grip of his hand. 'No. You're going to kill him.'

'Not if I can stop him some other way.' He was staring at her, knowing now that it was her father she was thinking of, not him, his pale eyes hardening, the softness gone from his voice as he said, 'You'll do as you're told, wait here – and if I don't come back, then you can join him and hunt down the fleeing remnants of East Africa's elephants.' He leaned forward, taking hold of her with both hands and lifting her bodily out of the Land-Rover. And when her feet were on the ground, he put his arm around her shoulders the way he had done with Karanja on the Baringo track and said gently, 'It's not your fault, Toto. Just wait here, and pray for us. Pray for both of us.' He bent his head down and kissed her forehead. 'Whatever happens, you mustn't feel you're to blame.'

He let go of her then, calling to Mtome and Mukunga and climbing in behind the wheel. The engine started, the two Africans piling in. 'Deal with that meat now,' he shouted. 'Then watch for the patrol. And keep hidden.' He gunned the engine and the Land-Rover went roaring off down the track trailing a cloud of dust. She stood there, not saying anything, not moving, just watching as he disappeared round the first bend. She stood there until the dust had settled, then turned slowly as though in a dream, her face pale and drawn, and in a small, vague voice she said, 'It's always been like that, all my life.' And I knew she was referring to van Delden going off and leaving her to wait.

'He'll get those elephants out of the gorge somehow,' Abe said. It was meant to soothe her fears, but the lack of conviction in his voice only increased them.

'How?'

He shrugged, smiling vaguely. 'I guess he'll find a way.'

'And the Army? What about the Army?' She was still staring at us, her fingers twining nervously. And then she laughed, a high, uncertain sound, and she smiled wistfully. 'The trouble is I love him. With all his faults, his obsession, his stupid, bloody obstinacy, his ruthless disregard for other people – I can't help it, I love him.' She sighed. 'Something he'll never know.' And she added bitterly, 'Even if he did, he'd never understand.'

There was nothing Abe or I could say, no comfort we could give her, the three of us just standing there in silence. 'Well, I guess he can look after himself,' Abe said awkwardly.

'Oh yes, he can do that all right.' She gave a false, bright little laugh. 'He's over sixty and never suffered anything worse than a few knife wounds and his shoulder mauled by a man-eater, so why worry about him, or about Alex? What is written is written.' She seemed to come to life then, moving quickly towards us, and in a firm practical voice she said, 'Come on, better get that meat over a fire before it's crawling with maggots.'

CHAPTER THREE

There was a strange atmosphere about the Mission, the wood of the buildings eaten away by termites and the forest moving in, the marks of animals and their droppings everywhere. As at the Lodge during the Conference, we were interlopers in a complex that had been built for a specific purpose, but here the sense of abandonment was overwhelming, our footsteps resounding in an emptiness that was full of the ghostly relics of a community dedicated to Christianity. And the disintegration of the fabric was not the result of war; it was time and the silent invasion of nature that had left its mark, so that I felt no sense of violation. But the sadness of all that hopeful endeavour wasted made it a strangely depressing place and I think we were all glad to get away from it, to the edge of the forest where we had a view of the road and the waterhole, and the Mission buildings were out of sight.

We got a fire going, and while Mary was dealing

with the remains of the meat, I walked across the open grassland to fill the plastic water container we had found in the abandoned kitchens. The area round the pipe was so thick with mud and the slime of animal droppings that before wading into it I removed my boots and socks and rolled up my trousers. It was hot in the sunshine, and when I had filled the container I stripped off my shirt and ducked my head under the pipe, sluicing the clear cool water on to the stubble of my face, letting it run over my back, thinking how marvellous it was that there should be water up here on Kulal when all this Northern Region was dying of drought. And afterwards I ran barefooted up the slope to the ridge above. Crouched among the rocks, I had a clear view of the road running in hairpins down the ochre-coloured shoulder of the mountain to the plain below.

I lay there for quite some time, the sun drying my bare back and all that empty, desert-yellow country hazed with heat, the mountains of the Mara shimmering in the distance. But though I strained my eyes against the glare, there was nothing visible, no movement except here and there the dancing whirl of a sand devil. It was all emptiness, no stir of dust from a moving vehicle, the road up the mountain empty, too. And having satisfied myself of that, I relaxed, enjoying the solitude, the feeling of being raised up on a pinnacle of unbelievable remoteness, a world apart untouched by man. And behind me the mountain with its primeval forest, the source of water and of the storms that lashed the lake. Lying there, I felt I didn't care if I never returned to civilization.

It was only gradually, and with a sense of reluctance, that I acknowledged the sound of distant shouting and turned my head. A small herd of buffaloes, black in the sunlight, stood motionless halfway between the forest and the waterpoint, their heads all facing towards the haze of smoke hanging over our fire.

I got to my feet, then sat down abruptly, conscious that I was alone and unarmed, cut off from the others. The calls had ceased, but the buffaloes remained with their heads up, all staring at the still figures by the fire. There was no suggestion of hostility, only an intent watchfulness, and they looked so ordinary, like long-horned cattle.

At last they moved, flowing in a black tide to surround the waterpoint, trampling the mud under their hoofs as they jostled each other to get at the source of the water. There was nothing I could do except sit there and wait for them to go. One of them, having drunk its fill, moved on to where I had left the container, sniffing at it with a wet nose, nuzzling my boots. Something moved on the edge of the forest, a muddy shape pushing through the leaves, and an elephant emerged, moving slowly with that soft, silent tread that seemed to cover the ground without contact. It saw the buffaloes and paused, fanning its ears, its trunk exploring the grass irresolutely. Then it glided slowly forward, and with much snorting and backing the buffaloes made room for it. The scene reminded me of Abe describing the salt lick at Tree-tops, for though both the buffaloes and the elephant demonstrated, there was nothing positively aggressive in their behaviour. The elephant was putting the top of its trunk to the pipe, sucking at the water, and then transferring it to its mouth, and when it had drunk its fill, it began spraying water over its head and ears until all the mud was gone and the forepart of its body glistened darkly in the sun.

It was while I was idly trying to count the buffaloes, wondering how long it would be before I could retrieve my gear, that I seemed to remember more than two figures standing by the fire. But when I looked again the fire was almost out, only a faint flicker of flame from the pile of dead ash, and no sign of Abe or Mary, or of anybody else. I tried to recall exactly what I had seen on turning my head at the sound of their calls, but all I could remember clearly was the shock of the dark herd standing there.

My gaze switched to the buffaloes again. They were on the move at last, drifting back towards the forest. But the elephant remained. It was kneeling now, a picture of innocent enjoyment, sucking at the pipe, and each time it curled its trunk up over its head the prismatic colours of a rainbow showed momentarily in the sprayed water.

The fire died and nothing stirred, the sun burning my bare shoulders. At last the elephant finished its ablutions and got to its feet. It had one last drink from the pipe, and then turned and ambled slowly off. The moment it had disappeared among the trees

I ran down the slope, put on my boots and shirt, grabbed the water container and made for the fire. The leafy fringe of the forest hung trembling in the heat, no animal emerged to face me, no sign of Abe or Mary when I reached the burned-out embers.

I stood for a moment, feeling deserted, but with the shelter of the trees to give me confidence I called to them, my voice loud in the burning stillness. There was an answering call from the direction of the Mission and then Mary appeared on the track, waving and walking casually towards me. 'Where have you been?' I asked her. 'Why didn't you wait for me?'

'We didn't know how long you'd be.' She was laughing. 'That bull might have stayed there all morning and we wanted to look at a map of Kulal made by Reverend Mallinson. It's in the house back there.' She took hold of one of the handles of the container, easing the weight of it as we walked down the slope to the track. 'Karanja turned up while you were enjoying the view.'

'Karanja?'

She nodded. 'Karanja and Dima, they both arrived together.' Her eyes were on the track leading down the shoulder of the mountain. 'If we'd known about that map . . .' She turned to me. 'You see, there is a way up out of that gorge. It's shown on the map, a game trail. Those elephants are safe on the mountain now.'

So there had been no point in van Delden going back down into the plain.

'You must have had a good view up on those rocks. Did you see any vehicle moving?'

'No, nothing.'

She shifted her grip on the container. 'Well, I hope to God he finds out in time... If he thought those elephants were still there and Alex was going in to get them...' Her voice trailed away. 'Are you sure you didn't see anything? No sign of the Land-Rover? Most of the track we came up must have been visible—'

'I told you, nothing.' I was still angry at having been left to fend for myself. 'Where's Abe? Why didn't he wait for me?'

'As soon as Dima mentioned this map he insisted on seeing it right away. Now, of course, he wants to go off into the forest and have a closer look at those elephants.' And she added, smiling, 'You were in no danger from that phlump and I was keeping an eye out for you.'

I asked about Karanja then. He and Dima had apparently stumbled into each other in the moonlight, following the elephants along a narrow game trail that snaked up the almost vertical side of the gorge. 'Did Karanja say why he was following them?'

'I didn't ask him.'

'But surely you must have—'

'He's rather full of himself at the moment.'

We had reached the track and she turned left, walking towards the missionary's house, her head bent, lost in her own thoughts.

'Didn't you ask him why he'd shot up your Land-Rover?'

'It wasn't my Land-Rover and he didn't know I was driving it.'

'What the hell's that got to do with it?' I said irritably. It didn't explain his motive, or why he had tried to stop the Land-Rover from turning those elephants. But when I said it was important to know what was going on in his mind, she turned on me angrily. 'So you don't care that I might have been killed.'

'Oh, for God's sake!' I wrenched the container from her grasp and transferred it to my other hand. 'All I want to know is why he did it. If the Army catches up with him he stands a good chance of being shot.'

'They could make him Minister in place of Kimani.'

I glanced at her, thinking she was joking. But she wasn't. 'You're serious, are you? His motive was political, a gesture to draw attention to himself. Is that what you mean?'

'Anything to do with game in this country is political. I told you that before.'

'But he's an African, a government employee. It's one thing for van Delden to take the law into his own hands—'

'Is it? He's killed two blacks and he's South African born. They'll never let him get away with that.'

'And what about Karanja? Going off to warn van Delden, shooting at Kirby-Smith—'

'Karanja's one of themselves and Alex is a white hunter. In opposing him he'll have the support of all those who believe in Africanization.'

'But surely—'

'Oh, it's impossible,' she cried, 'talking to you about Africa.' We had reached the gate of the missionary's house and she turned in quickly. 'Ask Karanja,' she said. 'Maybe he can explain it to you.'

The door of the half-ruined house was open and I could hear the sound of voices. They were in the room to the left, Abe and Dima standing in front of a map pinned to the wall. Karanja was seated at the missionary's desk, his rifle propped against the wooden arm of the chair, and as we entered he said, 'No. I don't go from here until I talk with Tembo.' There was a decisiveness in his voice, his manner indefinably different – more confident, almost authoritative. 'Is important I talk with him.' He saw us and swung round in his chair. 'You, Mr Tait, tell your American friend is dangerous for him to go into the forest alone.'

'No danger, Karanja, if you come with me,' Abe said. 'You know almost as much about elephants—'

'I tell you, I not coming. I stay here and wait for Tembo.' And he ordered Dima to the door to keep an eye on the track.

Abe turned to me. 'Come and have a look at this map. And you, Mary. Right now this is where we are.' He jabbed his finger on the paper. It was yellowed with sun and damp, the ink faded, but I could just make out the shape of the buildings and the track snaking up the mountain. All the gorges were marked, the tracks and game trails showing faintly, the broken line of the water-pipe, and right in the centre the peak itself, its height in feet written beside it. 'The elephants came up out of the gorge on this trail.' He traced the zig-zag line with his finger, and then he was pointing to a position due north of the Mission. 'That's where Dima and Karanja left them. The scale is an inch to the mile, so it's only just over three miles away. Say we make it in two hours, that's nine hours since they left them. They won't have moved far.'

'Perhaps they come down here for water,' Karanja said. 'In that case you see them without need to go into the forest.'

'There's water at kambi ya mawingo,' Mary said. 'There'll be other places, too.'

'Well, what do you say?' Abe asked me. 'If we find the Wandrobo then maybe you'll get your archaeological mystery solved.'

I shook my head, thinking of the elephant at the waterpipe, the two that had charged us the night before. 'Van Delden asked us to wait for him here.'

'He may not come.'

'If Tembo say he come, he come,' Karanja said.

Abe shrugged. 'Okay, Colin, you and Mary stay here with Karanja, I'll take Dima—'

'No.' Mary shook her head vehemently. 'I'm not staying here while you go off exploring the mountain.

'It will only be for a few hours.'

'I want to see those elephants, too, and now Karanja is with us—' She looked at me, her eyes sullen.

'If Abe is willing to go into the forest on foot . . .' She hesitated, then said angrily, 'What are you scared of? Dima will have a rifle with him.'

I hesitated, unable to explain to her the sense of uneasiness the mountain gave me, or tell her about Abe's wife and the feeling I had that his addiction to danger was very close to a death wish. But in the end I agreed. 'All right,' I said. 'I'll come.'

Karanja got to his feet. 'Is not good for us to split up.'

We might have wasted more time arguing, but Dima suddenly poked his head round the door. 'Patrol,' he hissed, and in the sudden silence we could hear the sound of a vehicle coming up the track. By the time we had gathered up our things and reached the gate it had stopped and a dozen or more African soldiers were running up the slope towards the Mission buildings. Abe darted back inside the house, and when he joined us on the track leading into the forest, he had the map of Kulal stuffed into the front of his bush jacket.

We went down the track as far as the swampy stream with its thick cane growth and there Karanja left us, going back to check the movements of the patrol. 'You said there were no vehicles down on the plain,' Mary whispered accusingly. 'Nothing on the road.'

'They must have been hidden by the shoulder of the mountain.'

A few minutes later Karanja came running with the news that the patrol was close behind us, following the track into the forest. He had us moving fast then, along a narrow game trail that climbed steadily upwards through the trees. It was the same trail he and Dima had followed on their way down to the Mission and shortly after noon we reached the spot where they had left the elephants. There was no sign of them now, only bushes and saplings, freshly browsed, and droppings that were warm to the touch.

Karanja paused for a moment, listening intently. But the forest was silent, a cathedral stillness, and he hurried us on, following the big footprints of elephants through a litter of broken branches that he hoped would make it more difficult for the patrol to follow us.

The trail broadened, the footprints increasing in numbers. And then the ground levelled out and suddenly we were in hot sun. It was a little glade full of butterflies and the quick darting of sunbirds, the grass falling steeply away, and across the green of foliage below we had a view eastwards into the Chalbi, the sand of the desert glimmering white like a great saltpan to a blue horizon hazed with heat. The tracks kept to the high ground and after that we were in thick forest again, amongst wild olive and other tall trees laced together with a liana tracery of rope-like strands.

'Where do you reckon we are now?' Abe stood with the map folded in his hand, holding it out for Karanja, who stared at it and shook his head. 'We come to gorge soon,' he muttered.

'And then?'

Karanja had his head cocked to one side, listening. 'Maybe if we climb down into that gorge nobody follow us there.'

'There's a game trail marked, but it zig-zags all the way, so I guess it's steep. Could elephants make it down a trail like that?' His mind was still on the elephants, not on the Army patrol following us.

Karanja shrugged. 'We go on,' he said tersely. 'Not far now.'

The trees became smaller, the forest thinning as we climbed, and suddenly there was light ahead, white and blinding. And then we were out of the undergrowth on to a green strip of coarse African grass that went rolling down a shoulder of the mountain, cascading over rock outcrops towards the distant blue of Rudolf. Directly ahead of us it ended, vanishing abruptly into space, and, across the void beyond, a great peak of rock, all greys and greens and the black of shadows, rose naked against a blue-white background of cloudless sky. An eagle skimmed across the face of it, poised like a speck of dirt on a colour slide, and in the foreground, on that green grass sward, round elephant turds lay like footballs on an empty soccer field. The eagle swooped and was gone. Something died with a distant cry and we started out across the grass to the edge of that gorge.

God knows how deep it was. Two thousand, three thousand feet? It was impossible to gauge, for there was nothing to measure height or distance by as we stood on a rock platform staring down to terraces of grass and undergrowth falling away into clefts of shadow, the bottom of the gorge invisible. Abe shook his head. 'No elephant could possibly—' But Karanja was pointing away to our right where a tumbled terrace of rocks had the brown earth of a beaten track threaded through it. 'Game trail,' he said. And then he was staring up at the peak opposite, his eyes slitted against the glare. 'Is there a trail marked up the far side?'

Abe pulled the map out, 'No. There's a trail running along the bottom of the gorge, that's all.'

'Maybe it go up the gorge and round the other side of Kulal.'

Abe shook his head. 'Up the gorge it crosses the height of land, then down along the shoulder of the mountain eastwards.' He looked up at the peak. 'That's no place for elephants.'

'I am not thinking of elephants, Mr Finkel.'

'What then – that we've got to go down and up the far side? Do you really think that patrol would follow us down into the gorge? It will be dark in a few hours.'

Karanja didn't say anything and Mary murmured, 'I wish Tembo was here. He's no way of knowing where we are.' She was staring at the far side of the gorge. 'Unless—' She turned to Karanja. 'Do you think he'd see a fire if we lit it high up, near the peak? There's no cloud. It would be visible for miles.'

Karanja looked doubtful. 'Is how we signal before we have walkie-talkie,' he admitted. 'But is dangerous.' Whether he was referring to the patrol or the mountain itself I wasn't sure, but I could sense a deep uneasiness.

'It's volcanic, so the rock will be bad in places.' Mary was staring up at the peak again, her hat pulled down to shade her eyes. 'I'm not certain about the last pitch, but up to that rock band just below the summit . . .' She turned back to Karanja. 'Do you think he'd see it?'

'Maybe cloud later.'

'Then hurry.' She was suddenly urgent. 'We'll find a way up. And if he sees that fire, then maybe it's not too late.' Her voice trailed away, his reluctance becoming apparent to her. 'At least there's a chance,' she said. 'If he's out on the shoulder of the mountain, clear of the forest.' And Karanja nodded uncertainly, his eyes troubled.

We started down then, into a tumbled litter of rocks, the trail falling steeply, twisting and turning down the buttressed face of the first of a number of ledges, and there were the slide marks of heavy bodies that had come this way before us. As we wound our way down deeper into the gorge it became hotter, occasional thickets of undergrowth hung drooping leaves in the windless air and there was an increasing sense of being shut in. A squeal from the shadowed bottom of the gorge stopped us momentarily, but we could see no sign of any elephants and nothing moved. A few moments later, coming out of a thicket below a sheer buttress of rock, we had a view right down the gorge with the same 'island' of rock we had seen the previous morning rising up out of the bottom, and the green of the steep meadow slopes was dotted with moving figures. Dima grinned. 'Nyani.' And as I focused my eyes in the sunglare, I could see they were baboons, crouched and moving on all fours, and there were young ones clinging to their mothers' fur.

The island looked nearer than it was, for we were now more than halfway down and my impression was of a great rock and grass plug blocking the gorge. Mary was searching the opposite face, which now seemed to rise up almost sheer, the peak of Kulal hidden by obtruding bands of rock. 'There's sure to be a game trail there.'

'Not for elephants,' Karanja said firmly.

'No, for kudu.'

'To hell with kudu,' Abe said. 'You find me those elephants.' And as if in response to his words a thin squeal came up from below us.

'Ndovu.' Dima nodded. But the squeal was not repeated, everything hushed and still in the lifeless air, only the coughing grunt of baboons made faint by distance.

It took us another half hour to reach the bottom, but though we could occasionally hear elephants, we never saw them. There was water in the bottom, actual running water that flowed in a channel that was deep in shade and twisted like a tiny canyon among cliffs and buttresses, and there were sudden expansive chambers that were flat and full of the debris of lush growth. The humidity was very high and the sweat poured off us. Karanja sent Dima on ahead, then stood staring up at the precipitous trail we had descended. Abe and I followed Mary's example, took our safari boots off and dabbled our feet in a pool. Small birds flitted in and out of the rock face. There was no sign of any patrol and the only sound was the faint rumblings of elephants, the snap of branches, from far down the ravine.

Dima came back after about ten minutes, his black splayed feet treading carefully the middle of the stream. He reported a well-used game trail with elephants on it, but not the elephants they had been following during the night. This was a small group of three cows and two almost fully grown calves, and he said there were more further down the gorge – he had heard them, but he had not seen them.

Abe wanted to go on, but Karanja had taken charge of us now and he was still worried about the patrol. The only way to be certain they were not following us down into the gorge was to climb to a vantage point on the opposite side. We sat there, chewing on some of the leathery elephant meat and drinking all the water we could absorb while we discussed it. The ascent looked difficult, sheer cliffs of rock interspersed with clefts full of boulders and tangled vegetation, and Abe had the sense to realize it was beyond him. In the end it was Karanja who made the decision. Dima would remain with Abe and the two of them would head downstream, keeping to the water all the time. Mary and I would go with Karanja and try to scale the side of the gorge. If the patrol did catch up with us, then ours would be the only tracks for them to follow, and by then we should be well above them.

I left my bag and all the film with Abe and as we started up the gorge he called to me, 'If you find an old city perched on the top, send word and I'll come and film it for you.'

'If it has pearly gates,' I shouted back to him, 'I'll have them opened so you can ride your elephant through.' It was a silly remark, nothing more, but I was to remember it later.

He was already splashing down the stream bed behind Dima. I saw him wave acknowledgement, then he was lost to view behind a buttress and we began casting along the north face, searching for a route up. But every cleft we tried proved impenetrable, all of them choked with fallen rock and vegetation. In the end it was the remains of stale kudu droppings that guided us. Mary spotted them, barely visible on a pile of detritus below a cliff overhang. The spill of rock and rubble led up behind the overhang, and after a few minutes' steep, almost vertical climbing from rock to rock we were out on a grass ledge with a mêlée of rock outcrops towering above us. It looked as though a demolition gang of giants had been at work on the mountain and if it hadn't been for the rare antelope that grazed there we would never have found a way. Their droppings were like signposts and both Karanja and Mary seemed to have an uncanny instinct that enabled them to follow the trail from one pale, dry-straw faeces to the next.

We were in the sun's full glare, the climbing hard

and exhausting, so that I was glad of the frequent pauses Karanja made to scan the far side of the gorge. Each time we stopped a new section of the trail we had descended became visible until at last we could see the lip of the gorge itself, a jagged line against the sun's glare. All this time we had seen no sign of movement anywhere on the trail.

The slope became easier for a while, our way winding through smooth battlements of rock, and when we paused again the sun was much lower and all the far side of the gorge was in deep shadow. Suddenly Karanja whispered hoarsely, 'Soldiers. Don't anybody move.' He would never have seen them if they had been on the trail, but they were on the skyline on the very edge of the gorge, figures moving in silhouette, climbing the rock outcrops and peering down.

We stood there, all three of us absolutely still, nakedly exposed in the slanting sunlight and very conscious that the gorge was so narrow we were within range of their rifles. Then Mary, who was standing only just above me, leaned cautiously down and gripped my shoulder. 'See them?' she whispered. 'Just starting down the trail.'

'Of course I see them.' They were leaping down the rocks, crawling out on to ledges, searching the trail.

'Not the soldiers, elephants – in the green of that first terrace.' Her face was close to mine, the voice husky with excitement. 'That's what they're all looking down at.'

'Ssh,' Karanja hissed from above us. 'Don't talk, don't move.'

I didn't see them at first. The sun was in my eyes and with the sides of the gorge all dark in shadow it was difficult even to detect the line of the trail.

'Almost level with us,' she breathed and slid her hand over my shoulder, pointing.

I saw them then, on the trail we had come down, where it twisted among the rocks, dropping steeply down into the gorge – brown-grey shapes plastered with mud moving cautiously. A trunk waved above a low thicket, a great head thrown back, and there was an elephant sitting on its haunches as though performing some ridiculous act at a circus. It was sliding on its rump, two great leg stumps thrust out ahead. It checked on the lip of a sheer drop, behind it a youngster squealing miserably with another squatting adult holding on to it with its trunk.

We stood there transfixed, incredulous, as the whole herd – seventeen of them – made that precarious descent to the sheer drop, made it safely and disappeared behind a buttress to lose themselves in a patch of forest thicket that clothed the next range. 'I wouldn't have thought it possible,' she breathed. 'Tembo has talked about them going up and down steep mountain paths, in the Aberdares and the Ngorongoro, but I never saw it so I never really believed it.' She was chuckling quietly to herself. 'The patrol hasn't a hope of getting down that gorge now, not with that herd blocking the trail. They'll have covered our tracks beautifully.' The elephants had started to browse now and she whispered in my ear, 'You counted, did you?'

I nodded, wishing to God I had my camera with me. If the sun had been behind us and that bloody patrol wasn't watching, what a picture it would have made – something unique, something I couldn't remember ever having seen on film before.

'I made the count exactly the same as last night.'

I nodded. 'Looks like Abe may meet up with his elephant after all.'

'I hope not,' she breathed. 'They'll be frightened and exhausted, and when they see there's water there—'

Karanja hissed at us for silence again and after that we didn't talk, just stood there watching the African soldiers on the lip of the gorge and the elephants slowly moving down the trail. I was thinking of Abe, imagining him relaxed by the side of some pool with his trousers rolled up and his feet in the water and those elephants suddenly looming up in the last of the light. I wasn't seriously worried. He had Dima with him.

We were stuck there on the side of the mountain for almost half an hour. Then at last the patrol gathered together in a group and headed back into the forest. But even when they had all disappeared Karanja insisted on our remaining absolutely still until he was convinced they really were returning to the Mission for the night. At last he moved, coming down to join us. 'Is getting late.' There was an urgency in his voice as he stared at the lengthening shadows in the rocks that surrounded us.

'We've got to get higher,' Mary said. 'High enough for Tembo to see it. And the sky is clear. There'll be a moon later. We can come down by moonlight.'

They stayed arguing for a while. Mary pointing out that the fire would not be visible from the Mission and Karanja still reluctant even though he was no longer in danger from the patrol. He was standing irresolutely, staring across the gorge at the trail opposite where the elephants were on the move again, performing their extraordinary circus act on the deep drop from one terrace to the next. Then he nodded abruptly, turning to face the mountain again, a stocky black figure clawing his way up. Following close behind him, I sensed his reluctance, the tension building up in him, and I knew he was afraid. The sight we had just witnessed was in no way remarkable to him. His imagination operated on a different plane, the old superstitions of his race more deeply felt than any miracle of animal behaviour. And as we climbed higher and higher, the world dropped away below us, the gorge, the long grass shoulders of the mountain, the dark green cap of the rain forest that lay like a mantle across its broad back, all visible like a topographical map rolled out now that we were nearing the peak itself.

'Bad place,' he muttered as I scrambled up to join him on a pinnacle of rock.

'How do you know? You've never been here before.' My voice came breathless, the altitude pressing on my lungs.

'No. But is what everybody say. Nobody like Kulal.

Cloud. Storm. Wind.' His eyes rolled heavenward as though at any moment he expected a hurricane to hurl itself at us out of the cloudless sky. 'Even Tembo don't like Kulal. Very dangerous mountain.'

The sun was falling into the west, lighting the surface of Lake Rudolf to a deep jade green, the cliffs of the distant Turkana shore a faded line of brown, and no breath of wind. Another hundred feet and we reached a broad ledge close under the rock band. There were clefts and deep gulleys choked with vegetation and the stunted growth of trees. We rested for a moment, watching the sun grow in size and the sky turn to an incredible, brilliant green as the red disc dropped below the earth's rim. The long flat mountain ranges beyond the lake were turning black, puffs of white cloud over the Mara suddenly taking fire, the sky deepening to purple as we began searching the gulleys for dry wood, piling it on the ledge.

Stars were showing before we had finished, and when it was too dark to gather any more wood, Karanja settled down to the task of getting the heap to burn. At first all he achieved was smoke, for the wood was green and damp, but gradually the pile warmed through and flickers of flame appeared. We had less than two hours before the moon rose and we sat there feeding it sticks, nursing those feeble flickers until at last the whole pile suddenly caught.

It went up with a roar then, showers of sparks lifting into the velvet darkness, the glow of it lighting the rock face. Shadows danced and flickered, our faces red in the flames. Karanja had fashioned a long branch into a sort of pitchfork with the panga, and when the whole pile was alight and blazing red, he began to spread the embers westward along the ledge so that from a distance it would have the shape of an arrow pointing down the gorge towards the lake. I never saw the stars go out one by one over the Mara. I was like a kid on Guy Fawkes night, intent on the bonfire we had created, watching the sparks riding the heat upwards into the night, the red blaze warming the rock behind us, our shadows looming large. It was exciting, wildly exhilarating – a roaring fire on the top of a mountain peak where nobody perhaps had been before us.

And then it was done, the signal arrow made in glowing embers that must look from the distance like the red of lava flowing from a newly opened volcanic vent, and we sat there, the three of us, watching it, feeling the heat of it on our bodies, enjoying a spurious primeval sense of power, the mountain conquered, ourselves the masters sending out our message to the world. I can remember Mary's face bright with flame, her dark hair falling to her shoulders, her slim hands held to the blaze, sitting there, cross-legged, the firelight dancing in her eyes. And Karanja with his white teeth showing in a grin, and his face, with its broad flat nose, no longer black, but a dark bronze red.

'You think he'll see it?' she asked him.

'If he is looking towards Kulal.'

'He must see it.'

Far to the eastward the desert began to reveal itself in a soft light like the loom of a distant city. There were no flames now, only the charcoal-hot red of burning embers, so that we saw the moon quite clearly as it came up over the edge of the Chalbi, a huge great Hallowe'en lantern, its slightly lopsided pumpkin face glowing orange as though lit from within. Karanja went to gather more wood. The moon was an African moon and he was an African, taking it for granted, but to me it was a strange unearthly sight as it rose up out of the desert like some ghostly phoenix to turn the far-off sands the colour of dried blood. Mary saw it differently, sitting there beside me, hugging her knees and staring entranced. 'It's beautiful,' she breathed and I thought I felt the mountain shiver as though with laughter. A spark flew and I heard the sound of the panga slashing wood deep in the cleft behind us. 'I wish he was here,' she murmured.

'Who? Your father?'

'If you like.'

It was on the tip of my tongue to ask which one, but I knew – knew also in that moment that she didn't think of him as her father. The heat of the fire that warmed our bodies was not for van Delden's safety, but only to draw him away from Kirby-Smith. I left her then and went into the cleft to help Karanja. There was something I had to ask him. And as he hauled at the branches of a half-dead tree, standing shoulder-to-shoulder in the dark of the cleft, I said, 'You don't like the mountain, do you?'

'No.'

'What are you scared of – devils?'

He looked at me and laughed, his eyes gleaming

white. 'Not devils, Mr Tait. Only this mountain that is a volcano has exploded many times.'

'Then why are you here?'

He turned, the panga hanging loose in his hand. 'I don't want the army to trap him in that gorge, and if he kills Major Kirby-Smith . . . either way is bad politically.' He shook his head. 'Is better I am with him.'

'What can you do?'

He shrugged, the lift of his shoulders barely visible in the shadowed glow of the fire. 'Maybe nothing. I don't know.' He stood there, a dim shape, very still, and he was frowning, his thoughts turned inwards. 'Is difficult for me. I am African and no influence outside of my country. I cannot write about elephants. But now that I have seen what is happening here, how they climb up out of that gorge, all together on this mountain and heading for Lake Rudolf . . .' He paused. 'He and I, we think alike now, and I have friends in Government. When they know I am also trying to stop this killing—' He was staring out to the darkness of the gorge and after a moment he said, 'Is part of our heritage and one day, maybe, I live to see those same elephants crossing Kulal again, but going the other way, going south into the lands they live in when I am young man, going to protected areas where the world can see them again. Quiet, dignified elephants living in peace and rearing their calves. Not fleeing half-starved and in terror, charging everything.' He shook his head, smiling to himself. 'Is a dream maybe, but that is what I hope.'

I didn't say anything for a moment, surprised at his depth of feeling, the way his words echoed van Delden's. But it was one thing to declare himself against the killing of elephants up here in the fastnesses of Kulal, quite another to put it into practice and if he started shooting at Kirby-Smith again . . . 'You'll get yourself killed,' I said. 'You may have political friends, but they're a long way away.'

'Okay, then I am killed.' And he laughed, his teeth shining white. 'But if I am killed, then it is reported in the press and everybody know that Karanja dies because he is opposed to the policy of extermination.' He was still laughing, as though death were of no account, and when he saw I was shocked by his acceptance of it, he slapped me on the back. 'No need to be afraid.' He didn't realize that what appalled me was the harshness of this foreign world where everybody seemed to walk with death looking over their shoulders.

We finished breaking up the tree and dragged the branches to the fire, but the dead wood did not burn and it was the moon now that lit the rocks, its light white and brilliant, the desert turned to snow. 'It's bright enough for us to find our way down,' I said. But Mary shook her head, huddled close to the fire, staring at the moon. Karanja, too, seemed transfixed by it, and suddenly I realized there was a circle of light around it and the air was colder, a damp breeze blowing. And even as we stared the moon's halo intensified, a great circle filling half the sky. The desert blurred and vanished, the bright moon dulled, and in an instant the halo was gone and the moon itself had vanished, leaving only a vague translucence. A damp cold touched my face and suddenly we were in cloud and everything dark, only the fire glowing red on the eddying curtain of dampness that enveloped us.

'Does that mean we're here for the night?' I asked and Mary nodded.

A blinding flash forked down the gorge, followed instantly by a crash of thunder that seemed to shake the whole mountain, and then the wind came, blowing out of the desert towards Lake Rudolf, and it began to rain. The rain was heavy for a moment and it was pitch black as we groped our way to the cleft. The noise of the thunder was incessant, flashes of lightning continually illuminating the rocks that sheltered us. Karanja curled himself up like a foetus, lying with his arms over his head, his eyes tight shut, moaning softly. The wind died and the air became charged with electricity. I could feel it tingling on my body as I crouched in the damp recesses of the rock listening to the storm advancing on us from across the gorge. It was like an artillery barrage, the noise deafening.

I crawled to the entrance, lying there with the ground shaking under me, watching through slitted eyes the super-charged currents stabbing at the rocks in sizzling, blinding bolts of brilliant electric blue. And in their reflected glare I saw the black belly of the cloud hanging over the mountain, writhing and contorting. An eye-searing bolt struck just below the feeble glow of the fire, the thunder of it mingling with split rock in one gigantic crash. The ground shook and the acrid smell of pulverized rock drifted up on an eddy.

But that was the worst and I lay there, listening, as the core of that electrical storm swept over the peak above us, the noise of it gradually lessening to the grumble of a barrage battering the further slopes. I crept out then to tend the fire, my body chilled by the damp air swirling round us.

Mary joined me just as I had coaxed the embers into a blaze and we sat as close to the fire as we could, watching its glow reflected on the dense cloud mist pouring like smoke up out of the gorge. Lightning stabbed behind the peak above us, the growl of thunder reverberating through the rocks. She rolled over, staring up at me, her eyes wide and luminous in the firelight. 'Frightened?'

I didn't answer, suddenly aware of her reaching out, her hand on my arm, pulling me down beside her. 'Well, I am,' she breathed, her face flushed, her lips parted and the glow of the embers in her eyes. 'Don't you know what to do when a girl is frightened?' There was a bubble of laughter in her throat, the hot glow of her eyes no longer borrowed from the fire, the passion of her nature overflowing. I felt the blood leap in my veins, the sudden appalling ache, and then her shirt was open, breasts bare, and she took my head in her hands, pulling me down, the open eagerness of her mouth reaching up to me. That kiss was like a flame running through me, the touch of her tongue, the feel of her hands tearing at my clothes, stroking me, and those breasts, the fullness of her flesh pressed against

mine. Some residue of puritanical ancestry caused me
to withdraw involuntarily, my brain flashing a memory
of Abe's warning. 'What about Karanja?' I breathed,
my lips buried in her hair.

'Karanja?' The laughter bubbled again. 'In Africa
mating is normal.' She suddenly drew back, staring at
me. 'You are normal, aren't you?'

'Yes.'

'Well then—' And after that I didn't care as we
sought the comfort and warmth we needed, the
reassurance of our physical existence. It wasn't love.
It was something wild, primeval, totally primitive, our
two bodies swept away by natural forces beyond control, and in the urge to imprint upon each other the
fact of our survival we seemed charged with the same
stabbing electrical currents as the air we breathed. It
was as though the storm had entered into us. With
passion we reincarnated the fury of it, and when we
had spent ourselves and were lying on our backs,
naked to the fire, there were stars overhead and the
thunder was a faraway grumble fading into the
distance.

For a brief moment the moon smiled down on us
from a ragged gap in the clouds, but then it was gone
and we were enveloped once more in a blanket of mist.
I slept fitfully and woke with the dawn. There was a
damp chill in the air, both of us lying fully clothed so
close to the burned-out embers of the fire that the
shoulder of my sweater was scorched brown. There
was no wind and the mist hanging thick round our
ledge made it seem as though we were imprisoned in

an empty void, nothing visible except the rock behind us reaching up into the clouds. I was lying there, my eyes searching the rock face, wondering what lay hidden behind that veil of mist, when Mary asked, 'Did Pieter van Delden ever make it to the top of Kulal?'

'No,' I said. 'He never came to this side of the gorge.'

'Well, now's your chance.' She jumped to her feet, tossing droplets of moisture from her lank hair, her arms hugged round her, staring upwards. But then Karanja said, 'We go down now.' Some time during the night he had come out of the dark womb of the cleft seeking the warmth of the fire. Now he huddled close to the dead embers, shivering with only a thin shirt, his black skin blue with cold, and all he wanted was to get back down into the gorge. 'You go on,' Mary told him. 'We'll follow.'

He shook his head, arguing that we had better go down while we could. But there were currents of air swirling the mist around us, a faint glimmer of sunshine. 'The cloud will clear soon,' she said. He seemed to accept that, so we left him there, trying to get the fire going again, and climbed up the side of the cleft where erosion had fashioned footholds in the rocks. It was easier than I had expected and above the rock band the slope was gentler, a chaos of mist-enveloped outcrops and boulders, the shattered debris of a mountain shaken by volcanic disturbance. The cloud thickened as we climbed and in the end neither of us was certain that we had stood on the actual summit of the mountain, for it was a nightmare of rock castles and gulleys all dimly seen through a thick grey miasma of moving cloud.

'So where's your ancient city?' Mary stood laughing at me, with her hair blowing in the clouds and her face glistening with moisture.

'Well, at least we're on the peak. I've seen it for myself.' I turned away, knowing now that no race of early men would be fool enough to build in such an area of instability. And since it wasn't Kulal, then it had to be Porr. It was the only other notable peak, and as we started down I was wondering whether I would ever get to that lone pyramid of a mountain halfway up Lake Rudolf. My mind on that, I lost all sense of direction. The cloudcap over the mountain had brightened now to a white translucent fog. It began to drizzle and we both of us stopped, realizing suddenly that there was nothing to guide us in that tumult of dim-seen rock shapes. The only certainty was that we were on the slope leading down into the gorge, and so we went on, until suddenly we found ourselves on the edge of a void. We had reached the rock band, a vertical drop falling into nothingness. We stood there, calling Karanja, our shouts lost in cloud and no echo of an answer. But a hundred yards or so to our left, beyond a pinnacle of shattered rock, we heard the sound of an answering call.

It was only when we reached the fire that we realized we were both of us shivering with cold. 'Better we go down now,' Karanja said, 'before the mist clears.' He was thinking of the patrol, which might well have started out from the Mission again at first light, but when I looked up at him and saw into his eyes there was a sudden flash of understanding between us. It wasn't just the patrol; we were both of us filled with the same urge – to get off that bloody mountain before it brewed another storm.

I think Mary felt the same, for she was on her feet at once, following close behind Karanja as he began the descent from that ledge. He moved fast, following unerringly the route we had climbed, and when we were about halfway down a breeze touched our faces, the mist lifting and brightening until it was a white intensity of trapped sunlight that was almost blinding. The far side of the gorge emerged first as a dark shadow, then as something visible but blurred. A moment later the mist vanished like smoke. The sun shone down on us and it was suddenly hot.

The abruptness of that transformation was startling, everything clean and fresh with moisture, and brilliantly clear as though we were looking at it under slight magnification. But the sun burned in a sky that was white, not blue, and it had a great circle of light around it. An ice halo, Mary thought. She had seen it once on Kilimanjaro.

We reached the bottom and turned downstream; no sign of any humans having been on the trail before us, only the track of elephants. We caught glimpses of that island of rock and grass coming gradually nearer until it seemed to block the gorge ahead, and every now and then the hot stillness was pierced with the cry of a baboon. We were right under that island with the wind on our back when there was a sudden roaring and squealing of elephants, a cry of pain, and then the crash of bodies in thick bush. Silence, and Karanja moving cautiously, his rifle ready in his hand. 'What was it – baboon?' I asked.

He shook his head. 'No, not baboon.'

And Mary said, 'It sounded human.'

Outcrops of rock now, the trail narrowing and everything suddenly very still, the heat oppressive. Karanja called softly – 'Dima! Dima!' We rounded a bend, the trail opening out again, a thicket of bushes on both sides of the stream, and suddenly there was Dima half-hidden behind a rock, his rifle pointed at us. He stood up at the sight of us, calling urgently, and when we reached him there was Abe lying at his feet, his face ashen, blood streaming from a gash in his head and his right hand at a grotesque angle. His eyes were open, a glazed look, so that for a moment I thought he was dead. But then his lips moved in a whisper: 'Is the camera all right, Colin?' He didn't seem to realize he still had it gripped in his other hand, cradling it on his stomach. And when I told him, he said, 'Take it, will you. There's about a minute and a half exposed, all close-ups.' He had closed his eyes, the sweat standing in beads on his face.

Mary came back from the stream, her handkerchief soaked in water. She bathed his head, then gently began rolling up the sleeve of his shirt. His arm looked as though it had been bit by a sledgehammer, the flesh all bruised, the bone broken just above the wrist. She straightened it with a deft, quick movement, the bone grating and his mouth opening in a thin scream. 'We'll have to splint it.' He had fainted and she looked up at Dima. 'What happened, for God's sake?'

The explanation came in a flood of Swahili and when he stopped she said to Karanja, 'He could have shot it.'

Dima shook his head obstinately. 'Patrol come quick if they hear gun.'

'Bugger the patrol,' she said angrily. 'He might have been killed. And that patrol, wherever it is, is out of earshot.'

'He don't know that,' Karanja reminded her. 'And if we are not coming down the gorge—'

'The calf winded us, is that what you mean?'

Karanja nodded unhappily and I said, 'What's this about a calf? A calf couldn't have done that.'

'No? Even at one year old they weigh about twelve hundred pounds, and that big calf of hers must be at least five; that's the average gap between births.'

'But what happened?'

She stared at me, exasperated that I hadn't understood a word of what Dima had said. 'It was the elephant he called Sally. They were holed up in the rocks there, waiting for us, and then this herd arrived and she was in the lead. She was right there in that open glade and he couldn't resist the opportunity. He crept down out of the rocks with his camera . . .' She turned to Karanja and asked him to cut some sticks to use as splints. 'Dima says he tried to stop him, but Abe wouldn't listen. The cow came right down to the water and the odd thing was she didn't seem to mind him. He was right there in front of her as she started drinking and then spraying water over herself. There was just the stream between them and he was crouched there, filming her when it happened. Her ears suddenly spread out, her head lifted, then she swung quickly round, facing up the gorge and trumpeting. That was when the calf came out of the thicket there, right behind him. It was obeying its mother's orders, trying to get back to her, and Abe was in the way. It sent him flying with a sweep of its trunk, ploughed through the stream and in an instant the whole herd was crashing away down the gorge.'

'It was my fault.' Abe's eyes were open again, his voice urgent as he struggled up on his left elbow. 'I was between the calf and its mother. I should have realized . . .' He sank back exhausted, his lips bared with pain. 'I forgot – she still had a calf.' And he added in a whisper, 'She was so quiet, so relaxed – until she scented danger. She seemed to understand I meant no harm, that I was unarmed.' He closed his eyes against the glare. 'I'm glad Dima didn't shoot,' he murmured. 'You can't blame the calf.' He reached out and gripped Mary's arm. 'Will it hurt much – when you splint it? I'm an awful coward.'

'You'll be all right,' she said cheerfully. 'It will hurt for a moment, that's all.'

But it took much longer than a moment, the three of us holding him down while he screamed and screamed. Then, thank God, he passed out and she was able to finish the job without him struggling all the time. She was covered with sweat as she sat back on her heels, staring down at the splint bandaged with strips of towelling. 'I hope it's all right. I've only done that with animals before, and usually we had an anaesthetic.' She looked round vaguely. 'How far is it to Loiyangalani? There's an airstrip there and if a plane came over . . . Where's that map?'

I found it in our bag. The oasis camp of Loiyangalani was a good six miles away. 'He can't walk that.'

'He'll have to. Or else we carry him. He has to be got to a hospital somehow.'

We started as soon as Abe recovered consciousness. I wanted to abandon all our gear, but Abe wouldn't hear of it and Karanja clung to the camera and films as though they were more precious than the plastic water container. Because of the elephants we were forced up on to a shoulder of the mountain, clear of the gorge, which gradually petered out below us. We moved slowly with many pauses. Abe light-headed and in pain, but doggedly staying on his feet, the heat increasing as the day wore on and the lake drawing gradually nearer.

Coming down off the lower slopes was the worst. It took us over an hour to cross an old lava field, the black rocks jagged and broken, the late afternoon sun beating up at us, dust blowing and the temperature in the high nineties. After that it was sand, long rolling dunes of it with isolated patches of thorn and furze. By then we had finished our meat and almost all the water, and Abe was barely conscious, stumbling along with two of us supporting him. But we could see the broken palms of the oasis now, the fire-blackened roofless buildings of the tourist camp and the remains of the Catholic Mission that Dima said had been run by Italians. And across the flat land beyond the palms, the lake stretched flat as a steel sheet to the jagged volcanic outline of South Island, the Turkana shore dim in the distance. There was not a breath of wind and nothing stirred along the lake's edge, no elephants, not even any sign of life around the huddle of conelike dwellings that had been the manyatta of the El Molo.

All the way down we had reckoned on the El Molo supplying us with fish, for this small lakeshore tribe had existed for centuries on the teeming marine life of the lake, particularly tilapia and the huge Nile perch. Now instead we would have to catch our own fish and Dima went on ahead with Karanja, the two of them rapidly lost to view as they loped off across the sands. We had glimpses of them later, after we had reached the shelter of the doum palms. Abe had fallen into a deep sleep, utterly exhausted, and Mary and I stood on top of the shallow escarpment on which the palms grew, looking out across the flats towards the sunset. Below us was the airstrip, the frayed windsock still hanging from its pole, limp in the breathless air, and the green line of a ditch carrying a trickle of oasis water out towards the deserted village, and beyond the manyatta two tiny figures were hurrying towards the flat burnished circle of the port. And when they had disappeared from sight behind the jetty, there was nothing moving at all except the birds flying in dark rafts close above the surface of the water.

The sun had set, everything very still, the sky a

violent purple, and out across the pale, almost luminous water of the lake, South Island stood black against the sky, a hideous, piled-up mêlée of volcanic vents and old lava flows. Years ago, I remembered a British expedition had landed two men there and they had never been seen again. When I mentioned this to Mary she named them – Martin and Dyson. 'Fuchs was the leader of the expedition.' And she added, 'Tembo has been over there several times, once on an El Molo fishing raft. There's a herd of goats there and the largest crocs he's ever seen. He says it's just about the most desolate place on earth.'

Night fell and with the stars came the mosquitoes. We dozed intermittently, bitten to hell. A wind got up, rattling the palm fronds overhead, the moon leering down at us, more lop-sided than ever, and then at last there were shouts and the two Africans were back with an old fishing net full of tilapia, all gutted and cleaned. We got a fire going and cooked them on sticks of thorn, holding them by the fins that fringed their flat bodies, and it was while we were squatting there in front of the blaze, sucking the flesh of the tilapia and trying to fend off the mosquitoes, that a dark figure suddenly emerged from the palms. Karanja grabbed his rifle and we all leapt to our feet.

It was Mukunga and he held something out to us, wrapped in a palm leaf and all bloody. 'Tembo send you present.'

'What is it? Where is he?' Mary asked.

It was crocodile meat and van Delden was camped about seven miles to the north of us in what Mukunga called El Molo Bay. I remembered it from the map, a shallow inlet opposite the small El Molo Islands. 'Me watch from hill of the dead. See smoke here.' He had a 15-cwt truck with him. 'You eat meat, then go with me. Loiyangalani no good – upepo now.'

The moon had gone, black clouds overhead, and the wind in the palms was like the roar of the surf breaking on a reef. Gusts blattered at the fire, the meat sizzling and Mukunga talking fast in Swahili, gesturing and laughing. He was telling the story of how they had got hold of the truck, and I sat there, listening to the roar of the wind and thinking of van Delden. At one point Abe said urgently to Mary, 'Ask him if he's seen any elephants along the lake shore.'

'Ndovu?' Mukunga nodded, and after listening to him for a moment Mary said, 'Yes. There are elephants in El Molo Bay, a whole herd, and more to the north. He says they're feeding on the lakeweed, lots of them wading in the shallows all along the shore.'

'Does Kirby-Smith know that?'

She nodded. 'Yes. Alex knows.' And she added, so quietly I hardly heard her above the shattering blast of another gust, 'He's moving the outfit up to Loiyangalani.' And she closed her eyes, sitting very still, not saying anything until finally Karanja doused the fire with sand and we walked through the palms to the truck.

PART FOUR

WARDEN OF THE NORTH

CHAPTER ONE

The moon was gone, black clouds hanging over the oasis as we headed north on a rough track, our own dust billowing past us in the gusts. We crossed a lugga, the track like the gateway in some ancient earthworks and after that the wind was less. There was vegetation here, thorn trees mainly, and small birds rose up from under our wheels, skittering away like grasshoppers in the headlights. 'Namaqua doves, I think.' Mary was leaning forward, her hand on Abe's shoulder. He was in the front seat and he half turned to her. 'This is one of the hunter's trucks, isn't it? How did he get hold of it?'

'Hijacked it.'

'Yes, but how? Did Mukunga say?'

She nodded, silent for a moment. I don't think she wanted to talk about it. To talk about it meant thinking about what happened now. But in the end she told us what had occurred after van Delden left us at the Mission. He had coasted halfway down the shoulder of the mountain to a point where he had a clear view down into the gorge and could get the Land-Rover off the track into the shelter of some rocks. Below them a party of hunters was moving slowly back to their vehicles parked in the flat scrub of country where the cliffs widened out. Later, from a different vantage point, they had watched the vehicles crawl across the plain below, and at the well, where the elephants had dug for water, two of the trucks had turned off and started up the track towards the Mission. The first was the Army 3-tonner carrying the patrol. 'They let that pass,' she said, 'then blocked the road with the Land-Rover and ambushed the second vehicle, which was following some way behind to avoid the dust stream.'

'What about the men in it – they were Africans, were they?'

'Yes, four of them. He dropped them off by the well.'

The moon had come clear of cloud and I could see Abe's face, dead white and frowning. 'At least he didn't shoot them.'

'What happened to the Land-Rover?' I asked.

'They ran it over the edge of the gorge.'

The track had become harder, the shoulder of a hill rising black to the left, a glint of water far ahead. Abe was holding himself tight. 'So what happens now, Mary? You said something about Kirby-Smith moving to Loiyangalani.'

She nodded, that look on her face. 'They were due

to break camp at dawn this morning. At least, that's what the hunters said.'

'To move up to Loiyangalani?'

'Yes.'

'Then why aren't they here? There's no sign of them and it can't be more than a day's journey.'

'The track probably. Mukunga says it's very bad where it crosses the lava fields by Sirimar. Earth tremors have destroyed several of the concrete ways the missionaries built to get their trucks over the worst of the boulders. Maybe they couldn't make it.'

Abe was silent then, knowing it was what she desperately hoped. We were running along the side of the hill now, close above the water, and it was shallow, more a marsh, with countless birds asleep like black stones. The headlights swung, the black stones turning to white and three pelicans pulled pouched beaks from under their wings in slow motion. A goliath heron, still as a post, lifted its razor-sharp head and there were storks standing one-legged in the mud. On the edge of visibility grey outcrops of rocks moved. 'Elephants?' but Mukunga shook his head. 'Kiboko.'

'Hippos,' Mary said. And then we had reached the lake shore and the moon was clear so that we could see islands pale beyond the wind-whipped water. The track ceased and we were on the beach, the truck bucking as it ground in low gear up a long promontory dotted with the cairns of ancient burials. 'Hill of the dead,' Mukunga shouted above the noise of the engine and the breaking waves. Then we stopped and van Delden was standing there like some prophet in a hostile desert of rock, his white hair blowing and a rifle, gripped by the barrel, lying across his shoulder. 'That you, Toto? I was afraid we'd lost you.' He spoke gently, a note of fondness in his voice.

'You didn't see our signal then? We climbed to the top of Kulal, lit a fire there.' She was nervous, her words coming in a rush.

He shook his head, his eyes fastening on Karanja. 'So it *was* you.' He didn't ask him why he had fired at Kirby-Smith's Land-Rover and then gone after the elephants, he just stood there, smiling, his teeth showing white in his beard. 'You stupid show-off bastard.' It was said affectionately, almost admiringly, and he seemed on the point of saying something else, but Mary interrupted him, explaining about Abe's arm. 'Has that plane been over here? We need to get him to hospital.'

'Army planes have other things to do besides looking for me.' He went over to Abe, examining the splint. 'A good job you did there. Anyway,' he added, 'nothing can land at Loiyangalani till the upepo dies down.'

The truck had a first aid kit and he gave Abe an antibiotic injection. After that we settled down to sleep, building little stone windbreaks for ourselves. The ground was very hard, the noise of the wind and the lake incessant, but I was asleep almost immediately.

I woke with the first of the light to the sound of voices, Mary arguing with van Delden.

'It wouldn't do any good.'

'You thought differently the other morning.'

'I was afraid you'd kill each other.'

'The situation hasn't changed.'

There was a long pause. Then on a note of forced cheerfulness she said, 'Perhaps he'll have turned back. Mukunga said the road was in bad shape.'

'We got through.'

'But with this wind blowing . . .'

'The wind won't stop him and he has enough men to rebuild the road where it drops down the lava escarpment to the shore.'

'He won't risk those refrigerator trucks on a road like that.'

'There's a back route. It was completed for the Mission early in 1973. One way or another he'll be here today.'

Silence then. Finally she said, 'All right, I'll try. But why is it always other people who must give way, never you?' Her words tumbling over each other, deep-throated and sullen. 'It's always been the same. Can't you ever see another man's point of view?'

'No, not in this.'

Another long silence, then he said: 'You tell him. Tell him to pull his outfit back to the South Horr Gap.'

'Why me? Why not talk to him yourself?'

That quick bark of a laugh. 'We've nothing more to say.'

'If you'd only talk to him reasonably. Not threatening, but trying to agree some limit—'

'You know that wouldn't work.'

'Because you hate him.'

'We don't speak the same language, that's all.'

'You hate him,' she repeated, her voice no longer sullen, but high and wild.

'That's enough, Mary.'

'No. No, it isn't. You've always hated him, ever since—'

The smack of his hand on her face, her shocked cry brought me to my feet. They saw me then, their dark dawn figures turning away almost guiltily and van Delden calling to me gruffly: 'Fetch some water from the lake, will you. I'll get a fire going.'

I went down the hill, my mind still on that scene, past the heaped rock piles of ancient burials, the light growing all the time and the water glinting pale, wavelets whispering in the wind. Was she right? Was it the hurt pride of a man who had lost his wife to another man? Inland, the shallows of the marsh mere were a still pale expanse, coots bobbing and waders busy at the edge. The pelicans had all gone, the storks too, but the herons were still there, motionless. And then I was remembering the Serengeti and how he had stood there at the Conference full of a deep anger, and I knew it wasn't that.

The lakeshore, when I reached it, was black lava shingle, the water tepid with an alkaline taste. I would have stripped off and waded in, but as I filled the jerrican something big swirled in the moving shadow of a shoal of fish and the surface of the water was whipped to a froth, leaping glints of silver. The sky was taking on colour now, a faint blue with thin wisps of cloud drifting like fog patches, but the islands close offshore were still dark silhouettes. I left the can and walked along the shore towards what looked like a dug-out canoe drawn up on a stretch of dark sand. Three logs lay stranded close beside it, but as I approached them they rose up on short legs and went sliding into the water, hissing angrily. The sand was gritty and just beyond the straight furrows scored by the crocodiles were the great rounded pug marks of a hippopotamus. The canoe was a raft of logs lashed together.

The clouds took fire as I climbed back up the hill, the light intense and luminous, a brilliance that was harshly beautiful. A blackened tin of water was already boiling and Mtome was squatting beside the glowing oven of stones, kneading posho into a dough. Mukunga plucking two Egyptian geese shot the previous evening. Van Delden looked up from cleaning his rifle. 'When the upepo stops blowing maybe I'll take you out in that raft.'

I shook my head, 'Don't bother.'

'You want to see Porr, don't you? You can't see it from here.'

'Not if it means going out into the lake on that thing.'

'It's safe enough when there's no wind. The El Molo use them for spearing perch. Have you still got that typescript with you?' And when I told him I'd jettisoned it on the mountain, he said, 'Pity. I'd like to have read it while we're waiting.' He put his rifle down and fished something out of the pocket of his bush jacket. 'This might interest you.' He held it out to me, a broken piece of pottery, badly pitted, but still showing the dark brown marks of a design.

'Where did you find it?'

'On that first island, in a fissure, and there were marks on the rocks; too faint to make out what they represented. Did Pieter van Delden get out to those islands?'

I shook my head, turning the fragment over in my hand. 'Is this part of a pot, do you think?'

'Keep it if you like. Take it along to the British Museum. They'll tell you. And there's more below the fissure, but all small pieces by the look of them. Maybe if you searched the other islands . . .' He stopped at a sudden outburst of bird cries and reached for his rifle.

We all turned, gazing down at the flat sheet of the mere where the birds moved restlessly. Something had disturbed them. Then, round the corner of the hill, an elephant appeared, moving slowly, its trunk exploring the mud and weed at the water's edge. It moved with a quiet, deliberate pachydermal dignity that seemed entirely at one with the primordial setting and I had a sense of timelessness; I could be back a million, two million years, back further perhaps to a time when the first ancestor of man inhabited the shore of this ancient lake.

'A bull,' van Delden said quietly.

Its back and head were plastered with mud, and the sun, coming up over the hill in a burst of heat that coloured the land a firebrick yellow, turned the animal from grey to pale ochre so that it merged into the background of sand and rock, barely visible as it shambled along the far edge of the marsh towards the lakeshore, an ugly gash across its shoulders. More elephants made their slow weary entrance upon the scene. I counted seven of them, all adults, moving in a stumbling silent rush towards the lake, which was now a brilliant sapphire blue. The islands off the shore were no longer vague humps, but clear and sharp in that bright light, all browns and reds with a frill of white where the wind broke waves against their base. The bull, a distant tide-rock shape standing in the lake, was spraying water, its trunk lifting and falling, its body already glistening black, the wound showing as an open slash of red.

'A lost world,' Mary murmured. And van Delden, looking at her sharply, said, 'This is their last refuge.'

'It can't support them.'

'Always some specious argument...' He turned abruptly away, talking to Mukunga in his own language and shutting her out as though afraid of losing his temper with her again. We drank our tea and ate our breakfast, and all the time I was conscious of the tension between them. The fragment of pottery van Delden had given me seemed suddenly of no importance beside that little group of tired gaunt leviathans all standing now in the lake and drinking thirstily. How far had they come, I wondered? From the Aberdares where the forest trees were almost cut down? Or Tsavo perhaps, across several hundred miles of hostile land peopled by man, their young all slaughtered, their numbers reduced? I picked up the piece of pottery and in a mood of sudden disgust I threw it on to one of the burial cairns where it shattered into fragments. 'You'd better show me how to use a rifle,' I said to van Delden. 'I've never fired one before.'

'Later,' he said. 'If you wish.' He was talking to Abe about the lake and its strange colouring, and I lay back, thinking about those elephants, the stones under me burning hot, the wind dying. Skeins of birds flew low over the lake, fish shoals dark like cloud shadows occasionally bursting into frenzied splashes of silver, and van Delden's voice murmuring gently in the heat: 'They say it's the algae. When the surface is calm, then it really is a jade green sea, all the mass of algae coming to the surface, a green skin of plant life. But with the upepo, it all sinks and the lake becomes hard and blue. Mostly, when I've been up here, it's been blue in the early morning, then the wind takes off and it turns green. You'll see – about noon it'll turn green.'

Mukunga said something, getting to his feet, and Karanja also rose. 'I go with him.'

'No. One is enough.'

But Karanja shook his head. 'Is better I go with him. When the hunting trucks arrive I think they still have the support of an Army detachment. Maybe I know the officer.' He shouldered his rifle, and without waiting for permission he went after Mukunga. The old man sat there, not saying a word, his eyes on the truck as it drove off, and I could guess what was in his mind. This was a different Karanja and he wasn't sure of him.

The truck disappeared beyond the line of the hill and he gave a little shrug, then turned to me. 'Okay, if you want to try a few shots, we've spare guns and plenty of ammunition.'

He had me firing at an old tin set on one of the burial mounds, and with the first shots the elephants were gone, lost to view behind a low rise. Van Delden, watching them, nodded his head in satisfaction. 'The further north they go the better it will be for them. I'd like to get them all off that mountain and headed north.' And he added, 'they've a long way to go before they get to the Ethiopian border. This lake is all of 180 miles long.'

I fired altogether about a dozen rounds, and with the last shots I hit the tin twice at a distance of 50 yards. 'Calm,' he said. 'That's the secret. You have to keep calm. Whatever's coming at you, just hold your breath, aim and fire, bringing the sights up on to the mark, steady and unflustered, just as if you were firing at that tin. Okay?'

The lake was already turning green, and not a breath of wind, the heat heavy and humid. Mary was splashing about in the shallows and I joined her, wading in with my clothes on. Her wet hair clung to her head, making it seem smaller, and I could see her breasts with the nipples poking at the thin wet khaki of her shirt. The water was tepid, the sun on it a blinding glare. Far to the north a toy elephant stood in a posture of levitation, its image raised by the lake's steaming heat. 'So now you're a crackshot.' She was grinning at me and I dived and grabbed her legs, tipping her up, and we played, laughing in the water till our eyes were sore and our heads burned with the heat.

I went up the hill then to see how Abe was, lying in the shade of the truck's canvas top which they had rigged up in the lee of a burial mound. 'Lucky devil!' he said. 'I'd give anything to be in the water.' It was airless under the canvas and he was sweating.

'Where's van Delden?' I asked.

'On top of the hill, keeping watch, and he's sent Mtome and Dima to guard the road. I don't think he trusts Karanja.'

'How's the arm?'

'Fine. It doesn't hurt too much.' He took his glasses off and asked me to wipe them. 'What do you reckon is going to happen?'

I shook my head. It was something I didn't want to think about.

'You realize Kirby-Smith has lost a plane, two trucks and a Land-Rover.'

'He can always call on the Army for replacements.'

He nodded. 'If it wasn't for the Army I'd say van Delden was waging a pretty successful holding operation.' I handed him back his glasses and he said, 'Sometime during the night he's going to dump me as close as he can to the oasis. Mary will be with me. I think he hopes she can persuade Kirby-Smith to pull his outfit back. A truce, in other words – a sort of modus vivendi. What's Mary think? Is that possible?'

'I doubt it. They were talking about it this morning and she didn't think he'd agree.'

'Nor do I.' He eased his buttocks on the stones. 'With luck I'll get evacuated. What about you? If it's a shoot-out — ' He was staring at me and there was real concern in his eyes. 'You'll have the camera, but if you've got pictures they consider damaging . . . I don't know, maybe you can trade the film for safe passage out of the country, but I wouldn't bank on it.' I thought I heard the sound of an engine, very faint and far away, and I ducked out from under the canvas shelter. The road was empty, but Mary was calling something from the lakeshore, and then the 15-cwt came into view with Mukunga driving, nobody else. It stopped beside her, and van Delden, halfway down the slope, called out, 'What's happened? Where's Karanja?'

'Gone off on his own,' she answered.

When I reached the truck they were still interrogating Mukunga and I had to wait some time before Mary explained that the old oasis touring camp had been occupied by an Army patrol and Karanja had gone down to make contact with the officer in charge. 'One of the trucks had a radio aerial and he was very confident the officer in charge would let him contact Army HQ. The last Mukunga saw of him he was holding his rifle up with a handkerchief tied to the barrel and walking straight towards the building that used to be the bar.'

'When was this?'

'About ten-thirty, just after Alex's outfit had established themselves in the Mission buildings.'

'Mukunga didn't wait for him?'

'Yes, but back at the truck, which was parked in the doum palms. He waited about half-an-hour, then one of the hunting trucks started down to the harbour and another headed out towards the airstrip. He was afraid of being cut off, so he came straight back.'

Van Delden was still talking to Mukunga, both of them gazing out across the shallow expanse of water to the bare brown slope beyond and the islands shimmering in the heat. Finally he nodded, looked at Mary and said, 'Okay, we'll shift camp. You get your patient ready to move.' He called to Mtome, gave instructions to Mukunga, then turned to me. 'You want to try paddling an El Molo fishing raft? Take it up along the shore there. We may need it.'

The raft, when I launched it, proved more stable than I had expected, but it had almost no freeboard and I hugged the shore, scared of deep water. Also it was difficult to steer until I got the hang of it, kneeling at the centre of balance and using the primitive paddle blade as a steering oar at the end of each stroke. I was almost out of sight of the hill of the dead before the truck began to raise its tell-tale dust stream. There was no wind now and in the passage between shore and island the water was flat, a dark, viscid green. Shoals of fish moved like cloud shadows and when I stood up, balancing myself carefully, I could see, far to the north, a heap of rock glowing white in the sun like the great pyramid of Cheops. And in a little bay about a mile away there were elephants standing in the water.

I began steering for the first of the islands, feeling free and full of a sense of exhilaration now that I was on my own in the immensity of the great lake. But I did not land, for as I glided into the shore long lizard shapes slid soundless and without a splash into the water. I had no rifle, no means of fending off crocodiles, and I turned the clumsy craft and headed back towards the shore, the heat making the blood pound against my temples.

The hollow in which they had parked the truck was a mixture of sand and rock interspersed with gravel, and it was all the same colour, ochre yellow washed out by the glaring heat haze. From the top of a rise we looked out across the mere with its bobbing coots to the hill where we had spent the night, and half an hour later an open Land-Rover with African soldiers in it appeared in a cloud of dust from the direction of Loiyangalani. 'They'll see our tracks,' Mary whispered, and van Delden nodded, 'So what happens then?'

'There are only four of them.'

Nobody spoke after that, the Land-Rover crawling along below the shoulder of the hill until it came to the lake. It stayed there for a moment, one of the men in it standing and staring up at the hill. He was not in uniform and van Delden, with his glasses to his eyes, muttered, 'Karanja.' The figure sat down again and the Land-Rover turned, moving back along the edge of the mere to the point where Mukunga had turned the 15-cwt off the track. It stopped there and we watched in silence as Karanja got out, stood talking to the driver for a moment, then turned and began walking towards us, his rifle gripped by the barrel and swung carelessly across his shoulder. The Land-Rover drove off, its dust gradually settling, nothing now below us but that solitary figure plodding steadily along the water's edge and up the slope, following the 15-cwt's tracks. Van Delden stood up, calling to him, and Karanja waved, coming straight towards us with something of a swagger, his teeth showing white in a broad grin. 'So what have you been up to?' van Delden asked. 'You look bloody pleased with yourself.'

Karanja nodded, still grinning. 'I think maybe the Army fly you out.' He sat down, rubbing the dust and sweat from his forehead.

'You made contact with the military commander, did you?'

'Ndio. I talked with him by radio. There is report of a band of Shifta moving towards Marsabit, so he don't want any trouble here. But first he must speak with Nairobi.'

'And what about Major Kirby-Smith? What about the elephants here on Rudolf? You knew I'd never agree to leave without some guarantee they would be left in peace.'

Karanja looked at him, not grinning now, just smiling quietly. 'But if Ileret is made a game reserve, I think you leave then.'

Van Delden gave that quick hard laugh. 'With you as warden, is that the deal?' And Karanja went into a high peal of laughter.

'Would Kimani agree to that?'

'Kimani? Kimani is finished, I think. After what you do at that Conference.' But he wouldn't even hazard a guess at Kimani's successor, still laughing in embarrassment and excusing himself by saying that he was not exactly at the centre of things here on the shores of Lake Rudolf. And though van Delden questioned him closely, his answers were evasive. All he would say was that Pat Murphy was the source of the rumours, having just flown back from Nairobi, and that Major Kirby-Smith was worried he no longer had full backing for his operation.

'He'll be ordered to stop it, is that what you mean?'

But Karanja shook his head. 'That will depend on who is made Minister in place of Kimani.' And he added, 'Is only talk at the moment you understand.'

He wasn't being devious and his laughter seemed a cover for his own uncertainty rather than any amusement at the situation. His relationship with van Delden was a very strange one now, the old subservience overlaid by a pushful self-confidence, and yet underneath it I sensed that nothing had really changed, the bond between them as strong as ever, so that I wasn't surprised at the deep concern in his voice as he said, 'Please, you take my advice. Do nothing. Perhaps tomorrow the Major gets a new directive.'

'In this country,' van Delden growled, 'things don't

happen as fast as that, and tomorrow he may kill enough elephants to fill those meat trucks of his.'

Karanja shrugged, as though to indicate there were other more immediate problems engaging his attention. 'Is not the elephants,' he muttered.

Van Delden reached out and grabbed him by the arm. 'What do you mean by that?'

But Karanja shook his head, wrenching himself free and getting to his feet. 'The Army don't want any trouble,' he said again. 'I am to tell you that and I have told you. They have mortars and machine guns and they know where you are.' He turned to Mary. 'You talk to him. Maybe he listen to you.' And he walked off, down towards the lakeshore, a suddenly impressive figure, solitary against the flat immensity of that jade sea.

'He's right.' Mary was leaning forward, her dark eyes pleading. 'Wait and see what happens.'

Van Delden said nothing, sitting there, his rifle across his knees, staring after Karanja, and I wondered what he was thinking. Was he seeing Karanja as I saw him, symbolic of the future here in Africa? Or was he resenting the passage of time, the change in attitudes? And Abe said quietly, 'If the cull is called off, then I hope to God he's stopped in time.' And I knew he was thinking of that elephant making her way down the gorge.

There was nothing for us to do now but wait, and after we had fed the afternoon passed slowly, a somnolent interlude, the heat intense and the lake a shimmering, blinding glare. We kept watch in turn from a crumbling outcrop, but no vehicle came down the track and nothing moved except the waders probing the mud at the mere's edge. I lay dozing, conscious of dehydration and the burning power of the sun, and all the time that sense of waiting heavy on my mind. At one point I remember studying van Delden through half-closed lids and thinking of Lear – that gnarled face burned brown by the sun, the long white hair lank with sweat. For Lear there had been nothing but disaster, and I wondered, my mind dulled by the heat and full of foreboding as the sun swung slowly across the brazen sky and sank towards the Turkana shore. And still nothing happened.

The sunset that evening was a purple flare like rich blood spilled across a pale blue-green ceiling. The lake turned red, then faded to the dull sheen of beaten metal, and with the dusk the birds came, pelicans, storks, geese, all manner of birds, singly and in flights. Two shots gave us a meal, and while Mtome prepared it, the rest of us laid out the net in the shallows and hauled in more tilapia. On the shore there, looking across to the fading shapes of the islands and thinking of the people who had inhabited this world thousands of years ago, I had a sense of frustration: to have come so far, and in van Delden's company, everything I had planned, and now I knew instinctively that this was the end of the road. Mary, standing barefoot in the water, caught my mood: 'You should have explored those islands while you had the chance. I'd have come with you.'

'We'll go tomorrow,' I said. But I was certain we

wouldn't. And so was she. She shook her head, staring out across the lake to where the first star showed in the dying green of the sky. 'Tomorrow I'll be at Loiyangalani,' she said, her voice a whisper, her face a pale oval against the dark of her hair. And suddenly I knew that deep down inside of her she was afraid.

'You could refuse to go.'

'No.' She shook her head, silent for a moment. Then she said, 'But there's nothing I can do. Nothing anyone can do.' And she turned abruptly away, heading back towards the fire that now glowed brightly in the dark outcrop of the rocks. I stopped to slip on my boots, wondering that she could walk barefoot over stones and gravel, and as I neared the fire I had a picture of dark African faces lit by the flicker of the flames and the old man sitting cross-legged, his great bearded head ruddy in the glow. It was a very Biblical scene, but Old Testament, not New. No man camped on Lake Rudolf could think in anything but Old Testament terms. This was eye-for-an-eye country, intensely primitive.

That night we took it in turns to keep watch and when Dima woke me, just after midnight, the moon was up and the lake so still it was difficult to tell where sky and water met, the reflection of the stars equally bright. The hill of the dead was almost white in the moonlight and below it the pale shape of the mere was dotted with the paler shapes of birds all fast asleep. It was a dead world, and lying in the hard hollow of the rocks, I had a sense of unreality, a feeling almost of disembodiment. There was no sound, no movement, everything frozen into immobility, no breath of wind and the air hot and heavy. I had time to think then, all the time in the world, but my mind seemed disorientated, incapable of concentration.

Time passed and gradually I became aware that the night was not entirely lifeless. Behind me, down on the lakeshore, shapes were shifting position almost imperceptibly. A hippo had its snout just clear of the water and there were crocodiles slithering on the dark volcanic sand. And towards the end of my watch several elephants appeared over a rise to my left, pale prehistoric shapes moving soundless through the moonlit landscape. They passed within a few hundred yards of where I lay, moving in a straggling line towards the lake. It was like a slow motion film with no sound track, and as they disappeared from sight a voice behind me said very quietly, 'If this could ever become a safe place you could walk among those elephants as you would among friends.'

'Was that how it was at Marsabit?' I asked, looking back at him over my shoulder.

He nodded, his white hair gleaming silver in the moonlight. 'I knew them all, and they knew me. Some I could go right up to and they'd touch my face with their trunks.' And he added in a hushed voice, 'It's a wonderful thing when an animal as big as that, and wild, gives you its confidence. It's like a revelation. Can you understand?'

'Yes, of course.'

'Hmm.' He sounded dubious. 'To understand that

is to understand the relationship of man and beast, the need they have of each other.' He was silent then, watching as the last of the elephants slowly disappeared into a shallow dip between two pale rock hillocks. 'Have you checked your camera?'

'It's okay.'

'You realize nobody has ever shot a film of an elephant kill being stopped.' He was staring at me, his voice suddenly urgent. 'It means a great deal to me, that it should be on record. And the future of these animals could depend upon it.'

'I've still got to get it out of the country.'

'Yes, well, we'll have to think about that. But after you've got the pictures.' And he nodded. 'Better get some sleep now. We start at four.'

But after what he had said sleep eluded me, my mind on what the day would bring. The world I knew seemed very far away, the harshness of this near-desert country all about me and the memory of those elephants gliding silent through the moonlight very vivid. Elephants. I could hardly remember when I had not been following their big footprints. I tried thinking about the night at Kulal, and romping in the warm waters of the lake, but it was all ephemeral. And that glimpse of Porr, the broken piece of early pottery I had discarded, nothing had any significance now, except this ghostly congregation of elephants. This was the day towards which we had been steadily moving, Abe and I two outsiders, spectators, caught up in a confrontation that was an extension of the arguments we had heard at that Conference. So long ago it seemed with the lake gleaming pale under the stars and Karanja snoring gently, his broad nostrils quivering.

Dozing, I was vaguely conscious of Mtome fanning the embers of the fire, of dark figures moving against the stars. The moon was half across the sky, lighting a bright path from South Island to the shore below us. No sign of dawn yet and I sat up and looked at my watch. Just after four and van Delden sitting on a rock, his beard limned in light, his head bent over an old Lee Enfield rifle, checking the magazine. Below me, Mary was stooping over Abe and I heard her say, 'A few hours now and you'll be able to get it properly set.'

'I'm okay,' he murmured. 'It's just stiff, that's all.' But his voice sounded tired. 'Any elephants passed during the night?'

I didn't say anything, nor did van Delden, and nobody spoke much as we sat there among the rocks drinking tea. By the time we had finished breakfast and loaded the truck, the first faint glimmer of dawn was showing behind the bulk of Kulal. Flights of birds were circling the mere as we drove round the edge of it, back on to the track, Mukunga at the wheel and van Delden sitting beside him. Karanja leaned across to Abe. 'When you see the Major, ask him whether Kit Kimani is still Minister. If he does not know . . .' He hesitated, then added firmly, 'Is important he does not do anything without authority. Tell him that.'

Abe nodded, but his eyes looked glazed and I wasn't certain he had understood. We were driving without lights, the bumps in the track unavoidable, and he was obviously in pain.

It was about six miles to the lugga and as we approached it the truck slowed. Van Delden had the glasses to his eyes, searching the line of drifted sand and rock outcrops. We ground our way through the empty stream bed, past the twin hillocks that formed a natural gateway, and then we were out in the open with the raised line of the doum palms away to our left, and all ahead the land stretching flat like a salt pan to the El Molo manyatta and the port. There was grass here, dry wisps overlaying a carpet of fresh growth, and above us the stars were paling, the dawn light growing.

We were about 500 yards beyond the lugga when the truck slammed to a halt. A light had appeared at the furthest extremity of the palm tree ridge. Mukunga switched off the engine and in the sudden silence we could hear doves calling. A hyena whooped up among the sand slopes we had crossed coming down off Kulal, the sound very faint and changing to an ugly chuckle. There was the snap of branches, something moving on the doum palm escarpment, then we heard the sound of an engine and headlights swung across the shape of the Mission buildings. Van Delden turned to Mary. 'Looks like they're on the move, so I'll have to leave you here.'

'He can't walk that far.'

'Then you'll just have to wait for one of their trucks to pick you up.' He had the glasses to his eyes, watching the headlights flickering in the palm tree boles. 'Hurry now, I can't wait here.'

She got out then and Karanja and I gave Abe a hand. His face looked very pale, his glasses owlish as they caught the dawn light. 'Okay?' I asked him.

He nodded, standing with his head up and his mouth set. 'I'll make it.'

A thin squeal sounded from the doum palms as we all turned our heads towards the ridge, but nothing moved and the sound was not repeated. Van Delden leaned out of the truck, his head turned to Mary. 'Try to make him see sense. Because if he doesn't . . .' He bit the words off short and told Mukunga to get going. 'Goodbye, Toto,' he called softly. Her answer was lost in the sound of the engine and all I caught was the emotion in her voice. It was in her eyes, too, staring at him, very wide. Abe, standing beside her, his arm in the sling she had made for him, said something and she darted a quick glance towards the palms. Only then did she look at me, but our wheels were already stirring dust as we swung round to head back the way we had come, and she turned away with a casual wave of her hand.

I was still staring after them, wondering why I had not insisted on going too, when Dima shouted something, pounding on Mukunga's shoulder and pointing towards the lake. A box-like object which could only be a truck was moving against the pale glint of the water, and there was another almost hull-down beyond it. They were both of them moving parallel to us, feeling their way slowly without lights.

Our speed increased and we scuttled for the protection of the lugga, bucketing across it and swinging sharp right to skid to a halt behind an outcrop. Van Delden jumped out, swearing softly. 'Get your camera.'

'It's too dark,' I said.

But he brushed my words aside, giving orders to the Africans and clambering up into the rocks, his rifle in his hand. 'Take them a little time to flush those elephants out of the palms,' he said as I joined him, lying in the shadow of an almost perpendicular rock. 'Dawn will come fast now and they need the light for accurate shooting.'

'You mean they're going to cull – now?' My mouth was suddenly dry.

'Yes, what else? Dawn's a good time.'

'What about Mary?'

'I tell you, it takes time to set up a big kill. They'll have reached the Mission before anything happens.'

But as the light strengthened and the hunters' trucks began to take shape in the flat country towards the lake, we could just see Mary, with Abe beside her, still standing on the track almost exactly where we had left them. Van Delden nodded towards the dim-seen figures. 'What are they waiting for?'

I shook my head, unwilling to tell him what was in my mind.

'Silly little fool,' he growled. 'They'll be in the way if they don't get moving.'

Karanja slid along the rocks towards us. 'What you do now?' But at that moment lights blazed behind the escarpment and we heard the roar of engines, headlights flickering on the tree boles. Trucks were moving on the sand slopes beyond and we heard the distant sound of men yelling, banging on door panels, horns blaring, followed by squeals and trumpeting – a terrible hunting-cry noise that ripped the peaceful stillness of that lakeside dawn to shreds. And down on the flats towards the lake the trucks we had seen moving into place in the half light were closing in, slowly, menacingly, the sound of their engines lost in the uproar.

For a ghastly moment I thought van Delden was going to do nothing. He lay there, shaking his head as though willing it not to happen, his gaze fixed on the doum palm escarpment. Dark shadows drifted through the tall curved stems, and then they were coming out, a whole herd with calves of various ages, sliding down the escarpment to the flat arid grassland below, not trumpeting, not making any sound, but moving swiftly, almost purposefully to their appointment with death. And in the lead, as they headed straight for the lake and the waiting hunters, was a large tusked elephant with a single calf beside her, tripping daintily – like a ballet dancer. The words flashed into my mind, Abe's words, and in that instant, my gaze switching to the two figures still standing on the track, I saw him start forward and Mary trying to restrain him. 'Oh God!' I breathed aloud. And van Delden, beside me, muttered, 'What's he think he's doing?'

But by then Abe's figure had detached itself and was running awkwardly. I thought I heard him shout-

ing, but I couldn't be sure, there was so much noise,
a thunderflash exploding and the trucks racing for the
end of the palms where they could come down into
the flat and complete the drive. Abe was still running
forward and Mary had almost caught up with him,
two tiny figures running in the pale dawn, and the
lead elephant had sighted them. She had stopped and
was standing, stiff-legged and uncertain, her head
moving from side to side, one foot scuffing the
ground. The calf moved ahead of her and she laid her
trunk across its shoulders, edging it to safety behind
her as she faced the two humans hurrying towards
her. The rest of the herd were bunching up behind her
now, adults presenting a solid front, the calves pushed
in behind, all of them alert to danger, thoroughly
roused.

I knew what was in Abe's mind. He was remembering what Karanja had done, up there on the Mara,
hoping to turn them towards us before the trucks
came down off the escarpment and began the final
drive to the killing ground. Van Delden knew it, too,
and he was already on his feet, running for the truck.
And as we piled into it, the engine bursting into life,
I had a feeling of panic, a dreadful certainty; Abe
knew nothing about elephants, only what he had read
in books.

We came out between the twin hillocks, the wheels
churning gravel as we hit the dip of the lugga, and
van Delden had the Lee Enfield instead of his double-
barrelled rifle gripped in his big hands. I was standing
in the back, holding on to the handbar, the cloud

hanging over Kulal glimpsed out of the corner of my eyes, tinged with red, and away to the right the hunters' trucks raising streamers of dust. Abe was motionless now, about 50 yards from the elephants, one arm raised above his head, and Mary had also stopped a little way behind him. I saw it like that, the scene set as in a still, very clear in the rapidly increasing light, everything motionless. And then the two trucks came belting round the end of the palms. There was an eruption of noise, the crack of a shot, flat and hard, the sound of it coming from a Land-Rover moving in from our right, and in the same instant the herd matriarch charged, not trumpeting, not making any sound, just covering the ground at great speed, the dust flying from her dancing feet. And behind her half a dozen others, big beasts with their trunks curled underneath their tusks and their heads high.

I saw Abe flung aside and Mary trying to run, engulfed in a grey mass. Another shot sounded, and another, a whole ripple of fire. One elephant checked, another down, but the rest of them kept going, driving straight for the Land-Rover and the two trucks now stopped and in the direct line of their charge. And it was in that moment I grabbed the camera, a reflex action, the need to do something, to blot out the scene I had witnessed. By the time I had it to my shoulder the elephants were in among the trucks and all was confusion, my impression blurred by the din of shots and squeals of rage, the camera whirring and everything seen through the eyepiece. Another elephant went down, rifles blazing and drifts of smoke, and one of the trucks backing away, but not fast enough. A thunderflash burst, but the elephants swept on, a grey tide engulfing it and the matriarch's flailing trunk smashing down on the driver's head, splitting his face open like an over-ripe melon. Tusks drove into the body of the vehicle, heads lowered, grey flanks heaving, and then the truck was on its side, with the wheels spinning and spurting sand, men running.

The cows stood there for a moment, bayoneting the truck with their tusks and trumpeting in fury, then broke, roaring and screaming, as the Land-Rover drove in furiously and bullets slammed into their hides. A shot right beside me, deafening, tracer streaming out on a flat trajectory to strike at the Land-Rover. More shots and the Land-Rover stopped, two men jumping out of it as an elephant bore down, raising it with her tusks, and another, a big bull I think, coming in from the other side, and the men running as it bore down on them. One man was picked up, flung in the air, the elephant suddenly on top of him, kneeling on him, crushing the life out of him, and then it rose, shaking its head at the bloodied pulp on the ground at its feet.

I ran out of film then, standing there dazed and shaking, realizing suddenly that we were stationary. Van Delden and Mukunga were firing over the bonnet, shooting lines of tracer, and the others had scattered, lying flat on the ground either side of us. One of the trucks from the escarpment was on fire, the other backing away with a flat tyre. More thunderflashes went off, but the elephants ignored them. They had re-grouped around their young and they passed within a hundred yards of us, taking no notice and moving swiftly northwards towards the lugga. By the time I had changed the magazine in my camera they were gone and only the dead remained, lying like low tide rocks, all still except one, which was thrashing its legs and trying to lift its head. And in the silence I could hear the gurgle of breath coming laboured from it wide-open mouth.

I sat down then on the tailboard edge, my knees shaking, my legs suddenly weak. The cloud over Kulal had thinned and was now a canopy of violent red. The sun was up behind the mountain, the palms of brilliant green, the earth blood-red and the lake blue, all bright, brittle colours in the sunrise, and van Delden walking slowly with bent head towards the curled-up khaki heap lying in the dust ahead of us. Exhausted and moving like an automaton, I scrambled out and followed him. Mary lay in a fallen heap, her head at an awkward angle, the neck broken. But for that she might have been asleep. All those elephants passing over her and no mark. It was unbelievable, and only the flies clinging to her eyes to show she was dead.

Van Delden knelt down, brushing the flies from her face. 'That fool American.' He closed the lids with his fingers, his hand quite steady and nothing else said, no expression of grief. It wasn't callousness. I knew that. It was just acceptance. The man who had been a father to her and had never really known her . . . 'You realize she loved you – very deeply?' My voice was hesitant, under compulsion and sounding strange.

He looked up. 'What do you know about it? About love and the pain of love?' And he added quietly, 'She was very like her mother – tempestuous, hot-headed, full of vitality and grabbing at life with both hands. Do you think I didn't love her?' He stared at me, no trace of emotion in the pale cold eyes, and his voice hard as he said, 'She's dead, and that's that.' He got to his feet, his big head turning to watch Kirby-Smith as he came limping towards us, and I saw his hands clenched on the gun he was still holding.

I don't know what he said to him because at that moment I heard a groan and a voice, very faint, calling me. It was Abe. He was about forty yards away, lying twisted against an old ant-heap. 'Is that you, Colin?' The blood bubbled in his lungs as he forced the words out, his eyes staring up at me, glazed and not seeing. His thin chest was so badly damaged he might have been in a road accident, the rib cage stove in, the white of shattered bone protruding through a dark mess of congealing blood that buzzed with flies. 'Is she all right?'

'Yes,' I said. 'She's all right.' I knew it wasn't Mary he was thinking of.

'They were shooting.'

'She got away.'

'It was those trucks, the bastards! She was charging them. Not me.' His voice was suddenly strong and he tried to sit up. 'Silly, I can't see her. I can't—'

He fell back with a gurgling cry, blood frothing in his mouth.

'Just lie still,' I said. 'Save your strength.'

But he didn't hear me, his lips moving, framing his wife's name, but no sound coming. His eyes closed and he gave a bubbling groan, his mouth spilling more blood. I think he died in that moment, but I couldn't be sure, never having seen anybody die before, and I called to van Delden. But he didn't hear me, his mind shut to everything else but the man facing him with one trouser leg ripped open at the knee and a lacerated arm '... your own child. God help me, I can't shoot you in cold blood—'

'You dumped them there deliberately.'

'Don't be a fool, man. Finkel had busted his arm.'

'You were using them.'

'He was injured, I tell you.'

'But Mary – to leave Mary there. Right where I was going to cull. You knew what was going to happen. You knew.' His voice was high, almost out of control, the two of them facing each other ablaze with anger, the body at their feet forgotten, and van Delden saying, 'You could have stopped it.' His voice was hard and full of menace. 'Instead, you fired. You fired at the lead elephant.'

'To turn them.'

'No. To start the cull.'

'If I hadn't had to shoot from a moving vehicle—'

'You'd have killed that cow, but it wouldn't have stopped the others. Don't you understand what those beasts have been through? They're so desperate now they'll charge any vehicle on sight.'

'We'd have stopped them if you hadn't interfered. Firing on our vehicles—'

I saw the gun come up, the flash of the barrel in the sun and I shouted something. But Mukunga was already there, his hand on van Delden's arm, and the old man suddenly came to his senses, turning angrily away. 'Get out of my sight,' he growled, shaking his head like a big bull uncertain what to do next. 'Christ Almighty! I should have killed you long ago.' He glanced briefly at Mary and his eyes passed on as though she were nothing now, his gaze fastening on a truck raising a cloud of dust as it came down the track from the Mission. It was an open 15-cwt. Kirby-Smith had seen it, too. His Land-Rover had been righted and one of his men drove it up to him, rubber flapping from the front tyres which had both been ripped open by the thrusting tusks. Mukunga was talking urgently to van Delden, Mtome and Dima gripping their rifles, eyes watching nervously as the Army truck approached. The hunting vehicles were sorting themselves out, one of them already under tow, and overhead the red of the sky was beginning to fade.

The Army truck slowed as it approached Mary's body, a young black officer standing up beside the driver holding on to the windscreen. It stopped and he stayed there for a moment, his gaze switching from the dead girl to Abe's body lying at my feet, and involuntarily I thought of Fortinbras, expecting him at any moment to make a speech. Instead, he shook his head, at a loss what to do in a situation like this. Slowly he stepped down from his vehicle, turning to Kirby-Smith as though seeking a lead. He said something in Swahili and Kirby-Smith nodded. Then suddenly they were all talking and Kirby-Smith's partner, Jeff Saunders, drove up in one of the hunting trucks to join in the angry exchange. Everybody was talking at once, all except van Delden, who stood there, not saying a word, just waiting.

Finally the officer turned to him. 'Where's Karanja?' he asked in English.

It was only then that I realized Karanja was not there, that he had not been with us in the truck when we had driven out from the lugga in our abortive attempt to head the elephants off. Van Delden shook his head, turning and looking back. The others also turned and following their gaze I saw a lone dark figure halfway along the track from the lugga, walking steadily towards us.

The officer got back into his truck and went to pick him up. When it returned Karanja got out. 'Very bad business,' he said, addressing Kirby-Smith, his voice high and trembling slightly, either with tension or suppressed excitement, I wasn't certain which. 'There will be no more culling please and you will withdraw your outfit to South Horr to await further instructions.' And when Kirby-Smith started to argue, Karanja cut him short. 'Those are the orders of the Military Commander.' And the officer beside him nodded.

It was Saunders who said quickly, 'Brigadier Osman doesn't control this operation. It's a political matter and Kit Kimani has given us—'

'Mr Kimani is not any longer Minister. There is a new Minister of Resources, Mr Abbas. That is what Lieutenant Elmi has just told me.' And he turned to the officer beside him, who nodded his head again and said, 'Ndio.'

'So you don't shoot any more elephants, not until I have spoken on the radio with Headquarters.' He turned to van Delden. 'I suggest you go back now to your old camp beside the lake and wait there. I will make endeavour to arrange safe passage for you out of the country. Okay?' And he added, 'I am sorry – about this.' He made a gesture that embraced the two sprawled bodies, then indicated the truck. 'This detachment is leaving now in support of the Army post at Marsabit. Maybe I arrange for you to go with them.' He turned to me. 'You took some film. I would like it please.' He was looking straight at me, his tone commanding, and when I hesitated, he said, 'Is not good what happens here is shown in the West, so you will hand it to me please.'

I glanced at van Delden, but he didn't say anything, his gaze turned inwards, his eyes blank. And as I turned away to get the film I heard Kirby-Smith say, 'Abbas. There was a Tanzanian called Simon Abbas, took over Tsavo East before the Ugandan Army moved across the frontier. Is that the man?' And Karanja nodded. 'Is why I tell you there will be no more culling without his authority. He has great interest in elephants.'

I got the film and when I came back with it Kirby-Smith was talking urgently with his partner. 'If they won't loan us a plane, then see if you can persuade Brigadier Osman to have Pat Murphy fly me to Nairobi. The sooner I talk to Abbas . . .' They were already moving away and van Delden, still standing by Mary's body, suddenly lifted his head and called out, 'Alex!' And when the other paused and turned to face him he said quietly, 'Where are you planning to bury her – here or in Nairobi?'

'How the hell can we bury her in Nairobi?'

'You could fly her down.'

'There isn't room in a Cessna.'

'Use one of your refrigerator trucks then.'

'No.' The suggestion seemed to upset him.

'All right then. Where?'

'It's nothing to do with me.'

'She's your child.'

'I tell you, it's not my responsibility. You brought her up. You caused her death. You bury her.'

Van Delden stared at him for a long moment, then he nodded his head slowly. 'All right. If that's the way you feel.'

We loaded both bodies into the 15-cwt and drove back to the hill of the dead. We buried them there on the stony slope that looked out over the little bay to the El Molo Islands. 'Dust to dust, ashes to ashes . . .' Van Delden knew the relevant passages of the burial service by heart, and seeing him standing there, white-headed and bearded, intoning the words of committal, I knew he had done this many times before. The dust we tossed into the shallow graves was volcanic dust, and the sun shone out of a clear sky, the heat blistering.

It took us the rest of the day, working with wet towels over our heads, to build the two cairns, and in the evening, when it was done, we sat over a brew of tea, watching the birds flight in to roost on the mere below us, the sun falling below the Turkana mountains and the first stars showing pale in the rapidly darkening sky. Nobody spoke, van Delden sitting silent and withdrawn, the three Africans squatting round the embers, a stillness settling on the land, and I found myself remembering Abe's thin, sallow face, the dark worldly eyes and the little twisted smile. I hadn't been brought up to believe in anything very much, but now, in this wild place with the stone cairns shadowy, above me, I knew there must be something – something to reach out for. He had possessed an inner strength. He had talked of love, and suddenly I envied him, his peace, the certainty of his beliefs.

Some time during the night Karanja arrived. He and van Delden were talking for a long time, but I couldn't hear what was said, only the murmur of their voices. I went to sleep again, and when I woke it was dawn and van Delden had gone.

I got to my feet, looking wildly round, realizing I was alone, the two cairns outlined against the sun rising behind Kulal. And then I saw them, four dark figures splashing through the shallows of the mere, and north along the shore a solitary figure kneeling on a log raft and paddling it across the still, calm surface of the lake towards a small group of elephants standing up to their bellies in the water. I stood there for a moment, staring at the white of his hair shining in the early morning light, the paddle flashing drips of water and fish breaking the surface ahead of him in glints of silver. It was something I shall always remember, that lone figure on the El Molo fishing raft paddling slowly up the shore of Lake Rudolf, heading north like the elephants.

By the time I had reached the bottom of the hill the four Africans were waiting beside a Land-Rover parked on the track above the mere. Karanja came to meet me, smiling and with something of a swagger in his walk. 'You sleep very deep, Mr Tait.' And on his shoulder he carried van Delden's double-barrelled rifle.

The sight of it, with the picture of that lone figure still vivid in my mind, shocked me. 'You let him go – unarmed.'

He shrugged. 'Plenty of fish. He live like the El Molo now.' And he added, 'He is Tembo van Delden and he is back with his own people. With the elephants.' Then, with something of a flourish, he said, 'The new Minister has appointed me Warden of the North. I look after all game in this region now. That is what I came to tell him, that he and his elephants are safe.'

* * *

Six hours later Pat Murphy landed me at Wilson Airport, Nairobi, and that same evening I boarded a flight for London. Since then I have been scripting a documentary on *The Building of the Canals* and in my spare time writing this account of the fortnight I spent in Africa. I have had no news of Cornelius van Delden, though I have written twice to Karanja, once care of his Minister, and have made enquiries at the E.A.F. Embassy. I have, therefore, no certain information as to his present whereabouts, or even whether he is still alive. But in my mind I see him still as I last saw him, paddling alone along the shores of Lake Rudolf against a background of elephants belly-deep in the water. My guess is he will remain there till he dies, a forgotten man, lost to anything but the world he knows and understands better than any other human being.

AUTHOR'S NOTE

My fascination with Lake Rudolf is of very long standing – a first meeting with Joy Adamson in 1960 at which she gave me a detailed description of this most extraordinary lake, which is part of the great volcanic fault of the Rift Valley. At that time politics predominated, and I felt very strongly that if I were to set a novel in that area I wanted to write about the underlying, enduring Africa that had survived the political winds of change. By 1972, however, friends I had met initially through my publisher, Sir William Collins, who has produced so many of the books on African wildlife, were warning me that if I wanted to see the last great game herds I had best come soon, before the pressure of population destroyed them.

The journeys my wife, Dorothy, and I made in Africa in 1972–73 began with Joy and George Adamson and Christmas spent at George's lion camp on the Tana River. His brother, Terence, was there, and

Ken Smith, the Game Warden, so that I could not have had a better introduction to animal behaviour. And our understanding grew as we journeyed north, a safari of our own under the guidance of Jonny Baxendale that covered a considerable area of the N.F.D., including the southern part of Lake Rudolf and camp established close to the summit of Mt Kulal. Later Richard Leakey flew us up to the northern part of the lake to visit his discovery site of the skull that put the origins of man back a million and a half years. Later still, we went south into the Serengeti, catching the migration in full swing, visiting Mary Leakey in Olduvai Gorge, Hugo van Lawick in the Ngorongoro Crater, and then out into the plains with Hugo and Jane Goodall to follow their Ghengis pack as the wild dogs hunted down a baby wildebeest.

To all these people, and many others, including Ian Player and Nick Steele in other parts of Africa, I am greatly indebted – for the time they gave to us, for their advice, assistance and the great fund of knowledge they imparted. And since this is a story about elephants, I must pay tribute to the work of Iain Douglas-Hamilton in the Manyara Reserve. During our travels in Africa we had the opportunity of observing the behaviour of these remarkable animals over long periods and at close quarters. But the proper interpretation and understanding of that behaviour would not have been possible without constant reference to *Among the Elephants*, the fascinating book written by Iain and his wife Oria.

For those readers who have a scientific interest in

animal behaviour I feel I should make it clear that, like the characters, the central theme of *The Big Footprints* is purely imaginary. I discussed it with Iain Douglas-Hamilton, but the circumstances of total disaster I have described are as yet outside anyone's experience. Nobody can say whether elephants have an inherited knowledge of safe areas, or whether, given the circumstances, they would undertake such a desperate migration. As to the presence of elephants on Lake Rudolf, though I saw none myself, and Ken Smith states positively there are none at the present time, they were certainly there in considerable numbers less than a century ago when Count Teleki discovered the lake. They were not only watering there, but also subsisting partly on the weed available in the shallows.

To what degree I have taken liberties with my subject only time will tell. And time is fast running out. There are believed to be not more than 120,000 elephants left in this part of Africa and the rate of killing has risen to some 20,000 a year. This appalling toll is mainly due to the rapid rise in the price of ivory, and I would beg my readers to remember that the purchaser of any ivory object is directly responsible for the protracted, lingering death of another elephant. No purchasers, no poachers – it is as simple as that.